# Warrior Pharaoh

# Other Books By Richard Gabriel

*The Memory of Egypt in Judaism and Christianity (2001)*
*Great Captains of Antiquity (2000)*
*Great Battles of Antiquity (1994)*
*A Short History of War: Evolution of Warfare and Weapons (1994)*
*History of Military Medicine: Ancient Times to Middle Ages (1992)*
*History of Military Medicine: Renaissance to the Present (1992)*
*From Sumer To Rome: Military Capabilities of Ancient Armies (1991)*
*The Culture of War: Invention and Early Development (1990)*
*The Painful Field: Psychiatric Dimensions of Modern War (1988)*
*No More Heroes: Madness and Psychiatry In War (1987)*
*The Last Centurion (in French) (1987)*
*Military Psychiatry: A Comparative Perspective (1986)*
*Soviet Military Psychiatry (1986)*
*Military Incompetence: Why the US Military Doesn't Win (1985)*
*Operation Peace for Galilee: the Israeli-PLO War in Lebanon (1985)*
*The Antagonists: Assessment of the Soviet and American Soldier (1984)*
*The Mind of the Soviet Fighting Man (1984)*
*To Serve With Honor: A Treatise on Military Ethics (1982)*
*Fighting Armies: NATO and the Warsaw Pact (1983)*
*Fighting Armies: Antagonists of the Middle East (1983)*
*Fighting Armies: Armies of the Third World (1983)*
*The New Red Legions: Attitudinal Portrait of the Soviet Soldier (1980)*
*New Red Legions: A Survey Data Sourcebook (1980)*
*Managers and Gladiators: Directions of Change in the US Army (1980)*
*Crisis in Command: Mismanagement in the Army (1978)*
*Ethnic Groups in America: The Italians and Irish (1978)*
*Program Evaluation: A Social Science Approach (1978)*
*The Ethnic Factor in the Urban Polity (1973)*
*The Environment: Critical Factors in Strategy Development (1973)*

\* \* \* \* \* \* \* \* \* \*

# Warrior Pharaoh

*A Chronicle of The Life and Deeds of Thutmose III, Great Lion of Egypt, Told in his own Words to Thaneni The Scribe*

Richard A. Gabriel

**Authors Choice Press**
San Jose New York Lincoln Shanghai

Warrior Pharaoh
A Chronicle of The Life and Deeds of Thutmose III, Great Lion of
Egypt, Told in his own Words to Thaneni The Scribe

Authors Choice Press
an imprint of iUniverse.com, Inc.

For information address:
iUniverse.com, Inc.
5220 S 16th, Ste. 200
Lincoln, NE 68512
www.iuniverse.com

ISBN: 0-595-17340-3

Printed in the United States of America

To Reuven and Ivria
and their Harvest

*and for*

John Gerard Finn
(1916-2000)
A very good man

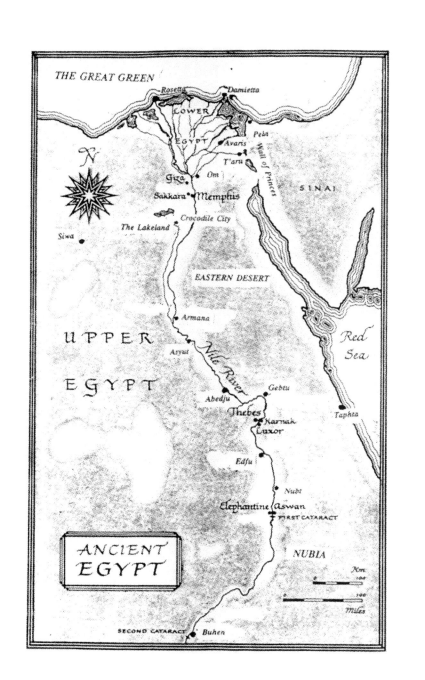

# One

I watched the boat carrying my son sail out of view as the captain set her course northward down the Nile toward the Delta and the open sea that we Egyptians have always called the Great Green. Merytre, the boys mother, my Great Wife, slipped her arm around my waist and pulled me close. Our eyes met and filled with quiet tears for our only son, Amenhotep, the guardian of Egypt's future, who sailed from us this day to lead an army in battle. He was eighteen.

One last look at the river. One last wish for him to be a child again. A deep sigh helped me rid myself of my sorrow. I walked from the palace balcony where I had stood so many times to address the people of Egypt. I am Pharaoh, keeper of the sacred land of *Kemit*, the Black Land, guardian of *Ta-Meri*, the Beloved Earth, the Great Lion of Egypt, and I will find little peace until my son returns in a year's time from the dangerous task of bringing the princes of Kadesh to heel. I had made him my co-regent a year earlier. Now I had given him the chance to prove his courage. The boy came from a long line of warriors. If blood is true, he will return to Thebes in victory. And then I can rest. And Egypt will be safe for another lifetime.

My hand brushed the remaining tears from my cheeks. At first I didn't see the old man sitting on the floor in the corner of the room. Then my eye caught the smile on his face.

"Thaneni, you old fool. Why do you sit in the corner like a dozing cat? Have you no respect for your Pharaoh! Rise you impudent bag of bones! How is it you dare to gaze upon the face of Pharaoh without fear."

The old man looked into my eyes and smiled broadly revealing a mouthful of missing teeth. The fine sand that invades everything in Egypt invades our food too and Thaneni's teeth had been ground to the gums from the abrasive action of the sand. The light from the windows gleamed off his shaven and well-oiled skull so brightly that it almost cast a shadow. From habit the old man sat cross legged on the floor so that his knees stretched the front of his linen kilt tight across his lap forming a flat surface that scribes used as a desk on which to place their papyrus and pens. He spoke in a tinny voice.

"Oh great Pharaoh, Strong Bull Arising from Thebes, I meant no disrespect. But these old bones have a life of their own. Once they find a comfortable place they are loath to move, Oh Powerful of Valor and Holy of Diadems."

"What are you doing here," I roared in mock anger. I had known Thaneni longer than any other person in Egypt. He was four years older than I and I was fifty two. By all experience we both should have been dead by forty like most Egyptians.

"Why do you clutter up my room with your worthless presence you old scribe. What is it you want?"

The old man's smile faded softly and his eyes met mine.

"I am here at your command, Oh Great Two Houses, to begin the writing of your history for the tomb painters and monument keepers and, of course"…and here he paused…"for the instruction of your son, the Prince Amenhotep, who will read your words when in his turn he becomes the Great Lion of Egypt." His voice softened. "But I see the sorrow of your son's leaving has taken you for the worse. Perhaps it is wise to begin tomorrow."

The old man began to shuffle his bones in an attempt to rise.

Thaneni was up to his old tricks again. I had met the wily scribe almost fifty years ago when we were both enrolled as apprentices in the House of Life of the Temple of Amun-Ra in Thebes. I entered the House of Life to be instructed in the sacred arts of writing by the Keepers of the Books. Writing was Egypt's most precious gift from the gods. The mastery of the pictures was given to the old ones by the Ibis-headed god Toth, Keeper of Wisdom. So it was that Toth became the patron god of scribes who labored in his name in the Houses of Life where writing was taught and the sacred books copied, relearned, and preserved. I was ten years old and Thaneni an older boy of fourteen when we met. As a youth I was shorter and smaller than most boys and have remained so to this day compared to most men. The other boys tormented me with names and blows, and once one of the priest-scribes even tried to mount me like a woman. It was Thaneni, a strong and wiry fellow, who came to my rescue and protected me until I could find within me the mettle to protect myself. We have been friends for a lifetime and no one in all *Kemit* could talk to me the way Thaneni did...and live.

"Why do you torment your Pharaoh? Do you think the absence of my son weakens the wrath of the Son of Ra against your impudent tongue! I am Menkeppere, Son of Horus, I am the Binder of the Nine Bows, the Smasher of Foreheads, the Scourge of the Asiatics, Slayer of Nubians, and Guardian of the Waters of Life!"

The bellowing voice brought no reaction from the old scribe. He lowered his head as if to get out of the way of my harsh words. Still he did not move nor speak.

"I am Thutmose and the spirit of the god Toth dwells in me as does the wrath of Horus the hawk. I have protected this Very Egypt for the last thirty years destroying her enemies and defending her allies. I have fought seventeen battle campaigns and brought to heel every manner of man from the Negroes of Nubia to the abominable peoples of the Mitanni at the Great Bend of the Euphrates. I am the third of my line, a warrior greater than my father and grandfather."

The old man had enough of the bellowing.

"Your voice has the ring of a braying ass! Stop this foolishness before you hurt yourself!"

The tone of voice was all too familiar, the voice of the older boy so many years ago correcting the younger so he wouldn't make a fool of himself. Before I could reply his voice reached my ear again, this time in a gentler way.

"Old friend, you are indeed the greatest Pharaoh that the gods of our fathers have ever given this Black Land. But you are a father and it is fitting that fathers should cry when their sons rush into harm's way with little experience and too full of the arrogance and confidence of youth. Your silent tears for your son mark your character. Great pharaoh you may be. But you remain always a father. Like all fathers, you will fear when the fates place your child in danger".

The old man was right. My anger ebbed like a fast tide and I found myself smiling at my childhood companion. Thaneni had been by my side for most of my life and had been witness to all my great deeds and failures. We had met because my aunt had seized the throne of Egypt first as co-regent with me, and then in her own right even proclaiming herself a male king! To get me out of the way I was sent to the House of Life in the hope that I would become a priest of Amun-Ra and forsake my rightful place in Egypt's history. From the House of Life to my service as a young officer in the army to recovering the throne and to the great battles that I fought for Egypt, Thaneni had always been there. Now that it was time for me to prepare a history of my reign for the tomb painters Thaneni would write that too. Perhaps he would even out-live me in this life and oversee the completion of my tomb hidden high in the cliff face of the Valley of Kings on the Western shore of the Nile in Thebes of the Dead. Somehow I thought that fitting.

"I see you have brought your writing materials."

The old scribe nodded. I remembered when I had been taught to write. I remembered the first day I was able to write something of my own, to express my own thoughts and not just copy the nostrums of others as young apprentices were trained to do. It was like being freed from a cage. I was literate and from that day for-ward I could make my thoughts known to others, mark my world in my own way, be who I became. And now the temple painters and relief carvers awaited the story of my life to be inscribed on the walls of the great temples at Karnak and Luxor. With Thaneni's help I will write my own annals, my own history for generations yet to be born. My tomb and the temples will stand for thousands of years as the pyramids have stood before them. And the ages will know the name of Thutmose the Third, Great Lion of Egypt.

# Two

My mother's name was Ese, a lesser wife of my father, Thutmose II. I was planted as a seed in her womb by Khunum, the god who fashions the Ka of human souls on his potters wheel. Her last red blood moon was near the end of the season of *Peret*, a cool and comfortable time of the year before the southwest wind overpowers the sweet breath of the north and brings a stifling heat to the city of Thebes. The time of my becoming in my mother's body is a barren time in Egypt. The Nile has already retreated to its narrow bed and continues to shrink for three more months. The land dies and there is no green to soothe the eyes from the glare of the red color of Seth, the god of death and decay. I had been fashioned on the potter's wheel only a month when the hot south wind began to blow driving before it the heat of the desert and making the air so hot that Egyptians dared go out of their houses only at night. The humid air is choked with fine dust borne by the force of the wind. It is impossible to escape the sand that invades every part of our lives.

The time of parched death, the season of *Shemu*, lasts for four months. The shrunken river has taken back its life exposing the bottom of the irrigation canals. Rotted plants and dead animals swollen purple from decay lie strewn in the muddy canals and about the fields. The heat and shallow water become home to green sticky scum that floats on the surface of what is left of the Nile's main channel. The once clear river is now a deep green and it lies almost still. There is no current to give it life. Only the wind stirs the surface. The water, too, seems dead, the consistency of thick poisonous soup. A heated stench settles over the land.

The land of Egypt is close to death. Were it not for the favor of the gods the Black Land would surely suffer the Curse of the Second Death and cease to be. But the gods are benevolent and Hapi, the goddess of the Nile, cares for the People of the Lapwing. The goddess of the Nile is a curious creature with her head of a hippopotamus and bearded face. Her breasts are huge and filled with milk enough for all. She is man and woman with both vagina and penis. This savior of Egypt lives far to the south in a great cave atop a mountain. There she sits with two large pitchers of water, one bright green and sweet, the other gray and heavy with the silt that floods life back into the parched lands of *Kemit*. These she pours into the Nile so that her people may plant and live another year.

It is a time when I am half formed, the season of *Akhet* when the waters of the Nile are renewed by the flood. I feel the first pulses of the Nile as they rise. The watery sack that holds me in my mother's belly grows cooler to my touch. Far to the south the first stirrings of the flood begin with slow waves. By the middle of June the streams are beginning to rise in Thebes while to the north six hundred miles away the Delta remains low and parched. At Elephantine on the border of Nubia and Egypt the priests are already measuring the strength of the flood. On the shores of the island whose huge grey boulders give it its name stands the small stone house with a measuring pole within it. The priests and government officials watch the water rise until it rises no more and then note its height. A good Nile measures 28 cubits at

Elephantine. Further north at Edfu it measures 24 cubits. It is measured again at Memphis where the great river enters the Delta. Here a Nile above 18 cubits is cause for alarm for it brings a devastating flood. Sixteen cubits at Memphis and the priests forecast a drought. Too high or too low and Egypt will starve.

The time of my birth was a good one for Egypt. The sacred Ibis, beautiful birds of black and white, foretold a good season as they moved down the river ahead of the flood that destroyed the reed beds where they feed on frogs and crocodile eggs digging them out of the soggy mud with their sabre-shaped bills. So reliable is their sense that the Ibis are renowned for their ability to predict the coming of the inundation. For this wisdom they are revered as gods. The timid streams of June are torrents by July as the mighty Nile renews its strength and spreads over the land bringing with it the rich black silt that fertilizes a soil close to death.

Within my mother's womb I am almost fully formed and I sense the change in the climate. The inundation—the Gift of the Bull—brings with it dampness and the air and earth grow heavy with moisture. All is hot and sticky like the inside of the womb that still holds me. Everywhere there is rebirth. The fireflies reappear to light the early dark of the Egyptian evening and the mosquitos search in swarms for blood. The swamps are alive with the croak of frogs, themselves an omen of fertility, and the jelly-masses of fishes' eggs writhe with the new life inside. All Egypt has become a womb as the people wait for the Nile to bring new birth to the nation itself. The rush of the Nile's waters are felt in my mother's womb. The opaque sack that holds me tears open and I issue forth from her body in a torrent. The Nile and I are one.

Khunum's seed burst forth from my mother in late September, the time of the height of the flood. She was fourteen, a year older than when most Egyptian women give birth to their first child. When her time came the birthing bricks were fashioned with the name of *Meshkhent,* the goddess of birth, inscribed on their face. As Ese waited my coming the birthing bricks were placed under her feet. For many hours she leaned back on her forearms raising and lowering her pelvis while I labored to be free of her womb until, my time come round at last, she squatted on the bricks and forced me from her. It was night. I am placed upon her chest and see for the first time the soft eyes of the woman who gave me life.

The temple priests entered the birthing room. A sharp flint knife severed my cord and I was wrapped in soft linen. The midwives stood aside, their task complete. Ese was a wife of Pharaoh and I was a royal prince. The Chief Priest of the Temple of Amun-Ra took me in his hands and brought his lips to my right ear, the place where the breath of life enters the body.

"Menkepper-Re," he whispered. Then again. "Menkepper-Re!"

"From this day you will be known as "Menkepper-Re," He in whom the spirit of Ra is made manifest."

The other priests lowered their heads before the new prince. Only now did I live, for we Egyptians believe that a person only has existence when he is given a name. Until that moment when the priest's words entered my ears I did not exist. Now I was Menkepper-Re, the name that I would be known by on all the documents and monuments of my reign. But I was both the son and grandson of a pharaoh and carried the dynastic name of Thutmose, "Him in whom Toth is born." It was the Ibis-headed Toth, god of wisdom, who carved the time on the birthing bricks that determined when a child was born. It was his familiar, the Sacred Ibis, who foretold of the flood. Toth, too, recorded the fate of the dead at the Last Judging, and he inscribed the number of years the king would reign on the leaves of the Ished tree causing it to bear fruit and bringing the king under divine protection. It was a noble name for a royal prince, even one who was not in line for the throne.

I lay in the darkness at my mother's side. Only the flickering light from the oil lamp on the table disturbed the night. I pressed against the linen swath that held me searching for the familiar touch of my mother's body that had nurtured me for so long. I stirred and Ese gazed down at me. She brushed the blanket from my face and her gentle smile warmed me. In a soft and tender voice she began to recite a prayer.

> May she flow away, she who comes in the darkness
> Who enters unseen
> With her nose behind her, her face turned backward
> Failing in that for which she came.
> "Hast though come to kiss this child?
> I will not let thee kiss him
> Hast thou come to injure him?
> I will not let thee injure him
> Hast thou come to injure him?
> I will not let thee take him away!

The prayer was to protect me from the Night Demon. Egyptians held the night in dread for that was when the dead walked among us. It was in the night when the evil we interred with the bones of men threatened us again. The female Night Demon moved among the living in the darkness with her head on backward as she tried to steal the essence of a newborn child.

As a child I heard this prayer many times from my sweet Ese, for a royal prince whose mother is only a lesser wife is always in danger. The Great Wife of Pharaoh can never be sure of any claim for her own son as long as other princes live. Princes who spring from the wombs of lesser wives were competitors for the throne. Their families and allies at the Royal Court could be ruthless. It was no secret that accidents and strange illness claimed the lives of many lesser princes. The Garden of Seclusion, the harem where the lesser wives and their princelings lived, was a cesspit of intrigue and murder. It was here that I spent the next few years of my life.

# Three

I was born during the feast of Amun-Ra, the largest and most sacred celebration in all Egypt. The feast marked the beginning of the new year and lasted twenty-four days. Pharaoh officiated at the celebration as Chief Priest of the Temple at Karnak and so it was more than a week after my birth before my father saw me.

"He looks a strong boy," my father said to Ese. I nestled next to my mother's body as she lay in the large bed. The great Thutmose, Pharaoh and Protector of Egypt, sat next to the bed holding my mother's hand.

Ese smiled.

"He is the son of a god, Oh Pharaoh, like his father. And like his father one day he will lead Egypt."

My father said nothing. He knew that many would think this child nothing more than the result of a night's pleasure with one of his lesser wives. The choice of kings was governed by more serious things than the wishes of women, and my father knew a hundred troubles had to be suffered before an heir to the throne could be chosen. Still I was his son, and his face seemed pleased whenever he looked at me.

"The boy has the nose of a Thutmose," Pharaoh laughed. "There is no doubting that nose!"

In a country that regarded thin noses as beautiful both my father and grandfather, the great Thutmose I, were cursed with wide hooked noses of great size. Pharaoh laughed again.

"It is a nose like the strong beak of the Horus!"

My father rose and walked toward the archway that opened on to the balcony. He stood there outlined in the rays of the sun that filtered through the linen curtain hung in the doorway letting the gentle breeze that accompanied the end of the day wash over his bare chest. The sun cast its rays around him and outlined his body in gold. He wore the short linen kilt common to men of all stations in Egypt. His feet were wrapped in leather sandals whose sides were almost high enough to form a military boot. The Pharaohs had the names and likenesses of Egypt's enemies painted on the soles of their sandals so that when they walked they ground the enemies of *Kemit* into the dust and were reminded of their duty to keep the nation safe.

From a heavy gold chain around Pharaoh's neck hung the great pectoral made of rare electrum and inlaid lapis lazuli. The pectoral was cast in the shape of the *Rekhyt*, the lapwing bird that was the most ancient symbol of the people of Egypt. The lapis lazuli was a deep blue, the color of the Pharaohs and of the stars. It is the color of Amun-Ra whose name means The Hidden One and who is the most powerful god in Egypt. My father wore the *Nemset*, the light crown of starched and folded linen whose stiffened ends tied at the nape of his neck. A gold band held the crown to his head. In the middle of the band shone the mighty *Uraeus*, symbol of the power of the God-King. The gold Cobra with red garnet eyes stood erect and coiled to strike the enemies of Pharaoh and Egypt. It was the ancient royal symbol of the snake goddess of lower Egypt. Of all the gods only Horus and Seth wore the fire-spitting snake on their foreheads. All who gazed upon the *Uraeus* knew fear and the power over life and death that Pharaoh wielded over his subjects and his enemies.

Great Pharaoh walked back toward the bed and bent over to kiss my mother on her forehead. In the mind of a child it was only a bright object, red and gold, and gleaming in the dying sunlight that washed the room in a deep yellow glow. Still, of all the things to be seen it was the cobra that held my gaze. As my father leaned over my mother his eyes looking only at her the great jewel came within reach. My tiny hand reached for it and I took it in my grasp, little fingers holding it tight. Pharaoh raised his head slowly to free the jewel. I wouldn't let go. Gently my father forced my hand from the gold cobra with the garnet eyes. He stood straight as a spear and seemed to me in that instant a giant. "So, little one, already you reach for the symbols of power." His voice was serious. "Do you think that is all that is needed to become Pharaoh and protect this land of *Kemit?*" The Great One sighed. "You have already learned that power must be seized. Perhaps one day you will also learn that it must be used ruthlessly to keep it." My father's eyes fell on Ese.

"So you think this is my heir?" he asked.

My mother's eyes went cold as black obsidian.

"He is your son, Pharaoh. Your blood flows in him as your spirit dwells in him. He is Thutmose, Menkepper-Re, and a true son of Horus like you."

She went silent, but her eyes never left Pharaoh's face. And then she spoke with a determination whose source only she knew.

"And one day he will be Pharaoh."

My father looked at Ese but said nothing. He shrugged his shoulders. I felt a gentle hand run over my face. When I opened my eyes Pharaoh was gone. Outside the sun had almost set. I was hungry and turned my face toward Ese in search of her breast. Her hand opened her soft linen gown and guided my mouth to her. I found her nipple and felt the warm sweet liquid flow into my mouth. In a few minutes I had drunk my fill and fell fast asleep.

I felt my mother's body move and was awakened from my sleep. She lifted me into her arms and carried me across the room to my crib and lay me down among the soft linen pillows. Webkhet stood next to the crib. Webkhet had been my mother's nurse when she was a child and served her still. Her hair was gray and thinning and her skin wrinkled. But the fire of a fierce loyalty still burned in her eyes marking danger to anyone who tried to harm her little girl.

"You must make haste Ese. Chancellor Paremheb waits outside. He comes on the instructions of Pharaoh. Hurry, girl! You cannot keep him waiting much longer. Get dressed!"

The old woman shook her head as Ese scurried around the room searching for her best robe. At last she settled behind her dressing table and applied her cosmetics. Her black eyes gleamed like polished gems against the background of the green malachite eye shadow. The red ocher applied to her lips made her mouth look like a juicy ripe fruit. One last glance in the polished copper hand mirror, a slight smile of satisfaction, and my mother was ready.

"Show the Chancellor in, Webkhet."

Webkhet opened the door and a large man walked through it. Paremheb was huge by Egyptian standards. In a country where most men were slightly over five feet the Chancellor stood fully six feet tall. His broad shoulders tapered to a narrow waist and his strong legs revealed the legacy of the rigorous marches of the former soldier that he was. He wore the long robe of a high government official and carried the *Sechem*, a short stick inlaid with gold that was the symbol of his office. He moved easily for such a large man and there was nothing threatening in his manner when he spoke.

"May Amun smile upon you gracious queen and your new son." He smiled. My mother nodded and returned the smile.

"I am here at the behest of Pharaoh who, I might say, is very much pleased with your gift of a son for him." He paused. "May I see the boy, my queen?"

My mother nodded and Paremheb walked to my crib and looked down upon me. The Chancellor turned back to my mother.

"Pharaoh commands that you and the boy be with him at the celebration of Amun in a week's time."

My mother's eyes betrayed no emotion even as she noticed the smile on Webkhet's face who sat quietly in the corner.

"For what reason does Pharaoh wish me and his son to attend the Feast of Amun? I am not yet long from being on the birthing bricks. My body not yet healed."

Paremheb spoke.

"It is my understanding that Pharaoh wishes to present his new son to the people of Egypt so that they may share his joy and know that the land of *Kemit* is truly fruitful of his seed. What better time to announce the birth of a son than at the Feast of Amun, the Hidden One who has brought prosperity to Egypt." Paremheb paused. "It is Pharaoh's command, my lady."

Only the tightening of the corners of my mother's eyes revealed her excitement. Webkhet was proud that her little girl had learned the ways of the powerful in hiding her true emotions and intentions.

"You may tell Pharaoh I am grateful for the privilege of once again being in his noble presence. And thank you, Chancellor, for your kindness."

Webkhet pressed her back firmly against the door that she closed behind the Chancellor and looked at my mother.

"Well my little girl what are we to do now?"

# Four

Paremheb escorted us to our place in Pharaoh's entourage. The royal court was assembled on a raised platform set on the riverbank next to the stone quay that lay at the end of the long colonnade connecting the Nile to the Temple of Amun and Mut at Luxor. Luxor was the dwelling place of Mut, Great Wife of Amun, who awaited the arrival of her husband as he travelled from his own Great House at Karnak three miles away. It was the feast of *Opet*, the beginning of the new year, and the whole population of Thebes gathered along the riverbank from Luxor to Karnak to watch the great procession of Amun and his truly begotten son, Pharaoh. For twenty-four days the people of Egypt drank, danced, and celebrated the renewal of the earth that the annual flood brings to their land and gave thanks to Amun and his son for protecting Egypt.

My mother cradled me in her arms and arranged my blanket to shade my face from the morning sun. It was late morning and already hot. A linen canopy over the platform protected the guests from the rays of the sun but many of the men and women had already placed the small cones of perfumed oil and beeswax on their heads. The heat melted the wax permitting the oil and perfume to run over their faces refreshing them and protecting their heads from the burning rays. We sat next to the Chancellor who seemed in a good mood and my mother did not question the presence of the armed bodyguard that stood behind us.

Ese was a lesser wife and had experienced the court and so was somewhat accustomed to the ceremony that accompanied Pharaoh. But she was still only a young girl and the grandeur of the ceremony of *Opet* was beyond her experience.

"Tell me, Chancellor, when is Pharaoh to arrive?"

The Chancellor cast his eyes in the direction of the road that ran along the river for three miles and connected the temple of Luxor with the complex at Karnak.

"The Great One is now at Karnak where he witnesses the removal of the statue of Amun from his golden shrine by the priests of the temple sanctuary. He will lead the great procession of the priests from the temple to the boat that will carry the Hidden One here to the quay at Luxor." He paused to look around as if to make certain all was in order.

"The boat itself is a beautiful thing, fully forty feet long and made from cedar timbers that come from the mountains of Lebanon. The holy barque is covered in gold so that it glows like the sun itself moving across the heavens. In the center of its deck is a shrine made of the most precious woods of fruit trees. The statue of the Hidden One is placed inside to ensure his comfort for the journey. The Golden Boat is towed by a royal flagship manned by high government officials who must see to its safe arrival under pain of death. Had I not more important matters to attend to today I, too, would be riding in the flagship as I have done so many times before."

Old Webkhet would have caught the meaning of Paremheb's words were she with us that day but it did not cross my mother's mind to wonder what work could have been so important to take

Paremheb away from Pharaoh's side on the most holy feast day of the year.

"Once Pharaoh has placed his father aboard the Golden Boat the shrine is closed and the priests assemble around it offering prayers to the Great God as he journeys on the river. Gangs of sailors pull the thick ropes attached to the flagship towing the great barge along the riverbank to complete the three mile journey. The barge floats among the hundreds of boats of the wealthy that accompany it to Luxor."

My mother seemed not to be paying attention. "Is there some water to cool my son," she asked. Paremheb nodded and motioned to a soldier. In a few seconds the soldier brought an earthen jug of cool water and placed it at my mother's feet. She dipped a cloth into the water and wiped my face. Wetting the cloth again she placed it on my forehead. She turned her attention to the Chancellor.

"Will Pharaoh join us soon," she asked.

"Look," he said standing and pointing up the road. "The Lion of Egypt comes!"

A great roar arose from the crowd lining the sacred road and the guests on the platform stood to catch a glimpse of the Lion of Egypt as his procession moved toward the quay. Beyond the crowd one could see the Golden Boat carrying the Hidden One on the river as it awaited its time to dock.

My mother stood with me in her arms trying to see the great procession. Pharaoh was dressed in a long white robe with golden sandals on his feet. The Keepers of the Person had done their task well. His face was white with powder. The red ocher on his lips made them seem larger than they really were and the black galena around his eyes made them look like they were on fire. He wore the red and white double crown of Upper and Lower Egypt, symbol of the unification of the two countries by Narmer almost two thousand years before. The false black beard tied up with a strap, the symbol of his maleness, stood almost straight out from his chin. His arms were crossed in front of him and in his hands he carried the crook and the flail, ancient symbols of royal justice and power.

My mother shifted position to see better. She could see him clearly now, this man whom she knew in a way that few others in Egypt did or ever would. A man she had seen made soft by passion and affection, a man who moved and shuddered as any other when he had finally possessed her. And yet as he was carried high above the crowd in the golden sedan chair on the shoulders of eight bearers arrayed in his robes of office he looked like no other man on earth. He looked like the Son of God that he was.

The procession drew closer to the quay. The fan bearers quickened their pace to cool the great king. Alongside the royal bodyguard pushed the crowd back to clear his way. To the front a hundred chariots accompanied by running infantry guards—The King's Braves—moved at a steady pace to keep the crowd at bay. On each side of Pharaoh's chair strode two tame lions held in check by their trainers who kept the thick bronze chains around the animal's necks tightly in their hands. The procession halted at the foot of the quay. The chair bearers lowered their sacred burden and the Lion of Egypt stepped onto the stone stairway that slopped downward and disappeared under the waters of the Nile.

The Golden Boat cast itself loose from its flagship and the sailors pulled hard on its lines until the vessel glided slowly to the quay and slipped sideways alongside the pier. At once the priests took their places around the shrine that held the holy statue. The Chief Priest bowed before it and reached inside to extract the painted wooden likeness of the Hidden One. Amun, great god head of imperial Egypt, had once been only a local god of Thebes. He was the god of the Theban princes and it was they who drove the hated Hyksos invaders from the land of *Kemit* fifty years before and who liberated Egypt from the Delta to the border of Nubia. The armies of Thebes conquered in the name of their city god and with their success came the ascendence of Amun as chief god of all *Kemit*. With every victory the kings of Thebes—the great Ahmose, Amenhotep, and Thutmose I—visited rich spoils upon the temple of Amun at Karnak until a great complex of buildings began to arise on the spot dedicated to the worship of Amun. Amun's priests believed that Thebes was the site of creation and that Amun had begotten himself from an egg on this very ground. We Egyptians called Karnak the *Ipet Isut*, the "Most Select Of Places." As my father stood in his god-like form on the Nile quay he did so to receive Amun himself who had come to visit his wife Mut in her dwelling place in the temple of Luxor.

Pharaoh climbed the steps and set himself upon the throne that had been prepared for him on the platform. His back was to me and my mother. Behind and to his left sat Pharaoh's Great Wife. Behind her arranged in the places of honor were the king's advisors, all except Paremheb who sat still further back with me and my mother. Below the Chief Priest led the procession carrying the statue of Amun up the steps. Directly in front of the throne the procession stopped and faced Pharaoh. My father resplendent in countenance and power rose from his golden chair. He placed the crook at his side and carried the flail in his right hand.

"Hear me, oh Amun, for I speak in the name of your children, the people of *Rekhet*. We are grateful for your gift of the Nile and for your strength that has permitted us to drive our enemies from the land of your temple. We honor you for without you we do not live." A great roar went up from the crowd. My father raised his hands. "We thank you for all your gifts and especially for the gift of my son!"

Paremheb rose, took my mother by the arm, and bid her rise from her seat. A few steps and she was standing in the presence of the Great Lion. Pharaoh looked magnificent and power flowed from him like glinting sunlight.

"Give him the child my lady," Paremheb whispered.

I could feel a trembling run through my mother's body as she held me before the god-king not knowing what to do. Her eyes moved from mine to those of the man who had created this child in her and decided that he meant no harm to the fruit of his own body. She raised me to him.

"Go, my son. Return to the father who made you."

And with this she smiled at her king.

Thutmose took me into his powerful arms and arranged my blanket so that he could see my face. His white face and high crown of red and white made him seem a fierce creature, truly the protector of all Egypt. He turned to the crowd and the priestly procession below.

"Behold, Oh Amun! Behold, Oh people of Egypt. Here is my son who was sent to me to serve the gods of *Kemit*. It is to Amun that I consecrate him this day. Smile upon him great Amun. Grant him your protection and make of him a servant of Egypt."

The noise from the crowd shook the mountains of the Valley of Kings across the Nile and the mountains sent the noise back again to its source and it washed over the multitude on the riverbank as a great wind. Amid great rejoicing and music the procession moved up the steps and toward the temple while my father sat upon his throne watching the priests of Karnak pass before him. His Great Wife, Queen Hatshepsut, was crimson with anger as she did her best to contain her murderous rage.

# Five

My public anointing as a royal prince was an important event and its significance was not lost on Webkhet who had learned the news even before we arrived back at the House of the Secluded after the ceremony. Not even the soldiers that accompanied my mother and me and the Chancellor served to put my mother on her guard. She was too happy to be wary, and it fell to the old crone to bring her to her senses. But my mother would not let her old nurse speak.

"Quiet! You old hen."

She laughed.

"It was wonderful. My son held in Pharaoh's hands and presented to the people of Egypt. Oh Webkhet, you should have seen how noble the little one was. He didn't cry or wriggle. The boy behaved like the son of a king that he is. You should be proud of us both, Webkhet. Your little girl has given birth to the next Pharaoh of Egypt."

Webkhet waved her hand in annoyance. "If he lives!"

My mother's smile vanished and her eyes flashed in anger. Before she could utter a word the old woman's hand moved faster than a coiled snake and struck Ese across the face with a loud slap.

"Come to your senses, girl! Are you without guile! Your son is in great danger. The boy is the son of a lesser wife. Do you think that Pharaoh's Great Wife, the Consort of the God, is going to stand by and watch her claim to power and the throne be taken from her?"

The old lady was shouting and out of breath.

"The queen is now your mortal enemy. Everyone who depends on her favor for wealth and office is your enemy. The next Pharaoh your son my be. But he will have to live long enough to claim his legacy!"

Paremheb was standing by the door listening. He had accompanied us from the celebration and had just finished giving the bodyguard its instructions. He took a deep breath and walked toward my mother who leaned over my crib sobbing. The Chancellor laid his hand on her shoulder and gently guided her to a chair. He motioned to Webkhet to bring him a chair and sat down opposite Ese. He spoke gently, but with a firmness that made it clear that what he had to say was important.

"My lady, your old bag of a nurse is right. You and the boy are in danger and that danger will not pass until the boy has grown to full measure and has been anointed by Pharaoh as his heir."

My mother wiped the tears from her eyes. She felt comforted by this strong man whose voice offered protection for her son.

"He will be Pharaoh's heir, then? Has he told you that is what he wishes?"

"I do not know my gracious queen. I am the king's Chancellor and he trusts me in many things. But in this matter he tells me only what he wishes me to know. The public announcement of his new son at the Feast of *Opet* surely had a kingly purpose. But, my lady, I truly do not know."

Webkhet grunted.

"Perhaps Pharaoh wishes to discover those who love his Great Wife more than him," Webkhet snapped. "He has been king for nine years and Queen Hatshepsut has produced only a daughter. The sacred line of the dynasty is in danger without an heir. If there is no son power falls to the queen who many say is already too powerful in the affairs of Egypt. To announce the existence of a son forces the powerful in the court to take sides. Then Pharoah will know where the treachery lies."

A tight smirk crossed Paremheb's face. The old women was a master of suspicion. Years of living around the nobility had taught her well. After a while servants become invisible and even the powerful loose their natural caution in their presence. This old woman had learned much from the loose tongues of her masters.

"My lady," Paremheb continued, "your nurse speaks the truth. The dynasty is in danger. There are terrible times to come, times in which your son's life will be in danger too. If the Great Queen produces no son in the next few years and the sickness that afflicts Pharaoh takes its toll, then only your son stands between the Great Queen and her supporters and the power they have. And then…"

Paremheb's voice trailed off.

My mother began to cry again. Webkhet took her in her arms to comfort her. The noise of conversation kept me awake in my crib and the sound of my mother's sobbing upset me. For some reason I did not cry. I lay there wide awake not knowing the meaning of the words that fell upon my ears.

"You speak of Pharaoh's sickness. What do you mean?" my mother asked.

"It is true, my lady. The priests are at a loss to explain it. All the sacred texts have been consulted and all manner of prayers have been offered. Nothing has made the sickness depart."

There was genuine concern in my mother's voice.

"What manner of sickness is it?"

Paremheb's voice struck a serious tone.

"Without warning his eyes roll and his tongue grows thick. His body shakes as a tree in a storm and he falls to the ground writhing as if in great pain. His advisors have been ordered to carry a small piece of wood on their persons at all times that they may place it in the king's mouth when the sickness is upon him so that he does not swallow his tongue or chew it off. When the madness passes, he falls into a deep slumber from which he cannot be awakened for many hours. When he awakens he remembers nothing."

My mother looked at Webkhet who wore an expression of worry upon her face. For a moment she wondered how much longer she would be around to care for the young woman that she had known since birth. She dismissed the thought. There would be enough time for that later. Right now it was important that her mistress understand the difficulty she was facing. Webkhet spoke to Paremheb.

"Your excellency," she began. "My mistress does not seem to understand the danger that she and her son must deal with. Perhaps if you could explain to her what part her son plays in this whole question of succession she would see her situation more clearly."

The Chancellor shifted his weight in the chair and turned his eyes toward my mother.

"Gracious Queen to understand why your son is in such danger you must understand the history of this great dynasty, the eighteenth in the history of the Land of Kemit."

From my crib I could hear Paremheb's voice change its tone as he began to tell the story of the warrior pharaohs of Thebes.

"This great land of Egypt was forged in the fire of battle more than two thousand years ago when Narmer, a prince of Upper Egypt, conquered the land of Lower Egypt and made our land one country under one king. For hundreds of years Egypt's greatness grew. The land of *Kemit* was protected by the great deserts on either side of the Nile. The Great Green to our north served as a watery barrier since none of the other peoples of the earth had yet learned to sail upon it. To the south, below Aswan, lay the land of Nub, or Nubia, the Land of Gold. Egyptian might kept the primitive peoples of Nubia in check so they could not threaten our nation. The gods saw fit to place Egypt on this earth where she was free from threats by other peoples. For two thousand years Egypt lay safe behind these natural barriers.

"And then two hundred years ago this land of our fathers fell prey to mortal danger. Far to the east in a land that was unknown to the Egyptians a warrior people fell upon our land the way a wolf falls upon sheep. Great Egypt was humbled and crushed under the heels of this strange people whom we called the Hyksos. They conquered all Egypt from the Delta to beyond our ancient capital of Memphis of the White Walls. The noble princes of Egypt were slain and their families reduced to slavery. The invaders established their capital at Avaris in the Delta and noble Egypt fell under the lash of the foreigner for more than three generations.

"Only the land from Thebes to Elephantine was not chained by the vile Asiatics. But seeing Egypt weakened by the foreigners, the Nubians overthrew their rightful Egyptian masters and regained the forts along the First Cataract of the Nile from which they threatened the Black Land. Only the warrior princes of Thebes and their patron, the god Amun-Ra, escaped the yoke of the Asiatics and the Negroes. A curse settled over the land of Egypt and its people."

From my crib I heard my mother's voice as she asked Webkhet to bring some refreshments. The sound of Paremheb's voice stopped as the old woman muttered aloud to herself in annoyance while she brought water, beer and date cakes to Ese and the Chancellor. The old woman shuffled back to her chair and sat down with a loud grunt. All was still in the room for a short time. Then Paremheb's voice again fell upon my ears.

"Seventy years ago a great warrior prince arose in Thebes with the blessing of Amun. His name was Sequenenre The Brave. He trained an army with new weapons and attacked the Hyksos. His first born, Kahmose, fought at his side. The war raged for three years and Sequenenre was killed. His son carried the fight along the Nile striking into the Delta and laying siege to the Hyksos capital. In his turn Kahmose was killed in battle so his younger brother, Ahmose The Liberator, took up the fight. The Egyptian people rose up in a mighty wrath, and Ahmose drove the vile Hyksos back across the Wall of Princes in the Sinai and destroyed their fortress at Sharuhen. At last this land of Egypt, the very place of man's creation, was again free. From that time it has been ruled by a strong line of warrior kings that knew how to govern and to fight.

"Ahmose was succeeded by his son Amenhotep who was called "The Bull Who Conquers." Under his rule Nubia was brought back to Egyptian control and the fortifications in the Sinai were rebuilt to guard against the Hyksos returning. Amenhotep reigned for twenty-five years, and during that time the government was reorganized. The local nobilities of Egypt's provinces were weakened so they could never again challenge the power of Pharaoh who governs all the land of Egypt. The militias controlled by these barons were disbanded and a national army loyal only to Pharaoh was created and given the task of protecting the country. The irrigation system was taken over by government officials and operated on a national basis so that all received a fair share of the precious water that is Egypt's lifeblood. Amenhotep installed the system of measuring the Nile flood and using it as the means for predicting the tax rate for the coming year. This great king first raised the cult of Amun to national status and bestowed upon the priesthood the spoils of his victories so that the construction of the great Temple at Karnak could begin.

"But Amenhotep had no son, and the bloodline of the greatest dynasty in Egyptian history was imperiled. In Egypt the succession of royal blood runs to the oldest son of Pharaoh's Great Wife. If the Great Wife has only daughters, they carry the true bloodline. Whomever Pharaoh chooses to be king must marry that daughter to keep the bloodline pure and unbroken. When Pharaoh chooses a son who is born of a lesser wife to succeed him, the boy must marry Pharaoh's daughter. In the past some Pharaohs even married their own daughters to keep the bloodline true. This custom is greatly misunderstood among other peoples who regard marriages with relatives as unclean. But of such barbarians nothing is to be expected.

"The Warrior Pharaohs of Egypt have always been mindful of having strong men succeed them. They also knew that their own sons were not always the best of men. The great dynasty of Ahmose was forged in war and the Theban kings were most concerned that he who led Egypt be a brave and competent man of arms. Near the end of his life Amenhotep chose a soldier to succeed him as Pharaoh. This man, Thutmose I, was a proven general and a distant cousin of the king so some royal blood coursed through his veins. To legitimize his rule Thutmose married Ahmes, the sister of Amenhotep. Thutmose became one of the greatest protectors of all Egypt.

"He first turned his armies on the wretched troglodytes of Nubia and brought them to heel. Raging as a panther, he struck at the king of the Nubians and destroyed his armies. He brought the king back to Thebes hanging him head down from the royal barge as it sailed the waters of the Nile. Thutmose turned his vengeance next on the vile Asiatic peoples who preyed on Egyptian merchants in the Lebanon and along the Orontes River. With a mighty army he marched through the land of the Rettenu and attacked the people of the Mitanni at the Great Bend of the Euphrates laying waste their villages and leaving behind a great stone pillar on which he inscribed a warning to the vile Asiatics that he would come again if they did not learn how to behave. Thutmose was a benefactor of the temples of Amun at Karnak. It was he who built the first temple to Montu, the Theban god of war, there. To protect his body after his death, Thutmose was the first Pharaoh buried in a tomb carved into the solid rock of the Valley of the Kings. The location of the tomb was carefully hidden by Ineni the architect who built it and who wished that is master's body sleep undisturbed forever in his House of A Million Years.

"The death of the Great Thutmose was a period of confusion for the royal dynasty. The king's two elder sons by his queen died before him leaving no heir. But Pharaoh produced another son by a lesser wife named Mutnofret, much as your son was sired by Pharaoh with you. The boy was called Thutmose, just as your son is named. To strengthen the boy's claim to the throne he was married to his half-sister, Hatshepsut, the daughter of Pharaoh and his queen. Hatshepsut is Pharaoh's Great Wife and sister. Should she be unable to produce a son, the line will pass to your son. And with that passage goes all the power and privilege she has obtained over these last nine years while she and Pharaoh have ruled Egypt."

Paremheb paused and looked deeply into my mother's eyes. In my crib I felt the silence.

"Gracious queen," he continued. "the Great Wife is not of a temperament to allow anyone to challenge her hold on the power she wields. With the public presentation of your son to Amun-Ra, he now stands between the Great Wife and all she values."

Paremheb sighed deeply, a trace of despair in his voice.

"My lady, you and your son live under the clouds of a gathering storm whose winds might sweep all before it, including your lives."

# Six

I spent the first five years of my life in the care of my mother and Webkhet. Egyptian children, even the son of Pharaoh, are left in the care of their mothers until they are five years old at which time their formal education begins under the direction of their father. In more usual circumstances I would have had my own nurse to look after me. But Webkhet would not hear of it. The old crone had transferred the deep loyalty she felt for my mother to me and would tolerate no interference from anyone in directing my young life. I came to love her very much. When, at last, her time came to sleep with the gods in the Fields of Marshes, it was an occasion of great sorrow for me.

Life in the Garden of the Secluded was pleasant and I remember those years with fondness and joy. Egypt's weather is hot and unless there was some good reason why children had to be dressed, they usually went about naked, boys and girls together without clothes. I sometimes think that it is our experience as naked children that gives we Egyptians our open attitude about sexual matters. No country seems to have so many sexual jokes or different words for sex. The public monuments are covered with sexual graffiti and Egyptians are great collectors of phallic symbols and pornographic art. Large sums are paid for aphrodisiacs.

Lettuce grown in special gardens is widely believed to loosen the inhibitions of women, and the perfumed smell of the Blue Lotus is said to be the best aphrodisiac in all creation.

The Garden of the Secluded is where Pharaoh kept his lesser wives and concubines. It is a world of women in which personal jealousies and dynastic ambitions for their offspring can lead to murder and maiming. More than one of the concubines had hot oil thrown in her face by a rival to diminish her beauty. Still others were poisoned. The struggle for Pharaoh's favor is vicious. Denied the ability to appeal to him directly, women turned their anger, frustration, and jealously upon one another often with deadly results.

Their allies in this incessant maneuvering for favor are the eunuchs who serve the women and tend to the daily affairs of the harem. Castrated men are naturally denied normal outlets for their frustrations and can become enthusiastic participants in the conspiracies of their female masters. Castration in Egypt is more complete than in other countries. Among the Retjennu and the Mitanni it is common to cut off only the testicles leaving the penis intact. To Egyptian thinking this is a job half done. After all, even if you take away a man's bow, he can still stab you with an arrow! Egyptian eunuchs have their testicles and their penis removed leaving only a stump with a hole in it through which the eunuch can urinate. The penis is cut so close to the body that it has no length and cannot be held when urinating. To the Egyptian mind this makes the eunuch more like the female in that he, too, must sit down to piss! It is no wonder that an angry eunuch can be truly dangerous.

I was too young to appreciate the dangers of the Garden. To this day I remember it as a place of beauty where my every whim was catered too. I was still a child and a prince of royal blood. The harem was located in a beautiful villa within the palace enclosure. Like everything else in Egypt except monuments and tombs, the building was constructed of sun-dried mud brick mixed with straw to give it strength. I often marvel at what we Egyptians are able to do with this building material. It suffices for a country that knows no rain. A single rainstorm such as I encountered in the mountains of Lebanon as a soldier could wash away whole buildings in Egypt. Perhaps that is why we build our monuments and tombs of granite. For a people obsessed with resurrection, it is only natural to worry about how long our legacies endure once we are gone from this life.

My playground was the large sprawling villa that housed the quarters of the lesser wives and concubines. The huge house was built upon a raised flat platform approached by steps and ramps. The inside centered about a large common living room with vaulted columns of palm logs running around the outside walls holding up the second floor. Above it similar columns supported yet another story. I often played with my friends in this great room. Sometimes I lay on my back looking up at the high vaulted ceilings watching the light stream through the clerestory windows high up in the eves. Sometimes a breeze moved a window curtain and the light played like a waterfall upon the room below. I lay naked upon the cool stone floor watching the light perform its colorful dance for no one but me while the cool air fell upon my body as a gentle linen handkerchief soothes the soreness of a sunburnt face. It was a delightful time for me.

We Egyptians love color. Perhaps this is to be expected in a land only a few miles wide surrounded by harsh deserts where all color is absent. We cannot get enough of it. We paint our bodies, our hair, and, naturally enough, our homes with it. We Egyptians believe that colors are manifestations of the essences of things, and colors have great meaning for us. Blue, the color of eternity and the gods, is our most valued for it brings serenity. Yellow, the color we always paint a woman's skin, brings comfort and warmth. Red is the color of Seth, of aggression, hatred, and death.

Only the embalmers wear robes of red. It seems natural that we color our walls with different hues as a way to capture the essence of what we are trying to recreate upon them. The walls of the Garden are completely covered in brightly colored paintings depicting all kinds of scenes from our life in Egypt. Hunting scenes are a favorite, as are large murals of the different kinds of animals that inhabit the Black Land. Many rooms are painted with scenes of swamps, the original gardens from which all life sprang forth upon the earth. We love our Nile that gives us life. Water is life to us and we can never be very far away from it without dying. So in our houses we paint pictures of watery life to remind us of how fragile our lives are, of how dependent we are upon this gift of the gods.

The villa stands within a walled compound connected to the palace by a single walkway that ends at a large door. The door is kept locked and guarded by two eunuchs—the Keepers of the Keys—who pledge their lives to keep the Garden safe from the sin of infidelity. The villa is surrounded by a formal garden thick with fruit trees. There are the usual fig trees and date palms, trees native to the Black Land and as old as Egypt itself. With the renewal of Egyptian imperial power by the Theban princes, Egypt has taken to itself from other lands new kinds of fruit. Now the gardens of Egyptian villas overflow with heretofore unknown wonders. Apple trees, plums, and pomegranates, even the incense bushes from Punt thrive here, providing Egyptians with a regular source of spice whose sweet odor we call "the sweat of the gods." The pathways that wind mysteriously through the formal gardens served the active imagination of my childhood. Many times I hid among the shadows waiting to attack a monstrous beast or human enemy as it wandered unaware into my ambush.

Of all the wonders of the Garden one of the most pleasant was the Sacred Lake. Placed at the far eastern end of the formal garden, the direction from which Horus rose on the sun every morning, the large T-shaped pool of water represents the original site of creation, the watery lake from which the sacred mound arose upon which Horus first alighted on a papyrus reed to begin the circle of life. At one end stands a small shrine where prayers and sacrifices are offered. I often waited there while Webkhet prayed to the gods for special favors. Sometimes she prayed for misfortune to befall her enemies! Every temple in Egypt has a Sacred Lake where the priests purify themselves by bathing in its waters before offering sacrifice.

In the Garden of the Secluded the watery pool is filled with plants and flowers. The Red Lotus, called "the blossom that came into existence at the beginning," is thought of as a symbol of long life. The waterlilies are magical. At evening they shut their petals tightly and retreat deep into the water so that they cannot be reached from shore. At dawn they are reborn and open their petals to catch the life of the morning sun striving upwards toward the light. Most beautiful of all is the Blue Lotus. The sweet sweaty smell of this magical flower filled my senses the first time I encountered it. It is a powerful odor that women regard as magical, and a sweet perfume is made from its blossoms. This flower also gave a blue dye that Egyptian women used to color the nipples of their breasts. Later, when I was a young man and aroused by women, I learned that the sweet sweaty smell of the Blue Lotus could be found again in the place between a woman's legs, a place I went often as a young man, although I cannot say in truth that it was the beauty of the Blue Lotus that always brought me there!

Egypt is a land of many wonders and in the Sacred Lake dwells a special fish. This is curious, for the priests and the nobles hold fish to be unclean and do not eat it. The priests regard fish so because it was an accomplice of Seth. When this angry god killed his brother, Osiris, he chopped his body into fourteen parts and scattered them in secret places upon the earth. Seth took his brother's phallus and fed it to the great Nile carp who swallowed it whole. But need usually wins out over religion so the common people eat fish. For some, the swamp people of the Delta, it is what they mostly eat. In the waters of the Sacred Lake dwells a sacred fish. We call it "the fish who gives rebirth." When this fish has young it spends several days protecting them until they can live on their own. If other fish come to eat them the young rush into the mother's mouth as if she is consuming them. Once the danger is passed the young are spit out and reborn into this world. This wonder is widely known. So much so that when a person lives at the favor of Pharaoh we say that "he lives in Pharaoh's mouth." It was my mother who taught me of this sacred fish and who warned that a great Pharaoh must also learn to spit when the time came.

For a young boy the most interesting place was the menagerie. Many wealthy families kept collections of wild animals on their estates. But the menagerie in the Garden was Pharaoh's personal zoo and he visited it often. His favorite were the two trained lions that accompanied him at formal occasions. In the thinking of Egyptians the lion is a solar animal, an animal associated with the gods. The new dynasty of Theban princes raised the lion to even greater heights, and it is regarded as an earthly manifestation of the sun god, Ra. The new Theban war god, *Sekhmet*, appears in the form of a lion as well. Only Pharaoh is allowed to hunt and kill the lion and no one else is permitted to keep one in captivity. From the beginning I was fascinated by the great cats and went to the menagerie whenever I could to see them.

The menagerie also held leopards, hyenas, gazelles, ibex, hares, and porcupines, all native to Egypt. From the land of the Retjennu and the Mitanni came the bear. From the incense countries near Punt came the baboon with its flashing teeth and the giraffe with its neck like a great tower. From Nubia we obtained sleek black panthers. The rarest of strange creatures, Negro pygmies, came also from Nubia. The pygmies were hunted and trapped in lands far to the south of Nubia itself, a place called the Pillars of the Earth where the end of creation can be seen. We Egyptians have a strange fascination for dwarfs of all kinds, and little people trained to sing or play musical instruments are common among the wealthy as pets. Black pygmy dwarfs are the most desirable and great sums change hands whenever they are bought and sold. They are strange beings these pygmies. It is their custom to wear a large hollow wooden penis strapped around their waist. The top of the wooden phallus pulls off and provides a vessel in which the pygmy carries his personal possessions and sacred items. The older the pygmy, the larger the penis until it becomes so large that its owner cannot walk unless the phallus is held with a string around the dwarf's shoulder to keep the thing erect and off the ground! It is a strange sight indeed and it sets Egyptians to shaking with laughter.

The pygmies were of interest to me on my visits since they were the only fully grown humans that were my size. They were not kept in cages like the other animals but generally allowed the run of the place. Control of the menagerie was in the hands of an obese eunuch named Nembet who was as merciless as the power of stone to crush flesh. His tongue had been partially cut as punishment for his part in some long forgotten harem conspiracy so that his speech, like a crushed and crippled leg, never knew when it would stumble. His eyes were yellow and the surrounding fat forced them partially shut giving his face a permanent squint. His body was soft and round like a rotten mellon and it wreaked of the odor of sweat. He was a pantomime of human ugliness, as evil as the nose of your enemy. One look at Nembet was to know the truth of the old proverb that one ought never to trust the son of a shit collector!

The Garden was my world and I was content within it. Like all children in Egypt I went barefoot. My head was shaved and oiled except for the long braided sidelock of black hair that hung down over the right side of my head. I wore few clothes. It was a time of great freedom and joy. Old men think of their childhood as "the time of the sidelock of youth," a pleasant time before the responsibilities of manhood required them to shave it off when a boy was twelve years old. I was unaware of any danger. My world was protected by my mother, Webkhet, and the military bodyguard that Pharaoh provided. But Paremheb's warning given so long ago was no longer loud in our ears. All of us had forgotten that to be Pharaoh's son in dangerous times was like sleeping with your hand on the belly of a lion.

# Seven

Iknew the old general better than I knew my own father. Of course when I first met him he was not yet an old general. He began as my guardian, then became my playmate and, finally, my friend. His name was Amenemhab and he was the captain of the bodyguard Paremheb assigned to protect me from the queen's ambition. Amenemhab was of that new breed of men in Thebes, men of common birth who had proven themselves fearless warriors and risen through the ranks by competence rather than birth and family connections. My guardian was just eighteen years old when he was awarded the rank of Captain of Fifty in the *Blood Of Isis* regiment, one of the elite units of the imperial army.

Amenemhab was the son of a farmer. He was conscripted into the army at the age of fifteen and assigned to an infantry company. He was a true son of the land and liked marching and living outdoors. Soon he was given command of a squad of men. His performance was noted by his superiors and again he was promoted in the ranks. It was the time of my father's campaign against the rebellious Nubians and Amenemhab's regiment was sent to the fight. One day his regiment came under attack and Amenemhab was wounded in his left eye. Blood poured from the wound, but the young soldier tore a strip of rag from his kilt stuffed it in his eye socket and ran back to the fight. He was like an enraged animal and lashed out with his *kopesh* sword killing the enemy one after another as a farmer cuts grain with a scythe. An enemy soldier rushed at Amenemhab striking him hard and forcing him to the ground knocking the *kopesh* from his hand. Amenemhab reacted with the instincts of a hunting animal and grabbed the enemy by the throat. Those who witnessed the fight said that he twisted the soldier's face up and pressed his head back to expose his throat. In a motion as quick as a hyena, Amenemhab struck and sunk his teeth into the soldier's neck. With his teeth stuck deep, Amenemhab shook his head from side to side like a panther shakes a hare trapped in its jaws. Blood spurted everywhere and turned the ground red. Still Amenemhab shook his prey until the soldier's body went limp and life vanished from his eyes.

In a single act of shocking violence Amenemhab's reputation was made known throughout the regiment. Soon the entire army knew of the episode and he was summoned to Pharaoh's field tent where his commander was forced to repeat the tale for Pharaoh and his officers. For his bravery Amenemhab was awarded the Golden Fly of Valor. The chain from which hung the fly cast of solid gold was placed around Amenemhab's neck by Pharaoh himself. Pharaoh assigned Amenemhab to his personal bodyguard until the Nubian campaign was finished. Back in Thebes he was reassigned to the *Blood of Isis* regiment. When Pharaoh needed a man of courage and loyalty to guard his son, he chose Amenemhab. Along with a bodyguard of hand-picked men of the same regiment, Amenemhab kept watch over me in the Garden of the Secluded for six years.

Whenever I saw him in the Garden I ran to him shouting, "Captain! Captain! Show me your eye!" He would stop and turn toward me. I rushed into his outstretched hands. In one smooth movement they grabbed me and raised me off the earth until I was staring the grizzled infantryman in the face.

"Show me the Eye of Horus!"

Amenemhab growled like an animal and raised the red colored eye patch that covered his wound. The socket of the eye was gnarled into a thick scar twisted from left to right. The skin around the scar was black like the tough mummified flesh of a cheaply prepared corpse. I poked the scar covered hole with my tiny finger pressing to find an opening. Whenever I did this Amenemhab roared.

"Now you have angered Horus with your probing. I will eat you like I ate the man who took my eye."

With this he pressed his face and jaws against my neck and pretended to shake me like a jackal shakes its kill. I screeched with delight half frightened that the bite might yet be real. Whenever Webkhet saw this she scolded the Captain. I learned then that even brave men have fears. Amenemhab's was Webkhet.

To a young boy Amenemhab looked like an old soldier even though he was not yet twenty. He was short and stocky and looked as difficult to move by force as the stump of a cedar tree. Thick powerful arms hung from muscular shoulders. It was said of him that no one in the army could wield the *kopesh* with greater power or deadly expertise. His hair was thick and black and he kept it closely cropped in the old style. Many military men favored the new Nubian style wigs with their rows of sausage curls and false waves. Such a device atop Amenemhab's head would have seemed ridiculous.

The skin on his face was older than the man's years, weathered thick and brown by exposure to the Egyptian sun. Already wrinkles appeared around his good eye. Unlike most Egyptian men, Amenemhab wore a full beard and moustache. Occasionally one saw a man with a thin trimmed moustache, but not very often.

The heat of the Egyptian climate made a full beard a dirty nuisance. Only Pharaoh was permitted to wear the long goatee as a symbol of his maleness. But even this was a false beard held in place by straps that tied up under the ears. Amenemhab's beard marked him immediately as different and earned him the nickname "the Asiatic." In the Egyptian experience only those people who lived far to the east beyond the Wall of Princes and the Sinai desert in the hills of Retjennu wore beards. For millenia we called these people Asiatics. Amenemhab covered his dead eye with a cloth patch dyed deep red, the color of Seth, the god who butchered his brother and scattered his mutilated corpse throughout the earth. The patch was held across the eye by a thin strip of leather that tied in the back of the head. The eye patch gave Amenemhab's face an evil look. When flushed with rage it must have been a terrible sight to those for whom it was the last thing they saw on this earth before being dispatched from this life by the work of Amenemhab's *kopesh*.

And yet I remember him as a gentle playmate, a man who always had time for the little boy who followed him around bothering him with childish questions. Perhaps he was kind to me because he loved my mother as the wily old Webkhet suspected. Maybe it was that the innocence of my childhood provided a soothing balm to a soul injured by battle and death. Whatever its source, the gentle side of Amenemhab was not revealed to many. He was to his depths a soldier, a natural fighter and slayer of men. And he could kill without mercy when circumstances called for it.

Amenemhab was with me that morning. The sun was not yet overhead and the Garden still rested in the shade offered like a cool gift by the fruit trees that provided it. I was sitting on a stone bench by the walkway waiting for Webkhet when I saw the old soldier.

"Captain! Captain!" I shouted. "Show me your eye!"

I ran toward Amenemhab with my arms outstretched expecting him to grab me and swing me over his head as he had done before.

"Not today my fine young prince," he said.

The momentum of my run carried me into his bare legs with a crash. Strong arms seized me and prevented any damage. I looked up and saw his large head and evil red eye patch staring down at me. His mouth widened in a smile.

"Not today, Thutmose. I have notice to report to my commander this day and I must make myself ready. Perhaps I am to be sent to another post." He paused. "So I cannot waste my time with the likes of you!" His voice betrayed affection, but it was lost in the mind of a little boy that could not have what he wanted.

"Take me to see the animals then!" I insisted. When Amenemhab did not respond I shouted, "I am a royal prince and you are a soldier! You have to do what I tell you!" There was defiance in my voice and its tone attracted Amenemhab's attention.

"Sometimes even royal princes cannot have what they want," he said. "And stop hanging your head like a pet monkey! You must learn to accept disappointment without anger. The disappointments of a Pharaoh are many. A Pharaoh cannot give in to anger and remain a good king." Amenemhab's voice trailed off. "You do want to be a good king someday don't you."

I looked at my friend, hung my head and said nothing. I was almost five and I wanted to go to the menagerie.

Amenemhab shrugged and was about to leave when he noticed the portly figure of the old crone barrelling down the pathway toward him.

"Oh shit" he said under his breath, "By the breath of Seth the old bag is upset."

Webkhet began shouting even before she reached us.

"There you are Thutmose! I have told you a hundred times not to wander off by yourself. I have been beside myself looking for you." The woman's toothless mouth moved angrily as she shouted in my face.

"I'm sorry," I muttered.

"And you!," she spat turning upon Amenemhab. "What are you doing here? Teaching him dirty habits again!"

Amenemhab looked at me and smiled. There was a mischievous gleam in his eye.

"I don't know what you mean," he said. "What dirty habits?"

Webkhet's eyes flashed.

"Don't pretend your innocence with me! Who else has been teaching Thutmose these oaths? He has taken to calling every eunuch he sees the "son of a shit collector"!

Amenemhab's large head rocked back and he roared with laughter. Animal dung was the staple cooking fuel in Egypt and there was money to be made organizing the collection and resale of dried shit. Some of the newly rich began their fortunes this way. It became common to insult a rich merchant by asking if he was the son of a shit collector!

The old woman shook her finger at Amenemhab. His laughter reverted to a smile and he was about to protest his innocence again when Webkhet turned her attention toward me.

"I am told by the eunuch Nembet that you wish to visit the animals this morning," she said smoothing my sidelock against my face.

"Yes! Yes!" I shouted. "Let's go see the animals and Nembet too, that son of a shit collector!"

Amenemhab broke into laughter again and moved off down the path toward his quarters. Webkhet grabbed me roughly by the arm.

"Enough of that you imp! Keep quite or I will feed you to the animals." She delivered a gentle slap to my bottom and pushed me along in the direction of the area of the Garden that housed the royal animals.

Nembet was waiting for us at the door.

"Good morning madam," he said bowing deeply. It was an empty gesture more of contempt than respect. He straightened up.

"I am honored that the prince has come to visit the animals." He bowed again this time in my direction.

"Yes, yes," Webkhet said absently trying to move things along. "The boy wants to see the lions again."

The eunuch nodded. "Follow me," he said and waddled toward the door leaving a strong odor of unwashed sweat and feces in the air.

Webkhet muttered to herself, "By all that is holy, he smells like the son of a shit collector!"

The corner of the outer walls of the Garden formed the two inner walls of the animal compound. Two additional walls completed the large rectangle constructing an enclosure within the larger grounds of the villa. We entered the animal compound through a large wooden door that Nembet neglected to shut behind us. A smaller door to our front led to the area where the cages were located. I had been here many times so I was not frightened by the noise the animals made when we first entered. The smell of animal waste and the decayed remains of uneaten meat that was food for the beasts hung heavy in the tepid air. I walked quickly ahead of Webkhet. She sighed and quickened her step to keep up with me. I ran to the lion cage in the center of the row. The beasts were curious and came close to the bars. Webkhet moved quickly to my side afraid that I might put my fingers through the bars. Her concern led her not to notice that Nembet was no longer with us. Only the sound of the door closing caught her attention. In an instant she realized that we were alone.

She grabbed my hand. I felt the strength of her grip and knew something was wrong.

"Stay by me," she said, "And do what I tell you."

For a few seconds all was still as even the animals sensed Webkhet's tension.

The stillness was broken by the loud crash of a door being opened and slammed against the wall. The sound frightened the animals and terrifying noises erupted from their throats. The large cats paced nervously and pawed at the air. Baboons at the far end of the enclosure bared their teeth and banged their chests. The sound of heavy laughter joined the noise of the animals. My eyes followed Webkhet's as she sought its origin coming to rest on the figure of Nembet. He was perched on the catwalk that ran completely around the room high above the cages. The great crash was made by the slamming of the door that led to the catwalk from the second floor outside the inner wall.

"Nembet! What is the meaning of this nonsense. Stop your laughing and get your fat ass down here or the boy's father will have your feet nailed to the front gate of Thebes."

Webkhet's voice showed no trace of fear. Only a slight tremor in her hand revealed her concern. She tightened her grip on my arm.

"Alas, you old crone I cannot do that! It is too dangerous for one so fat as me. I present too much of a temptation to the animals who look at me each day like I were a succulent meal. No, you witch. It is too dangerous for a man in my position to risk my life when there are wild animals loose."

I was more confused than frightened.

"What is the son of a shit collector doing?" I asked.

"Shuush, little one. Be quiet!"

I could see Webkhet was trying to find a means to escape. But from what I wondered. The animals had calmed down and there was no one else in the room except Webkhet and me.

I saw it before Webkhet did, the movement of a small black figure out of the corner of my eye. At first I thought it was an animal and my heart raced. It darted between the cages and I could not see it clearly. For a few seconds there was no sound. Quiet. Suddenly the figure jumped on top of one of the cages and stood there looking up at Nembet who was lowering a knotted rope over its head.

The pygmy's skin was as black and oily as scribe's ink. He stood on the cage looking down at me, a broad smile upon his face as if we were playing a child's game. If such a creature was capable of understanding, I must have appeared puzzled to him while I stood there holding my nurse's hand.

We were about twenty feet apart. Nembet's rope dangled over the pygmy's head. He grabbed the rope with one hand and with the other reached down and pulled the wooden peg from the latch that held the cage door shut and threw open the door. He grabbed the rope with both hands and pulled his knees up with the rope between them until he sat on the large knot tied at the end of the rope. The pygmy on a string rose slowly as Nembet began hauling in the rope. Webkhet grabbed me in her arms and backed towards the door. Her eyes never left the door to the open cage. Webkhet shoved me behind her putting her body between me and the nameless danger.

For several minutes the narrow corridor formed by the row of cages on one side and the enclosure wall on the other was empty. At first I could only sense the movement of the great cat as it moved noiselessly among the cages seeking to make sense out of its sudden freedom. Again quiet. Then without a sound the great cat was standing in the middle of the corridor. Its pale yellow eyes narrowed to the thickness of a knife blade. Those eyes forced themselves into my consciousness, and with the awareness of the panther's existence came fear. There was death in those eyes. But there was also a terrible beauty. I learned that day never to hate a thing for doing what it was required by the gods to do.

Nembet's laughter cascaded over us as he pulled the pygmy to safety. As soon as the little fellow reached the catwalk he scampered along it to the stairs that led to the doorway and disappeared from view. The obese eunuch waddled along behind until he too was gone. Only the sound of the door being closed and locked disturbed the silence.

Webkhet remained still as stone. Ten feet away the panther stared into the eyes of its prey. I could hear its breathing. It sounded like the gentle disturbed purring of a cat in heat. No other animal made a sound. Perhaps it was their fascination for a new kill. At last man was the prey. To see the hunter hunted is rare in their world. In their quiet no animal wanted to miss the spectacle. The silence scratched my ear like a dagger and time seemed frozen in stone.

Webkhet's clothes were soaked with sweat. To my young nose she smelled old. There was no trace of the sweetness that mixes with the sweat of young women that I came to treasure when I reached adolescence. So tightly did Webkhet hold it in her claw that my hand went numb. The panther's skin glistened in the light, its muscles slowly rippling with every patient movement. Its head moved slowly from side to side, nostrils widening and closing as it smelled the air for danger. Webkhet and I remained motionless. There was nothing else to do. Later in my life when I was a soldier, whenever I saw a prisoner being led to an uncertain fate I recalled my feelings on this day. I know that sense of absolute helplessness in my soul. I learned it from the beautiful beast whose savage eyes paralyzed me with fear.

And then the panther took a deep breath and the tension went out of its muscles. The animals's ears twitched and lay back. The pale yellow eyes slowly widened and lost their knife edges. The beast circled once around itself and lay down on the earthen floor facing us, its paws crossed regally one over the other. It gave us one last look and produced a great yawn revealing the sharp white teeth that could penetrate the skull bone of its prey. The great cat's eyes narrowed once again, this time in sleep. Gently it lowered its sleek head upon its paws and appeared to doze.

I cannot say how long the animal lay dozing, but it seemed a long time. Perhaps an hour. Webkhet tried the locked door several times, but only succeeded in attracting the attention of the great cat. This forced her to stop and remain silent and motionless once again. So we waited, Webkhet, the panther, and I.

Without warning the door flew open and slammed against its hinges making a great crash. The figure of a man rushed by us and came to a lurching stop between us and the great cat. The panther was instantly awake. Its muscles flexed as it crouched to receive its attacker. From out of the beast's mouth came a roar like that of a waterfall. Its teeth flashed like highly polished knives. Its ears twitched ominously as the great cat prepared to hold its ground against this new threat. I could smell the odor of urine as Webkhet's fear made her water loose.

I recognized the man at once. It was Amenemhab, and in his hand he held his deadly *kopesh* ready to tear the cat apart. Like the cat Amenemhab stood low in a crouch to receive the attack. His eyes, too, were narrowed and focused. Slowly he twisted the blade of the short sword back and forth catching the light in a glint reflected off the blade. Again and again he sent the reflection off the blade in the direction of the panther's yellow eyes. At first the cat followed the light. Then, quickly, it regained its sense of purpose and stared straight at Amenemhab trying to paralyze its enemy with a pitiless stare. Amenemhab held his ground but made no effort to advance.

"Get the prince and the old bag to safety!" he shouted over his shoulder. His eyes did not leave the animal's face.

I felt a strong grip seize me around my waist and pull me through the door. Webkhet followed me a few seconds later. I looked up into the hard face of a soldier of my bodyguard. The door remained open and I could see Amenemhab and the panther locked in an untouching embrace as they stared across the space that separated them from one another.

Amenemhab made the first move. Slowly he raised himself from the crouch and lowered the *kopesh* almost to his side. It was a gesture calculated to signal the great cat that he meant it no harm. The panther stared silently, its eyes locked on the human to its front. Amenemhab took a slow step backward. Again the panther did nothing. Another step backward, a pause, then another. It seemed to me that for a moment the great cat permitted its shoulder muscles to relax. A second later it, too, straightened its body from the crouch, The animal's head moved back and forth sniffing the air for renewed danger. It found none and allowed its eyes to widen slightly releasing Amenemhab from its deadly gaze. My guardian moved slowly backward toward the door in a slow continuous motion until he reached the portal. More relaxed now, Amenemhab allowed himself the luxury of a great smile that revealed two rows of good teeth, rare for an Egyptian even at his age.

"Well, my friend," he said. "Perhaps we will fight another day when one of us has a clearer advantage."

Amenemhab offered a slight bow to the great cat and raised his *kopesh* in salute as if to an honored enemy who he knew would kill him if he could. The black cat sniffed the air again and a low growl issued from the panther's throat. It stood erect and turned away. A second later Amenemhab came through the door like a desert wind and snatched me up from the floor. He was angry as Seth and his breath was hot and smelled from tension.

"Come with me!" He roared. "You too you bag of old bones," he yelled over his shoulder. "You will be lucky to escape the anger of your mistress when she finds out what has happened."

Webkhet was exhausted and could barely stand.

"And you, you little fool," he yelled at me. "This day you are likely to witness your guardian's feet nailed to the gate of Thebes when your father hears of this!"

# Eight

It was night before things calmed down. My mother, Webkhet and I were taken to Ese's apartment in the Garden and kept under guard. It was now early evening and no one had been allowed to enter or leave since late morning. Once he was certain I was safe, Amenemheb sent a messenger to inform the Chancellor of what had occurred. The news quickly brought Paremheb to see for himself. He ordered the bodyguard strengthened. Then he and Amenemhab left to attend to the important business of finding the culprit.

They had been gone all day when the door opened without a knock. Amenemhab and Paremheb entered the room and quickly covered the distance between the door and the couch where my mother and I were waiting. Both men remained standing. They looked tired and worried. Through the open doorway I could see soldiers guarding the corridor.

"Gracious queen," Paremheb began. "There is no time to explain. You must make yourself and the prince ready for an audience with Pharaoh at the palace. He has commanded that you and the boy be brought to him this night."

My mother looked at Webkhet. A short nap had done nothing to drive the look of exhaustion from the old woman's face. She nodded her head as if granting permission to Ese. My mother glanced at her nurse and nodded back. Without a word Ese began fixing her makeup and wig. She wanted to look her best for the great king.

"Am I going too?" I asked, my squeaky child's voice sounding terribly out of place among the serious tones of soldiers and chancellors. I wanted to go desperately. Although the Garden was within the palace compound, I rarely saw my father and then only when he came to visit my mother. There were but a precious few memories of him and me together. Even so, he was Pharaoh and I was his son, and I loved him as a son should. Amenemhab squatted down on one knee. He smelled of sweat from the day's work. His eyes were red from fatigue and worry. He answered me in a firm voice.

"Yes, my prince. You may be assured that you will visit the Great One this night. You'd best be on your good behavior. Pharaoh has much to think about because of you."

I didn't understand what Amenemhab was talking about. In my child's mind the events of the morning in the animal compound had been a great adventure, a thing of dreams and nothing more. For my life I couldn't begin to understand why Pharaoh would have much to be concerned about.

"I am ready," my mother said rising from her dressing table. As always in my eyes she looked a great beauty. Webkhet placed a heavy cloth shawl around Ese's shoulders. It was two months past the end of the flood, a time when the weather in Egypt turns cool in the evening. Amenemhab led the way.

A squad of soldiers preceded us down the path toward the door that separated the Garden from the main palace. Soldiers walked beside and behind us, a military escort provided by the men of my bodyguard. They took the attempt on my life personally, as if it were their own failure. The guards were tense this night and would have quickly killed anyone who they thought might have meant us harm. The Keepers of the Keys opened the door and we made our way into a great open courtyard longer and wider than any enclosure in all Egypt. Only the temple at Karnak was grander than Pharaoh's palace. But even at Karnak the courtyard was smaller than the magnificent open space in which we now stood.

The huge courtyard was paved with polished red granite slabs quarried in Aswan and moved to Thebes on special ships. Each piece of smoothly polished stone was four feet square and fitted so tightly against the slabs around it that it was impossible to slip a sheet of papyrus between them. Quarrying granite with wooden wedges and stone hammers was hard and dangerous work. Many a workman had lost an eye to the stone chips that flew from the stone while the workmen coaxed these beautiful slabs from the surrounding rock. The stone pavement ran hard against the enclosure wall that ran around the entire temple complex forming a rectangle more than two hundred yards long and a hundred yards across. The outer wall was thirty five feet high and more than twenty feet thick and was covered with white stucco made from gypsum mined from the ancient lake bed near Memphis called the Fields of Salt. At the end of the courtyard nearest where we stood was the main gate, the formal entrance to the royal palace of Thebes. Over forty feet high, the gate was framed in stone and covered by rare black granite slabs dragged on sledges from the eastern desert whose parched red sands ran the distance down to the shores of the Sea of Seth. Enormous doors of Nubian mahogany swung on lintels fashioned from cedar logs harvested from the mountains of Lebanon. Bronze straps and pegs held the tongue and grooved wood together in the shape of a perfect rectangle. The gate itself opened on to a large sloped stairway that led down to a stone quay that ran along the Nile.

We entered the courtyard through a door in the wall that formed the right side of the courtyard. A bright moon floated in the night sky illuminating the courtyard as if it were still daylight. At intervals along the wall and from posts placed throughout the enclosure at fixed spaces were brightly painted columns of tall thick palm logs from which hung oil lamps whose wicks produced a flickering light. We approached the great stone ramp that led steeply upward to the first of three brick platforms upon which the rooms and offices that constituted the temple complex were constructed.

The royal palace of Thebes was not only the official residence of the king. It was as well a vast complex of residences, workshops, audience halls, military barracks, temples, shrines, and government buildings from which high officials governed the empire of the New Kingdom. At the end of the stepped ramp that led to the third level was the Great House of Pharaoh. In ancient times the word "Pharaoh" meant "great house." It was only in more recent times that the title came to mean the king himself. Above the magnificent entranceway to the residence hung the great balcony, the *Smeshed*, from which all official proclamations were read and from where Pharaoh addressed his people on state occasions. The third level housed a number of audience halls of various sizes. The largest of these was a clerestory hall connected to the throne room by a long row of columns through which Pharaoh walked to receive foreign dignitaries and important guests. Every room in the palace was painted with murals depicting the usual Egyptian themes of hunting, economic life, and creation. But the wide walls of the formal audience hall were covered with brightly colored portrayals of Pharaoh's magnificent deeds. The common theme of these brightly hued murals was Pharaoh as a warrior prince, the Smasher of Foreheads, trampling his enemies into the dust or otherwise reducing them to submission and death. It was here that representatives from the lands that surrounded Egypt awaited Pharaoh's presence. While they waited they could contemplate the power of the great Lion of Egypt whose den they had entered.

We were met at the bottom of the stone steps by the commander of Pharaoh's military guard. He dismissed our bodyguard and escorted us up the stairway that led to the formal audience chamber. The commander was a grizzled army veteran of many campaigns who wore the Gold of Valor around his neck. The visible scars on his legs and arms were evidence enough that this was no garrison soldier. He was in command of Pharaoh's personal bodyguard. The *Eaters of Hearts* was one of the oldest regiments in the imperial army. Originally it had been Thutmose I's regiment when he was only a general and before he became Pharaoh. During his reign he kept the regiment close by him in battle and in peace and regarded it with special affection. His son, Thutmose II, my father, served with this regiment as a young man. When in his turn he became Pharaoh, he kept the unit as his bodyguard. Its name was instantly recognizable to every Egyptian.

We Egyptians believe that the heart is the true site of all human intellect, will, and emotion. Upon our deaths we are judged by Ma'at, the Goddess of Truth, before a gathering of divine judges who sit in the Great Hall of Souls. Ma'at takes our heart in her hands and places it on one pan of the balance scale. In the other she places The Feather of Truth against which our hearts are weighed. If we are pure and truthful in our lives the scales will balance and we are permitted to pass into the Field of Marshes where those who have died before us dwell. But if the scales do not balance Ma'at grasps the untruthful heart and throws it to the demon called the *Eater of Hearts*. The demon's head is as a crocodile, its body like a lion, and it possesses the haunches of a hippopotamus. Once the heart is consumed the human essence of the person is lost forever and he suffers the worst fate that can befall an Egyptian, the Second Dying from which there is no resurrection.

Pharaoh's bodyguard is rightly feared for like the true *Eater of Hearts* they bring with them the fearful promise of certain oblivion.

We were led into the great hall and down its entire length and through another large doorway at the far end that led to the throne room. We passed through the open doors. The doors were covered in gold leaf and inlaid with ivory and lapis lazuli so that even in the dim light of the flickering oil lamps the great doors glittered as if in daylight. My eyes lingered for a moment on these beautiful things and I was not paying close attention to where we were going. Without warning the bodyguard and the others suddenly halted in their tracks. In a jumbled movement the little group knelt upon the ground, stretched their bodies forward, and pressed their noses and foreheads against the cold alabaster tile. Caught unaware, only I remained standing. My eyes rose to embrace the sight of Pharaoh, Great Lion of Egypt, standing in front of his golden chair, legs apart and arms folded. He stood alone at the top of the stairs that led to the raised platform upon which sat the great throne of Egypt. His eyes blazed with anger and he looked like an animal about to pounce.

Except for two bodyguards posted off to the side of the platform the magnificent throne room was empty. When he spoke Pharaoh's voice echoed off the hard plaster walls and fell harshly upon our ears.

"Rise!" he commanded. "I wish to see your eyes when you tell me why my son was almost killed today!"

The anger in his voice produced a visible shudder in Webkhet. Even my mother pressed her forehead more tightly against the cold stone floor. Until that moment I had never heard my father's voice raised in anger. It sounded like the roar of a great beast. It was the roar of the Great Lion of Egypt. None of us moved.

"Have you no ears! Rise! I command you!"

As if kicked from behind, the members of our little group clattered to their feet and stood fearfully before Pharaoh. Not knowing any better only I looked at his majestic face. The others stood with eyes cast downward daring to look only at the floor. It was an old Egyptian belief that anyone who looked directly into the face of Pharaoh, the son of the sun god Ra, would be consumed by the brightness of his light. It was one of those old ideas that still governed the behavior of men whenever they stood in the presence of their gods. For millennia those brought before Pharaoh knelt with their noses and foreheads "kissing the ground." No word could be uttered in the Great One's presence without first repeating the long list of formal titles that Pharaoh bore with him in this life. The din of the endless noise of empty phrases made even important conversation with the head of state impossible. My grandfather was the first to do away with the court custom that those in the presence of Pharaoh kiss the ground, although on public occasions the crowds of common people still did it. Thutmose I was a soldier accustomed to directness in speech and manner. From his day members of the court were required only to kneel in Pharaoh's presence and to speak clearly and loudly. High ranking military officers were accorded the privilege of touching only one knee to the ground before rising and speaking while standing. The Theban princes were soldiers whose victories over the Hyksos were fresh in their minds. Such men preferred the practicality of the field tent to the empty rituals of a royal court.

The Great Lion slowly walked down the stairs and stood before our group. He put his hand on Ese's shoulder. Her eyes rose to meet his and there was concern for her son in them. Pharaoh smiled gently.

"Do not worry, Ese. The boy is unharmed." There was softness in the great man's voice as he comforted the mother of his child. His eyes fell upon me.

"Well, young man," he said much like any father. "You have given us a fright. We'll have to see what must be done to prevent such nonsense in the future."

He placed his hand on my shaven head and then tugged playfully on my sidelock, an old Egyptian gesture of affection.

"Hold on to this Thutmose," he said tugging the sidelock again. "Once you cut it off your life changes for the worse." Then the Great Lion turned to face Paremheb.

"Tell me, Chancellor, why events so completely escaped your control." He paused. "Then tell me what you intend to do about it."

Pharaoh's voice was cold and emotionless, and the discomfort it produced flashed across Paremheb's face. The two men had served in the same regiment as young officers and knew one another. In those days Paremheb had shown himself a capable staff officer. When my father assumed the throne, Paremheb seemed a good choice to oversee the state administration as Chancellor. Paremheb always thought of Pharaoh as his old comrade. But even he knew at this moment that he had come within a hair's breadth of being executed. Only the fact that I had escaped unharmed kept him alive. Now, as he told my father of the day's events, Paremheb knew that another mistake would cost him his life.

Paremheb began to tell my father the story of the morning's happenings. When he told of my rescue by Amenemhab, Pharaoh looked hard at the man who saved his son. He seemed to be weighing some great question in his mind and for a time said nothing. Then, as if he had resolved an impasse, Pharaoh spoke.

"It seems I have reason to be grateful to you again, Amenemhab. Your loyalty is of great value to me and your deeds are surely worthy of honor. You have the gratitude of your Pharaoh and all Egypt for what you have done this day."

Amenemhab's body relaxed and he let his breath out as noiselessly as he was able. As captain of the bodyguard, Amenemhab was personally responsible for my safety. It was his negligence that placed me in jeopardy to begin with. Undoubtedly Pharaoh was aware of this. Still, he permitted the man to escape shame and punishment. Perhaps Pharaoh knew that loyalty is never stronger nor more dependable than when it rests in shame and must call such shame honor. Pharaoh had made certain that he could depend on Amenemheb's loyalty absolutely, not a trifling thing in dangerous times.

Pharaoh listed intently as Paremheb told of how Nembet, the swollen obscenity of a eunuch, was found by Amenemheb's men cowering in a corner of the eunuch's quarters. The Chancellor personally oversaw Nembet's torture. Creatures like Nembet serve only the master of the moment, and it did not take long for the man to tell Paremheb what he knew. And after he did the pain went on and on until his tormentors were convinced that the eunuch had nothing left to tell.

"Does the man still live?" Pharaoh asked.

"Yes, your majesty," Paremheb answered. "Although it is not certain he will live more than a few days unless he is attended by the physicians."

"See to it Paremheb. I wish him to live a while longer so that I may see the son of a swine impaled on a stake outside the eunuch's quarters as a warning to other seditious fools who participate in these harem conspiracies."

Paremheb nodded, "Yes, Oh Great One."

The Chancellor did not think it strange that Pharaoh failed to ask about the pygmy. Such pets had no humanity, no ability to think beyond that of a trained monkey or dog. If the pygmy removed the peg to the panther's cage, it was because he was trained to do it. It was ludicrous to think of the dwarf as having any importance in this matter. The little fellow had been found playing gleefully in the garden. Enticed with some food, the little creature walked quietly back to his cage.

"What else have you learned? Who is behind this infamy?" Pharaoh asked.

Paremheb continuéd.

"The eunuch gave us the name of a woman named Iutenheb who he says drew him into the conspiracy. She gave him three rings of gold as payment and the promise of an estate when the boy was dead."

"Who is this woman?" Pharaoh was getting impatient.

"Great king I must tell you that this Iutenheb serves as a lady to your Great Wife." Paremheb paused. Pharaoh's eyes narrowed like a jackal sensing its prey. The Chancellor continued.

"This woman is a distant relative to the queen's chief advisor, Senenmut the Commoner, who governs the affairs of the queen's household."

Paremheb stopped talking. He sensed the king's anger even though the great man had not spoken a word. For a few seconds he watched the color of Pharaoh's face change as his skin flushed. Pharaoh remained silent even as his eyes revealed the strong emotions that were being held in check.

"As soon as we discovered who she was," Paremheb went on, "the guard was sent to arrest her. Alas, Great King, they found the woman dead in her apartment, her throat cut from ear to ear. Whoever set this plot murdered the person who could have led us to him." He stopped speaking for a few seconds and then added..."or her."

Pharaoh's harsh gaze fell hard upon Paremheb and he was rooted to the spot. The Chancellor understood the risk he was taking. And for what seemed to me a long time Paremheb stood as still as death. Silence descended upon all of us as we awaited Paremheb's fate to befall him. At last Pharaoh spoke.

"What is it you are saying Paremheb?"

The Chancellor remained quiet. His face was ashen with fear. He said nothing. The fruit in his throat moved up and down nervously and he rolled his tongue desperately searching for a drop of moisture to wet his parched mouth.

"Do you accuse the Great Wife of being behind the attempt to murder my son?"

Pharaoh's voice was smooth and without a trace of emotion. There was no surprise in the timbre with which he formed his words. One might have thought that the Wise One had already permitted these ideas to escape his own thoughts.

"Well, speak up! Tell me what it is that you believe."

Now his voice rose as if challenging Paremheb to measure the conviction with which he held the thoughts he had just spoken. As he spoke Pharaoh flung his arm outward extending a finger in Paremheb's direction. It was a gesture designed to shake the confidence of any man, and the movement with which it was delivered was as sudden and as quick as the strike of a cobra. From somewhere Paremheb found his courage.

"Great king, I do not know who took the first step down this path of treachery. But it is unlikely that the woman Iutenheb could have begun this treachery by herself. What has she to profit from it? Nothing. And now she is dead. It is certain that someone else in the court, someone of position and influence, murdered her to keep her silent."

The Chancellor paused and took a deep breath to steady his nerves.

"The fact that this woman's relative is a powerful figure at court and placed in the queen's household cannot be ignored except at great peril, Great One. Guilt must fall heavily upon Senenmut the Commoner. Beyond this, there is only suspicion."

Pharaoh was lost in his own thoughts and he seemed not to hear Paremheb's final words. It was as if he had already resolved the matter and had begun to think about other things. I stared at the great man who had sired me. I had completed my fifth year two months earlier. In all that time I had seen my father only a few times. Now, as he stood before me, I marveled at how magnificent and noble he looked. In the more than five years since my birth Pharaoh had sired no other children with his royal concubines. The Great Queen remained also without another child. She had born Pharaoh a daughter three years before my birth, but there had been no other children. The Great Wife was past thirty in years, older than Pharaoh. Soon her red moon would come no more and the chance to bear an heir for Egypt would be lost to her for all eternity. Of course my death would guarantee the queen's power for as long as she lived. And if she outlived my father, she still held legitimate claim to the royal lineage. She could remarry, perhaps Senenmut who was rumored to be her lover, and continue to rule Egypt with the commoner as her consort. All this required, of course, my demise.

Then Pharaoh spoke.

"Leave this matter to me. I shall see to it in my own way." He paused and looked around as if searching for a word that wouldn't come. He looked at me and the Great One smiled. He stretched out his arms.

"Come boy," he said. "Stand by your father and let me see how tall you have grown since you were an infant in your mother's arms."

A feeling of joy came over me. I looked up at my mother who smiled back at me. She loosened her grip and let my hand slip from hers. I ran from her into my father's arms.

# Nine

I stood on the lip of the stone quay that formed the hard edge of the harbor of Thebes listening to the sound of the water caressing the piers. The early morning air felt cool on my skin. It was three months after the inundation had reached its peak and the crop of the planting season was already seeded into the black soil that is the gift of the Mighty Bull. For the last month the Nile had been gradually relinquishing its watery grip on the bottom land along the riverbank drawing back unto itself the life-giving fluid that filled the irrigation canals. It was the time of year when the Nile retreats to its main channel where the river's flow is shaped by the contours of the unseen valley and rocks that lie deep below the surface. The current flows strong as the Nile makes its way downstream to empty into the Great Green.

It is a good time to make the journey to Memphis. The steady current and the deep water will make the voyage easy on the backs of the oarsmen. The wind still blows from the north stronger than during the time of the flood, but not so strong as to overcome the current that will bear us like a floating log toward our destination. The wind will be in our face and we will not need the large sail. The headwind helps when the river narrows and the current grows stronger. Then the small topsail can be raised and the force of the wind against it will slow us making it easier for the helmsman to steer the boat. But if we do not leave Thebes soon the wind will begin to blow from the southwest bringing with it sandstorms from out of the western desert. The combination of strong current and a wind at our backs makes it difficult to control the boat. It is the time of year when shipwrecks are common, when the tranquil Nile turns into a silver serpent devouring boats the way a water snake devours small frogs.

The journey from Thebes to Memphis is almost six hundred miles. But the Nile runs like a slash of molten silver for another six hundred miles to the south of Thebes where it begins at the confluence of two smaller rivers near the Pillars of the Earth. Over thousands of years the force of the river rushing to the sea cut a deep gash in the surrounding desert highland wearing the earth away for hundreds of feet slashing a deep trough in which the river could always find its way. The annual inundation forces the water out of its banks and covers the flood plain forming a rich and fertile valley in which we Egyptians have lived for thousands of years. South of Aswan in Nubia the Nile is constrained by sandstone cliffs that restrict the width of its flood plain to five miles or less in most places. But once the river passes the First Cataract, the land broadens and the valley opens out to twenty miles and even thirty in some places before it reaches the broad expanse of the Delta. All along the Nile's banks one sees terraced fields planted with crops. Beds of papyrus and shallow marshes remind one of the first Marsh of Creation. They are home to the hippopotamus and crocodile. Here man must take his place among other creatures, animals and birds, and live in harmony with them if he is to flourish.

But the Nile is not everywhere at peace with itself. The great force of the rushing water that carved the fertile valley did not succeed in pushing back the land at every place. At the edges of the

valley are the steep cliffs that mark the top and sides of the original sandtable before the Mighty Nile washed its innards to the
sea. These limestone cliffs are eight hundred feet high in places
and run almost five hundred miles along the river's length. In
places the earth has won out over the river and the corrosive force
of the rushing water remains trapped in narrow stone sluices
through which it must travel if it wishes to gain the sea. Here the
cliffs hug the water's edge so tightly that there is no riverbank at
all. The stone walls rise straight out of the river's bottom and
reach five hundred feet above the water's surface. The route from
Thebes to Memphis is marked by several of these stone canyons
and our captain is aware of the great danger they present to his
boat and his precious cargo. The journey to Memphis promises to
be an adventure for a young boy not yet six years old.

The waves made by the movement of the boats sloshed against
the huge stones that formed the quay and made a gentle and relax-
ing sound. Along the dock the sailors set to work loading provisions and cargo on the boat that will carry me to Memphis. The
boat is the *Shining Horus*, one of the transport vessels of the new
Egyptian navy, and she is carrying a shipment of chariots for the
army garrison at Asyut. Chained securely in her hold is a cargo of
slaves destined for the papyrus beds in the Lakeland. The harbor
at Thebes is one of the best in all Egypt. Here the Nile is almost a
half mile wide and quite deep providing sufficient room for many
boats to maneuver at the same time without too much risk of a
collision. Thebes is the capitol of the New Kingdom and there are
always plenty of boats to fill the harbor.

Today is no exception and the harbor is crowded. I can see a
richly painted funeral boat push off from its berth. On its deck is
a wooden coffin carved in the shape of a man. Painted on its cover
are wide silver wings that wrap completely around it so that the
god Osiris appears to embrace its contents. The coffin holds the

mummified remains of some soul who has departed this life. It rests on a wooden platform for its journey and is accompanied by two shaven-headed priests murmuring prayers over the deceased. The corpse is being transported to the great cemetery on the west bank of the river. The rise of Thebes as the capitol has brought with it a new burial place for the pharaohs, and with that has come the desire on the part of many who can afford it to be buried near them in the new cemetery. The dead are brought from all over Egypt to be entombed here. The place is becoming over-crowded and the residents of Thebes have begun referring to the west bank of the Nile as Thebes of the Dead! I catch a glimpse of the captain's face as the funeral boat glides by. He looks bored. He has made this trip so many times that even death seems to have no meaning for him. It is merely business, a trade in traveling corpses that earns him a tidy sum.

I am excited by it all! This is my first trip on the mighty Nile and I will be going without my mother and Webkhet. I am more than five years old, the time in Egypt when male children leave their mother and nurses and begin their education under the guidance of their father's hand. Were I not in danger, I would have been sent to the Temple of Amun-Ra in Thebes to be instructed in the knowledge of the gods and the nature of this world. Then I would have gone to the House of Life to learn to read and write. But there is no way to keep me safe in Thebes. So I am to be sent far beyond the reach of the Chief Wife, to the Temple of the Ka of Ptah in Memphis, where I will be safe and can be instructed by the priests until I can return to Thebes.

My head is filled with all kinds of visions of adventures to come. For a moment the sound of familiar voices draws my attention. A few feet away my mother, Webkhet, the Chancellor, and Amenemhab stand speaking with one another. Then they are silent as if my presence has enforced upon them some quietness that I don't understand. If I look at my mother's face when she doesn't see me watching, I see a look of sadness that changes to a forced smile when she sees that I am looking at her. It is as if she is trying to hide her feelings from me. Webkhet's eyes are the eyes of an old woman watching her grandson going off to battle. They cry out with the twin fears that she will not live to see his return or, even worse, that she will survive only long enough to learn the news of his death. Of them all, the old crone seems to be having the most difficult time of it.

Paremheb pays me no mind. I am a responsibility he will be glad to be rid of. He talks to the captain of the bodyguard in the brusque manner of a military man. The captain is responsible for my safety during the voyage. He and his men are from the *Eaters of Hearts* regiment, the personal bodyguard of the king. They all look as fearless as they are disciplined. Although I cannot hear all of Paremheb's words, I have no doubt that he is putting the fear of Seth into the captain and reminding him of the fate that will befall him and his men should anything happen to me.

From where I am standing it is difficult to see Amenemhab. He is busy chatting with some fellow I do not know. He presses a copper ring into the fellow's hand payment for something or other. When he turns around and sees me he smiles. With a wave of his hand he calls me to him and I run to embrace my old friend. I rush at him as I have done so many times before.

"Captain! Captain! Show me your eye!" I yell. Strong arms grab me and lift me off the ground and twirl me over his head only to set me down gently in front of the old soldier who has kept me safe all these years.

I can't keep myself from giggling as Amenemhab stoops down on one knee so that I am staring into his face. The beard and eye-patch make him look as fierce as ever. But there is a broad smile on his face and it is an affectionate smile.

"Well my young prince today is the start of a great journey. Today you begin your education as befits a royal prince."

He used his good eye to wink at me as if we were conspirators in some intrigue. I smiled broadly and blinked both eyes for I had not yet mastered this trick of closing one eye and not yet the other. Amenemhab reached out and adjusted the shoulders of my shirt.

"You will need this," he said. "The nights are cool on the river at this time of year. The shirt will keep you warm once Horus has flown beyond the western desert at the end of the day and taken his warming rays with him."

I nodded. "How long will it take for the boat to reach Memphis?" I asked.

Amenemhab raised his eyebrows as if puzzled, his mind working to provide me with an answer.

"About thirty risings and settings of the sun I should think. It is almost six hundred miles to the City of the White Wall. With a fair current and no headwind the boat should make twenty miles a day." He paused and looked at me. "Is that a long time for you?"

I shook my head but said nothing. At my age a month was a lifetime! Perhaps this voyage was not such a grand idea after all. Perhaps the sadness and concern that I had seen on the face of the adults had some meaning. For the first time since my father explained the reason for the voyage I realized that I would leave behind all the people who had shared my life. Of course it never entered my head that my departure would leave a void in their lives too, but then children never really comprehend the feelings of adults. It was as if a cold chill had blown over me. I felt only what I felt, and what had begun in my mind as a great adventure was, without reason, turning into sadness. It was this sadness that Amenemhab now saw on my face.

"Will you and Ese come and visit me at the Temple of Ptah?" My voice was low and I was suddenly near tears. "Will Webkhet come too?"

Amenemhab tried his best. "Perhaps, my prince. Memphis is not beyond the stars. We will make every effort to visit you if life and the gods permit." It was not really the answer I was looking for and disappointment must have shown on my face.

"Thutmose," Amenemhab began, "sometimes even a prince as young as you must endure things that he wishes were not so. Perhaps this is one of those times."

His voice fell off and he grew silent as if trying to hold back a sadness he did not wish me to see. When he continued his voice was steady.

"My prince, a warrior must learn about the world in which he lives if he is ever to have any hope of mastering it. In this there is often hardship. But there is also great joy in learning of wonders you have never dreamt of. Above all you must learn of Egypt. For how can a prince rule his people with justice unless he first learns of their land and their gods?"

His eyes narrowed as if he was trying to keep them from becoming moist.

"Thutmose, you are a prince of Thebes, and if the gods permit one day you will rule this land of *Kemit*. Now is the time of your preparation, of your becoming a prince fit to rule."

I had been looking into the face of my friend as he spoke. Now my eyes turned away from his and my chest was tight with emotions I felt but could not explain. I rushed toward Amenemhab and hugged him around his legs. I hung on to the old warrior and began to sob.

Strong arms grabbed my shoulders and pushed me away. I stumbled backwards almost falling to the ground.

"No!"

The word rang out like the crack of a lightening bolt and its sound drew the attention of the others standing a few feet away. I stood still and silent as I stared into my old friend's eyes, eyes that had suddenly gone cold.

"No, my prince." Amenemhab said firmly. "It is not fit for you to act in this manner." His voice had that edge to it that officers reserve for correcting subordinates.

"You must be strong or all about you will be weak. You must live this day and all the others, even in hardship if needs be, for it is only in bearing your duties can you convince other men to follow you onto whatever dangerous paths lie in your future."

And then the captain of my bodyguard, the soldier of the *Blood of Isis*, and the man who had slain an enemy with his teeth looked straight into my young eyes.

"You must do what is asked of you because there is no choice given you. If you would learn to rule, then you must first learn to obey."

My troubled mind sought comfort in my mother's eyes as children have for all time. There were only tears as she looked upon the face of her son, a son who had grown too fast and would leave her this day. Never after this day would her son be a boy. Events had conspired to ensure that. Her heart felt pain as she tried to drive from her mind the dangers that might lay in wait for him. Webkhet's face said nothing. She raised then lowered her shoulders in a shrug as if to tell me that now was as good as any time for me to resign myself to my fate, as good as any time to grow up and learn that in this life many burdens must be borne no matter what. Paremheb smiled at me and turned his back. He was glad to be rid of me. I had been nothing but trouble and worry to him since I was born. The sooner I was out of his sight the better.

I stood silently looking at those who meant the most to me. For the first time that I could remember, I felt alone. It was a feeling that I would come to know well over the years. With time I would learn to endure it without much discomfort. I looked at Amenemhab. His face had lost none of its firmness as he looked back at me. Years later, when I asked men to put their lives at risk in battle, I often thought of this day when first I learned of the power of resignation. There are times in this life when there are no choices given, when all courses carry with them difficulty, fear, and danger. In these times the greatest danger is paralysis of the will, the inability to find the courage to suffer your fate. I was, it is true, only a boy about to leave his parents for the first time. Still it was enough pain for me.

Amenemhab looked at me and his good eye twisted upward in his familiar wink. A sly smile crossed his lips and his face softened. He turned away for a moment so that I could not see what he was doing. Suddenly I heard the sharp high pitched bark of a dog. Amenemhab stood up and turned toward me. In his arms he carried the sleek gray form of a puppy, a rare *slughi*, the most prized dog in all Egypt! The animal's snout came to a long rounded point, the only part of the beast that was black. The rest of him was a soft gray like the color of the clouds that reflect the dying sunlight at early evening. The sleek body ended in a pair of strong muscular hind quarters atop which began a bushy tail that made a complete loop before coming to rest on the dog's back. The large ears stood straight up and looked much like the triangular shaped sails seen on pleasure boats. The animal was not native to the Black Land, but came from the lands beyond the Great Bend of the Euphrates where the fierce Mitanni dwelled. The Hyksos brought the *slughi* to Egypt where it quickly became the favorite pet of the nobility. The breed was a favorite with embalmers, too, who wore dog masks while they conducted the ceremony of cleansing the corpse. Amenemhab handed the animal to me. I took it in my arms. Nothing could stop the smile on my face.

"You see, young prince, now you are not alone. This brave animal will be your companion in your travels and will keep you safe until you return to Thebes."

The old warrior was smiling, the stern visage of the disciplined soldier was gone.

"Is he really mine!" I said almost with a screech.

Amenemhab nodded. The other adults seemed for a moment somewhat less sad than they had been.

"Does he have a name?"

"His name is *Kera-Ra*, Thutmose. It means "He Whose Face Looks Like Ra." A fitting name for such a noble dog, don't you think?"

I nodded my head. Amenemhab was right. Here was a loyal companion who would share my adventures. I had *Kera-Ra* for many years, years which in so many ways shaped me. And always the dog was at my side, always loyal, always asking little but an affectionate pat on the head. It is too bad that people cannot be more like dogs. The world would be a better place.

The sound of the drum attracted the attention of everyone on the quay as the procession approached. Shaven headed priests from the Temple of Amun in Luxor walked in pairs ahead of the sedan chair waiving their sticks to keep people back from the line of march. Behind the chair were other priests holding fans and palm fronds. Four Nubian slaves, their sweaty bodies glistening in the sunlight, carried the sedan on long poles that rested on their strong shoulders. The platform had posts in each corner to support a green linen canopy and protect its occupant from the harsh sun. Curtains hung from the sides of the canopy. Usually lowered for privacy, they were tied back giving everyone a clear view of the important person who rode in the chair.

The procession approached the quay and stopped. With a grunt the Nubians lowered the platform and stepped away. The priests

quickly formed a corridor through which the honored one might
pass. Amenemhab stood at attention focusing his gaze on the figure descending from the chair. The Chancellor moved quickly to
the end of the priestly corridor and waited. *Kera-Ra*'s ears pricked
up and he sniffed the air trying to make sense of the commotion.
He wiggled a bit in my arms. From where I stood I could see
clearly the man whose arrival was causing so much fuss. It was
Ra-hotep, the Chief Priest of the Temple of the Ka of Ptah.

He was dressed in the long white linen robe that Egyptian
priests wore. A single shoulder strap held the garment in place and
a linen shirt provided protection for his arms. A cloth cowl covered his head. A leopard skin draped over one shoulder hung low
enough to be tied at the waist. The tail of the leopard was
arranged in such a manner that it hung from the priest's buttocks
making it appear as if he had a tail too! With a deliberate motion
Ra-hotep threw back the cowl revealing his shaven and oiled
skull. The sunlight glanced off its roundness and created an aura
of cleanliness that was exaggerated by the spotless white of his
robe. In his right hand he held the long wooden walking stick that
was the symbol of his office. He moved slowly along the row of
priests nodding sanctimoniously as he went, exuding a bearing of
mystical holiness and religious authority. He was not a tall man,
no taller than the average Egyptian, and underneath the robes
could be seen evidence of a body grown too plump for its own
good, a testament to many years of rich food. He reached the end
of the row of priests and nodded to Paremheb who bowed slightly
more out of formality than genuine respect. His eyes shifted and
his face made a gesture as if to acknowledge my existence. I
looked at the old priest and nodded in respect. Well, I thought,
this is the man at whose hands I will receive my education.

I had met Ra-Hotep a month earlier, after he had been summoned to Thebes by my father. I was present when Pharaoh told

the priest that he intended to place his only son under the protection of the Temple of Ptah and that Ra-hotep himself was to have responsibility for my religious education in the temple at Memphis. For the first time I heard the details of the attempt on my life as Pharaoh instructed Ra-hotep in the dangers I faced. Memphis was chosen because it was far from Thebes. The henchmen of Queen Hatshepsut who my father believed to be behind the attempt on my young life could not reach me there. The inner temple complex was completely closed to visitors, so with due diligence my safety could be assured. The Temple of Ptah in Memphis was the oldest religious center in Egypt and its priests renowned for their knowledge of science as well as the sacred texts. There was no place better to educate a future king.

I remember, too, how easily the noble bearing of this temple priest had been shattered by fear when Pharaoh spoke of the consequences that would befall Ra-hotep and his priests should they fail to protect me from evil. All would be impaled, said Pharaoh, and their relatives and families forced to finish their lives as laborers in the gold mines of the eastern desert. Any priest who was particularly derelict would be hanged head down with his feet nailed above the temple's doors until he suffocated to death. But all this was nothing. Pharaoh looked the priest in the eye and told him that his corpse would be thrown to the jackals. Ra-hotep's name would be stricken from every place where it now resided. For us Egyptians this was worse than death. Without a mummified corpse safely preserved in some tomb and with our names removed from this life, Egyptians believed that we suffer the Second Death, the place from which no resurrection is possible. As I watched my father speak to the old priest I learned that a king's word becomes reality by threat and promise. He can fail to make good on a promise, but he must never fail to make good on a threat.

Now as I stood looking at Ra-hotep I realized that Amenemhab was right. There was no real choice for me to make. There was only a need to discover some way to make my fate of value to me. All life is experience. The trick is to learn from that experience, to draw from it the lessons that lessen the dangers that one must inevitably confront as long as one walks above the grave. As I thought about this I heard the stern voice of the *Horus*'s captain fall on my ears.

"We are ready to depart, Holy One" he said in the general direction of no one in particular. The *Horus* was an imperial ship-of-the-line and manned by professional sailors in military service. Its captain had every intention of departing on time. The tone of his words reminded us all of just that.

The body guard boarded the boat and I followed. Ra-hotep crossed the gangplank and took his place next to me at the bow rail. On shore tears rushed to my mother's eyes as her old nurse pulled her close to comfort her. Amenemhab waved and the smile on his face betrayed the true affection that he had always held for me. The captain barked commands. The crew moved about like talented spiders along a familiar web. Slowly the oarsmen backed the boat away from its berth until the bow was clear of the quay. The large wooden oars flashed in the sun as they dipped into the water and pulled the boat across the river's surface. In a few minutes we were some distance from shore. The helmsman brought the boat about and pointed its bow downstream. The current seized the hull and held it in a grip that was to last for the entire journey. I stood at the rail and looked at those left behind. Already it was difficult to make them out from the others on the quay. I waved one last time. I felt the arm of Ra-hotep fall gently across my shoulder. I looked up at the old priest who looked straight ahead in the direction of the shore. No tears fell from my young eyes. I was very proud of that.

It was just past noon and the sun was high in the sky. Across the river from Thebes I could see the wall of gray mountains turned almost red by the rays of the sun. Beyond the first wall of mountains lay another. Concealed between was the burial place of the Theban kings. The mountains held their tombs carved in solid rock hidden in secret locations to protect them from thieves. Amenhotep was the first to have his tomb set in the valley. Thutmose I was buried there and my father's tomb was already being constructed somewhere in the same valley. Beyond the valley itself, atop the third row of limestone mountains, I saw the stone peak that sloped like a great pyramid like the ones outside Memphis that marked the tombs of the ancient kings. The peak watches over the valley like a great stone beast set there by the gods to protect the tombs of their earthly sons. This great natural pyramid and the graves of the Theban warrior princes have already given this place its name. The people of Thebes called it the Valley of Kings. I wondered if, perhaps, someday I, too, will carve my tomb deep into one of the gray mountains where my body can be kept safe for my Ka forever.

The riverbank between the mountains and the Nile in western Thebes is deep green and fertile, and from the boat I can see the two mortuary temples that sit peacefully upon the land marking the place where the Ka of the great kings Amenhotep and Thutmose I are cared for by the temple priests. My father's temple is almost completely built, although the village where the construction workers lived while building it is still there. In the old days before Thebes ruled Egypt, these temples were connected to the tombs themselves. But the Hyksos invaders plundered the tombs of the kings in lower Egypt. Now the princes of Thebes hide their tombs in rock. But the Ka of Pharaoh must still be provided for so the mortuary temples stand alone on the riverbank far from the tombs themselves. No longer can they be used by thieves to find the location of the royal tombs.

The sound of the water rushing by the hull was lulling me to sleep. The air was cool and the ship smelled of water soaked wood. Overhead the rigging slapped against the mast held to the main deck by a step that permitted the tall pole to be raised or lowered in a few minutes. Ships sailing downstream with the current had to remove their sails while those sailing upstream needed them and the wind at their back to overcome the force of the current. I thought it clever of us Egyptians to invent a way to remove the mast so quickly. The sailors scampered over the ship paying attention to their tasks while the captain stood his post at the rear of the boat. The *Horus* had two steering oars, one on each side, and the captain controlled the boat by giving orders to each of the two helmsmen who manned the oars. In the bow I could see the pilot lookout responsible for warning the captain of floating obstacles. Sandbars, too, were a great hazard in some parts of the Nile and the shallows near the cliffs often ran swift. It wasn't uncommon for a boat to run aground in these places. The lookout yelled that there was a floating log ahead and the captain ordered the helmsmen to change course. It was all done with naval precision born of an experienced captain and crew who knew the river well.

We had gone three miles when Ra-hotep reappeared from the deckhouse and made his way to the rail where I had remained since we left the quay. Toward the rear of the boat several of my bodyguards were already sick from the rocking motion. The *Eaters of Hearts* regiment was infantry to its core and it was doubtful that any of my guards had even been near a boat since joining the army. The old priest stood beside me and gave me a warm smile. The tone of his voice was level like that of a teacher about to begin a lesson.

"It is never too early to begin your education, Thutmose," he said evenly. "All education requires rules. And the first rule is that I will call you Thutmose and you will call me Teacher." He paused. "Do you understand that?"

I nodded that I did.

"Good," Ra-hotep said with some delight. "The second rule is that you must always listen to what people tell you. Your ears are your most important way of learning next to your eyes. It has been said it would be more fitting if the ears of a student were on his back so that he will learn quickly when beaten with a stick. So, Thutmose, you must learn to listen to those who know more than you do. At your age that is just about everyone."

Again I nodded and again I said nothing. Better to keep one's mouth shut, I thought, until I learned more about this man.

"Finally, you must always ask questions when you do not understand. It is truly a foolish student who pretends to know an answer when he does not. More wrongs have been done by men who refused to admit they did not know what they were doing. So always ask, Thutmose, always ask what you do not know." He paused for a moment. "Are the rules clear?"

"Yes, Teacher. The rules are clear."

The old priest's face lit up in a smile. He was delighted. I felt as if I had passed some sort of test.

"Good! Good!" he said. "Let us begin today."

With that he extended his arm and pointed in the direction of a cluster of buildings standing on the river's east bank.

"That is Karnak, the temple of Amun-Ra where the great god of Thebes lives and is worshiped," he said. "It used to be quite small, but the princes of Thebes rule and conquer in the name of Amun and have lavished upon the temple huge sums that are used to construct a great temple. Ahmose the Liberator, Amenhotep, Thutmose I and your father have all contributed temples and rooms to the complex. The great pylon gate was built by your grandfather, a great warrior and servant of the gods." Ra-hotep paused. "If the princes of Thebes rule long enough and Egypt can be kept safe from the barbarians who prowl her borders, someday this temple at Karnak will be a true wonder that men will marvel at for all time."

I listened in silence. I understood what the old priest was saying. When I became Pharaoh I, too, lavished large sums upon the temple and I, too, built great buildings. But priests are not always sufficiently of this world for kings to make good use of them. A king must always be wary of the power that priests possess over the people. It was a lesson I learned with great difficulty. It is always wise to keep a heavy hand on those who disdain the goods of this world. They are not easily dissuaded from dangerous actions by the usual methods. But they, too, are just men. And like all men can be brought to heel with the proper whip.

I was getting hungry and a plate of dates, bread, and roasted goose flesh was brought to me. I consumed it quickly and washed it down with beer from a clay cup. No expensive pottery here, I thought. Only the usual dishes and cups of wood and clay used by the crew. We had been on the river for more than five hours and the sun was setting behind the far sandstone mountains in the West. The captain gave the order to put in to shore and the *Horus* slipped silently against the riverbank and came to a stop. It was growing dark, and no captain sailed the river at night. There was too much danger from sandbars and rocks. Besides, we Egyptians dread the night. It is a time when the demons walk among us. Better to spend the hours until daylight sleeping around a fire on deck after a good night's meal. Ra-hotep did not object to my sleeping on the deck with the rest of the crew. Wrapped in a blanket to ward off the night chill I fell deeply asleep and slept without dreams.

The morning came early. I was awakened by the sounds of the crew making ready to get underway. The captain's voice sounded like the bark of an angry dog as he directed his crew to their tasks. We were already moving downstream by the time the suns rays crept over the eastern horizon and Ra again bathed the Nile farmlands with his lifegiving warmth. This day's journey would end in the town of Gebtu halfway through the Great Bend in the river where the Nile swings east for thirty miles before turning back upon itself for almost the same distance and moving northward again. There are places where the river is shallow and the crew have to man the oars to pull the boat over the sandbars. At Ra-hotep's urging I decided to spend the day exploring the *Horus* and learning all I could about her.

The *Shining Horus* was one of the new naval vessels of the kings of the New Kingdom. Made of yellow pine imported from Syria, she was fifty two feet long and twenty three feet wide with a mast of thirty-three feet made of double lumbered logs lashed and pegged together for strength. Every bit of strength was needed for the mast to hold a yard twenty feet long without snapping in a brisk wind. *Horus's* steering oars were sixteen feet long and she carried twelve ten foot power oars for moving against the current. Her sails were folded and wrapped out of the way, but her mast remained upright. Looking up from the deck I could see the second yard that held a smaller sail that could be swung on a ring to catch the wind. Forward on the main deck was the special nest where the lookout pilot was posted to watch for treacherous waters. In the middle of the boat stood a wooden deckhouse that was being used as Ra-hotep's and my living quarters. Usually it contained the ships cargo and other necessary supplies along with the captain's quarters. Below the main deck was a small hold into which our cargo of a dozen slaves had been crammed with little in the way of fresh air or light. The chariots we carried were dismantled and stowed in piles of parts lashed to the deck. The bow and stern of the *Horus* were high off the water and made landing against and pushing off from the riverbank easier. Even a boat as big as the *Horus* had no keel. A hogging truss of strong rope cable ran through the boat connecting the stern with the bow providing longitudinal rigidity. Without this truss the boat would break in two in rough water.

I learned from Ra-hotep that from the earliest times we Egyptians had built boats with which to sail the Nile. Originally these were made of lashed together reeds that grow in abundance in our land. Later palm wood sawed into planks was used with the planks held together by strong linen rope. Propelled by sail and current on the Nile these boats served Egypt well for millennia as long as we did not venture upon the Great Green. When Ahmose drove the Hyksos from our land he used strongly built boats to move his armies. Much had been learned about building boats from the peoples who lived along the coast of the Great Green in the land beyond the Sinai. The Theban princes needed a large navy to protect the new empire. They needed ships that could sail upon the open sea and carry bulk cargoes of soldiers, food, chariots, and horses. These ships had deck beams that passed through the hull and were deeper in their drafts for stability in rough water. The deckplanks of these ships were grooved and fitted to one another and held together with wooden pegs. The Theban princes gave Egypt its first real navy, one that could move the armies even upon the stormy waters of the Great Green.

I spent the day watching the sailors go about their work while the *Horus* moved silently downstream. Once, I poked my head down the open hatch to see the slaves, but was chased away by one of the sailors. From time to time we passed a boat going the other way. When this happened the sailors on the *Horus* laughed and made crude gestures toward the sailors on the passing boat who had the difficult task of rowing upstream when there was little wind. Otherwise the journey to Gebtu was uneventful. By day's end when we docked at the quay I was feeling quite proud of myself at having grown comfortable living on the boat.

The harbor at Gebtu was very busy for so late in the day. It seemed that every commercial boat on the river was seeking a berth for the night. Those unable to secure a harbor berth tied up to the riverbank. Still others rode the night out at anchor. Ra-hotep tells me that Gebtu is an important trading town. It guards the road to the Red Sea that lies more than a hundred miles to the east. The port of Taphta is Egypt's main opening to the east, and goods are carried overland by pack train to Gebtu where they are loaded aboard boats for shipment to the cities. The road also connects the Nile Valley with the quarries at Rehanu and the gold mines of the eastern desert at Eshuranib. Caravans ply the route to the mines and the Red Sea making them prey for the *Ente* bandits that control the hill country. Since ancient times Gebtu has been home to military garrisons that patrol the road and keep it safe from bandit attacks. Our captain tells us that the army has captured some of the bandits and that they are to be executed in the morning.

It is less than an hour since sunrise and the crowd is forming to watch the execution. Ra-hotep and I stand near the edge of the circle that the soldiers have formed with their spears and shields to keep the crowd back. Gebtu, like most Egyptian towns, does not have walls, and the crowd has gathered at the edge of the settlement where the buildings give way to a shallow marsh. The soldiers have no difficulty keeping the people in order. There is an erie quiet. The morning air is cool and still. It is not a good day to die.

"Here they come!" someone shouts. Those nearest the edge of the circle stretch their necks to see. Three pairs of human beings chained together are led into the clearing. They are dressed only in loin cloths and their bodies are bruised from being struck with sticks. No doubt they have been beaten to secure information about their fellow bandits. One of the bandits drags his leg behind him kicking up a small cloud of dust in the morning air. He seems in great pain as he stumbles to keep up with the others. Curious that a man should care about arriving at his place of death on time!

The commander of the guard gives the order to prepare the prisoners, and two soldiers bend the arms of each of the *Ente* behind their backs and over a short thick wooden pole. Their upper arms and forearms are tied with rough cord. This method of tying prisoners is peculiar to the Egyptian army. Years later I saw it used many times whenever my armies captured prisoners. The poor wretches are forced to their knees. Quickly other soldiers take their posts beside each prisoner and draw their deadly *kopesh* swords.

"Teacher, I cannot see," I said tugging at Ra-hotep's robe.

Ra-hotep looked down at me. "Are you certain Thutmose that you wish to see what is about to happen?" There was a pained look on his face as if he was thinking whether to grant my request or not.

I nodded. "Yes, Yes! Lift me up. I want to see!"

"As you wish young prince." He paused then muttered under his breath, "Perhaps it is time." Ra-hotep's bare arms appeared from under his robe and he lifted me around the waist. I put my arm around his neck as he held me to him.

The soldiers stood at the ready. Each executioner grabbed his victim by the hair and pulled it straight up and back exposing the neck. The rush of blood through the thick neck veins swelled them until they looked like the bodies of headless snakes. The strong grip on the victim's hair forced their eyes open and they were made to stare into the face of Horus. It was the last thing they would see in this life. The executioners kept their eyes on their commander who raised his hand at the ready. In a quick movement the commander dropped his arm and the blades of half a dozen *kopesh* slashed deeply into the prisoners' throats.

I was amazed that there was not a single cry of pain from any of the *Ente*. Their eyes had the look of surprise, like those on a gazelle when it is struck by the hunter's arrow. I remember thinking how like animals we were when it came to dying. The slash of the sword produced an instant spurting of blood from the neck. The soldiers had expertly positioned themselves so that the blood flowed out and down falling harmlessly on the warm sand rather than on the soldier's clothing. There was no struggle. For a few seconds the blood flowed strong and hot. And then just as suddenly as it had begun, it slowed to a trickle. I could see the bodies go limp as the life ebbed from them. The only thing keeping the bodies upright was the strength of the executioner's grip on their hair. One by one the soldiers released their grip and stepped back. One by one the lifeless bodies of the bandits fell to the ground coming to rest face down on the warm brown sand. The soldiers kicked sand over the spilled blood until the earth had done its work and there was little trace of the precious fluid that once coursed through the veins of six human beings.

From somewhere in the crowd I heard the retching of a troubled stomach as it expelled its contents in a vomitous rage. Ra-hotep looked into my face. His eyes searched as if trying to determine what was going through my young mind now that I had witnessed the death of a human being. Curiously, I felt little, although I do not know if that was because of my young age or because there was something in me that made me cold to such events. I truly do not know. Ra-hotep said nothing as he lowered me to the ground. The crowd was drifting away and in a few minutes only a small knot of spectators remained. Ra-hotep took my hand and began leading me back to the boat. For a second I resisted.

"What is it, Thutmose?" Ra-hotep asked.

"What will they do with the corpses," I asked with a detachment that seemed to disturb my teacher.

Ra-hotep let out a deep breath.

"They will be thrown into the marsh where they will become food for the fish and crocodiles" he answered. "Is there anything else you wish to know?"

Ra-hotep's voice was edgy. Somehow I had disappointed the old teacher, but I did not know why.

The *Horus* made good time down river. By day's end we put in along the riverbank for a good meal and a night's sleep. The boat was underway again by sunrise, and at midday we slid past the town of Junet Tantere where I saw the great temple of Hathor resting majestically on the riverbank. Its sandstone walls glinted beautifully in the noon sun and Ra-hotep told me it is the oldest temple of Hathor in all Egypt.

Our captain barked new orders and the crew rushed to their stations. For the first time I saw the oarsmen tie themselves in their seats and slip the large oars through the rope loops that serve as oarlocks. The *Horus* rounded the curve of the Great Bend. For the next thirty miles the river is shallow, rocky and full of sandbars. Because the river narrows the current flows more quickly. The captain ordered the small sail hoisted to the top of the mast. He will use the headwind as a brake and to quicken the response of the boat to the steering oars. He wants to clear the shallows by nightfall. For the next six hours he and the crew will do their difficult work in unison to avoid becoming stranded on a sandbar or suffering an even more serious mishap.

Ra-hotep urged me to go forward and stand with the bow lookout. The man has the eyes of a falcon and he continually shouts instructions to the captain who stands at the stern giving orders to the helmsmen. I kneel at his feet looking through the bow rail, my untrained eyes searching to find the dangers that the lookout sees so easily. He has no time for me except to mutter for me to stay out of the way. After a while I learn the trick is to look for the water's surface to change color. A light green surface means shallows and sandbars. Dark spots amid a deep green can hide boulders that could crush a ship's hull. Always the trick is to stay in the deep water where the oars and steering rudders can bite deeply and steer the boat around obstacles.

For hours the crew worked under the command of the captain who, more than any other, seemed to feel the tension of keeping the boat safe. By the end of the day the oarsmen were exhausted and the men who worked the topsail ropes had worn out the leather pads strapped to their palms to prevent burns. We pulled into the little town of Hut only moments before Horus disappeared over the horizon. Our captain did a fine job in seeing us through the narrows. The crew was given an extra ration of beer for its performance.

Two day's sail and we arrive at Abedju, one of the holiest place in all Egypt. It is here that the great god Osiris is buried. A large temple marks the place. The temple is surrounded by cemeteries that are considered to be the most desirable places to be entombed. It is here where the first pharaohs of Egypt are buried. There is a brisk trade in death. From the rail of the *Horus* we can see the funeral boats that bear the bodies of the dead from all over Egypt carried here to be buried in the same ground as Osiris himself. Our captain maneuvers carefully to avoid hitting these small boats and more than once the relatives of the deceased are given an earful of abuse directed at a boat that came too close. The tombs and the temple can be seen from the water. At night they are illuminated by the light of torches that keep the grave robbers away.

It is early evening when we go ashore. Ra-hotep wishes to visit the temple and bathe in its sacred lake. It has been more than a week since he has purified himself in sacred water and he tells me he is feeling unclean. Abedju makes its living off the dead, and the temple priests charge a tidy sum to officiate at the entombment of the deceased. Still, Abedju is a place of pilgrimage to the grave of Osiris. The pilgrims are drawn, too, by the regular reenactment of the slaughter of Osiris at the hands of his brother Seth. After he has bathed, Ra-hotep and I attend the reenactment. My teacher says it will be the beginning of my religious studies.

It is late and I am tired. My mind cannot follow the subtleties of the play that is being performed in front of me. What sticks in my head is the story of Seth and Osiris, brothers who fought over the dominion of the earth. Seth hacked the corpse of Osiris to pieces and scattered his body throughout the earth. Wherever a piece of the body was found buried, there a holy place sprung up. Abedju is the place where Osiris's head is buried. In my tired state the whole story strikes me as ridiculous and I wonder to Ra-hotep why the pilgrims come to hear such silliness. The old priest responds that faith is its own justification. That the world soon wears down the mind that seeks for truth only in what it can see or touch. I do not understand and fall asleep. When I wake it is morning and the *Horus* has already been underway for two hours.

Ra-hotep brings me a large loaf of bread made from emmer wheat for breakfast. The loaf is shaped like a turtle and the depression in its middle is filled with honey and dates. Next to this the radishes that the sailors eat and even the dried goose flesh that we have been eating is poor fare. Ra-hotep sits down beside me and watches me eat.

"Did you sleep well, Thutmose?" he asks.

The honey is sweet to my taste and I hardly hear him. "Yes," I answer and take another bite of the emmer bread. My clay cup holds a tart beer, the favorite drink of all Egyptians. Egyptians also drink wine of course. The finest grapes come from the vineyards in the Delta. It is said that the hated Hyksos made the best wine. But beer is best, and there is an old proverb that says "Bitter is the day without beer." The beer from my cup is cool and thin and cleanses my throat of the honey's thick sweetness.

The boat follows the channel as it snakes close to the western shore. Ra-hotep points out over the rail to some farmers working the land. He draws my attention to a device that they are using to raise water from the river and to lift it to the irrigation canals that nourish their fields.

"Do you know what that is, Thutmose?" he asks.

Before I can answer he adds. "Do you know why it is so valuable an invention for the land of *Kemit*?"

I am too busy eating to answer. I lift my cup to my mouth and Ra-hotep's hand stops me from drinking.

"Pay attention, Thutmose." The sternness in his voice forces my interest.

"No Teacher. I do not know."

"Listen, then," Ra-hotep said. "That is a *shadouf*, and it is a gift of the Hyksos invaders that they left behind. Look at the two stakes driven into the ground. They support that long wooden beam that has a weight on one end and a big leather bucket at the other. See how the farmer dips the bucket in the river."

Ra-hotep stopped speaking until I looked over the railing at the farmer.

"A full bucket would be too heavy to lift. But the weighted beam makes it easy to lift the bucket and swing it up half again as high as the stakes that hold it in the middle. With this device one man can do the work of twenty in the old way."

"But why do we use the things of the hated Hyksos," I asked. "Did they not invade this Black Land and put a curse upon it for many years? Why do we not be rid of all that is of the Hyksos?"

Ra-hotep ignored the question.

"Look at the farmers in the fields. See how the boys pull the plow to break up the earth. They use the new plough with upright handles made of light wood. In ancient times only those farmers who could afford an ox could till the land. Now the new plough can be pulled through the earth by any farmer's son. Many more farmers can till and plant so that Egypt is rich in food and will never again know famine unless the gods will it so." Ra-hotep paused. "That new plough was also a gift of the vile Hyksos. What do you think of that?"

The puzzled look on my face must have spoken volumes. I was about to say something when Ra-hotep cut me off.

"The lesson, Thutmose, is that you must never be afraid to learn from others. Even from your hated enemy. The world is full of mysterious things and no man has solved them all. Never take pride in your ignorance. Search for knowledge everywhere, even among those who oppose you. Never permit hatred to cloud your thinking. Always see things as they are. A prince cannot afford illusions."

Ra-hotep looked away casting his eyes toward the opposite shore. Suddenly I saw his face pucker in a hideous manner like he had tasted something foul. He shook his head so violently that his cheeks fluttered. He turned his head away and spat.

"What is it, Teacher?" I asked.

"Look!" he said pointing behind me. "Look at that!"

He spat again, this time giving off a whining sound that sounded like the cry of a captive bird.

I turned around. The sailors were snickering at Ra-hotep's manner. All I could see were some fishermen casting their nets in the river in hopes of a catch. "What is it?" I asked again.

Ra-hotep was almost sick. "Those fishermen!" he said with alarm. "Fish are unclean! They are not to be eaten by civilized people!" The sailors laughed for much of their diet consisted of fish!

The captain roared with laughter.

"Do not be concerned, Oh prince. Most of the common people of Egypt eat fish every day. It is another gift of the Nile. Without them we could not feed the navy!"

I looked back at Ra-hotep. He sat there shaking his head in disgust. The captain spoke again.

"The priests think fish are unclean because Seth cut off Osiris's prick and fed it to the great Nile carp who swallowed it whole! These great fish weigh five hundred pounds and must be hunted with spears, for no net can hold them."

The captain stopped speaking for a moment. When he resumed he had an impish look in his eye.

"Perhaps the priests don't eat carp because it tastes like a prick!"

The captain roared with laughter and his crew laughed openly along with him.

"Of course," he said pretending to be serious, "since they go without women you'd think that priests should be able to tell the difference between the taste of a fish and the taste of a prick!"

The crew convulsed into laughter. Even one of the soldiers of my bodyguard could no longer contain himself and laughed loudly.

Ra-hotep was furious. He rose and walked angrily away and disappeared into the deckhouse. I sat there not knowing what to do. I had just had my first encounter with the religious mind and it left me confused.

# Ten

We were twelve nights on the river, almost half-way to Memphis, when the *Horus* put in at Asyut on the west bank. Here the Nile narrows and the desert encroaches upon the river forming a natural desert plateau connecting the river with the Libyan plain. For centuries this area has been a major route of invasion from Libya. Asyut has been a military town for as long as the pyramids have stood. It is home to a large walled fortress and a full division of imperial troops, almost five thousand men. The division commander was standing on the quay to provide an official welcome. Quarters had been prepared for us within the fortress and we were invited to dinner.

The commander's name is Mersu and he is one of the corps of professional soldiers to whom the New Kingdom has entrusted its fate. Short and stocky he moves like a muscular donkey. His voice is pleasant enough, but has an edge to it that comes from being accustomed to command. During a meal of roast goose, bread, and wine Ra-hotep and the commander talk amiably about life in Asyut. Mersu tells us that he is pleased to receive the chariots that the *Horus* has brought. The desert rocks are hard on the machines and keeping them in good repair is a constant problem. It will take a day to assemble them and they will be immediately put into service patrolling the desert roads.

"Its the damned Libyans!" Mersu said pouring another glass of wine for Ra-hotep and himself while I busied myself with eating a plum. Plums were a new fruit for Egypt at the time and were somewhat hard to come by. They were imported from Syria and were very expensive. Mersu had come by a shipment as payment from a caravan leader whose mules were fed at imperial expense. My tongue chased the sweet juice from the purple jewel as it ran down my chin. Ra-hotep gave me a dirty look. Mersu smiled broadly and laughed.

"The boy eats like a soldier," he said. "Good. Good. Do you want another?"

Ra-hotep glared at me. "Not until you learn to eat like a civilized person!" he snapped. Having made his point Ra-hotep steered the conversation back to the Libyans. "Tell me, general," he said, "what is the military situation in Asyut."

Mersu sat back in his chair and his voice was serious.

"The damned wooly-heads are always causing trouble. Small bandit raids happen often and the caravans to the desert oases can never be sure when they will be attacked."

Mersu paused and sipped some wine from his cup.

"Its more a nuisance than anything else," he said with a sigh. "There are enough Egyptian troops in Asyut to make sure that no real trouble starts."

Ra-hotep nodded. "I see," he said pleasantly. The wine had gone to his head and he was loosing interest in the subject.

Mersu continued.

"You see we have the advantage. The terrain here is flat and the ground hard packed. It is ideal chariot country. The chariots give us the advantage in speed and range over the Libyans who raid mostly on foot. What transport they have is provided by donkeys.

Every day our chariot troops patrol the roads and roam the desert searching for the bandits. Whenever we find a bunch of wooly-heads we run them down and herd them into the open desert. The sun does the rest."

The old soldier let out a deep belch and smiled. He looked satisfied like someone whose world was completely understandable, a world of no complexity.

"It will take a half day at least to unload the chariots tomorrow," Mersu said. "Perhaps you and the boy would like to ride along with one of the patrols."

I perked up immediately. Ra-hotep was less than excited. I was beginning to learn that physical exertion of any kind held no value for the man. Sensing the priest's resistance and my excitement, Mersu pressed the attack.

"If you have any fear for the boy's safety," he said, "I will personally lead the patrol and the young prince can ride with me."

He had the look of a conspirator upon his face.

"What say, Oh prince, would you like to get your first taste of chasing wooly-heads in the desert?"

"Yes, Oh Yes!" My voice had that high pitched squeal to it that lingered until I was twelve years old. I hated it. It made me sound like a child. Here I was being invited by the division commander to hunt bandits and all I could do was squeak like a mouse! I regained control of my excitement and tried to sound grown up.

"I would very much like to ride the chariot," I said. "What time do we leave?" I looked at Ra-hotep ready to argue with him if need be, but the old man said nothing. Mersu took his silence as agreement.

"Good. Then its settled. I shall have my aide call for you at your quarters one hour before sunrise." Mersu poured himself another cup of wine and raised his glass in a toast. "To you, my prince. Good hunting!"

The sky was gray in the time before sunrise. Ra-hotep, Mersu's aide, and I walked from our quarters down a narrow alley that opened upon a large parade ground. Barracks surrounded three sides of the open area forming three sides of a square. The barracks square was the center of military life, the place where parades, marching practice, weapons drill, and formal ceremonies were held. It was also where public punishments were pronounced and carried out. The warrior princes of Thebes had seen to it that the Egyptian army was renowned for its discipline, and the army relied as much upon the whip to motivate its soldiers as it did upon good commanders.

At the far end of the square I could see Mersu standing in front of his chariot. Another soldier had already mounted the vehicle and was holding the reins that controlled the bits in the mouths of two beautiful horses standing side-by-side in a double harness attached to a single wooden pole that ran between them. The end of the pole had a wooden cross brace forming a T-bar attached to it that fit snugly under and against the chest of each animal. The horses were of that rich reddish brown color that resembles African mahogany. Their ankles were white in stark contrast to the reddish brown of the rest of their legs. One horse named *Beloved Of Amun* had a white diamond blaze on his forehead. These horses were specially bred in military stables for use by high ranking officers in the chariot corps. They stood over six feet tall and their muscles rippled beneath their skin with even the slightest movement of their bodies. Their eyes were large and clear and seemed to possess a permanent stare as if trying to anticipate what next to do. From time to time one horse would flare its nostrils in a loud snort and push against its partner. The cool air was easy in the animals' lungs as first one then the other stomped the earth with a hoof as if to stretch its muscles in preparation for the day's work. I walked close to the animal nearest me and ran my hand along its flank. The skin felt smooth and the creature smelled like moist leather.

"Good morning my prince," Mersu said with a wave of his hand. "Good morning Holy One," he added almost too nonchalantly. He had a sarcastic smile on his face.

"Are you ready to hunt the wooly-heads?" he asked turning back to me.

"Yes, general" I said. "I have thought of nothing else all night."

The old soldier smiled again. "Good, good." He paused and turned to the soldier in the chariot.

"This is Sinwe," he said. "He is my driver and shield bearer. He gets me close to the enemy and I kill them!"

He roared with laughter and I saw Sinwe laugh with him. These two had been hunting one enemy or another for a very long time together.

"If anything happens to me you can rely on old Sinwe here to get you back safely." Mersu paused. "He's very good at running away." The general burst into laughter. It was an old joke between these two professionals, one that Sinwe had heard and endured a hundred times.

Mersu looked impressive arrayed in his battle uniform. A bronze helmet resembling the War Crown of the Pharaoh marked him as a general and it sat regally upon his head held in place with a leather chin strap. Body armor fashioned from small overlapping bronze plates two millimeters thick covered his body from neck to waist. The coverlet protected his arms to the elbow. Like Mersu's helmet, his body armor was richly decorated in painted designs of red, yellow, and blue. Tough leather boots reached above his ankles and the thick soles provided good traction on the chariot's wooden floor. Leather wristbands and gloves protected the forearms and hands from the snap of the bowstring and permitted a firm grip on the composite bow that rested quietly in its case attached to the side of the chariot. A thick leather belt around Mersu's waist held a *kopesh*, a reminder that even chariot officers were expected to dismount and fight like common infantry once the battle was joined. As I looked at Mersu dressed for battle he looked all business, a professional soldier who would kill in the wink of an eye if circumstances warranted.

Twenty chariots, each carrying a driver and an officer, stood assembled in a line off to our right. The commander of the squadron was a Leader of Twenty, typically a young officer holding his first or second command. Mersu would ride with this unit today, but command remained with the young officer who would have to perform under the watchful eye of his superior. Grooms tended to the squadron's horses as they awaited the order to begin the day's patrol. At the end of the day when the grooms cooled and fed the horses there would be treats of dom dates and figs for these fine animals. The grooms had a look of pride in their eyes as if the horses were their children. Like grooms everywhere, they resented being required to trust their charges to soldiers who might get them hurt. I remember thinking that it was a wise chariot officer who took the time to listen to a groom about how to treat a horse.

"I think it wise, my prince, if you were to ride with me" Mersu said. He turned toward Ra-hotep, "Holy one, perhaps you would care to ride with the commander of the squadron." Ra-hotep was not enthusiastic about any of this and grunted annoyingly as he walked toward the commander's chariot and silently climbed aboard. Mersu turned to me.

"Well, my prince, shall we climb up on this old war chariot of mine?" I smiled broadly as he lifted me up to the vehicle. Across the center of the machine slightly towards the front was a wooden bar that ran completely across the chariot from one side to another. About two inches thick, it was strongly attached to the chariot's side. Hanging from its center was a thick leather strap. From each end of the bar where it attached to the sides hung a leather thong in the form of a looped slip knot. Mersu saw that I was trying to determine what purpose these devices might serve.

"The center pole is called a belly bar," he said. "The warrior wraps the strap around his body and leans against the bar when the chariot is at full-speed. This helps him keep his balance in a rough ride and steadies his aim with bow or javelin."

I nodded as if it all seemed so obvious. What was obvious was that I had much to learn about this fighting machine.

"What are those loops for," I said pointing to the leather slip knots that hung from each far end of the belly bar.

Mersu answered the question seriously as if he were instructing a young soldier.

"Those are leg loops," he said. "The archer slips one leg through the loop and pulls it tight. They serve the same purpose as the belly bar, to provide steadiness when the chariot is at high speed."

"Do I have to wear one," I asked trying not to sound excited.

Mersu smiled. "We will let you try it out once we get into the desert." He paused. "After all," he grinned, "we can't have you falling out of the damned thing now can we!"

The general turned to Sinwe.

"Ready you old fart!" he said with a laugh.

"After you, my lord" Sinwe said sarcastically. I could see that Mersu was having a good time. It had been months since he had ridden with the troops. Garrison duty in peacetime dulls the edge of an old soldier but not his appetite for the hunt. I could see the excitement rise in Mersu's eyes as he yelled to the commander of the squadron.

"Are you ready, Captain?" He waved at the commander.

"Yes, general," came the reply.

"Very well," Mersu yelled in return. "By Seth, what are you waiting for! Get these troops moving! No one has yet earned his pay this day!"

With a wave of his arm the Leader of Twenty signalled his squadron to fall into a line of column two machines abreast and to proceed at a walk to the main gate of the fortress. Mersu and I watched the vehicles move into column with a precision born of practice. Their wheels disturbed only a light dust as the chariots and the horses moved out at a walk. Mersu smiled.

"Now there's a young lad who knows his animals," he said. I looked up at the general.

"Always give the horses a chance to get warm. Walk them first. Let them get used to the air in their lungs. Many a good army horse has been ruined by some young show off who pressed them to break gait to a gallop too soon."

Sinwe snapped the reins on our horses and they, too, moved off at a brisk walk. The chariot lurched forward and the large wheels turned with a surprising smoothness on the hard packed earth underneath. Mersu pressed his body against the belly bar out of habit and I hung on to the thing with both hands. I was tall enough to see past the horses and could see that we were falling into the rear of the column. Somewhere in the pack was Ra-hotep riding along being thoroughly miserable. I was having the time of my life. As we passed through the main gate that opened out to the western desert my heart was pounding with excitement.

The squadron moved along the dirt track that led into the desert. The Libyan desert was a mystical place for Egyptians. We believed that it ended far to the west where the gates to the under-world stood. The western desert was where Horus ended his life each day with the setting sun, only to be resurrected and to rise again in the east the following day. The sun had cleared the horizon and was beginning to turn the sand into a frying skillet. We had not been on patrol more than a half hour and already I was soaked to the skin with sweat.

Mersu took the heat in stride and did not seem to be suffering from the weight of his metal armor although he had removed the heavy helmet and stored it on a peg. He must have sensed how warm I was.

"Would you like some water, young prince" he asked as neutrally as he could. I guessed he didn't want to embarrass me by my need for water so early in the patrol.

I was truly thirsty but decided to wait.

"No, general. I will drink when the others do." Young as I was I was beginning to find some enjoyment in trying to behave as an adult or, what is not the same thing, not to behave as a child.

Mersu seemed pleased by my answer. He changed the subject. "How do you like our fine Egyptian chariots?"

I smiled and nodded in approval. "Tell me," I said. "Have we always had such fine vehicles for our armies?"

Mersu shook his head.

"No my prince," he answered. "The chariot is another gift from the vile Hyksos that we took when we drove them from the land of *Kemit.* For more than two thousand years before the invasion we Egyptians had no vehicles at all for we did not know of the wheel. Our armies were little more than militias who fought with simple bows, spears and clubs. In battle we wore no armor or helmet nor carried the *kopesh,* for all these things we did not yet know."

I listened with great interest as Mersu continued.

"Egypt was protected by the great deserts on either side, the Great Green to the north, and the cataracts of the Nile to the south. She was sealed from invasion by these gifts of nature. For two millennia we fought only the wooly-heads and the Negroes of Nubia who, like ourselves, were armed with the same primitive weapons of war."

Mersu stopped talking and squinted to see what was happening up ahead. For some reason Sinwe had not kept pace with the squadron and we had fallen behind. The column of chariots had stopped and was waiting for us to catch up.

"Pay attention, Sinwe," Mersu said in his official voice. "Don't let the squadron get too far ahead. We have a royal prince with us. If something should happen I don't intend to have to fight the wooly-heads alone!"

Sinwe said nothing but snapped the reigns to prod the horses to move along. The chariot lurched forward and I strengthened my grip on the belly bar. Mersu continued talking.

"It must have been a terrible time," he said, "when the Hyksos came to this Black Land. Our armies were slaughtered in days. And when it was over the Asiatics sat upon Egypt from the Delta to Memphis for almost two hundred years."

The old soldier paused and looked toward the horizon as if trying to see back into time in the eye of his imagination.

"But how was it possible for such a vile people to bring the people of Egypt to their knees? The Asiatics are barbarians still and my grandfather's armies crushed them again and again! How could Pharaoh's great armies be so easily defeated?" There was an edge to my voice that I did not put there.

Mersu smiled broadly.

"You are riding in the answer my prince!" His voice was enthusiastic as he realized that I was genuinely interested in what he was saying. "Our armies stood on the desert plains only to be slaughtered by the Hyksos and their chariots. Their archers mounted on the vehicles slaughtered our footsoldiers from great distances. Until that day Egyptian soldiers had never seen a horse much less a chariot. Even when our soldiers mustered the courage to stand and fight, the horses and chariots smashed into our ranks with great force shattering them into helpless pieces. The archers now put down their bows and struck our men with javelins as the chariots pressed in upon our footsoldiers from all sides. When our men could suffer the slaughter no longer, they broke and ran across the desert casting their weapons away. It was then that the real killing began. On foot our soldiers could not outrun the chariot. Skilled drivers guided the machines close to the running soldiers. The javelin thrower now became an archer again. The driver brought the machine close and the archers killed the soldiers with easy shots from the bow. Thousands of our soldiers were slain in this way until, at last, great Egypt could bleed no more and surrendered to her new masters."

It was a fantastic tale, one that I had never heard before. It was a tale with many lessons. Even at my young age I sensed that no army could stand against the power of a chariot force in the hands of a competent officer like Mersu. In the hands of our warrior kings of Thebes the horse and chariot had regained our freedom. If Ra-hotep was here he would have been proud of me for what I said next.

"General" I said trying to muster some authority in my voice "tell me more about this machine of yours."

For the next ten minutes I listened silently as Mersu explained the important parts of the chariot to me. Watching the old general was like watching a proud man explain his work to an apprentice. And I was an eager apprentice indeed! Mersu drew my attention to the wheels and axles first. He told me how the original Hyksos machines had the axle in the middle of the riding platform, a design that made the chariot unstable at lope or canter speed. We Egyptians were clever enough to move the axle to the back of the platform. It gives our machines greater balance and we can charge ahead at the full gallop and still keep the machine upright. The wheel, too, was improved by our commanders. The Egyptian wheel has six spokes instead of four for greater strength and lighter weight. The wheel itself is made of individual sections notched, glued, and fitted together for strength. The rim is of hammered bronze held to the wood with studded nails whose square heads extend beyond the metal's surface and give the wheel excellent traction. The entire machine is made of wood and leather and the fighting platform is constructed of Syrian pine. The wooden front and rounded sides are of soft pliable palm wood that is native to Egypt. The wheels are made of hardy cedar. Completely assembled the Egyptian chariot can be carried across streams and other obstacles by only two men with little effort.

I could tell from the way he spoke that Mersu was proud of the way the Egyptians had improved the vehicle. Like many Egyptian commanders, he had given his machine its own name much as one would a horse. Printed neatly on the side were the words *Battle Animal*. Having known Mersu for only a short time, I could not have agreed more that this name was fitting. Each squadron in the division had its own colors painted boldly on the front and sides of their machines. When at full gallop with their guidons streaming from flexible poles and the dust blowing up in great clouds, a chariot squadron was an impressive sight indeed.

The sun was still at a shallow angle in the sky when the chariot carrying Ra-hotep pulled next to us. Even at a trot it was difficult to communicate while the machines were moving. Finally Sinwe pulled back on the reins and we slowed to a halt. Mersu leaned over the side and spoke.

"What is it, Holy One?"

Mersu was not used to addressing anyone but his military superiors with formal respect. It was easy to see that he did not like it even when he was required by circumstances to do it. I said nothing although I guessed what Ra-hotep wanted.

"General," the priest said, "it is getting late. We must return soon or the boat will not be able to make sufficient distance before nightfall to justify the day's sail. It is mid-morning and it will take us yet an hour to return to the fortress. We must start our way back soon."

Ra-hotep's voice was irritable. He had not enjoyed the morning patrol as I had. Mersu did not appreciate the priest's tone and I could see that it took some effort to keep his tongue civil.

He looked at me and shrugged. "As you wish, Holy One," he said evenly. "Turn around, Sinwe," he said. "Make good for the barracks."

In a single motion Sinwe snapped the reins and pulled the left one hard. The horses took a few steps backward and then quickly began a turn to the left. Sinwe snapped the reins again and the horses moved into a brisk trot. As we passed Ra-hotep's chariot facing the other way Mersu smiled at the priest and raised his hand open palm in the manner of the Egyptian military salute. Ra-hotep was no fool and saw the look of satisfied sarcasm on the old general's face as he realized that he would be forced to follow Mersu's machine all the way back choking on the dust from our chariot.

Sinwe coaxed the horses into a brisk trot. All the time we had been on patrol the horses had moved at a walk. It was good sense in the desert to conserve the horses' strength until it was truly needed. I gripped the belly bar a bit more tightly when Mersu spoke.

"My prince, perhaps you should slip one leg through the leg loop and make yourself tight to the bar." The old general winked at me.

He had read my mind! I wanted to see the horses run and feel the machine as it moved at battle speed. Quickly I put my leg through the loop, tightened it, and hung on. My face must have had a grin on it. Mersu asked if I was enjoying myself.

"How fast can it go general?" I asked knowing right well that the general knew what I was trying to do.

"Quite fast, my prince." "Sinwe!" the general said with a shout. "Take the horses to a lope!"

Sinwe nodded and snapped the reins. In an instant the machine sped up and I could feel the power of the wheels as they spun faster. The bronze studs on the metal rimmed wheels clawed into the earth and grasped it more securely with each revolution. I felt the vibration of the wheels' motion over the packed ground in my hands. I clung to the belly bar.

It was all in a day's work for Mersu who, I recalled thinking, looked like he had been born on the thing. He pressed his weight forward leaning against the belly bar. Both hands were still on his hips as the chariot raced over the desert sand. Out of the corner of his eye he saw me looking at him as I tried to work up the courage to let go of the belly bar. Again the general read my mind.

"Give it a try, my prince. The leg loop will keep you from falling out the back." He paused and grinned broadly. "After all, the point is to be able to shoot the bow and throw the javelin from the chariot, not just to ride around in the damned thing!"

Slowly I leaned forward and released my grip on the belly bar. At first my legs were a bit unsteady, but I caught my balance. Both hands were free! It would take practice, but once a soldier caught on he could wield his weapons with deadly effectiveness from his perch on the chariot. Suddenly I became aware of the sounds around me. The horses' hooves pounded into the ground like the sound of a strong wind blowing fruit from the trees. The leather reins that controlled the horses were slapping up and down along the full length of the animals' back making sharp wet sounds. But it was the clatter of the wheels on the hard ground that made the whole machine shake, giving off a creaking sound that felt like the wood would break scattering it and us in a thousand pieces. I turned around and immediately saw that whatever was behind us was lost in a thick cloud of dust. How did the drivers see when they were in the heat of battle? My throat was dry and my nose filled with dust. I tried to wet my mouth, but no spittle came. It was like chewing on cloth.

It was too noisy to talk. I caught sight of Mersu who was looking down at me. He nodded his head as if to ask if I were alright. I grinned widely and nodded back. His hand moved forward and he tapped Sinwe on the shoulder. Sinwe snapped the reins and the horses leaned forward and dug their rear legs into the ground. Their bodies were wet from sweat as they broke their gait from lope to canter. The machine flew like the wind across the desert. For the first time I wondered where Ra-hotep was, only to realize that I didn't really care. I was enjoying and testing myself at the same time, something I learned to do with some regularity as I grew older. But for now it was enough that I was a royal prince of Egypt thundering across the western desert in the chariot of a general and having the time of my life. There was no fear, no second thoughts, no desire not to repeat the experience. I have wondered since then if it was on that wild ride that I first knew that I would be a soldier.

We roared through the open gate of the fortress and Sinwe brought the machine to a halt. Mersu was laughing heartily as he helped me free myself from the leg loop and dismount. We were both covered with a thin dust that mixed with the sweat of our bodies and covered us in a caky gray slime.

"Come, my prince. We must wash off." He led the way to the long rectangular box filled with water. It was the horse trough where the animals drank. The general looked at me and winked.

"Here is where soldiers wash at the end of the day," he said and immediately stuck his large head under the water. His hands scooped water over the back of his neck. He straightened up and shook his head sending water over me. With his hands he rubbed his forearms clean. With one last motion he bent over the trough and filled his scooped hands again throwing the water over his head in a last rinse. Then he turned to me and stretched out his hand toward the trough.

"Your turn, my prince." he said with an impish grin.

Behind us Ra-hotep arrived and for a second I turned from Mersu and looked at my teacher. He dismounted and walked toward us apparently upset by something. Mersu looked from Ra-hotep to me. "Well," he said. "Here comes civilization." I smiled back at him as I turned toward the priest hurrying toward me. When he was almost upon me I turned from him and plunged my head into the water in the horse trough. It was cool and refreshing. I raised my head from the water and let it drip over my clothing as I followed Mersu's example and scooped water over my arms. The water filled my ears so I could not clearly hear what Ra-hotep was saying. It was enough that when I finished washing with the horses I turned toward him and saw the look of displeasure upon his face. For a moment I thought the old man had had another taste of fish.

Mersu ordered Sinwe to drive Ra-hotep and me to the dock where the *Horus* was waiting to continue our journey down the Nile. Ra-hotep was still covered with the dust of the desert when we arrived and he kept our captain waiting while he bathed in the river to rid himself of the smell of dirt and animals. I went aboard to check on *Kera-Ra* who had been left in the care of one of my bodyguards. The animal rushed toward me, his tail wagging excitedly. In a graceful movement he leapt from the deck into my arms. The dog seemed to be trying to lick the smile from my face as he poked his snout here and there about my head. I played with the dog for a few minutes until I heard the captain order the gangplank hauled in. Ra-hotep had finished his bath and had finally graced the ship's company with his presence on deck. Our captain shook his head in mock disgust and barked out orders to get underway. I stood at the rail with *Kera-Ra* in my arms watching the *Horus* back out of its berth under the power of her oars. A few minutes later and we were on our way downstream again.

The distance from Asyut to Menat is fifteen miles. Here the river widens and the current seems swifter as indeed it is. Three miles south of Menat the river suddenly swings west in a tight loop before swinging back again to the east where it makes another loop before resuming its northerly direction. Menat sits at the top of the second loop. The town is the last place for a boat to put in before attempting to negotiate the twenty miles of swift water that lies downstream. Our captain planned well and we reached Menat shortly before dusk, time enough to tie up to a wooden pier and prepare ourselves for the next day's journey.

Before setting sail the next morning Ra-hotep and I paid close attention as the crew lashed down everything on deck. Our personal baggage stored in the deckhouse was also tied down. The *Horus* slipped its pier with no effort as the strength of the current swiftly caught the bow of the boat and threw it downstream. The captain ordered everyone to tie a safety rope around their waists and attach the other end to the mast or bow rail. I found a short length of rope and tied it to *Kera-Ra*'s collar. I wrapped the other end around my hand for a secure grip. We were on the river for only a short time when the dull throbbing sound of rushing water reached my ears. Looking at the riverbank I could see that the Nile was giving up its width as it had been for the last few miles. The sound of rushing water grew louder while the Nile grew ever narrower until it seemed that I could reach out and touch the riverbank. The boat rounded a slight bend and suddenly the riverbank transformed itself into a solid wall of rock. Massive cliffs higher than the walls of the Temple of Luxor rose straight up from the water's edge, their stone legs rooted deeply in the hard earth beneath the surface. A few seconds later the *Horus* gained speed with the current and plunged between the sheer sides of the stone chute that trapped the river for the next twenty miles.

The captain prepared the crew for a rough transit. The lookout was lashed to his nest overlooking the bow shouting one warning after another to avoid rocks, shallows, and sandbars. The oarsmen lashed themselves to their seats with strong rope. Their oars stuck straight out from the ship's deck. At the command of the captain, the oars were to be used to keep the *Horus* from slamming into the cliff walls on either side of the rushing river. The helmsmen manned their steering oars at the stern. The captain stood nearby trying to anticipate the treacherous river's next move.

The boat rocked violently as the turbulence sometimes raised the steering oars completely out of the water leaving the boat to float freely with the current. Ra-hotep was nowhere to be seen. He had gone inside the deck house some time earlier. Lashed to the forward rail with my safety rope I had a good view of what was happening. The noise of the rushing water grew louder the further we penetrated into the narrow watery space that coursed between the cliffs. The height of the cliffs blocked the light that reached the bottom making it seem like dusk on the river's surface where the *Horus* was doing its best to stay afloat. Seconds later the boat was struck from the side with a great force that turned its bow sideways to the flowing water. The *Horus* rocked forward then back then forward again threatening to roll over. For what seemed like a long time it moved sideways with the current. Just as suddenly as it had begun the sideward force stopped and the boat's bow straightened and followed the current downstream again.

It was a frightening event and for a few seconds I thought that we might all be thrown into the water. Later I was told that the sideward force was a strong gust of wind that struck the top of the

cliff. The stone face of the cliff directed the force of the gust downward toward the bottom of the gorge. The speed of the wind
increased as it fell toward the base of the cliff. Once it struck the
water's surface the gust shot across the river at great speed. The
last gust turned the *Horus* almost completely around and threatened to roll her over. I tightened my grip on the rail and wondered
what I would do if things got worse.

In the next instant *Horus* lurched to the left, this time so
strongly that in the blink of an eye we were moving downstream
backwards! The helmsmen worked the steering oars with great
effort, but they were useless. The roar of the water against the
rocks made it difficult to hear and I was trying to make out what
the captain was yelling to the oarsmen when the force of the
impact threw me to the deck. A second later I crashed into the rail
and almost lost my grip on *Kera-Ra's* leash. When I raised my
head from the wet planking all I could see was a wall of stone. The
boat had crashed sideways into the cliff throwing cargo and bodies everywhere. Were it not for the safety ropes some of the crew
and bodyguard would have been thrown into the river. I struggled
to my feet and held on as tightly as I could. I saw the oarsmen
extend their oars and push hard against the cliff sending the boat
backwards. Another half turn and the *Horus* was pointing her
bow downstream.

From where I stood I could see the worried look on our captain's face. The wind had shifted from out of the north completely
around to the southwest as it often did this time of year. Behind us
a desert sandstorm was racing across the open dunes driving a
great wind in front of it. That wind was blowing over and behind
us. It was lashing us with strong gusts that raced down the cliff
walls and smashed into our boat. At the same time the wind was
pushing us from behind, making the bite of the steering oars too
shallow for good control. One did not have to be an experienced

sailor to realize that trapped as we were in the narrow gorge it would be only a matter of time before the *Horus* rolled over or was smashed against the cliff walls. Not even the most experienced captain could fight these dangerous conditions for the next twenty miles and hope to emerge unscathed.

The key was the wind, as I never forgot. A boat moving downstream at the same speed as the current has sufficient steerage only so long as the current is not too fast. The greater the speed of the current the less effect the steering oars have on the direction of the boat. When the steering oars cannot hold, any sideways force from the wind or from turbulent water can force a boat sideways and throw it out of control. I watched our captain shout his orders and I realized that he was ordering the mainsail raised to catch the following wind pressing against our back. A few minutes later and the bright green mainsail was tight against the first yardarm, its halyards tied firmly to their rail pins. The sail filled with the brisk wind in a great billowing motion that was accompanied by the snap of the thick linen unfurling itself to the following wind. A second later the mast made a loud creaking sound as its twin timbers strained against the force of the sail. Almost instantly the *Horus* seemed to have been taken into a firm hand. Her bow straightened true to the current and the steering oars bit deeply into the water. With the wind at her back and her sails full the boat gained speed until it was moving faster than the current. As long as she maintained her forward speed the *Horus* was under control.

The danger now was sandbars, and the captain warned his bow pilot to keep a sharp eye in his head. For the next ten miles our captain beat back the river's every challenge until the cliffs that had hidden our vision of the world beyond the riverbank dropped away. In their place was a long strip of fertile land running along the east bank of the river and stretching away almost five miles to the horizon. With no stone walls to contain it any longer the Nile once more spread out and gave up its fury in the way a bird suddenly calms itself after a few moments of being given its freedom from a cage. In these gentle waters I knew the *Horus* had seen us safely through the danger. It was late afternoon as we glided smoothly against the riverbank to tie up for the night.

The crew had worked hard all day and the captain showed his gratitude by having a hearty meal prepared. Half a dozen live geese were strangled and roasted over an open fire on the riverbank. The mud oven was put ashore and emmer and barley bread was baked fresh. Jugs of beer quenched the thirst of the crew and the captain passed out a few bottles of wine to the men to go along with their usual ration of beer. Ra-hotep emerged from the deck house shortly after we docked. He seemed a bit disheveled as if he had been ill. *Kera-Ra* went from person to person begging scraps. When he had eaten all he could, the animal curled up at my side and went to sleep. It was night and the crew was exhausted. The hot food relaxed us and made the pleasures of sleep irresistible. One by one the crew drifted off where they lay along the riverbank or on the deck. Even Ra-hotep had a difficult time keeping his eyes open and soon excused himself to return to his bed in the deckhouse. One of my bodyguards brought me a blanket to ward off the night chill. I lay down on the deck with the dog by my side. The stars shone brightly in the night sky. Soon the fire flickered low giving up its life with little resistance. I stared into the glowing coals. Their warm glow made my eyes heavy until I could no longer keep them open and, finally, fell asleep.

I rose early and watched the crew cast off the lines that held us to the riverbank. By the day's early light I could see the cliff walls a mile back up the river. But here the land was flat and wide. We sailed along for almost ten miles before the open fields narrowed again against a rocky riverbank. In the distance, perhaps five miles away, a ring of mountains formed the horizon. The mountains began as a continuation of the cliffs along the riverbank but then jutted inland and formed a semi-circle that surrounded the fertile plain on three sides with the Nile itself forming the fourth. In places the mountains were more than five hundred feet high. The sun rising over the eastern mountains colored the plains a rich green. The land was one of the most beautiful places that I had seen in Egypt. I walked along the deck to where the captain stood.

"Good morning, captain" I said pleasantly.

The captain nodded, "Good morning your highness," he replied. The captain was young to have such responsibility, no more than twenty or so. But then I remembered that in Egypt most men died before they were forty. Young he may be, but he had already lived more than half his life.

"I have not yet seen Ra-hotep this morning captain. Have you seen him? He looked a bit ill yesterday."

The look of satisfied sarcasm on the sailor's face was unmistakable.

"I think you will find him in the deckhouse, Oh prince." He grinned an evil grin. "He will not leave the deckhouse until we are past this place." His arm made a wide arc to indicate the flat plain of the east bank."

I was puzzled. "Why?" I asked.

"Better to ask him," he replied in a serious tone. The captain was tired of the conversation and had more important things to attend to.

I started to walk away. "One more thing, captain" I said turning back. "If it is not too much trouble can you tell me what they call this place?" I tried to show my irritation with the captain's impudence. But as always my voice just squeaked.

The sailor turned toward me and let out a sigh to show that he expected this to be the last time I would bother him today.

"This place is called the Plain of Amarna, and its said to be the most accursed spot in all Egypt."

*Kera-Ra* jumped at my dangling hand as I walked toward the deckhouse. The animal was in a playful mood and demanded attention. I stopped and scratched the dog behind the ears until it rolled over exposing its stomach. I was only a few feet from the door of the deckhouse and I wondered what Ra-hotep was doing inside. It was beyond the time when he usually made his appearance in his priestly robes nodding sanctimoniously to all who looked in his direction. This morning he was nowhere to be seen. I decided to beard the beast in his den. Why not? I was a royal prince after all. And though I had used them rarely preferring to sleep on deck with the crew my quarters were also in the deckhouse. I left *Kera-Ra* to his own entertainment and walked to the deckhouse door, knocked and without waiting for an invitation opened it and went in.

The smell of incense—"the sweat of the gods" as we Egyptians called it—was so overpowering that it almost made me sick. The window curtains were pulled tight so the air hung heavy with the heat and smell. What little light there was came from two small oil lamps in the corner. It took my eyes a few moments to get used to the dark. The incense was making my eyes run. My eyes adjusted to the dim light and I saw Ra-hotep kneeling in front of a small shrine tucked into the far corner. His back was toward me and the cowl from his priest's robes covered his head. His voice was a soft murmur. I could not make out what he was saying. I stood just inside the doorway wondering what to do. A few minutes wait produced nothing. Ra-hotep was still murmuring in the corner. I decided he must be at prayer. I also decided that I was sufficiently curious to interrupt him.

"Teacher," I said loud enough to give the man a start. "Are you ill? I did not see you on deck this morning and came to look after you."

My voice seemed to startle the priest. He quickly turned around to see who was speaking. Even in the dim light Ra-hotep recognized me. He turned back to the shrine as if to return to his prayer. Instead he made some sign with his hands, slowly peeled back the cowl from his head, stepped back and bowed. The ritual complete, he walked toward me put his hand on my back and followed me out the door. We stood in the bright sunlight for a few seconds adjusting to glare of the daylight and the cool morning air.

"Thank you for thinking of me, Thutmose. I assure you I am in fine health. But it was considerate of you to check on me."

He turned his gaze toward the plain. He stared at it for what seemed a long time. A shudder ran through his body. Ra-hotep looked at me and a forced smile appeared on his face. I remember thinking to myself, "Something is frightening this man," although I could not guess what it might be.

"Teacher," I said with genuine enthusiasm, "Do you not think this is a beautiful place? I asked the captain what it is called. He called it Amarna." I paused for a moment. "It is a strange word. What does it mean teacher?"

Ra-hotep was better now but he was still ill at ease. Again his eyes turned toward the open plain. For a long moment he stared at the mountains while remaining silent. Not knowing what else to do I stood with him and stared in the same direction. After a few minutes Ra-hotep spoke.

"This is the most accursed place in all of Egypt," he said. "Have you not wondered why a place of such beauty has no farms or villages in which men live and till the land? Have I not taught you to look closely at the things around you, Thutmose? Do you see any cattle? Are there any wild game to be had?" He stopped speaking for a few seconds. "Listen! Tell me what you hear." I looked at him and made a motion as if I was listening to something. Ra-hotep fell silent. After a few seconds I spoke.

"I don't hear anything teacher," I said. "What is it I am searching for?"

Ra-hotep's voice was serious now. "Where are the birds, Thutmose? Why are there no birds in the sky to fill the air with their voices." He stopped. "Have you ever been in a place in Egypt where there are no birds to be seen or heard?"

I stood as silent as the absent birds, for I did not know what my teacher wanted me to say. He had asked me many questions but in a manner that suggested he already knew the answers to what he asked of me. I sensed that Ra-hotep was frightened and as he told me about Amarna I understood why.

Ra-hotep spoke slowly. There was pain in his voice as if he were recalling painful memories.

"In the days following the invasion of the Hyksos the plain of Amarna became a vast killing ground, a tortured cemetery where Egyptians were butchered and torn open and forced to endure unspeakable horrors. Some were buried alive, others were allowed to rot upon the earth. It was the time we remember as the Great Bloodletting."

My teacher stopped speaking long enough to examine the expression on my face. It was an expression of grave interest. Satisfied that this lesson would not go unlearned, Ra-hotep continued.

"It was after our armies had been defeated by the Hyksos. Thousands of our soldiers who were captured were brought here to Amarna for execution. Many were beheaded, their bodies left upon the earth to rot until the crows and vultures picked them clean. When the army was destroyed along with its officers there was no force left to stop the Hyksos in their killing. To consolidate their rule in the Delta many members of the nobility in lower Egypt were taken here in chains and slain. Their lands were confiscated and the eldest children hunted and killed to remove all heirs and claims to the property. These lands were then given as rewards to Hyksos soldiers."

Ra-hotep's words had grown heavy as if he were weary of the tale he told. It was his heart, I think, that was heavy and what he told me next was sufficient to shock any person who served the gods of This Egypt.

"But of all the sacrileges," he said letting out a deep sigh that sounded like it came from the man's bowels, "the most terrible of all was the slaughter of the priests and the sacred Apis Bull. Hundreds of priests were taken from their temples by force and transported by ship to meet their death on this beautiful plain. So many Holy Ones died here that it was said that even the birds no longer came to Amarna to feed on the dead for those that did and ate of the flesh of the Holy Ones died. It has taken Egypt almost four generations to recover from the death of her priests."

My teacher was struggling to hold his emotions under control. I could see that the horror of which he spoke upset him very much. Yet he had not lived to see it. He was not yet born when the great slaughter occurred. And still he spoke as if he had witnessed it. It was as if Ra-hotep was able to recall living a life he had not lived, perhaps in the same way that as I was to learn much later men often recalled suffering wrongs they had not suffered or hating peoples who had never done them any harm. I was learning that memory was a slippery thing. My thoughts were interrupted as Ra-hotep spoke again.

"Amarna is the place where the god's themselves cry out for vengeance at the death of one of their own. It was here that the Hyksos slaughtered one of the great gods of *Kemit*. The vile Hyksos were Asiastics and worshiped foreign gods. Our gods meant nothing to them save perhaps as a means of demonstrating to Egyptians that Hyksos power knew no bounds. The sacred Apis Bull of Memphis, the earthly manifestation of Ptah, was taken from the Temple of the Ka of Ptah and brought to the evil plain of Armana. Here among the stench and decay of thousands of unburied corpses left to putrefy in the heat the Great Bull was staked to the ground like a common steer, slowly tortured and killed! Its sacred body was then butchered and the meat roasted and eaten by the common soldiers of the Asiatics!"

There were tears in Ra-hotep's eyes.

"And then," he said with great sorrow, "the Temple of the Ka of Ptah was desecrated and became a stable for the horses and livestock of the vile Asiatics."

My teacher spoke of how the killing went on for more than two years until Egypt could bleed no more and the dominion of the foreigner over lower Egypt was complete. When the killing was finished, Amarna was abandoned to its dead. Many came to believe as Ra-hotep did that the Plain of Amarna was accursed forever.

"You see, Thutmose, there is good reason why this place has no villages or cities. It was here that a great wound was inflicted upon Our Egypt. It was here that an Egyptian god died while manifesting himself on this earth. No one dares to tread here for fear that whoever does will be cursed and polluted by the remains of the poor souls who lie buried a few inches beneath the desecrated soil. The gods themselves stand ready to avenge themselves on anyone who violates this sacred place. The gods will destroy whoever builds here."

It was a fantastic tale and it frightened me. I thought about what Ra-hotep had said as I watched the Plain of Amarna slip by the bow rail for the next ten miles. To his credit my teacher stood with me although I could see that he was in great pain. That evening I could not sleep as visions of the terrible slaughter preyed on my mind. I tried to imagine what it must be like to die without resurrection, what it might be to suffer the Second Dying. But I could not, and in the end sleep overtook me and I slumbered soundly quieted by the rocking motion of the boat as it swayed at anchor. By morning's light my somber mood had passed. I had worried enough about Amarna. I stood on the deck of the *Horus* warmed by the morning sun. My thoughts turned from the past to what lay ahead. We were still ten days from Memphis.

The next few days on the river were uneventful. The Nile flowed broad and deep with few obstacles for our captain to concern himself with. The river's west bank was rich and fertile and populated with farms. The east bank belonged to Seth and ran hard against the stony dirt of the eastern desert. From time to time boulders and cliffs clung closely to the riverbank blocking our view of the lands beyond. Not that there was much to see. On the east bank the desert sands ran as far as one could see beyond the river. It was a harsh land whose value was marked mostly in mines and quarries that gave up their precious treasures at the cost of terrible hardships and many lives. In ancient times military conscripts and condemned prisoners worked these mines. Now it was slaves like the ones we carried in the *Horus*'s hold that labored under miserable conditions until their bodies gave out and life fled from them.

I sat by the rail watching the water slide beneath the hull. *Kera-Ra* stretched out next to me trying to take some coolness for his body from the deck. It was always amazing to me how the animal could appear to sleep so soundly and still keep its ears alert for danger. For a second the dog's ears twitched once then again. Suddenly *Kera-Ra* sat up. The animal was instantly awake. Its eyes focused on the space between the deck hold and the wooden hatch cover. The cover had been left half-open to permit air and a little light to filter below deck. I saw the dog's eyes narrow and watched as the animal slowly cocked its head from one side to the other trying to catch the faint sounds that attracted its attention.

"What is it *Ra*?"

I spoke softly not wanting to startle the animal. The dog shot me a quick glance but immediately returned to its original position. I stroked *Ra* on the back of the neck.

"Do you hear something?" I grabbed the animal's collar and pulled back on it to straighten the dog in the sitting position. One of my bodyguards had told me that this was the position from which a well-trained dog began the hunt. *Kera-Ra* was only a puppy and as far as I knew had no training at all. Still, it was fun to pretend. The dog straightened up and strained his ears as I held him to attention. Leaning down next to *Ra*'s face I whispered in his ears.

"Go, *Ra*! Catch what you hear!"

I released the collar and struck the animal softly on his haunches. To my surprise *Kera-Ra* was on his feet and running in an instant. The animal bolted straight for the open hatch. A few seconds run brought him to the opening. The dog stopped and peered over the edge into the darkness. He cocked his head to one side and began to bark.

I reached the dog in a few seconds and pressed my hand over its snout to quiet its barking. I knelt next to the hatch and stared into the dim light of the cargo hold. Only a sliver of light cut through the darkness and it was difficult to see. With some effort I moved the hatch cover back and light and fresh air poured in. The cargo hold was small, perhaps no more than ten feet long by five feet wide. It was low enough so a man could not stand without bending his neck. With the hatch closed the little room was stifling and a man could die from the heat. I peered over the edge and looked down into the faces of twelve human beings who looked on the edge of death.

They were slaves. The look of despair on their faces spoke clearly to their awareness of a terrible fate. From my perch above them I could hear the sound of low moaning like a man in pain that had attracted *Ra*'s attention. The men's bodies were strewn about the floor. Some slept, others knelt with their backs against the walls, still others lay face up with their arms shading their eyes. One leg and an arm of each of these wretches was chained to a metal ring on the wall or on the deck, an arrangement that permitted some movement of the limbs. I judged from the thick black hair on their heads and their beards that they were Asiatics. Surely they were not Egyptians, and their light skin made it impossible for them to be Nubians whose skins were like ebony. The stench that rose from the place forced me to turn away and gasp for fresh air. For a second I thought I might vomit. When I turned back *Kera-Ra* stood by my side peering into the hold. For a moment I wondered what he made of this sight of humans treating other humans like animals.

My thoughts were broken by the sound of a gruff voice.

"Careful, Oh prince, or you might fall in and join the wretches!"

I felt the pressure of a hand on my back and for an instant did not know if it was to prevent my falling or to push me over the edge. I looked over my shoulder and saw the grinning face of the *Horus*' lookout. He smelled like a dead fish and the odor of his breath in my face stank like rotten gooseflesh. The man needed a bath.

"You should be more careful your highness. One slip and you would have fallen among the bastards." He had that evil grin on his face. "Then no one would have been able to help you." He paused and looked at me distastefully as if daring me to respond.

"And if I had my bodyguards would have hanged your body from the mast's yardarm." I paused and smirked my best smirk of disdain. "No one would have forgiven the man responsible for the death of a royal prince of Thebes."

The smile disappeared from the lookout's face replaced by a look of anger that bordered upon rage. Had I not been who I was, he would have struck me. But this was a man of the world, a man used to responsibility and discipline. And he was no fool.

"Ah, yes," he said. "As always, Oh prince, you are right." He paused and gave me his best sycophant's smile. "I have many things to tend to," he said. "Be careful near the open hatch and don't get too close to those Asiatic bastards. They're a tricky bunch those people are. Can't be too careful." He walked away toward the bow. I sat there in the sunlight looking into the hold with *Kera-Ra* at my side. Having found what it was looking for. the animal had calmed down. I recalled that when I had first seen the slaves being brought aboard at Thebes I asked Ra-hotep about them.

"Slaves are new to Egypt," he said. "Before the New Kingdom only a few of the nobility kept slaves and the number in all Egypt was very small. The land was tilled by farmers on small plots and the merchants and artisans worked in their shops with their sons. Building the great tombs and temples was a religious duty and done willingly by military conscripts and skilled stonemen. What slaves there were were curiosities more than anything. What could a slave do that was not already done willingly by a proud people?"

I recalled being confused by my teacher's answer for it seemed to me that Egypt was Egypt for all time. If the ancients had done without slaves, why did we need them now? Ra-hotep saw the confusion on my face.

"I see, Thutmose, that you do not understand," he said pleasantly. "The New Kingdom is not the Egypt of the old ones," he explained. "The Theban princes have forged an empire out of the fire of the Hyksos and brought with it many changes to this land of *Kemit*. Now the land is arranged into great estates owned by the nobility. Even the temples have great lands and huge herds of cattle. On such large farms using slaves to till the land is very profitable. The warrior pharaohs have need for large numbers of slaves to build and maintain the many fortresses that guard Egypt from Nubia to the Wall of Princes in the Sinai. Even the worship of the gods requires slaves when it is done on so grand a scale as at Luxor and Karnak. The temples require many slaves to construct and maintain. The quarries work overtime and the mines are required to produce greater amounts of their treasures to meet the needs of the wealthy and the foreign markets."

Ra-hotep stopped speaking for a moment to see if I was still listening. He nodded his approval at my paying attention.

"So, Thutmose, Egypt has changed greatly since the vile invader was driven from our land. It is just such an Egypt that you will someday be expected to rule. You serve yourself and your people well to learn all you can about her before you become pharaoh."

All this went through my mind as I sat on the edge of the hold looking at the slaves below. Sinub, the commander of my bodyguard, must have seen me sitting there for quite some time before he came over to me.

"Good morning my prince," he said pleasantly. He stood over me for a few seconds waiting for me to respond. I finally looked up at him and smiled. He knelt beside me on one knee his hand on the hilt of his *kopesh*. Sinub was a professional soldier and not one to trust an enemy even when he was chained in a ship's hold.

"You are deep in thought, your highness. And you seem troubled."

His voice was level and without emotion. The man could hardly keep his eyes still as they rapidly took in all elements of his environment constantly searching and assessing danger. When the eyes lingered for a few seconds it was always on the open hold that held the slaves. It was as if he expected one of them to attack. He seemed a good enough fellow, and the thought entered my mind that he might know something about the slaves.

"Tell me, Sinub, are these slaves the Hyksos that I hear so much about? Are these the defilers of our land and gods?" I asked.

Sinub shook his head. "No highness. The Hyksos are long gone from Egypt driven beyond the land of the Lebanon where they cannot cause more trouble." He looked into the hold again. "These are Asiatics," he said. "They are the peoples who live beyond the Sinai far to the east along the coast of the Great Green all the way to the Lebanon and beyond the Orontes River."

"Why do we call them Asiatics," I interrupted.

Sinub shrugged either because he did not know or did not think my question of any importance.

"Perhaps it is because they come from the east or perhaps it is because their skin is different in color from ours. I do not truly know, highness. We Egyptians have always called the peoples of the east Asiatics in much the same way as we have for thousands of years called the people of Nubia the Vile Kush or the peoples of the Mitanni the Abominable Kheta."

Sinub shrugged again as if to let me know he had no more to say on the subject.

"I see," I said even though it made no sense to me. "Are these slaves soldiers taken in battle?" I asked.

Sinub looked over the edge and examined the slaves below for a few moments. He shook his head. "It does not seem so," he said. "They look more like the wandering herders who travel over the desert with their flocks. These shepherds are always getting in trouble in one way or another with the border authorities. But I don't think they are soldiers," he said.

A low moan rose from the hatch and I turned to see what it was. One of the slaves was looking up at me. There was a pleading look in his eyes as he held me in his stare. I should have turned away, but for some reason I did not. I looked at the man trying to keep my face expressionless. The slave moved his hand to his mouth in the manner of a beggar begging food. His tongue ran around his lips in a gesture of thirst. I saw his mouth move and the language that came from it was strange to me and had no meaning. But the language of human suffering was clear enough and pity arose in my breast.

"Sinub," I said. "These men suffer like animals. See to it that they are given barley loaves and water. It does Egypt no honor to treat even slaves in this manner. What good will they be if they cannot work once they get to She-Resy?" It was, of course, not a real question and Sinub knew immediately that it required no answer from him.

He turned his face toward me and his eyes met mine for only a few seconds. There was nothing in them, no doubt, no fear, no questioning. One course was as good as another. He shrugged as he did before, rose to his feet, and walked off to find bread and water.

I looked into the face of the hungry slave. There was neither hatred nor anger in his eyes, only the look of pleading resignation, the expression of a man totally at the mercy of other men who, in different times, might have forced them to change places with him. I put my hand to my mouth in the manner of a person eating trying to make him understand that bread was being brought to fill his hungry stomach. The Asiatic mimicked my motion as if to let me know he understood. And then a broad smile forced through parched lips spread across his face. He bowed in a gesture of thanks and submission and raised his hands to me in the Egyptian sign of the Ka. My heart was moved and I smiled warmly. Then I turned away.

Three day's sail brought the *Horus* to the west bank city of Henun Nesut. It was mid morning when we arrived and I had slept late. A breakfast of turtle cakes and dates filled my stomach as I stood on the rail watching the boats in the harbor. The harbor was crowded and we had to wait for more than an hour before our boat was given a berth at the main pier. The harbor here is always filled with boats, for Henun Nesut is the major port for shipping the produce from the Lakeland, the richest agricultural land in all *Kemit*, to markets up and down the Nile. Our captain has stopped here to unload our cargo of slaves and oversee their transhipment to the city of Sobek Nut which lies across the stone mountains and near what we Egyptians call She-Resy or the great southern lake that forms the Lakeland.

I saw Ra-hotep standing near the gangplank watching the crew lower a ladder into the boat's cargo hold. From where I stood I saw that my bodyguard had been pressed into service as guards to make certain that the slaves gave no trouble. Obviously Ra-Hotep had agreed to this arrangement and now stood at the gangplank watching the slaves being led from the boat. The poor wretches had chains and shackles on their legs and their arms were tied behind their back in Egyptian military style. Ra-hotep was talking with the *Horus's* captain. It was impossible to hear what they were saying, but the captain's pained facial expressions suggested that he was not pleased with whatever Ra-hotep was saying to him. A few minutes later the captain waved his hand in resignation and stalked off down the gangplank. Ra-hotep stood there a few seconds and then turned and walked toward me. He had a broad smile upon his face that years later I came to associate with men who had won their way.

"Good morning, Teacher" I said with genuine good feeling for the old priest. After almost a month of living together on the river I had come to have a high regard for Ra-hotep. There was almost no question for which he did not have an answer. He was pious and served the gods in the Egyptian manner and from time to time even showed a flash of humor, although in my mind he seemed overly serious in almost everything he did. I had come to believe that he liked me and had every intention of keeping me safe while he labored at his task of pushing back the folds of ignorance that still draped around me like a heavy cloak. Most important Ra-hotep had come to have a true affection for me, one I believed I could rely upon in difficult times.

"It is that, Thutmose. Yes indeed, it is a good morning."

Ra-hotep was dressed as he always was in his white priest's robe, sandals, and walking stick. His head was freshly shaved and oiled to protect his scalp from Ra's burning heat. The bright sunlight made his white robes even brighter and it hurt my eyes to look directly at him. Ra-hotep saw my discomfort and smiled.

"Perhaps you might do better to use your hands to shade your eyes from the glory of Horus," he said. "We can't have you going blind, now, can we?"

Ra-hotep watched me block the sun from my eyes and nodded approvingly.

"Good," he said. "I have a surprise, Thutmose," he said. "I have spoken with our captain and he has agreed to allow us to accompany him when he delivers the slaves to the town of Sobek Nut." He paused for a second. "Do you know what Sobek Nut means, Thutmose?" he asked.

The expression on my face must have revealed quickly that I had no idea what it was.

"It means," Ra-hotep continued, "The City of Crocodiles. It lies in the heart of the Lakeland. It is here that Sobek himself, the great crocodile god, is worshiped. Only in one other place, in Nubit just above Elephantine, is Sobek revered as a god and his temples held sacred," he said. "Are you ready Thutmose to meet your first crocodile?"

I could hardly keep from running as Ra-hotep and I followed the captain down the gangplank on to the pier. Ahead the slaves were shuffling along at the urging of their guards towards another berth where a small boat was tied up. The boat was about half the size of the *Horus* and not an inch of her was clean. Her deck was stained from the remains of her last cargo and even her sails were dirty and patched as they lay piled lifelessly in a careless heap at the foot of her mast. Beneath the dirt I could make out the name *Falcon* painted in bright red on her bow. On deck Ra-hotep and I could see our captain bellowing at the captain of the *Falcon*. It turned out to be about money as it usually was when it came to business around the docks. Our captain was trying to hire the boat at the usual rate to transport the slaves to Crocodile City. The *Falcon*'s captain, naturally, wanted more. As was usual in such matters the argument resolved itself into splitting the difference. Ra-hotep and I arrived at the gangplank just in time to see the two captains seal their deal with a handshake, although neither of them seemed very pleased about it.

A few minutes later the *Falcon* pushed off from the pier and cleared her berth with the help of her oars carrying the slaves, Ra-hotep, myself, our captain, and three bodyguards with her. An hour's rowing brought the boat to the entrance of a natural canal that branched from the main Nile like a small river. The current flowed eastward toward a range of stone mountains five miles away. The canal was barely a quarter mile across but sufficiently wide to permit two boats going in opposite directions to pass each other without difficulty. Cliff walls hemmed the river in on both banks allowing the impression that we were moving inside a tunnel. I was surprised that the current was as weak as it was especially so since a glance back over my shoulder left me with the thought that the water was flowing downhill even as it ran straight for the mountains that blocked the horizon. It was an unnerving experience and I was glad to see Ra-hotep making his way toward me. "Are you enjoying yourself, Thutmose?" he asked. There was a lightness in his voice that I had not heard before. Perhaps it was because we would reach Memphis in a few days and Ra-hotep could return to more familiar surroundings.

"Yes, Teacher," I replied trying to match the good mood that Ra-hotep was enjoying. "But is not this river a strange place," I said. "The water is trapped tightly between the cliffs and yet it flows slowly. When I look backward along the river it seems that the water is flowing downhill as well." I paused to give Ra-hotep a chance to see the confusion on my face.

"Very good, Thutmose," my Teacher said. "You are learning how to learn by trusting what you see and think. And," he paused for effect, "you are right in everything you observe." He pointed toward the mountains in front of us. "The land behind the mountains is lower than the level of the Nile. In ancient times when the Nile flooded the water sought a way through the mountains to reach the lower land beyond so it could rest comfortably on the land. Many times the Nile tried to breach the mountains until, finally, it wore a narrow gorge through which its waters ran tightly against the stones. At last the force of the water broke through and flooded the plain beyond the hills. Once free, the Nile continued to flow to the gorge and fill up the lands beyond the mountains."

Ra-hotep paused and looked at me.

"This canal runs downhill through the gorge. Once we pass beyond the mountains you will see the Lakeland. It is very large, almost a thousand square miles of rich farmland and marsh. Far to the east is the She-Resy, the Great Lake, that is sixty-five miles across. Five hundred years ago a pharaoh named Amenemhat built sluice gates and dams to control the flow of water from the lake so that the land below would always have sufficient water to

grow crops. The Lakeland is one of the most beautiful places in all
Egypt. Each time I see it I think of the Field of Marshes in which
the resurrected dwell after death. I believe that this is how the
earth looked during the time of creation."

I stood at the deck rail for the entire five hour journey waiting
for our entrance into the Lakeland. Ra-hotep's description of the
place had stimulated my imagination and I didn't want to miss
anything. At last the *Falcon* approached the opening that led
through the mountains to the Lakeland and the City of
Crocodiles. The passage was uneventful, and once beyond the
mountains the river widened as the cliff walls fell away to dark
bottom land.

Never have I seen a place so wet and green! Marshland
stretched away from the river for as far a I could see. Ahead the
dark green of planted land filled the entire horizon. There was no
place where there was not life in abundance. The Lakeland was
even more wondrous for this was the time of year in all Egypt
when the Nile took back her water from the land. But here the
water lay trapped in a great depression of the surrounding land
and could not flow back. If the water began to disappear into the
sunlight, Amenemhat's sluice gates were opened and water poured
from the Great Lake over the land keeping it alive all year round.
Ra-hotep was right. This must have been what the earth looked
like at the dawn of creation.

The *Falcon* glided slowly to a stop against the pier. This was
Crocodile City where the slaves were unloaded and turned over to
their new masters. The Lakeland always needed new slaves. There
was much planting and harvesting to do on the large estates. The
huge papyrus beds were a valuable crop and they required constant
tending. But the marshes and farms held dangers for those who
worked the land. Evil spirits that lived there made men ill. Many
died of fever. Many were killed every month by the crocodiles that

infested the Lakeland. There were so many of these monsters that the city was named in their honor! So the wealthy who owned the vast estates needed a constant supply of slaves to replenish those who died or were eaten. I watched the slaves trundled together down the gangplank and handed over to their new owners. These were Asiatics, I thought. Desert people used to sand and parched hills. I wondered what was going through their mind as they looked about at their place of confinement. It must have been frightening.

I followed Ra-hotep as he led the way to the great temple dedicated to Sobek, the god whose earthly form was the crocodile. As always Ra-hotep wanted to bathe in the temple's sacred lake and cleanse himself. I waited in the company of one of the temple priests, a rather skinny fellow with the unlikely name of Sihathor. It was a curious world indeed when a man named after the goddess Hathor could be found serving as a priest in the temple of Sobek! Sihathor was a young man, perhaps not yet twenty. He told me that the crocodile had been worshiped in the Lakeland since the ancient times when the god himself had allowed the sweat from his body to pour onto the land of *Kemit* filling it with the moisture of life from which the great Nile itself was formed. It was the crocodile, Sihathor said, that made the marshes teem with life. The green of the god's skin is seen in the color of the plants and grass that are signs of life in the earth. The priest said that in ancient times the crocodile provided the hides from which the breastplates and helmets of Pharaoh's armies were made. So thick is the animal's hide that no arrow or spear could pierce it. Sobek cleanses the earth by killing and eating that which is decayed or evil. Without the crocodile, Sihathor said, there would be no Lakeland. It was an interesting tale and for all I knew probably as true as any. As I grew older I gained respect for all the gods of

Egypt, for in each one men found something of value with which to enrich their lives.

Ra-hotep joined us looking refreshed.

"Tell me, Holy One," he said respectfully to Sihathor. "Is this not the time of year when Sobek is brought to the temple to receive his sacrifice?" Ra-hotep glanced at me and smiled thinly. I said nothing.

Sihathor nodded, almost bowing as if to acknowledge his own lesser status. "Yes, my brother. It is indeed that time." Sihathor's eyes fixed Ra-hotep with a stare. Perhaps he was impressed with Ra-hotep's knowledge of another cult's practices. Perhaps he was also suspicious. "Why do you ask, Holy One?" Sihathor said.

"Does this ceremony not require that men go forth into the Lakeland and seek out Sobek to bring him back to the temple," Ra-hotep said ignoring Sihator's question. Ra-hotep continued to speak without waiting for the priest's response. "I am responsible," he said with authority "for the education of my young prince of Thebes who has been placed in my care. It would be most valuable if my young charge could witness the capture of the Great Crocodile." He paused, "With your permission, of course."

A smirk crossed Sihathor's face. "I will ask that the Chief Priest grant your request," Sihathor said with a formal nod. His meaning was clear: he had no intention of asking the Chief Priest to grant anything.

"Good" Ra-hotep said sternly. "And please tell him that Ra-Hotep, Chief Priest of the Temple of the Ka of Ra, will be in his debt."

The young priest's eyes widened in surprise. It was clear that this was the first he realized who he had been talking to. With a deep respectful bow Sihathor rushed off to obtain the permission of the Chief Priest of the Temple of Sobek for me to accompany his men on the crocodile hunt.

Early next morning Ra-hotep and I boarded the small boat that the men of the temple used to hunt the crocodile. It was more of a raft than a boat, constructed only of reeds lashed together with rope. Another rope pulled up the front to form a make-shift bow. There was no stern to the raft and very low sides. The thing was no more than twenty feet long and seven feet wide. It was so small that the six man crew used paddles instead of oars to move it about. The crew, myself and Ra-hotep were all that could fit on the unsteady craft. Not a single bodyguard accompanied me. When I mentioned this to Ra-hotep he merely remarked that there was no room. "Besides," he added, "there will not always be bodyguards around to help you even in times of danger."

A crocodile hunt is not something to be taken lightly and the men chosen by the Chief Priest to capture Sobek had lived all their lives in the Lakeland. Here near misses and crocodile bites were daily occurrences. The fact that none of these men yet bore the mark of the crocodile's teeth came as a testament to their ability to hunt the beast. I learned from one the leaders of the group that he had been hunting crocodiles for many years. His name was Hetepet. He laughed when I asked him about the hunt and held up his arms and hands for me to see that he still had all of his parts! In truth, he said, he hunted crocodile eggs. This was no easy task either since the mother kept close watch on her nest buried in the warm sand along the shore. Sometimes she guarded them for as long as three months. Even when they hatched, the old hunter said, he had seen a mother crocodile take her young in her mouth and carry them to the water so they would not be eaten by other animals.

Finding a nest of eggs was the least difficult part of the hunt. When the nest was found the hunter had to stay close and avoid the mother crocodile until the young hatched. Working with another hunter to divert the beast's attention, Hetepet gathered up as many young crocodiles as he could and stuffed them in a cloth sack. When I inquired why he did this he told me that many pilgrims came to Sobek Nut to pay homage at the Temple. The young animals were killed and mummified and then sold to the pilgrims who left the stuffed crocodiles in the temple as an offering to the great god. It was good business, he said. When it was not the season for crocodile eggs to hatch, the mummified ones could be purchased from a temple priest and resold to new pilgrims!

Hetepet was a strong man and had worked around the water all his life. He was as home on it as in it and did not appear to be concerned about the task of capturing a live crocodile. We both knelt on the floor of the boat facing each other. He was a jovial person. If he worried at all, it was not evident in his manner.

"What you say is of interest to me, Hetepet. Please tell me more about this great beast that the people of the Lakeland worship as a god," I said pleasantly. Hetepet smiled broadly, pleased that a member of the nobility was taking notice of him and his life.

"The crocodiles are everywhere in the Lakeland, in every marsh, stream, and swamp. They are part of it the way the birds are part of the sky. Men who choose to live here must accept that," he said, "and never expect the beast to change its habits. It is man who must change his habits or risk being eaten!"

He laughed at this thought although it was for my benefit. Hetepet went on.

"The crocodiles of the Lakeland are the largest in all Egypt. Some are more than twenty feet long. Their hide is so tough that bronze metal tipped spears will not penetrate it. Better to use the obsidian tipped spears that were used by the ancients. On land the animal is very fast and for short distances can run down a man. More than one poor fool has gotten too close only to find that the animal was faster than he was. They bask in the sun with their mouths open appearing to be asleep. They will remain motionless for hours until some unsuspecting animal wanders too close and then…SLAAAP!" Hetepet suddenly brought his hands together in a loud sharp clap to demonstrate the quickness of the beast's jaws grabbing its prey.

Ra-hotep heard the sound and turned quickly in my direction. He stared at us for a few seconds and then turned back to what he was doing, apparently deciding that I was in no danger. Hetepet looked at me as if to ask permission to continue. I smiled at him and nodded my head that I wished to hear more about crocodiles.

"In the water the crocodile is an excellent swimmer. The force of his tail moving slowly from side to side propels the beast silently on the water or under it. The animal has a keen sense of smell and excellent hearing. Crocodiles can hear the distress of a stranded animal for great distances. Nothing brings them together in one spot so quickly as the sound of a steer struggling to free itself from the mud. I am sure you have seen the great jaws of the crocodile," he said. "But remember that the beast cannot chew well. Those great jaws are for trapping and holding its prey. Once in its grasp the crocodile draws the prey down with it beneath the surface until water enters its lungs and it drowns. Even then the skin of a steer is too tough for the crocodile's teeth to tear. The beast will force its drowned prey under a log or even the riverbank and leave the animal there for several days until the water softens the carcass enough for the animal to take big bites of the carcass and eat its fill."

I listened intently as Hetepet told of this great beast. Looking around at the boat my mind's eye tried to imagine a beast as long as the boat! It did not help that Hetepet told me that any hunt must be quickly concluded before the sound of the beast's thrashing brought other crocodiles in search of easy prey. Hetepet excused himself and went back to join the others in preparing their equipment. As we drifted along following the main channel of the giant swamp, I could not help but wonder if Ra-hotep's idea of joining the hunt was a sound one.

One of the men shouted at Hetepet and pointed out over the right side of the raft. All eyes turned in that direction. The large bull crocodile appeared to be snoozing in the warm morning sun as he took up most of the space on a flat rock that rose upward from the water to dry land. The sun warmed the rock and the crocodile rested upon it absorbing the heat into its body through its tough skin. The animal's hide was gray-green and broken into sections that resembled wooden shingles on a roof. They appeared to overlap much like a soldier's body armor. The long snout rested fully closed upon the rock and here and there teeth stuck upwards from the bottom of the snout overlapping the upper lip of the animal's top jaw. The animal's eyes were half closed as if it were asleep. But to Hetepet's trained eye the beast looked fully awake and ready to kill anything that came within range. The adult male crocodile stretched out to its full length and Hetepet guessed that it was almost eighteen feet long, big enough for a god.

Hetepet instructed Ra-hotep and me to move to the center of the raft and to stay out of the way. He handed me a dagger.

"If something goes wrong and you find yourself in the water with the beast use this to strike him in the nose. The snout is very sensitive and a good stab there will usually make the crocodile retreat," he said. He must have noticed the concern on my face. "Don't worry, Oh prince. There is no danger."

As Hetepet turned back to his crew I looked at Ra-hotep who had a strange look on his face. Perhaps he was wondering why Hetepet hadn't given him a dagger as well.

The raft glided silently toward the rock where the crocodile lay. One of the men lowered himself into the water and I could see him silently making his way along the bank toward the rock. In his hand he carried a thick wooden pole with a metal ring at the end. Through the ring passed a long leather thong that formed a slip-knot noose at one end. Several feet of leather ran back along the pole and wrapped around the other end. I could see the man with the noose quietly approach the beast from behind.

Hetepet and another man moved to the side of the raft as it moved closer to the rock. The other man held a thick stick. Hetepet was armed with only a length of rope about two yards in length that he wrapped tightly around each hand. The raft came to a slow stop against the sloping stone. Hetepet and the other man leapt onto the rock landing only a few feet from the beast. My heart began to beat rapidly as fear filled me with dread! I looked around for Ra-hotep only to find his eyes were as tightly drawn to the drama playing out in front of us as mine. Out of the corner of my eye I saw the man with the noose move behind the animal and prepare the snare. In only a heartbeat the animal came awake and lifted its head and snout from the heated rock. The man with the snare moved with the quickness of a cheetah. In one motion he was straddling the beast and slipping the noose over its snout, pulling it tight around its neck. The animal began to react when the second man struck the crocodile sharply on the top of its snout. Its attention diverted, the beast swung toward its tormen-tor and snapped. Its giant jaws opened and closed so quickly that my eye did not see the complete movement. The thrust missed its target as the man danced away loosing his balance and tumbling into the water.

Hetepet was upon the creature like a jackal. The beast's jaws were tightly closed from its missed attempt at the man with the stick. Hetepet dove straight for the beast's snout with his chest landing on top of it. His hands moved swiftly around and around the snout as he tried desperately to wrap the jaws closed and secure them with the rope. But the animal was enraged and swung its huge head from side to side trying to free itself of the object that clung to its head. Hetepet hung on for his life and shouted loudly at the man with the noose to use his strength and raise the animal's head and pull it as far back as he could. Lifting itself up on its legs the crocodile swung its powerful tail to swat the man straddling it. Fortunately he saw it coming and jumped away permitting the tail to swing harmlessly underneath. Regaining his footing the man with the noose pulled back with all his strength. For a second the crocodile appeared to be winning the test of strength when suddenly its huge head snapped back until it could move back no further. Hetepet was on his feet in an instant tying the rope around the animal's jaws. Two men jumped from the raft with coils of rope. In a few minutes the great beast was bound snout to tail with its powerful legs wrapped tightly against its body.

Ra-hotep and I had watched the capture from less than ten feet away. My body was soaked with sweat as if I, too, had thrown my body upon the beast. My nostrils were filled with the smell of the swamp, that damp musty smell that seems to accompany rotting plants. The insects, too, now intruded upon my skin and the loud buzzing of the pests around my head irritated me. Why had I not noticed the sounds and smells of the swamp before this? Had my mind been so given to the anticipation and then the events of the hunt that all else was shut from my consciousness? Perhaps.

I stared at the jaws of the great beast. Its eyes were fully open now examining everything around it. They glared with the yellowish hatred of a trapped animal planning its revenge. Hetepet and the others had done their job well. The paddlers maneuvered the raft close to the rock and with a great effort the men lifted the crocodile god onto the reed deck. The beast stretched almost the complete length of the raft. There was no place to go where I was not within an arm's reach of the creature.

We arrived at the temple pier to a cheering crowd. The croco-dile was lifted onto the pier and the temple priests examined the beast and pronounced it acceptable. I spotted Sihathor among the crowd of priests, but our eyes did not meet. It was just as well, for the man had a demeanor about him that I did not like. The priests paid Hetepet two gold rings for the beast. A crew of temple work-men placed the animal on a wooden platform and carried it away to his sacred place in the Temple of Sobek in the City of Crocodiles.

That evening Ra-hotep and I attended the ceremony in which live birds and animals were fed to the great beast amid ritual, praying, and rejoicing that once again the great god had seen fit to come among his people and share their sacrifice. Much to my sur-prise Ra-hotep seemed bored by the grisly proceedings. Then I remembered that we were only two days sail from Memphis and the great temple of Ptah that Ra-hotep called home. I looked at the old priest and tried to share his enthusiasm for a city I had never seen. I had come far in the last month, but my heart remained in Thebes.

# Eleven

Ra-hotep was going home to his beloved Memphis. He stood at the rail for the entire day it took the *Horus* to make its way from Henun Nesut to Dashur where we put in for the night. The sun moved slowly toward the western horizon casting its diming rays across the Egyptian sky turning the thin layer of clouds violet. Rahotep stood motionless on the deck and stared contentedly into the dying day enjoying the peace of a man who, away from his roots too long, returns at last to his hearth. Dashur was the southern boundary of the great necropolis of Memphis, and the old priest had made the half-day trip from Memphis many times to officiate at the funerals of the powerful. From Giza in the north to Dashur, a distance of twenty miles, the Memphis cemetery was the largest and oldest in all Egypt. For two thousand years the kings of ancient Egypt were buried here, first in flat *mastabba* tombs and then after a thousand years in pyramids so enormous they required twenty years to construct. Surrounding the royal graves were thousands of others, the tombs of retainers and high officials who wished to serve their pharaoh even in death. And for all that time the priests of the Temple of the Ka of Ptah presided over the funerals and tended the graves.

I tried to follow Ra-hotep's eyes as they stared off in the distance. Quietly I made my way next to him. There was a broad smile on the old priest's face as if he recognized an old friend.

"There, Thutmose, do you see it?" Ra-hotep's arm swept the horizon. His finger shot out to locate the precise spot he wished me to see. "There," he said "can you see the pyramid?"

A few seconds of searching and I found it. Ra-hotep watched my face and saw the look of recognition on it before I could say anything.

"That, young prince, is the Red Pyramid of King Snofru and it has stood there for more than a thousand years!" It was said with great pride as if Ra-hotep himself had built it or was in some other way responsible for the monument.

It was a remarkable edifice. In the dying light the red granite from which it was constructed grew redder and gleamed all the more brightly in the shallow sunlight that precedes the dying of the day. Ra-hotep's voice was almost solemn in its tone of respect.

"This is the true Egypt, Thutmose, the place of the Old Ones. Egypt was a thriving country and Memphis its capital a thousand years before Thebes was a village. The necropolis of Memphis was where our greatest kings built their pyramid tombs, their Houses of a Million Years. A short way down river at Saqqara is the oldest place of royal burial in all Egypt. The great pyramid of Djoser stands there, planned and constructed by Imhotep, the man who first invented the way for constructing stone buildings. So great was his gift that he was consecrated a god and all Egypt worshipped him." Ra-hotep stopped speaking and stared off into the distance again.

The light was almost gone and all along the quay I could see flickering lamps appearing in the growing darkness. I watched Ra-hotep stand his post until Horus had ridden from view beyond the western sky. It had been a long voyage for me and tomorrow I would arrive in Memphis. I had no idea how long I would have to stay here or under what circumstances I would be recalled to Thebes. Whenever I thought about my circumstances I became troubled and tried to push these thoughts from my mind. Tonight was my last night aboard the *Horus* before she put in at Memphis and I began my new life. These thoughts raced through my mind as I looked at Ra-hotep standing at the rail looking off into the distance. In the dim light I could barely make out the smile on his face and the tears of joy that ran from his eyes.

The next morning came early. I slept little in anticipation of the day's events and arose from my bedding in the deckhouse long before dawn. It did not surprise me to find Ra-hotep already on deck sitting in a chair staring toward the eastern horizon as if beckoning Horus to arrive. The old priest was dressed in his usual white robe and seemed to be lost in thought.

"Good morning, Teacher," I said. Ra-hotep turned toward me and a thin smile appeared on his face. He was relaxed. "I see the excitement kept you from a good night's sleep as well," I offered.

Ra-hotep nodded knowingly.

"You may be sure of that, Thutmose. But sometimes it does a man good to be so excited by something that he cannot slumber. It assures him that he is alive and not worn by the regularity of the world." He paused. "Of course, at your age excitement with the world comes easily." His voice trailed off as if in thought.

I did not know what he meant and said nothing. Ra-hotep began speaking again.

"Memphis is more than my home, Thutmose. It is Egypt itself. It was the first capitol of a united country. When the great Narmer brought Upper and Lower Egypt under one crown, he chose a site for his capitol where the two countries touched one another. Here he founded the great city of Memphis, "The Place Which Binds The Two Lands." Memphis remained the center of *Kemit* for more than a thousand years until the Hyksos came and made the land bleed. Even the invaders could not ignore this great city. For two centuries they lived in it and kept a large garrison here. Though the Theban princes govern from Thebes, they still maintain residences here and visit the hunting grounds as though to touch the source of all that is truly Egypt."

Ra-hotep paused and looked at me for the first time since he began speaking. I nodded to show that I was listening. He returned to peering into the grayness of the early dawn.

"It was Memphis that gave This Egypt its first gods. Ptah, the oldest and most powerful god, is called the Ancient One. For thousands of years he was the first god of Memphis. Ptah, who fashioned the world as creator with his heart and tongue, with word and thought, is found in every heartbeat of creation, in every sound. It is Ptah who brings together in his one person Nun and Naunet, the masculine and female natures. It is Ptah who is truly the "Sculptor of the Earth." Ra-hotep's voice changed becoming harsh, almost angry. "The gods of Thebes are but children compared to the great Ptah!" The old priest almost spat the words. "One day all will worship Ptah...One day," he said. "One day." Ra-hotep's voice trailed off into an erie silence.

The crew was awake and the sun shone brightly upon the *Horus'* deck. The boat had been home to me and *Kera-Ra* for almost a month and I used some of the morning to take one last look around for memory's sake. The voyage had changed her. To my eye she seemed older, her sails a little less bright, her deck a bit more weathered, her ropes a dirty yellow. It was as if the voyage had seasoned her, somehow worn the newness from her and forced her parts to wear themselves in until they worked comfortably together. I, too, felt different, older perhaps, and a bit more certain of some things than others. It even seemed to me that *Kera-Ra* had grown, although his youth was very much evident in many of the things he did as I am sure it was in me as well. Yet, I was different. That much I knew although I couldn't tell you just how.

The noon sun was high in the sky when the *Horus* sailed within sight of Memphis. The city appeared to me much larger than Thebes even as it pressed against the river as all Egyptian cities do. It lay on the Nile's west bank and sprawled for three miles up and down the riverbank. Behind it, against the western horizon and to the north, the peaks of two giant pyramids gleamed white in the bright sun. A small hill rose from the otherwise flat landscape on the north side of the city. Upon it sat the Citadel of the White Wall, a giant fortress constructed by Narmer the Unifier. Ever since it had stood guard over the approaches to the city. As our boat pulled closer to the shore, Ra-hotep tugged my sidelock to get my attention.

"There, Thutmose, is my home," he said pointing to a large walled enclosure that sloped upward against another hill. "That is *Hikuptah*, the Enclosure of the Temple of the Ka of Ptah, the holiest place in all Memphis and, perhaps, even in all Egypt." He took a deep breath and let out a loud sigh. His body relaxed as if it had just given up the weight of a heavy burden. A broad smile coursed across his face and he ran his hand over his shaven head. "Home," he said barely above a whisper. "I am home."

The pier was crowded with shaven-headed priests dressed in sparkling white robes that had come to welcome their Chief Priest. Ra-hotep walked down the gangplank with great dignity bestowing his best sanctimonious nod upon all who approached. He betrayed not an ounce of emotion to his colleagues some of whom wept openly upon seeing him again. Still Ra-hotep remained unmoved even when his immediate subordinate, Parshepses, who led the priestly congregation in his absence, knelt before him and kissed the hem of his robe.

I remained on the deck of the *Horus* until Ra-hotep climbed into a sedan chair and was borne off in the direction of the Enclosure on the shoulders of eight priestly novitiates. My bodyguard and I reached the bottom of the gangplank and were greeted by Parshepses who apologized that there was no transport for me. No one had been informed of my presence in advance of my arrival. Sinub, the captain of my bodyguard, was not pleased with this state of affairs and made it clear he was in no mood to listen to the futile excuses of this troublesome priest. With a soldier's directness Sinub commandeered one of the new wheeled wagons that hauled cargo on the docks. Despite the driver's objections, within a few minutes we were on our way tagging along at the end of the procession bearing the honored Ra-hotep home to the Temple of Ptah.

Less than a half hour later the procession moved solemnly through the main gate of the Great Enclosure. The walls were thick as military battlements and the gate more than thirty feet high. Tall flagpoles stuck out from the top of the gate from which flew brightly colored flags. The central feature of the Enclosure was the Great Temple itself. It occupied a huge amount of space and dwarfed the remaining structures with its size. Once inside the gate I judged the Enclosure to be two hundred yards wide. Its rectangular shape suggested that it was much longer than it was wide, an impression that was later borne out by experience. To the left of the gate and back along the wall was a large stone house with a penned enclosure running around it on three sides. This was the House of the Apis Bull, among the holiest places in all Egypt. Along the same wall but far to the rear of the Enclosure was the Embalming House where the sacred animals were prepared for mummification and eternal life. Along the right wall stood the priest's living quarters. Arranged like military barracks, they were little more than bare rooms that held a bed, a night pot, and a wash basin. The Chief Priest's house was in the Temple itself. I guessed it had been many years since Ra-hotep had lived in such sparse accommodations himself. Examining the priest's quarters made me wonder what living arrangements had been prepared for me. I was, after all, a Theban prince and could not reasonably be expected to live like an ascetic.

The procession came to a halt in front of the temple. Ra-hotep emerged from his chair and stood at the base of the steps for a few moments before climbing the stairway and disappearing into the temple's cavernous gate. Out of the corner of my eye I saw Parshepses scurrying toward me, the worried look of the harried bureaucrat on his face.

"Oh prince," he shouted. "I beg your forgiveness for this indignity!" He wiped his sweaty brow with the sleeve of his robe. "It is not proper that a prince of Thebes should be carried in an animal cart!" There was a look of desperate exasperation on his face.

There was no good reason not to permit this little silly fellow not to suffer.

"Let us say, Parshepses, it is not a good omen that my visit to the Enclosure should begin with the stench of animals." I gave him my sternest look. "I trust the rest of my stay will be more pleasant. You will see to that, won't you Parshepses?" I asked with a sneer in my voice.

The priest bowed deeply and wiped his sweaty face again. "Yes! Yes! your highness. You can be sure that this insult will never happen again." He continued bowing and a wry smile crossed my face. Out of the corner of my eye I saw Sinub wearing a thin grin. He was pleased to see the priest squirm.

"Very well, Parshepses. Enough of this in the hot sun. I assume that you have been able at least to find suitable quarters for me?" It was a question that did not require an answer although

Parshepses immediately began to bow again. "Good," I said. "Now take me to them."

My quarters turned out to be a guest house that stood in the middle of a row of priest's cells that pressed tightly against the side wall of the Enclosure. It was a two story Egyptian house similar to what a merchant might live in. The first floor had the usual common living room with a bedroom and other rooms off to the sides. The second floor was more pleasant with a large bedroom opening up upon the inevitable Egyptian balcony. Even on this hot day the interior of the room was cool. The walls and columns were painted in the usual Egyptian manner. I was pleased to see that the bedroom was equipped with a bed and not the woven reed mat that the priests slept on. Egyptian beds are quite comfortable. My bed had a wooden frame with a footboard but no headboard. A mattress of folded linen rested firmly upon latts of leather stretched across the frame rails. A padded wooden shoulder rest richly carved with the image of an Apis bull on it is a comfortable place to rest one's head. The head rest is much cooler in the heat than pillows.

The dining room was equipped with the usual complement of small individual tables that meals were served on. There was only a single slant backed chair in the whole place. Visitors would have to use the wooden stools familiar to any Egyptian household. The absence of a dining table often surprised visitors to Egypt. Egyptians ate from small individual tables. Except for farmers who ate most at the beginning of the day, Egyptians ate their main meal in the evening. The alabaster tableware of the nobility, so thin that one could see through it, was nowhere in evidence nor was there any of the new glass tableware that was all the style in Thebes. In its place were simple utilitarian cups, bowls, and plates fashioned from clay. Only the cups had any decoration on them, a strange sign I did not recognize.

Parshepses followed me from room to room as I inspected my new home anxious to please but ever fearful that I would find something not to my liking. In truth the place was as sparse as the military quarters of an officer which, when compared to the splendor of the royal palace in Thebes, was bare indeed.

"It is not what I expected," I said as sternly as I could trying to keep my voice from squeaking. "These are not living quarters befitting a prince of the royal house of Thebes." I fixed the priest in my stare. "And, Parshepses," I said sneeringly, "They will not do!"

The priest began shaking where he stood. He muttered incomprehensivably and continuously wiped his head which seemed to have an endless supply of sweat upon it. I said nothing and let the man stew in his own juice. Without warning a booming voice filled the room.

"To the contrary, Thutmose, they will have to do!"

The powerful voice reached my ears like a clap of thunder and its force seemed to linger for long after the words were spoken turning the silence that followed it ominous. I turned around to see the impressive form of Ra-hotep standing in the center of the room. He looked refreshed and his priestly robes gleamed more than I had ever seen before. His body seemed to stand straighter, his head was larger, even his eyes glistened with a renewed force. It was as if my teacher had drawn strength and renewal from being within the temple. I looked upon him and I thought for the first time since I had met him that Ra-hotep was a man of inner strength, a man not to be taken lightly.

Ra-hotep walked toward me. He stood before me like a tower so close that I had to lean my head back to look up at him. He nodded to Parshepses who scurried from the room like a mouse grateful to be free of a cat.

"Thutmose," Ra-hotep said. "Your father has entrusted me with your education. Education does not rest only in learning about things. It also requires that you become other than what you are now as a boy. To do this you must learn to deny yourself and to force yourself to endure hardships. You must learn to persist when others cease, to fight on when others surrender. Remember, Thutmose, as a prince you must be strong or all around you will be weak. Do you understand?" he asked.

I nodded. "I think so, teacher."

The fiery little prince who had taken some sport in tormenting the frightened Parshepses was gone replaced by the respectful student who stood in fear and awe of his teacher.

"Very good," Ra-hotep said. "It is upon your father's instructions that this place has been prepared for you. He wishes you to learn how others live. It is his wisdom that deprives you of the comforts of a prince so that you may learn how unimportant they really are. You are sired by a line of strong warriors, Thutmose, and warriors must learn to suffer want." He went silent for a few seconds and fixed his eyes to mine. "This is your first lesson."

It was *Shemu*, the time of the year when all Egypt suffers under the drought, the time when the land dies until reborn by the flood that is the Gift Of Hapi. It was a poor time to travel and my education was confined to learning about the city of Memphis and the Great Enclosure itself. I wandered about the Enclosure from time to time looking at things I did not understand. At the end of the day Ra-hotep would visit me and ask me about what I had seen. He answered all my questions and the next day I would repeat my travels learning how to observe the world about me.

One day in the early afternoon I was walking along the south wall near the House of the Apis Bulls when my ears were struck by the sound of a terrible wail like the noises made by women at funerals. It began with a single voice, but within moments it was joined by others until the disturbing noise completely filled the courtyard. Sinub was walking with me and his hand moved instinctively to the handle of his *kopesh* while his eyes searched for danger. We drew nearer to the House of the Apis Bull. Suddenly the door flew open with a force that carried it into the wall with a great crash. Screaming priests, some with their hands over their ears, tumbled from the doorway in confusion. Sinub drew me behind him as the hysterical priests ran past. In minutes the alarm spread and what seemed like the entire congregation came running past us rushing through the door of the sacred house and into its consecrated sanctuary.

Sinub slid the *kopesh* into his belt. There was no danger here, he decided. Only the noisy bleating of frightened priests. He stepped aside to clear my way. I walked cautiously through the doors of the temple not knowing what to expect and followed the sound of wailing down the hall directly behind the doorway. The interior was dimly lit by oil lamps. I made my way carefully through the narrow corridor that ran along the outer wall until I was completely engulfed in the sounds of mourning. A doorway connected the corridor to a large room filled with white-robed priests. They were gathered around a sunken pit in the center of the room. There appeared no order among them so it was easy for me to make my way from the doorway to the edge of the pit without being noticed. The sunken enclosure was almost half as large as the room itself. Two ramps ran down into it from either side. One led to the front hall, the other to the back of the room that opened upon a doorway leading to the outside coral. Except for where the ramps met at the top of the enclosure, a bronze rail ran around the entire pit. This was the sacred home of the Apis Bull, the Holy of Holies of the great god Ptah.

I moved cautiously through the crowd of priests until I was able to see over the rail into the pit. On the floor below lay the body of a great bull, its eyes wide in the surprise of death. A rivulet of moisture ran from the animal's nose. The smell of fresh shit filled the place and I could see that the animal's anus had opened and allowed the beast's vile contents to escape onto the floor. The sacred bull still wore the brightly colored vestments with which the priests adorned the animal each day. The gold leaf that covered its horns looked a deep tarnished color in the dim light as did the red paint that adorned the sacred animal's hooves. Even in death the great bull was magnificent.

The arrival of Ra-hotep caused great commotion. The wailing grew louder as the priests tried to outdo each other in a public demonstration of their grief, especially so now that their superior was present. The wailing sounds were trapped by the stone walls of the temple and flew round and round never seeming to decrease in intensity. The din was deafening and I put my hands over my ears to gain some peace. Ra-hotep reached the rail, turned to the crowd, and raised his hands. Without a word the priests went silent as all eyes fell upon my teacher. He looked into the pit lingering long enough to perform a few ritual signs that I did not understand. As he turned back toward the crowd his eyes caught me in their web. For just an instant there was a look of distress on the old priest's face. This was sacred ground and no unconsecrated person was permitted to enter it. My presence was a sacrilege. Without a word Ra-hotep regained his composure and turned toward his fellow priests.

"My brothers," he began. "The great bull is dead, drawn home to his father to spend eternity among the resurrected."

One by one the priests lowered themselves to their knees.

"In the moment of death the Ka of the Apis Bull entered the body of another animal somewhere in Egypt. Soon he will rejoin us."

Ra-hotep paused for a few seconds. I could see the priests kneeling before him were beginning to make ritual signs with their hands until the whole congregation seemed in motion. Ra-hotep presided over whatever was happening in silence. At last he raised his hands and spoke.

"Prepare the embalming house to receive the god," he said with great solemnity. "Let us begin our days of mourning."

The priests rose and filed out into the sunlight. Ra-hotep turned and walked the few steps to where I stood now alone in the empty room.

There was sternness in his voice as he spoke.

"Remain behind until all have left, Thutmose. It would not be pleasant for other's to see you in the sanctuary." His arm appeared from under his robe and he pointed toward the door at the rear of the sunken pit. "Once I have departed you may leave through that door," he said. "It leads outside. No one will notice you."

My teacher took a few steps, stopped, and turned back to me. "Observe well, Thutmose. I shall have much to explain to you at our lesson this night."

That evening Ra-hotep instructed me in the story of the Apis Bull.

The Apis Bull is born of a cow struck by lightning the instant when the seed of the god is implanted in the animal's body. The bull is made known to the priests by its distinctive marks. The sacred animal is black, and upon its head is a white blaze in the shape of two pyramids joined together at their bases. There is upon its back a mark in the shape of Horus the Falcon. Two white hairs run along the otherwise completely black tail, and under the bull's tongue is the mark of a scarab beetle, the ancient symbol of creation. Only one Apis Bull walks the earth at one time and he is kept and worshiped at the Great Enclosure in Memphis. When the animal dies, its soul is instantly transported into the body of another Apis bull still in its mother's womb. It is the task of the priests of Ptah to search the country and find the new bull.

My teacher was at great pains to explain that the worship of the Apis is much different than the worship of other animals by other cults. The Apis is not just a representation of the god as in other cults. The Apis *is* Ptah himself, his glorious soul reincarnated in animal form, given as a gift to his priests so they may worship him and know their faith is justified. Ra-hotep noted with pride that Ptah is the most ancient god worshiped in Egypt, as old as Osiris himself. Ptah and the Apis have been worshiped in the Great Enclosure for as long as time was recorded on the pyramids and even before. He was, Ra-hotep assured me, the oldest and most powerful god in all Egypt. Someday, he said, even those simpletons in Thebes would realize that.

The death of the Sacred Bull was a major event in the life of the priests of the Great Enclosure and for the next two months preparations were made for the burial of the animal. Groups of priests roamed the countryside outside the city and in the cattle ranches of the Delta in search of the reincarnated bull now having taken the form of a newly born calf. I watched as a procession of priests carried the dead bull from the sunken pit to the embalming house at the far end of the temple enclosure. I asked Ra-hotep if I could witness the manner in which the animal was prepared, but he refused. The ceremony of preparation, he explained, was among the most secret rituals in the worship of Ptah. It was restricted even to most priests. The temple had its own special priests who prepared the Great Bull for his eternal life. I could observe the procession of the bull to its final place of rest in the desert at Saqqara if I wished, Ra-hotep said. Two months later the funeral preparations were almost complete.

It was the time of the inundation and the waters of the Nile rose on their regular schedule to renew the parched earth and give it life again. The Apis had died at a propitious time, when the Nile's waters were in abundance. Otherwise it would not have been possible to entomb the great animal for another year. Mummification of the great beast required almost two months to complete. But without a tomb to place the sacred animal at rest, the Apis would have remained unburied in the embalming house for another year. The waters of the Nile must be full before it was possible to float the Apis' great sarcophagus down the river to its final destination at Saqqara. All was in readiness for the funeral when one day the engineers arrived at the temple gate.

Ra-hotep greeted the foreman of the engineers and the two talked privately for more than an hour. Like the others, I stood aside waiting for something to happen. After a while Ra-hotep called Parshepses to him and gave him instructions. The priest ran off to insure that whatever Ra-hotep had requested was done. Then my teacher waved to me, beckoning me to come to him. He introduced me to the chief engineer, a man named Webaoner who was in charge of delivering the great stone casket in which to bury the mighty bull.

"I have asked Webaoner to take you with him to examine the sarcophagus of the Great Bull. You are to direct your questions to him in a polite manner as befits a royal prince."

This latter was no doubt for Webaoner's benefit.

"Above all, Thutmose, be careful! I do not relish the thought of having to inform your father that you met your end crushed under a great stone."

Ra-hotep took his leave of the chief engineer and the two of us were alone. The man looked down at me and smiled.

"Come along," he said, and the two of us walked out of the gate followed by Sinub my trusted protector.

I followed Webaoner down the hill toward the harbor where we boarded a small boat for the short trip up river to Saqqara. The man was thin as a reed. The legs that hung down beneath his kilt seemed more sticks than limbs. In places the loose skin of age hung limply from his arms. Altogether he did not look fit to lift a small stone, never mind to be master of a quarry. On the way

Webaoner told me that he was from the Valley of Rehanu on the road between Gebtu and the sea. He followed his father into the quarry business. The family had specialized in carving sarcophagi for the interment of the dead for longer than anyone could remember. Webaoner bragged that their quarries in Aswan produced the finest black granite in all Egypt. He was fond of saying that the dead deserve only the very best.

The boat was nearing Saqqara when Wabaoner pointed at a hugh black object that appeared stuck fast against the riverbank.

"There, Oh prince, is what we have brought the priests of Ptah."

From where I stood on the deck of the small boat I could see what looked like a giant stone block that was as black as the skin of the Apis bull itself. The great stone appeared to float on the surface of the water without support. When we sailed closer I saw the large raft of logs and reeds that held the thing up. Thick ropes lashed the granite block to the raft. Webaoner said they kept the stone from shifting during the trip. Our boat slipped next to the raft and tied up against the riverbank.

Webaoner saw my fascination with his work and a broad smile broke out upon his face. Death is, after all, a dismal business and there are few occasions for laughter when you are selling someone a coffin. Rarer still is the opportunity to openly express pride in your work without insulting the mourners. It is true, I guess, that a well-prepared corpse is still a corpse!

"Well, my prince, what do you think of the work of my quarrymen?" he asked.

I was so taken with the size and color of the giant coffin that I barely heard his question.

"It is amazing," I said honestly. "How large is it truly?" I asked with obvious pleasure in my voice. Webaoner was still smiling as he answered.

"The coffin itself is more than twenty feet high and twenty-five feet long. It is carved from a single piece of black granite. It took almost a year to free the block from its bed."

He looked at the confusion on my face.

"You don't think we wait for the bull to die before we begin work on the coffin do you?" The expression on my face revealed my ignorance and Webaoner laughed loudly. "No, no," he said. "It takes hundreds of craftsmen more than three years to fashion such a beautiful coffin as this. First the block must be cut, then shaped, then hollowed out, its lid fashioned from yet another piece of stone and, finally, it must be polished and smoothed." He looked at me and laughed again. "It was ordered for this bull four years ago" he said.

I nodded pretending I knew that all along.

"As you see, Oh prince, quarrying stone is very hard work." He paused a moment. "If you have never worked in a quarry it is difficult to imagine the heat and dust that engulf the workers. The dust is so thick sometimes that from the top of the quarry the bottom cannot be seen. Only the sounds of the hammer and drill betray that work goes on below. The workers wear rags over their mouths and noses. There is a water boy who moves fom man to man bringing water with which to wet the rags. Still the dust fills one's lungs and many die early from the illness that chokes the air from the body. Some workmen are blinded by stone chips that fly off the ends of the chisel when the stone is shaped. Sometimes the drills used to open channels in the rock cast bits of stone at such great speed that they penetrate the body like shot fired from slings. It can be miserable work and many die each year from accidents." Webanoer sighed. He knew his business well, I thought to myself.

I was curious.

"How was it possible to cut such a great stone from the earth?" I asked taking no notice of the human cost that might be involved.

"The first thing that must be done is to cut slots in the rock around the outside of the stone. This is done with chisels and copper-tipped drills and requires much time. For a stone as big as this one," he said, "hundreds of chiseled slots are needed. When that is done wooden wedges are soaked in water and driven into the slots with hammers. The water makes the wooden wedges expand and they press against the stone with sufficient force to crack it. When the stone splits it makes a sound like the clapping of hands togther." Webanoer brought his palms together and a loud SLAAP! split the quiet air.

"Then," he continued, "the important work can begin. Sledges, rollers, and rockers are used to move the stone and hundreds of workers are sometimes needed to pull on the thick ropes and drag the heavy weight across the ground. Copper saws to cut the stone and chisels are used for detailed work. A good chisel man is worth his weight in grain. When it is ready to be polished, pumice and quartz sand are worked across the surface with wooden trowels until the stone is so smooth it shines in the sun." Webanoer smiled. "As I said, Oh prince, it is not easy work."

I stepped from the boat on to the raft and walked slowly around the giant stone casket. It was truly a wonder that we Egyptians could fashion such an object. It was equally wondrous that we could move it from Aswan to Memphis, a distance of almost a thousand miles! Could any other people on this earth perform such a great deed I wondered. My hand moved easily over its smooth polished surface. If I stood back from it a few inches I could see my image in the stone as in the face of a copper mirror. Even in the mid-day heat the large stone was cool to the touch. A faint odor of moisture reached my nostrils as if the stone had taken within itself the Nile's smell during the long journey upon the river. Webaoner stood aside watching the expression on my face.

"How much does it weigh, Webaoner," I asked. "Surely as much as the pyramids themselves" I said excitedly.

"Not that much to be sure, Oh prince. But enough to make the living envious of the dead!" he said with a smirk. "The body of the tomb weighs 160,000 pounds or eighty tons. The lid is two feet thick and weighs almost ten tons," he said. "That," and here Webaoner's voice filled with pride, "is heavy enough to insure that no grave robber will violate the tomb of the Sacred Bull."

I shook my head in a combination of agreement and amazement. And then it suddenly struck me that moving this giant stone on the water was one thing, moving it overland to the burial place at Saqqara was quite another! Again ignorance stood out all over me as I turned to Webaoner with my question.

"How in the name of the Great Montu are you going to move it from here to the desert?" I asked.

Webaoner's eyes widened with pleasure and a broad smile broke out upon his weathered face. It was the look of a man who loved his work.

"It is not easy, my prince. But if the Temple keeps its promise and provides us with a thousand men to work the tow ropes we should have no trouble."

The broad smile turned into a relaxed grin.

"The great coffin must be moved three and one half miles from the river to its location in the Cemetery of the Great Bulls. More than half of that distance is over land now covered with the flood. The raft will float inland for as far as it can go. In those places where the water is too shallow to support the raft, the workmen will dig a temporary canal. Hundreds of workers pulling ropes will move it down the waterway until the next shallows where we will dig another canal."

Webaoner saw my eyes brighten as I grasped the idea of what he was saying. He stopped talking for a few seconds and smiled his broad smile. Then he nodded his head as if to confirm that he knew what was in my mind. I nodded in return enjoying the discovery of a new idea. Webaoner continued.

"When we can go no further on the water we will use the mud," he said. "Using ropes and large wooden rollers the width of the stone itself the great coffin will be pulled from the raft up onto the rollers. The slippery mud makes sliding the stone over the rollers easier and the rollers prevent the stone from sinking too deeply into the soft earth. In this way the stone can be moved until the edge of the desert is reached."

I shook my head knowingly as if I knew what he was going to say next although I knew nothing of the sort.

"Now is when we will need a great number of workers to man the tow ropes. The hard desert sand works against the smooth turning of the wooden rollers upon which the stone sits. It will not be as easy as pulling it through the slippery mud. But a thousand men pulling on a score of thick linen ropes can move the pyramids if only a few inches at a time," he said. "It will require almost as much time to move the stone over the last half mile of desert sand as it takes to move it the first three miles from the river. But a month ought to be long enough so that the coffin will be in place in time for the funeral."

I listened to Webaoner with renewed respect. The frailness of the man's body was nowhere to be found in the workings of his mind or the determination of his will. He had taught me that a difficult task is only difficult when you do not understand it. The key to success is not strength, but intelligence. And Webaoner knew his work and his intelligence made it possible to accomplish his task. I thought to myself that it must have been men such as these who first conceived of and then built the great pyramids, men who first gained victory over their intellects before forcing their bodies against the heavy loads.

For a few minutes we both stood there on the raft examining the great stone as if it were some huge beast that required taming. It sat upon the water as if by magic waiting to be goaded into life by the hand of man, the same hand that had torn it from its bed and moved it a great distance so that it could live a life far different from that intended by its natural creator. Webaoner's voice cut through the silence.

"Would you like to see where the burial will take place?" he asked in a reverent tone. "It is only a short distance and I can have one of our carts take us there." I guessed the reverence in his voice was for my benefit, perhaps because he thought that I would require it. Webaoner had been around death far too long to regard it with either fear or reverence. Death was death. No more no less. Reverence was something he offered to those who he thought wanted it or, perhaps, needed it. As for Webaoner the seller of coffins he required neither for himself.

The trip to the burial site was uncomfortable. Egyptian wagons were far less developed than Egyptian chariots and the four-wheeled wagons were unstable in the soft desert sand. More than once I thought we would turn over and fall to the bottom of the tall dunes to be buried forever by the sliding sand. The driver brought the wagon to a stop a few feet from the crest of a ridge of dunes and Webaoner and I dismounted from the clumsy machine. The sand was heavy around my feet as I plowed through it making my way to the top of the ridge. It seemed to have no effect on Webaoner who moved without any visible effort. A few minutes of hard walking and we arrived at the crest of the dunes. I was unprepared for what I saw before me.

From the top of the ridge I looked down upon a large area of deep green vegetation rising from the middle of the desert sand that surrounded it on all sides. A wall perhaps ten feet tall completely enclosed the field and held back the drifting desert from overwhelming the barrier. I learned from Ra-hotep that work crews labored constantly to keep the sand at bay. Without their efforts the desert would have overwhelmed the protective wall within a few months. The green field was rectangular in shape. I guessed it to be almost a mile long and a half mile wide. From my perch on the dunes I could make out what looked like small stone black boxes arranged neatly in rows. By my rough count I reckoned there were more than a hundred of them. Puzzled, I turned to Webaoner.

The look on my face must have told him all he needed to know. He didn't wait for my question.

"This is the Cemetery of the Great Apis Bulls, he said." "Those black boxes you see below are the giant stone coffins in which the bulls are buried." He paused for a moment. "Each of them is as large as the great coffin that waits on the river." He let his eyes sweep the horizon. "This is a very holy place, my prince."

His arm moved across the panorama before us as if to draw my attention yet again to what lay before me.

"The priests of Ptah have buried their sacred bulls here in black stone coffins for more than a thousand years. And for all that time they have tended the cemetery and kept the sands from reclaiming the land for Seth." His voice was serious. "It is a remarkable testament to the power of religious faith," he said softly.

A thousand years of Egypt's history lay at my feet. The power of Egypt's gods was truly great, and for the first time I understood why the Theban princes lavished such riches on the temples. To bind the gods to human endeavors makes men capable of great deeds. Ra-hotep was right when he told me that faith was its own justification. True enough. But faith molded by the hand of a powerful prince can make men move mountains.

Webaoner drew my eye to what looked like a stone tunnel that emerged from the desert sand just beyond the cemetery wall.

"That is the end of an underground canal that runs from the cemetery to the Nile more than three miles away," he said.

A look of astonishment appeared on my face.

"For all but the three months of *Shemu* the Nile flows easily into the mouth of the canal, its life-giving waters reaching the cemetery without difficulty. During the summer months when the river is low and without current, the priests of the temple use the *shadouf* to raise the water to the canal's mouth. This is done throughout the day and night. Never is there a time during *Shemu* when the priests are not working the water lifting device. Without their labor the green would turn to dust and the desert sands would overrun the holy place and deliver it into the hands of Seth. And then the sacred cemetery of the Apis Bulls would be lost for all eternity."

He paused and took a deep breath and slowly let the air escape from his body.

"But," he said, "as long as there is a Temple of Ptah there will be someone to watch over the sacred bulls."

For the next month I watched as Webaoner and his workmen labored to move the magnificent stone sarcaphagus to the place chosen for it in the Cemetery of the Apis Bulls. True to their promise, the temple provided the thousand workers. When the Nile floods the farmers cannot work the land and are available for other labors. It is during the time of the flood that most of the work on Egypt's great temples and monuments is accomplished, for only then is there sufficient manpower available. In about the amount of time Webaoner had predicted the great stone coffin reached its destination and was prepared to received the body of the Great Bull.

The funeral procession was a sight to behold. Thousands of mourners pressed against the outside walls of the Great Enclosure waiting for the bier to emerge from the temple so that they might accompany the Great Bull to its final resting place. Inside hundreds of priests, noblemen, and high government officials stood in solemn prayer waiting for Ra-hotep to emerge from the temple where the last prayers for the sacred animal were being offered by the priests. I stood by the doorway where I could watch the proceedings. My bodyguard stood close by. At last the Chief Priest emerged from the shade of the temple entrance to the sound of the voices of Ra-hotep's fellow priests raised in song. Behind him came a column of singing priests accompanied by music played on harps, lutes, oboes, and trumpets. A single large drum beat out a doleful cadence to measure the pace of the procession as it wound its way from the temple through the waiting crowd and out the main gate.

Next came the Apis Bull held high on a platform of gilded and painted wood carried upon the shoulders of a dozen priests. The animal was mummified in the kneeling position, its huge body wrapped tightly in the finest white linen. The linen formed a canvas upon which painters had portrayed the facial features of the great bull as he was in life. The sacred markings on the animal's forehead, back, and tail were accurately represented for all to bear witness that this was truly the body that once held the glorious soul of Ptah. Tied between the gilded horns was a large sun disk of solid gold representing the spirit of Horus, and around the animal's neck hung a large ebony scarab on a chain of precious electrum. It was truly a funeral fit for a god.

I watched as the procession moved through the Enclosure gate and the crowd of commoners filled in behind it to follow the Sacred Apis to the cemetery. I decided not to take part in the procession, wishing instead to remain behind and explore the Great

Temple in whose doorway I now stood. The Great Temple had stood for a thousand years, and although I had been living across from it for almost six months, I had never ventured inside. I was not certain that it was not forbidden as it had been in the House of the Apis Bull. Sinub was bored and seemed grateful when I gave him leave to go into the city for his entertainment. The temple complex was deserted and no danger could be reasonably expected. Besides, the other guards were never far away. I watched Sinub walk down the steps and make for the main gate and the road to the city. I turned to enter the door that sealed the main temple from the outside world and found myself face-to-face with Parshepses the worrisome priest.

"Are you not attending the burial of the Sacred Bull majesty?" Parshepes said with a tone of surprise in his voice. "It is a ceremony that happens only rarely, perhaps only every fifteen years or so. Once found and brought to the temple, the Apis Bull lives longer than other bulls you know."

The priest's words sounded like nervous chatter. I had already decided that the man was a weakling easily upset by common events. Still, simple courtesy required a reply.

"No, Holy One," I said deliberately using the term of respect for the man in hopes of putting him at ease. "I wish instead to learn more about the temple and its priests so that I may better understand them."

The man's eyes widened. Perhaps he saw an opportunity to do the temple a good deed by getting in my good graces. As I looked at him standing in front of me I recalled some of what Ra-hotep had told me about the Egyptian priesthood. Parshepses' shaven head forced me to recall that priests shaved their head daily. In fact their bodies were supposed to be clean of every hair in every crevice of the body.

"Tell me," I said in a somewhat regal tone as if I meant to command him, "why is it that priests shave their heads?"

Parshepses was taken somewhat aback. Perhaps he did not expect such a personal question. Still he smiled and bowed happy to be in the role of teacher that he had seen Ra-hotep perform with me so many times. His voice had an even and rather formal tone to it.

"It is Egyptian belief that to possess a man's hair is to possess his whole person, to seize his essence. That is why many of the monuments of our pharaohs show them holding their enemies by the hair. The priests of Ptah shave their heads as a symbol of their complete subjection to the gods. What we remove from our bodies no earthly man can possess."

As he spoke Parshepses began to walk slowly down the temple steps. I followed first from courtesy and then out of interest. The more I listened to this nervous priest the more I appreciated his knowledge of his profession. Besides, it is always valuable to learn the motives of men different from you.

I nodded my head in understanding as the priest went on to explain that shaving one's head was not so difficult. More painful was the way in which other hairs of the body were removed. Parshepses told me that hot candle wax was poured over the hairy areas of the body. It was then allowed to cool and harden until the hairs became stuck in the wax. Then, as strange as it seems, he told me that the priests tore the wax from each other's bodies tearing the hair out by the roots that held it in the flesh! Sometimes, he swore, the pain seemed like fire on the skin and blood poured from where the roots had been! It did not sound very pleasant, although to endure the pain in silence was regarded by the priests as a sign of piety.

We walked together as he spoke and I listened. Soon we approached the Sacred Lake, the pool of water in every temple that represents the first water of creation. To the priests of Ptah it was the water of all life and being. Priests were required to bathe in its cleansing waters four times each day to purify themselves before prayer or before caring for the statue of the god within the temple sanctuary. After each cleansing the priests adorned their bodies with fresh robes of white linen. We stopped by the waters of the pool and stood in silence for a few moments enjoying the shade of the trees that protected the pool from the burning sun. Parshepses seemed at peace or at least he was not as nervous as he usually was.

From time to time during my stay in the Enclosure I had seen women leaving the temple, often in the evening. It was with some delicacy that I raised the matter with Parshepses.

"Holy One, is it not true that priests of the Ka of Ptah have taken an oath not to be with women in the way other men are?" I asked.

Even at my young age I was aware of the sexuality of men and women thanks, no doubt, to the open attitude with which we Egyptians regarded such matters. Of course to go without women at my age, as I recall thinking, was of no consequence.

Parshepses did not seem particularly surprised by the question coming as it did from a mere boy. "Yes, Oh prince, we have taken a vow to remain celibate. Without the distractions of the flesh we are better able to serve the wishes of Ptah." The priests words were spoken with deadly honesty.

"But then," I said "are not the women in the temple concubines of the priests as they are in the royal house or the houses of the nobility?" It was an honest question.

Parshepses smiled.

"They are not concubines your majesty. They assist in the cere-monies. The voices of women are pleasing to Ptah and their chants and songs are pleasant even upon the ears of old priests." He paused while examining my face to see if I believed him. Satisfied, he continued. "The women are called the Chantresses of Ptah and are the daughters of pious families who wish to please the Ancient One."

My stomach rumbled and I realized that I had not eaten since early morning. The excitement of the funeral had upset the daily schedule and no one had brought me food to eat. The hunger that seemed suddenly upon me made me recall that Ra-hotep had told me that Egyptian priests avoided certain foods. The incident on the boat with the fish and the captain's obscene humor reminded me of that! Fish, mutton and pork are forbidden,although once a year on the Night of the Pig even the nobility eats pork. The pig was unclean because it is regarded as a familiar of Seth. Nor do priests eat onions, peas, garlic, leeks or beans. Of all these vegetables beans are held in the greatest disgust for they produce embarrassing rumbling sounds deep with the body accompanied by the expulsion of foul odors from one's anus. Egyptians are addicted to purges to cleanse their bodies of the decayed matter in their bowels. They also believe that all blood vessels begin and end at the anus. Perhaps they might think it strange that the most holy among them invent rituals and prohibitions so that they could pretend the anus didn't exist!

I thanked Parshepses for his company and took my leave of him. I was hungry and in search of food. I returned to my quarters and ordered a servant to bring me some meat, bread, and beer to feed my body. I sat upon a couch and let my spirit grow calm. My stomach rumbled reminding me once more of my mortality and dependence upon natural things. In a few minutes the servant appeared with a plate full of slabs of meat. Rolls made from emmer and barley bread were place next to my plate and the servant poured a hearty wine into my cup. The meat and bread slid easily down my throat and quieted the rumbling. The wine quenched my thirst and left a strong taste in my mouth. The sounds and sights of funerals were still fresh in my mind. At that moment I felt great joy in being alive. While there is much to be done to please the gods, there is very much to be said for enjoying the things of this world as well.

It was the night marking the seventh year of my birth, the season of *Akhet* when the Nile has finished flooding and the fields are renewed, that the great fire occurred. I was awakened from my slumber by the sound of shouting voices below my window. Within seconds of my waking, Sinub entered my bedroom making certain no harm came to me. He walked to the balcony and surveyed the scene below. I dressed quickly and joined him there.

There were shouts of "Fire! Fire! coming from everywhere as the priests scurried about half asleep adding to the panic. At first I thought the Temple was ablaze and then, perhaps, only a small building somewhere within the Enclosure. Owing to the slope of the land on which the Enclosure was built it was possible to see beyond the wall from the balcony of my quarters. While others ran about in panic below, Sinub and I watched the flames light up the horizon with an orange glow. The fire was burning across the river on the east bank.

"Its the shipyard," Sinub said calmly. "The shipyard's on fire."

Sinub and I raced down the stairs out into the courtyard. The priests were no longer shouting and scurrying around. Once they realized that the fire was not within the Enclosure, many seemed to loose all interest and returned to their beds. The two of us ran to the stables and hurriedly harnessed the donkey to the small cart and made straight for the harbor. The trip took only a few minutes. The streets were clear of other carts, but a steady stream of curious people were making their way to the docks. Across the river the fire burned brighter than ever as it seemed to be spreading from one source of flame to another. I was wide awake now and the smell of smoke reached my nostrils producing a heady feeling. I looked around for Sinub. He had found a boat that was transporting volunteers to help fight the blaze. With a wave of his arm he beckoned me towards him. I broke into a run and jumped straight from the pier onto the deck of the boat. Sinub caught my arm as I hurtled by and steadied me with his strength. We looked at each other for a moment and then both of us broke into giddy laughter excited by the confusion around us.

The oarsmen shoved the boat away from the pier and put their backs into rowing the vessel across the river. On either side of us I saw other boats carrying more volunteers. Across the water the flames leapt into the night sky making it seem almost daylight. A thick smoke hung just above the water unmoved by any wind and made it difficult to see. From time to time I could see small groups of men gathering near the foot of the fires. These I judged to be sailors carrying buckets of water to throw on the flames. Otherwise there was nothing but confusion everywhere.

The boat slid through the smoke and for an instant it was difficult to breath or see. Sinub reached over and tore a piece of cloth from my shirt soaked it thoroughly in the water and tied it over my mouth. He threw a handful of water into my eyes. In a few seconds I could breathe and see again. I noticed the wily soldier had already tied a wet rag over his mouth. For what seemed like a long time the boat glided through the smoke. Then without warning its bow crashed into a wooden pier at a steep angle, slid off, and came to a stop alongside the quay. Seconds later we were standing on the quay. From out of nowhere came a blast of heat that almost stole my breath. The haze made vision difficult. Up ahead I could make out Sinub's form as he extended his hand to me. I grasped it tightly and he pulled me along side.

"Stay close by me, my prince. This night is filled with adventure and danger. Use your wits and follow me." With that he was off as I tried desperately to keep up.

Sinub made straight for a group of sailors off to our left. Many of the other volunteers from the west bank knew nothing of fighting fires and milled about in confusion waiting for someone to give them direction. The sailors were organized into brigades to carry water from the riverbank with which to quench the fire. It seemed to me that there was little chance of extinguishing the raging flames. It would be more profitable to try and prevent the fire from spreading. The officer in charge of the sailors may have reached the same conclusion, for he ordered the sailors to let the fire burn and to begin wetting down the roof of the brick building nearby. For hours people ran back and forth trying to contain the flames. There was nothing for Sinub and me to do. From time to time we joined a bucket brigade hauling water. Sinub thought the sight of a royal prince dragging buckets of water to quench a fire was ridiculous. Sometimes I caught him standing there watching me and shaking his head in disbelief. All night the confusion reigned. By morning's light I could see that our efforts were useless.

The burnt out hulks of three wooden ships looked like blackened skeletons as they rested in chars on their construction platforms. Two construction huts made of wood that the workers used for resting and escaping the sun were burnt to their brick foundations. Beyond them in a straight line along the flat riverbank the next two partially built boats suffered only minor charring and discoloration. The three ships further down the line were unharmed. Fortunately someone had once had the foresight to locate the sail storage building far enough away from the construction piers. Otherwise acres of precious linen sails and coils of rope would have gone up too. Sinub and I sat next to one another staring at the wreckage. Our faces were dirty and my shirt had several small holes in it where hot cinders had burnt their way through to my skin.

Sinub offered a tired smile as he grinned at me.

"Ah, my prince, another night of pointless adventure. The shipyard burns and we sail across the Nile to watch it!" He laughed. "For all the help we were we would have been better to stay in the Enclosure."

Sinub shook his head in disbelief. I laughed softly.

"Yes, my friend, it seems likely that we have not succeeded in this line of work." The remark struck Sinub with humor and he threw his head back and roared with laughter.

"What is this place, Sinub," I asked. "I know you called it a shipyard. But it seems quite large to be simply a place where merchants build boats."

Sinub smiled and nodded his head in agreement. "It is not a merchant's shipyard, my prince. It is a shipyard of the royal navy. This is Pharaoh's shipyard where the boats that sail upon the Great Green are constructed." He paused and examined the damage once more. "There is going to be heavy price to pay for whoever is responsible for this," he said seriously. "I would not want to be in his place when the commander of the yard is called to account."

Ever the soldier, Sinub was thinking about the harsh punishments commonly meted out to military officers who failed in their duty. He sighed deeply and rested his head on his forearms.

"Tell me more, Sinub," I insisted. "Are there other shipyards to fashion Pharaoh's ships?"

"Only one other," he answered. "At Taphta at the end of the road that leads from Gebtu to the Sea of Seth. There are no materials in the eastern desert from which to construct sea-going ships that can survive the voyage to Punt and the Horns of the Earth. But Taphta is Egypt's only opening to the eastern waters. So construction materials are carried overland by military escorted caravans and the boats are built right on the water at Taphta."

"Is the yard at Taphta as large as this one?" Sinub was showing his weariness and I knew he wanted to sleep. But I was fresh with excitement. All around me was new to my experience. I had no intention of going to sleep. Sinub would have to find the strength to stay awake. The weary soldier slowly raised his head from his forearms and his mouth widened in a deep yawn. He shook his head violently so that his cheeks flapped as he loudly let out his breath. Sinub rubbed his eyes while he talked.

"The Memphis shipyard is the largest in all Egypt. Memphis is close to the Great Green and it is easy to obtain materials by boat. Most of the wood comes from Syria and Lebanon and can be shipped right up the Nile most of the year. The flax fields of the Delta are a handy source of cloth for sail and rope and the large farms and cattle ranches offer ample provisions of grain and meat for the voyages on the open sea." He paused and yawned again. "Besides, the people of the Delta and this area have been in contact with the coastal peoples beyond the Sinai for generations. Some of them are even the descendants of the Hyksos. These people know how to build large ships and the shipyard makes good use of them."

Sinub yawned again and muttered something. He lay down on the ground in a heap and was fast asleep in an instant. Perhaps it was Sinub's bad example. But suddenly I felt very tired myself. From within came the beginning of a deep yawn and I could not muster the strength to stifle it. Perhaps, I thought, a short nap might be useful. I lay down on the riverbank and closed my eyes. The smell of smoke lingered in my nostrils and in the distance I heard the faint sound of voices as their owners went slowly about the business of cleaning up the mess. A deep breath ran through my body and a warm wave of relaxation trickled over me. I was satisfied with myself that day and there is no greater potion for sleep than self-satisfaction.

Ra-hotep had been at Saqqara presiding over the funeral of a nobleman when the shipyard caught fire and it was several days before he returned to the Enclosure. At first I was eager to inform him of my adventures, but seeing the old man changed my mind. He would be angry, I thought, and there was no point getting on his bad side especially so since I wanted his permission to visit the Temple.

My teacher entered the room with his usual pious bearing and sat down on the couch. He seemed tired from the trip and let his breath escape in a sigh of relaxation.

"Well, Thutmose, I see you have been up to your tricks during my absence. Do you think it wise what you did?" The smirk of satisfaction on his face was unmistakable.

I stood there dumbstruck! How in the name of Montu did Ra-hotep know about my presence at the shipyard fire? The thought raced through my mind that it was fortunate indeed that I had decided not to deceive him about my presence there. Otherwise I could only imagine what punishment might have been visited upon me.

"Well, Teacher..." I muttered nonsensically. My voice trailed off to silence. I lowered my head and my eyes fell upon the floor. It was, I thought later, a ridiculous performance and certainly not one befitting a royal prince of Thebes!

Ra-hotep let my silence envelop us both for a few moments. Then he spoke.

"My prince," he said. "You must take care not to place yourself in danger when there is no point to it. The very idea of a prince of Thebes passing water buckets is incomprehensible. There is suffi-cient danger in this world, Thutmose, and you shall no doubt have your share of it." He paused and a slight smile appeared on his face just enough to soften it a bit. "From now on be careful. Always use your intelligence." His voice was familiar now, its tone one I had heard a thousand times whenever Ra-hotep instructed me in my lessons. "Otherwise," he said, "There will be no more lessons!"

I nodded respectfully and let my eyes rise from the floor and fall upon Ra-hotep's face. His voice and the relaxed look on his face told me that he had said enough about my irresponsible behavior at least for this day.

"Teacher, may I ask you something?" My voice was steady although I suspected some tone of contrition was evident in it.

Ra-hotep nodded his head. "What is it Thutmose?" he asked suddenly alert.

"I have been here for almost two seasons and have endeavored to learn about the Great Enclosure. Much have I seen and remembered and all of it of great value." My voice was still steady and I was pleased with my performance so far. I plunged ahead. "But, Teacher, I have no knowledge of the Great Temple itself." I stopped speaking again, waiting for some reaction from Ra-hotep. Nothing. I gathered my courage. "I am a prince of Thebes. One day I shall be expected to serve the gods. I think it is time that I be instructed in the ways of the Temple so that I may have that knowledge to guide me." I looked straight at Ra-hotep's eyes and waited for a reaction.

He stared straight back at me for a what seemed at long time as if he was mulling over my request. Had I been a merchant or commoner the request would have produced ridicule. The priests of Egypt served the gods, not the people. Their worship in the great temples was reserved for the powerful. The common people had their local gods to look after them. On the occasion of important religious festivals the common people were allowed to attend as members of respectful crowds of worshipers. Lesser persons were never allowed inside the great temples themselves. My request was somewhat irregular even for a royal prince. My lineage permitted me to enter the temple sanctuaries. I was, after all, Pharaoh's son, in a sense already the offspring of a god. But I was a prince of Thebes, a worshipper at the shrine of Amun-Ra in whose name my ancestors liberated this land. It would certainly have struck some that my interest in the worship of Ptah was a bit peculiar. All this ran through my mind as I waited for Ra-hotep's answer.

He rose from the couch and walked to the balcony. The bright sun fell upon his robes and set them ablaze in white fire. Ra-hotep stood in silence looking out over the Enclosure permitting the sun to warm his body. He stood there for a few minutes before returning to the room. He walked over to me and spoke in a deliberate manner.

"We will begin your lessons tomorrow, Thutmose. Perhaps it is time you learned about the house of the great Ptah." He frowned at me. "But," he said, "you are too young to understand the mysteries the gods require. We will confine your learning to the temple itself. One day when you are older perhaps you will still wish to learn of the mysteries of Ptah." He smiled formally. "Who knows?" he added mockingly. "There is always the chance that even a prince of Thebes may decide to return to the worship of the gods of his ancestors."

I was waiting for Ra-hotep at the bottom of the steps of the Great Temple. Morning prayers were over and the priests filed out of the temple and past me down the great stairway to begin their day's duties. The staircase began at the open space inside the main Enclosure gate and extended perhaps a hundred feet along the courtyard before making its way upward to end on the large stone landing in front of the Temple's huge gateway. Both sides of the staircase were lined with red granite pedestals upon which lay painted stone statues of the Apis Bull portrayed in the kneeling position. The sides and rails of the staircase were made of limestone from the quarries at Terofu across the river from Memphis. The steps were polished granite, the same red stone taken from the quarries at Aswan and used in Snofru's Red Pyramid. A visitor passed through the main gate of the Enclosure into an open area perhaps a hundred feet square to be met by the foot of the great staircase. Its upward slope forced the eyes to follow its ascent until they fell naturally upon the twin towers at the top of the staircase that formed the massive stone gateway that guarded the entrance to the holy temple itself.

Ra-hotep's voice broke my concentration. I turned and saw him standing in the doorway of the gate dwarfed by its great size. I waved my greeting and began running up the stairs with all my speed. As I often did I made the run a contest with myself to see how rapidly I could cover the distance. I was two months into my seventh year and my body had grown thin and gangly. But my muscles responded quickly when I called upon them. Much better now than when I arrived. The baby fat that surrounded me for so long was also gone. Unlike Ra-hotep, I relished physical exertion and engaged in it whenever the opportunity presented itself as it did now.

I was almost out of breath when I reached the top of the stairs. Ra-hotep greeted me with a smile. "Good morning, Thutmose" he said pleasantly. "I trust you are ready to begin your lessons?" I moved my head up and down in agreement while I gulped for air. "Yes, Teacher" I said breathlessly. "Good, good" Ra-hotep said and started down the staircase. I followed behind him until we reached somewhere in the middle. Ra-hotep stopped and turned back to draw my attention to the hugh temple gate that stood like a fortress above us. He pointed to the gateway.

"All temples in Egypt are aligned with the sun running lengthwise east to west," he said. Their gateways face east as a symbol of the eastern horizon to greet the arrival of Horus each morning. Every morning Horus arrives above the main gate and travels above the central axis of the temple throughout the day until in the evening the dying rays of the sun god pass beyond the back wall and can be seen no more."

I listened intently but could not take my eyes from the gateway itself. The twin towers were at least forty feet tall, higher than the walls of the Enclosure itself. One tower represented Isis and the other Nephthys, the goddess wives of Osiris and Seth. Wooden flag poles on which flew colorful banners stood upward from the top of the towers. The height of the flagpoles was such that a visitor approaching the Enclosure from a great distance first saw the flags and the temple gate. A tall obelisk made of smooth black granite stood before each tower. The points of these monuments were covered in gold that caught and reflected the sunlight like fiery torches. The towers were joined in the middle to form a lintel beneath which swung massive doors that opened upon the entrance to the temple behind them. Passing through the gate cool air shaded by the gateway fell upon us. It was quickly replaced by the light of a blinding sun as we emerged into the open courtyard on the other side.

Ra-hotep and I passed into the light of a spacious forecourt open to the sky. Around the outside walls stood double rows of stone columns, their capitols shaped like closed lotus flowers. The columns were completely covered in painted scenes of Egyptian life and the life of the gods. It was in this forecourt that the public ceremonies of the temple were celebrated. During my time at the Enclosure I saw it filled to capacity with worshippers on more than one occasion. The size of the open area was impressive. I calculated it to be thirty yards across and the same distance wide. Horus' rays filled the courtyard and warmed the granite paving blocks beneath our feet. I could feel the heat from the stones through my sandals and I thought to myself that this was no place to walk without sandals unless you wanted Horus to cook your feet like slabs of meat!

From where I stood I could see the ramp leading to the next level across the courtyard. We walked slowly into the light and my senses took in every aspect of the Great Temple. Ra-hotep noticed my concentration and kept silent as we walked to the foot of the ramp. Then Ra-hotep spoke.

"Did you know, Thutmose, that the floor plan of every temple in Egypt is exactly the same?" He paused. "Some are larger than others, of course, but the design is the same." A quizzical expression came over my face.

"Why do you think that is so, Thutmose?" he asked.

This was not a rhetorical question and Ra-hotep expected an answer. "I do not know, Teacher." I added, "I cannot even guess for it seems impossible that it should be so."

I shrugged my shoulders in what had, of late, become my favorite expression for demonstrating my ignorance.

The old priest frowned.

"I assure you that it is so" he said with a snap in his voice. "Otherwise, young man, I should not have told you that it was!" Silence stood between us for several moments then Ra-hotep continued. "It is so because of the power of faith to move men's minds. Every temple is laid out in similar fashion because the gods themselves revealed what they wanted their houses to be in the tale of creation." He waved his hand for emphasis. "Every temple is the same because every temple reconstructs the original mound of creation from which all life sprang forth." Ra-hotep took a deep breath. Obviously teaching theology to the young was not always a pleasant task. He walked slowly up the ramp and I trailed after him.

The ramp led to another great hall that was about the same size as the forecourt and was filled with painted stone columns that ran from floor to roof. Never in my life had I seen such thick columns. It seemed to me that they must have measured twenty or thirty feet around. Great barrels of stone piled atop one another mortared tight and painted bright colors took up most of the space in the great hall. Inside was dark and cool. The only light came from small clerestory windows high above the floor. On some of the columns censers shaped like bowls hung from bronze holders shaped like human arms in which incense smoldered filling the still cool air with an acrid smoke. In this part of the temple everything seemed larger. Even the walls seemed thicker than those at the front of the temple. As we walked across the columned hall between rows of thick columns I could not escape the impression that the walls were closing in upon us. The dim light made the columns and walls appear to narrow at the far end of the room. The closer we came to the ramp leading to the sanctuary the darker and narrower the room became.

At the top of the ramp I turned and looked back from where we had come. The dark hall seemed far below us while the forecourt appeared very far away. It was as if we were standing upon a small hill while everything else receded from us. We stood at the ramp leading to the sanctuary, the holy of holies where the great god Ptah dwelled. The floor of the room sloped upward toward the sacred barque that held the statue of the god within it. The barque stood more than eight feet tall and looked like a gilded rectangular box. Two small doors set four feet off the ground marked the chamber in the middle of the shrine where the god resided. A mud seal with blue cord running through it attached to each of the door handles made it impossible to open the doors without breaking the seal. Ra-hotep told me the barque was made of the wood of fruit trees, an ancient Egyptian symbol of life. The barque itself was richly decorated in paint, gold, lapis lazuli and ebony and truly looked like the sacred enclosure of a god.

The only light in the room came from the flicker of oil lamps and the hazy glow of the incense pots. There was no movement of air, and the odor of incense overwhelmed my senses. For a few moments I choked on the smoke and feared that I couldn't catch my breath. Our path had taken us ever upward through the temple. Each room was higher than the previous one. We moved from the bright light of the forecourt to the mysterious darkness that surrounded the god himself. Overhead Horus moved on his daily journey. At dawn he cast his rays over the great temple gate. Later he warmed the forecourt and by late morning his light fell through the clerestory windows to brighten the columned hall. At noon Horus stood straight overhead, his rays falling upon the holy sanctuary as if to warm Ptah himself. By the end of the day Horus took his warmth and light with him into the night and the sun disappeared over the west wall of the temple compound. And every day that Horus made his journey, the path above the temple was the same. Thus it had ever been since the dawn of time.

I stood in awed silence as I studied my surroundings with reverence. I felt Ra-hotep's hand touch my arm. I tilted my head upward and looked into the face of my teacher. He, too, stood silent out of respect. For a few minutes the two of us stood there staring at the sacred barque. I saw Ra-hotep's lips move as if in prayer, but no words reached my ears. Then he made a deep bow, looked at me, and slowly backed away from the shrine. I followed him as best I could. We walked backwards until we reached the head of the ramp leading down to the columned hall. Ra-hotep straightened his body, turned, and walked out of the sanctuary and down the ramp.

Neither of us said a word to the other until we reached the open forecourt. There Ra-hotep sat down on a stone bench and breathed deeply. The sun fell upon him like a gentle breeze and warmed him. A brief shudder ran through his body until the warmth had done its work. I stood by my teacher and waited for him to speak.

He began slowly, his voice softened by religious reverence. There in the bright Egyptian sunlight Ra-hotep told me the story of creation.

"In the beginning, Thutmose, darkness and chaos ruled the universe and the earth was covered with water. After many years the water receded and a single mound of earth was revealed. This was the place where the first god who took the shape of a falcon alighted on the earth. A single stalk of reed sprouted from the ground and upon it the god alighted and began life on this earth. The god constructed a wall of reeds around this single stalk upon which he perched while he did his work. This perch was the center of all creation and it is represented by the temple's sanctuary. The mound on which the stalk grew was the highest point in all creation for much of the world was still covered with water. So the sanctuary room is higher than all the others just like the mound itself. As the gods were mysteries to us, so the temple requires the person to move from the light to the mystery of darkness."

He stopped speaking and looked around the courtyard. He closed his eyes and lifted his face allowing Horus' rays to fall upon it. It was as if he was reliving the creation by telling me its story. A few moments later he lowered his face and opened his eyes. His voice was still full of reverence when he spoke.

"So the temple is the same everywhere because the story of creation is the same everywhere," he said. "Our faith informs our minds and we build our temples in this manner because it is how the gods wish it to be." He looked at me a moment and then smiled as if he had just proclaimed a great truth. I stood there in silence watching the look of peace upon my teacher's face.

How was it, I thought, that some men can find such wonder and certainty in things when others cannot no matter how much they search? Was it not Ra-hotep himself who taught me to observe, to use my intelligence and seek knowledge from all I encountered? Why could I not see what Ra-hotep saw when he worshipped the gods? Why did they hide themselves from my consciousness? Even as an old man I never answered the questions that Ra-hotep raised in me that day. Perhaps it was all a grand illusion, a trick of the senses. Perhaps. But if so, Ra-hotep had taught me well. A prince ought never to have any illusions.

# Twelve

It has been more than a year since I left Thebes. After all this time Memphis has not replaced Thebes in my heart. Memphis was held prisoner by the Hyksos for two hundred years and bondage makes people different. Many of the peoples' customs are strange to me, and the residents are cautious in dealing with those they do not know. Even when I travel among them only with Sinub so they do not know I am a prince, still they remain cool to strangers. The invader's yoke has long been cast off but the wounds it wore upon the shoulders of the people of this city remain, and these wounds touch much of what they do.

For several weeks I have been without interest in anything. I awake almost as tired as when I took to my bed the night before. The sun shines as it always does in Egypt, but inside my mind all is gray. I am lonely. Memphis remains a place of no warmth for me. There are no boys my age with whom to share adventures and I am surrounded by adults who see the world much differently than I am yet able to see it. Each time the temple receives a government official from Thebes I hope that he has brought a message from my father calling me home. Each time I am disappointed. There has not been a single message from Thebes in more than a year and I have begun to feel that I am abandoned.

My eyes and heart miss Ese who gave me life and with whom I spent the warmest moments I remember. Webkhet and Amenemhab are often in my thoughts. Sometimes I cannot recall their faces. A strong fright comes over me and I am truly alone.

Ra-hotep has been gone from the Enclosure for two weeks and there is little to do. I am in a dark mood and nothing pleases me. I have no playthings like other fellows my age to amuse me. There is no mother or father to see to such childish things. Once I asked Ra-hotep if it was time to teach me to read and write. I can only write my name and recognize a few words. If I cannot read, I have no way to learn by myself. Even my education depends upon others. Ra-hotep tells me that I am still too young. He promises that next year we will begin our lessons. I am terribly disappointed. Another attempt to bring some part of my life under my will fails, and the gloom within me grows.

It was in the midst of this unease that I awoke one morning not feeling well. The day was bright and the coolness of the early morning lingered in my bedroom. But the pleasant air did little to soothe the pain that surged throughout my body. My limbs were heavy and my joints ached. It was difficult to move and it was with great discomfort that I made my way across the room to the table and poured myself a cup of water from the jug. The water ran smoothly over my tongue and I could feel its coolness as it slid down my gullet and into my stomach. I drank all the water in the jug and still my thirst did not depart. The pain grew worse and my legs barely held me in the effort to return to my bed.

I lay upon the mattress feeling the sweat pour from my body until my clothing was soaked with moisture. My head felt hot as the surface of an incense bowl. I felt the sweat run in little rivulets from my face into my hair and felt as if I was being cooked from the inside. Without warning the room above me moved in a slow dizzying circle. I gasped for air and swallowed hard to clear my head of the thick fog that enveloped it. The more I tried to force the illness from me the thicker the fog became.

And then the room around me grew suddenly cold as if possessed by the shades found in the depths of old rock tombs. At first the coolness felt comfortable against my heated skin, but its pleasing touch passed through my skin and came to rest deep within me turning everything cool and then very cold. My body shivered once, stopped, and began again, this time more violently until I was shaking from head to foot. I reached for the thin blanket that covered me during the night and pulled it over me. My lips quivered and my teeth chattered against one another producing a sound like the chattering of monkeys. I lay there in cold pain even as my skin was burning. The gray mist inside my head permitted little light to pierce its curtain. I felt my will slipping from me as all my efforts to resist the illness faltered in the dim glow of fading consciousness. The last thing I remembered was the worried face of Sinub staring down at me. I passed peacefully from the light into the darkness.

It took all my strength to push back the heavy weight that lay upon my eyes. I forced them open and bright light flooded in. I could see nothing of where I was. Blue-white flashes blocked my sight and produced stabbing pains inside my head. I pressed my hands against my eyes to bring back the darkness and rid myself of the ache. Slowly the bright light turned a dull gray and the pain receded. I rubbed my eyes for a few seconds and again found the courage to open them.

The room was small and brightly lit by a large window through which Horus found his way. Two chairs stood at the foot of the hard and uncomfortable bed. The small table against the side wall held a water jar and several cups. Through the haze I could make out a small shrine in the rooms's far corner. A wooden pedestal held a painted wooden statue of *Sekhmet*, the goddess who reigned over illness and healing. She was the patron saint of the *Wabau*, the profession of special priests who studied the healing arts and who petitioned the goddess to bestow cures upon the sick. Whenever I tried to sit up my head began to pound. I lay there in my misery wondering where in the name of Seth I was.

Sleep had almost overtaken me when the door opened and in walked a pretty young girl dressed in a linen dress of such sheer cloth that it was almost possible to see through it to her bare form underneath. The garment was tied behind her neck with two small strings of cloth that left much of her chest and all of her back exposed. It clung tightly to her body accentuating her breasts and narrowing at the waist so that her hips formed a bulge where the rest of the garment slid tightly over her legs. Upon her head she wore the usual black wig favored by Egyptian women. Long curls draped over the nape and sides of her neck while the top of the wig shaped like a rounded cone came to an end in a set of bangs just above her eyes. Around her neck was a small necklace from which hung a gold statuette of the goddess of healing. Two bracelets of ebony graced each arm. She moved quietly trying not to awaken me. She carried a tray whose contents were hidden by the cloth that covered them. Through my one open eye I watched her glide across the room and place the tray upon the table. She turned to the statue of *Sekhmet* bowed her head and muttered a short prayer. Having pleased the deity, she walked over to the side of my bed and placed her hand upon my forehead.

The girl smiled down at me.

"Hello," she said. "Are you feeling any better?" Her voice was soft and carried with it a sense of caring that I had not heard since I had left Ese.

I sat up and tried to speak. My voice came out raspy and uncertain as if it had not been used for some time.

"Yes, thank you," I managed before having to clear my throat.

She smiled warmly. "That's good," she said. "For a while we thought that you might never awake."

Her voice had such a pleasant lilt to it that the meaning of what she said was lost upon me. She stopped speaking and lowered her eyes in a false coyness that I was later to find common in Egyptian women. She was perhaps fifteen years old, old enough in Egypt to be married and bear children. She was about the same age as my mother when she brought me into this world.

"My name is Lanata," she said. "And I have kept watch with *Sekhmet* for these last five days in your name. I am pleased to see that the goddess has seen fit to drive the demons from your body and to make you well."

What a beautiful name I thought. Lanata, an old Egyptian name that means "daughter of the waters." How fitting for a people that lived their entire lives upon a river to see even their children as the gift of the Nile. I rubbed my eyes and tried to clear my head. "Thank you," I said. "My name is Thutmose." I could see by the look on her face that she knew who I was. "Where is this place and how long have I been here," I asked as pleasantly as I could manage for my head still hurt.

"You are in a special room where the sick are cared for in the Enclosure. You were brought here five days ago when all the prayers of the priests had failed to drive the sickness from your body." She paused and a serious frown crossed her face. "To be honest, Tabu did not think you would live to see many more days." She smiled again and the seriousness passed. As with so many women she feared seriousness was not a trait that endeared her to men.

Now a frown appeared on my face. "Who is Tabu?" I asked. It was a strange name and one I had not heard before.

"He is my father," Lanata answered, "and the physician who saved your life with his magic." There was pride in her voice. "He is a lector priest of the Temple and without his healing arts it is quite likely that you would be dead!" The pride was replaced now by an edge that seemed to invite confrontation.

Now I was truly confused. "But I thought that temple priests took no wives," I said. The confusion was evident in my voice. "So how can this be?" The question floated in the air as if I was talking to myself.

Lanata's pleasant face broke into a wide grin and she giggled playfully. "For a prince you do not know very much," she said. "He is a lector priest not a real priest. He spends only one season a year at the temple away from his family and wife. When he is here he tends to the worship and study of *Sekhmet*. For the rest of the year he practices as a physician in the city and applies his cures and medicines to the afflicted." She paused for a few seconds. "Many say he is the best physician in Memphis."

I nodded my head and it began to throb again. I was getting better but I was still nearer to illness than to health. It would take more than the warm voice of a pretty girl to drive what was left of the sickness from my body. As I lay there I wondered what had caused me to become ill. What god had I offended? What demon had taken hold of me? I had no answers for such questions. I felt sick.

Tabu walked into my room with all the certainty of a man of science which as a priest-physician in Egypt he most certainly was. He was a short man with a body that ran to fat. His head was completely shaved in the manner of a priest, although in Egypt it was quite common for men in all walks of life to shave their heads. His dress was unremarkable and were it not for his eyes which bulged from their sockets nothing would have distinguished the man from any other. Wheat does not fall very far from the stalk, and it was difficult to believe that this toad-like fellow could be the father of such a beauty as Lanata. Yet stranger things have happened.

"Well, Oh prince, Ra-hotep will be happy to learn that you will see the next sunrise although I confess there were times when I had my doubts." He spoke rapidly and his body seemed as tight as the string of a lute. It was as if he could not stand still. "Your body suffered a serious fever. For a time we thought it was the demon worm in you but my examination could find nothing." He fell silent while his hands pressed upon my stomach looking for the gods know what. "See," he said absently, "there is no demon worm." His fingers shot out and grabbed the lids of my eyes pushing them back in a single motion. "Good, good," he muttered. "The fluid in your eyes is clear." Tabu stepped back. "Open your mouth," he ordered. Without thinking I opened my mouth. Two fingers pressed against the inside of my mouth forcing it open so far I thought I might never succeed in shutting it again. "Good, good," the physician said again to no one in particular. From the corner of my eye I saw Lanata pressing her hand over her mouth to stop her giggling. Whatever discomfort I was suffering, Lanata was having a pleasant time.

At last Tabu removed his fingers from my mouth and wiped them on the bedclothes. When he spoke it was with certainty.

"Another day or so of rest and you will be able to return to your quarters, Oh prince. Until then my daughter will see to it that you are comfortable and have what you need." He stopped talking and looked at Lanata. "She is the best assistant I have ever had," he said. Tabu smiled at his daughter who smiled back in the way only daughters can. "I trained her myself." With a quick hug from Lanata and a short bow in my direction Tabu the physician whirled out the door as quickly as he had arrived.

For the next two days Lanata took care of me. She obtained fresh bedclothes, brought meals from the temple kitchen, saw that the water was fresh and even on one occasion asked if I wanted a bath. This I chose to refuse mostly out of my own embarrassment.

One night the fever returned and my body ached with renewed pain. Lanata wiped my forehead and gave me water to comfort me. Still the pain increased. At last she took a thick brownish liquid from a small bottle Tabu had left for just this emergency. She poured it into a spoon and then poured it down my throat. The taste was bitter-sweet and the fluid stuck to the inside of my mouth like honey. I lay back upon the bed. Soon I felt the painful throbbing in my head recede and then disappear. My limbs relaxed and a strange comfort overcame me. I was whole again and I felt my mind begin to form the dream images that had been absent ever since I left Thebes.

In my softened slumber the faces of Ese, Webkhet, and Amenemhab appeared to me in pleasant guises and their vision brought me peace. Laying there on my bed I felt as I had never felt before. Then among the visions already in my head I saw the face of Lanata. Her arms reached out and wrapped around me as she lay her cool body next to mine. Her tiny hand stroked my forehead, her lips brushed against my cheek. Warmth rushed through my body and I felt strangely tense and calm at the same time. The smell of her body was as the sweet perfume of the blue lotus. All this I saw and felt that night. I drifted off to sleep unsure if it was real or a dream. When I awoke in the morning there was no one next to me and Lanata was gone.

I was fully recovered by the time Ra-hotep returned from his journey. He listened intently as I told him about my illness, Tabu, Lanata and the strange dream. When I had finished he rose from the chair and stretched producing a great yawn. He was weary from his journey and I could see that he required some rest.

"Why do you think I had such a dream, Teacher?" I asked. Ever since the dream I had been concerned. Never had my mind been so strange to me than in the dream.

Ra-hotep sat down in the chair again and rubbed his eyes. "The dream was produced by the drug," he said. "From your description of the liquid given you I believe it was the new medicine that comes from The Valley in the Lebanon near the River of the Dogs. It is drawn from a beautiful red flower that has a gray bulb at its base. The farmers cut the bulb until it bleeds a liquid that looks like thick milk." He paused for a few moments and rubbed his eyes again. "When the liquid is heated it becomes thinner and turns brown in color. I am told it is a remarkable potion. It banishes pain and relaxes the muscles. Egyptian physicians use it to aid women in childbirth." The old priest took a deep breath. "The drug also relaxes the mind and permits visions to enter it. Oftentimes these visions make no sense. At other times they help relieve the pain that we carry within us." He smiled. "From what you have told me of your dream Thutmose it may have helped your pain too." The expression on my face told him he was right. I nodded in agreement and said nothing. Despite the illness nothing had really changed and my somber mood returned from time to time. It was no help that I wanted to know more about the mysterious Lanata whose image filled my memory thoughts.

Ra-hotep watched me in silence as the expressions of unspoken thoughts came and went from my face. "I see that you remain troubled, Thutmose." There was kindness in his voice, like a father speaking to a son. I raised my head and looked into his eyes but said nothing. "I have thought about our conversation on this subject that we had before I left on my journey." He paused. "Perhaps you are correct in your feelings. In any case let me give it further thought for a few days. Maybe then a solution will suggest itself."

I spent the next two days searching for Tabu and Lanata among the many rooms and offices of the temple complex. Parshepses made inquiries and told me that Tabu and Lanata had left the

Enclosure. Tabu's term as lector priest was finished for the season and he had returned to his practice in the city. Parshepses assured me that perhaps in a few days it might be possible to find the whereabouts of his office. Ra-hotep, too, seemed to have vanished for he was nowhere to be found. Then at the beginning of the third day I was walking across the courtyard and saw Ra-hotep making his way toward me from the opposite direction.

"Good morning, Teacher," I said. I was glad to see the old man and let my voice inform him that this was so.

"Indeed it is Thutmose," Ra-hotep answered. He smiled broadly. "I have good news, young prince. In a few day's time it will be the Feast of *Heb-Sed*." The troubled look on my face brought his speech to a stop. I hadn't any notion what the Feast of *Heb-Sed* was and that fact must have been written all over my face.

"Ah!," he said. "I see that I must pay more attention to your education in these matters, Thutmose, especially so since this feast is usually celebrated only in Thebes itself." His voice grew serious. "The Feast of *Heb-Sed* is celebrated whenever the priests of Amun believe Pharaoh is in need of restoring his health and strength to prolong his life. The temple celebration calls upon the gods to protect the king, to restore the life in the Mighty Bull so that he can serve Egypt and his people." Ra-hotep's voice stopped speaking for a few moments. "The priests of the Temple of Amun-Ra proclaimed the feast to be held at the next half moon and I have arranged for you to perform your first temple sacrifice in honor of your father."

I was worried that Ra-hotep's words held hidden meanings.

"Is my father ill?" I asked directly.

Ra-hotep bit his lip before answering. "Yes, my prince," he said. "He has been ill for some time, although few know of his sickness beyond his closest advisors and the temple priests who pray for his health."

Slowly I nodded my head more in resignation than understanding. "Where am I to perform my first sacrifice Ra-hotep?" I asked.

The old priest saw the anguish in my eyes. It was the first time I had called him by his name since we met.

"The ceremony must be performed in the presence of the Ka of the king. His body walks the earth, but Pharaoh's essence lives in all the former kings of Egypt. The Ka resides in all the mortuary temples of the great pharaohs. You shall perform your first temple sacrifice in the mortuary temple of Cheprin at the base of the great pyramid in Giza." Ra-hotep looked directly at me. "You need not worry so much about your father, Thutmose. The illness that grips him has held him for a long time without killing him. It is not likely to kill him soon."

I nodded my head slowly. That was good news.

"Besides," Ra-hotep continued, "*Heb-Sed* is a celebration of life, of the renewal of power and strength. It is an occasion of joy." The old priest fixed his eyes on me and drew my attention to his face. "As you have such few friends in Memphis, or so you say to me, I have invited Tabu and his daughter to attend the ceremony."

My eyes widened and a look of surprise crossed my face.

"That is," he said, "unless you wish me not to."

And then Ra-hotep winked at me! It was the perfect thing to do. The face of Amenemhab rose in my mind and I could see his broad smile as he winked at me. It was the first gesture of affection among men I had known. Seeing it now lightened my spirit and drove the grayness from my mind. My face broke into a happy grin and I saw Ra-hotep's face relax at my joy.

I was prepared for my first sacrifice by Parshepses who tutored me in the ceremony and its meaning. The sacrifice was to be offered to the Ka of the Pharaoh Chefrin in his mortuary temple. The Ka of a man is his vital essence and has a separate existence from his body. When Khnum makes the child on the potters wheel, he fashions an exact spiritual double of the child at the same time. While the man dwells on this earth his Ka waits for him in the hereafter. Upon the king's death he is reunited with his Ka. As the body requires nourishment during life, so the Ka requires spiritual nourishment after death. This nourishment—or its essence—is provided each day in the mortuary temple of the deceased. Here a Ka priest places food or sacrifice upon a table in front of the statue of the Ka. Each tomb has a false door through which the king's essence passes each day to receive the nourishment offered him by the priest. Thus it has been for thousands of years. The day of the ceremony began with a thorough cleansing of my body in the waters of the Sacred Lake of the Temple of Ptah. Ra-hotep and Parshepses accompanied me on this special occasion. My head was shaved and my sidelock made proper. A new white priest's robe was given me and sandals trimmed in gold adorned my feet. Guided by Ra-hotep and Parshepses, I walked solemnly down the great staircase and into the sedan chair waiting at the bottom. Ra-hotep climbed in after me. A great crash of cymbals signalled the start of the procession. I felt the chair sway and we were suddenly lifted from the ground. Six pairs of priests hoisted the carrying poles to their shoulders. The drums sounded a loud cadence and the whole procession began to move at a steady pace. We passed through the Enclosure gate and the trumpets took up a slow marching song. Soon the procession was marching and swaying to the tempo of the trumpet and drums as we made our way down the hill to the boats waiting for us in the harbor.

The procession attracted little attention from the common folk. The priests were always celebrating something or other and the people of Memphis had long ago learned what ceremonies were important and which were not. No crowds hindered our movement and we reached the harbor in a short time. Three boats waited to carry the priests to the mortuary temple at Giza. The journey on the river took little more than an hour. I sat on a chair next to Ra-hotep on the center deck of the first boat from where I could see our boat approach the shore. Even from five miles away the great pyramid tomb stood like a giant beast astride the desert. It stood between the pyramid of King Chufu, Chefrin's father, on its right and the pyramid of Menkaure, Chefrin's brother, on its left. The edifice reached high into the sky where it came to a perfect point. Covered with white plaster the great tomb gleamed so brightly in the sun that it hurt the eyes to look directly upon it.

Ra-hotep saw my eyes widen as they examined the great tomb. He pulled on the sleeve of my robe to get my attention.

"Tell me, Thutmose, which of those three pyramids is the tallest?"

From this distance it was difficult to tell. "I do not know, Teacher," I said.

Ra-hotep looked at me and smiled. "That is the correct answer, Thutmose. For the differences are slight so as to make something appear other than it is." I shrugged my shoulders in my usual expression of ignorance and Ra-hotep continued. "Chefrin's pyramid, the one in the center, is slightly smaller than Chufu's," he said. "But Chefrin wisely built his tomb on higher ground so it appears much taller than it is. It is a trick you should try to remember. Always exaggerate your strength."

A good lesson indeed, and one I learned to appreciate as I grew older.

"How tall is the tomb Teacher?"

Ra-hotep stayed silent for a few moments. His eyes closed and I could see him trying to recall what he knew about the grand edifice. He opened his eyes and spoke." Each side of the tomb is almost six hundred feet long. From the ground to the top is almost five hundred feet." Ra-hotep watched as the magnitude of the pyramid made itself known in my mind. I raised my eyebrows

in surprise and shook my head from side to side in an expression
of disbelief.

"To look at the smooth surface one would not know that the
great tomb is made from many individual blocks of limestone that
are hidden underneath," he said. "Can you guess how many
blocks, Thutmose?" Ra-hotep said with a laugh knowing full well
I could not. "The number is truly amazing," he said. "Underneath
the heavy coat of white plaster are two hundred and fifty thousand limestone blocks each weighing two and one half tons!" My
teacher leaned back and watched the look of surprise upon my
face. Ra-hotep always liked to surprise me with knowledge. It
meant, he once told me, that I had not grown too proud or arrogant to stop learning.

The sun felt pleasant upon my body though I was grateful for
the linen canopy that protected me from its harshest rays. It was
morning and Horus had not yet burst forth in his full power upon
the earth. The boat moved closer to the river bank as it prepared
to put in to shore. The closer it came to the riverbank, the less I
could see of the surrounding shore above the bank itself. All at
once the river bank fell way permitting a stone boat landing to
come into view. Two small temples stood side by side above the
quay. Lying on the desert sand next to one of the temples was the
most unusual statue in all Egypt, the Great Sphinx.

It was truly a wonder to behold this enormous statue with the
body of a lion and the head of a man. My reaction brought a wry
smile to Ra-hotep's lips. I stepped from the boat onto the quay
that lay at the feet of the huge stone beast. Its great head loomed
over me like a giant cloud more than fifty feet tall. I had never
seen such a statue and turned to Ra-hotep as the usual cure for my
ignorance.

"What is it, Teacher?" I asked tilting my head back in an effort
to see the top of the great head.

Ra-hotep grinned and shrugged his soldiers. "It is only a curious statue," he said with some sarcasm. "Only that and nothing more."

"But surely it has some significance for it rests at the foot of a tomb of a great pharaoh." My voice actually sounded like I knew what I was talking about although nothing of the sort was true. "Why does it stand like a sentinel in the desert if not to please the gods?"

My teacher smiled again. "Not everything has a hidden purpose, Thutmose. Sometimes things just are what they are." The furrow of a frown appeared on Ra-hotep's forehead. "If you look closely you will see that the head of the beast is made from a different stone than its body. During Chefrin's time a great natural stone stood here. Someone had the idea to carve the likeness of the Pharaoh in the great stone. As this is the place of Pharaoh's tomb it made sense. Later, no one knows when, the body of the lion was constructed around the great head of Chefrin. The lion is Pharaoh's solar animal so casting the body in the shape of a lion would also have made good sense. The result was the sphinx that you see before you. It has stood here for as long as pharaoh's tomb."

He stopped speaking and watched my eyes examine the statue and the rest of the enormous complex that was Chefrin's tomb. When he saw that I had finished he continued.

"The beast was brought into being to please the eye of some architect nothing more. It has stood for over a thousand years and for all that time the mortuary priests have kept the sands from burying the great beast." He shook his head in disgust. "Vanity! Nothing but vanity brought the beast here. It was the will of man, not the gods." His arm swept over the panorama before us. "It is more trouble than it is worth," he said.

The procession formed behind us on the quay. Again the drums and cymbals sounded and again the trumpet took up the march.

This time Ra-hotep and I led the procession forward toward the valley temple. The valley temple was the place where the corpse of the pharaoh had been received by the embalmers and where it had been prepared for burial in the great pyramid. It was connected to the mortuary temple at the base of the pyramid by a long covered causeway made of granite. The mortuary priests had opened the door so that the procession could pass through it and into the causeway itself that began at the rear of the temple. I stood in the entrance and looked down the long stone corridor that extended for more than two thousand feet to the base of the pyramid. The floor and walls were polished smooth and the light from the torches that hung on the walls glistened brightly against them producing an erie flickering glow. At Ra-hotep's urging I started down the corridor. This time only the snap of a drum accompanied the procession as it followed behind me while I led them to the mortuary temple and the place of sacrifice.

We were greeted by the priests. Each day for a thousand years priests had fed the Ka of the deceased pharaoh offering food and drink and the sacrifice of animals. Each time the Ka had come through the false door that bore Pharaoh's life-sized image and consumed the essence of the offering nourishing him as he enjoyed his afterlife. I stood before the offering table while the procession moved around me so that all found places from which to watch the sacrifice. The last of the priests made their way to the back of the temple. From the corner of my eye I saw Tabu and Lanata standing at the rear of the group. The priests were packed together so tightly that they reminded me of the way Nile fishermen stuffed their fish into a small wicker basket. Without warning the drum stopped its funereal beat and all was still.

A mortuary priest stood silently behind the offering table, his eyes fixed on Ra-hotep and me. A nod from Ra-hotep and the priest turned his back to us. A moment later he faced us again. In his arms he held a young antelope. The animal's limbs were carefully bound together. Rich vestments of cloth and painted leather adorned the creature and the odor of perfume wafted from its hide into my nostrils. The antelope's nose was wet from its heavy breathing. I saw its sides rise and fall as it strained to catch its breath. The animal's eyes were wide with fear and in them I saw that look of stark terror that later in my life I saw so many times in the faces of soldiers as they met their deaths at the hands of my army.

The priest moved forward a few steps and placed the antelope upon the offering table. Lying on its side the animal strained to keep its head off the table. It was as if it wanted to witness its fate and look its executioner in the eye. I stared at the helpless creature and my legs weakened. I felt the strong need to urinate and beads of sweat appeared upon my forehead. Ra-hotep pressed his body against my side to steady me. Instinctively I lifted my head to look at him. He stared straight ahead and my eyes could not join his and draw his attention to my plight. Now the mortuary priest stepped around the table and offered me the long knife with which to kill the antelope. I wiped my hand against my robe to rid it of sweat so that I would not drop the knife. Its hilt was made of bronze and felt curiously cool against my skin as the palm of my hand wrapped tightly around it.

I raised the instrument in front of me until I could see the blade. It was made of polished flint. The flint knife was the instrument of ritual and sacrifice and had been given to us by the Ancient Ones. It was used to transfix the evil of Seth. Nothing could stand before its power to protect him who wielded it. The flint blade was used to circumcise males when they reached the proper age, and it was a flint blade on Horus's spear that was used to slay the Ass of Seth before battle. The knife I held in my hand may well have been a thousand years old, brought here by the first mortuary priests of

Chefrin's Ka. It had been witness to thousands of sacrifices. This day when I offered my first sacred sacrifice of an animal to the gods was no different to it than many others in which it had been the instrument of death. Only the hand that held it was different. Today the hand that held it was mine.

The eyes of the antelope seem to carry the sorrow of the world in them as they stared up at me. Suddenly my bowels felt loose. Were it not for Ra-hotep's presence at my side I should surely have run from this place. Again I looked to him for comfort and again he stared straight ahead to where my eyes could not reach him. Whatever else, Ra-hotep had decided that I would walk this path alone. My mind raced to the edge of panic and I used all my will to force it to slow down. Think! I heard myself saying. Remember what Parshepses taught you! I focused my mind as best I could on the task at hand and tried to ignore the pitiful sight of the gentle animal's tongue heaving in and out of its mouth as it fought for air.

As deliberately as I could I placed my hand around the creature's snout and pulled it back away from its chest. I felt the animal struggle against my hand and my body was struck by a wave of weakness. My hand tightened over the animal's mouth while I pulled its head back exposing the thick jugular veins on each side of its long smooth neck. With the knife in my hand I reached around in front of the creature's neck and placed the blade gently against its throat. I raised my eyes to the face of the mortuary priest standing across from me. For the first time I saw the bulges on his neck and face left from an illness called the Tumors of Kenntu. I knew the sickness was fatal. I stared into his face and thought that the ugly priest was as doomed as the poor animal that lay helplessly tethered beneath my knife.

The priest nodded his head and I drew the flint knife sharply across the antelope's throat. The razor-like blade bit deeply and easily into its neck. The sudden pain made the animal tense against my arms. I held the creature fast and in a few moments felt its strength expire against mine. A second later its struggle ceased and I felt the weight of its head against my hand. Gently I lay its head upon the table while its lifeblood flowed into the channels cut there to gather the blood into a pot below the table's surface. I placed the flint knife carefully upon the table. My fingers moved over the animal's face. With a gentle touch I closed its eyes. When finally I turned from my task I saw the look of sorrow on Ra-hotep's face as if some important innocence had been lost this day. I had seen that look once before. For a few moments I could not recall where. And then I remembered. It was at Gebtu, when the soldiers executed the bandits. Only then I had not felt the loss. As I looked at Ra-hotep he understood that today was different. And the loss I felt was very real.

It was a week later while I sat in front of my quarters dozing in the shade of the balcony when I saw Lanata again. She was exquisitely dressed in her wig and a white linen dress that swayed gently about her as she walked toward me. As she came closer, I could see that she had taken great pains to arrange her make-up. The black mascara of her eyelashes stood out starkly against the deep green powder applied around her eyes. White powder with just a hint of yellow tint set off her face from the black wig and the lipstick made her mouth seem wet and ripe. Around her neck she wore a necklace of multi-colored faience beads and the twin ebony bracelets that I had noticed on her before graced her slim arms. I rose from my chair as she approached and was rewarded with a wide smile.

"Good morning, your highness," Lanata said cheerfully. "I am glad to see that you are well," she added and extended her hand to me.

I took the slender fingers in my hand and looked at the beautiful creature before me. The smell of perfume reached me and it immediately reminded me of my dream.

"Good morning, Lanata" I blurted out nervously. The timid sound in my voice was unmistakable. It did not please me that a Theban prince felt ill at ease in the presence of a young girl.

The two of us said nothing for a few moments as we stood there looking at one another. My silence was rooted in my own embarrassment and Lanata's, I suppose, in the fact that I was a prince and she the daughter of a physician. It is not common for people of such vastly different stations to talk so easily.

Lanata placed her finger to her lips and trapped my face in her eyes. "I have been sent by your teacher to find you and bring you back to him," she said. "He and my father are waiting for you now." She paused and smiled gently. "Ra-hotep would like you to join them as soon as you are able." Lanata lowered her eyes a bit and looked up at me through her black lashes. The gentle smiled broadened until her face gleamed.

"Do you know what they want me for?" I asked.

Lanata shrugged her shoulders. "No," she answered.

"Will you walk with me to Ra-hotep's office?" I asked.

She took a step closer to me. "Yes, of course," she said pleasantly. "We can talk a bit along the way."

Ten minutes later Lanata and I walked into Ra-hotep's office. I greeted my teacher and the physician Tabu respectfully. Lanata said nothing and sat down upon the couch behind her father. The three of us exchanged greetings and then Ra-hotep spoke.

"I trust you have met Tabu the physician," he said to me. "He is a lector priest of the Temple and an authority on the sacred books and prayers that govern health and illness." My eyes shifted to Tabu and I offered him a slight bow of my head to acknowledge that we had met before. He returned my gesture with an even lesser bow. Ra-hotep continued.

"Each year at this time when the last crops of the harvest season are gathered from the ground before the arrival of the season of *Shemu* the good physician travels to the Delta of the Nile to gather herbs and medicines. With these he fashions compounds that treat the many sickness that afflict our people. He is a man of great skill and wisdom and has much to teach others, Thutmose." He paused. "He is probably the best physician in all Egypt."

I smiled and bowed my head in Tabu's direction again to acknowledge that I appreciated Ra-hotep's description of the man's reputation. Tabu returned the nod.

"I was not aware of the physician's reputation, Teacher, only of his skill with which he drove my own illness from me" I said. A frown appeared on my forehead as I wondered what it was that Ra-hotep was really up to. He most certainly did not invite me here to meet a physician I had already met.

Ra-hotep saw my frown. "I think it would be a good idea if you were to accompany Tabu on his journey this year," he said. "It won't be a long journey, perhaps only a few weeks, and it will have much to teach you." He paused and looked from me to Tabu. "The good physician has already graciously agreed to take you along." Ra-hotep shifted his eyes to Lanata. "Besides," he continued, "you will be safe in the competent hands of Sinub and I am sure that Lanata will help make your journey an enjoyable one."

I remained silent for a few moments wishing to conceal my excitement. Whenever I did this Ra-hotep always smirked as if he knew what I was up to although I can never remember a time when he openly disapproved.

"Perhaps it will be very valuable as you suggest Teacher," I said. Without willing it my eyes glanced at Lanata who had a smile upon her face. "When do we leave?" I asked. "In two days," Tabu said. It was the first words he had spoken since I entered the room. "I have hired a small boat and all is prepared for the voyage," he said. "It will be a great honor, Oh prince, to have you accompany us. And in return I shall show you things that you could not learn even from the sacred books!" He reined in his enthusiasm as quickly as he had loosened it.

I turned to Ra-hotep. "As always, Teacher, your advice is best."

Two days later I said farewell to Ra-hotep as our boat pushed off from the quay at Memphis and headed downstream toward the Nile Delta.

From Rakote on the edge of the Libyan desert in the west to Sile where the green fields touch the bleak sands of the Sinai in the east the Nile Delta is more than a hundred miles across. Twenty five miles north of Memphis at Khem the mighty Nile splits into two main streams. One flows northeast and gains the Great Green at Rosetta. The other which we will travel twists and turns back upon itself so many times before rushing into the sea at Damietta that its length is twice the distance to the sea than as the crow would fly it. Between and on either side of these two great channels are hundreds of smaller streams, rivers, and canals that run off the main channels. These criss-cross the flat Delta plain forming a web of waterways that gives life to the ground. Marshes and swamps abound and dams and irrigation canals have turned large tracts of wetland into the most fertile farmland in all Egypt. Here is where cattle are raised in great numbers and the emmer wheat and barley grow in abundance. Birds, insects, hippopotami and wildlife are everywhere to be found.

The Delta is the home of the *Sochete,* the mysterious People of the Swamp, who live deep in the marshes on floating rafts and reed houses on platforms. They live by hunting birds and trapping animals rather than farming. The *Sochete* have great knowledge of magical plants and potions that grow in their swamps whose very waters are said to possess magical powers. We are headed for the town of Busiris four days sail from Memphis. It is a town where the *Sochete* come to trade and where Tabu the physician comes to purchase magical plants and potions for his patients.

Our boat slid by the old city of Om. Tabu and I sat on chairs with a small table between us upon which Lanata had arranged a light lunch of figs, bread, and wine. Upon the riverbank the tall walls of the city came into view. I drew Tabu's attention to them. He looked over his shoulder and nodded as he took a long drink from the clay cup that held the cool wine.

"That's Om," he said. "It is one of the oldest cities in the Delta and where some of the most ancient sacred books were first written. For centuries the sacred Phoenix ruled here as a familiar to Ra, the god of the sun." He popped a fig into his mouth. "Do you see those walls Thutmose?" he asked. "They are double walls built of strong brick." I shaded my eyes from the sun to see better. Tabu continued. "Those are Hyksos walls! For generations we Egyptians had nothing to fear from invaders and so our cities had no walls to protect us. All the major cities of the Delta were easily overrun by the invader. For two hundred years they sat upon this land and they fortified every major city in the Delta with great walls which still surround them." He shook his head in disgust as if blaming some long dead pharaoh for the Hyksos presence.

Tabu and I sat together eating and making pleasant conversation. From time to time I caught sight of Lanata as she moved around the deck attending to her father's needs.

"Tell me," I said, what is it like to be a physician?"

Tabu smiled and swallowed a bit of bread. "It is rewarding work at times. At other times it leaves me feeling helpless. *Sekhmet* is a capricious goddess it seems." He leaned back in his chair and the wine seemed to relax him. He was a pleasant man and I liked him although I did not know what to make of his bulging eyes and nervous manner.

"I am a priest-physician, a *Wabau*, who tends to the sacred books on healing and the prayers to seek the intercession of *Sekhmet*, the goddess of illness and healing. For each illness there is a prayer that if performed properly will drive the illness from the afflicted. But..." and here his voice trailed off. He sipped his wine and replaced the cup on the table. "I am also a man who knows what he sees. There are many illnesses and injuries for which prayers are useless." He watched my eyes to see my reaction. "Many things can be healed with certain herbs and other medicines. As for injuries, there is nothing mysterious about them at all." He paused. "Did you know that the ancient texts show how to open the skull and remove the pressure from inside to cure an illness?" I shook my head in response. An expression of interest must have crossed my face for Tabu warmed to his subject.

"The ancient books show how to cut into the chest and let the green ooze of the demon escape from the lung!" He sipped more wine. "I tell you the ancients had many practical skills that we no longer have." He shook his head. "The temple priests are interested only in prayers to the goddess. They do not know the miracles of the ancient texts and no longer practice them."

The expression on Tabu's face was that of man who was ridding himself of an anger he had carried for a long time.

"So," he said with a deep sigh, "I watch the *Swenew*, those who are not priests but who heal the sick and repair injuries without prayers. I have learned much from them that is practical. There is much to learn that is not in the sacred books. That is why I come to the Delta. It is where I find the herbs and ingredients for poultices to heal the sick and repair broken limbs and cut hands." He paused and looked at me. "Sometimes what your senses show you is more important than what your mind tells you," he said.

The next day we sailed into Khem where we stopped for a short while to obtain provisions. Here the great Nile splits into two branches. Our boat steered hard to the right bank and soon we were in the main channel that led to Damietta and the open sea. The next evening found us at Kem-wer where The Great Black Bull is worshipped as the local god. We tied up there for the night and were invited to dine with the manager of one of Pharaoh's Fields.

His name was Nachtem, and he managed one of the many large agricultural estates that belonged to Pharaoh. When Nachtem learned that Tabu was a physician he offered us accommodations for the night if Tabu would agree to examine some of the slaves who had fallen ill. Over dinner I listened as Nachtem told us about the estate.

"The place is enormous!" he said with pride. "I am responsible for the crops and livestock on over two thousand acres of prime land. The farms in middle and upper Egypt are but small parcels compared to this," he said "And if I may say so myself not just anyone can make such a large farm work as well as this one does." A servant brought beer and wine and Nachtem poured cups for us all. I spoke while he was still pouring the beer into my cup. "Do you use slaves to do the farm labor? Are they difficult to control?" I asked.

Nachtem shot a glance at Tabu who raised his cup to his lips and said nothing. Nachtem sighed and let his shoulders fall.

"Oh yes, my prince, there are slaves here, but only a handful at present." His face became serious. "They are not good workers and are always getting into difficulties with other workers. I use them because they are sent to me for that purpose. But I would not miss them if they were gone." He paused. "When it comes to farming it is always better to use farmers! They love the land and treat it with respect. What does some captured Asiatic bedouin know about farming? And what does he care?"

It suddenly dawned on me that I had never been on a farm in my life! All my existence was spent in palaces, temples, gardens and, now, religious enclosures of one sort or another. I knew nothing of how Egypt fed itself. Tabu saw the puzzled look on my face as I ran that thought over in my mind.

I turned toward Tabu and then to Nachtem.

"Then you do not own this farm?" I asked. He nodded that I was correct. "Then who does and what do you do here?"

Nachtem sat back in his chair and began to speak.

"Long ago, even before the Hyksos fell upon our land, those who tilled the land were held by the nobility as if they were cattle. They had no rights and many were not even given names. Each year the tax collectors registered the peasants in the same manner that they registered the farm animals."

Nachtem searched my face for a reaction to his words.

"The wars against the invader destroyed the old nobility, and the new princes of Thebes created a state in which the practice of treating farmers like animals was abandoned. In its place Thutmose I introduced the idea of Pharaoh's Fields and gave the peasant his own land to farm. Some estates were divided into strips of arable land sufficient for a farmer to feed himself and his family and to produce a small surplus crop to send to the state granaries. Then Pharaoh caused each farmer to be given legal title to his land. For the first time in our history the farmer owned his land and could pass that ownership to his son. State surveyors marked each strip with boundary stones and the clerks recorded who owned the land. Each year the farmers had to sign a document that they had not moved the boundary stones. The farmer worked his own land and paid his taxes in crops and livestock. The rest he kept for himself. Of course Pharaoh kept large estates like this one for himself. Ever since Egypt has never been without food for her people." He paused and a frown crossed his face. "And we have never needed slaves to do it," he said with disgust.

The slaves caused problems, Nachtem said. "They belong to the state but we have to feed and care for them. They are branded and assigned to the mines, military camps and even the temples to do whatever work is required. But now the temples and the nobles use the slaves and force the free farmer from his land by refusing to share seed and equipment. Many farmers sell their titles for rings of precious metal. Piece by piece the farms are bought up and worked with slaves at a tidy profit for the nobility, thank you!" It was a subject Nachtem felt strongly about. "If it is not stopped it will be only a short time before the nobles own everyone again!" His tone was venomous and I saw Tabu's eyebrows rise in surprise.

The next morning I accompanied Tabu and Nachtem to the slave quarters. Nachtem was surprised that Lanata came along until Tabu told him that his daughter was also his medical assistant. We approached the small mud brick building where the slaves slept. It had no windows and the doorway had no door in it. Each night the slaves were chained to the walls to prevent escape. They slept at the ends of their chains on reed mats thrown over soiled straw. We could smell the place long before we reached the doorway.

Everyone inside was sick and the stench of vomit and feces was terrible. Tabu ordered the slaves released from their chains and carried outside into the sun. Tabu recognized all the signs of canal fever. He explained to me that farmers working barefoot in the irrigation ditches often caught this illness. Their bodies ran hot with fever and sometimes they coughed up blood. It took weeks for the illness to depart, and when it did it often left a man so weakened that he could no longer work the fields. Tabu bent over the pain-racked body of one man and used a small stick to force back his lips so he could see into his mouth. Tabu bobbed his head from side to side as he examined the man's teeth. "They're not bad," he said. "He certainly is no Egyptian!"

Tabu told me that the sand in our food and the sweets we Egyptians loved wore out our teeth at an early age. Many people spent the last few years of their lives in constant pain from aching teeth. Some were even driven mad by the pain. Whatever else was killing the poor suffering slave, he could take some comfort that he had good teeth! I saw the expression on Tabu's face change as his eyes caught sight of another slave lying upon the ground a few feet away. Tabu raised his hand to get Lanata's attention. "Fetch my instruments," he said.

Lanata returned with Tabu's medical bag and took her place with Nachtem, Tabu and me who squatted over the body of the sick slave. The poor fellow moaned and turned his body from side to side in obvious pain. Tabu reached into his bag and took out a small bottle of the brownish liquid that he had given me when I was sick. He poured a generous portion into the man's mouth. In a few minutes the man stopped moaning and fell into a heavy sleep. I remember thinking it was probably the only peace he had felt in several days.

Tabu removed the slave's shirt. "There," he said pointing at the slave's naked stomach. "Look closely Lanata" Tabu ordered. "You are about to see something remarkable." A red raised welt ran completely around the man's chest and stomach. It looked as if a thin rope was hidden beneath the slave's skin forcing the skin upward. "Watch" Tabu said. He placed his finger near the end of the welt and pressed gently against it. Suddenly the welt moved in the way a snake might move when covered with a cloth. Tabu pushed it with his finger again and again it moved. He looked at me. "Do you know what that is Thutmose?" he asked with a smile.

I was too astounded to answer and merely looked at him stupidly. Tabu went back to his work.

"Hand me my knife Lanata," he said softly. Lanata pulled something from the instrument bag and handed it to her father. Tabu unwrapped the cloth and took from it a small lancet. He held it up for me to see. "It is a common swamp reed sharpened at one end," he said. "And it makes a perfect scalpel." He pressed the knife against the head of the welt and made a small cut an inch across. Tabu then made two parallel cuts along the sides of the welt. Finished, he wiped the reed lancet clean and rewrapped it in the cloth. We were all crowded closely around the stomach of the slave who slept soundly through it all. I caught sight of Lanata's face. She was watching her father's hands with intense interest and had no time for a smile. Tabu laid his finger on top of the welt near where he had cut the flesh and pressed down gently. The welt moved under the pressure. To my amazement something began to force its way out of the opening that Tabu had made with the lancet.

Its face resembled a serpent except that its jaws appeared always to be moving in a chewing motion as if the creature were eating its way through the flesh into the daylight. Two small black pits at the top of its head I took to be its eyes stood out against the brownish green flesh that covered it in a way that made me think of the water snakes of the Lakeland swamps. Tabu pressed further behind the opening and more of the horrible creature chewed its way out of the opening until fully four inches of its head and body lay upon the stomach of the slave for us to see.

"That, my friends, is the demon worm."

Tabu spoke with the unemotional detachment of the physician that I would often encounter later in my life. It annoyed me then just as much as it does now.

Tabu explained that the worm entered the body where it lived off the food that nourished the person. Over many months the worm grew longer. Usually the creature preferred to live under the skin as on the belly of the slave. Sometimes, Tabu said, the worm turned inward and ate deep into the person until it consumed the heart or the liver. Once, he told us, a woman came to him with a worm that had moved along her neck until it burrowed deep behind her eyes cutting the tunnel to the soul through which our eyes are able to see. I stood there listening to Tabu tell a tale that I would not have believed had I not seen the worm for myself. Then, from deep within my mind, I recalled his words when he examined me in my sickroom when he thought I might be infested with the demon worm. My eyes caught sight of Tabu who had cut the head from the beast and was now slitting the flesh along the sides of the entire welt removing the creature as he went. The man was whistling a tune as he worked! Suddenly my stomach moved upward and I felt the surge of half-eaten food press against the back of my tongue.

The farm was pleasant and we were in no rush to be on our way so we accepted Nachtem's invitation to see his prize bulls. Cattle raising is a major industry in the Delta for only the Delta possesses sufficient land to allow the animals to graze. Large pens segregated into individual stalls keep the animals from fighting with each other. A dead bull is no good to anyone, not even the rival that killed it. The men who tend the animals regard them as pets and every animal has a name affectionately bestowed upon it by its shepherd. Some of the animals even had their hooves shaved and painted!

Most of the Nachtaem's bulls were Zebu oxen and were pure white with large red and black patches. The patches looked like they had been painted on for some special occasion. The bright colors against the white hides gave the animals an air of festivity. I was looking over the collection of animals when I saw a fantastic sight. In the middle of the corral stood a large black bull with a red belly and red ankles! The animal's muscles rippled when it moved and its huge head swung from side to side as it snorted and bellowed at another bull in a nearby pen. What caught my eye was the animal's magnificent horns. Painted bright gold, one horn was bent downwards while the other pointed out and upwards in its normal position making it look very much like the paintings in Egyptian tombs and temples. I drew Nachtem's attention to the animal and asked how the bulls horns had become so deformed.

Nachtem laughed. "We Egyptians are skilled breeders of bulls," he said. "But no one could make a cow give birth to a bull with horns like that." The shepherds overheard my question and were laughing to.

"No, Thutmose. No god made that bull. That is the work of man." He explained that one had only to cut the horn of the animal when it was young and shave the inside of the horn's curve. When the horn grew back it would naturally grow downward and away from the head leaving the animal with one horn up and one horn down. "Besides," Nachtem said. "Who cares about horns! As long as the cow doesn't care and the bull makes more cattle!" The herdsmen roared at the joke and I felt a bit silly for it all.

A short walk brought us to a large pasture filled with cows and steers. The cows, Nachtem explained, were sacred and were fed clover or hay. Steers, on the other hand, were an important product raised for export and domestic markets and were permitted to graze in large herds. The brands on their haunches marked these cattle as belonging to the army. They were, Nachtem said, butchered with a special knife that was curved and blunted at the top so that the blade formed a small hook. This instrument permitted a skilled butcher to skin the animal without piercing its hide. The hides were then sold to leather and furniture shops. The army sometimes bought the hides to make shields.

As we rode around the farm in the small donkey cart I sensed that Nachtem was a happy man doing the work he loved most. He was taking me to see the harvesting of the wheat and flax. It was the time of the harvest and he wanted to make sure the crops were in before the onset of the parched season. The donkey towed us briskly down the road that ran between two large fields. One was planted thickly with emmer and barley the other with Egypt's other important crop, flax. Nachtem saw the man standing in the middle of the road before I did and brought the cart to a stop.

"What is it Sim," Nachtem said. He was clearly irritated.

The man said nothing but threw a look over his shoulder in the direction of another man standing at the head of a herd of pigs.

"We must cross over."

There was no anger in his voice.

"Oh very well, Sim. Go ahead." The man smiled and waved to his companion. Within seconds a large herd of pigs crossed before us and continued on into the wheat fields. The wheat was at full height and the animals disappeared below the stalks of waving grain. Sim ran a few steps to the head of the herd. His companion brought up the rear. It was a hilarious sight. Two pig herders waist deep in wheat leading a group of pigs that only they could see! Nachtem and I watched them until they were almost across the field and out of sight.

"Pig herders! What an abomination! I swear they are Seth's handmaidens those two. Pigs themselves in human guise!"

Nachtem explained that pigs were the familiars of the evil Seth and those who touched them or raised them were also abominations. If a priest or a nobleman so much as touched a pig or a pig raiser he had to bathe in the Nile with all his clothes on to wash off the sin.

I was puzzled. "Who would raise pigs if there was no one to buy them for food," I asked. "It doesn't make much sense."

Nachtem shrugged and a smirk crossed his face. "What you say is true. Once a year even the nobility of Egypt is permitted to eat pork and that is on the Night of the Pig when the animal is sacrificed to Osiris and the full moon." He looked around at the fields and took a deep breath. "For the rest of the year," he said, "Who knows?" He snapped the reins and the donkey broke into a trot carrying us down the road.

The road ran along the top of a dike separating the two fields on either side. The mid-afternoon sun hung like a giant orange disc suspended above deep green fields that ran endlessly to the horizon. Palm trees dotted the landscape and every here and there a clump of twisted sycamores spread their leafy branches in front of the sunlight casting shadows on the ground. The heat coaxed the moisture from the ground and turned it into a fine mist that covered everything with a humid dew. The languid surroundings promised sleep and the clop-clop of the donkey's hooves on the packed earth beat out a restful cadence that made it difficult to keep my eyes open. As if in a dream the sound of sweet music drifted through the haze. The delicate hum of the lute brought with it a woman's voice carrying the sound of a beautiful song. It was as if *Renenutet* herself, the goddess of the harvest, was calming the earth with her voice.

The music came from near the small house where farmers were bringing bundles of wheat to be threshed. The lute and song helped to break the monotony of the work. Egyptian farmers harvest emmer and barley with a wooden sickle with a blade of flint. The tops of the stalks are cut off and brought here for threshing. Later the stalks themselves are cut and used for hay. The heat was oppressive and the work tedious. But the music seems to relieve the burden.

Nacthem and I walked the few yards across the road to the flax fields. There was no music here for the work was very hard and required considerable strength to perform.

"Not as easy as cutting wheat," Nachtem said. "Want to try it yourself?"

I smiled and nodded. "But you must show me what to do." Nachtem smiled and led me to the end of a row of flax plants.

"The important thing is not to damage the plant," he said in an officious tone as if he were training a new worker. "Grab it with two hands near the top like this." He half-squatted and grasped the plant from both sides with his hands. "Pretend you are strangling a duck for dinner" Nachtem laughed. "Now, using your legs pull straight up until the roots come out of the earth." He gave a slight groan for effect and pulled the gathered flax stalks out of the moist ground.

"There!" he said. "Now you try it."

Some grunts and groans later I managed to lift a single flax plant from its anchor and then only after I had bent its shaft.

Nachtem smiled. "Not too bad really. You need more practice that's all." He explained how the seeds were raked off with wooden combs and saved for next year's planting. Then the stalks were soaked in water for several days to soften them so that the woody stalk opened and the long thin fibers inside the plant could be harvested. These were twisted to make thread that was woven into linen cloth.

Nachtem had his servants prepare an evening meal of goose, birds eggs, fruit, bread and fine red wine made in the vineyards of the eastern Delta. Over dinner he offered a toast to our health and wished us a safe journey. I slept well that night and awoke refreshed. Two hours after sunrise we were on our way again headed for the small town of Busiris.

A full day's sail brought us to Busiris just before nightfall, none too soon to escape the vast clouds of insects that plagued the early evenings in the Delta. A servant that Tabu recognized met us at the docks and took us to a small house on the edge of town. It was fully dark now and the servant's torch provided only scant light to examine our surroundings. The house was clean and comfortable and an acceptable meal was prepared for us. Over dinner Tabu told us that the house belonged to Temhet, the leader of the *Sochet*, the People of the Swamp. They rarely left their homes deep within the marshlands except to trade. Temhet kept this house at the edge of Busiris for merchants and other guests. We would meet Temhet and the others in the morning.

I woke to the early sun and stood before my bedroom window wiping the sleep from my eyes. My head was clouded and my nose felt plugged. The humid air of the Delta seemed to fill my head with water until it felt like a swamp! I gathered my wits slowly and had to look twice before believing what I saw. Across the narrow street that ran under the window was a large cemetery! I had slept all night across from the dead without a covering on my window to protect against the Night Demon! I was furious. What fool would put the soul of a Theban prince at such risk! I dressed quickly and headed down stairs to confront Tabu.

The physician was seated at a small table across from Lanata having breakfast. I walked quickly up to Tabu and shouted my anger at what he had done. He listened in silence and without expression. Across the table Lanata's eyes flashed in anger. She did not appreciate my shouting at her beloved father, Theban prince or not. When I had finished Tabu smiled and offered me a chair at the table. He pushed a plate of dates and bread in front of me.

"There is no need to be concerned, your majesty," he said evenly. "You were never in any danger from the evil ones." He frowned as if to suggest without saying so that he had some doubts as to the existence of these demons. "There are no humans buried in that cemetery so there are no souls to wander the dark." Tabu's eyes looked directly at me. "You see, my prince, that is an animal necropolis. In fact it is the largest and oldest animal necropolis in all Egypt." He smiled. "You have little to fear from the mummified remains of cats and birds I assure you."

The sarcasm was unmistakable and it struck deeply at my pride. Lanata's face still wore an angry look. There was no comfort for me in those eyes this morning! Tabu continued.

"Busiris is a small backwater of a town and it is ideally suited as an opening on the world for the Swamp People. They do not worship the normal gods of Egypt. Their gods are all around them in the birds and animals that they live with. They mark their festivals with the sacrifice of animals who are then brought here to the necropolis and buried." Tabu leaned back. "They are an interesting people and you will do well to pay attention when we visit them today."

The sound of the door opening behind us drew our attention immediately. A short man stood in the doorway with the light to his back. Behind him I could see other men. All of them were of slight stature, smaller than the average Egyptian. The man in the doorway wore only a leather kilt, a loin cloth really, similar to what the crewmen on the *Horus* wore. Tabu rose from the table and walked over to him.

"Temhet!," he said. "I greet you with great joy old friend."

With that he put his arms around the little man and drew him close in gesture of affection. From where I sat I saw the little man's arms embrace Tabu and both men slapped each other on the back several times before loosening their embrace. The men exchanged a few words that I could not make out. Tabu nodded his head and turned to Lanata and me still at the table. "It is time to go," he said, and waved us after him as he followed Temhet out the door.

Temhet and Tabu chatted as they walked the few yards to the riverbank. Tied against the bank was a small reed boat like those the ancients sailed on the Nile thousands of years ago made of bundles of reeds lashed together with rope and sealed with pitch. It was similar to the boat with which we hunted the crocodile in the Lakeland. Were it not for its upturned bow held in place by a taut rope, the boat would have been easily mistaken for a raft. We boarded without difficulty and the poleman pushed us from the bank and turned the boat downstream. A short time later we made our way into a small tributary of the Nile and soon we were traveling across a large wetland that seemed to go on forever and become greener and thicker with each passing hour.

The humidity was uncomfortable and the swarms of insects unbearable. From time to time Temhet and Tabu stopped talking and looked back at me and laughed. They seemed to be enjoying my discomfort. Lanata was still angry from the morning and bore the discomfort of the journey in stony silence. At last Tabu motioned to me to join him and Temhet on the bow. The old chief said something in a strange language and bowed deeply. Tabu translated and told me that he had informed the chief of who I was and that he said Temhet was honored to have such a noble person visit his people. I smiled at Temhet and bowed in return. A broad grin broke out on the old man's face and I noticed that for his age he still had good teeth. I looked at Tabu who said, "No sand!" Temhet said something to Tabu again and the physician nodded. He turned to me.

"He wants to know if you want to hunt birds," he said with a smile. I nodded while Temhet continued to smile.

I had seen the scene many times painted on walls and columns of Egyptian houses. Temhet stood like the noblemen in those murals with a weighted throwing stick in his hand. The other hand held a live bird by the feet. The hunter shook the bird gently to get it to screech and attract other birds. As I watched Temhet instruct me in how to hunt birds I saw the familiar painting reenacted before me. Temhet shook the duck by the feet and it screamed in fright. A few shakes and screams was all that was needed. As if by magic several curious ducks scurried from behind stumps of reeds to investigate the commotion. Temhet stood very still all the while gently shaking the duck to keep it screeching. The ducks cautiously approached the boat. In the wink of an eye the weighted stick shot out from behind Temhet's head where he had held it in readiness. Two and one half turns and the instrument fell directly upon a duck's back as the stick crashed into the still water with a great splash. The decoy screamed in horror and the other ducks scurried over the water half running and half flying. When the water calmed itself both the duck and the throwing stick floated on its surface.

With great pride Temhet presented me with the bird and I thanked him. My own attempts at hunting ducks proved fruitless. To be truthful, the writhing of the decoy frightened me and I never succeeded in holding it correctly. The accursed duck screeched whenever it wanted to and not when I wanted it to. Eventually a few other ducks wandered into range, but my aim with the throwing stick left much to be desired. The throwing stick is very heavy although it does not appear so until one holds it. It takes considerable practice to make it find its target. I managed to miss every duck I aimed at and I was happy for the thing's ability to float. Otherwise I should have used up every throwing stick on the boat without killing a single bird! Tabu tried to remove my embarrassment with his good humor and the suggestion that I try the boomerang or the bow with the blunted arrows to kill the birds. I respectfully declined. I had limits to how much humiliation I was prepared to endure for a meal of roast duck!

The journey required almost the entire day to complete and it was late afternoon before we approached the village of the People of the Swamp. Their huts were constructed of reeds and rested upon platforms to keep them off the water. Tabu told me that the platforms were high enough so that when the inundation came their houses would not be washed away. They lived on birds and fish and other small swamp animals. Goats were kept for milk. I even saw a few pigs, although Temhet said that they were not welcome because they attracted crocodiles. The People of the Swamp had lived deep in the Delta swamps for as long as there had been an Egypt. Their language and gods were strange although I suppose they thought the same of mine.

I was thankful for the smoke of the small fire that kept the insects from tormenting us even more than they were. We sat around the flame eating roast birds and drinking a thin beer. Tabu and Temhet were talking to one another. Lanata had lost her coolness with the heat of the journey and now chewed lustily upon the wing of a roasted pigeon. Her perfume had worn off and she had not replaced it when Tabu told her that it attracted more insects than men and that we would all be grateful if she could forego it for the time being! I sat there in silence looking around at my erie surroundings not knowing where in Seth's name I was.

Out of the darkness that trapped the circle of firelight came a small figure with the feathers of a bird upon his head. In his hand he carried a leather bag tied at the top with a draw string. He sat down next to Tabu directly across from me. Tabu and the man exchanged greetings in the strange tongue of the Swamp People. A moment later the man opened his leather bag and pulled from it several small pouches of leather and placed them side by side upon the ground in front of him. He looked at Tabu and smiled broadly. Tabu's face glowed in the dim light of the fire with excitement and gratitude. Whatever it was, this is what he had come for.

After a while Tabu turned to me and spoke.

"These are the herbs and ointments that I came for," he said. "The *Sochet* have no gods that they cannot see and there are no priests who make their livelihood interpreting the minds of the gods." He stopped for a moment and poked the fire with a short stick. "No temples of medicine where priests study theology more than the body, where they listen to the ramblings of the mind more than the offerings of their senses." He stopped again as if searching for the proper words. "Often they reject out of hand what appears before their very noses because it disagrees with their notion of the what the god's desire. Here among the *Sochet* there are no invisible gods and so there are no invisible illnesses." He stared into the fire as if in deep thought. "I have learned much from them and they have given me medicines that are not found anywhere else in Egypt" He sighed. "Mostly they taught me to keep an open mind. There are many strange things in the world, my prince, and no man knows them all."

I shook my head in agreement. Why had Tabu found it so difficult to come to this realization? It was one of the rules that Ra-hotep had taught me from the very start. I smiled to myself. Perhaps I wasn't as unlearned as I sometimes thought.

We stayed among the Swamp People for only a day. We returned to Busiris by evening of the next day and spent the night in Temhet's guest house. I slept better knowing the cemetery held only animals. But for caution's sake I hung a curtain over my window. In the morning our boat set out upon the river. Two hours later we passed by Tjebnutjer on the west bank. Just beyond the city the Nile suddenly regains its width. Its path still twists and turns as it had since we entered the eastern channel at Khem, but the width and current of the river conveyed the impression that we were moving downstream with greater speed. We spent the next night aboard our boat. I lay upon my mat unable to sleep. From somewhere a cool breeze that seemed somehow unfamiliar kept the night comfortable. There was a strange smell, almost a taste, in the night air. I was uneasy and waited for the coming of the morning light.

The morning came and filled me with apprehension. The warm sun was gone. In its place was a thick layer of dark clouds that raced across the sky along a brisk cold wind that danced upon the Nile and turned its surface unsettled. The strange smell of the night before was stronger now. I took a deep breath and felt the faint taste of salt on my tongue. Our boat moved with the strong current. Standing on the bow I felt the headwind upon my face and sensed it growing stronger by the minute. I turned and saw Tabu and Lanata sitting together in the middle of the deck. I walked back to where they sat.

"It is a strange morning Tabu," I said. "What do you make of it?" I tried to sound self assured.

Tabu looked at Lanata who was clearly frightened. "I don't know," he answered. "Probably nothing." He shrugged. "We are very near the Great Green. It is only an hour's sail to the open sea. Perhaps that has something to do with it." He smiled at Lanata and pulled her close to him.

For the next hour the boat barely made headway against the increasing wind. The Nile's current turned back upon itself and white-tipped waves pressed against the bow of the boat and slowed it even more. The water's surface became turbulent. The boat rocked from side to side while the water beat against the hull. Behind us a thick ceiling of gray clouds stretched to the horizon. Up ahead the clouds had turned black. Off the starboard bow I could see Damietta and I felt the steering oar bite deeply into the water and try to force the front of the boat toward shore. Twenty minutes more and we would have reached the harbor.

A loud crash echoed across the blackened skies with such force that I thought it had deafened me. The wind, already forcing the boat beyond the control of the helmsman, suddenly increased. It made a howling noise as it moved over the boat and the frightened crew. Our little vessel pitched up and down while the crew tried desperately to lower the sail. The sun had fled the heavens leaving only a darkness which descended all around us. Within a few seconds I could not see the shore a half mile away. A bright jagged streak of light raced across the heavens accompanied by a tremendous crash and then was gone. The whole event stunned my senses. I was struck still as if carved in stone. I barely recovered from the first flash when a second and then a third fell upon the horizon making it bright as day for a few seconds before the darkness reclaimed the sky. The booming noise that followed was frightening. I looked for Tabu and Lanata and saw both of them upon the deck holding on to each other for dear life. I grabbed the bow rail with all my strength and hung on.

Suddenly water poured out of the sky and fell upon everything around us. I had never seen such a thing before. Later, during my campaigns in Lebanon and the mountains I encountered rain many times. But this was my first storm. It never rains in Upper Egypt and only rarely along the seacoast of the Delta. But the rain that fell upon us that day was beyond what anyone who lived on the coast had ever seen. For more than an hour water fell from the skies. Sometimes it blew straight across our boat in wind-driven sheets. At others it fell straight down with such force that it stung my skin.

The boat rose and fell on the serpentine waves and pitched from side to side as the helmsman lost the bite of the steering oar in the violent churning water. The wind was driving us toward the stone quay of Damietta harbor and there was no way to control the boat. Through the darkness and rain our little boat drifted up and down and side to side without steering or direction. The crew had given up trying to steer the craft. Most hung onto anything they could find to steady themselves. From time to time the jagged light flashed around us followed by a crash like that of giant cymbals. Each time there was a strange odor as if the air had been cooked. I made my way to Tabu and Lanata. I was bending over them trying to shout above the noise of the wind and steady myself against the heaving deck when the force of the crash hurled me hard against the rear rail. An instant later I was in the water.

Instinct brought my head above water. Without thinking, I moved my arms and legs to stay afloat. I saw the stern of the boat a few feet in front of me. But it disappeared in the wall of water that crashed over my head. I surfaced and caught sight of the boat again. This time the waves and the wind worked in concert and the boat smashed violently against the stone pier. Wooden planks came loose from the stern just above the waterline. In seconds the stern was full of water and the vessel's bow pointed skyward as it began to slide beneath the surface. A piece of broken planking floated toward me. I grabbed it wrapped my arms around it and hung on.

The water was full of cargo boxes, pieces of broken wood, and people. I looked around for Lanata and Tabu and saw the boat disappear beneath the waters of the river. Again and again the wind and waves drove people against the cruel stones of the pier. Several times I saw crew members smashed head first against the pier and float limply away as the water carried them out only to smash them against the stones a second time. The rain fell harder and the waves grew stronger. I was becoming tired and my grip on the life-saving plank was weakening. I knew that if I released the plank I would surely be lost. With all my determination I hung on and waited for the storm to end.

From behind a powerful arm grabbed me around the chest. A voice from out of the roaring water said "I have you, my prince. No need to worry." It was Sinub's familiar voice, the same combination of anger and annoyance that marked his tone whenever something unpleasant had to be done. Sinub had seen me fall over the stern. Instead of following me into the water he wisely jumped to the pier. There he commandeered two men and a rope and ran along the quay searching the water for me. When the boat slipped beneath the surface he saw me close by it. He jumped into the water tied to the end of the rope. Now he had me in his firm grip while the men on the pier pulled us both to safety. A few minutes later we sat on the pier watching the confusion as men scrambled for their lives against the angry river. It was not a pretty sight. I saw several crewmen slip beneath the surface. Another I saw torn to pieces as he was smashed again and again against the stones. Men ran up and down the pier tossing ropes to those who had the strength left to grab and hold onto them.

It rained heavily and the wind blew strongly for another hour. And then it stopped. The darkness lifted and the clouds drifted apart permitting streaming rays of sunlight to reach the earth. The anger left the Nile and the river became tranquil again. Sinub and I searched for Tabu and Lanata. A crowed of people from the town gathered along the quay and made it difficult to find anyone in the confusion. We searched the water with our eyes for a long time but found nothing. Then Sinub made his way through the crowd to the far end of the pier. Suddenly I heard his voice calling me. I ran to him as fast as my legs would carry me.

I was not prepared for what I saw. A small knot of people gathered around a figure kneeling on the pier. Sinub stood over the man and I made my way toward him. As I approached I saw that it was Tabu kneeling beside a still form. The sound of his tears reached my ears and a great fear fell upon my mind. Tabu's back was to me and I placed my hand upon his shoulder. Tabu turned toward me and the expression on his face told me that something terrible had happened. I looked down at the figure lying before Tabu. It was Lanata.

She looked peaceful lying there, her beauty undiminished by the small bruise that discolored the side of her head. Tabu held her hand and wept openly for the life of his only child. One by one the group of people drifted away until only Sinub and I remained with Tabu. Lanata's features looked like fine alabaster, and I could not take my eyes from her delicate face. She had nursed me through my terrible illness and was my friend. Now she was dead and would laugh with me no more nor taunt me with those soft eyes. When I was older and had lost comrades in war I often thought of Lanata whenever the news of a friend's death was brought to me. It was never any different then than it was that day. One never becomes accustomed to it. The pain is never any less.

# Thirteen

The priest moved noiselessly from corpse to corpse while the soldiers from the Damietta barracks arranged the bodies from the shipwreck upon the stone quay. The boat's home port was Memphis and it was unlikely that there would be any relatives willing to pay for the funeral services of the dead. Still one never knew about these things so the priest went from corpse to corpse anyway. Tabu cradled the dead Lanata in his arms. Off to one side Sinub was talking with one of the soldiers. The crowd was gone leaving the quay quiet. The soldiers finished their work and waited in a group for their commander to finish speaking with Sinub. Neither Tabu nor I heard the priest approach.

"Forgive my intrusion," he said, "But I want to express my sorrow for your loss."

The sound of the priest's voice pierced through Tabu's sobbing. He looked up and saw the shaven-headed prelate in red robes standing before him. The sight of the red garments sent a shiver through Tabu's body. He pulled Lanata tightly against him and began to wail in grief. Tabu's crying caught Sinub's attention. He moved the few steps toward us and squatted next to me. Tabu's despair wounded my heart and I used every bit of the power of my will not to break into tears myself. As always Sinub remained impassive.

The priest spoke. "It is a terrible time for you, my friend." His voice was low and even but lacked any emotion. It was as if he was speaking words in a well-rehearsed play, as if he had spoken the same words many times before in exactly the same manner. Tabu held Lanata tightly and rocked her back and forth in his arms.

"Your grief is understandable," the priest said. "But you know she is not truly dead. She is being prepared to fly to the Field of Marshes and her glorious afterlife. It is a land that is just and fair and without trouble." He paused waiting for Tabu's sobs to lessen. At last Tabu went silent and looked up at the priest.

"You are a priest of Anubis?"

Tabu's voice quivered as he asked a question to which he already knew the answer. The priest nodded respectfully. A thin smile crossed his lips for a second and then was gone, buried in the false expression of compassion for a man and his daughter that he had never met. Tabu shook his head slowly from side to side and returned to looking at the pale face of his daughter.

I tugged at Sinub's shirt to get his attention. "What kind of priest is this man?" I asked in a whisper. "I thought that all of them were the same." The red-robed priest must have heard me and shot me a quick glance of disapproval as if I were interfering with his important business.

Sinub smirked. "He is a priest of the dead, Oh prince. An embalmer. Only they wear the red robes, the color of Seth."

Sinub paused and shook his head in disgust. He was a soldier and had seen the dead buried on the battlefield many times. To him there was nothing so useless as a corpse. To spend all the time and money it required to embalm and bury a body was pointless as far as he was concerned. It was a fanciful habit for rich officers.

"Don't be fooled, my prince. He is just drumming up business. Tabu's sorrow is only an opportunity to increase the temple's wealth."

The priest knelt down on one knee and talked to Tabu in a whisper that made it difficult for me to hear what he was saying. As he spoke Tabu's sobbing subsided. From time to time he nodded his head as if agreeing to something. At the priest's urging Tabu slowly lowered Lanata's body to the ground. The priest helped him to stand and steadied him with one arm. The other arm made a quick waving motion as if the priest were signaling to someone. Within seconds three men appeared from nowhere. Two of them carried a litter. As we watched Lanata's body was wrapped gently in a white blanket and lifted upon the litter. The third man moved in front of the bearers and began to lead them in a slow cadence to the sound of a wooden rattle. The man shook the rattle more vigorously as he moved it away from his body and slowed its sound whenever he brought it toward him. The sound began as a gentle whisper gradually rising in strength and pitch to the noise of a strong wind caught in the branches of a willow only to fall back to a whisper again. It resembled, so Ra-hotep told me later, the sound of the Ba of the deceased taking wing and hovering over the body. The priest placed his arm around Tabu and walked with him behind the litter. Sinub and I fell into line. Together we accompanied the beautiful Lanata to the embalmers where she was to be prepared for her next life.

Our little procession moved through the temple gate and into the outer courtyard. The mortuary was a large brick building with steep stairs leading to a pillared entranceway at the top. With a deliberate pace we climbed the stairs bearing with us the burden of the litter and the sorrow in our hearts while the sacred rattle filled the air with its mournful sounds. The procession slowed and stopped. When Tabu saw the figure standing at the top of the stairs he burst into tears. If the priest had not steadied him he would have collapsed. I stepped to the side to see why we had stopped and my eyes fell upon a sight that might have frightened even old Amenemhab, that eater-of-faces! Guarding the gateway to the mortuary was Anubis himself, the god of the dead!

The chief priest of the mortuary stood there in his crimson robes. Over his head he wore a wooden mask of the jackal Anubis. The long black dog's face ended in a tapered snout that wore a thin smile of resignation upon its lips. The high pointed ears stood straight up, the better to hear the last cries of the dead. Red garnets against yellow backgrounds cast a pitiless stare from the jackal's eyes that shone against the crimson linen headdress. The red robe hung from the priest's shoulders all the way to the ground in the manner of high government officials. Beneath the open robe I saw the green kilt held around the priest's waist by a belt fashioned from the skin of a cheetah. Gilded sandals adorned the priest's feet. In his hands he held an open scroll from which he read.

We listened in awed silence as the god-made-flesh read from the sacred scrolls welcoming the deceased to the mortuary temple in preparation for her life in the Marshes of Creation. It had always struck me that we Egyptians rarely acknowledged that someone was dead. Instead we used all sorts of phrases to deny ourselves the reality of death. Ra-hotep once told me that this was so because it helped us endure the pain of so great a loss. The idea that the deceased were not dead and that we might once again join them in a better life was comforting, he said. But when I asked if he truly knew that the dead did not die, my old teacher shook his head. He did not, he told me, but was willing to wait until he, too, passed beyond to find out.

As Anubis read from the sacred scroll two priests appeared behind him. They walked the few steps to the litter and walked around it spreading incense over Lanata's body. One of them pulled the blanket from around her face and anointed her lips with myrrh to remind the deceased of the sweet fruits she would soon enjoy in the afterlife. A strange expression came over the face of the other priest when he looked at Lanata. It was almost an expression of desire, as if this priest wanted to possess her. I looked at Sinub who was glaring at the priest in angry disgust. Sinub would not take his eyes off him for a long time. It struck me that Sinub was threatening him with some grim punishment for an unknown crime. The whole episode left me puzzled.

Our procession moved ahead again, now led by Anubis himself. We passed into the mortuary temple and down a short corridor finally stopping before a door. One of the incense priests opened it and we entered. Lanata's body was placed upon a wooden table. More incense and more prayers. All the while Tabu sobbed heavily at the thought of leaving his child. At last Anubis ordered us to leave. Tabu was hysterical and taken in strong hands by Sinub who spoke to the physician in comforting tones. At last Tabu calmed himself. He stood over Lanata for one last while and gazed deeply upon her face as if trying to carve her visage into his memory. He bent over her face and kissed her gently on the forehead.

"Goodby, my precious one."

His words were barely audible through his sobs. The priest placed his arms upon Tabu's shoulder and led him from the room.

Sinub and I followed until the four of us made our way out into the sunlight. Anubis had disappeared as had the two incense priests. The red-robed priest spoke to Tabu and the two of them walked off no doubt to settle the cost of the funeral arrangements. Sinub raised his hand to his eyes squinting into the sunlight searching for something. We stood there together for a few minutes. From where we were on top of the stairs I saw a troop of four soldiers moving at the double come through the gate. Quickly they climbed the stairs and halted in front of Sinub.

One of the soldiers spoke. "Good day, sir. We are sent here under your command."

Sinub smiled and saluted smartly. "Very good, sergeant," he said. "Bring two of your men and follow me." He walked off quickly and the soldiers followed. Left out of everything, I trailed behind.

Sinub led the soldiers through the door down the corridor and stopped before the door leading to the room where Lanata's body lay.

"I want this room guarded day and night for three days. No one is to be permitted to enter without my written permission. Is that clear sergeant?"

The soldier snapped to attention. "Yes sir," he said.

Sinub continued. "You can use the other soldiers as a relief. But at no time is the room to be left unguarded for the next three days." His voice was firm like that of a man accustomed to command. The sergeant nodded.

Sinub turned to me. "Are you ready to leave, Oh prince?" he asked. I looked at him but said nothing. "Perhaps you wish a final few moments with Lanata," he said. I thought about it for a moment and then shook my head. "No. Its alright. Perhaps we had better go."

He shook his head and offered a thin smile. "As you wish, your highness. Perhaps it is better that we return now to Damietta where I have made arrangements for the three of us to stay until the funeral preparations are complete and we can accompany Lanata's body to Memphis." Sinub paused. "I assume that is where Tabu will wish to bury his only child." There was a softness to his voice that I had never heard before. Perhaps the death of a child moved even Sinub, but I could not say for certain.

The commander of the barracks at Damietta provided suitable quarters for the three of us and we settled in for what was to be a long stay. It took seventy days for the embalming process to be completed. Then Tabu had to contract for a funeral boat to make the journey to Memphis with Lanata's mummy and the three of us aboard. As things turned out it was four months after the ship-wreck before I saw Ra-hotep and Memphis again. The barracks commander sent a messenger upriver with the next boat so that Ra-hotep was informed of what had happened and would not expect my return until the flood was again at its height.

Tabu was still too upset to be much good at anything so Sinub and I took to overseeing the funeral arrangements. This required me to learn new things, some of which burdened my mind for many years. Fortunately Sinub turned out to be as good a teacher as he was a soldier and he helped me along the way. My education began the next morning at breakfast. It was just Sinub and I. Tabu was exhausted and remained in his bed.

I munched on some figs and bread. Sinub was ravenous and swallowed bread and roasted gooseflesh like a hungry wolf. When he had eaten enough to calm his angry belly I asked him about the events at the mortuary.

"Tell me, Sinub," I said. "Why did you post guards around Lanata's body?" I paused. "And why for three days?" I added.

He stopped eating in mid-bite. His eyes narrowed in anger and he coughed up a short laugh that sounded like a snort. "To keep that perverted bastard of a priest from having sex with her, that's why!" There was anger in his voice. He took a quick drink of beer and slammed the clay cup on the table. "Did you see how that incense priest looked at Lanata when the blanket was pulled from her face?" He spat the words out. "The bastard couldn't wait! Sick son-of-a-bitch!"

Sinub's words stunned me. My voice stammered. "Wha...What are you...you saying?" I couldn't get the words out. "Do you... you...mean that he was going to...to."

Sinub's angry reply cut me off. "Yes, Oh prince. That's exactly what I mean."

"But...but...Lanata's dead!" The words came out in an expression of surprise like I had just discovered the fact that Lanata had died. "It's unbelievable!" I found myself shaking my head in disgust.

Sinub poured himself another cup of beer. "Well this is one girl he won't get!" He took a swallow from the cup and bit off a piece of bread to go with the gooseflesh.

"But why guard her for three days?" I had barely formed the words before I wished I hadn't said them. Sinub looked at me as if I were a numbskull. He spit a short laugh and shook his head.

"Because, my prince, in three days time Lanata will no longer be attractive to any man, not even as evil an animal as that priest. In just a short time the Egyptian heat will take its toll and her body will start to decay. The odors from her insides will overpower all else. Still her body will not be so decayed as to be beyond repair by the priests of Anubis who will earn a tidy sum for their skills."

He paused and looked at me to see if his words were causing me pain. I tried to show him that they were not, although I do not know how successful I was. Sinub continued.

"It is a common practice for the families of young girls who have died to keep their bodies at home until they are partially decayed and no sane man would try to mate with their corpse. We will have no complaint from the embalmers about the guard. They understand that we understand." He rubbed his eyes. "But my prince I do not think that Tabu the physician is up to overseeing the embalming of his daughter."

Sinub looked straight into my eyes probing for weaknesses in my spirit. "Perhaps," he paused for a moment, "it is something that you might do for your friend. If you wish I shall be by your side." I returned Sinub's stare. To say no would reveal the pain and fear that I felt at the prospect of witnessing an embalming. Slowly I nodded my head in agreement although no words came to my throat. Sinub took another gulp of beer.

"Good," he said and swallowed deeply.

Two days later Sinub and I went to the mortuary. The red-robed priest was named Tepet and, as Sinub had said, he offered no objection to our having posted the guard nor to the suggestion that I witness the embalming. I was, after all, a Theban prince of the royal family. It would be fitting, Tepet said, for me to gain the knowledge of how Egyptians prepared their dead. Someday I would be pharaoh and the knowledge would serve me well. As the priest spoke I had no sense of the prophecy that hung in his words. With matters settled, Sinub took his leave to dismiss the guard.

The priest grinned at me as I sat across the table from him. "Would you like a cup of cold water before we see Lanata," he asked. I shrugged and shook my head. The priest nodded and leaned back in his chair. The thin smile on his face reflected the coldness in his air of self-assurance. I did not like him.

"Perhaps it would be of some use to your highness if I told you something about what you will witness over the next few days." His voice was self-assured and calm. Too calm. Like the surface of a deep pond that hid the danger that lurked beneath the surface. "For instance," he continued, "what you will see in the embalmer's parlor is not something that we Egyptians have been doing for very long. In fact, we owe much of the demand for mummification to your ancestors, the kings of Thebes." He paused for a few moments. "It was they who made mummification popular." Tepet smiled as he watched his words take hold in my mind.

Before I could answer he spoke again.

"The *idea* of mummification is very old, but not embalming itself. The first mummy, of course, was Osiris. I am sure you recall from your religious instruction that Osiris was killed by his evil brother, Seth, and his body cut into pieces and scattered upon the earth."

I moved my head slightly to indicate that I was familiar with the legend. The priest smiled and continued.

"When Isis gathered the parts she magically bound them together with cloth strips making the first Egyptian mummy. Isis then became a bird and wrapped Osiris in her wings and brought him back to life. She gave him the gift of resurrection. It was that idea, of preserving the body for life in the hereafter, that we Egyptians have always held so precious."

Tepet looked at me and offered a smile. "Do you understand, Oh prince?"

This time I was not going to be intimidated like some school boy. "Of course I understand," I said. My voice had a hard edge to it and the lilt of anger rested just beneath the surface. "There is no need to treat me like the feeble-minded!" I paused for a few seconds. "Go on with your story" I ordered.

The red-robed priest bowed his head in submission, but the thin snake-like smile on his face remained unchanged. He spoke slowly.

"In ancient times we buried our dead in the hot dry sand and let nature remove the moisture from the body. Then about a thousand years ago we began to wrap the body in plaster and linen before placing it in the ground. It was only a few hundred years ago when we began removing the organs before burial. It was a primitive procedure where linen cloth was placed inside body and covered with gum or resin. Sometimes even sawdust was used instead of linen." Tepet shook his head. "Of course no such thing will be done to Lanata." Again he smiled the thin scar of a smile. I was beginning to truly dislike the man.

"But why is it you say that the Theban princes were the first to insist on complete mummification?" I asked. Tepet gathered his thoughts. I tried to imagine my grandfather demanding mummification from some embalmer. It was a silly vision and made no sense.

"The warrior kings of Thebes thought of themselves as the sons of gods and it befits a god to live forever. To make this possible the embalmers tried new techniques to preserve the god's body." Tepet paused. "There was also another reason," he said. "To escape the fate of other pharaohs at the hands of grave robbers the princes of Thebes no longer were buried in the hot sand that preserved the body. Instead they demanded rock tombs high in the mountains of the Valley of the Kings. These tombs were cold and damp and made the bodies decay. If the princes of Thebes were to live forever, they required completely mummified bodies. This is why the priests of Anubis became experts at preservation." Tepet sat back in his chair with a look of satisfaction on his face.

For a few minutes I sat across from this priest of death saying nothing. I attempted to form images in my mind to portray what Tepet had told me. The more I tried the more they eluded me. I was learning that some things cannot truly be imagined until they have first been experienced. There was a growing concern within me that the realities of Lanata's embalming might be too horrible for me to bear. Suddenly the snake-like smile on Tepet's face revealed its full meaning. He was counting on my being unable to witness Lanata's embalming! The red-robed bastard had every intention of reducing a prince of Thebes to a frightened child! Amenemhab's words returned to my mind.

"*Sometimes even a prince must suffer,*" he said. "*Learn to endure!*" I knew that it was good advice. Did I have the courage to face it? It took only a few seconds to make up my mind.

"Tepet," I said. "Perhaps it is time for us to begin." A frown creased the priest's brow. "Perhaps it is time for me to see Lanata now."

His body stiffened a bit as he rose from his chair. Again the serpent's smile and again the smooth emotionless voice.

"As you wish, Oh prince."

It was a brief walk to the corridor and the door to the room that held Lanata's corpse. Two mortuary assistants accompanied us. The air inside the mortuary was warm and a strong smell of incense wafted through the corridor. The incense was coming from a large censer bowl resting on a stand in front of the door. Tepet's hand reached for the door latch and pushed the door open.

"Do you wish to enter or shall I instruct the assistants to remove the body to the embalming room?" he asked. His face was without expression as he awaited my answer.

Even here, outside the room, the stench of putrefying flesh was beginning to overpower the incense and my stomach felt uneasy.

"I shall see her," I said. Mustering all the courage I could, I walked the few steps past Tepet into the room.

Lanata lay on the wooden table much as we had left her three days earlier. Except for her face the blanket covered her completely. The bruise on the side of her head was darker and her skin had turned waxy gray. Her lips seemed swollen and dark spots had begun to appear where her eyelids covered her eyes. I reached forward and brushed my hand against her cheek in one last goodby. As my fingers moved lightly over her face my fingernail caught a small pouch of skin. To my horror the skin came away from her face revealing an oozy substance underneath. Her flesh was the consistency of overripened fruit, and the slightest disturbance caused it to burst. I withdrew my hand and wiped it against the side of my kilt as if to rid myself of some disease. The strong odor of death and decay was everywhere. The more I stared at Lanata's corpse, the stronger the stench became until I feared it would cling to my very being for all time. As years passed I came to forget what I had seen here but, strangely, I never forgot the odor of death.

The sound of Tepet clearing his throat disturbed my thoughts and I was glad for the interruption.

"If you wish, my prince, I will have the assistants move the woman's body to the embalming parlor," he said. I nodded in agreement and walked out of the room. A few minutes later the two assistants emerged carrying the corpse on the litter.

Tepet and I followed them down the corridor. They passed through a large doorway midway down the hall that opened in on a large room with a wooden table in its center. Standing at the head of the table was a priest, his head covered in the jackal mask of Anubis. Four assistants stood off to one side. One of these carried a large censer from which clouds of incense billowed filling the room with gray smoke. Against the far wall stood a solitary figure dressed in white. I could not make out what he held in his hand. Whatever it was he moved it nervously through his fingers. At the foot of a table was a smaller table. A collection of knives and instruments rested upon it. Next to the table was a wooden trunk. Four stone jars, each one adorned with a cover representing the head of an animal or a person, stood on the table. Next to the jars was a small tray of magical amulets artfully arranged around a carved stone scarab beetle, the Egyptian symbol of creation. The room was well lit by lamps that hung from special stands that could be moved to provide the best possible light.

The assistants placed Lanata upon the table and left. Anubis began to speak. Reading from a special scroll he intoned instructions and prayers over the corpse. When he was finished he stood arms folded and watched the proceedings begin in silence. Tepet and I stood to one side. One of the assistants motioned to the figure standing against the far wall. Tepet spoke to me in whispered tones preserving the solemnity of what was about to take place.

"That is the Opener," he said. "He will begin the ceremony of embalming by making a long incision along the left side of the body. He uses a special instrument called the Ethiopian Stone whose blade is made of obsidian."

I watched the man approach the corpse. Two assistants removed the blanket. The dress was cut with a sharp blade and removed from the body. Even in the smokey haze I could see the large purple and blue spots that had appeared on Lanata's white skin. Her fingers and toes were colored like dark grapes. Lanata's beautiful alabaster complexion was gray.

The Opener walked around the table and stopped at Lanata's side. He pressed the knife against her skin and in one swift motion drew a deep slash on a diagonal across her belly from her rib cage to the top of her thigh. He stepped back bowed in the direction of Anubis and walked from the room. From where I stood I could see the open wound. Strangely, I thought, it did not bleed.

One of the assistants moved next to the corpse. In one hand he held a small bronze knife. He slid both hands into the gash in Lanata's side. Expertly his free hand located the intestines while the other guided the knife against the tissue that held them to the body. From the movement of his upper arms I guessed that he was cutting the organs free. In less than a minute the assistant pulled the intestines out through the incision. Instantly the room was filled with the odor of decaying flesh and feces. The man holding the incense bowl blew on it to force the perfumed clouds from it more quickly. The intestines were passed to another assistant who examined them carefully before putting them into one of the open jars on the top of the trunk. Again the assistant's arms moved guiding his hands as they roamed inside Lanata's corpse. This time the swift cuts of the knife freed the liver. The greenish-gray organ looked like sickness itself as it was passed to the other assistant who placed it in a second jar.

I could see that the cutter was having some difficulty with his knife. He had both hands inside the body and was struggling to make the knife cut laterally under the ribs. There is a strong muscle that separates the lungs and heart from the lower organs, and the assistant was having a difficult time cutting through it. After a few minutes work when the movement of his arms suggested he was wielding a saw more than a knife, the assistant reached deeply into the upper body so that even the muscles of his upper arms disappeared into the gash in Lanata's side. One last tug and he was rewarded with a pair of fine pink lungs. These, too, he passed to the other assistant. Finally the assistant moved his knife one last time and removed the stomach. When the work was complete, the Anubis priest said a prayer over the jars in which the organs had been placed.

I was doing my best not to be sick and summoned all my strength to keep my face impassive. From time to time I saw Tepet looking at me as if taking my measure to withstand all this. Somehow I managed not to vomit or to run from the terrible scenes in front of me. I remember thinking that perhaps the worst was over.

"Do you see those jars at the foot of the table?" Tepet said to me. I saw the assistant filling the jar with a white powder. "That is a special salt that comes from the Fields of Salt near the Lakeland," Tepet continued. "It is used to dry the organs until all moisture is gone from them."

I nodded and swallowed hard.

Tepet continued. "Can you see the lids on the jars," he said.

I managed to speak. "Yes," I said.

"Each organ of the body has its own guardian among the Sons of Horus. The lid for each jar is carved in the image of these guardians. Look closely."

Again I summoned my courage. At the end of the table the assistant was rolling Lanata's organs in a tray of natron salt before replacing them in their jars. It was a truly horrible sight and it seemed to have no effect at all upon the assistant who was holding Lanata's insides in his hands. Tepet's voice crashed through my mind.

"Notice," he said, "that the image of the ape guards the lungs, the jackal the stomach, the man guards the liver, and the falcon the intestines. For all eternity these fine Sons of Horus will protect these organs from evil." The priest's voice seemed filled with pride as if what he was telling me was important beyond measure. All I could do was shake my head.

From across the room I saw the other assistant move toward the table. He stood facing Tepet and me. From the small table he picked up an instrument that looked like a metal spike whose end had been hammered into a flat bent spoon. The assistant looked across the table at me and bowed his head slightly to acknowledge my presence. Then he drove the instrument up into the corpse's nostril until it could go no further. With the palm of his hand he struck the base of the metal spike forcing it through the obstruction. When almost the full length of the spike had disappeared into the corpses' nostril the assistant twisted it from side to side. Satisfied, he withdrew the spike bringing with it a spoonful of what looked like grayish porridge. For more than an hour he drove the spike into the corpse's nose again and again each time withdrawing the gray mash until he had filled a small pot with it. I could hardly believe what I was seeing. My mind went numb. Whatever visions of Lanata I possessed were driven from me to keep from going mad. And then the voice of Tepet.

"See, Oh prince, how the head is filled with this useless gray mash." The man was almost laughing. "The heart is left within the body so that it may be weighed at the last judgement because it is where all intellect and feeling are located." He paused. "This gray mash has no purpose."

I stared at what was left of Lanata. The assistant's shoveling at her nose had split it open. The skin above her lip was torn and pushed upward so she wore a twisted smile that exposed her top row of teeth. It was the grimace of tortured death, of someone who was still suffering though physical pain was absent. The pressure against the corpse's nose had forced open one of Lanata's eyes. It had turned a dull yellow as it stared silently at nothing. The opening in her side was wide enough to place an arm through, and the force with which the assistant worked his will had torn a gash across the lower chest forming a great loose flap that could be opened or closed at will. Through it all the Anubis priest repeated prayers and instructions to guide the gods and the assistants in their work. And when they had finished the beautiful Lanata was reduced to the ugliness of an open sore. The anger and rage I felt threatened to overwhelm all else! Could I have gotten my hands on one of the instruments I would surely have buried it in the chest of one of the miserable assistants. So, too, for the Anubis priest and Tepet. I stood there in silence consumed by rage and grief at the destruction of beauty. Again I heard the voice of Tepet in my head.

"They will move her now," he said.

I looked at him, but words would not come. The smile of the serpent returned to his face. He beckoned me to follow him as he walked from the room. As if I was without a will of my own, I followed him, perhaps even grateful that I was out of that terrible place. A short walk brought us to another room. Tepet opened the door and I followed him through the entrance. There was no incense here and the stench of wet spoiled meat clung to the stones like paint. Stone coffins three feet deep were arranged in two rows from the front to the back of the room. There must have been at least thirty of them. Each coffin was filled with a strong smelling liquid. A thick brownish scum floated on top. I took a few steps closer and looked in. This was the worst of all! Beneath the surface of the water I saw a naked corpse, its loosened skin floating from its bones.

"In the name of Seth what is this place," I muttered and sank to my knees in defeat. I had no idea such things existed and my will was worn to nothing. I could resist no further. Slowly I raised my head and stared into the smiling face of Tepet the serpent, the priest of the dead, violator of women, and would-be destroyer of my sanity. Even as I knelt there I wished only to kill this vile creature and rid the earth of his kind before they befouled us all with their beliefs.

Tepet stood over me for a few seconds. Then he stooped, put his arms under mine, and raised me to my feet. He would give me no respite. I had asked to see the embalming and promised Tabu I would look after Lanata. And now this priest of Anubis was going to see to it that I did. His voice entered my head like a dagger.

"This is the beginning of the preservation. The corpses remain in a bath of palm wine and natron salt for ten days. After that they are taken to another place where their bodies are covered with dry natron salt for another forty days." Tepet stopped speaking long enough for me to raise my head and look at him. Now that he had my attention he spoke again.

"It is over for now, my prince." His voice was comforting. I marvelled at how this man could call forth whatever emotion the situation of the moment required.

"Forty days from now I shall come for you to bring you here again to watch the final preparation of the beloved Lanata."

The way he said "the beloved Lanata" dripped with contempt. He paused to make certain his meaning was not missed. Even in my weakened condition I remembered the vicious tone of his voice.

"I trust that you will report to Tabu the physician that all has gone well with the preparation of his daughter." His face broke into a hideous grin as he gave me an exaggerated bow, walked past me, and disappeared into the corridor.

A few minutes later I found my way out of the mortuary and into the bright sunlight of the Egyptian day. It was hot and the heat felt good on my body. I wished for it to purge my garments of the smells and sights of death. Perhaps it would be so for nature has many wonders. Yet as I walked through the gate onto the road that led to the barracks, I knew as certainly as I knew my own soul that nothing could ever rid me of the images I had seen this day.

There was nothing else to do but wait. The embalming would not be finished for two more months. I took comfort in the fact that I would not have to endure any more horrors for a while. Of course the account I gave to Tabu was much different from what I had witnessed and he seemed to take solace in the care and dignity with which the priests were treating his little girl. As the days passed Tabu's spirits rose a bit each day. Sinub and I passed the time exploring the military base at Damietta and going for long walks along the coastline of the Great Green. The ocean air was new to me and its cool breezes helped drive the terrible images of Lanata from my mind. The breezes kept the insects away and I passed many a comfortable evening sleeping on the beech. The sounds of the waves calmed me a great deal, and I slept more deeply than I had in many months. The stench and heat of the parched summer that made the Nile Valley miserable at this time of year was nowhere in evidence. For the first time in my life I passed *Shemu* in comfort.

I emerged from the cool ocean amid the slapping waves and made my way to where Sinub was waiting for me on the shore. We had been in Damietta for three weeks and Sinub was growing bored with his surroundings so I was pleased to see the smile on his face. He was in a good mood and he waved to me as I walked toward him. The sun was already hot and I was completely dry by the time I reached him.

"You take to the water like the great carp of the Nile my prince," Sinub said with a laugh. "Perhaps you might serve in the navy when you are king, like Kamose who moved his armies against his enemies by boat." He smiled broadly and I could see the relaxed expression on his face.

"Nile carp indeed!" I said with mock indignation. "Ra-hotep would have your hide for comparing me to a fish!" I laughed. "You know how much he loves fish, don't you?" Sinub roared with laughter and my face broke into a happy grin.

"I come with good news, my prince." He paused. "A troop ship leaves Damietta in a few days for a short voyage to Pela. It carries a regiment of troops to relieve the garrison there. I have already spoken to the captain and he would be delighted to have us aboard. Pela is a few days sail down the coast and the boat will sail upon the open sea. I thought perhaps you might be interested in seeing a royal ship-of-the-line going about its work."

A broad smile broke out upon my face. "What a delightful idea," I said. "When would we leave?"

"In two day's time." He lowered his eyes and his voice became serious. "We would be back in time for you to visit the embalmers on the appointed day," he said. He shook his head as if he were tired. "Perhaps it makes good sense to take Tabu along with us. He is better, but still he wears his sorrow like a painful yoke."

My voice took on the same respectful tone.

"What you say is true. I will talk to Tabu and request that he come with us." I paused. "The ocean air and salt might do him some good."

Tabu thought the voyage a good idea and agreed to come along although in all truth he did not show much enthusiasm. I knew there were those who never recovered fully from the death of a child. It passed through my mind that Tabu might be one of these. I tried not to judge too quickly for I knew nothing about the special pain that comes from such a loss. I resolved to keep an eye on Tabu and to see how he struggled with a burden that only a father could suffer.

We boarded the troop ship at the naval pier in Damietta. By the time we arrived the *Spirit of Battle* was packed from stem to stern with soldiers and their equipment bound for the garrison at Pela. The boat was easily more than a hundred feet long and forty feet wide. Except for its size, it differed little from the *Horus* that had carried me to Memphis more than a year ago. Double steering oars rose from over her stern and an enormous mast and sail gave her power upon the open sea. The Nile ran in its main channel this time of year and the south wind was little more than a vapor. The short distance from Damietta to the open sea would be made under the power of the *Spirit's* oars.

The captain greeted the three of us with a salute and welcomed us aboard. His mate showed us to our quarters in the deckhouse. We stowed our baggage and returned to the open deck to see the crew scurrying around making ready to get underway. In less than half an hour the *Spirit of Battle* rounded the point where the Nile empties into the ocean. Here the winds changed becoming stronger and more variable. A series of sharp commands from the captain and the topsail turned to catch the wind. A few minutes later the mainsail raced for the top of the mast and billowed before the breeze the heavy canvas snapping against its stays. I felt the boat surge forward as she gained speed driven by the steady wind. Another command and the bow swung outward away from the shore and headed toward the open sea.

I stood next to Sinub who examined the soldiers with the eye of the military professional that he was.

He shook his head and smiled.

"Conscripts," he said, "Mostly new recruits off to their first duty." He snorted the now familiar laugh. "Most of them will be sick within the hour," he said. "The movement of the boat over the waves makes them dizzy and they loose the contents of their stomachs. To my eye the soldiers looked healthy enough. They were a bit crammed in so that all the available deck space was taken up with their bodies and equipment. Their sergeants moved among them checking their food sacks and water bottles. Pity the recruit who had misplaced his rations! There would be nothing to eat for three days and the promise of a good beating to boot for being careless. Some of them looked frightened. Even to my eye all of them looked very young to be soldiers of the king.

I asked Sinub about this.

"Most are fourteen years old," he said. "They are selected from their villages to serve one year of military service. For most of them it is the first time away from home. Even the month of military training and barracks life has not made soldiers of them, not really. They will grow into soldiers over the next year as their officers and sergeants see to their training and discipline." His eyes examined the faces of the men before him. Sinub sighed. "I must be getting old myself," he said. "They do seem younger than I remember them."

Sinub had just finished speaking when I heard the harsh sound of someone losing control of his stomach. A few seconds later another soldier vomited, this time on the other side of the deck. Another stood up holding his stomach and took a few steps to make his way to the rail. Almost immediately a sergeant struck him with a stick and sent him reeling back into the ranks.

Sinub smiled. "Now that's a sergeant who knows how to handle troops!" The pride of the professional was in his voice. He looked at the puzzled expression upon my face. Hitting a man with a stick did not seem to me the way to lead men anywhere. Sinub saw my face and guessed what I was thinking.

"It is not as harsh as it seems, my prince." Sinub's tone was that of an officer instructing a subordinate. "If you allow one man to make it to the rail soon another will follow and then another and another until half the regiment is gathered on one side of the boat. Then the boat will tip over and drown them all!" He laughed. "Never wait for a situation to get out of control. Recognize what is happening and put a stop to it quickly." He shook his head and smiled. "Yes sir! That's a damn good sergeant."

I stood there feeling very stupid. The sounds of repeated vomiting coming from the troops did not help. The crew of the *Spirit* had transported troops before and when the vomiting stopped sailors appeared with buckets of water that they threw over the soldiers to wash the vomit from the decks. By the end of it all the soldiers were not only sick but soaking wet as well. All this and we had not been upon the sea for more than an hour!

We never lost sight of land and by my reckoning were never more than three miles from shore. The large transport moved over the water remarkably well for its size and could cover the distance to Pela in two and a half days. By foot the journey took ten days. It didn't take a military genius to see the value of a navy that could transport large numbers of troops, chariots, and horses by sea. The warrior princes of Thebes had given Egypt its first real navy.

Sinub and I stood at the bow watching the sun disappear over the *Spirit's* stern. The faint glow of the remains of a dying day colored the sky behind us a dull pink. Up ahead the night's darkness had already begun to reclaim the sky for its own. I could begin to make out the faint twinkle of distant stars far to the west. Behind me Horus passed to his death leaving the burning stars of the goddess Nut the only light in the sky. The stars grew brighter with each minute and it seemed they grew larger as they descended around us until the blackness that enveloped us from horizon to horizon was lit by large lanterns giving off crystal bright light. A cool breeze caressed my skin. I heard the sounds of the mast creaking under the strain imposed upon it by the canvas sail. Crewman moved expertly in the dark as they went about their business making the ship ready for its night passage. The dim light stole the features from the soldiers sitting on the deck so that to my eye they appeared as one solid mass of shadow that could easily be mistaken for any other cargo. Slowly the *Spirit* made her way across the tranquil sea.

I was taken with being at sea in the dark. My every sense was sharpened by the experience. The old Egyptian fear of the darkness seemed groundless. Instead I was excited and turned to Sinub who stared silently out to sea lost in his own thoughts.

"It is more beautiful and calm than I imagined," I said. "Never have I seen such a night. Never have I been surrounded by so many large stars." Sinub heard the excitement in my voice and smiled.

My words were lost in his silence. He seemed to find it difficult to tear himself from the calm that embraced him as he stared across the sea. I could almost hear his heart beating in the silence. Then he took a deep breath and let it out slowly. The sigh awakened him.

"Yes, my prince. It is something few Egyptians have ever seen or would believe, to be upon the Great Green at night." He gestured with his head toward the shadowy mass of soldiers on the deck. "Many of the new soldiers are frightened to death this night. They fear the Night Demon as they have all their lives." He shrugged. "The sergeants will have to keep careful watch tonight. Some of the soldiers will lose their nerve and try to leave the ship to get back to shore." The look of surprise on my face made Sinub grin. "Don't worry," he said. "Come morning light they will be so glad to be alive that they will loose their fear of the darkness the second night." He paused. "And then they will have conquered their fears. For a while they will strut about like real soldiers." Sinub gave out a short laugh and turned back to the open sea.

I stayed awake for as long as I could that first night lost in its beauty and, to be honest, my satisfaction that I too, like the young soldiers, had controlled my own fear of the night. Eventually I made my way to the deckhouse and to my sleeping mat. Sinub and Tabu were already asleep. My head felt comfortable upon the headrest. In a few minutes I stood upon the edge of sleep, that time when the images of dreams begin to form as a thin mist in the consciousness. This night no dreams came. Instead a gentle peacefulness enveloped me and carried me slowly into a restful slumber.

The rest of the trip was uneventful. In the early afternoon of the third day *Spirit* tied up to the quay at Pela. Tabu joined us while Sinub and I watched the troops disembark and reform in ranks on the beach. The quay stood alone connecting the sea with the desert sands. For the entire morning the *Spirit* had sailed past a desert shoreline where nothing green lived. I had mentioned this to Sinub at the time.

"It is the Sinai," he said. "The great desert that separates Egypt from the Asiatics who live along the coast and in the mountains of the hill country. Beyond them are the Mitanni and the Lebanon."

Now that we had docked at Pela I was surprised to find that there was no town here at all! Sinub saw the confusion on my face and sighed.

"This is the landing quay for Pela," he said. "The town itself, if you can call it that, lies about three miles inland." He pointed into the desert. "You can see it from the top of those dunes over there." I was about to ask him why anyone would put a town in the middle of the desert when he spoke again. "Pela is a military camp more than a town. It guards the coastal road that runs through the Sinai to the border. Along the same road leading to the Delta but beyond Pela is Migdol and then Sile, all military towns with strong garrisons. An army coming down that road would have to first reduce those towns before it could move into the Delta. And that would take time," he said. "And in the time it took, large reserves of troops could be rushed to the rescue by land and sea."

His eyes scanned the horizon as if he could see the advancing army in his mind. Sinub's silence was broken by the sharp voices of officers and sergeants forming their troops into ranks. More commands, more voices. The soldiers shouldered their equipment turned their ranks toward Pela and upon command marched off. A few minutes later the last of them disappeared over the hill of dunes.

Early the next morning the *Spirit* took aboard the regiment from Pela and prepared to transport them home. These soldiers were different from the conscripts. They moved with confidence and a prideful gruffness that military life can sometimes bestow upon a young man. They had been at Pela for a year and in that time had been honed to a warrior's edge by their officers and sergeants. Some who had been the youngest and weakest among them when they arrived had changed and grown stronger. Others had failed and would forever remain weak men. Most had simply grown up, taken their own measure, and fulfilled what was asked of them, if often with complaint. A few had found that they liked military life and decided to become professional soldiers. Some of these would live to regret it when they discovered that the storm of battle was far different from the life of a soldier in garrison. Others would pay with their lives for their decision. Still, all in all, life went on for soldiers as it did for everyone else. As I watched the *Spirit of Battle* prepare itself for the return trip I thought to myself that I was very fortunate to be in the company of these men who stood guard over this Egypt even if it was for many against their will.

The return voyage was pleasant and we arrived at Damietta in due course. The sea air seemed to have been of benefit to Tabu whose spirits were better every day. A few days later Tabu came round to see me.

"Sinub tells me that you greatly enjoyed our visit to the *Sochete* and that you were interested in the plants and herbs that were given me." Tabu's voice and body seemed well rested.

I answered pleasantly for I had truly come to like this man whose nervous nature belied a calm if fragile heart.

"Yes, Tabu. Sinub tells you the truth. I would like very much to learn about your secret herbs and plants." I paused. "Who knows the future?" I said with a smile. "Perhaps I will become a physician like you."

Tabu bowed as if he took my jest seriously. "Well, my prince. If you wish I will teach you about these things. I may even tell you some of my healing arts." He smiled broadly. "Even a future pharaoh should not mistreat his patients," he said.

For the next two weeks Tabu and I spent each day together while he told me about the special plants and ointments that had the power to heal. He purchased some writing papyrus and drew pictures of the plants and their leaves so that I might recognize them when I came upon them. And he taught me how to use the natural things provided by the gods to heal injury.

"Honey and beer are the two greatest cures," he said. I thought he was joking and laughed at his words. "No, your highness," he said in a serious voice. "You know that we Egyptians are always suffering some cut or other. Workers on the public buildings are frequently hurt and there are always the crocodiles! They are a public menace!" he shouted. "In most villages women are forbidden to wash their clothes on the riverbank lest they be attacked by the beasts. No, my prince, we Egyptians have many injuries from which a good physician can make a tidy living." He laughed at his own words although what he said was true enough. Tabu continued.

"The Ancient Ones bequeathed us an old text called the Book of Bites and in it they taught us how to treat cuts and crocodile bites with honey and beer. First you must wash the wound thoroughly with a strong beer and make sure there is nothing foreign left under the skin. Then fill the wound with plenty of good quality honey. The wound itself should be closed only partially by using the shortest thorns from the Acacia tree. Pass the thorns through each side of the wound and wrap thread around the ends being careful not to pull the wound completely closed. That way when the body tries to expel the green poison it can pass safely through the spaces and out of the body. Finally wrap the wound in fine linen and hold it to the arm or leg with the sticky gum from the Acacia tree or Syrian pine. After a few days the honey will suck the moisture from the wound and take with it any poison that is present. In two or three weeks the wound will heal completely."

He leaned back in his chair with a satisfied look on his face.

I shook my head in mock disbelief. The last two weeks of listening to Tabu had taught me that he was an educated man from whom I could learn much. He had created in me an interest in plants and animals that I carried for many years. Later, when I was pharaoh and my armies ranged to the end of the civilized world I ordered them to seek out and bring back to Egypt any new plant or tree that they encountered. In this way I introduced many new plants and even animals to Egypt. No matter how pressing the matters of the day were I always maintained my interest in plants and trees and always made time to wander through my personal garden of rare plants. All this I owed to Tabu the physician who stood before me now with a sad look upon his face.

"Tabu, what is troubling you." His mood had changed so quickly that I did not know what to think. "Why do you look so sad when a moment ago you were gay?" My eyes searched his face and I saw his lips quiver as he choked back tears.

"I am sorry, my prince." There was despair in his voice. "But today I must meet with the owner of the funeral boat to make arrangements to carry my daughter to Memphis." He rubbed the tears from his eyes. "It makes me sad to think of her death. I am grateful to you for insuring her the proper dignity and treatment at the hands of the priests of Anubis." And then he did the strangest thing. He reached across the table to me and took my hand. He leaned forward and kissed it in a sign of respect and affection. "Thank you," Tabu said. "Thank you for caring for my little girl."

I did not sleep all that night thinking of Tabu's pain and Lanata's corpse as it lay in the embalmer's tent covered in natron salt for the last seven weeks. It was, I knew, time to return to the embalmer's parlor and its inhuman horrors. All night long I was restless and unable to sleep. I rose early and greeted the dawn in an ugly mood. This time I would take Sinub with me. If I had no choice but to deal with the foul Tepet, there was at least no need to do it alone.

With Sinub by my side I walked into Tepet's office. The smell of death and potions hung in the air. All the incense in the world could not conceal it. I saw Sinub sniff the air and recoil at the odor. The place had seen so much death and dissection that even the stones were unfit to be used by the living. Tepet rose when we entered the room. "Ah, your highness," he said and offered a bow that made a mockery of any notion of respect. "I trust you are well." His eyes glanced at Sinub. "And who is your companion?" he asked with a trace of suspicion in his voice.

I ignored the question. "I have come to see that arrangements are progressing in the proper manner." I forced as much coldness in my voice as I could. "I trust that all is satisfactory and that you have done what you are being paid for." The contempt in my voice was deliberate. Tepet's eyes darkened at my words and a furrow creased his brow. Still he managed the snake-like smile that seemed his most common gesture.

He took a deep breath. "Everything is as you say, Oh prince. Indeed, if you wish, you may inspect things for yourself. It is time to remove the corpse from the salt and begin the preparation of the body for wrapping." His voice made a mockery of any idea of sincerity. "Perhaps," he said, "you would care to follow me." With that Tepet walked passed Sinub and me and out into the corridor. We followed Tepet down the corridor and into the room where the corpses were submerged in stone tubs of preservative. As I passed down the row of tubs I caught sight of the cadaverous features of corpses in the brownish-green solution. Their faces were swollen and bulbous. One corpse's eyes were open and another's tongue protruded from its half-open mouth. The odor of the solution was vile. Sinub pressed his fingers to his nose to rid himself of it. None of this had any effect on the evil Tepet who crossed the room to a door at the far end, opened it, and disappeared through it.

To my surprise the door led to the outside into a walled compound with no roof. Small tents made of sail canvas were arranged in two neat rows. Tepet walked to one of the tents and stopped in front of it. He turned toward us.

"Your Lanata has been well cared for, I assure you," he said. "Would you like to see her?" Tepet smiled. "She is to be moved to the embalming parlor."

He did not wait for me to answer but turned his back and began unlashing the rope that held the tent flap closed. It took only a few moments for Tepet to open the flaps and push them back over the sides. Through the opening I saw a pile of salt that completely filled the tent. Tepet saw the look of confusion upon my face and spoke.

"She is here, Oh prince, of that I can assure you," he said in an almost jovial tone.

Tepet turned and with his hand began brushing the pile of salt from the center to the sides. Gradually the shape of what seemed like a lump of brown leather began to emerged from the center the pile. A few more swipes of Tepet's hand and I could make out the shape of a chest and legs. When he brushed the salt from her face I thought I would fall unconscious. What lay before me was no more Lanata that it was the shrunken old hag it appeared to be! Her skin was loose and wrinkled and drooped limply from the bony sticks that were once her limbs. Lanata's beautiful hair hung like dried straw from the top of her scalp. Much of it was missing. A thin scar remained where her thick sensual lips had been, and her eyelids fell deeply into their sockets with no eyes beneath to give them support. Her fingernails and toenails appeared to have grown even in death giving her hands and feet the appearance of the talons of a diseased bird.

I felt a sense of revulsion deep within in me. If I could I would have killed the evil priest where he stood. My head pounded in pain as blood coursed through it as if under great pressure. My ears rang and I felt dizzy and weak. I forced myself to look at the lump of skin and bones that had once been Lanata. To treat the dead as Tepet and his criminals did was a sacrilege, an offense to Khunum who fashioned our bodies on the potter's wheel. What mother could watch her child become like this? What husband could witness his wife being embalmed without losing forever his memories of her? In my dreams would the face of Lanata ever be as it had once been or would I carry with me her portrait as she lay before me this day? This evil priest had stolen a very precious thing from me. On the spot I swore I would someday have my revenge on the likes of Tepet and his priests of the dead.

I held on. The steadiness of my voice surprised me. "I presume you and your embalmers are prepared to begin the final preparation." It was a statement that carried with it the hint of a royal command. Tepet bowed slightly in response but said nothing. "Good. Now I want you to tell me exactly what will be done with Lanata from this day until she is ready to return to Memphis with her father."

Tepet nodded and began to speak in the solemn tones of the practiced voice of an experienced charlatan.

"She will be removed from the drying tent this day to the preparation parlor. There my artists will begin to rebuild her body. The inside of her belly and chest will be covered with a mixture of resin and oils and allowed to harden forming a cavity into which linen rags and sawdust will be stuffed to give the body some form. The skin on her face will be slit and salt ash carefully placed inside until the firmness of her face returns."

He paused and looked at me. I looked straight back at him and nodded. Tepet continued.

"Now the artists make the body look as it did in life. First the corpse is painted. Lanata's skin will be painted pale yellow. The lips are made life-like with ocher and rouge applied to the cheeks. Eyes of black and white stone are placed behind the eyelids and the usual green and black cosmetics of Egyptian women are applied to the eyes. The fingernails and toenails are painted as well after the fashion of most Egyptian women. Then the body is ready for wrapping."

The priest paused.

"Perhaps it would be of interest for you to see the place where the final wrapping takes place. It is cooler inside than out here."

As much as I hated this toad, his suggestion permitted me to depart this cursed courtyard. I wished to be free of the sight of Lanata lying in salt. I nodded and Tepet led us out of the heat into the dimly lit rooms cooled by the stone walls. A long table stood in the center of the room. Several wooden blocks lay upon its surface. Rolls of linen bandages were placed on top of another small table that held what looked like cooking pots. The three of us stood before the long table. Tepet began to speak.

"The body is placed upon these wooden blocks to make it easier to pass the bandage rolls under it during the wrapping. Before wrapping begins a number of sacred amulets are placed on the body. Then the first wrapping is applied in a spiral fashion." He made a gesture like a spiral with his finger. "Now the artists apply a coat of sticky resin that will harden with time. A large sheet is placed over and around the body and then another layer of linen bandages. These, too, are covered with resin before the last layer of bandages is applied." Tepet pointed to a pile of cloth bags on a small stool. "The body is then wrapped in one of these special linen bags and the bag stitched tightly around the corpse. Then the body can be sent to the family." To Tepet it was all in a day's work, all so matter-of-fact, all so common, and his voiced expressed exactly what he felt about it all. It was the only time since I had met him that he had said exactly what he felt.

"When will all this be finished?" I asked.

"In about a month's time," Tepet answered. "Just sufficient time for you to have a coffin made to carry the body to Memphis."

A week later Tabu and I went to the coffin maker's shop to select a casket for Lanata's corpse. The popularity of mummification under the New Kingdom brought with it a new industry in ready-made coffins. The merchant explained to Tabu and me that the body was placed in a first coffin made of a thick cartonnage.

All the prayers of the dead and appropriate spells were already painted on its surface. Of course there was sufficient space to place a copy of the Book of The Dead if one wished but this would add to the cost. The coffin fit snugly into a second coffin made of richly painted wood. The merchant assured Tabu that his daughter would rest in the care of Isis' silver wings just as Osiris had so long ago. To insure this the outer casket had Isis's large silver wings painted around it as if embracing the form of Tabu's precious child. Tabu inquired about the features of his daughter. She was, he told the merchant, the most beautiful girl in all Memphis. Her features were very distinct and her eyes...her eyes were the most beautiful of all. Could the merchant capture such beauty on the coffin? For without it the gods themselves would be deprived of the pleasure of looking upon her for all eternity. The merchant assured Tabu that he understood completely. The coffins came from the factory already adorned with female faces upon them. But, and here the merchant give his solemn promise, he would hire an artist at his own expense if Tabu would but describe his daughter's features to guide the painter's hand. That way, he said, the coffin would be perfect. Tabu embraced the merchant in a gesture of thankful understanding and promised him he would return in a day or two with the description of Lanata. The merchant waved farewell and Tabu and I walked from the shop into the sunlight of the bright Egyptian day.

It was more than a month later when Lanata's body was placed aboard the funeral boat for the trip to Memphis. I stood with Tabu and Sinub watching the priests lower the coffin onto the platform on the rear deck. The coffin merchant was there, too, but stood off to one side in well-rehearsed reverence for the deceased. A few more prayers and a final blessing and the sons of Anubis, too, took their leave. Only Tepet turned and looked back. Our eyes met, but no words passed between us to lessen the mutual dislike that we had developed over the last four months. Tabu drew near to his daughter's coffin and placed his hand gently upon it. He choked back his tears and suffered the pain that I had come to believe would never truly end for him. Sinub walked to the bow and stood there alone. The captain waved his hand and the oarsmen pushed us away from the quay. A few minutes and we were in mid-channel. The captain gave the order to lift the sail into the brisk north wind that would return us to Memphis in two weeks time if all went smoothly. I did not miss Damietta. It had been a place of no joy and considerable pain for me. The boat slowly gathered speed before the wind. I looked upon the city for one last time. Even then I knew I would never return.

Hapi had renewed the Nile and the river renewed the land of Egypt. Everywhere we passed life was evident. The hippopotami were abundant and the sky was filled with birds. Even the crocodiles seemed to surface in unusually large numbers. Along the riverbank the farmers worked to prepare the land for planting. It was my favorite time of year, the time of my own birth. Like all the other princes of Thebes I, too, was a son of the land of Egypt. Somewhere in the middle of our journey I passed my eighth birthday, old enough in most families to be sent from home to learn a trade or profession. My life had no such direction. For all the learning I had gained from Ra-hotep and my own adventures, no clear avenue for my life could yet be seen. Memphis was better than Damietta, but neither city was my home nor ever likely to be. My home was in Thebes and my heart longed to return there.

The boat pulled along the quay and my heart grew happy when I saw Ra-hotep and Parshepses standing there. I waved vigorously to draw their attention. Parshepses saw me first and pointed me out to Ra-hotep. A broad smile crossed his face and he waved to me. I was happy to see my teacher and the nervous priest who always tried so hard to please. The boat slid alongside the quay and slowed to a stop. I didn't wait for the gangplank to be lowered. I leapt over the side landing upright on the stone pier. Sinub shook his head as if to show that nothing I did really surprised him anymore. I ran the few steps to where Ra-hotep stood waiting and stopped before him.

"Well, Thutmose, I see you have made it back safely. You gave us all a fright when the messenger told us of your shipwreck. I trust you will tell us more about what happened in Damietta after you have had time to rest." The pleasant tone of his voice went well with the smile on his face. Ra-hotep was glad to see me and it stuck out all over him.

"It is a great pleasure to see you after all this time, Teacher." My voice sounded to me like that of an excited child happy to see its parent. In many ways I realized even then that Ra-hotep had been as much of a parent to me as anyone. "I have much to tell you, Teacher, and even more to ask you, for I have seen many things whose nature I do not truly understand." Ra-hotep smiled. At least I had not become so arrogant that I had stopped learning. My teacher was pleased.

"Parshepses will attend to your luggage. I have arranged a cart to take us to the temple." He paused and looked at me with genuine affection. "I have made sacrifice to the gods in thanks for your safe return, Thutmose."

I smiled at the old man.

"I did not relish the thought of having to tell your father that you lost your life in a shipwreck." He seemed genuinely relieved. "Besides, if anything had happened to you, you would have missed your surprise." Ra-hotep had the look of a conspirator on his face.

"What is it, Teacher? What surprise?" I realized I was begging but couldn't help myself.

"You will see soon enough, Thutmose. Now sit there and tell me about your adventures on the Nile."

The donkey cart clattered up the hill pulling all of us and our baggage the short distance from the quay to the gate of the Great Enclosure of Ptah. It was just as I had left it more than four months earlier. My eyes wandered from place to place as I tried to locate this and that in my memory. I was not paying attention and took no notice when we stopped at the foot of the great staircase. I was climbing backwards down from the cart when I heard the booming voice.

"You must do better than that, my prince, if you ever expect to bend Egypt to your will."

The voice bounced off my ears and a vision of its owner came immediately to my mind. There was no mistaking the strong timbre of that voice. And yet for a few seconds I could not bring myself to believe it. I stepped from the cart onto the stairway and turned in the direction of the voice. There, dressed in his uniform standing at attention with his hand raised in the salute of the Egyptian army, stood Amenemhab my old guardian and friend.

At first I could hardly believe my eyes. A shiver of delight ran through me. My eyes widened and my face burst into a broad smile. Suddenly I was running toward him shouting at the top of my voice.

"Captain! Captain! Show me your eye!"

Amenemhab burst into laughter and his huge head and bearded face rocked backward while the sound of his voice bounced over the stones. I was upon him in a few seconds and leapt from the ground expecting the old soldier to catch me and twirl me around his head as he had done so often before. My weight caught him by surprise, and instead of finding myself flying over the ground Amenemhab lost his balance and crumpled backward into a heap with me lying on top of him. It was great fun and both of us rolled around in each other's arms laughing at the top of our lungs.

"Enough! Get off me!" Amenemhab yelled. "This is no way to treat a colonel in the army of Pharaoh!" The anger in his voice was feigned, but it was a signal that rolling on the ground was not what colonels or the son of pharaoh ought to be doing.

Amenemhab sat on the step and I stood before him. "By the soul of Osiris you have grown," he said.

I smiled broadly. I was eight years old, enough to begin work and only four years away from when Egyptian men usually married. Over the last year I had lost my chubbiness and my limbs had taken on a strength that pleased me. My legs were muscular and I had discovered that my endurance was greater than most people my age. I was still short and I often worried about my height. As things turned out it was my nature and nothing could be done about it anyway. But when one is young such trifles often seem important.

Amenemhab stood up. "Come," he said. "Let us sit and talk together. I leave in the morning and there is much that we old friends have to tell each other." He draped his arm over my shoulder and the two of us walked toward the guest house.

Amenemhab and I dined alone that evening. After a meal of roast birds and beer we dismissed the servants so that we could talk in privacy. Amenemhab had been promoted to colonel at the direction of my father and given command of the string of fortresses known as the Wall of Princes that guarded Egypt's Sinai frontier. It was an important command, and if he did well the odds were my old guardian would become a general. He seemed pleased by this turn of events, although there was something in his voice that made me uneasy.

Amenemhab raised his cup to his lips and drank. He placed the cup down on the table and looked straight into my eyes.

"I am sorry to bring you the news, my prince, but your old nurse, Webkhet, has gone to mingle with the gods." He paused and waited for my reaction. "You will see her no more until you, too, join her in the Fields." Again he searched my face for some emotion.

I answered as coldly as I could.

"You mean Webkhet is dead, don't you?" Amenemhab raised his eyes in surprise at my directness. I continued. "I have seen enough of death these past months to have earned the right to call it by its proper name. Webkhet is dead!" I paused and caught my voice rising in anger. "She will come no more. So be it!" My eyes fell upon Amenemhab's face. There was a look of sorrow as he returned my gaze. He knew something had happened to me. Whatever it was it had taken what was left of my childhood from me. And for that my old friend was sad.

Amenemhab poured himself another cup of beer. "I have more news," he said, "news that I am sure will be more to your liking." He sipped from his cup. "You are instructed by your father to return to Thebes at the earliest possible time." His eyes flashed. "I trust that is the news you have been waiting for these two years," he said.

My face broke out in a beaming grin and I could hardly contain my joy. Thebes! I was going home! Home to my father and Ese! Nothing in the world could have made me happier at that moment than the thought of going home.

Amenemhab reached across the table and grabbed my arm. There was a serious look on his face. "There is more," he said. "Now listen carefully for what I am about to tell you is very important." I straightened myself in my chair and stopped smiling. I felt uneasy at what Amenemhab was going to say. I hung on every word as he began to speak.

"Pharaoh is ill, Thutmose, very ill. He fears for his life and for yours. When you were born he acknowledged you as his son, but not as his successor. Now the time has come to affirm your claim to the throne. It is his wish that you succeed him." He stopped and a deep frown appeared on his forehead. "But there are dangers, great dangers that you must face. The queen will not easily give up her power. She has no son of her own through whom to rule. But if you are dead the bloodline of succession falls to her and she may rule as queen in her own right until a marriage to a new pharaoh." He paused. "When you return to Thebes you will be in danger of being killed. You must return in secret, my prince, and your presence in Thebes must remain secret until Pharaoh himself reveals it."

I shook my head to let him know I understood. Amenemhab then outlined his plan. Sinub would be told of the danger. Then he and I would travel as common people back to Thebes. All signs of my rank or status were to be removed before the journey began. Ra-hotep was to be sworn to secrecy as well. Upon my arrival in Thebes, Sinub and I were to go directly to the Temple of Amun-Ra and seek out the Chief Priest. He was appointed to his post by my father and his loyalty was not in doubt. Sinub was to seek out the officers of Pharaoh's bodyguard, his old regiment, and obtain help in keeping me safe. When this had been done, I was to send a message to Pharaoh through the Chief Priest to inform him of my whereabouts. Pharaoh would then tell me what to do.

Amenemhab finished speaking and drank deeply from his cup. He was uneasy with these things and was doing his best not to show it. He wiped his mouth with the back of his hand and stroked his black Asiatic beard.

"Well, my prince, things get complicated wouldn't you say?"

I nodded but said nothing. Amenemhab produced a small leather pouch and handed it to me.

"Inside is a gold medallion bearing the cartouche of Pharaoh. Present it to the Chief Priest when you meet him. It will serve to identify you as being who you say you are." Amenemhab's voice became deadly serious.

"This is dangerous business, my prince. You must take the greatest care or you will forfeit your life. Would that I could be with you. But I have not been with you for the past two years and you have done well. Except for Sinub and some of the bodyguard, there will be few in Thebes you can trust. Always be on your guard and watch what you say."

He paused and there were the beginnings of tears in his eyes.

"Remember always, my prince, that you are Egypt. And it is into your hands that your father commends her care and safety."

Amenemhab and I talked late into the night until I was exhausted and he was drunk. At last we took to our beds only to be awakened in a short time by the morning sun. Over breakfast Sinub was taken into our confidence. I could tell from his expression that there was no question of his loyalty nor had there ever been. Ra-hotep, too, was told and assured us of his concern and silence on the matter. Later the three of us accompanied Amenemhab to his boat. He and I embraced as we said our farewells. I stood on the quay until I could see Amenemhab and the boat no more. My heart was heavy with sadness. As things turned out it would be many years before I saw him again. I turned from the river and walked toward Ra-hotep and Sinub who stood waiting a few yards away. The smile on my face was false, but as I spoke it was all the confidence I could muster at the moment.

"Well," I said, "we had best begin making our arrangements."

I paused and looked around at the city that had held me for so long.

"It is time," I said. "Let us leave this place and return to Thebes."

# Fourteen

We arrived at the docks in Thebes at dusk. By the time the crew tied the boat fast to the pier the dying light had surrendered to the evening darkness and the dockworkers were already lighting the lamps along the quay. Sinub and I had considered making the last leg of our journey on land, but rejected the idea. The city's gates were always posted with sentinels and it was not unusual for them to ask for identification from travelers injudicious enough to be abroad at night. After careful thought we decided that travel by boat offered the best chance of an unnoticed arrival in Thebes. We took no chances, though. Before leaving Memphis we traded our fine clothes for those of ordinary merchants. Even our sandals were of the rough-hewn variety. Sinub had carefully packed away any insignia of his rank or service and replaced his beloved *kopesh* with a small dagger that he easily concealed in his belt. Much of our baggage had been left in Memphis and we carried only what few clothes and other things we truly required. Even these were packed in well-worn valises that Ra-hotep had purchased for this purpose. During the voyage we kept to ourselves and spoke only rarely with the crew and the few other passengers. Whatever else the passengers may have

thought of us, it was unlikely that they suspected they were traveling with the son of Pharaoh and his military bodyguard.

We waited until the other passengers had gone ashore. The
crew was busy with making the boat fast for the night when Sinub
and I walked down the gangplank carrying our own baggage like
two common travelers. A brief walk along the quay and a short
climb up a steep flight of stairs brought us to the street above. I
followed Sinub as he led the way in the darkness. Neither of us
said a word. The street was narrow and dark and there were few
people on it. The walls of buildings and houses on either side
made the night even darker and what few lamps I could see threw
only a dim light. Ahead of me Sinub stopped at an alley and
looked around to see if I was following him. Having assured himself, he stepped into the alley and disappeared from my sight. I
reached the alley a few seconds later and turned down it. I saw
Sinub's shadow at the other end and moved toward him. He
waited for me to catch up then both of us stepped into the street.
Off at a diagonal from where we stood was a two story building
with a half-dozen large lamps lighting the front. The double doors
of the entrance were wide open. From the inside came the sounds
of music and laughter. Above the door was a sign that read *The
Blue Crocodile*.

Sinub looked carefully down the street before starting across. I
followed closely on his heels as he made for the entrance. *The Blue
Crocodile* was an inn and Sinub had chosen it because the officers
of the *Eaters of Hearts* regiment frequented the place. One of
these officers, a colonel named Djet, was the commander of
Pharaoh's bodyguard. Sinub found the proprietor and arranged to
rent a room for a week. The proprietor was a scrawny evil looking
man who seemed the personification of corruption itself. When
Sinub wanted only one room I saw a smirk cross the proprietor's
face as he looked from Sinub to me and back again. It had become

quite the fashion of late for members of the wealthy classes to have sex with young boys. There was no mistaking the proprietor's look that said he thought that was exactly what was going on here. Sinub did nothing to correct the innkeeper's thoughts.

The innkeeper's assistant showed us to our room on the second floor. It was small and sparsely furnished with a bed, table and a few chairs. A single window looked out onto an alley that ran back from the street. There was only one way in and one way out and that was down the front stairway that led from the main floor. The door itself was sufficiently strong to make forced entry difficult and a bronze bolt and slip permitted a reasonable degree of security. Sinub examined all these features one by one.

"This will do for our purposes, my prince. We shouldn't be here more than a few days in any case," he said. He began to unpack our bags. The *kopesh* was wrapped just as Sinub had left it. He removed it from the valise and laid it upon the table covering it with a single cloth. Here it would be out of casual sight but easily available should it be needed.

"Are you hungry?" he asked.

I smiled and nodded my head vigorously. "Thirsty too."

"I will get us something to eat," he said. "Stay here with the door locked until I return." His voice was serious. "Do not open the door for anyone but me, my prince. Is that understood?" It was not a question as much as an instruction. I nodded. "Good," he said and closed the door behind him.

Sinub returned with a tray of food and beer. We sat across from each other at the small table and ate in silence. When we had finished Sinub pushed his tray away and stretched offering an audible sigh.

"It is time for bed, my prince. Sleep well. The next few days may be difficult for us both," he said.

We remained at the inn for the next week. For four days I was not permitted to leave our room. Sinub stayed with me most of the time. But as each evening neared and darkness approached he would leave the inn for a short time. I learned later that he ventured close to the military barracks near the palace compound in hopes of spotting Djet. Each night when he returned he checked on me and then went downstairs and took a small table in a corner of the main room. Sitting in the shadows Sinub waited. When the last guest left Sinub rose and returned to the room. After a few days of being left in my room for so many long hours I asked Sinub if I might accompany him downstairs. At first he refused. But when he saw that I was determined to have my way he relented. And so the next night I joined Sinub in his place at the table in the shadows.

The *Blue Crocodile* was crowded and noisy. Groups of sailors and workmen sat on benches at long tables drinking beer and wine. Laughter and conversation filled the place with so much noise that from time to time the musicians put down their instruments and took a respite from their efforts. In the far corner a few women sat alone talking and primping their hair and face makeup. They wore dresses of the sheerest linen so that their colored undergarments were clearly visible. The nipples of their breasts were dyed blue. One woman sitting cross-legged at the end of the table pulled her dress high up upon her thighs revealing the small tatoo of the god Bes that was the symbol of her profession. The evening was far too young to expect any customers. And so the ladies sat with one another chatting and waiting for the wine and beer to create the illusions and fantasies for which the minds of men were infamous. Then it would be time to sell one's wares and at a pretty price too!

Sinub touched my arm to draw my attention. I turned and saw him gesture with his head in the direction of the door. A stocky fellow stood in the doorway looking over the crowd. He moved carefully through the noise and commotion making his way to an empty table a few feet away. He seemed unaware of our presence and sat down with his back to us. Shortly a barmaid brought him a cup of beer and a plate of bread and meat. Hunched over his meal he ate his food noisily and with his head down. I looked at Sinub. We sat watching the fellow until he finished eating and ordered another cup of beer before leaning back in his chair to relax.

Sinub rose from his chair and motioned me to stay put. He moved silently across the short space separating the two tables and approached the fellow from behind. In one swift motion he placed his hand on the fellow's shoulders and at the same time moved into his field of vision to permit the fellow to see him clearly. I gathered from Sinub's caution that it was never a good idea to surprise a soldier from behind unless, of course, you intended to kill him which, in any event, was not what Sinub was up to at all. From where I sat I could see and hear everything that transpired between the two.

"Well, Djet, I see you are still up to your old habits," Sinub said. His voice was even and pleasant as if addressing someone he knew well.

The fellow was taken by surprise at Sinub's appearance for only a moment.

"Sinub!" The fellow's voice was almost a shout. He stood and grabbed Sinub by the shoulder in a gesture of friendship.

"How long has it been? A year? Two?" To anyone who bothered to notice the scene was a familiar one, two old friends meeting again. Sinub smiled at the fellow.

"Why don't you join my nephew and me," he said and gestured toward me with his head. "Come on. I'll introduce you."

The two of them walked the few steps to the table and sat down. The fellow sat with his back to the crowed while Sinub sat off to his side allowing the shadows to fall over his face. He had a good view of the inn's entrance. Unless one looked closely, it was almost impossible to see the three of us in the dimly lit corner.

The pleasant expression on the fellow's face vanished instantly and his eyes darkened as they focused on mine. Even in the dim light I could see that he was lighter skinned than most Egyptians. His hair was closely cropped and he was clean shaven as was the rule for men in Egypt. He was short and stocky and he had huge hands that were attached to muscular arms. Together they looked quite capable of snapping a man's neck like a dry twig. Sinub spoke first.

"This is Djet," he said. "Colonel and commander of Pharaoh's bodyguard. He has come to help us stay alive." The last few words hung in the air. I looked at Djet and bowed my head to acknowledge his presence and my gratitude. Djet nodded back but said nothing. Sinub continued.

"I presume that Pharaoh has spoken to you of this matter, Colonel?"

I noticed Sinub's use of Djet's military rank. Sinub had been second in command of the bodyguard before leaving Thebes with me two years earlier. Although the two were peers in every respect, Djet still outranked him.

Djet again nodded. "Yes. I have been instructed by Pharaoh to insure the safety of his son for as long as is required. My loyalty is to the king and his wishes. Should anything happen to his son I am prepared to pay with my life." Here he paused and looked at Sinub and me as if trying to gauge whether we understood the importance of what he had said.

"The threats to the boy's safety are not yet clear," he continued. "My guess is that they might come from anyone near the queen by people seeking to curry favor and position with her. So the threats have as yet no direction. That makes them at once unlikely to succeed and still the more difficult to predict and deal with should one of them get close by fortune alone." Djet paused and looked at me. His face gave nothing away. "Our best defense is secrecy. If we can keep the boy's presence in Thebes a secret for as long as possible and then house him somewhere where he would not be expected to be, we ought to succeed."

Sinub listened intently nodding in agreement from time to time but being careful not to interrupt. When Djet took a deep drink of beer from his cup Sinub spoke up.

"We cannot stay here much longer," he said. "Have you a plan and a place where we might be safe if only for the time being?" It was said matter-of-factly with no sign of worry in his voice.

Djet's voice was low and serious.

"It is Pharaoh's wish that the boy be taken as soon as practicable to the Chief Prophet of the Temple of Amun here in Thebes. Once there other arrangements can be made." He paused and drew in his breath. "I can move safely between the palace and the temple without suspicion," he said, "and I also have opportunity to be near Pharaoh so that any messages or instructions can be easily passed. It is best for you to remain here for the next day or two. No need to come downstairs anymore now that we are aware of each other's existence. Stay in your room. I will come to you in a day or so with the rest of the plan." It was not a request. Djet's voice made it clear that he expected Sinub and me to follow his instructions. And for the next two days we did just that.

The knock on the door was followed by the familiar sound of Djet's voice. He spoke barely above a whisper. Sinub opened the door. Djet moved quickly through the open doorway and into the room. He skipped any pleasantries and came right to the point.

"It is time. Pack your valises and make ready to depart. Make sure that you leave nothing behind. Nothing." He turned to Sinub. "Have you settled your accounts with the innkeeper?"

Sinub nodded noting that we had paid for the entire week in advance. "Good," Djet said, "One less thing to worry about."

Sinub and I hurried with our packing and in a few minutes we were ready. I noticed Sinub slide his *kopesh* in his belt. Djet noticed it as well.

"You'd best pack that thing Sinub," he said. "There is no need for it and its presence will give you away if you are stopped by even the dumbest policeman." He smiled. "Besides," he continued, "we have three guardsmen with us. I personally selected them and they can be relied upon to do what they are told and to keep their mouths shut."

Sinub wrapped the *kopesh* in its cloth and placed it in the valise.

The three of us walked out of the *Blue Crocodile* and into the street. Djet led us a short distance before turning into one of the innumerable alleyway between houses that mark the failure of Thebes to have developed according to any plan whatsoever. Thebes is full of alleys and only an accomplished police officer or thief is likely to know his way about with any certainty once the main streets are abandoned. Djet, it seemed, was having no difficulty negotiating the maze. In a short time we entered a small courtyard where the three guardsmen dressed as merchants were waiting for us. Together our little group set out to make its way to the Temple of Amun Ra.

The temple itself was more than two miles from the *Blue Crocodile*. A third of that distance was within the confines of Thebes itself. The rest was through open country over a single road that ran from the city to the village of Karnak where the temple was located. It was still early evening when we left the city and began our travel along the road. Traffic on the road was light but enough so that our group did not seem out of place being where it was. It took us more than an hour to make our way to Karnak and to the temple. We arrived at about the time most Egyptians were making ready for bed.

In those days the Temple of Amun was not the great structure that it has become. Compared to the Temple of the Ka of Ptah in Memphis is was but a village hut! The building was small and stood off by itself on a flat piece of ground that was not even enclosed by a wall. I could make out the single pylon gate that my grandfather built and the two obelisks that stood before it. There was no great hall of columns, only a simple open courtyard that led to the sanctuary. Even the sacred lake was but a puddle surrounded by a brick border and no enclosure walls. Amun was a local god and a temple of some sort had always stood on this spot. But it was only with the rise of the Theban princes who conquered in his name that Amun had become a national god. Even so, his temple at Thebes remained a simple affair for many years. When I became Pharaoh I lavished great sums on it and had two more pylon gates constructed as well as a great colonnaded hall, and several small temples. Behind the central court I built a Festival Temple. Within it stood a botanical garden with a large hall upon whose walls I caused to be carved representations of exotic plants, birds, and animals in honor of Tabu the physician who had first inspired my interest in these things.

Our little group made its way in the darkness up the unpaved path that wound to the temple. We approached the pylon gate and stopped. All was still. There were no guards or priests about. For a few minutes we stood in silence as if waiting for something to happen. From out of the darkness a whispered voice broke the silence.

"Welcome to the Temple of Amun." There was a trace of nervousness in the voice. A small man stepped out of the shadows. "I am Intef, Priest of Amun, and assistant to Mentuhotep, Chief Prophet of the god himself. In his name I bid you welcome."

Djet examined the man. He had sworn his life against mine and he was taking no chances. For a few moments he said nothing. Then in a low and emotionless voice he spoke.

"We come to see the Chief Prophet," he said. "He is expecting us as I am sure you know." His voice trailed off while he waited for a reaction from Intef who smiled and bowed to acknowledge that Djet was correct in his assumption. Djet continued. "Take us to the Chief Prophet," Djet said. "It is important that we keep him waiting no longer."

The assistant bowed. "Please follow me," he said and walked through the gate. Sinub, Djet and I followed. The three guardsmen were left outside with instructions to remain in the shadows and do nothing to draw attention. Intef led us through an open courtyard lit only by the stars through a portico and down the outside corridor formed by the inner and outer walls of the temple. The door to the room was closed and Intef knocked loudly. A strong voice came through the door in response. "Come!" it said. Intef pushed on the handle and the door opened smoothly. Sitting at a desk across the large room was Mentuhotep, Chief Prophet of the Great Amun, First Father of the God, and servant of Pharaoh who had made him all these things.

Mentuhotep motioned with his hand for us to enter. Intef led the way and we took chairs that had been set for us in front of the desk. Mentuhotep was a fat man with two chins. His body filled the slant-backed chair to overflowing. Puffy forearms and fatty hands poked out from under the sleeves of his robes. His shaven head extended his forehead and made his head look even larger than it was. Sacks of extra white flesh hung from under each eye and he had the largest ears I had ever seen on a human being. If he resembled anything it was a large frog. When he spoke his eyes stared straight ahead and above the person to whom he was speaking. There was no life in those eyes, they rarely moved when he spoke, and they eyes offered no expression at all to his words. He was the first blind person I had ever encountered and I could not take my eyes from his. The three of us sat silently in front of him as Intef whispered in his ear. Finally he spoke.

"I trust you had a safe journey and that outside of our little group no one knows of the prince's arrival and presence in Thebes?" His voice was flat and his eyes stared into eternity.

"That is correct Chief Prophet. All is according to plan. The son of Pharaoh has arrived safely and sits before you, his secret kept from all but our eyes." Djet paused and looked at Intef. He was not pleased that yet another now knew of my presence. Even the guardsmen were not told who they were escorting. Now a priest of unknown loyalty had been let in on the secret. An assistant with the trust of the Chief Prophet could move anywhere he wished without suspicion. He was, too, the logical successor to the Prophet, especially so if he were to do the queen the favor of killing Pharaoh's son! Intef was positioned perfectly to become an assassin and Djet did not like these new developments one bit. Later he took me aside to warn me to be especially wary of Intef. Mentuhotep's words interrupted my thoughts.

"What I say now are the words of Pharaoh. What I command you to do he commands you to do."

Still the vacant stare, still no emotion in his voice. It was as if his soul were also blind. I remember wondering how was it that my father had come to place such trust in this man? I made a promise to myself to find out. Mentuhotep continued.

"Djet, you will return to your post as commander of the guard and continue to keep our king safe. As you will learn, he is ill and I fear that his sickness may tempt his enemies to move against him." He paused. "You must be vigilant, Djet, or the blood of Egypt will be on your hands."

Djet nodded and offered a slight bow of respect for the man who was speaking to him.

"When you are needed again I will send Intef to you with my instructions. You are to obey him as you would me. Do you understand?"

"Yes, Chief Prophet," Djet responded. I saw his eyes flash with anger and suspicion as he glanced quickly at Intef.

Then the Chief Prophet turned to me and stared over my head as if he was looking at the wall behind me.

"It is your father's wish, my prince, that you remain within the confines of the temple for as long as is necessary. Here we can keep you safe. Your identity will be kept secret even from the other priests. As far as they will know you are the son of a wealthy merchant from Memphis who wishes his son to be educated and taught to write in the House of Life. I have also let it be known that you are a religious fellow and that you might consider entering the priesthood. This will raise you up in the eyes of the other priests and they will treat you with respect." He paused and I did not know whether he was waiting for me to speak or not. For a few moments I sat there in silence.

"What of Sinub?" I asked. "Is he to remain with me?" I glanced at Djet who nodded his head in approval of my suggestion. Sinub, as always, said nothing and awaited his orders like the good soldier that he was.

"It is a good suggestion, my prince," Mentuhotep answered, "and one that we would be well to listen to. We can tell the others that you are ill and that Sinub must be with you to oversee your health and treatment. He will, of course, assume the demeanor of your servant. He seems a clever fellow and should have no difficulty doing this."

I glanced at Djet who nodded again. Later I saw him talking to Sinub in an ernest tone. I guessed that he was telling him not to trust Intef. Sinub was nodding his agreement. Like most soldiers Djet and Sinub shared a suspicious regard for the nobler motives of men. It was a good lesson but, alas, one that took me years to truly learn.

The Chief Prophet stood up. The meeting was over.

"Intef will show you out Djet and then take the prince to his quarters that he will share with Sinub. Be on your guard, Colonel. The assassins may hide in the clouds themselves and the fate of Egypt rests on your courage and wits." The Chief Prophet bowed his head in the general direction of Djet who returned the gesture.

I turned to follow Djet, Sinub, and Intef out the door when Mentuhotep spoke.

"If you please, your highness, I would be most honored if you would stay a few moments. There is something I wish to discuss with you."

I stopped and turned back to my chair. Mentuhotep sat down again and gestured in the general direction of the chair in front of his desk. I sat in silence and listened to the sound of Mentuhotep's labored breathing as his enormous body gasped for air. It was some minutes after the others had left before I finally spoke.

"What is it you wished to say to me, Chief Prophet?" I said.

Mentuhotep shook his head slowly.

"It is not so much I who wish to speak with you, Oh prince, as it is someone of much greater importance."

He took a deep breath and struggled to his feet. Reaching to his side his hand found the walking stick that had been leaning against the wall for all this time. Using the stick as a brace, Mentuhotep moved from behind the desk and walked by me to the door.

"Please remain here for a few minutes, my prince. I shall return shortly."

He found the door latch, opened the door, and left leaving it slightly open. I looked at the opened door for a few seconds then turned around in my chair to wait.

It was late and for the first time I was aware that I was tired. I tried to stifle a deep yawn, but was overcome by it instead. My eyes wandered aimlessly over the empty room and my mind began to calm itself as it does when I am sleepy. And then I heard words carried on a voice of thin reeds.

"It does my eyes good to behold you again, my son."

In my dreamy state the words did not immediately carry their meaning to my consciousness. I turned toward them more because of the sound than their meaning. I stood up and turned in the direction of the voice. Standing before me was my father, the Great Lion of Egypt.

The sight of him turned my legs to stone so that I could not move. My heart beat rapidly within my chest and I felt a rush of blood to my head. I was suddenly very warm. Beads of sweat appeared on my brow. I wanted to run to him and grab him the way I did the last time we had seen each other. But that time now seemed long past. I was a child then and he was only my father. Now I was older and had seen some of the world. I had learned much about Egypt and the god-king who ruled it. I was no longer the child at his father's knee. I was older now and he was Pharaoh, and I could never reverse either of these facts of both our lives. And so I stood like any other Egyptian in the presence of the son of god who was his king, and like them I trembled.

Pharaoh stood framed in the doorway looking at me. His face bore the expression of a man in pain. He moved slowly toward me as if unsteady on his feet. In the silence I could hear him breathing as though it required a great effort. Closer the great king came until he was standing in front of me. He was, I thought, much thinner than I remembered him. Too thin, almost frail of body.

The black eyes still flashed with intelligence and vigor, but they seemed to have sunken into his skull. The deep set eyes forced his great nose forward giving his face the appearance of Horus. The linen crown upon his head affixed with a gold band shone with the dignity of his office. The garnet eyes of the *Uraeus* serpent remained ready to strike at all who mustered the courage to challenge his will. He was, after all, Pharaoh and the power of life and death rested firmly in his hands. He was still a man to be reckoned with.

His face broke into a wide grin revealing a set of teeth stained and worn with age. He looked down upon me standing there before him.

"Well, Thutmose, you certainly seem to have grown since last I saw you." He paused. "Have you grown so old that you cannot give your father a proper greeting?" With these words he stretched out his arms and called me to him. In an instant I was in his arms as he held me in a tight embrace. We held each other for a few moments like any other father and son.

"I must tell you how it warms me to see you again, Thutmose," he said. "I have missed you very much. Now that you have returned to Thebes there is much we have to say to one another. There is also very much that has to be done over the next few months." His voice was pleasant and the expression of discomfort had vanished from his face. He leaned back in the chair. "Now, my boy, you must tell me all about your adventures since you have been away."

I could hardly contain the excitement in my voice while I told my father all the things that had happened to me since leaving Thebes more than two years earlier. In recounting my story I realized that much had happened to me in so short a time. Much had changed within me. How differently I now saw things! For the first time I was gratful to have learned the lessons of the world from such men as Amenemhab, Sinub, Ra-hotep, and Tabu.

Different men would have, no doubt, taught different lessons. But the lessons I learned from these men served me all my life. I had, as I told my father, been witness to things that children rarely witness, and I told him how they sometimes pressed upon my mind. And as I spoke I realized that whatever childhood I had been granted had long since fled and would never return. Somehow, standing there in the presence of my father recounting my adventures, the loss of my childhood did not seem to matter.

My father listened to my tale without interruption. From time to time he would smile broadly or furrow his brow in worry or disappointment. Throughout my tale he kept his eyes on my face as if searching it for something. When at last I was finished he seemed pleased.

"You have done well, Thutmose. You are a son to be proud of." There was a firm pride in his voice. He looked at me and nodded approvingly. A broad grin slowly widened across his face.

"And you father?" I asked. "Have you been well and is all well in Thebes and in Egypt?"

He rested his head in his hand and took a deep breath. The grin disappeared and the furrow in his brow deepened.

"All is not well with Egypt, my son. There are evil forces that seek to capture her and rule her for their own profit and gain." He paused and leaned back in his chair. For a few seconds he seemed lost in thought. Then he spoke again.

"Thutmose, you must realize that you are in great danger. More so since you have returned to Thebes." He looked carefully at me waiting for some reaction. I hid my feelings as best I could.

"I have learned that from listening to Djet and Sinub. But it is not clear to me why it should be so," I said.

Calmly he began to explain.

"You are my only son Thutmose and my heir. There are no male heirs except you. When you are named Pharaoh, Queen

Hatshepsut ceases to be queen. But should I die and you be killed, then the line to the throne resides within her alone and she may rule until she remarries or until another marries her daughter and becomes Pharaoh." He stopped speaking for a few seconds and caught his breath. "I must arrange your appointment as my heir in such a way that your life will not be forfeit. Even then it will be a gamble. The queen has used her influence to place her friends in high positions. Any one of them might strike you down to seek her favor. Until events can be planned properly, you must remain here in the care of Mentuhotep. You are safe as long as your presence in Thebes remains secret."

I nodded my head in agreement. "To my eye," I said, "this man Mentuhotep seems a strange creature." I paused to see how my words set with my father. "Why is it that you trust him as you do?"

My father's eyes focused narrowly upon my face.

"Do you say this because of how he looks or because he is blind, Thutmose?" It was not a pleasant question and the unpleasantness was clear in the tone of my father's voice. "Mentuhotep is heir to a distinguished family. His father was an important and trusted officer in your grandfather's army. I have known of him since I was a young man. He served for many years as a judge in our courts and always his loyalty to Pharaoh was beyond reproach." He paused. "But all this aside, Thutmose, why should he be worthy of my trust in such an important matter? It is a good question."

I sat silently trying to follow my father's reasoning, wishing that I had not asked the question to begin with. Pharaoh went on.

"He was among my most trusted advisors at court for many years, one of those closest to Pharaoh called *The Honored Ones*. As Mentuhotep grew older he grew closer to the gods in his soul. One day he came to me to ask if I would appoint him to be a priest at the Temple of Amun. I could not refuse such an honored and loyal man. The position of Chief Prophet has always been too important to leave to mere priests. As the Pharaohs before me, I selected a trusted courtier who had already had a successful career at court. And that, Thutmose, is the true answer to your question. I trust Mentuhotep in this matter for the simplest of reasons. All he has he owes to me. This is so much so that any one who would steal his loyalty for their own cause could never trust him completely nor he them. Like many men he is trapped by his own history. Only I could release him from his bonds and then only by his death."

As I listened to my father's words I realized that he was a wise and cautious king, a man used to weighing the motivations of other men against their public actions. Once again I looked upon my father's face with the awe of a child. And the great man looked back upon me with a slight smile. For he saw that I understood what he said to me, and in that spark of my intelligence he saw himself.

We sat across from each other for another hour talking and laughing. Somewhere during that time I realized that our time here was the longest we had ever spent with each other since I was born. My father was pleased with me. Sometimes when I was speaking to him he seemed to stare at my face as if trying to carve a picture of it in his memory. Whenever he did this it seemed he was not listening to what I was saying at all. He was watching me, studying me, as if I was some precious amulet that could bring him good fortune or protect his life. It was, I confess, a pleasant feeling.

And then it was time for him to depart.

He rose from his chair and threw his arms around me. "Be careful, Thutmose, for you are the future of Egypt." He looked down at me. "Do as Mentuhotep instructs you. Now that you are in Thebes we will see each other more often." He breathed a deep sigh. "Important events are to be set in motion shortly, my son, that will have great consequences for your future." He paused. "Leave these matters to me and see to your learning here at the temple." He took another deep breath and let it out slowly. "May the gods protect you my son as they watch over Egypt."

He moved toward the door. As if by magic it opened upon his approach and the Lion of Egypt passed through the doorway. With the door open I could see into the corridor. There, holding my father's cloak and walking stick, was Paremheb the Chancellor. He draped the cloak over my father's shoulders that suddenly seemed to droop under the weight of the cloth. My father took the walking stick in one hand and leaned heavily upon Paremheb's arm with the other. He had done his best to conceal his illness from me. But as I looked upon him now without his knowing it was clear that the Lion of Egypt was very sick. And as with other powerful and feared animals grown weak, the knowledge of his weakness attracted the jackals.

It was Mentuhotep's first instruction that I should be immediately enrolled in the House of Life and be taught to read and write in a proper manner. The instruction I had received in Memphis was hit and miss. When Mentuhotep quizzed me in reading, I failed miserably. "We cannot have a future king who cannot read his own edicts!" And so I was enrolled in the House of Life, the temple school that taught writing. It was more than that, of course. The House of Life earned large sums for the temple making copies of legal documents and works of literature. Its most profitable product was copies of the Book of the Dead. These were large scrolls of complex signs, prayers, and spells that instructed the deceased how to prosper in the after life. Originally these spells had been used only by the kings. But in modern times the wealthy paid large sums to bury their dead with the same words of advice that the gods originally reserved for their mortal offspring.

The other boys in the school lived with their families and came to class in the morning and left at the end of the day. Most were the sons of the nobility and they easily accepted the story that I was the son of a Memphis merchant who had sent me to study for the priesthood. There were also a few boys who were not of good families. One, Thaneni was his name, had been sent by his employer to learn to keep books and handle the written records of his employer's company. Thaneni was an orphan and older than the rest of us. He was quiet and kept mostly to himself.

Classes were taught by a priest named Khufu. He was a strict disciplinarian who believed that "the ears of a boy are on his back. They only listen when they are beaten!" We were drilled each day in learning the signs that made up the written language used in daily commerce. Writing, Khufu told us, was the gift of the god Toth, "the baboon with shinning hair and amiable face," who gave the Ancient Ones the divine words. Actually Toth gave us the pictures of things. By arranging these pictures in certain ways we could tell a story with them. These pictures were very old and were found among the tombs of the earliest pharaohs. Long ago we Egyptians found drawing these pictures very cumbersome for every day use. So we began to abbreviate them by using fewer marks for each one. The complete pictures are still used, of course, in tombs and for sacred texts or official decrees, but the new system of writing with the fewer marks came into wide use. That is what we were studying at the House Of Life. Scribes write mostly in this new language and only a few undertake higher study to learn how to write with the pictures the way our ancestors did.

Once we had memorized the marks we practiced getting them to mean things. Each day the students copied three pages of written material. Mostly we copied exercises from our textbook. These were fictitious letters supposedly written by an ancient scribe that contained lessons on wise conduct and good manners and morals that a scribe ought to observe. Other material consisted of sample letters that were most commonly used in daily business or government regulations. With reed pens and cheap ink we practiced our craft over and over until we had memorized the marks. Papyrus was expensive so we practiced on clay slates or even pieces of broken pottery. Each student was required to keep a daily copybook that he had to present to the teacher upon request. This permitted the teacher to check on the student's progress. It was slow going and it was weeks before I could recognize the written version of even the simplest word.

During the first few weeks Thaneni and I became friends. Having no family of his own and bound for service to another, the other boys ignored him. I was smaller than the other boys and was often the butt of jokes and pranks. Most of the boys were from wealthy families and had known one another even before they entered the class so it was normal for them to band together in their jokes and jibes against the two boys who were strangers to them. And so it was that Thaneni and I leaned upon one another.

Thaneni was a wiry fellow and not given to patience with the silliness that sometimes overcomes school boys. Once he was challenged by a group of boys over something or other and flew into a rage striking two of the boys so hard in the face that he caused their noses to bleed. On more than one occasion he rescued me from the teasing of the other boys. Usually I managed to get in one or two good blows at my tormentors before Thaneni came along and separated the combatants. As the weeks passed we became friends. Thaneni was a commoner and I knew little about the common people of Egypt. I took whatever opportunities arose to get him to talk about himself. Once I asked him about his family.

"Not much to tell," he said. He had a raspy voice and when he was angry it sounded like two stones being rubbed together.

"My mother died giving birth to me. My father was a laborer in the glass factory. He raised me as best he could until the illness took him too. By then I was apprenticed in the same factory. One day the owner approached me with an offer to teach me to read in exchange for my promise to work for him as a scribe and keep his accounts. It was a good opportunity to get away from the heat and danger of the glass furnace. So here I am. When my lessons are finished I am indentured to the owner. Then its back to the glass factory." He said it all in a pleasant tone and even with a smile. It was clear that he expected little else in life. People from his station in life did not hope for much it seemed.

The weeks passed one by one and I turned my attention to my lessons. I had not heard anything further from my father and thought it wise not to bother Mentuhotep with any inquiries. Sinub remained in the background as always. After a while it was as if he had become part of the furniture in that no one ever questioned his presence no matter where he turned up. Thaneni and I passed our leisure time playing board games and exploring the temple. In those days Karnak was but a small village and there was little to entertain two adventurous boys. Thebes itself was more than an hour's walk away. No matter. It was unlikely that I would be able to slip away from the watchful eye of Sinub for very long in any case. I came to see that the temple was chosen as my hide-away precisely because it was isolated. But after almost six months of enforced confinement I yearned for some change in my routine. And then as if my wish had been granted by the gods themselves the isolation of my existence was shattered.

It began one evening when Mentuhotep knocked on the door of my room. I let the Chief Prophet in. He ambled slowly almost painfully across the room and sat down with a heavy sigh in one of the two chairs. Sinub sat at the small table finishing his meal. His eyes were alert and he took in every word.

"I bring you good news, Oh prince. Pharaoh arrives this evening with his advisors

to spend the night under the temple roof. He wishes to make a special offering to the Hidden One in the morning. A large group of other invited guests will travel from Thebes at first light to be in attendance as well." Mentuhotep paused and took a deep breath, leaning a little in Sinub's direction. Before he could continue I spoke up.

"Will I be permitted to visit with him this evening?" The excitement in my voice must have been as obvious to Mentuhotep and Sinub as it was for me.

The Chief Prophet shook his head. "No, my prince. It is not Pharaoh's wish that this be so." The words were spoken with a deliberate finality. "In truth, my prince, I know not your father's purpose in coming here this night nor, I confess, his desire to make special sacrifice to the god in the morning." He shrugged. "But I am not the Lion of Egypt and do not pretend to know the mind of the king." There was genuine puzzlement on his face. He rose and leaned on his walking stick. "Who knows," he said. "Perhaps things will seem clearer in the morning."

I slept fitfully that night and it was not until a few hours before the dawn that I fell truly asleep. I was awakened from my slumber by a rude shaking accompanied by Sinub's voice.

"Wake up!" he said. "It is almost light. Wake up, Oh prince."

Each entreaty was followed immediately by a hard shake of my body. At last I opened my eyes and rubbed the sleep from them.

"What is it?"

Even my befuddled mind could see it was not yet dawn. I shook my head to clear it and yawned deeply. Slowly Sinub's face came into focus. Across the room I saw Intef standing with his arms folded watching my every move.

"Awake, my prince. We must hurry!" There was genuine urgency in Sinub's voice.

I tumbled from my bed and threw water from the basin over my face. Quickly I changed into my regular clothes and sandals. My stomach growled and air flew from my anus like a strong wind. In a few minutes I stood ready to follow Sinub and Intef to wherever it was they were taking me.

The sun rose over the Temple of Amun and Pharaoh arose from his bed. His arising each morning was a sacred occasion equal in importance to the rising of the sun. Then began the Rite of the House in which the king was washed by his attendants with water from the temple's sacred lake. These waters symbolized the primordial waters of Nun and creation itself. His bathing in them made Pharaoh "born anew" in the same way as the sun itself is born anew each day. When this had been done two priests entered the chamber of the king. One wore the mask of Toth and the other of Horus. They anointed Pharaoh with oils and adorned him in his sacred robes. Finally they presented him with the royal insignia of his office. This morning in the Temple of Amun Mentuhotep and Intef wore the masks of the gods.

The small courtyard of the temple was crammed to the walls with dignitaries and invited guests. The Great Wife and the king's most important advisors—the *Honored Ones*—sat in the front row facing the sanctuary. Behind them were important public officials and the leaders of Thebes' most noble families invited personally to participate in the special offering that Pharaoh made today. The Lion King entered the courtyard and a hush went over the crowd as a hundred heads bowed low in respect. Silently but with a renewed strength in his stride He Who Is Egypt walked slowly through the crowd. He paused at the steps leading to the sanctuary and turned around to face the gathered assembly. No eyes rose to meet his save those of the Great Queen Hatshepsut whose loveless stare was met with a wry smile on the Lion's face. He nodded to her, turned, and walked up the steps. Toth and Horus followed in the footsteps of their brother god and entered the sanctuary hidden from view of the crowd.

The sanctuary was dark and smelled of incense. I stood within its walls watching my father make his way up the few steps toward me. My heart beat rapidly like that of the antelope I had sacrificed in Giza. Off to the side almost invisible in the dim light stood Sinub. He was shaking like a leaf in a strong wind. He feared for his very soul as he stood in the presence of the gods before him. Thoughts of sacrilege ran through his mind, of having his heart eaten by the *Eater of Hearts* on judgement day. But fear or no fear Sinub stood his post. I saw his hand tighten around the hilt of the *kopesh* under his belt.

The Great Lion followed by Horus and Toth walked solemnly to the front of the shrine that held the statue of the Hidden One. Pharaoh reached for the clay seal on the door and broke it with a twist of his wrists. In this he had "opened the sky" for the god. He Who Is Egypt fell upon his knees and his fellow gods followed. Pharaoh began to recite the Hymn of Morning Worship. "Wake in peace," he said. "As the goddesses of the two crowns wake in peace." Pharaoh rose and opened the door of the shrine revealing the statue of the Hidden One, the Great God Amun in whose name all is accomplished and made manifest in this world.

I could not believe my eyes as they fell upon the statue of the god. Later, when I was Pharaoh, I performed this ceremony many times, but never once with the same sense of awe, wonder, and fear that a I felt at the moment of encountering the Hidden One for the first time that day. The king's hands closed round the statue and brought him forth from his shrine. He cradled Amun in his arms and went through the motions of feeding, washing, and clothing the god. Then he placed jewelry upon the statue and rouge upon its cheeks. With great respect the Hidden One was returned to his home and the doors closed. The clay seal was affixed to the door.

From somewhere the great crash of cymbals filled the courtyard with noise, a signal that the offering was accomplished and Pharaoh was about to fill the room with his godly presence. Usually Pharaoh would leave the sanctuary backwards, bowing as he went, using a palm frond to erase his footprints from the floor. But this time the Great Lion stood erect and walked toward me until I stood before him. My body was soaked with nervous sweat and my stomach threatened to rebel at the overpowering smell of incense. My skin was taut with goosebumps and my leg would not stop shaking. I stared at my father almost paralyzed with fear.

"Easy, my son. I am your father and there is nothing to fear."

His voice was serious, but its tone was warm as he tried to calm my fears.

"Today your life will change forever and you will bear the cause of Egypt upon your shoulders. It is a difficult burden. When you come to curse me for placing it upon you as the years pass, remember this day when we stood together before the Hidden One and pledged ourselves to the lonely task of kingship." He smiled thinly and sighed as if he were truly sorry for what he was about to do.

"Give me your hand, boy," he said extending his to me. I took his hand in mine and felt the gentle squeeze of affection that men sometimes reserve for one another. I looked into the face of the Great Lion. There was no fear. There was only the certitude of doing what had to be done.

"Now, my son, shall we permit Egypt to meet my true heir at last?" He smiled broadly and winked. "Come," he said, "Let us show Egypt her next king!"

We passed through the doorway of the sanctuary into the light of the courtyard and stood at the top of the steps looking down upon the gathering of nobles and advisors. Horus and Toth stood beside us. There was not a sound from the assembly. The look of surprise on their faces turned to shock when Pharaoh spoke.

"Hear me servants of Egypt!"

His booming voice filled the chamber like a strong wind carrying all other sounds before it.

"This day I have made special offering to the Hidden One to seek his guidance and blessing. Guided by his hand I was brought to this place to find my only son and to fulfill the command of Amun that my son be made my heir to the throne of Egypt."

A sound like air being sucked from an opened tomb rose all at once from the crowd. The assembly murmured and rustled like a great beast trying to free itself. Pharaoh stood in mighty splendor listening to the sound grow in strength until it fell like a wave over the room.

"Silence!"

His voice was like the roar of the lion and it struck the ears of the crowd with great force and stunned them into obedience. They pressed against each other like frightened goats, their eyes wide in terror at the thought of the wrath of the Mighty Lion. Off to one side a few people continued to murmur. Pharaoh brought his walking stick down hard upon the granite floor with a loud crack. A glance in the direction of the group and it, too, went silent.

"I am Pharaoh, the servant of Amun and Protector of Egypt. This day I declare my only begotten son, Thutmose, to be my regent and to rule with me over this Black Land until the time of my death. I command my scribes to write my wishes in the official records and to carve my command in the stones of the temples throughout the land." Pharaoh's great voice went silent. He found the faces of Hatshepsut and Senmut before him and fixed their eyes with his powerful stare.

"Let all who would disobey Pharaoh's wishes be hunted down and put to death by fire!"

Again the crowd pressed upon itself seeking safety from Pharaoh's words. Senenmut's courage could not withstand the fear of my father's vengeance and his eyes fell upon the walking stones in fear. But I saw clearly that Hatshepsut's glare had not weakened. Her eyes flashed with anger as she looked directly into my father's face without intimidation. Pharaoh's glance fell upon me and for a second our eyes met. There was concern in those eyes. And as I looked from my father's face into the eyes of the queen, I knew that my life would never be the same from this day forward. And that as long as she lived, I had much to fear from this woman.

# Fifteen

Living in the palace seemed strange at first. It was a huge place with many halls and rooms and housed not only the quarters of the royal family but the center of government as well. Military barracks, government offices, workshops, audience halls, and rooms for important guests all competed for space in the giant complex. The large number of people required to run the government came as a surprise to me. There were people everywhere and a constant coming and going of staff and visitors all with an air of self-importance as they scurried about like rodents seeking cheese. The complex had three residential palaces. The king lived in one, the queen in another, and the third was used from time to time to house foreign dignitaries or other important visitors. I was given an entire wing in my father's palace for my own use. Soldiers from Pharaoh's personal guard were posted at key points in and around my quarters to insure my safety. As always, Sinub and his deadly *kopesh* remained my constant companions.

I lived my early life with Ese and Webkhet in the Garden of the Secluded and I had visited the palace itself only a few times, but even those memories had dimmed. Now as I wandered through the Great House I marveled at its beauty and wealth. The floors were of polished pink granite. Each slab of stone fit so tightly

against the one next to it that it was difficult to see the seam.
When sunlight fell upon the floor it turned the pink stone lumi-
nous so it resembled translucent labaster. A person walking there
appeared to be walking on a thin layer of floating mist instead of
hard stone. Great columns were everywhere, some holding up the
roof lintels, others merely decorative. All were painted in bright
colors against which rows of carved hieroglyphs stood out seeming to shout their stories to passers-by and beckoning them to stop
and listen. Some of the massive pillars were quarried from a single
piece of stone. Others were constructed of several large stone barrels placed one atop the other and covered with mortar and plaster. The walls were decorated with murals depicting the usual
Egyptian themes of creation, hunting and everyday life. Light and
color were everywhere vibrant with life and beauty in contrast to
the actually cavernous design of the place itself. Where it not for
these things the Great House might easily have been overcome by
the heavy gloom reminiscent of a tomb.

The furniture served its purpose even though it was, I thought,
far too large and opulent to be of practical everyday use. Tables
and chairs made of the finest cedar and pine were inlaid with
ebony brought from Nubia. Carved heads of animals adorned the
ends of chair arms and seats were woven in fine wicker or covered
with thickly tufted cloth cushions. The couches were uniformly
uncomfortable as were the eating tables which seemed to me the
only items that were smaller than they should have been. The cups
and dishes from which I took my meals were carved from stone,
alabaster, limestone and even rock crystal, a far cry from the common clay I had grown used to in Memphis. The new glass plates
were just coming into use and from time to time my meal would
be served on them. The glass was translucent, more like alabaster,
a result, I was told, of the manufacturing process in which impuri-
ties remained in the glass after it was spun from its clay core. One

of the servants told me that when foreign dignitaries stayed in the palace they were served with utensils made of gold and electrum, an alloy of gold and silver. Egypt has no silver of its own and so it is regarded as the most precious of metals. Its use in dinnerware was probably designed to impress the dignitary with Egypt's wealth. As for myself I confess to finding all of this luxury ostentatious and bothersome. Later, when I was Pharaoh I discovered that I could not rid myself of it. For while I found it valueless, many others thought it of great worth and in diminishing it I risked diminishing them. And so I learned to live with it.

I spent a few days becoming accustomed to my new surroundings before I summoned Sinub and told him I wished to see my mother. It had been so long since I had set eyes upon her that I wondered whether the vision of her I carried in my memory was truly as she was. Of all those I had left behind two years earlier, it was Ese that I missed most. She had given me life in the way that Hapi gives life to the Nile. Many times I cried the tears of a young boy separated too soon from his mother. Now that I had returned I was eager to see Ese again, to fill my eyes with her presence and bask once more in the affection she felt for her only son.

"Sinub," I said. "It is my wish that my mother be brought to me here in the palace so that I may again look upon her face and she upon her son." I paused for a moment. "Can you make it so?" I asked.

He was sitting on one of the uncomfortable couches. He raised his eyes and looked at me. "That will not be possible, my prince," he said. "As a lesser queen she is only permitted in the palace at the request of Pharaoh." He paused. "Now is not a good time," he said.

I shot him a puzzled glance and a look of annoyance passed over my face. Before I could say anything Sinub spoke again.

"The Great Wife has forbidden her presence and Pharaoh has more important business to tend to than to settle the quarrels of two women." He looked at me in earnest. "To anger the Great Wife further may put Ese in danger. Up to now the queen has been content to ignore your mother. It is not wise for you to bring Ese to the attention of a vengeful wife. Better that you should go to her. There will be a lifetime of opportunities for you to see her in the future. But for now it is better to be cautious."

Sinub, as always, made sense and I took his advice.

It was early that afternoon when Sinub and I approached the gate that led through the wall to the Garden of The Secluded. A loud knock and the big wooden door swung open guided by the hand of one of the eunuchs who guarded the entrance.

"I am Thutmose, son of Pharaoh, and I have come to visit my mother."

I did not wait for a reply and walked through the door onto the pathway beyond. Sinub followed. The huge eunuch said nothing. He bowed as I passed and closed the door behind us. I walked down the pathway and past the bench on which I had waited for Amenemhab so often. It brought a smile to my lips and my mind danced with pleasant thoughts of the old soldier now guarding Egypt's frontiers in the Sinai. I owed much to him, and having returned to the garden where we first met I felt even more grateful. The small pool where Webkhet had taught me about the ways of the blue lotus and other plants seemed unchanged. Even the shadows cast by the trees were familiar. A short distance ahead I saw the doorway to my mother's apartments. I turned to Sinub and placed my finger to my lips as a signal for him to be quiet. I covered the short distance to the door silently. A broad smile beamed from my face as I knocked on the door and waited.

I waited a few seconds and knocked again. The sound of the bolt slipping from the latch reached my ears and suddenly my heart began to beat quickly. I stood there shaking. Then slowly the door opened and I was looking into my mother's sweet face. At first a look of confusion appeared on her face. For the briefest of moments her eyes moved over me. A second later they grew wide with excitement. Her mouth opened as if she wished to speak. Although I saw her lips move, no sound came forth. She held me fast with her gaze and I could not take my eyes from her beautiful face. And even when I saw her tears, still I could not take my eyes from her. When the words finally came they flew forth from me like a burst of wind.

"Mother," I said, "I have come home!"

Ese rushed to me and threw her arms around me in a loving embrace. "My son! My son!" The words came forth in tearful joy. "You are home at last!"

She held me for what seemed a long time. I felt her shudder against me as she let her tears fall freely. Then her embrace relaxed as she stepped back and pushed me in front of her to see me better.

"You bring joy to my eyes, Thutmose. Let me look at you."

She let go of my hand and stepped back. "You have grown into a fine boy."

I stood there smiling like a fool, saying nothing as I basked in the warmth of my mother's affection. Her face was beaming. What creases showed in her skin could as easily be put to her joy as to her age. My mother was not quite twenty-five years old, middle aged by Egyptian standards, and still a very attractive woman. Yet a few strands of gray had begun to appear in her dark hair and the skin on her hands seemed dry and wrinkled. She attended to her make-up each day and seemed radiant for her efforts under her perfectly set black wig. As always she wore the whitest linen dresses and her jewelry was selected to attract the eye to her neck and arms, features that Egyptian men held in great value when it came to judging a woman's beauty. Looking at her there before me

I saw that she was every bit as beautiful as I remembered her. I cannot say what she thought of me for she never said. But judging from the expression on her face and the lilt in her voice I guessed that she was well pleased.

She took my hand and led me into the house. We sat at a small table and Ese called to a servant for bread and beer. A few minutes later an older woman appeared and placed the food in front of us before bowing and disappearing without saying a word.

"I see you have a servant," I said. I lowered my voice in respect. "I was sorry to hear that Webkhet has gone to live with the gods." I caught myself using the old Egyptian phrase trying to ease the burden of my words upon my mother's memory.

Ese shook her head and sighed. "Yes, I know," she said. "I think of her often and I do miss her so."

She took a deep breath and held back the tears. In an instant her attitude changed and she lowered her voice almost to a whisper. "Be careful what you say," she said. She looked over her shoulder and her eyes searched the room. "When Webkhet died they sent me this woman, Lila, to be my servant. I don't trust her. I think she spys for the Great Wife. Say nothing of importance in her presence." Ese looked at me and I nodded that I understood.

We snacked on the food and chatted about all sorts of things. Mostly my mother amused me with stories of Webkhet and me when I was an infant. Needless to say I recalled nothing of their substance but sat there enjoying the pleasure of my mother's company content just to be with her and to see that she was happy and safe. At last she stood up.

"Come," she said. "Let us walk about the Garden and remember good things."

She held onto my arm as we strolled slowly from place to place talking pleasantly about this or that thing that we came upon. We reached the stone bench next to the pathway and Ese sat down and motioned me to sit next to her.

Her eyes darkened and her face became grim.

"I have heard that your father has named you as his regent. The whole palace was buzzing with stories about what the queen would do now that your father has placed you in direct line for the throne." I shook my head to show her I understood. "But as regent you are only that. The Lion of Egypt must still name you as his successor or upon his death your position may yet be taken from you." This was something I did not know. I said nothing and Ese went on. "Your father is very ill, Thutmose, and has been near death several times. I am concerned that he will pass to the gods without having made his will clear that you are to be Pharaoh. You must go to him, my son, and tell him of my concern. Press upon him that the time is now for him to act." There was fear and warning in her eyes and her voice filled with emotion. "I fear for you my son."

I watched her speak and wondered why she did not go to my father with her fears. "I fear for my life as well," she said. "I cannot leave the Garden and have spies in my own household!" It was clear that she took the affront personally. "Each day your father grows weaker, each day his will fails him more, and each day he becomes more dependent upon those around him. Power to the ambitious is like raw meat to jackals, Thutmose. Pharaoh's illness tests the loyalty of his advisors. Some already think of an Egypt without him and wonder of their part in it."

She paused and spat. The anger in her voice was unmistakable.

"Few besides Paremheb remain loyal to your father, my son. The rest are the queen's men. Hatshepsut has been queen for a long time and has been responsible for the careers of many in the court. Over the past year she has replaced one minister after another with men loyal to her, men who now owe their futures to the favor of the Great Wife. Even some of the younger officers of the bodyguard have been replaced. There are only a handful of men, Paremheb among them, whom she dares not challenge openly, at least not yet."

She reached over and took my hand in hers.

"Thutmose, my son, it is my fear that your father will die shortly without making his wishes clearly known. Without Pharaoh's testament concluded you remain only regent upon his death. And in that case Hatshepsut will rule as queen for as long as she wishes."

I lowered my eyes and shook my head in anger. Here I was, son of the Great Lion of Egypt, and still I was hostage to the threats and plots of others. Would there never be an end to it? How long must things move in crooked lines before the path becomes certain? I was angry at them all for trapping me in a game where I was the weakest player, where everyone's ambitions centered upon me or my death. I was most angry for the absence of trust in my world, a world created by others and in which I was forced to live. I would do as my mother asked if for no other reason than I knew not what else to do. But the lessons were slowly dawning. I could no longer rely upon others to make my way safe. From now on I must use my own sense, my own guile, and I must learn to recognize an adversary when I encountered one. In this there was no greater adversary than the sickness that was killing my father. I had to see him before it took him and with it my right to the throne of Egypt.

It was a few days later when Djet came to me late one night. I suspect he had chosen the time deliberately when the palace was asleep. Even spies had to rest sometime. Djet knew he could rely upon the loyalty of the guardsmen who protected me. He had, after all, selected them himself.

"It is as you say my prince. Pharaoh is ill and those around him use the excuse that no one is permitted to see him because of it. He is closed off from much that goes on about him in his name. Few of the old ministers are left and new faces abound. The king is weak and accepts the explanations given him. He signs edicts without knowing their contents. Even the few ministers he recognizes are now of doubtful loyalty as they seek to secure their positions by currying favor with the queen." Djet spat. "Even some of my young officers have been replaced with others whose backgrounds I do not know. I am to protect the life of the Lion with men whose own loyalty I cannot trust." He spat again in disgust.

Sinub and I listened to Djet and watched the anger grow inside him. At last Sinub spoke. "Are there none left who can be relied upon to serve Egypt?" he asked. The expression on my face asked the same question. Djet frowned and raised his eyes in thought.

"Only one would I trust. Paremheb the Chancellor. He serves Egypt." Djet paused. "Perhaps, my prince, if you approached him directly he could bring you to Pharaoh. I would trust no other of the swine that gather now like hungry piglets at the body of a dying sow!"

It was, he knew, a terrible thing to say. But men like Djet whose lives are founded on loyalty and honor do not take likely to those who lack it. Especially so when they strike at the object of loyalty itself. Watching Djet's anger boil over I knew that even Pharaoh was not immune from his criticism. A good leader would have laid the question of his succession to rest long before this. Djet the soldier and bodyguard did not like things unsettled. In confusion there was always danger, and Djet's anger was directed at that danger. And so the plan was for me to go to Paremheb and ask him to help.

But events often move beyond one's control. Before I arranged to meet with Paremheb the fates arranged that I should chance upon Nefurure, daughter of the Great Wife and my father, my half-sister. In fact, chance had little to do with it as Nefurure sought me out in my apartments one day. It was the first time either of us had laid eyes upon the other.

"I am pleased that we have met at last," she said. Her voice was soft and not unpleasant. She stood in the vestibule dressed in the usual Egyptian shift. As one would expect she was well made-up. Her wig was of the new style with long rolls of curls hanging from each side. The hair was colored blue highlighted by a gold band that ran in front. Upon her head she wore the traditional cone of perfumed oil. The heat from her body was slowly melting it and streaks of scented oil ran down the sides of her face. I had always thought the custom, while understandable in Egypt's hot climate, a curious one. Once, many years later, I inquired where it came from. The custom is, it seems, of Nubian origin. Not surprising, really, since we had been dealing with the Nubians for at least the past thousand years! Nefurure was short even for an Egyptian woman. Judging from her thick thighs and large ass she had a hearty appetite for good food. Nonetheless she presented her self as a pleasant woman eager to please with her beauty and manners.

"I agree," I said. I tried to keep any emotion from my voice. She and I were half-siblings but every sense I had told me that this was her mother's daughter and that I should be as wary of the pup as of the bitch.

Nefurure walked across the room and sat down upon the couch. I guessed her to be about twelve years old, an age when women commonly marry and bear children in Egypt.

"I guess you know that our father is very sick," she said. "Have you seen him lately?"

I said nothing and offered a smile to show that I recognized the trap.

"No, I guess not," she continued. "The physicians do not allow him many visitors. They say it makes him weak." She smiled back at me. It was the most insincere smile I had ever seen cross a human face. She and Tepet would have made a good pair!

I wondered how it was that this woman knew so much about our father when he was not permitted visitors. Perhaps from her mother's spies. At least it was safe to assume that. Nefurure smiled at me again no less insincerely this time.

"You must look like your mother," she said. "There is nothing of our father in you." And then she launched into a long statement about how her mother was always the king's favorite and that he had only taken up with my mother on a whim. Of course, it wasn't my fault that Ese came to be with child but, after all, it was really quite silly for me to ever think that I was really a welcomed child of the king. From time to time she stopped talking to see my reaction. Each time I sat impassively and said nothing. It was unclear to me what purpose she had in mind with such talk. So I just sat there and watched her ramble on.

"It is our law that the road to the throne of Egypt lies through the womb of a woman," she said. It was an old proverb and had a number of meanings, some of them obscene! "The bloodline runs through my veins and the veins of the Great Queen. You are regent and nothing more! When the king is gone, you will go with him." The harsh edge to her voice was designed to intimidate. This was one woman who had learned her lessons at her mother's feet. There was strength in her and ambition and, I suspected, a ruthlessness her words merely hinted at.

"So, darling sister, you have come to meet me for the first time and in less than a few minutes you threaten me with oblivion." I paused and shook my head to indicate my disbelief although, I confess, that, too, was feigned. "What is to be gained by such talk? If, as you say, all is arranged, then you have nothing to worry about. I will be abandoned at my father's death, you will be married to some noble and become queen." I smiled. "Then tell me, Nefurure, why are you so troubled?"

She folded her arms and sat straight up. Her dark eyes peered at me from under thick eyelashes and her face went into a childish pout.

"There is no need for the queen in any of this," she said. Her voice was venomous. "She has had her day and now it is mine!" Nefurure's voice rose almost to a shout. She glared at me. "Don't you see, you stupid little boy! We, not her, hold the future of Egypt in our hands. All that is needed once Pharaoh dies is for you and me to marry. Once that is done the bloodline is established again in you. I am your queen and Hatshepsut and her commoner lover are driven from power forever."

My mouth almost fell open from surprise. Nefurure was a true "serpent of the Nile" with blue nipples and perfumed breath to entice the victim close only to sink poisonous fangs into its veins. Once struck, death came slowly but it came with certainty. Nefurure was proposing an alliance with a cobra! The stunned expression on my face must have passed for a state of deep thought. My dear sister sat quietly looking at me waiting for my response.

My mind raced in all directions at once! The depth of her betrayal was impressive. She was proposing nothing less than an alliance against her own mother! Why not? The stakes were sufficiently high, no less than the crown of Egypt itself. Was not such a prize worth abandoning any human loyalty? It was a proposition designed to test the moral strength of the strongest men and it threatened to overwhelm me. I felt my knees shake and my legs grow weak. I was out of my depth and I knew it. Somehow I had to extricate myself from this conversation before I sealed my own doom by saying something whose harm I could not even begin to calculate.

"It is a fascinating idea," I said with as much strength in my voice as I could muster. "But surely there is much to be thought about before I give you my answer." I paused and watched her eyes deepen as suspicion crossed her face. "You have taken me by surprise, my sister, and now you must allow me the time to think over what you have said." I could see the look on her face as I struggled to get away. It was the look of a hungry hyena anxious to consummate the hunt and swallow its prey.

Suddenly she smiled. The crease on her face formed by thin lips gave her the look of a sly serpent. I half expected her tongue to shoot forth and taste the air. But when she spoke it was with a pleasant tone in her voice.

"As you wish, Thutmose." She rose from the couch and moved toward the door. "But do not take too long. You are standing in a running stream and all about you is changing." Nefurure's smile disappeared. "I have offered you a boat, brother. Don't be too stupid to take it."

The discussion exhausted me and I flopped down on the couch to gather my thoughts. Djet and Sinub emerged from the next room where they had been listening to it all.

"The little viper puts her mother to shame," Djet exclaimed. "Let that be a lesson to you, my prince. Be wary of ambitious women!"

Sinub grunted his assent. "The old tale is true," he said.

I looked at him with a puzzled expression on my face. "What old tale?" I asked.

Sinub glanced at Djet and both men smiled as if conspirators in what was about to be said. "In ancient times," Sinub began, "there was once a powerful Pharaoh who angered the gods. To punish him they struck him blind. In great fear he prayed to the gods to lift the curse. To teach him a lesson they set him to a test. If he could find one faithful woman in all Egypt, the gods would

return his sight." Sinub glanced at Djet again. There was an impish glint in his eyes.

"What happened to him?" I asked.

"As the story goes, my prince, the Pharaoh set his ministers to
the task of finding a faithful woman in Egypt. The search went on
for years and all the while the king remained blind. At last an aged
advisor suggested he travel outside the Black Land. Pharaoh took
the advice and found a faithful woman in the first one he encountered outside our borders." Sinub paused. "It is a good tale, my
prince. Be wary of Egyptian women. Their perfumed breath often
conceals poisonous fangs!"

Djet laughed at Sinub's words.

"That woman is as devious as a fox. In return for marriage she
promises you the throne. You are already regent and have the
right to rule with the queen should your father die. Nefurure has
no claim unless you marry her and her mother abdicates. And, my
prince, I assure you the Great Wife will never step down unless she
is removed by force."

Sinub nodded his head.

"The daughter promises you what she cannot give. Your real
enemy is the queen. Her daughter can be safely ignored for now,
although I confess I would not turn my back on her for too long.
Only the gods know what plot she will set in motion next!"

I was grateful for Djet's advice and for Sinub's loyalty. These
two men were my only allies while I tried to survive the snakepit
that was the royal court. My father had spoken highly of
Mentuhotep. I wondered if he, too, could be relied upon to help
me. Perhaps so. But his blindness made him a questionable asset
and there was always the suspicious Intef who, if Djet was right,
had to be watched closely. The more I thought about the whole
situation the more complex and confusing—and dangerous—it

became. My head began to hurt and my stomach burned. I was weary of going around in circles in my own head.

Djet's words cut through my mood. "I have spoken with Paremheb, my prince."

Paremheb! Of course! In my confusion I neglected to add him to the list of allies. He was a strong man and deeply loyal to my father. I was grateful for Djet's clear mind.

"He shares our concerns, your highness, and has agreed to come to you and offer his counsel." Djet paused. "He must be careful for there are many in the court who wish him dead. If the queen learns that he stands with you, she may strike against you both." He paused. "There is need for great caution, my prince."

Djet's words were said in deadly earnest. I had come to trust the man's nose when it came to danger. "What do you suggest, Djet?" I asked.

"Let me arrange the meeting for some late night. I still control the guard and will arrange the postings so that only loyal men are on duty. That way no one but trusted soldiers will see the Chancellor arrive and they will keep their mouths shut."

I nodded my head in agreement.

"It may be some time before Paremheb can come to you. He knows that he is being watched. There is no point to a secret meeting that is not secret. On this we must trust him, for the greater risk is his."

Djet was right, of course. For the next ten days I kept to my normal routine. Then one night as I returned to my quarters I noticed that there were only two sentinels guarding the corridor leading to my apartments. Sinub, too, noticed the absence of the others. As we passed the guardsmen Sinub nodded to them.

"I know these men. They are ours." Sinub said. "This is Djet's work." His voice changed tone. "Unless I miss my guess you may expect Paremheb tonight."

It was very late and all but one of the lamps had consumed their oil leaving the room in heavy shadows cast by a dim light. I dozed in my chair while Sinub sat by the door like a guard dog. I caught the movement of his body rising from the chair before I heard the sound of a soft knock. Sinub's hand moved automatically to the hilt of his *kopesh* as he moved toward the door and pressed his ear to its wooden surface. A second knock, garbled words spoken through the door, and Sinub slid the bolt back and stepped back. A second later it swung open and Paremheb walked quickly into the room and closed the door quietly behind him.

He acknowledged Sinub's presence with a brief nod and moved across the room and sat opposite me. For a few moments his eyes examined his surroundings for signs of danger or betrayal. He turned to me and spoke.

"It has been a long time since we have seen one another, my prince. I am pleased to find you in such good health." He paused. "I wish we had more time, your highness, but every minute spent here presents a danger to us both. Djet has told me that you wish to see your father. Is that true?" His eyes focused upon me like a cobra upon a bird. Paremheb searched for signs of strength or weakness.

"That is correct Chancellor." The use of his title was deliberate. I was no longer the little boy who had caused him so much difficulty. I was Pharaoh's son and he was a government official. Although I needed him, there was no point in putting off the issue of who was superior to whom.

"It is my wish that you arrange for a meeting with my father at the earliest time. It is important that my enemies do not know of this meeting." I paused and stared into his eyes for a moment. I felt my heart beating but my brow was dry. The nervousness I felt left me.

"Your father is very ill, Oh prince and…"

My words cut through his.

"I know of his grave condition." My voice turned harsh as if my impatience had reached its bounds. "I also know that the fate of Egypt is at great risk and that steps must be taken to ensure that my father's wish that I succeed him is carried out." I paused and took a deep breath. "Paremheb, my father always held you in high esteem. He rewarded your successes and forgave you your faults. Now it is your turn to return the favor to your king. Will you do it?"

Paremheb's eyes glared at me. His voice was barely under control when he spoke.

"I have always served Egypt and its king, first as a soldier then as a minister."

He shook his head and almost spat the breath from his lungs.

"Nothing has happened to change that! Nothing could happen to change that!"

Paremheb eyes flashed with anger at me.

"You insult me with your presumption, my prince. And I take offense. You would do well to remember that you are not yet Pharaoh and..." He let his voice drop..."Unless you have more friends than you need in this perilous time, you would be wise to keep the few you have."

It was a stinging rebuke. It was stupid to attempt to force this man to my will. All I had to do was ask for his loyalty and he would have willingly given it. Once again I had failed to distinguish an ally from an enemy and I moved quickly to correct the mistake.

I smiled. "As always, Chancellor, your advice is wise. Perhaps that is why you served my father so well." I let my voice drop. "And that, Paremheb, is why I need your advice now." His face softened and the anger in his expression lessened. "Our enemies are Egypt's enemies. They would deny the nation her rightful king and subject *Kemit* to the rule of a woman!" Paremheb nodded in agreement. "This must not be," I said. "Egypt must have a king, and it is my father's wish that I be that king."

Paremheb rose and stood before me. "What is it you wish of me, my prince? You have but to command me in your service and I shall obey."

"Then sit, my friend, and give me the benefit of your counsel, for these are dangerous waters in which we sail and you are the only experienced helmsman that Egypt can rely upon." I pointed to the chair across from me. The loyal soldier took his seat and waited for me to ask of him what I required.

"Can a meeting be arranged with my father in such a manner that only those who keep faith with us will know of it?" I asked.

Paremheb thought for a few seconds. "It will take some planning and I shall need Djet's help in arranging the guard, but it can be done. Of course, Pharaoh is too ill to travel. If we are to succeed in keeping our efforts secret we shall have to go to him in his apartments." He stopped speaking and a look of concentration passed across his face. "The meeting must take place late in the evening when fewer of the queen's spies are about." He sighed. "But if Djet can arrange for loyal guardsmen to be on duty that night, we can do it." A thin smile creased his lips. Paremheb enjoyed being useful to someone again and I could see the pleasure on his face.

Over the next few minutes I explained to him what I intended to do at that meeting and asked his help. From what I could judge he thought the plan a good one or in any case probably the only one open to us. Sometimes one faces the dilemma of having only a single alternative. In those times one must press forward or lose the battle.

"Do you think Mentuhotep can be trusted," I asked.

Paremheb squinted and shook his head. It was gesture of uncertainty. "There is no reason to believe that he cannot be, my prince." He shrugged. " The truth is that it doesn't matter very much. You need him. Only he can lend the sense of legitimacy to your words when the time comes. So you must rely upon him or forego the game from the beginning." It was the practical advice of an experienced soldier. There are, after all, few certainties in anything we do in this world. I would have to content myself with Mentuhotep's past loyalty and my father's high opinion of him.

"Will you see to the necessary documents, Paremheb?" It was more a request than a question and Paremheb nodded his head as he agreed without saying a word.

"How many will be present?" Paremheb asked. "The fewer the less risk of discovery" he added.

I thought for a moment. "Five I should think," I answered." A smile crossed my lips. "Not too large a crowd to save a country," I laughed. My attempt at humor relaxed Paremheb. From across the room I saw Sinub smile as even he let down his guard for a few moments.

We talked for a few more minutes and then Paremheb took his leave. He would examine the comings and goings of Pharaoh's ministers and doctors and choose the right time for the meeting. If Mentuhotep was to attend I needed at least two day's warning so that he could travel to Thebes and await my summons. The man was blind for Seth's sake, and was not likely to go unnoticed even in a large crowd! In my mind I thought it humorous that any plot should have blind conspirators. But often reality exceeds the imagination. At least Mentuhotep would not have to be told much in advance to play his part. As I lay on my bed waiting for sleep to come I mulled that fact over in my mind and was grateful for this small favor.

More than two weeks passed and still I received no word from Paremheb. During that time I sent one of Djet's guardsmen with a message to Mentuhotep asking him if he would be willing to come to me at a moment's notice should I send for him. To remind him of his loyalty to my father, I enclosed the gold cartouche with the name of Pharaoh inscribed upon it that Amenemhab had given me in Memphis. Mentuhotep had not questioned my identity when we first met and had never asked to see it. Now I sent it to the Chief Prophet in the hope that his loyalty to my father would come to me as a gift. I was pleased to receive his reply. He said he would come to me when summoned any time day or night. I could only hope that he would heed my advice and tell no one of my request.

It was during this time that I met Ineni the architect, the man who constructed my grandfather's tomb in the Valley of the Kings. He came to my apartments one afternoon with a young man not much older than me. The young man's name was Puemre and was Ineni's youngest son. Neither age or youth served to reduce Sinub's suspicions and he demanded proof of who they were. To my surprise Ineni produced a gold cartouche exactly like the one I had been given by Amenemhab. When I questioned him he told me that Pharaoh had told him to present it to me as proof of the words Ineni was to speak to me. I showed the old man to a chair and sat opposite him.

"Tell me, Ineni, when did you see my father and is he well?" The old man's eyes avoided my gaze and he shook his head. His loose skin shook like the baggy fur on the back of an old dog and spittle flew from the corner of his mouth.

"He sent for me two days ago, highness." The old man paused. He did not like bringing bad news. "I am sorry to tell you that your father is very ill, highness. From what I could see of him in so short a visit, his illness takes a heavy toll of him each day." He said all this without looking at me and in a tone of voice that was solemn and honest.

I reached across to him and touched his arm. "Thank you for what you have told me," I said. I changed the tone of my voice in an effort to be pleasant. "So what is it you wish of me old man?" I smiled at him and his eyes brightened.

"It is your father's wish that I escort you to his tomb so that you may see how he is prepared to live forever in his House Of A Million Years."

As the old man spoke I saw Sinub's body tighten. His eyes found mine and he shook his head as if to say, "too dangerous!" I looked at Ineni.

"Your grandfather was the first of the Theban kings to be buried in a rock tomb in the Valley of the Kings," he said. "Your father will be the second. Many years ago he instructed me to design his resting place. Pharaoh was pleased with the plan. Workmen have been busy at its construction for more than five years. Now that it is completed he wishes you to see it before it is sealed forever." Ineni's voice broke and tears welled in his eyes.

I reached across and gently touched the old man's arm again to comfort him.

"Does your son study architecture?" I asked. It was said pleasantly to take the old man's mind from his grief. Ineni's head rose and a smile managed its way through the gloom. "He is a good son," he said. "He has talent for design and construction. In truth, it was Puemre who oversaw most of the construction of Pharaoh's tomb. My age has left me weak and my eyesight is too poor even to drop a plumb line accurately. So I must rely on the strength and senses of my son."

There was affection for the boy in the old man's voice that reminded me of my father's voice when he listened to me tell of my adventures in Memphis. Many years later when I had a son of my own I learned that all fathers who love their sons speak in the same voice.

Sinub was still shaking his head when I told Ineni that we would come for him and his son sometime in the morning of the next day. I had refused Ineni's offer to arrange transport and to depart at a specific time and place. Ineni was innocent enough, so innocent in fact that he might not even be aware that he was leading me into an ambush. Sinub arranged with Djet for a military escort. At mid-morning of the next day I sent one of the guardsmen to fetch Ineni and his son while Sinub and I waited at the palace gate.

It was a short walk from the gate to the quay where a boat waited to take the four of us and the four guardsmen across the Nile to the western shore and Thebes of the Dead. The river is a half mile wide at Thebes, and the ship's captain did not bother to unfurl the sail for so short a journey relying instead upon the backs of his oarsmen. We were met on the western shore by two more of Djet's soldiers who obtained one of the new coaches to carry us to the Valley of the Kings.

The coach was called a *Kat'ana*, which is the Asiatic word for "horse," two of which were harnessed in the races to pull the coach along. The coach was little more than a rectangular wooden box that sat on four wheels. Three wooden benches ran crossways through the wagon. The driver and his assistant sat on the first bench while Ineni, Puemre, Sinub and I sat on the other two. The wheels were standard six spoke chariot wheels with molded bronze hubs lubricated with mutton fat. Mounting the box directly over the wheels made for a rough ride. The *Kat'ana* was really designed for hauling military cargo, usually with oxen on the reins. But this particular one was drawn by horses and was equipped with a cloth canopy to keep the sun from broiling our heads as we made the overland journey to my father's tomb.

The guardsmen ran alongside weapons at the ready as the *Kat'ana* bounced along on the unpaved road that ran the two miles from the riverbank to the foothills of the limestone mountains that stood between us and the Valley of the Kings. The road ran through green fields thickly planted with crops. My mind wandered as I thought of my father lying ill in his bed. Soon he would make his way along this same road. Then he would be carried upon a great sled drawn by hundreds of officials who took him to his final rest next to his father. It was almost noon and the sun beat down mercilessly upon our little group. The guardsmen kept pace with the slow moving wagon. Sweat poured from their faces and the strain showed in their eyes. Up ahead the mountains rose straight up, more like cliffs than mountains, and their pinkish color contrasted sharply with the green fields that pressed against their base. Our driver pulled to a halt at a place where the road took a sharp right turn and ran parallel to the mountains. Here the green ended in a flat open plain that ran north and south for several miles. I ordered that the soldiers be given water from a near-by well and that we all rest for a short while before continuing on.

It was here on the plain where the edge of the grass met the lifeless desert that my ancestors constructed their mortuary temples so their Ka could be kept by the priests for all time. Here Amenhotep I had constructed his mortuary temple after ordering his body to be buried secretly in the harsh hills beyond the first range of mountains. So successful had his architect been at hiding the location of Amenhotep's tomb that even the government officials whose job it was to know such things were uncertain as to where it was. Some distance down the plain was Thutmose I's temple. It was a simple affair as these things came to be, and quite befitting a man who spent his entire life in the military and lived in spartan simplicity even after he came to the throne. Off to the side I saw my father's temple. It was grander than both his ancestor's and yet nothing that would cause great comment in this land of the New Kingdom. My eyes strained to take in the widest possible view of the things that spread out before me, the mix of past and present, of old and new, and of what was alive and what was dead. A shudder ran through me and for an instant I felt cold. And then it passed and I returned to the others.

There was little point in continuing our journey in the wagon. The ground was rocky and broken and the fastest way to travel was to make our way on foot. We walked along a path that led from the plain toward the mountains before us. It was hard going and the sun was hot. I worried about the effect of the difficult travel on Ineni. His son held a sun shade over the old man's head. From time to time he poured water onto a cloth and wiped his father's face with it. The tomb workers used this path regularly to transport materials and supplies to the work site, but the hard ground had resisted making the path smooth. It was wide enough to accommodate a small wagon but not much more. I wondered to myself whether the funeral sled could make its way over it without getting stuck.

The harsh desert was full of limestone rocks that had grown hot in the sun and now threw their heat from the earth so that our feet and legs were burning. At last we reached the place where the path wound its way through the first wall of bare stone hills. The hills rose steeply on each side of the path and provided some much welcomed shade. We stopped in the narrow cut seeking a respite from the broiling sun and drank water and took a short rest. To my eye even the trained and hardened elite soldiers of the *Eaters of Hearts* regiment were suffering. To my surprise Ineni was no worse off than the rest of us and seemed to be taking the whole thing in stride. Sinub, as always, sat impassively without complaint.

It took only a short while for our party to make its way through the narrow pass. The pass opened out to a wide space between the first row of mountains and a second row of smaller hills and ravines that ran across the front of us. This was the Valley of Kings. A broad path ran directly before us connecting the West Valley burial sites with those in the East Valley. All around were hills of solid rock, sufficient space for hundreds of royal tombs for future generations of Egyptian pharaohs. My grandfather's tomb lay in the deepest reaches of the West Valley. My father had ordered Ineni to construct his tomb in the same location. My father had visited his tomb on a few occasions when it was being built but had never seen it since it had been completed. For some reason I did not understand he wanted me to see it before it was sealed forever from human eyes.

We walked along the road in the blistering sun for almost a mile before we came upon a cluster of huts and workshops built by the workmen who labored on my father's tomb. Constructing tombs was big business and it was not uncommon for workmen to move their entire families to the work site and take up residence for as long as it took to complete the tomb. Several foremen recognized Ineni and Puemre and came running to them. We were given water and taken to a place out of the sun. Ineni spoke to one of the workers and soon beer, dates and bread appeared on the bench table at which we sat. We ate and drank and refreshed ourselves. Ineni's eyes were wide with excitement. He seemed to have recovered quickly from the long walk. There was renewed energy in his speech. His arm swept across the sky as he gestured toward the cliffs behind me.

"There it is my prince." I saw his eyes move from my face to the cliffs. I turned and looked at the sheer wall of solid rock that rose straight up from the sandy desert floor. Its peak was at least seven hundred feet high. Along its sheer face was a wooden stairway that ran in zig-zag fashion from platform to platform ending at an opening in the rock face three hundred feet up. Timbers held only the first set of stairs from the ground. Above that holes drilled into the cliff face had been filled with timbers driven deeply into the rock to anchor each set of stairs leading one after the other up to the tomb entrance. Workmen scurried up and down the stairs carrying materials and tools. Ineni saw my eyes widen in surprise.

"Like his father before him, your father wished his body to be safe from grave robbers for all eternity. Once the tomb is sealed and the stairway removed, it will be impossible for thieves to climb to the entrance. And as time passes and the tombstone weathers against the rest of the cliff face even the entranceway will be difficult to see from the ground." Ineni took a deep breath. "It will truly be a House of a Million Years, my prince, and the Great Lion will lie within it safe for all time."

I smiled warmly at the old architect.

"What you have wrought here is beyond my imagination," I said. "Truly you have served Pharaoh well." My eyes moved to Puemre sitting next to his father. "And you, Puemre, did you have much to do with this?" It was a friendly question. The boy just shrugged and said nothing. His father spoke instead.

"The design and measurements are his." There was great pride in his voice. "The boy is a better architect than I am," he said. "In a few years he will be the best in all Egypt, my prince." He paused and smiled slyly. "You could do no better than my son in finding an architect for yourself."

I could not stop myself from laughing. The sly fox was seeking a position for his son! And none too subtle about it too! But why not, I thought? Someone has to oversee my building projects when I am Pharaoh. Pharaohs have always built grand buildings and temples as a way of insuring their memory in the hearts of the people. And so architects have always occupied a place of special reverence and respect in Egypt. The first of these great builders, Imotep, planned and constructed the pyramids more than a thousand years ago. It was he who taught the Egyptians the skill of building in stone. So remarkable were his achievements that he was made a god and is worshiped to this day.

"It is an idea worth thinking about," I said. Ineni's eyes widened and he offered a slight bow of his head to show his gratitude. "Now I would like to see the tomb."

Ineni stayed behind claiming the climb was too much for him. Sinub was not unhappy when I ordered him to remain where he was and enjoy his beer. He offered no resistance to my suggestion. To his professional eye there was no realistic chance of attack here. What danger there was came from my own clumsiness in that I might miss my step and fall from the stairway. Sinub read my thoughts. "Be careful on the stairs, my prince," he said and went back to his beer and bread.

The climb to the opening in the cliff face was steep and difficult. I wondered how the workmen accomplished it with such ease. Their bodies were lean and muscular and deeply browned from so much time in the sun. I was learning that the construction business was not for the weak of body or heart. Once, I looked over the side of the steep stairway perched precariously against the rock-face with only scant means of support and my stomach fluttered with fear. I made it to the top by fixing my gaze at the step above me until I stood safely inside the opening in the cliff face. I tried not to think about how I would make my way down again.

The opening was quite large, perhaps ten feet square. A few paces inside and we stood at the foot of stone stairs leading upward along a corridor carved in solid rock. At the top of the stairs the corridor widened to twenty feet high and across. Puemre saw the look on my face and spoke.

"The corridor gradually descends from this spot to a distance of almost three hundred feet into the rock, your highness. On these walls the story of the Great Lion of Egypt is told in beautiful murals so that he may look upon his great deeds for all eternity."

His voice was solemn and respectful as he tried to strike a balance between the pride he felt in his work and the respect for the dead that he felt I required.

Lamps hung from fixtures all the way down the corridor. In their light I saw the brightly colored murals that recounted the story of my father's life and his reign as pharaoh. The arched ceiling, too, was covered with paintings. Many of these scenes I had seen before in the murals of the palace, government buildings, and temples. Art in Egypt was funereal not freely decorative and most paintings were generic in theme and content. The artist had little chance for innovation. As Puemre and I walked down the painted corridor the whole schema took on a familiar sense. At the far end a group of artists were putting the finishing touches on a painting. I watched as they applied the grid to a wet plaster wall so that standard forms of humans and animals could be traced with unerring scale. Once the outlines were done, a relief sculptor chiseled out the backgrounds from behind the figures giving the forms the appearance of rising from the wall itself. Then came the painter who filled in the details with standard colors for each part of the figure. No creativity was asked for nor given. The painter worked with a length of wood whose end had been pounded to a pulp to make a soft brush. The colors were held to the plaster with a colorless mixture of beeswax and nut oils mixed in the paints. It was style without variety, form without movement. It was the perfect art form to be enjoyed by a corpse.

The corridor led to an open door through which we entered the antechamber. The room was cavernous and its rounded ceiling rose no less than thirty five feet from the floor. Like the corridor this room was covered with paintings. The place was more like a court than a room. Just inside the door lying on its side was a thick slab of polished stone. "What is that?" I asked.

Puemre spoke instantly only too happy to demonstrate his skills. "That is the plug for the doorway, highness" he said. "When the tomb is finally sealed the doorways to each room will be sealed with a custom fitted stone." He paused. "This one weighs ten tons."

"And this antechamber?" My eyes wandered around the great hall as I spoke.

"It will be filled with those things from Pharaoh's life that he will take with him to the Field of Marshes to enable him to live a pleasant life. It will be filled with beds, tables, chairs, chariots, all types of food, jars, and many other things that he will need to live as a king among kings." Puemre stopped and looked around. "I hope there is sufficient space for it all," he said. "If not," he shrugged, "we will use the annex." He led me to a small door at the far corner of the room. Its plug, too, lay on the floor. Puemre pointed into the darkness beyond the door. "This is the annex to the antechamber. It gives us more room if we need it." He smiled. "Besides, we have to put the *ushabtis* somewhere!"

I pursed my lip to show my confusion. "*Ushabtis?*" I said. "I do not know of this thing."

Puemre smiled. "It would be foolish to send the king to eternal life without his servants. If we sent his mortal servants with him soon there would be complaints and a shortage of good servants in Egypt!" He laughed at his own joke. "For we Egyptians form is substance and substance is essence. So we send *ushabtis* with our kings to serve them forever. We send them with small wooden carvings of all they will need. For your father there will be hundreds of wooden soldiers to protect him. Carvings of boats and chariots and *kat'ana* to carry him wherever he wishes. Slaves and servants carved in wood or stone will go with him, and even his favorite animals. Of course they will not come to life until he has reached the Fields of Creation. But when they do they will be of great use to your father."

At the far end of the antechamber off to the right was a wall of pillars. The doorways between them gave the impression of a colonnaded wall with many entrances. Up close these pillars and doors turned out to be only paintings cleverly placed upon a plaster facade. Behind the false wall was the real wall with the door that led to the burial chamber. The burial room was about half the size of the antechamber but, strangely, possessed a higher ceiling. The flickering lamps threw sufficient light for me to see the huge rock sarcophagus standing in the center of the room. Its lid rested against the back wall. Puemre saw the expression of wonder upon my face and spoke.

"It is quarried from a single block of granite. Its lid alone weighs two tons. It was shipped here by boat from the Aswan quarries." He paused as if pondering what to say next. "It has sat her for more than a year," he said respectfully. My eyes met his and I nodded to show I understood his meaning. Puemre bowed his head in solemn respect for the Pharaoh's soul. He walked to the far end of the room and pointed to yet another doorway.

"This, highness, is the treasure room where the treasures of the king will be placed. It will be filled to the ceiling with gold and other precious metals, fine linen and clothes, the best wines and beers, and precious stones from all parts of the world." His voice was excited. "The treasury can only be reached by removing the great stone plugs in all the other rooms first." He smiled. "That is no easy task even for an architect with sufficient men and equipment. No grave thief could do it." He said it with a confidence that only the technically proficient seem to have. For the rest of us, the world rarely appears so certain. Live long enough and anything seems possible. Even the removal of heavy stone doors by a grave robber.

We retraced our steps to the opening in the cliff face. My eyes took several minutes to adjust to the bright sunlight. We were three hundred feet above the ground and the only way down was on the wooden staircase that now seemed to me to be made of thin straw! My stomach turned. I would not be able to avoid looking at the height by staring at the steps above me. They were all below me now. With each step I was reminded of how high up I was. I tried not to show my fear.

"Shall I go first," I said. It seemed to me that false courage screamed in my words.

"If you wish, highness," Puemre said. "But perhaps it is best if I go first. That way I can clear any loose dirt or tools that careless workmen may have left on the stairs." He smiled.

Clever fellow, I thought. He knows I am frightened and is salving my pride with a silly excuse. I remembered thinking he might make a good royal architect after all! "Yes, perhaps you are right," I said grateful for the excuse not to lead the way. Step by step I followed Puemre until we stood safely upon the solid earth and could breathe easily again.

It was past the time when the sun is highest in the sky and our little group began the walk to where the green met the desert and where the *kat'ana* waited to carry us back to the Nile and the boat to the east bank. I was tired as were the others and few words passed among us as we put one sandal in front of the other covering the distance over the desert sand as best we could. My thoughts wandered to the tomb and the magnificent house prepared for Pharaoh's corpse while Pharaoh himself stood on the brink of his earthly oblivion. The journey had been an interesting diversion, but it had changed nothing. I and the throne of Egypt were still at risk and the one man who could help me, my father, lay at death's door while sending me on an inspection of his tomb! These thoughts danced in my head made fuzzy by the heat. Live long enough and nothing surprises you! I was still a very young man and already the truth of those words was becoming clear to me, and I marveled at how difficult it was to accept one's fate.

We arrived at the palace before Horus rode to yet another death in the western sky. I bathed and dressed and prepared for dinner. I had just seated myself at the small table when Sinub strode into the room with Djet following behind him.

"I am sorry to disturb your meal, my prince, but Djet has important news."

I looked to Sinub and then to Djet. His face was flushed with excitement and he was plainly nervous. It was a trait that did not become him and it did little to calm my own fears.

"Your highness the time has come at last," he said. I could hear the sound of his heavy breathing. It reminded me of an impatient animal ready to pounce. "Paremheb came to me this morning. You are to prepare yourself for the meeting with Pharaoh in two nights time. I am to place loyal men around Pharaoh's apartments to make certain that we are not disturbed by unwelcome visitors. With your permission I shall dispatch a guard to accompany Mentuhotep to the *Blue Crocodile* where he can hold himself in readiness for your summons. He will be told only that you require his presence. Nothing more. The fewer who know of the details the better. My men will deliver the Chief Prophet to the royal apartments and should have no difficulty passing through the guards. I am to tell you as well that Paremheb has prepared the necessary documents."

Djet stopped speaking. He began to relax in the manner of a schoolboy who had just finished reciting a memorized text for his teacher. The soldier was accustomed to more direct skirmishes. I could see in his face that he disliked being used as a messenger. Officers, after all, had their pride. It was a trait I encountered later on in my own senior officers. The same general who expected instant obedience from his subordinates often bristled at even the most minor direction from his Pharaoh. It seemed to come with the breed.

Djet left having accomplished his mission and I sat down to wait. No matter how many times I went over it in my mind I discovered nothing more I could do to move events any faster or to increase the chances that our plan would succeed. In fact the chances were good that it would succeed. The number of conspirators was small, five in all. Large enough to possess the resources we required and small enough so our secret would not get out. The next two days, I knew, were critical. If our enemies were to find us out it would be now. Once the meeting was completed we would have the advantage, and there would be little the queen or her advisor could do but accept their fate. I did not sleep very well that night as I rehearsed over and over again what I would say to my father. Time and again I examined each detail of the plan until I convinced myself it must succeed. The next day dragged by slowly and I busied myself with minor things. I had not left the apartments since Djet's visit. Another night and then the final dawn. I awoke well rested and strangely calm. Before another dawn came either Egypt would be safe from its enemies or the five of us might be dead.

It was late when the light from the Star of Sothis beamed through my apartment window. The rising of the star was the signal that Paremheb set for us to gather in the royal apartments by separate routes. Sinub extinguished every lamp in the room. Noiselessly I slipped the door open and looked down the corridor that led across the palace to the royal apartments where my father lay waiting. Djet's men had done their work. Only half the lamps that usually lit the hallway were aflame. At the far end of the corridor two guards stood their posts. Sinub and I approached them silently from the shadows. We passed before them without a word

and walked on until we reached the top of the grand staircase
that led down to the palace's central court. Moving with our
backs pressed against the corridor wall we hid our movements in
the deep shadows. A few moments later and we were across the
open space. We passed through the two sentinels guarding the
entrance to the corridor that led to Pharaoh's apartments. Here
more lamps were alight and I could see that for the entire length
of the corridor. Each doorway had a guard posted before it. We
moved quickly. As we approached the end of the corridor
Paremheb suddenly appeared before us. He stood with his legs
apart and arms folded in typical military fashion. The door to his
right was open. I approached and sensed the presence of the Lion
inside. A slight bow was all the recognition I received from
Paremheb. I managed a silent smile. The soldier walked through
the doorway and I followed.

Djet had already arrived and rose at my entrance into the room.
I nodded to him but said nothing. Paremheb moved across the
room and stood in front of a door at the far end. Sinub sat down
and I stood awkwardly in the middle of the room. A heavy silence
hung over the chamber as each of us was caught in his own
thoughts. Minutes passed slowly and soon it seemed to me that we
had been in the room for a very long time, although in truth it
probably was only for ten minutes or so. The sound of knocking
at the door filled the room with crashing noise or so it seemed to
the ears of men fraught with tension at what they were about to
do. Paremheb moved quickly across the room and opened the
door. Mentuhotep stood in the dim light, his bulbous body and
head taking up almost the entire space in the doorway. In one
hand he held his walking stick while the other to my horror rested
on the arm of his loyal assistant Intef! Djet groaned.

It was a colossal error! No one had remembered that because
Mentuhotep was blind he required his assistant to travel anywhere

outside the temple! I stood there in shock imagining my plan failing a piece at a time. My mind raced to the edge of panic. In one single stroke we had put the entire plan at risk.

Djet's eyes moved from me to Paremheb and back again and it seemed from the expression on his face that he might have been contemplating killing Intef where he stood. I saw him shake his head in disbelief and let out an audible sigh. Paremheb's face wore a similar expression, a mixture of disgust and concern. He looked at me and shrugged his shoulders as if waiting for me to tell him what to do. While we tried in silence to decide what to do about Intef, the priest led his superior into the room and found him a place on the couch next to Sinub. Intef straightened up, folded his arms, and stood behind the Chief Prophet. At least Djet had not told Mentuhotep the purpose of the meeting so it was unlikely that Intef knew either. It was even possible that Intef did not know that he was even in the king's apartments. Certainly his escort would not have told him. In the dark of the evening combined with the corridor's dim light Intef might only know that he was somewhere in the royal palace but not where. It was a risk, of course, but one worth taking if for no other reason than that there was no choice!

I rose from my chair and looked at Paremheb. "Perhaps it is time, Chancellor, " I said. "Will you escort the Chief Prophet?" The expression on his face told me he understood my intentions. I turned to Sinub. "Intef will remain here with you until we are finished." Sinub nodded and rose from the couch and took up a position near the door. Intef said nothing and remained where he was. Paremheb bent over the Chief Prophet and offered him his arm. "Please come with me, sir" he said. Mentuhotep stood up and took Paremheb's arm and walked with him into the adjoining room. A few seconds later I followed. Djet came after me closing the door behind him leaving Intef and Sinub alone in the outer room. We walked across the connecting room to a door at the far end. Paremheb knocked softly and from the other end I heard the sound of a voice so weak it sounded like a muffled rattle.

"Enter."

Paremheb slipped the bolt and led us into the room.

There on the large bed propped up by pillows lay the Great Lion of Egypt. It had been only two months since I had last seen my father. The sight of him now sent a shiver through my body. His body was mostly skin and bones. The skin that covered his chest was stretched tight against the bones of his rib cage. Whatever muscle had once lived beneath the skin had long since been consumed by the illness that was killing him. My father's arms looked more like twigs than limbs. Discolored skin hung limply from where once powerful muscles had responded to his will. His neck seemed like a single bone supporting a cadaverous skull whose most prominent feature was a jaw bone extended outward forcing my father's mouth into a permanent grimace. Lips made thin by disease no longer shaped his mouth and his missing teeth permitted deep hollows to form in his cheeks. Eyes barely flickering with life had sunk deep in their sockets so that his cheekbones appeared to stretch themselves taut against his flesh. All this made the great Thutmoside nose look even larger and gave his face the appearance of a sick vulture awaiting its own death.

Pharaoh motioned us to him. His hand reached out and touched mine. It was more a claw than a human hand and I almost drew my own back in disgust. But I did not and Pharaoh pressed his hand in mine.

"My eyes delight in you again, Thutmose" he said. "I am glad that you have come." He looked around the room and nodded to Mentuhotep. "And you, Chief Prophet, I am grateful for your presence. Much of what we do will depend on you." Mentuhotep stared over my father's naked head into space and simply nodded that he understood. Then Pharaoh looked at me with a father's worry.

"Thutmose, my son, the time has come for me to name you as my successor. Paremheb has prepared the necessary documents for my signature."

He lifted his arm as if to call Paremheb to him but let it drop against the bed clothes. He was too weak. Paremheb saw the gesture and understood my father's wishes. From a small leather case he produced a document written on expensive papyrus. He held it out for Pharaoh to take.

My father shook his head. "Give it to the boy." I took the document in my hand and began to read it. It was of few words. My father had sworn that I was his only son and heir and that on this day it was his last testament that I should succeed him as Pharaoh after his death. I finished reading and looked at my father.

"I will do my best to rule Egypt with justice and power and will keep your memory always before my mind and before the people of this land." My voice was choked with emotion and tears where not far from my eyes.

Paremheb took the document from me and placed it upon the leather case. He held it in front of my father and handed him a pen. The Lion made a great effort to sit up and took the pen in his hand. His eyes were half closed as he squinted to see the place for his signature. Then he signed it and handed it back to Paremheb who placed the document in the leather case. The Lion took a deep breath and began to speak.

"I have, Chief Prophet, just signed my last testament in which I name my son my lawful and only successor. I say this so that you may hear what your blind eyes cannot see. You are my witness along with Paremheb. I command you to bear witness to the truth of my last wishes for the people of Egypt." He paused and again breathed deeply. The sound of rattling liquid came from his chest.

"Do you understand my old friend?" Pharaoh's voice was full of affection for the man for whom he had done so much and from whom he now expected final payment. Mentuhotep's blind eyes filled with tears and sobs burst forth from his huge chest. Puffy hands covered his eyes and he wept openly for his friend who lay dying before him.

"Yes, Great One!" It was almost a scream. "I will bear witness for your son!" He broke into tears again and Paremheb led him from the room. Djet stood rigidly at attention all this time trying to control his emotions. Nothing in his life as a soldier had prepared him for this. To be sure death was no stranger to his experience. But the death of his king was beyond anything he could imagine. He turned his face from the living corpse before him and followed Paremheb and Mentuhotep from the room and left my father and me to say our farewells in private.

I stood at side of the bed looking into my father's face. The lids of his eyes seemed to weigh heavily upon him, and he closed his eyes as if trying to escape their weight. It was the first time I had seen my father without his linen crown. He wore his thin hair closely cropped in the old fashion. His hair was gray and receded deeply around his forehead. Only his breathing disrupted the quiet of the room, a shallow breathing that made thin sounds in his chest whenever the air escaped his lungs. To my young eye he did not appear troubled by the nearness of death. There was instead a curiously tranquil expression in his face, a peaceful sense of quiet tiredness of a man seeking to sleep and rest before seeing another dawn. Looking at him I did not know if I should disturb his slumber or not, if it was slumber at all. And so I just stood there, quiet, looking at his face in a way that I had never been able to do when life flowed strongly in him.

And then I left. I never saw my father again after that. Two weeks later Thutmose II, the Great Lion of Egypt, passed to the

Fields of the Marshes to dwell forever with the other gods and Egypt was plunged into three months of official mourning led by Hatshepsut, my father's queen.

I spent the first few days after his death with my mother sharing our grief at the passing of the man who loved us both. Each night I returned to my quarters in the palace where I slept only fitfully. Sinub remained at my side more alert now than ever. Paremheb was occupied with the funeral arrangements and traveled from the palace to the embalmer's temple almost daily. I had not seen nor heard from him in more than a week when Djet burst into my apartment in a rage.

"Paremheb is dead my prince!" His face was flushed. He swallowed hard and gulped for air as he sought the words to give voice to his anger.

"The bastard sons of Seth have assassinated him!"

He stood before me in a boil. He swung his arms against the air as if trying to strike a phantom. Djet's body was tense as stone but he could not stand still. He began to pace back and forth in front of me. Sinub and I waited for him to get a grip on his rage and calm down.

Sinub moved quickly to the open door that Djet had left behind him and looked into the corridor. Satisfied, he closed the door, crossed the room and stood next to me. Djet moved in front of him and Sinub's arm shot out and caught him by the shoulder.

"Easy colonel," he said. "Get hold of yourself." His voice was stern but still that of a subordinate addressing a superior officer. "Tell us what happened." His eyes moved from Djet to me and back again. "What happened?" he said.

Djet sat down and rubbed his eyes. "He was attacked and killed this morning. Stabbed in the heart and in the eye." Djet shook his head and let his breath escape in a great rush. "It was near where the embalmers are doing their work. Paremheb had just stepped from his sedan chair when three men rushed him. The porters said he was taken by surprise and was dead in seconds." He looked at me. "The assassins escaped. The porters were so shocked at the attack that no one thought to follow after them." Djet's face had returned to its normal color but the tension in his body betrayed his lingering anger. "The bastards!" he shouted. He stood up and began to pace back and forth across the room.

Sinub's eyes followed his superior officer and then turned toward me. The expression on my face must have revealed the confusion and fear that filled my mind. Who could have killed him? Who gained by his death? I had not a single answer to these questions. The assassination of a major government official right in the capitol was serious business. Whoever his enemies were, they were powerful and well-placed. And if they could strike at the Chancellor they could strike at anyone. They could strike at me.

Djet stopped pacing for the moment and stood with his arms folded saying nothing. "Have you searched Djet's office and apartments?" I asked. It had finally dawned on me that whoever ordered Paremheb killed must have had a very good motive for doing so. Someone may have learned about the meeting with Pharaoh. Paremheb's death removed one of the important witness to my father's decree that I be his successor. If that was true, then all who were present that night were in danger. As dramatic as Paremheb's death was, it would be meaningless without destroying my father's last testament. The document had been entrusted to Paremheb for safekeeping. Now that he was gone I had to find it. Without the testament my claim to the throne was impossible to enforce on a court packed with the queen's men.

My question brought the flush of anger back to Djet's face. "Yes, my prince," he said. "I myself searched his office." He paused and lowered his eyes as if confessing to a failure. "Nothing," he said. "I found nothing of importance. Wherever Paremheb hid the testament, he took the secret to his grave with him."

I took a deep breath and sighed. I rose from my chair and walked slowly over to the window. The air was hot but it felt good as it caressed my face. "Is there any reason to think that the testament may have fallen into the hands of our enemies?" I was beginning to have dark thoughts and my voice reflected my somber mood. Neither Sinub or Djet spoke. It was, of course, a pointless question. Without the testament in my possession, my claim to the throne was based on little more than my own words and the witness of Djet and Mentuhotep. It did not matter if my enemies possessed the document. What was important was that I did not possess it. It was unlikely that even the testimony of the Chief Prophet would force the queen and her ambitious followers to give up the throne of Egypt. It was a dark time. I instructed Djet to continue his search. When he left I sat down upon the couch and fell into a deep gloom that lasted well into the evening.

It was very late when we heard the knock on the apartment door. Sinub was instantly alert. He approached the door with his hand on the hilt of his *kopesh* and opened it carefully. In the dim light of the oil lamps two guardsmen stood at attention with their shields and spears drawn back against their bodies. I rose from the couch and made my way toward the doorway. A tall figure dressed in the long robe of a high government official stood behind the bodyguards. The smoothness of his shaven head was disturbed by a band of cloth tied around his forehead and knotted at the back of his skull. The extra cloth ends hung from the knot down to the base of his neck. His feet were covered by the softest sandals and he carried the staff of his office in his right hand. The man's eyes were small, almost like beads, and deeply set. Strong bones formed the ridges of his eye sockets providing plenty of purchase for bushy eyebrows to take root. His was a common face that could be found on any corner in Thebes. And that was as it should be, for Senenmut was born a commoner who had worked his way into the confidence of one government official after another until he stood before my door as the most trusted advisor of the Great Queen Hatshepsut.

I stood in the open door and addressed my self to him. "What is it that you wish Senenmut?" I permitted my annoyance to make itself plain in my voice. "It is late. Most honest men are already asleep. What could be so important as to require your presence at my door at so late an hour?" It was not a question as much as it was an attempt to dismiss him. I had little to gain by a conversation with the toady of my sworn enemy. I glared at the man trying to intimidate him.

Senenmut was an old hand at this game and merely smiled in amusement at my antics.

"I do apologize, highness. But I am sent by the queen herself." He paused and a smirk crossed his lips. "The Great Queen is not one to be ignored when she makes a request." It was as if he was sharing a private joke and he gave out with a short laugh. "This hour I am to bring you to an audience with the queen."

I started to speak in a loud voice to protest when Senenmut's voice cut me off before I could get a word out. He extended his hand toward me with his palm outward as if to form a wall to my very words.

"There is, I'm afraid, no choice offered you by her highness."

His tone was almost ominous like a man who had run out of patience. An angry look crept over my face. Sinub had been standing behind me and the change in Senenmut's voice caught Sinub's attention. He moved next to me. He stared straight at Senenmut his hand on the hilt of his *kopesh*. There was no mistaking the threat.

Senenmut was not intimidated. I extended my arm to my side as if to block any further advance by my bodyguard. Sinub stared straight into Senenmut's eyes. The advisor ignored him and looked at me with an expression on his face that told me to stop this foolishness and get on with what had to be done this evening. He was right, of course, there was no choice.

"I shall take Sinub with me," I said. It was a statement of independence to masque my capitulation.

Senenmut smiled and nodded.

"There is no need, of course. You will be perfectly safe." He shrugged. "But if it puts you at ease, highness, your bodyguard may certainly accompany you at your pleasure." He paused for a moment and glanced at Sinub. "It would be much better if you could instruct him to remove his hand from his weapon unless he is prepared to use it. That way he will not be attacked by some overzealous guardsman trying to protect the queen." He flashed a cynical grin at Sinub then turned away and led us down the long corridor toward the queen's apartments.

Queen Hatshepsut sat on a large chair that looked every bit like a great throne. She was perched upon a platform from which she could look down upon the rest of the room. Senenmut escorted me across the room and stopped at the bottom of the steps. He lowered his eyes and bowed deeply in a gesture of respect. I ignored the gesture and stood where I was.

"Well, my boy, we meet at last."

A grin of satisfaction spread over her face and she leaned forward to get a better look at me. I had no idea of how I appeared to her. But to me she seemed a formidable presence. Much of what I had seen in her daughter, Nefurure, was chiseled in the stone that was the original. She was large for a woman, taller and heavier than my father whose half-sister she was as well as his wife. Dark eyes against dark skin gave her a Nubian appearance, but her thin upturned nose was typically Egyptian and her most beautiful adornment. Above all she radiated confidence and strength. This was not a woman to be taken lightly as, I guessed, my father had learned. And why not? She was the daughter of a great general, my grandfather Thutmose I. Strength ran in the breed. It was only necessary to witness her bearing to sense that she had no intention of giving up her position no matter what the cost.

I stood there not knowing what to say. "What is it you wish of me?" I muttered at last. It was a question without guile, for I had absolutely no idea why I had been summoned.

She smiled and her face looked for an instant like that of a cat who has cornered a mouse.

"Though you are not of my body, you are still the son of my husband. His appointment of you as regent before his death makes you a member of the royal family now that Pharaoh is gone." A pleasant almost sincere expression crossed her face. "Your mourning is felt by me as well, Thutmose. You must believe that," she said. It was as if she were a mother talking to a son.

I looked at her unwilling to avert my eyes lest I betray my fear that I would reveal my own weakness before her in that instant. I felt trapped. I was alone with no allies. And here I stood before the queen of Egypt listening to her tell me of my fate. It must be what it feels like to be a condemned man...or a mouse cornered by a cat.

"Because you are regent I expect you to fulfill your official duties at the funeral of the Great Lion. Senenmut and his staff will advise you as to what you are to do." It was said without harshness but without question either. Out of the corner of my eye I saw Senenmut offer a slight bow as a smirk crossed his face. "And when Pharaoh is placed in his tomb and laid to rest for all time, then you and I will speak again." Her eyes probed my face for any sign of a reaction. I did the best I could to hide the uncertainty I felt in my bones.

I kept my silence, bowed slightly, and turned to leave. I had taken but a few steps when Hatshepsut's voice fell upon my ears once more. This time there was sarcasm in her tone as she called to me.

"Before you go, Thutmose, there is someone I want you to meet."

I turned around to face her just as she clapped her hands with a loud crack that echoed off the walls of the chamber. To my left I caught sight of a door opening and turned my eyes in that direction. Intef entered the room dressed in the white robes of his profession. He carried the *"sekhem* with two eyes," the short staff inlaid with gold and lapis lazuli that was the symbol of office of the Chief Prophet of the Temple of Amun-Ra. The priest glanced at me but would not meet my eyes. He remained off to the side of the queen looking at her in silence.

Hatshepsut's eyes lit up. The cat was toying with her prey and having a good time of it. "I believe you know Intef?" she said. I said nothing. "Come now. Surely you must know each other! Why it was only a few days ago that he was telling me how it was that so many people thought you might make a good king." Her voice wore the false face of mock surprise. "Why would anyone say that unless he knew you?" she said her voice dripping with venomous sarcasm.

I wished only to be free of this woman and her evil words. But even that was beyond my power. I looked at Intef who stared straight ahead. Senenmut had moved to where he stood next to the queen. He looked down on me with a wry smile. He was, after all, a commoner and had in his time witnessed many of his class humiliated and oppressed by unjust officials and nobles. Perhaps he saw my plight in much the same way except this time one of the tormentors was being tormented. No matter how high they rose, men like Senenmut never forgot their origins. Even when they had become nobles themselves they took special pleasure in watching the high-borns suffer torment, more so when the torment was visited by the high-born hands. In their world it was what passed for justice for a thousand slights that went unpunished.

Hatshepsut turned her eyes toward Intef. "I am sure Thutmose would rather hear it from you Intef," she said. Her voice was cold. "Tell him!" she shouted.

The commanding sound of her harsh voice took the priest by surprise and at first he said nothing. Gathering his wits he stumbled over his words until, finally, he was able to speak clearly.

"It is with great sorrow, Oh prince, that I tell you that your teacher, Mentuhotep Chief Prophet of Amun, is dead." Intef bowed his head and spoke in a solemn and respectful tone. And in my bones I knew it was false.

The look on my face must have revealed my surprise. I saw Senenmut's lips form a thin smile as he glanced in the direction of the queen. She sat upon her great chair with an easy confidence watching Intef's face flush and the veins in his neck swell. Always Intef averted his eyes from mine. Even when I asked him about Mentuhotep's death he did not look at me.

"The Chief Prophet was found dead this morning," he said. "I went to bring him to prayers and found him dead." Intef's face was crimson with guilt. His words had the hollow ring of someone who had badly rehearsed his part and could not wait for the play to be finished so he could escape his deserved embarrassment. Intef was as guilty as man's first sin was old. But had learned the first rule of betrayal, that a man who lies can be as comfortable and successful as one who tells the truth provided he just keeps on lying.

I looked at the queen. The look of satisfaction on her face was unmistakable. She made no effort to conceal her feelings. And then, as if in a vision, my mind made some sense of it all. It started when Intef stumbled upon our meeting with Pharaoh. Mentuhotep trusted him and must have told Intef about Pharaoh's testament and the Chief Prophet's intention to swear to Pharaoh's wish to place his son on the throne of Egypt. To further his own ambitions Intef found his way to Senenmut. In return for his appointment as the new Chief Prophet, he told him about the testament. Senenmut then had Paremheb killed. The Chancellor had the testament in his possession and thus was the most dangerous of the conspirators. Paremheb's assassination was the signal to Intef to poison Mentuhotep. Senenmuts' men may even have found Paremheb's copy of the testament. But it was of no consequence now.

I had failed and now I stood before my enemies. I would find out soon enough what fate Hatshepsut had in store for me.

# Sixteen

For the next three months there was nothing to do but wait. Pharaoh's body was in the hands of the embalmers who prepared it for entombment in the same hideous manner that I had seen them prepare Lanata's mortal remains. All Egypt waited for the embalmers to complete their task and deliver the mummified corpse of the Lion of Egypt so that it could be properly honored and then, at last, sealed in stone for eternity.

From time to time I made an appearance at court at the command of the queen. During these appearances I was always seated to the right and behind the Great Queen. The chair upon which I sat was small lest anyone mistake it for a throne. I was never spoken to nor permitted to speak. There had been no coronation to enthrone a new pharaoh. The queen made it clear to the court that I held only the title of regent, nothing more. Hatshepsut continued to rule as co-regent, a situation that in past times lasted until the regent came of age and assumed his place as pharaoh. Hatshepsut ruled in the name of the next pharaoh. But it required eyes as dead as Mentuhotep's not so see that Hatshepsut would never relinquish power to me unless she were dead!

The precarious nature of my circumstances was adequately revealed one day when Djet came to my apartment. The queen had permitted me to remain in my old quarters. Djet entered and walked to where I sat gloomily staring out the window into the dying sun.

"I hope you are feeling well, my prince," he said.

His voice was low with his own gloom. I turned to him and smiled, but did not rise to greet him. In truth I was surprised that he was still alive. His role in the conspiracy had not gone unnoticed nor had the queen forgiven his loyalty to me.

"I have sad news, highness." He paused and bit his lower lip as if in pain. "I have been removed as commander of the royal guard." He shook his head in disgust. "Her highness no longer trusts me and I am to be sent to another regiment. Some of my officers are to be sent with me."

His eyes had a sadness in them that I had seen before in injured animals. It was not that he did not understand his fate. Only that he had not yet come to accept it. For a man like Djet acceptance was always more difficult. His breeding pressed him to fight until he could fight no more. But slowly even he had to admit that his fate was no longer in his hands. Not wishing to add to Djet's gloom, I tried to put a pleasant tone in my voice.

"Where are you to be sent?" I asked.

"Buhen!" he answered. "Its off to some god-forsaken Nubian outpost guarding the second cataract of the Nile." He shook his head. "Nubia!" His voice rose to a shout. "Who can suffer the place."

Djet's anger had turned into a self-mockery of sorts that he focused now on his next posting. As a young officer Djet had fought in two campaigns in Nubia. More than once he had told me what a terrible place it was with its sandy brown earth and no trees. Still it was better than a shallow grave in the eastern desert, a fate that might have befallen him had the queen taken a harsher view of his questionable loyalties. After all, Paremheb and

Mentuhotep had both been eliminated. There was no doubt that my step-mother would resort to murder if need be. To her credit she had some sense of proportion in assessing the danger her enemies posed to her. And in Djet's case he was just a loyal soldier who backed the wrong horse. Not a capital offense certainly, but not one that could be overlooked.

Sinub sat on the couch while Djet and I spoke. Now he rose and walked over to Djet and placed his hand on the shoulders of his fellow officer. As he did so his eyes sought me out.

"And so, Djet," he said with a false smile, "is there no news of my fate?" He looked at me again and smiled as if to assure me that things were alright. Djet glanced over his shoulder at Sinub and then turned back to me.

"I am afraid, my prince, that Sinub is to be sent away as well," he said. "He is to be posted to Siwa and the garrison there."

The mention of Siwa provoked a grimace on Sinub's face and his eyebrows came together producing a deep furrow across his brow. Siwa was one of the most barren places in all Egypt! The Siwa oasis located deep in the Libyan desert was one of a string of five oases that ran along the rim of the border between Libya and Egypt. Unlike other oases where fresh water pools and wells made it possible to live a civilized existence, most of the water at Siwa came from warm springs that turned the place into a steaming insect ridden marsh where no respite from the blazing heat could be found no matter what the season of the year. The place had no economic or agricultural value at all. The oasis was garrisoned by a small number of troops who kept watch on the Libyan nomads. The troops were also jailers for this dismal oasis had long been used as a place of exile for trouble makers and others who fell from favor in the court. Prisoners were forced to live in miserable conditions and tend the marshes for whatever might be coaxed from them. It was a miserable posting and Sinub could not be blamed for believing that he had suffered a harsh punishment as the price of his loyalty to me.

Within a week my loyal allies had departed Thebes I was alone with my fears. The days passed slowly and the weeks seemed like months for an existence that no longer had much meaning. Except for the few command appearances at court, I rarely was permitted to venture beyond my apartments. Sinub's departure for Siwa left me without a bodyguard and it did not take long for me to realize that I was completely defenseless. Should the queen decide that my death served her interests, my demise could be accomplished in a matter of hours. This sense of vulnerability made a strong impression on my mind. It was many years before I truly rid myself of it. My circumstances made it difficult for me to retain my faith in the dream that one day by right I would rule Egypt. I had many nights when sleep would not come. I discovered, too, that the enemy of one's will is despair. Had the imprisonment gone on much longer I would likely have abandoned my dreams altogether.

Almost three months passed since my father's death before the embalmers finished their work and the preparations for the funeral were complete. It was the end of *Akhet*, the season of inundation, and my father was laid to rest a few days after my ninth birthday. Senenmut came to me bearing instructions as to how I was to conduct myself during the funeral ceremonies. In truth there was little for me to do but take part in the procession and sit where I was told to sit.

The ceremonies began with the presentation of my father's body at the gates of Thebes. Large crowds gathered to watch the priests of Anubis carry the sarcophagus from the Nile quay to the city's main gate. A procession of priests moved to the slow cadence of the funeral drum. Between each beat the air filled with the shooshing of sistrum rattles that made a sound like a strong wind struggling to escape the embrace of a thick willow. It was the sound of Pharaoh's *Ba*, the winged creature with the body of a bird and a human face that hovered over the coffin seeking its place of rest in the tomb. Slowly the procession made its way over the short distance up the hill to the city gate. Tears streamed from the eyes of the people of Egypt in great torrents that day and the wailing voices of women filled the air with sorrow.

From my seat on the raised platform that held the queen and her trusted advisers I watched the procession approach. A blue cloth canopy with painted white stars protected the assembly from the sun. I sat behind the queen at the far end of a row of chairs occupied by her advisers. Senenmut sat directly behind Hatshepsut where he could reach her ear should he be required to whisper advice. Off to Senenmut's right sat the vile Intef, murderer of Mentuhotep, and now Chief Prophet of Amun-Ra. A military guard surrounded the assembly and pressed the crowd back upon itself for a considerable distance to provide room for the casket to be laid at the feet of the queen. And then the drum went quiet and the sistrum ceased its serpent's hiss. The great container of death was laid upon the earth of Egypt so that my father might look one more time upon Thebes and feel the touch of the Black Land upon his body. A great wail went up from the crowd and the noise crashed over us like rushing water.

Had I not known of the hideous remains that the casket concealed perhaps I, too, might have wept. But whatever was left of my father's essence had long since fled, and visions of Lanata's mutilated corpse would not leave my mind. It was the first time I had seen one of the new style coffins, although it had some of the features of the one that Tabu had selected for Lanata. The coffin was formed from linen and wood in the shape of a man. What were supposed to be my father's features were painted on the face. To my last memory his face was that of a sick old man and the features painted on the coffin resembled no one I knew. Painted silver wings—the *Rishi* of Horus—went completely around the coffin to symbolize that the deceased already lay in the embrace of the great god. Texts of the Book of the Dead were carved upon the casket lid while the complete set of spells were inscribed on the Book itself that lay inside the coffin at the feet of the deceased. The beautiful container was itself a facade, merely the outer shell of two more coffins within it, each more beautiful than the other. Beneath the outer coffin lay another more richly carved and painted and inlaid with precious woods, lapiz lazuli, silver, and gold. This, too, held still another coffin that held the mummy itself. The first coffin of the Great Lion was fashioned of solid gold inlaid with precious stones. The death mask, too, was of gold and electrum, perfectly fashioned by craftsmen to be as lifelike as possible. If I could have seen it perhaps here I would have found the face of my father as I once knew it.

The Chief Prophet stood and raised his staff and a heavy silence fell upon the crowd. Intef was enjoying his new authority. He exaggerated his every movement as he made his way from the platform to where the body lay upon the earth. An assistant handed him an incense pot suspended from a chain. Intef walked around the body allowing great clouds of incense to fall from the swaying pot upon the coffin. He anointed the body with the touch of "the *sekhem* with two eyes" and led the priests in the recitation of prayers for the dead. The priestly murmur died gradually as the prayers were completed. Intef moved a few paces and stood at the head of the coffin looking up at the queen. He murmured something I could not make out and the queen rose from her chair. As if on cue, the rest of the assembly rose. Hatshepsut made her way down the stairs and over to the coffin. The rest of us followed not quite knowing what to do. Intef bowed deeply to the queen. He turned and gestured to the priests who then raised the coffin to their shoulders. Intef made his way to the head of the procession. With a wave of his hand he started to lead the priests, musicians, pall bearers and the assembled nobles back down the road that led to the quay.

The royal barge lay at anchor alongside the quay. The honor guard, assembled from the men of the *Eaters of the Dead*, the royal guard, snapped to attention as the procession approached. Oarsmen stood rigidly at their posts, oars raised in naval salute. The vessel's captain waited at the foot of the gangplank to escort the body of his pharaoh aboard. The *Star Of Two Countries* lay at her anchor gleaming in the sun. It was the largest and most beautiful boat in all Egypt. Over a hundred and sixty feet long her external hull planking was richly painted in bright colors and complex designs. Her deck was polished to a bright shine. On a platform behind the prow of the boat stood a life sized painted statue of the Mighty Bull of Egypt trampling his enemies under its hooves. Upon command the oarsmen sat in seats attached to the gunwales and slid their oars through oarlocks made of rope. The mast was a single timber of Lebanon cedar to which was attached a great crossbeam almost forty feet in length around which the huge blue sail was carefully wrapped. The large deck house had plaster walls. Brightly colored paintings and tapestries decorated the interior. Even the small booths for the captain and the helmsman were decorated like small chapels. The raised quarterdeck usually held the thrones of the king and his queen. For this journey one of the thrones had been removed to make space for the coffin.

The priests carried the coffin up the gangplank and placed it reverently upon the quarterdeck. With deep bows they relinquished their burden and took up places behind the statue of the Mighty Bull. Senenmut walked by the queen's side and steered her to her place at the head of the coffin. Ever the clever one

Senenmut arranged for the queen's throne to be removed so that Hatshepsut sat upon Pharaoh's throne as she escorted the body of her husband across the Nile! A muffled noise ran through the assembly of advisors when they saw Hatshepsut assume her place on the great throne. The murmur was quickly silenced by a snarling glare cast in the direction of the group by the obviously annoyed queen. Hatshepsut turned and resumed her demeanor as the grieving widow. A thin smile creased her face as her eyes caught mine. It was the expression of someone who had achieved a great ambition and cared nothing for what it cost.

The *Star Of Two Countries* carried Pharaoh with great dignity on his last journey across the Nile. The oars barely rippled the surface of the mighty river as they dipped beneath the water and pulled the great boat closer to the quay on the west bank. Even the wind was still, and it seemed to me that there were no birds in the air. It was as if all creation had paused to watch the passing of the great king. The far bank was lined with people for as far as the eye could see. Behind the quay were thousands of others standing along the narrow road that connected the river with the mortuary temple. The road through the mountains that led to the tomb itself was closed and guarded by soldiers. Pharaoh would be lifted to his tomb just before sunset so his place of final rest would be seen by as few people as possible.

The *Star* pulled alongside the quay and the crew made fast her lines. The gangplank was lowered into place coming to rest on the stone without a sound. At the word of the Chief Prophet, the pall bearers lifted the coffin and carried it from the boat and up the riverbank. There the great sled awaited its burden. With great reverence the body of Pharaoh was placed upon it like a precious relic upon an altar. The procession began to assemble along the road that it would travel bearing Pharaoh's coffin to the mortuary temple for the ceremony required for the great king to begin his life among the gods.

The death of a king is an important event and the enormous size of the official procession reflected this fact. There were several thousand people who had come to honor their king. The time required to prepare Pharaoh's corpse was sufficient so that thousands of important people had been able to make the journey to Thebes in time for the funeral. The important noble families of Egypt were there, as were the richest merchants and high government officials. Generals and members of the diplomatic corps travelled from their postings to attend the burial. The chief priests of every temple of every god in all *Kemit* were assembled. Even a gathering of foreign princes and lesser kings were present. All expected to take part in the great procession. Organizing the march so as not to slight important guests required the talent of a general. It was, of course, too important a task to be left to military men so Senenmut and his henchmen had seen to it.

The procession formed along the riverbank running from the road back from the river. This permitted each segment to join behind the other and follow the head of the great snake as it led the way along the road to the mortuary temple two miles away. The queen and the official party took seats in a shaded pavilion near the funeral sled until it was their time to join the line. Each element of the great parade passed before us as it made its way one by one down the road.

First in line came the chariots, units of the king's personal guard. The machines had been newly painted for the occasion and each one carried a driver and archer in full battle dress their polished weapons glistening in the bright sun. The chariots were pulled by pairs of white horses with carefully braided manes. Reins painted gold and cross braces colored deep blue contrasted brightly with the pale white of the animals' skin. The machines moved in pairs past the great sled bearing the body of their fallen sovereign. Battle pennants dipped in honor before the bier as the machines passed in review.

Next came the infantry marching along in slow cadence, spears and shields at the ready. Behind them the archery units with their brightly colored bow cases and arrow quivers slung from their shoulders. Then the famous "Braves," elite soldiers known for their courage to undertake dangerous missions. A contingent of Nubian mercenaries resplendent in bright tribal dress and head pieces contrasting brightly with their dark skinned bodies came next. The Nubian irregulars were masters at hit and run tactics and fought alongside the army against the raiders of the eastern desert. Contingents of these Nubian soldiers had served in the Egyptian army for more than a thousand years. Even when they were required to fight against their fellow countrymen in the many wars between the two countries, the Nubians' reputation for loyalty to their commanders was untarnished.

A delegation of visiting priests walked behind the Nubians. The expressions on their faces portrayed their great unhappiness with their place in the procession. They had been told they would be near the front and naturally assumed it was a position of honor. When it turned out that they were marching in the dust of soldiers and chariots, their disappointment turned to anger and then to despair. It seemed it was always so with priests. They were men accustomed to respect and deference in their own temples. But here in Thebes at the funeral of a king even the most respected priest of a temple outside the capitol was likely to be regarded as just one more troublesome guest. Still they came walking through the dust of the soldiers and chariots that covered their shaven skulls with a thin gray film and stuck to everything it touched.

Pharaoh's menagerie followed the priests. Cages carried on the shoulders of bearers had poles sufficiently long so an angry cat did

not reach one of the bearers with a swiping paw. Scores of animals
were carried past their master in final respect. The last of the great
beasts to pass were the two trained lions that my father loved so
much. Both walked regally along restrained only by a thin chain
held by their handlers. There was no ill-discipline in their passing,
only a sturdy dignity and sense of strength that set them apart
from all that had already passed. Clear eyes set deep in magnificent skulls took in all about them as the beasts' widened nostrils
sniffed angrily at the air. When, at last, they reached the bier, one
of the great cats stopped next to the coffin. Its huge maned head
turned toward the sled. I saw the beginnings of panic well up in
the eyes of the animal's handler. The lion took a few steps toward
the coffin and sniffed it. Its ears stood straight up and its eyes narrowed as if searching for prey. Again the beast sniffed the air. In a
graceful movement the animal's head snapped back as it threw its
full power into its lungs and let loose with a mighty roar that
echoed off the Theban hills like thunder. Its eyes widened and the
beast shook its mighty head as if in anger at the death of its master. And then the great cat walked on and took its place among the
mourners who had come to honor their king.

The band broke into a dirge as it approached the bier. The
paced Thump!...Thump!...Thump! of the funeral drums beat out
a mournful cadence whose echo bounced off the mountains with
great force. Rows of tambourine players beat their instruments in
time with the smaller snare drums that struck at the half beat
between the thumps of the funeral drums. Next came the trumpets
with their shrill voices filling the air with a sound like the screech
of the desert shrikes that inhabited the mountains of the Valley of
the Kings. Low sounding oboes and pipes gave forth with a deep
wailing that calmed the ear and lessened the harshness of the
trumpets. The last to pass were the scores of women with clappers
and rattles that filled the air with the hiss of a rushing wind.

Their's was the most sacred sound. The cadence of the rattle was broken at regular intervals by the sharp snap of the clapper giving a murmured sound like the beating of the wings of Pharaoh's *Ba* as it hovered above his coffin.

But to me the mixture of sounds and cadences fell harshly upon the ear. It was as if each section of instruments had badly memorized some pattern of sounds with little regard for the sounds of the others. The result was more sound than music, more noise than harmony, more thumping than rhythm. Later when my armies brought musicians from other lands to my court, I learned that Egypt had no system of musical notation like other peoples and that each musician memorized what he was taught to play. No wonder, then, that the group of musicians at my father's funeral provided little in the way of genuine comfort to the mourners or the deceased!

The throngs of professional mourners took their places in line and started to move toward us. With thousands of Egypt's people burdened by sorrow at the death of their king it seemed strange that it was necessary to hire professional mourners at all. The mourners were women and there must have been a hundred of them walking along the road, their bodies swaying from side to side so as to give the impression of being on the edge of fainting from grief. Their blue dresses tied tightly around the waist flowed in sensual patterns toward the ground. The women were naked from the waist, and hundreds of shapely breasts bounced from side to side and up and down as the great collection of females moved their bodies in a sensuous dance of mourning. Curiously, the women wore no wigs. Long black hair was permitted to hang over their faces and shoulders in a symbol of grief. The mourners wailed as they passed the bier. They threw fistfuls of dirt in the air and the wailing grew louder and louder. Some clawed at their breasts while others pulled at their hair as if trying to pull it from its roots. The noise became a frenzy the closer they came to the coffin and some had to be restrained by the guards from throwing themselves on the great sled that held Pharaoh's earthly remains. Even the most cynical could be forgiven for failing to remember that the mourners were professionals hired for the occasion. All in all it was a magnificent performance, no doubt well worth whatever it cost.

My eye was drawn to a movement in front of me. Senenmut leaned over and whispered in Hatshepsut's ear. She nodded and rose from her chair. As if on signal, the other officials and guests rose from their seats. Not knowing what else to do I stood also. The queen made her way to the front of the great sled. One by one the guests filed past Senenmut and took up their positions behind the queen. When it came my turn Senenmut placed his hand on my shoulder and pulled me aside nodding politely to the next person in line who walked down the stairs and took his assigned place. In a few moments only Senenmut and I remained on the platform.

"Please, your highness," he said in a voice that was not unpleasant "let us both find a seat." He led me to the back row of chairs and sat down beside me.

"As you see the Great Queen will shortly lead the procession bearing her husband to the mortuary temple." He smiled. "The others will help pull the sled!" He gave out a short laugh. Even I smiled at the thought of high ranking nobles and government officials trying to move the enormous vehicle over the road by their own power.

Senenmut looked at me and spoke. "The queen will lead the way by herself, for it is important for the people of Egypt to see who it is that truly governs this land." He said it without any harshness in his voice. There was no threatening tone, only the air of certainty as if what he said was already carved in stone and impossible to change. I looked at him and said nothing. It was not the time to engage in a debate about who was the true ruler of Egypt.

"Look," he said. "Here come the great bulls."

Ten pairs of pure white oxen were led by their handlers into position in front of the sled. The horns of the animals were painted gold and their yokes brightly painted in red and blue. The animal's noses were pierced with metal rings which their handlers used to control the beasts. Each pair of animals wore a double yoke over their broad shoulders. Thick ropes ran from the yoke rings back between each pair of beasts where they were tied to the yoke rings of the oxen behind them. In this way the power of twenty oxen was harnessed to haul the sled. It took only a few minutes for the teams of oxen to be brought into position. Now the guests and officials took up their places alongside the oxen where they could be seen to be helping pull the weight of the great sled. My eyes fell upon the vile Intef who jostled others for a place at the head of the line. As with much in Egypt, form is often regarded as substance. Everyone knew that the guests were not really pulling anything. Nonetheless it was a great honor to walk with the oxen *as if* one were pulling the weight with them.

I sat beside Senenmut watching the priests make the tow lines fast to the sled. The great bier was a large rectangular wooden box ten feet long and six feet across. A thick wooden post ten feet high in each corner supported a canopy made of fruitwood with a curved interior. The inside the canopy was painted the deep blue of the night sky. Bright white and gold stars adorned the sky so during his journey my father could gaze upon the face of Nut, the goddess of the eternal heavens. Outside, the canopy was richly painted in bright designs of many colors. Each post was carved and painted in the form of giant papyrus stalks. The platform upon which the coffin rested was constructed of pine wood and inlaid with precious ebony and fruitwoods. Paintings of the gods of Thebes—Amun, Montu, and Mut—adorned the sides of the platform and told all who looked upon them that Pharaoh's presence among the gods was already accomplished. Green pennants flew from the top of each post. Green was the color of creation and life. Its presence on the bier was symbolic of the new life and resurrection that Pharaoh would enjoy in heaven. The bier and coffin rested upon a large wooden sled that moved over the ground on runners. As the oxen pulled, teams of workman poured rivulets of wet desert clay in front of the runners to lubricate them and make the sled move easily. In some places wooden rollers were placed before the runners and the sled dragged over them. It was the way for thousands of years that we Egyptians moved the great stones with which to construct the pyramids and our temples.

The ropes went taut and the oxen strained against the yokes. Workers moved around the sled pouring clay and water on the ground. Priests with censers moved about the sled bathing it in clouds of incense from their fiery pots. At first nothing happened. Then the great sled lurched forward and the procession of the bier got underway at last. Senenmut turned to me.

"It is time for us to take our places," he said. I stood next to him in front of the platform watching the sled move slowly before us. Behind the sled a group of white-robed priests waited to fall in behind the bier. Suddenly my eyes widened in surprise. Standing before the priests was Nefurure! The sled passed before us and I felt Senenmut's hand on my shoulder.

"Here, highness, is where we will take our place." He led me next to Nefurure. "I assume you two know each other?" he said with a smirk. The man's ability to sense things was incredible. He most certainly knew about the meeting between Nefurure and me and had bided his time until just the right moment to take greatest advantage of what he knew. I looked at him and shook my head in amazement and disgust. Nefurure's eyes glowered with anger and she spit at Senenmut's feet.

Senenmut walked behind us as my sister and I trailed behind the coffin sled, the perfect portrait of the king's two children. And that, indeed, was precisely the point that Hatshepsut wished to convey to her subjects. Children! The chosen regent of her husband was only a child and therefore not yet fit to rule. Hatshepsut, the Great Wife and queen, would rule in his name and in his stead until the poor boy was old enough to do it himself. Of course, no one could really say what might happen in that time. It was in the hands of the gods to determine when the regent might assume the throne. Nefurure, as always, carried the womb through which future pharaohs would enter this world should something happen to the child-regent. It was all very uncertain, of course, and all that could be done had been done. In the meantime Egypt had her queen and the fate of Egypt was in her hands.

The procession was already a mile long and still more of it was to come. The priests of Amun who walked behind me were followed by another sled. This one was smaller than the one that carried Pharaoh's coffin and was pulled by four men dressed in the bright red robes and jackal masks of Anubis, the god of the dead. A small figure wrapped in a hooded robe lay on its side upon the sled, its legs drawn up to its chest. This was the *tekenu*. In ancient times the sins of the king were transferred to another by means of ceremony. When the king was laid to rest this other was slain on the spot and buried in the king's tomb. The *tekenu* represented the sins and evil-doings of the deceased, and was offered to the gods as punishment for his evil deeds. Of course the *tekenu* was no longer slain. But if the gods demand punishment before the deceased is allowed to pass to the Marsh of the Reeds, the punishment falls upon the *tekenu*.

It was hot. Before I had walked only a short distance my throat was dry. I called one of the servants who moved up and down the line bringing water to the participants. He brought cool water from a jug. A wet cloth refreshed my face. The procession halted far up front and I found myself on top of a small rise from which I could look back over the rest of the procession still forming behind me. From where I stood I saw the great canopic chest being carried on the shoulders of more than twenty bearers. The large wooden square chest was covered with bronze and gold and contained the mummified organs of the deceased, each carefully sealed in an alabaster jar. The lid of each jar was fashioned in the figure of one of the four Sons of Horus whose presence protected the organ from harm. A statue of Isis fashioned of bronze and leafed with gold stood on a small platform on each side of the chest. Priests with pots spread clouds of incense before and behind while the pall-bearers suffered in the hot sun under the weight of their burden.

Next came hundreds of servants carrying household goods to fill the antechamber of Pharaoh's tomb. There were beds and fine linens, all kinds of *ushabtis*, model soldiers, animals, and boats, chairs, tables, chests of dinnerware, gold cups, and fine clothing, all for the use of the king in the life hereafter. In the middle of the long line of servants came the royal treasure hauled on sleds drawn by squads of soldiers. Gold masks and figurines of various types carefully wrapped in cloth and placed within gold and ebony chests filled the treasure sleds. Thousands of gold, silver, and copper rings of many *deben* weights were placed in bulging linen sacks so that all might see the wealth of Pharaoh. This great wealth would be sealed forever in the tomb's treasure room so Pharaoh might be able to live as a king among kings in the next life.

The white oxen strained at the ropes pulling the great sled and the procession began to move again. It required two hours for the sled to reach the mortuary temple. Standing upon the temple steps watching the pall-bearers lift the coffin from its platform I could see the entire length of the procession stretching as far back as the Nile. Like a giant serpent whose head had been cut off but whose body still writhed, the funeral procession continued long into the night. I stood with Senenmut and Nefurure off to the side of the assembly of guests watching Hatsepsut stand at the top of the stairs and prepare to receive her husband. The pall-bearers moved with a deliberate slowness that bordered on ritual. Then suddenly the steps were filled with hundreds of *Muu* ritual dancers wearing strange headdresses of reeds and dancing to the sound of the tambourine and sistrum rattle. They danced alone, snapping their fingers and keeping rhythm with their instruments. Their bodies jiggled and swayed. They used brooms fashioned of reeds and rushes in movements that swept away any spirits that might hinder the passage of the Great One into the temple.

All this commotion swirled around Hatshepsut who stood silent and motionless exuding as royal a air as she could muster. She was, after all, of a strictly practical bent. While she approved of ritual and ceremony as long as it had a purpose she could measure, she was not fond of noise or movement that seemed to be committed solely for its own sake. And so she stood her ground glancing around from time to time as if searching for the temple priests who would assist in making the body of her husband ready for life in another world.

The pall-bearers placed the coffin on the small platform just outside the temple doorway and stepped away. Intef, Chief Prophet of Amun, stood before the coffin dressed in his white robes. The skin of a leopard hung from his shoulders drooping low over the priest's back and bound around his waist. The tail of the beast hung so that it appeared that the priest himself had a tail. To adorn the priest in the skin of a leopard was among the

oldest practices of the Egyptians. Its presence on the body transformed the priest as if by magic into a *Setem* with the power to
transfigure the dead into living beings so that they could live anew
in the afterlife. He did this by performing the Ceremony of the
Opening of the Mouth.

The priest began the ritual with great reverence, circling the coffin and sprinkling it with holy water from the Sacred Lake of the
Temple of Amun. Again and again the priest walked around the
coffin permitting the smoke of the "sweat of the gods" that rose
from the incense pot to fall gently upon it like the thick mist that
sometimes rests over the Nile in the winter evenings. At the foot of
the coffin two priests placed a lamb upon its side, its limbs bound
for sacrifice. The *Setem* raised the flint knife to the sun seeking the
blessing of its rays and then lowered it to his side. He grasped the
neck of the lamb and pulled it back exposing its throat. With a
quick cutting motion he severed the animal's veins. The blood
poured forth into a bowl held by another priest who carried the
precious fluid into the temple where it was used as an offering to
the *Ka* of the deceased. The slaying of the lamb caused a grand
silence to fall upon the crowd.

And now the pall-bearers moved to the coffin and raised it so
that it stood before the entrance of the temple as if it wished to
enter by itself but had not the strength of its senses to do so. The
Opening of the Mouth restored the power of his senses to the
deceased so that he might live again and eat and drink and make
love in eternity the way he did in this life. The coffin stood in
silence for what seemed a long time when from within the temple
came the low groaning sound of a dying animal. The groan grew
louder into a terrible bellow that bounced off the temple walls and
shot forth from the entrance like a great wind. Again the animal
bellowed and again the blast of sound crashed over the crowd.
The animal's painful wail made many feel uneasy. Some cried out

in fear. And then only silence again. Deep within the temple in the room called the Sanctuary of the Knife, a great ox had been tethered for sacrifice. Its veins were slowly and precisely cut so its throat could scream forth its pain in a great bellow. While the animal screamed, priests collected its blood in alabaster basins for presentation to Pharaoh's *Ka* as had been done with the blood of the lamb. Now that the beast was dead a priest severed the left foreleg of the animal, the symbol of earthly strength and power, and presented it to the *Setem* standing before the upright coffin.

The priest extended the bloody limb toward the coffin and shook it as if to force the life and strength of the animal into the corpse itself. A carpenter's plane was then handed to the priest. The wood of the coffin protected the corpse from the magic to open its senses. The priest touched the plane to the ears, eyes, nose, lips, hands and feet of the coffin to symbolically scrape the wood away so that the senses themselves might be touched and released to live again. And so it was that the priest brought forth a special metal knife with a blade in the shape of the tail of a fish. And with this sacred *peseshkef* the priest anointed all the senses of the body magically restoring the senses of the corpse to life. As he touched the organs of each sense, the priest spoke the sacred words: *"Take your head, collect your bones, gather your limbs, shake the earth from your flesh! The Gatekeeper comes out to you, he grasps your hand, and guides you into heaven."* At last it is done! Pharaoh lives again! He enters the tomb certain of the promise to rise from the dead and dwell among the gods!

In ancient times the Opening of the Mouth was performed at the tomb. But the wish of the warrior princes of Thebes to keep the location of their tombs secret led to performing the ritual at the entrance to the mortuary temple. Though thousands of mourners gathered about the temple, only a select few would accompany the coffin of the Great Lion to the tomb itself. From where I stood I could see that the road that led through the mountains and the Valley of the Kings was lined with soldiers. A military honor guard and a small body of officials would accompany the sled on its final journey.

The road to the Valley had been improved since I was last here and the narrow places in the mountain pass had been widened to accommodate the sled. The journey of two miles required more than two hours to complete. At last the small procession arrived at the mountain where Puemre had carved Pharaoh's House of A Million Years. A final blessing from the vile Intef and the coffin of the Great Lion was handed into the care of Puemre's strongest workmen who carried it up the wooden stairway to the tomb entrance. The burden was heavy and it took the workmen more than an hour to lift their load to so great a height. As I watched the coffin raised higher and higher I thought the stairway looked as rickety as it did when I climbed it. I should not have been surprised if the stairway, workmen, and coffin came crashing to the ground. But it was not so and my father's coffin made its way safely to the entrance. A short time later Puemre watched as the heavy stone lid of the sarcophagus slid into place sealing my father forever from the sight of human eyes. It would take another few days to put the stone plugs in the tomb doors and seal the entranceway first with rubble and then with stones and plaster. While the plaster was wet the official seal of the necropolis guard was set in it. The seal portrayed Anubis holding nine bound captives at his feet. And for as long as there was an Egypt Anubis' guards would stand their posts at the base of this mountain as they had stood their posts at the tomb of my grandfather buried in this same valley.

It was late afternoon when we took chairs and were carried back to the Nile for our crossing to Thebes. I rode with Nefurure. Neither of us said a word for the entire journey. I welcomed the quiet and the chance to be alone with my thoughts while I tried to sort out what might lie before me in the coming months. I was regent, that much was accepted by all. But I was not Pharaoh, and as long as there was Hatshepsut I would not be. While I was by no means certain it seemed unlikely that Hatshepsut's interests were served by my death. Quite the contrary. With me alive the thin fiction of her acting as regent remained plausible. Sooner or later something would have to be done with me. Even Senenmut would find it difficult to explain the delay in my regency within a year or two. For the present, however, I was reasonably safe.

But what was to become of me in the meantime? Was I to be allowed to remain in the palace under conditions of house arrest? I could, I suppose, be placed in some dark prison or locked room in the basement of the palace and dragged out from time to time as the occasion demanded. And what plans did Hatshepsut have for her daughter who, after all, carried the womb from which the next pharaoh would emerge? My head grew weary with all these thoughts, the more so with no friends like Sinub and Djet from whom to seek advice.

It was dusk once more when the *Star* approached the quay at Thebes. I was exhausted and wished only to make my way to the palace and seek the comfort of my own bed. I walked down the gangplank and over to the waiting chair. I turned and looked across the Nile into the face of the dying sun. In a few minutes Horus would disappear behind the mountains. I had watched the sun set over these mountains many times in the last few months. But tonight was different. This time when Horus raced beyond the mountains he carried with him the soul of my father. I drew a breath and from deep within me came a feeling of profound sorrow. My father was dead! And like every son who has suffered this loss I suddenly felt terribly alone.

The next few months were torment for me. Alone in my palace apartments without friends or visitors the days passed slowly. I pondered my fate and sent requests to Senenmut for us to meet, but they were never answered. I passed each day alone with no human contact except for the brief periods when servants brought my meals. Often I fell into a deep gloom that lasted for days upon end. Sometimes I convinced myself that things would shortly change or that I would be sent to some other place and the gloom would pass. When my wishes did not happen, I plunged back into the gloom again. And so it went until one day Hatshepsut sent for me.

I was escorted into the room by two guards. I had come to this room to visit my father almost three years ago before I left on my journey to Memphis. It was a large room with richly painted walls and smooth pavement. Beautifully painted columns decorated with hieroglyphic text ran along the outside walls supporting the massive clerestory ceiling. The wide staircase at the far end of the room led to the raised platform upon which sat the thrones of Pharaoh and his queen. A picture of my father standing before the great throne of Egypt legs apart and arms folded smiling down at me flashed through my mind. It was, I realized, one of the clearer portraits of my father that I carried with me. Now my eyes caught sight of Hatshepsut sitting upon her throne. Standing beside her was Senenmut The Commoner. The great hall was silent except for the sound of my sandals as I made my way to the foot of the stairs.

The queen's voice echoed as it boomed through the empty hall. "Well, well, my boy! It seems that we have not spoken in such a long time." She smiled at me and glanced at Senenmut who smiled too. "No need to stand there, Thutmose" she said pointing down at me. "Come here, my boy." She patted the seat of the empty throne next to her. "Come sit next to me."

I climbed the steps and stood before her. My gloomy mood was still with me and anger filled my mind. I had come to hate this woman who toyed with me as she and Senenmut shared their little joke. My face felt flushed and my palms were wet. Had there been a dagger in my hand I should surely have plunged it into Hatshepsut's heart! But, of course, there was no dagger. I cleared my mind of these pointless fantasies and tried to focus on her words.

Hatshepsut's face broke into a sly grin. "Do you not wish to sit upon this throne of Egypt?" she said sarcastically. Her hand pointed absently to the gilded chair to her left. Her eyes searched my face for weakness. I tried to offer her no clue to my feelings. My silence bothered her and her smile vanished. Furrows appeared on her brow. Her eyes narrowed.

"Have you nothing to say, Thutmose?" She paused and glanced at Senenmut. "Do you not wonder what is to become of you?" Hatshepsut leaned back in her chair and waited for me to answer.

There was no fear in my voice when I spoke, only a sense that I was prepared to accept my fate, a resignation that must have been all too evident.

"It is over, my queen." Hatshepsut's eyes widened for a second at my use of her title. I could have called her aunt or even mother, for in a strict sense she was both. But her official title seemed far more appropriate under the circumstances.

I hoped my voice sounded sincere. "It is finished!," I said. "You are the Great Queen and I am your nephew. There is no more to it than that." My words spoke the truth. I was without allies and without prospects of attracting any. Whatever the wishes of my father might have been, his testament remained lost. No government officials owed loyalty to me. My only two friends among the officers of the army had been banished to remote postings. What I wanted was to escape with my life and be gone from the imprisonment of the palace.

The great queen smiled. "But, Thutmose, you are still regent are you not?" The question was only sarcasm. "Do I not rule in your name?" Again, sarcasm.

"You rule because you are queen, not because I am regent," I said. "And when you are finished the throne will pass to the first son of Nefurure and whoever it is that you select for her husband. But even he will not be Pharaoh until you are finished." I paused. "I wish only to be left alone and to continue my education." I looked at her with as much sincerity as I could command under the circumstances. "Perhaps I will become a physician, like Tabu and tend to the wishes of the goddess *Sekhmet*. It is honorable work."

Senenmut's eyes narrowed as he took the measure of my words. I hoped he credited me at least with seeing things as they were. The queen's silence struck me as ominous as she, too, glared at me with narrow eyes. The silence was deafening! My fate rested in the hands of these two expert conspirators, at least one of whom was a murderer. And all they could do was stare at me and be silent! It was not a comfortable feeling. At last Senenmut spoke.

"And where, oh prince, would you continue your education?" It was said seriously. The time for humiliation was over. The victors had accepted their victory. And, I supposed, they had decided to permit me to live. And rightly so for a murdered Pharaoh's son gained them nothing except piece of mind and raised too many embarrassing questions. I chose my words carefully.

"Perhaps I could return to Memphis and continue my studies with the Chief Priest of the Temple of Ptah. One Tabu resides in the city. He is a physician of great reputation and I have made his acquaintance." I paused and lowered the tone of my voice. "And Memphis is far from Thebes," I said.

A wry smile crossed Senenmut's face. "Indeed it is," he said as the smile was quickly replaced by a frown. "Perhaps it is too far, my prince. After all, your aunt may worry with you so far from home." The new smile on his face was a false as the one it replaced. "The idea is sound, but someplace closer to Thebes might be advisable."

Hatshepsut nodded her head at Senenmut's words as if to agree but without saying so. I stood there expressionless, sharing the silence with nothing more to say. I had pleaded my case for permitting me to leave the snakepit of intrigue that was the royal court. Since my father's death I had come to believe that I lacked the talent for the habit of betrayal that was necessary to survive here. It seemed to me that power had a point when one already possessed it. The struggle for it, however, was another matter. And if one was not careful the process of obtaining power warped its future exercise so that however noble one's goals may have been at the beginning, the necessity for harsh means allowed them to become false aims or deferred forever. The truth was that Senenmut and Hatshepsut were more nicely fit for the game than I. Perhaps Egypt was in better hands after all.

And so it came to pass that I was sent to the Temple of Amun in Thebes to continue my education. Memphis, it turned out, was too far and Senenmut preferred having me at hand under the watchful eye of Intef the murderer who, after all, owed everything to the queen. I was given a small staff of servants to look after my needs and a suitable allotment of gold, cooper and bronze rings of sufficient *deben* weight to cover my expenses. There was, of course, no need for me to visit the palace any more and my comings and goings at the temple were reported on regularly by Intef and his spies. But life in the temple was not unpleasant, and my time in Memphis served me well in adjusting to my new surroundings. I was grateful for the respite from the defeats of the last year.

I made up my mind to turn my attention to my education which, it seemed to me, was sorely deficient.

I was pleased to learn that Thaneni, my old friend and protector, was still in residence at the temple and immediately sought him out. I found him giving lessons to novice scribes.

"Well, old friend, I see that you have escaped the glass factory!" It was said with pleasant sarcasm and I could not stop myself from laughing as I spoke. Thaneni heard my voice and turned toward the doorway where I stood. A broad smile broke over his face and his eyes widened in happy surprise.

"By Toth's beard, is it really you Thutmose?" He put down his pallet and rushed toward me catching me up in his embrace. Over his shoulder I could see the faces of his young students and the surprised look on their faces that such a harsh taskmaster as Thaneni had within him even a trace of human feeling. He swung me around and put me down. Then he stepped back.

"Where have you been?" His voice dropped low almost to a whisper. "There were rumors that you had been killed or sent to the desert after your father died." His voice was serious. And then just as suddenly it reverted to its original lightness. "But the gods kept you safe I see." He winked at me as if to say, "Watch what I am about to do." He turned and addressed his students. "Quiet, unruly swine!" he yelled. The serious expression on his face had the desired effect and the novices dropped their eyes in fear. "The lessons for the day are finished!" he exclaimed. "Go forth from my sight and do not return until tomorrow when, perhaps, I will be able to look upon your faces again." In an instant the students rose and rushed from the room glad to be free of Thaneni's harsh words.

We walked together into the courtyard, two friends happy to see one another again. "It was not so long ago that you and I sat where the novices sit." I smiled at my friend. "Now you are a teacher!" I shook my head in comic disbelief. "How are such things possible? How is it that you remain here? I have been gone for more than a year's time, enough for you to be keeping books for the glass maker!"

Thaneni grinned.

"You speak the truth, Thutmose. As events have it my patron died only a few weeks ago. With him dead I was released from my indenture and so I had no place to go. A priest of some influence knew of my skills and thought I would make an adequate temple scribe. One has to eat, you know! So here I am instructing novices in a skill that I myself have barely mastered." He shrugged in a gesture of amusement at the fates. "And you, my friend? How is it that you are here?"

We walked through the courtyard into the garden and I recounted for Thaneni my tale of the events that conspired to bring me here. He listened intently nodding his head from time to time to let me know he understood what I was telling him. When I finished he looked at me in earnest and spoke.

"So you will stay here for the time being?" he said. "What will you do?"

My shoulders shrugged. "Exactly what I told Senenmut I would do. See to my education. My reading and writing are dismal. When I have repaired those, perhaps I will take Tabu's advice and study medicine." I shrugged again. "After that, who knows?"

We spent the day together discussing all sorts of things. It was my idea to engage him as my personal tutor so as to improve my reading skills as quickly as possible. With a position as tutor to the regent of Egypt Thaneni would be free from the prospect of having to depend upon the kindness of the temple priests for work. And I would have a companion I could trust. So began a friendship between two young men that has lasted our entire lives. Even now as I speak these words it is Thaneni who writes them down and preserves them for the ages.

Under Thaneni's guidance my reading and writing skills improved quickly. Within a few months I could accomplish both with little difficulty. One day I suggested to him that it seemed like a good time to begin my studies in earnest.

"To do that you will need to make the acquaintance of Ka-Aper and plead for his help," Thaneni said.

A puzzled look crossed my face. Thaneni smiled as he anticipated my question.

"Ka-Aper is the temple librarian. He is the Keeper of the Sacred Books. Only he can grant you permission to use them in your studies."

A silly grin appeared on my face. "Ka-Aper," I said. "What an appropriate name for a keeper of books." Thaneni smiled too. Ka-Aper's name meant "He Who Keeps The Ka." It was difficult to imagine a more appropriate name for a librarian!

"Well," I said, "if you think my skills are up to it, perhaps we should visit this Ka-Aper and see what he thinks of my suggestion."

Ka-Aper was as ancient as the pyramids. Never had I seen a human being as old as this man. He moved around his office shuffling his feet in very small steps so only the front of his sandals were worn while the heels looked unused. This manner of walking I took to be a way of maintaining his balance. He walked and sat in a perpetual stoop and unless he was clasping a book to his chest his arms hung straight down from his shoulders. Ka-Aper's body was as thin as a stick and his robe seemed so large for his body that its folds of cloth hid most of what little physical presence there was within them. His shaven skull capped an emaciated face and sunken features that resembled death itself. He had not a tooth in his head, and when he smiled spittle gathered at the corners of his mouth. When he spoke moist bubbles formed at the corners of his lips. The voice that belonged to the body was thin as a reed, as if his breath originated no lower than the top of his throat. If his lungs had any function, his habits and oversized robes hid it well.

Ka-Aper greeted my suggestion politely and immediately questioned my skills and determination to read the sacred books. The books themselves were very old and I would be permitted only to examine the copies. Of course, until I had proven myself a trustworthy student even the copies might only be read in the library. There was to be no question at all of my taking them from the room. The medical texts, Ka-Aper made clear, were among the oldest works in the library. Two of the surgical treatises, although copies themselves, were more than four hundred years old. The originals were more than a thousand years old! Ka-Aper explained that this presented a problem. These old books were written mostly in hieroglyphs and ancient ones at that. How did I, he wanted to know, expect to make any sense of their contents? Thaneni came to my rescue by pointing out that he had studied hieroglyph writing and could make his way through most texts. As my tutor Thaneni would be by my side to help me comprehend the books. Ka-Aper seemed pleased by this. After more questions the old man agreed that I might read the medical books provided I took due care with them.

And so began more than a year of study. Each day Thaneni and I made our way to the library to read the old books. Thaneni had no interest in medicine and spent most of the time reading things he felt would be more useful to an aspiring scribe. He read the great works of Egyptian literature and poetry and became quite fond of poetry. He even began trying his own hand at it reading it aloud to me from time to time. For the most part, I must admit, it never sounded particularly good to my ear. I most enjoyed Thaneni's recounting of the great religious myths that lay at the base of our civilization. Egypt is, after all, a country fascinated with death and the preparation for it. Listening to Thaneni explain the ancient myths, the fascination made somewhat more sense than it had before. All in all, Thaneni turned out to be quite a helpful tutor. I credit Thaneni's conversations and recitations as being among the most enjoyable and useful elements of my own education.

My only experience with medicine had been at the hand of Tabu the Physician. There were times during my studies when I wished he were present to see my amazement at what I was learning. More than once I promised myself that I would visit him when the time was right. But then I would think of Lanata and push the idea from my mind. I was surprised at how disturbing the memory of her death still was to me. Sometimes the sadness that came over me whenever I thought of her forced me to interrupt my studies for the day. Still there were pleasant memories from that time. Among the most pleasant was Tabu's willingness to share with me the secrets of his special herbs and ways of healing.

Much of the practical bent with which Tabu approached the art of healing I found in the old medical texts. Indeed, the more ancient the texts, the more practical and expedient their contents were. Egyptian doctors in ancient times knew about the pulse and called it "the sound of the heart." They regarded fever as a sign that something was wrong in the body. Scalpels were used to lance boils and cut open wounds that had healed badly and became green with putrefecation. Bleeding could be stopped by heating a knife and pressing it over the wounds. To close a wound linen thread was used to stitch the sides together. Sometimes bandages with sticky gum on them were used instead of linen thread. My researches taught me that we Egyptians had learned early on to deal with broken bones of all kinds. An army without helmets that used the mace as a weapon suffered quite a few skull fractures after all. The workmen who constructed the pyramids and temples often suffered injuries from the heavy stone. The ancient texts showed how to lift the broken skull from the soft matter inside and bandage it. Broken arms and legs were set between two pieces of flat wood and wrapped in bandages covered with starch to stiffen the splint and keep the limb from moving. And there was even Hesy-Re, the Chief of the Teeth, a physician to a Pharaoh who lived more than a thousand years ago! It seems that his king had terrible teeth that pained him with great torment. Hesy-Re removed the teeth only to find that there was putrefecation under the jaw bone. To remove this the physician used a small drill to make two holes in the bone that permitted the putrefecation to drain away. At last when all was healed, Hesy-Re, with the help of a talented goldsmith, fashioned a gold denture with ivory teeth that fit perfectly in Pharaoh's mouth. So relieved was Pharaoh to be free of his pain that he lavished estates and gold upon the physician.

The more I discovered about the talents of the ancients the more I wondered why Tabu had told me that physicians no longer studied the medical texts of these great healers. And the more I examined the profession of physicians, the more it seemed that Tabu was correct. Medical training was in the hands of the temple priests, few of whom ever ventured forth to treat a patient. It was not unlike being taught how to build a pyramid by an engineer who had never constructed one! With no practical experience, it was not surprising that the priests placed their attention on the spells that were used by the ancients to accompany their treatment of the sick and injured. Only in modern times the spells had taken the place of practical treatment. Now physicians learn to recognize the signs of certain illnesses and to choose from among the many spells and prayers the correct one that will convince the goddess *Sekhmet* to heal the patient. A physician like Tabu can treat many illnesses as the ancients did. But the modern physician specializes in treating only those illnesses of a single organ. Even the old knowledge of special plants and herbs is no longer used. Instead, all sorts of compounds are mixed together to conjure potions with which to heal the sick.

It was not, it seemed to me, a state of affairs that worked very well, but one that I have been powerless to change even as Pharaoh. What I have been forced to do is ignore it. I leave the priest-physicians to their spells and prayers for it is always a good rule never to anger the powerful when they are content to be ignored. To care for the soldiers of my army I place practicing physicians with no formal education on the government payroll. These are the *Snuwu*, men who have learned their healing skills through practical experience at the hands of other physicians. In a curious way, I guess, it is a memorial to Lanata who had learned the healing arts from her father's hand. These healers are less interested in spells and prayers than in doing the things that keep wounded soldiers alive. And so it is that my armies carry with them trained *Snuwu* to care for my soldiers after the battle. Their skills have saved many men. On the march their knowledge of what wells and springs to drink from, among other things, has saved many soldiers from illness.

As much as I enjoyed my study of medicine it was only a short time before I realized that I was not cut out for it as a life-long work. My interest in plants and herbs stayed with me for a life-time. But after a few years, little of my foray into the field of medicine remained with me. Strangely, I followed Thaneni's lead and began to read literature and theology. I was particularly taken with the tales of great kings and their exploits in battle. Narmer, the Great Unifier, the king who forged the state of modern Egypt in battle was a particular favorite of mine. Another was Hor-Aha, "Fighting Hawk," the great warrior pharaoh who first took up arms against the Libyans. I spent hours reading of the brave exploits of the early warrior princes of Thebes. The bold Seqenenre who drew first blood against the Hyksos and who was surrounded in battle and slain with spear and axe. It took five wounds to finally kill him. His sons, Kamose and Ahmose, lived in Egypt's recent memory as the men who broke the back of the Hyksos yoke and drove them into the desert. It was men like these that stirred my emotions. None of them had lives easier than mine. None of them succeeded without difficulty. When I thought of their exploits my mind wandered back to that day in Asyut when Mersu had taken me for my first chariot ride! I remembered thinking then that I wanted to be a soldier like him. And so as the months passed I read more and more of military exploits until it was only a matter of time before I decided to enter the army and begin my life's journey in earnest.

I had passed my eleventh birthday by more than two months when I reached this momentous conclusion and decided that it was time to forego the things of childhood and take my place among the men of Egypt. Most boys my age had been at work in shops or fields for at least three years. Sons of the nobility had finished their schooling in reading and writing and were enrolled in the professions of their choosing. Boys my age were already being selected by the conscription teams to serve in the army. Soon they would make their way to the military training camps and from there to their units where they would spend a year serving as Pharaoh's soldiers. And so it was time. Whenever I looked into a mirror I saw before me the face of a man who still wore the side-lock of youth. More and more I came to dislike that symbol. One day I approached Thaneni with the suggestion that I pass the ceremony that would mark me as a man for the rest of my days.

It is not merely shaving the sidelock that marked one as a man in Egypt. It is circumcision too. It is, I suppose, a curious custom, one that is only practiced in Egypt, although I was told years later that some of the peoples who live under the protection of the Egyptian empire also hae adopted circumcision. It is a custom practiced mostly by the Egyptian nobility to mark them apart from the peasants and other commoners. In some ways, I suppose, it is a test of character, of one's ability to endure pain. It had been practiced since ancient times even by the earliest pharaohs. A special knife was used to circumcise the son of a pharaoh, not the usual flint blade used by others. This sacred knife was fashioned of a metal harder than bronze that could be sharpened to an edge thinner than that found on any razor or sword. So durable is this magic metal that it could not be melted in the furnaces of bronze factories. It is the rarest metal known to Egypt and has never been found in any other land. The metal comes from within a rock that has suffered a great heat, as if it came from the sun itself or somewhere in heaven. This sacred metal, it is said, came from the stars! So deeply is this believed that the hieroglyph for this knife and for "star" are the same!

But my sidelock was shaved with a common razor and my circumcision performed with the flint knife, for I wished no public ceremony that would attract Hatshepsut's suspicion. She ruled in the fiction that I was a minor child. It was unlikely that she would be pleased by a public performance marking my entry into manhood. And so with Thaneni's help and that of Ka-Aper my sidelock was shaved and my circumcision performed on the shore of the Sacred Lake of the temple one bright day. Since then I have seen the scene of circumcision painted on the walls of many tombs and it was as it had been done to me. I stood in front of the physician who kneeled before me. I required no others to steady me against the pain. As a sign of courage I placed my hand upon the physician's head, the other upon my hip, and stared straight ahead. I felt the knife bite deeply into my flesh and the pain surge through my body. And when it was done the lingering pain did not matter, for it reminded me that I was no longer a youth. For better or worse, my life was now my own.

The wound healed quickly. In less than a month I was prepared to ask Hatshepsut to take my leave of the temple and enter military service. Thaneni had grown bored with life in the temple and thought it a great honor that I asked him to come along with me as my tutor and scribe. We discussed how Hatshepsut might be convinced that it was in her interests to permit me to leave Thebes. There was, Thaneni suggested, always the possibility that I might be slain in battle something the queen, no doubt, would find very attractive! While we sought a clear plan of action, events took their own turn and I was summoned without warning into Hatshepsut's presence.

Much had changed in the nearly two years since I looked upon the face of Hatshepsut and her toady, Senenmut. The two of them had driven the last of my father's officials from the government and replaced them with men whose careers rested upon their continued favor with the queen and her advisor. Senenmut was now the most powerful man in all Egypt. Even the vizier, Hapuseneb, walked with caution around him. Senenmut was the queen's only confident and, as events later showed, her lover as well. He was the Chief Steward of Amun, Steward of the Barque, Overseer of the Graneries of Amun, the Fields of Amun, the Cattle of Amun and the Gardens of Amun. He was also the queen's Chief Architect and Overseer of Public Works. There was not a single government position that escaped the grasp of his authority. It was said that Senenmut controlled Egypt and Hatshepsut controlled Senenmut!

Thaneni and I were made to wait in the ante-chamber of the throne room until the queen was ready to receive us. Unlike my last visit, there was an air of deliberate formality to this audience whose purpose I could not explain. The murals portraying the great deeds of my father on the chamber walls had been replaced. Thaneni drew my attention to them as we awaited our summons.

"Thutmose," Thaneni said. "Come here and look at these paintings. They tell of the birth of the queen."

I walked over to the wall and examined the mural in great detail. What I saw brought anger to my eyes. The mural portrayed the story of Hatshepsut's birth. Her mother, Queen Ahmose, was shown in the embrace of the Hidden One himself. Next to Queen Ahmose were all the gods of childbirth including the ram-headed Khnum, the frog-headed goddess Heqet, and the seven fairies of Hathor. It was as if Hatshepsut had been chosen by Amun himself to be Pharaoh! The mural implied that Amun was her father! Another panel showed Hatshepsut crowned queen as a child by her father, Thutmose I, in full view of the royal court implying that he, too, recognized her divine origin and her claim to the throne. Nowhere was there mention that my father had even existed! Thaneni was the first to regain his wits.

"In the name of Osiris, Thutmose! The woman is claiming to be Pharaoh by the will of Amun!" He paused and shook his head. "It is sacrilege!" His voice trailed off and he went back to staring at the mural.

I could not find the words to give voice to my anger. For Egyptians the forms of things are their essence. That is why we never carve images of animals that are exactly lifelike. To do so is to risk that the image will become the animal itself, that its form will prompt its substance to live. And so it has always been with paintings and carvings in tombs and temples. The form becomes the essence and being of a thing by its mere portrayal. Hatshepsut's portrayal of herself as the Son of God spawned from the loins of Amun himself had, in the act of its portrayal, become official history. No doubt this version of her rise to the throne of

Egypt had been copied in the ante-chambers of other government buildings and in the temples of Amun and others throughout the land. In this way Hatshepsut the woman had become Pharaoh. On each side of the portal leading to the throne room had been painted a life sized portrait of Hatshepsut along with the royal titles and names that she assumed. And so from this time forward she was to be known as *Horus Wosretkau* or "She Who Is Of The God Horus," the King of Upper and Lower Egypt, *Maatkare* who is "The Truth That Is The Soul of Ra", and *Khnemetamun Hatshepsut*, "She Who Embraces Amun, The Foremost of Women." All that she did not claim was the title of Mighty Bull.

The great gilded door swung open and a servant beckoned me to enter. Thaneni remained where he was, for his presence was not required. I walked quickly to the stairs at the foot of the throne and cast a glare upward at the figure of Hatshepsut who sat above me. As my eyes fell upon her I thought for a moment that my anger betrayed my vision and caused me to see things that were not so. But my eyes beheld the truth! Hatshepsut sat upon the great throne of Pharaoh in the middle of the platform so that there was no empty place where the queen's throne had once been. There was only one throne and Pharaoh sat upon it! She wore the great red and white double crown upon her head. Her gowns and make-up were as if she were a male! So there would be no mistake she wore the ceremonial beard upon her chin tied up behind her head to keep it in place. Hatshepsut's hands held the scepter and flail and the garnet eyed *Uraeus* stood erect upon her forehead and glared fire every bit as powerful as if it were worn by a man!

I drew myself to my full height. "I am here at your command, my queen. What is it you wish of me?" There was a strength in my voice that I had heard only a few times before. At last the high pitched sound of my child's voice had departed from me.

My words drew an angry reaction from Senenmut who spat his words at me.

"How is it you dare to address Pharaoh so! He who sits before you is Egypt! Has all your education gone for nothing, my prince?" Senenmut's voice changed from anger to suspicion. "Or perhaps it is only that your loyalties lie elsewhere." He paused. "It is unwise, my prince, for you to behave so poorly in the full view of the royal court."

At that an angry murmur rose from the assembly of advisers that stood to the side of the stairs. They had already made their peace with the new order of things and why not? Profit was profit and power was power. It did not really matter whose hand had to be kissed to obtain it. As I looked at them it struck me that these were men who long ago ceased to wrestle with their consciences over what needed to be done to secure their offices. Pharaoh's wish was their wish. Why did things have to be any more complicated than that? The trick, of course, was to survive and prosper. And these men were masters at it.

My eyes met the narrowed glare of Senenmut and held it for a few seconds. Then I turned from him and spoke to Hatshepsut. "I am here at your command, highness. What is it you wish of me?" I stood as straight as I could and waited for her to answer.

Hatshepsut sat above me with all the regal bearing of someone accustomed to ceremony and power. She placed the flail and scepter upon a small table and sat back upon the throne. Her hands grasped the chair arms like the claws of a regal and dangerous cat. For a few seconds she looked down upon me in silence. It required all my discipline not to avert my eyes from her gaze. At last the great queen spoke.

"I am pleased as always to look upon you nephew. I see that you have shaved the sidelock of your youth." A smile rose from the corner of her lips. "I see, too, that you wear your hair in the old style," she said. Before she could continue I heard the sound of my own voice blurt forth.

"It is the manner in which my father wore his hair."

It was a stupid thing to say and the look of anger that appeared instantly upon Hatshepsut's face made me wish I had never spoken those words. Senenmut shook his head in disgust as if to say that I had learned nothing of etiquette or politics from my studies. Another murmur rose from the advisers who gave voice to what they thought the queen wished to hear. Hatshepsut's eyes narrowed, her smile vanished, and she spoke with a venom in her voice that left no question as to her hatred for me.

"I care as little for you as you do for me, nephew. You have always been a thorn in my sandal since the day you first drew breath. You would have served me better dead than alive. But, alas, you live. And for the first time since your birth I have use for your miserable life." The smile of a cobra crossed her face. "I trust you will not deny me what I am about to ask." The smile vanished. "Not if you wish to see the sun once more!" The sound of drawing breath rushed from the assembly of advisers. Senenmut merely snickered at my fate. The powerful torment the powerful. How wonderful, he must have thought!

To be truthful I had no idea what my aunt was about to ask of me. I can only say now that what she asked I would never have dreamt in a million years!

"You are Egypt, highness. You may command of me what you will." The words were said more in fear than reverence and had the unfortunate quality of being true. For a thousand years there had never been an alternative to accepting the command of Pharaoh except death. And whatever else was true, I had every intention of getting out of this place with my skin.

Hatshepsut's face broke into an insincere grin. "Good," she said. "Good." She summoned Senenmut to her side and whispered in his ear. He nodded as she spoke. Finished, she waved her hand absently and Senenmut retired to his place at the side of the throne. The great female looked at me for a few seconds. And then she spoke.

"Now that you have shaved your sidelock and become a man, Thutmose, I am prepared to exact of you a man's burden." She paused and the words fell upon my confused mind lending no clarity to my thoughts whatsoever. I stood there looking up at my aunt, waiting. "Thus it is Thutmose that I command you to marry Nefurure and to sire an heir that will rule the land of Egypt!" The woman's face was beaming with pleasure. She glanced at Senenmut who was smiling too. "Do you understand, nephew?" she said. Her voice cut through me like a knife.

I could hardly believe my ears! I was going to be forced to marry the vicious Nefurure and for the most pragmatic of reasons, to sire an heir to the throne of Egypt. Not that such things were unheard of. The fact that the path to the throne lay through the womb of a woman had often required such arrangements throughout Egypt's history. After all, paternity is always uncertain! When reasons of state are at hand it is perhaps best not to inquire too closely. Hatshepsut knew her history, too, and had every intention of revisiting her own fate upon her daughter. Hatshepsut was the daughter of Thutmose I whose legitimate sons died before him. His only living son, my father, he had sired with a concubine in the same way that my father sired me with Ese. So, like me, my father had no claim to the throne unless he was married to a woman who carried the womb of Egypt within her. That woman was Hatshepsut. And now Hatshepsut intended for me to marry Nefurure whose womb was Egypt and sire a child with her who would in his turn be the heir to the throne.

I stared at Hatshepsut in silence. But it was as if I could read her thoughts. Should I sire a son and he be proclaimed the legitimate heir to Egypt, he would still require a regent to rule with him until he came of age. No doubt Hatshepsut intended to be that regent. And what was to become of me? Once the child was born my claim to the throne was further diminished. If need be, harsher steps could be taken. As I stood there looking into that vile face I had to confess that it was a perfect plan, one that guaranteed that Hatshepsut would remain on the throne of Egypt for as long as she lived!

At last I was moved to speak.

"Great highness," I began "I am prepared to serve Egypt as you request." Hatshepsut's breath relaxed and her mouth turned up at the corners into a sly smile. "But if this marriage is to be as you will it, then perhaps it is also wise to consider another solution to the problem." The woman's eyes narrowed like a cat who had spotted a dog. The expression on her face gave nothing of her feelings away. She said nothing and I continued. "I will marry Nefurure and sire an heir for Egypt. But when this is done you in return will permit me to leave Thebes and enter military service as an officer in the service of Egypt. It is my wish to pursue this service as my career." I stopped speaking half expecting Hatshepsut to interrupt. Senenmut, too, stayed silent although he and the queen exchanged suspicious looks. "That way, highness, you shall have both your heir and the throne of Egypt and I shall be free of this court and its intrigues for all time. I will be free to make my own life, content to remain a regent far from Thebes and the throne of Egypt." Hatshepsut glanced at Senenmut whose narrowed eyes and furrowed brow spoke of his mulling over my proposal in his mind. I saw in his expression that he was not truly convinced of my intentions and measured them against other courses that might be taken. Hatshepsut, too, said nothing. But I sensed in her a willingness to be rid of me once and for all, to remove any lingering cloud of suspicion that my presence cast upon her claim to the throne. For what seemed a long time the room was quiet. Then Hatshepsut spoke.

"What you propose has merit, nephew," she said and grinned at Senenmut who did not return the gesture. It seemed to me that he still had his doubts. But not even the powerful Senenmut dared to disagree with his patron in public. And so he shrugged his shoulders and said nothing.

"And so it shall be. You will wed Nefurure in the coming months. When your first male child is born then, nephew, you may be on your way." Suddenly she smiled and her voice snickered. Even Senenmut was taken by surprise. "I expect to find you at your work until there is a child. By Isis's breasts I will have no more females born of this line!" She paused. "And you will work until the drilling is done. I am sure Nefurure will not object." Her smile broadened. "It will serve the young witch right!" With the wave of her hand the audience was finished and I was dismissed. I turned and walked from the room while behind me the cackle of laughter fell upon my ears.

Being married to Nefurure turned out not to be so bad after all. She was almost fifteen at the time of our joining, by Egyptian standards past the time when she should have already been wed and made with child. Because of this she came to the marriage if not with enthusiasm then with a sense that it did not have to be a torment either, and she tried mostly to be pleasant to me. As for me life with Nefurure was at least more comfortable than my room in the temple and, need I say, filled with many more pleasures!

At twelve I had no experience with women's bodies and had to rely completely on Nefurure's skills in this area. The circumstances of my tumultuous life up to that point had made it impossible for me to visit the Blue Houses with the Ladies of Pleasure as many young Egyptian males my age had already done. Fortunately for me, Nefurure's skills were considerable and I have always looked back upon our time together with fondness. As my first woman she became the standard by which I later came to judge the abilities and performance of other women. To my surprise it was many years before I discovered another of such expertise and enthusiasm. I have no idea to this day whether Nefurure would have made a good wife. My own thinking is that she was too much her mother's daughter to be anything but the viper Hatshepsut was. Still, in those years when we were both young and our bodies cried out often to be touched and satisfied, it sometimes seemed that being able to possess her body at will might be worth the risk. But then our bodies relieved themselves and the tension passed in a burst of pleasure and I saw the world more clearly and thought better of it.

And so the months passed. Thaneni was given quarters of his own at the palace and we saw each other regularly. Thaneni was a good friend and tried to give me advice on dealing with women. He subjected me as well to terrible taunts about my being "the royal stud," telling me once that he had grown quite accustomed to the luxury of the palace thank you and he would not mind at all if I continued to fail to get Nefurure with child so he could continue to enjoy his new life! Thaneni was, after all, a factory worker's son. But there was an element of truth in what he said. Each month Nefurure watched for her Red Blood Moon to appear. To us Egyptians, when the moon no longer came upon her it was a sign that Khunum had fashioned a child upon his potter's wheel and implanted it in the woman's body. Four months passed and still her Red Blood Moon came round to her each time.

One evening after we had taken our meal and were sitting on the balcony enjoying the cool evening breeze, Nefurure told me she was feeling ill. Her brow was moist and her skin warm and I thought it wise that she be put to her bed immediately. She fell quickly into a troubled sleep, unable to keep from thrashing about as if some great beast possessed her and was struggling to escape from her body. Throughout the night I bathed her body with wet cloths trying as best I might to keep the fire on her skin from consuming her altogether. At last, near dawn, Nefurure fell into a deep slumber.

That morning I summoned the royal physician to examine her. He arrived quickly enough and we both sat outside Nefurure's bed chamber waiting for her to awaken. The physician was one of the more ancient temple priests and had spent his life in the study of the sacred books. To my eye he looked tired, as if he had been rudely awakened from his own sleep by my summons, and was not particularly happy to be here so early in the morning. I engaged him in conversation and described as best I could the signs of the illness that afflicted Nefurure.

"What manner of illness do you think it is, physician?" I inquired. I tried to conceal my worry and keep a civil tone. I was by no means certain that this old man would be of any help in treating Nefurure.

"It is difficult to tell without examining her, highness." His voice struck that bored tone that physicians often reserve for patients. "There are many reasons why bad spirits come to inhabit the body." He was not warming to his subject at all. "I should be able to discover what spirit has entered her when I examine her." He paused and his face opened in a cavernous yawn. His arms reached upward to the ceiling and he arched his back producing a cracking sound in his old bones. For a second I thought he was himself suddenly possessed. But the gyrations were only his manner of stretching his body in the morning and in a few moments the old physician returned to his normal pose.

"Do not worry, highness. Whatever the evil, the powers of the goddess *Sekhmet* are far more powerful. I have spent my life in the study of spells and charms to bring forth these powers and cure the sick." He smiled the smile of one who has truly come to believe his own faith. It was not a trait I found terribly reassuring.

The mark on the shadow clock was approaching eleven, and still the physician and I sat in the outer room awaiting a sound from Nefurure. At last I stood up.

"Perhaps I should look in upon her. It is very late for her to remain in her bed." I paused and looked toward the closed door that led to Nefurure's bed chamber. "Please wait here physician," I said. "I shall awaken my wife."

The room was dark, the light from the day's sun kept from it by the drawn shutters on the windows. I quietly made my way to a window and drew back the shutter to permit the light to enter. A strange smell struck my nostrils. I turned toward the large bed where Nefurure slumbered. A shaft of light cut through the darkness and fell upon her upturned face. Though it shone strongly upon her eyes it did not awaken her. I sat down softly upon the bed and placed my hand upon her brow expecting to feel the heat from her skin. To my surprise her brow was cool. Her face, too, was cool, and her skin felt waxy and clammy as my fingers moved gently over her features. She was, I remember thinking, quite pleasant looking if not beautiful. My eyes fell upon her breasts pressed tightly against the sheer bedrobe that she wore. As if struck by a clap of thunder, I realized that there was no movement in her chest. Nefurure was not breathing!

Without thinking I grabbed her by the shoulders and began to shake her calling her name in panic.

"Nefurure! Nefurure! Wake up!" I pulled her body against mine and felt her head hang limply from her neck. "Wake up!" I cried again and again. Still no life flickered inside her.

The sound of my shouting brought the physician to my side. With a professional hand he took Nefurure from my arms and laid her gently upon the bed. He stood over her examining my wife with his eyes.

"There," he said pointing to a large dark stain that started at the bottom of the bed and reached upwards toward Nefurure's legs. The physician glanced at me. The serious look in his eyes told me that there was something terribly wrong. He grabbed the bed covers and pulled them back. Nefurure lay in a pool of her own blood. The stain covered her legs from below her hips and had dried to a dark crimson. My eyes widened in shock at the gruesome sight. I looked helplessly to the physician for an explanation. He, meanwhile, searched her neck veins for some signs of the life of the heart. Finding none, the physician pushed back the lids of Nefurure's eyes to search for the last spark of the soul only to find emptiness. At last he stepped back and reached for the bed clothes pulling then over Nefurure's still body. "She's gone," he announced and turned toward me.

The words stammered from my mouth. "Is sh…e…she dead?" I asked. I could not hide the tremor in my voice. I looked at the physician with wide eyes. "Why…why…did she die?" I felt a terrible sadness inside as I spoke.

"Her womb has burst," he said, "The life that flowed in her body escaped the canals that held it until there is no more life within her." He paused. "Perhaps it was because Khunum placed within her only a half-formed child." The physician shook his head. "It is difficult to know always why the gods do this." His voice fell off in a somber tone. The priest seemed truly to suffer sorrow for the death of so young a woman. He turned to me.

"With your permission, highness, I shall inform the queen of her daughter's passing." He waited for me to nod my assent and then went on. "It will be left to others to make the final arrangements." The old physician walked over to me and placed his hand gently upon my shoulder. "I am truly sorry for your loss, highness," he said. "It is the will of the gods." I felt his hand slip from my shoulder and heard the sound of his sandals as he shuffled across the room and out the door leaving me alone with Nefurure's corpse.

It is curious how often we fail to see behind the formality required of our stations in life and discover the true soul that resides deep within us. And so it came as a great puzzlement to see how Nefurure's death drove Hatshepsut to the brink of madness. When she was told of her child's death, the sound of her wailing could be heard throughout the palace. Her fingernails clawed at her garments rending them to shreds. Hysterical eyes rolled backwards in her head. She pulled clumps of hair from her scalp. Senenmut and the physicians gathered around her, but could not stop the painful writhing of her tormented body which she beat with her own fists as if she, somehow, was responsible for the death of her own child. Hatshepsut ran from her apartments to her daughter's bedroom. She burst past me and looked upon the dead fruit of her body in great sorrow. Tears streamed from her eyes. In a gesture of loving gentleness she sat upon the edge of the bed and cradled her child in her arms. She rocked the babe back and forth kissing her face and brushing the hair from her daughter's silent eyes as if her mother's love alone could breath new life into Nefurure's soul. But, of course, it was not to be, and after some time Hatshepsut laid her daughter upon the bed and brought the covers over her. The queen turned to me and her eyes fell upon my face. Great pain shown from them. There was, too, an expression of sorrow and powerlessness, of being at the mercy of forces that one could never understand. It was, I learned later in my life, an expression common among those who had lived to see their children die, a vulnerability born of the betrayal of the gods themselves who held the power to prevent death and yet, for unknown reasons, delivered upon a parent the cruelest death of all, the death of a child. I learned, too, that those who suffered this loss carried that feeling with them until the end of their days.

My own sorrow at Nefurure's passing was bearable. We had known each other only briefly. As I look back upon it, she bequeathed me many pleasant memories. I was, of course, sorry for her passing, but it changed nothing of importance in my life. The embalmers came and took Nefurure away and I spent the next few months waiting for them to finish their grizzly business so that Nefurure might be properly buried. Thaneni and I spent many hours planning what we would do once we left Thebes and entered upon a career in the army. Then one day Senenmut came to see me.

"I see that you are bearing up well under the circumstances," he said. It was not meant as sarcasm but a statement of simple fact. Senenmut was not one to waste time on pointless sentimentalism.

I nodded and offered a pained smile.

"Thank you, Counselor, for your concern. It is, of course, a difficult time for all of us." I paused. "How is my aunt? Has the great queen recovered from her sorrow?"

Senenmut shrugged as if to indicate that he was powerless in such matters.

"Your aunt still carries great sorrow in her heart." He shook his head slowly from side to side in a gesture of resignation. "But her heart will heal in time," he said. He raised his head in one quick movement and focused his eyes upon my face. "Well," he sighed, "there is important business to tend to. Shall we get to it?"

My mind raced as I tried to think what Senenmut was about. As always, his intentions eluded me until he chose to tell me of them. This time was no exception. I brought a serious expression to my face and permitted my voice to rid itself of any emotion that might betray my feelings.

"By all means, Counselor. Let us discuss your concerns."

Senenmut's face offered a smirk as if he were tolerating a silly pupil trying to conceal something from his teacher.

"It is this, highness. It is the queen's wish that you depart Thebes as soon as possible and that you not be present for the funeral of her daughter." He reached inside his robe withdrawing a papyrus envelope. Senenmut handed it to me. "It contains a letter to the commander of the Wall of Princes in the Sinai informing him that you are a royal prince and that you wish to enter military service. He is instructed to see to your training as an officer. When that is complete and he feels you are competent to assume your duties you are to be assigned to a posting in the eastern desert." He stopped speaking and looked straight into my eyes. "Is this not what you wished?" he said. Senenmut stared at me searching my face for some clue as to what was in my mind.

I met his gaze and smiled. Senenmut's suspicions were aroused, but he was guessing! The great conspirator did not really know! And I wasn't going to betray my only advantage if I could help it.

I nodded my head as I spoke.

"Yes, Counselor, it is what I wished." My voice was even and steady. I detected no trace of the excitement I felt. I rose from my chair to let him know that we had nothing more to say. "I shall require about a week's time to make preparations. Of course adequate financial arrangements will be made for me I presume?" Senenmut bowed his head to assure me this would be the case. "And I shall take my servant and scribe with me as well." It was said as a matter of fact and Senenmut did not object. I walked with Senenmut to the door. He turned toward me and spoke.

"I wish you well highness in your chosen calling. I am sure you will make an excellent officer." He smiled. "But you would be wise to remain far from Thebes and the court." Senenmut sighed. "The truth is highness that you lack the abilities for the exercise of power. Better to spend your life following the orders of others!"

A quick nod of his head, a final snake-like smile, and Senenmut walked out the door. It was many years before we saw each other again and by then the wheel had turned. The queen's counselor would come to regret his words. But although he did not know it, he had done me a great service. I was being sent to the Wall of Princes where Amenemhab was in command! Senenmut had just delivered me into the hands of the most loyal friend I had in Egypt, a friend who in time would help me take my revenge.

# Seventeen

The voyage from Thebes to Memphis took thirty-two days and was less eventful than my first journey down the Nile. Except for a brief episode when *The Wild Bull* became lodged on a sand-bar, the journey was comfortable and without surprises. Thaneni and I passed the time reading history books and swapping tales about what military life was like. It was aimless chatter since with the exception of my stay in Damietta neither of us had ever been on a military post in our lives. Our only inkling of what life was like in the *mesha* or army came from one of the letters that our instructors made us copy when we were learning to write. The text purported to be the advice of a father to his young son who wanted to join the army. In it he tells how officers beat the men who are treated no better than donkeys. The food is terrible and soldiers are made to sleep on the ground without mats. Days are long and the work hard often without sufficient water. At the end the letter warns the young man that he would be much better off learning to write and becoming a scribe because "they are hon-ored among all men." Thaneni and I agreed that the whole thing was made up to make scribes look good. Besides, I was going to be a soldier on any account. If military life proved harsh well, then, I would have to adjust to it. There was no thought of turning back now.

Memphis was much as I remembered it, a bustling port that accommodated the heavy flow of commerce on the Nile. The quay was crowded with boats loading and unloading their cargoes and *The Wild Bull* had to wait until a berth was available before it could put in. From offshore I could see the hill that rose steeply above the city. The great Enclosure of the Ka of Ptah stood almost at the top. Above it, commanding the crest, was the Citadel of the White Wall the great fortress built more than a thousand years earlier by Narmer to enforce his unification of the Delta with Upper Egypt. The Citadel was the headquarters of the Army of Ptah, "Plentiful of Valor," and the first stop in my military career.

Thaneni and I made our way through the narrow streets of the city heading for the Citadel. Before I left Thebes Senenmut suggested it might be wise for me to introduce myself to the commanding general of the Army of Ptah and inform him of who I was and that I intended to train as an officer. Senenmut provided me with a letter of introduction and, to my surprise, a Hawk Seal to ease my way. The Hawk Seal was a small statuette of the god Horus fashioned from silver, the rarest and most precious of all metals available in Egypt. Pharaoh gave the seals to those on special missions. It required government officials to heed all requests of him who possessed it as if the requests were from Pharaoh himself. The seal marked me as someone of importance and with it I could travel throughout the empire commanding whatever aid from government and military officials that I might require.

Ever the scholar, Thaneni could not resist telling me of the history of the army as he had learned it from his readings.

"You know Thutmose," he said, "it amazes me how we Egyptians take our guidance more from the past than from the future."

I smiled and said nothing trying to encourage him to go on, although the one thing that Thaneni never required was more encouragement to tell you something he thought was important.

"Here we are in Memphis where an Egyptian army has been stationed in the same place for more than a thousand years!" There was a tone of wonder in his voice. "Not only that," he went on, "but the headquarters has been in the same building for all that time!" He shook his head. "Only Egyptians could have done such a thing!" he said.

Now that Thaneni had pointed it out to me I had to admit that it was a singular accomplishment. But then in a country that had been sealed from the outside world by its deserts and mountains for so long it was not surprising that innovation was not among its most common practices. The more I thought about it the more I recalled Ra-hotep's lesson that it was the Hyksos invasions that finally brought Egypt out of its isolation and forced it to confront the world beyond its borders. And the primary instrument for dealing with that world was the Army. Thaneni's voice pushed through my thoughts.

"Even the disposition of the forces is the same as it was when Narmer first deployed them to keep Egypt unified," Thaneni continued. "He placed an army in Thebes, the *Army of Amun, Mighty of Bows*, to guard Upper Egypt and keep the Nubians in line. Here in Memphis he posted the *Army of Ptah, Plentiful of Valor* to keep a strong hand on the conquered Delta and protect it from the Libyan raiders." Thaneni stopped talking for a few seconds to see if I was listening. I nodded to show that I was paying attention. Encouraged the way a good teacher is by a student who appears interested, Thaneni continued.

"Of course the enemy has changed. The Delta has long been pacified and the Libyans are only a nuisance. Now the enemy comes from across the Sinai among the peoples of the land bridge and the mountains near the Lebanon. So the Army of Ptah guards the cities from Memphis to the Wall of Princes on the Sinai frontier. Every large city along that route has been strongly fortified and has a troop garrison within it. Memphis itself holds only the headquarters and a small contingent of troops. Even the reserves of the *Mighty of Bows* are deployed below the city itself ready to rush to whatever point of attack might need reinforcement." Thaneni sighed. "It is a good plan for Egypt," he said. "And like so much in Egypt it, too, is a modern application of a very old idea."

At last we found our way to the Citadel. The garrison was surrounded by a high wall covered with bright white plaster that gleamed in the sun. When the sun struck it at just the right angle the glare made it almost impossible to look directly at it. It had been called the Citadel of the White Wall for more than a thousand years. The sentries at the gate accepted our story and allowed us to pass. From inside the garrison appeared to be a large open rectangle with many smaller buildings built against the outside walls. In fact there were so many buildings that it was difficult to imagine this as a place where troops were quartered. Only parts of the original parade square remained uncluttered with stalls and buildings, the single reminder of the time when this was a fighting fortress. Now it was a headquarters filled with scribes and staff officers with only a few combat soldiers to stand guard duty. A passing officer provided us with instructions to the offices of the commanding general. Thaneni and I took only a few minutes to make our way there.

The general's name was Ahmose. As he sat back in his chair reading my letter of introduction it was not difficult to imagine that he had been named after the great warrior pharaoh if only because of his hard looks. The general was a tall powerfully built man with broad shoulders and a great barrel chest. His short dark hair and thick eyebrows gave his face the look of an angry bear.

He was one of those rare men who truly looked like a killer. The furrow in his brow seemed permanent, and he had the habit of sucking his teeth as he concentrated on the words in front of him. At last he placed the letter upon the desk and leaned back in his chair and took a deep breath.

"I am at your command, highness."

His voice was formal like that of a thousand government officials I would come to know in my time. It was the voice of the compliant bureaucrat confronted with his superior and wishing only to accomplish what was requested of him so that his superior would go away and he could get back to doing what he was doing.

"Will you need anything while you are in Memphis?" the general asked. His eyes narrowed in expectation as he waited for my answer.

I offered him a smile as I spoke. I truly did not wish to cause difficulty for him or anyone else.

"Perhaps a few days lodging for me and my scribe until we are on our way again."

The general nodded. "That is easily accomplished," he said. "But, highness, how do you intend to make your way to the Wall of Princes? It is almost a hundred and fifty miles and most of it is overland. You can make your way to Om by boat. After that you will have to travel by foot or cart unless, of course, you are willing to take the canal."

I looked at Thaneni who looked back at me. In our ignorance we had just assumed that the Nile ran to wherever it was we had to go. Now, confronted by my own stupidity, I squirmed uncomfortably in front of the general. I looked at him and shrugged my shoulders. Better to admit my foolishness right away rather than try to conceal it from someone who clearly knew what he was talking about.

A broad smile crossed the general's face. It was a smile I would come to know well during my training as a young officer whenever I made an error in the presence of my superiors. It was the smile of indulgence, a way of telling the young officer that he had missed the lesson, failed to observe the obvious, and, as a consequence, placed himself in a position that was avoidable had he but thought clearly. It was usually followed by some scathing comment about one's stupidity and, eventually, by a solution to one's difficulty. For obvious reasons General Ahmose skipped the usual crass comments and offered me a solution.

"Might I suggest, highness, that I provide you with an experienced officer to aid you in your journey and to see you safely to your destination? He can arrange for transport and lodging along the way." He paused and offered a wry grin that bordered on sarcasm. "Perhaps he can offer some helpful information as well. After all, if you are going to become an officer, it might be a good idea to get a jump on things by starting to acquire an officer's eye for terrain and fortifications." He searched my face for a reaction. I smiled and nodded my agreement.

"Good," he said. "I shall have one of my aides take you to your quarters. In a few hours one of my officers will come there and make himself known to you." The general stood up. The meeting was over. General Ahmose reached across the desk and handed me my letter. "I hope you have an interesting journey," he said.

I stood up as if on cue. "Thank you, general," I said. I turned and made my way to the door. From over my shoulder I heard the general's voice, stopped, and turned around.

"The Wall of Princes is one of our more important garrisons, highness. It is commanded by Colonel Amenemhab. He is good man and a fine soldier. Will you convey my best wishes to the colonel for me?"

For a second I almost blurted out that I had known Amenemhab for many years, but caught myself in time.

"Yes, general. It will be my pleasure to convey your words to the colonel."

Our quarters were standard military fare for Egyptian officers of lower rank. Royal prince or not, apparently General Ahmose had taken me at my word that I wished to be a soldier and billeted me in the usual quarters for young officers. Two beds occupied the opposite walls between a single window under which stood a small table holding a pair of wash basins and water jugs. A bare wooden chest for keeping personal belongings rested at the foot of each bed. A single sheet and blanket lay folded upon the thin military mattress. The common latrine was outside behind the billet and consisted of little more than a small area walled on three sides. A slit trench ran across the enclosure fronted by a knee-high wooden hand-rail that soldiers grasped on to as they leaned their asses over the trench to defecate. All in all it was certainly not the royal apartments at Thebes!

From the window I could see the old parade ground now crowded on all sides by buildings and offices that reduced its once spacious dimensions to a small square barely sufficient to hold a single regiment on parade. Yet in my mind's eye I could imagine it when it was its original size, when thousands of Egyptian troops and their weapons filled it from end to end and officers reviewed the soldiers of mighty Egypt. It was on parade grounds like these that Egyptian soldiers from time immemorial had been awarded the Gold of Valor for courage in battle. From here raw recruits marched off to their first war, visions of glory and death turning in their minds. It was to these parade grounds that the bloodied regiments returned carrying the corpses of their officers and the wounded with them, limping home to rest and heal and prepare for the next battle. On this parade ground warrior pharaoh's of times past took command of their armies and led them personally into the cauldron of deadly combat. Some, like the brave Sequenenre, never lived to return, leaving behind only their legacy for another generation and the promise that Egypt would always find warriors to shield her from the enemies that threatened to overwhelm her and force her to carry the oxen's yoke. And so it was from that window overlooking sacred ground that I felt for the first time that special attachment to my country that had for generations motivated Egypt's men at arms. It was the first time, too, that I began to think of my life as part of something larger than myself.

Thaneni found a servant and sent him off to *The Wild Bull* to transport our luggage to our quarters. We washed and refreshed ourselves and set about thinking how we might get something to eat. It was late afternoon and we had not eaten since breakfast aboard the boat. I was about to say something to Thaneni when a knock came at the door. Thaneni rose and opened it.

"Yes," he said. "What is it?"

Standing in the doorway was a young officer dressed in the sleeveless tunic and kilt of a military uniform. Thick soled sandals wrapped with leather thongs to his knee marked him as infantry as did the *kopesh* and ball-handled dagger that hung from the wide belt around his waist. His close-cropped hair framed his pleasant features as he stood there with one hand raised palm out-ward in the standard military salute. He could not have been more than two years older than I was.

"Good afternoon, sir. My name is Sunusret. I have been sent by General Ahmose to see to your needs."

He paused and dropped his salute to his side. He relaxed his position of attention and stood with legs spread in a pose similar to that which I had seen my father strike on several occasions. In one hand he carried a rolled scroll.

I rose from my chair.

"Welcome, Sunusret. My name is Thutmose and this is my companion Thaneni. We are on our way to the Wall of Princes for military training. I am grateful that you have been assigned to travel with me." I smiled to put the man at ease. "We can certainly use your help and experience in these matters," I said glancing at Thaneni.

Sunusret's eyes narrowed as if trying to determine what to do next.

"Well, sir, I will try to live up to your confidence in me." He said it as if he meant it, and it struck me that given his age it was unlikely that he had seen much military service. As it turned out Sunusret had finished his own officer training barely a few months earlier. Memphis was his first staff posting. "Have you eaten yet?" he asked.

Thaneni and I shook our heads.

"Well perhaps we can begin with some food." A broad smile crossed his face. "The first lesson a soldier learns is to eat when he can!"

We followed him to the officers' mess and sat down to a meal of emmer bread, roast goose, dried fish, radishes, and honey cakes. Beer and wine helped to wash it all down. The food was much better than I had expected. Sunusret pointed out that we were in the officers' mess of a major command headquarters with scores of high ranking officers and government officials to please.

"It is far different when you are stationed away from Memphis I can tell you." He spoke with an authority that I was not certain he truly possessed. "And I am told that the food is truly terrible on the march even when you are fortunate to receive any at all." He laughed as he said it and I could tell from his tone that he was trying to determine how informal he would be permitted to become with us. I decided to put him at ease.

I looked at Sunusret and smiled broadly.

"Sunusret, we are going to be spending several weeks together and in pretty close quarters at that." Sunusret nodded that he understood. "And the truth is that I hope to learn quite a bit from you that might help me in my own training when I finally get to the Wall of Princes." I glanced at Thaneni who nodded his head too. "What I suggest is that we drop this military formality, call each other by our names, and try to make the journey as pleasant and as valuable as possible." I paused. "What do you say, Sunusret?"

Sunusret shrugged. "That would make the journey very pleasant indeed," he said. "It shall be as you wish." And with this he broke into a broad smile as did Thaneni and I.

Sunusret produced a scroll and unrolled it upon the table. Using the basins and water jugs, he held down the upturned corners. It was a map of the Nile Delta showing all the important fortresses and military roads from Memphis to the Wall of Princes on the Sinai frontier. Thaneni and I gathered around Sunusret and stared at the map.

"Here's Memphis," he said pointing with his finger "and here's the Wall of Princes." He moved his finger out to the edge of the map placing it on the large bare section marked "Sinai." He paused while Thaneni and I examined the map more closely. A few moments later he began to lay out the route we would travel.

"I suggest that we travel from Memphis to Om by boat. It is the quickest and easiest way and there is nothing of importance for us to see between here and there." I followed his explanation on the map.

"From there we will travel overland to the town of Nay-Ta-Hut, the first major fortress that guards the road to Memphis. Nay-Ta-Hut is called the "Hyksos Fort" because they built it." Sunusret glanced at me and saw that he had my attention. It was part of Ra-hotep's legacy that I remained interested in anything left behind by the Hyksos invaders. Sunusret went on. "The Hyksos garrison here was very large. It was intended to keep control of Memphis and to be the first line of defense against any Theban army that tried to liberate the city." He paused. "Very good strategic thinking actually." His voice had a complimentary tone in it. "I think you will be impressed by the size of the fortification. It is five hundred yards square and sits almost astride the main road. The walls are massive and very different from the kind of walls we Egyptians build."

I raised my eyes. "What do you mean," I said.

Sunusret smiled. He enjoyed my questions because they allowed him to cast himself as the more experienced officer explaining the situation to his peers.

"In Egypt we build straight walls. The ground is almost always flat or can easily be made flat so we build straight up. The Hyksos knew how to build a wall that followed the rolling terrain to take advantage of the shape of the ground itself."

He paused and waited until I nodded that I understood before going on.

"The Hyksos knew how to slope a wall. The walls at the Hyksos Fortress are straight up on the inside of the enclosure but slope steeply outward on the outside of the wall. It makes scaling or knocking them down very difficult." He smiled and again there was an expression of admiration for the talents of the enemy. "I don't know for certain," he continued, "but I am told that the new forts along the Wall of Princes had been redesigned to incorporate these features in them. Perhaps when we get there we can see if it is so."

He glanced at Thaneni.

"I forgot to mention it but it is only about twenty miles from Om to the Hyksos Fort. The garrison there is very large and quarters and food ought to be good. The fort holds the main units of the strategic reserve for the whole Delta region. These are the fellows who will come to the aid of the Wall of Princes if it is attacked."

Sunusret straightened up and stretched. Thaneni and I continued to study the map laid out before us. After a few minutes I asked, "Where do we go from there?" Sunusret turned back to the map.

"After Nay-Ta-Hut we travel two days to Bast, the City of Cats, and the key to the defense of the Delta." He paused and took a breath. "Come closer," he said "and follow my finger on the map." He pointed to Bast. "Do you see how Bast sits at the junction of two important avenues of advance?" He placed his finger on the spot on the map. "The two major cities and fortresses to the northeast are Tanis and Avaris here and here." He moved his fingers over the cities. "Avaris was the Hyksos capitol. It was destroyed in the war of liberation. We have been rebuilding it and restoring its fortifications, but much remains to be done. Tanis escaped destruction so we were able to take over the Hyksos fortifications with only minor repairs. These two cities hold large Egyptian garrisons and would bear the brunt of any attack from the northeast." Sunusret looked at me and Thaneni. "Notice," he said, "how the road back from these fortresses runs through Bast and then on to Memphis. It is from Bast that our reserves would deploy against the attack."

As I listened to Sunusret explain the deployment of Egyptian troops to protect the Delta I was impressed. This was, after all, a young officer, only a few years older than me, and his knowledge of military matters seemed very good. Thaneni, ever the scholar and historian, was impressed as well. Later I learned that what Sunusret was telling us was drilled into the head of every Egyptian officer. Their superiors wanted each officer to clearly understand his mission and obligations and their instruction began with a comprehensive understanding of Egyptian strategy. Sunusret drew my attention to the map again.

"Look here, Thutmose," he said pointing with his finger. "Do you see that narrow strip of land running from south of Bast eastward out to where the desert sands of the Sinai begin?" He stopped speaking while I looked closely at the map. Thaneni stood behind me and looked over my shoulder. After a few moments of searching I found the strip.

"That's the Goshen Valley. It connects the main Delta with the frontier fortress of T'aru. The valley itself is fertile, but the large area to the northeast is harsh desert as is the land to the south. What this means is that the Goshen Valley is a natural invasion corridor. An enemy must either come through here or risk the hazards of the desert. It is no accident that where the valley meets the Sinai, at T'aru, we have built a large fortress. T'aru is the key around which the Wall of Princes is constructed." Sunusret stopped to see if I understood. After a few more moments of studying the map I nodded. "So," he continued. "After we leave Bast we will travel through the Goshen Valley. There are plenty of small forts and strong points along the way to stop at and rest and get food."

Thaneni and Sunusret began to talk about something or other and drifted off to sit in the chairs across the room. I was fascinated by the map and remained slouched over it trying to learn as much as I could from its features. This was the first military map I had ever seen. Much to my surprise I seemed to have an almost natural talent for imagining the features on the map in my head. Later, when I commanded my own armies, others would say of me that as a commander I had the "gift of the inner eye" when it came to comprehending the way the various parts fit into the complete battle. Somehow my mind formed patterns from what to others seemed nothing more than a series of isolated events so the deployment of the enemy's armies was always easy for me to predict. With a little practical experience, once a commander discerned how the enemy arranged his armies it was not very difficult to sense what his intentions were. I was thankful to the gods for having given me this ability and always tried to use it well.

I studied the map with intense interest. I was impressed at the sophistication of the Egyptian strategy to protect what we called "our sore shoulder to the East," the eastern frontier that rubbed against the hostile tribes, city-states, and great powers that could threaten Egypt with invasion from that direction. Sunusret and Thaneni moved back to the table and stood next to me while I continued to examine the map.

"It is a very well thought out plan of defense," I said to no one in particular. Then turning to Sunusret I said, "Don't you think so?"

The young officer nodded his head and shrugged. "I guess so," he said. Then he smiled broadly. "One more gift from the Hyksos!"

My eyes widened in surprise. "What do you mean?" There was an edge to my voice. "What other gift did these invaders leave to Egypt?"

Sunusret's eyes narrowed and his voice grew serious. "Exactly, Thutmose" he said. "And once they invaded Egypt they had to hold it against a counter-attack from Thebes." He paused. "Look at the map. The avenues of invasion and retreat are precisely the same."

I looked down and tried to form an image in my mind. Sunusret continued.

"The Hyksos system of forts and roads was pointed at Memphis and Thebes. But the forts controlled the same important ground no matter who was using it." He paused and an image of what he was saying finally began taking shape. "So when the Egyptians drove the Hyksos from our land, we occupied the same fortresses and roads. Only now our armies faced outward instead of inward like the invader's armies!"

At last the image that was struggling to emerge in my mind took form and I saw clearly what he was describing. Indeed, the positioning of Egyptian armies to protect Egypt was simply the reverse of the positioning of the Hyksos armies to invade Egypt! I was learning the valuable lesson that the land itself often made the choice of tactics and strategy inevitable or, at the very least, greatly restricted the choices available to the commander.

Late that night after Sunusret and Thaneni had gone to bed I continued to study the map by the light of an oil lamp. It was as if I could not leave it! I examined every fortress, canal, river, and swamp portrayed in front of me and tried to deduce its importance in some fictitious battle that I might fight. I was excited by it all and my mind would not cease forming images. At last I had found something that truly interested me, something that seemed to come to me without great effort. When finally I crawled into bed sleep came slowly as images of forts and soldiers continued to turn in my head until they faded and I slipped into slumber. My last thoughts were of the days to come. I was anxious to get on with my training and become a soldier.

Two days later the three of us boarded a boat for the half-day voyage to Om. From there we intended to make our way overland to the Hyksos Fort at Nay-Ta-Hut and stop at the garrison there. Our boat was a large flat-bottomed barge that wallowed in the water like a wounded hippopotamus. This was especially so when it was packed to the gunwales with new recruits being transported to Nay-Ta-Hut for basic military training. Space was at a premium and Sunusret's officer's uniform did not obtain much in the way of privileges for us with the result that we sat upon the quarterdeck with the conscription officers surrounded by a sea of youthful faces that occupied every square inch of deckspace below us. One fellow, Neb by name, was the Scribe of the Recruits and in charge of making sure this cargo of human material for the army reached its destination safely. Neb seemed a pleasant fellow and I struck up a conversation with him.

"You seem to have your work cut out for you," I said evenly opening the conversation. He smiled at me and sucked in a deep breath.

"You do not understand the half of it," he answered. "Not many of these boys are here because they wish to be. Oh sure, some are," he paused, "but not many. One of the reasons the conscription teams visit the villages during the time of the flood is that there is little work and the prospect of military service often appears attractive. Usually its the families who try to convince one of the boys to join the army for a while. One less mouth to feed you know."

It was my first awareness of the plight of the common Egyptian soldier. I had not known that they were forcibly taken from their villages. The few officers like Djet and Sinub I had known were volunteers. It had never entered my mind that the common soldiers were simply taken from their families. I said as much to Neb.

"Its not quite that bad," he said. "And unless there is a war going on most of these lads will spend their military service in frontier garrisons or working on the repair of dikes and bridges. Some of them will even be put to work in quarries or public buildings. Its not really quite so bad." His voice fell off as he turned his face upward and closed his eyes allowing the rays of the sun to warm his face.

I waited a few minutes without speaking not wanting to disturb his pleasure. When he opened his eyes and turned back to me I spoke.

"How often are the conscripts gathered?"

I hoped Neb would tell from the sound of my voice that I was interested in learning about his occupation. The tone of his voice when he answered suggested that he did.

"Egypt's greatest military advantages are her manpower and her ability to feed herself. The Black Land yields much with little effort. Even her people are fertile so that we have many times the number of men we need for military service. At the middle of every flood the conscription teams move over the land visiting each village in Egypt. Usually the team has a scribe, a man skilled in detecting illness, and a few soldiers to enforce the conscription law. The young men of each village are assembled and examined. Those that are fit could all be taken. But, of course, this is never done. It would make no sense to take too many workers from one village and make it impossible for the village to work its fields. Instead we ask first for volunteers. Only if we cannot get a few this way do we actually conscript what we need." He lowered his voice. "Of course we do our best to make the choice seem like a good one. But in the end the young man has to come with us anyway."

I nodded to show him that I understood and how interested I was in what he had to say.

"How many men are taken each year?" I asked.

"In the old days the army took one male of each hundred for service. But today…" Here he stopped speaking and shrugged to show that the circumstances were beyond his control. "Today we take about one man in every ten." He paused and moved his head from side to side in almost a playful manner. "It makes sense, though. Egypt has many more enemies now. Her frontiers are longer and she needs more men to man the garrisons that protect us from the Nubians. Too,…" and here Neb showed that he really knew his business, "the armies are fully manned and ready to fight at a day's notice. That takes manpower. We are fortunate that the gods have blessed Egypt with these resources."

I looked around at the human cargo covering the barge's deck. I gestured toward them with the sweep of my arm.

"They do not look very happy," I said.

Neb laughed. "No," he said. "I guess not. But soon they will adjust to their new circumstances. Before you know it a year will have passed and except for the few who take to military life and stay on as professionals most will return home safely and richer for the experience." He frowned. "That is unless there is a war and then…" his voice trailed off.

I chatted with Neb for a little while longer. He told me that recruits were called *Nefru* and that each year they were assembled either at Memphis or Thebes to begin their military service. From there groups were sent to large training centers just as this group was being sent to Nay-Ta-Hut. Here the healthiest and most intelligent of the lot were formed into *sekheperu* or drill companies and given further military training before being sent off to their units to become *menfyt* or seasoned soldiers. The rest were sent as manpower to work on the public buildings, quarries, bridges and other construction projects. Once the *menfyt* arrived at their regiments they received more training in the military arts. My mind went back to when I sailed from Damietta to Pela aboard the *Spirit of Battle* when it was transporting new soldiers to their posting. I remember thinking then, as young as I was, that those fellows seemed more like boys than soldiers. As I examined the faces of the recruits before me, they seemed even younger to me now.

The barge put its cargo ashore at Om without incident and Sunusret, Thaneni and I watched as the recruits were herded to one side by a group of sergeants and a single officer whose task it was to make sure the conscripts reached Nay-Ta-Hut by nightfall. It was almost twenty miles by foot and it was now just before noon. A march of this distance would take almost seven hours. Each recruit was given a cup of beer and a chunk of bread to eat where he stood. In a very short time the sergeants assembled the recruits into a column four abreast. By rough count I made the group to be about two hundred men. A soldier posted himself at the head of the column carrying a military standard from which hung red and white ribbons, the national colors of Egypt. The sergeants posted themselves at intervals along the sides of the column. The chief sergeant barked a command and the standard bearer raised his standard high enough so that each man could see it. He held it aloft for a few seconds and then dropped it quickly giving the signal for the column to march off. And shuffle off they did without any pretense of keeping in step. The sergeants descended on the rabble with a verbal barrage to force them to march in step. Abuse and obscenities filled the air while frightened conscripts tried desperately to keep in step. And so it went as the column began to make its way to Nay-Ta-Hut.

None of us paid any attention to the cart until it was almost upon us and the driver brought his horse to a halt. Watching the column meander down the road Thaneni, Sunusret and I had wandered into the middle of the road.

"By Seth's ass are you going to stand there all day!" the driver shouted from his perch on the driving bench of the *ka-tana*. The horses' carefully braided mane and the red and white pennant flying from a pole on the wagon made the vehicle immediately recognizable as belonging to the military. The driver was a young officer of the same rank as Sunusret.

"What's the hurry? If you are trying to catch up with that rabble you will not have far to go." Sunusret's voice showed annoyance. Now that he saw that the driver was of the same rank he was determined not to be pushed about by this fellow.

"Just the same," the fellow shouted, "I have to catch up. I really would be pleased if you three moved out of the way." His tone of voice was what often passed for civility in the army. At least he was trying not to make matters worse.

Sunusret's voice lightened. "What is your regiment comrade?" he asked in a light hearted voice. There was a broad smile on his face.

"*Sobek's Nose*," came the reply.

"And a good name too for a regiment stationed in the Delta," Sunusret answered.

The driver laughed.

Sunusret moved next to the horse and stood below the driver's bench. "I take it you are going to accompany that bunch to the Hyksos Fort?" He grinned broadly as he spoke and the driver nodded.

"What about giving me and my two friends a lift? I'm posted with the Memphis garrison and escorting these two to T'aru." Sunusret paused. "What say Sobek's Nose? Will you do your brother officer a favor?"

The driver shook his head and grinned. "Why not," he said. "Its a long ride and I can use the company. Anyway when the sergeants' feet get sore they try to make me drive them too. This way we'll all have a good laugh and they can well learn to take care of their own feet!" He waved to Thaneni and me who had been standing off to one side while the driver spoke to Sunusret.

"Climb aboard," he said. "Hold on to your asses. The benches have no cushions and the road is full of bumps." He looked over his shoulder as we clambered into the bare wooden wagon. The reins snapped loudly against the horse's rump. In a second we were on our way, the tag end of a recruit column bound, hopefully, for better things.

The trip to Nay-Ta-Hut took the full seven hours and then some so that it was dusk by the time the column made its way through the main gate with the three of us, the driver, and the wagon bringing up the rear. I was sore and tired and needed water badly. My throat was parched from the dust kicked up by the column's marching feet. We made our way to a water trough in front of a row of barracks and drank our fill. I soaked a cloth and wiped my face and arms and waited while Thaneni and Sunusret did the same.

The fortress was an enormous enclosure with walls more than thirty feet high running five hundred feet to a side of a great square. Scores of barracks constructed of mud brick were packed side by side along the outside walls. Barns for horses that pulled the chariots were located at the far end of the enclosure. Next to them were the workshops required to construct and repair the machines. Officers' quarters were located on either side of the main gate next to the administrative and command headquarters. The parade ground formed the center of the compound and was enormous compared to the one I had seen at the Citadel in Memphis. This one could easily hold ten regiments at the same time and rightly so, for this garrison was a fighting fort with troops trained and ready for a fight should they be ordered forward.

At Sunusret's suggestion we found the headquarters building where we sought lodging for the evening. The officer in charge said he was sorry but he could find nothing for us. The garrison was at full strength and thousands of new recruits were arriving daily and had to be housed as well. He suggested that we find an inn in the town. It was almost dark when we finally found one that would rent us rooms. After placing our baggage in our rooms we washed and went downstairs to eat.

*The Ram's Head* was a typical soldier's inn complete with cheap food, wine, and beer and a collection of women who provided entertainment and companionship. Seth himself only knew how long the place had been here, but Tay-Na-Hut had been a soldier's town for a very long time. Wherever there were soldiers there were inns like this with their thin fare and beckoning women. Both, of course, could be had for a price. We ordered meat, bread, and wine and ate ravenously for it had been a long time since we had last eaten that day. The food comforted my belly. Little by little a warm glow crept over me until I felt relaxed and a bit sleepy. I could see that Sunusret and Thaneni were beginning to feel the same way. The three of us sat back in our chairs. Sunusret poured wine for us all.

"It has been a tiring day," I said to no one in particular. "Even the thin mattress on our bed will feel comfortable tonight!" My words brought laughter. I looked around the place and shook my head. "Not much to look at," I said with a smile.

Sunusret nodded his head. "But enough for a soldier with a little money and some time on his hands," he said. He gestured toward a table in the corner. "There you have it, Thutmose." I turned toward the table behind me. A short plump woman with a blue wig was sitting on the lap of a soldier stroking his hair and whispering in his ear. There was a broad smile on the soldier's face as he rubbed the girl's haunch with his free hand. I turned back to Sunusret with my eyebrows raised and a sly grin on my face.

"I see what you mean my friend," I said.

Thaneni laughed. I could tell from his words that he had had to much to drink. "Perhaps we ought to purchase one of those for you Thutmose?" he said pointing to the woman on the soldier's lap. His eyes had an impish gleam to them and I could tell that Thaneni was having a joke at my expense.

I shook my head and grinned. "Not on your life!" I said and broke into laughter. "Besides," I said, "She looks just fat enough for you, my friend! I prefer them with a little less meat on their bones!" The three of us broke into a loud round of laughter at the whole business more from the wine than from the wit of my words.

At last fatigue got the better of us and we climbed the steps to the second floor and our rooms. I was exhausted and it was an effort to remove my clothes before falling into bed. Unlike the night before, sleep came quickly and with it dreams of scattered images of the long day's events. After only a short time, I tumbled into a deep slumber and rested my body and mind.

The next day dawned hot and humid as did all days in the Delta during the flood season. We ate breakfast and headed back to the fortress in search of transportation to Bast. As luck would have it a small boat carrying a recruit drill company was on its way there and we obtained permission to travel with it. Usually the route from Nay-Ta-Hut to Bast was by road. But during the flood the waters of the irrigation canals overflowed their banks turning the fields into shallow lakes that could be crossed by shallow draft boats powered by polemen and small sails. In the dry months the journey would have taken two days. By boat we reached Bast in a day.

Bast was a large city renowned throughout Egypt for the great temple in which the local lioness goddess, Bastet, was worshiped. Soldiers knew it as just another military town while generals saw it as the key to the defense of the Delta. It sat at an important crossroads and could defend against attacks from the northeast or the Goshen Valley. Much to my surprise the town's fortifications were not impressive. Even its central citadel was small.

"That's because the troops are deployed at smaller fortresses throughout the countryside," Sunusret explained. "The idea is to delay the enemy for as long as possible until reinforcements can arrive from Memphis and Nay-Ta-Hut."

The town was surrounded by large estates. Sunusret explained that these were gifts from Pharaoh to distinguished officers who had retired from military service. Thutmose I, my grandfather, began the practice of giving his best officers twelve *khet* of land free of tax from which to draw a living after leaving the army. These estates were located near large military garrisons and a brisk trade grew up between them and the garrisons in food and supplies. Many of the sons of the soldiers who grew up near the garrisons entered military service as well. And so it was my grandfather's practice of awarding his soldiers farms that made it possible for a soldier to spend his life in the military and still have a respectable retirement. It was the beginning of Egypt's professional officer corps. When I became pharaoh I, too, awarded these farms to my soldiers, but only on the condition that their families provide at least one serving officer for as long as they held title to the property. It was a practical arrangement and one that persisted to this very day.

We spent only one night in Bast and in the morning were on our way again. It was sixty miles from Bast to T'aru. We traveled by rented boat along the canal that connected the two cities and provided the water that gave life to the lush green fields of the Goshen Valley. We had not traveled ten miles on the canal before coming upon one of the smaller forward fortresses at a village called Sopdu. The fortress itself occupied a rectangle of ground perhaps only fifty yards long by thirty yards wide and was surrounded by ten foot high walls that fell straight from the top parapet without a single degree of slope. The corners of the rectangle were rounded, a feature that prevented the corners from crumbling under the weight. The walls were constructed of bricks made from Nile mud mixed with straw for strength and baked in the sun. The pattern of brick work was typically Egyptian in that the broad flat sides of the bricks were laid alternately with the narrow sides of the other bricks. The main gate formed a perfect arch where the bricks on the inside of the arch were notched and fitted together to form a half-circle. Thick wooden doors opened inward toward the main parade ground. I guessed the whole enclosure could hold barely two companies of men.

Our boat glided slowly over the canal's calm waters and a few
soldiers waved to us from the ramparts. As the little craft pulled
even with the front of the fort, Thaneni and I squinted into the sun
trying to get a better look at the fortifications. From behind me I
heard Sunusret's voice.

"Thutmose, look at the far corner of the upper wall." I turned
my head and shaded my eyes with my hands. Again Sunusret's
voice fell on my ears. "There," he said stretching out his hand to
point out the direction where I should look. "Over there! Can you
see it?" he asked.

My eyes searched the far wall until I saw what looked like two
dark pieces of thick canvas hanging side by side from the top of the
wall. I drew Thaneni's attention to them and he shaded his eyes to
get a clearer look. I stood staring at the objects for a few minutes
unable to make out what they were. At last the boat's progress
brought me closer to where I could get a good look. I could hardly
believe my eyes! I turned to Thaneni about to speak when he, too,
recognized what he was seeing and blurted out an oath.

"By Seth's great balls! What have they done to those men!"

The look of shock on his face was met by my own look of horror at what I had seen. We both turned to Sunusret who was staring at the wall shaking his head in anger.

I turned back to the sight before me, still uncertain of what I
was seeing. Hanging from the fortress wall were the bodies of two
men whose feet had been nailed onto a wooden board fixed to the
outer wall. Their bodies hung like slabs of spoiled meet grown rotten from the heat and the sun. The corpses' skin was black like
overbaked bread. Their arms hung limply from their sockets.
Bloated stomachs and what was left of their faces were covered by
a cloud of black flies. The flesh on their lower legs had been eaten
away so only bone connected their knees to their feet through
which large holes had been made by the metal spikes that had

been driven through them into the wood. Not much flesh remained to hold the feet to the wall. It would be only a few more days before that, too, was weakened by decay and finally gave way and the corpses fell to the ground.

"Sweet Isis!" I cried out. "Sunusret what has happened here? Why are those two men hanging there like dead animals?"

There was a sound of outrage in my voice. It was a bad habit of mine to become outraged over something upon first impression without waiting for an explanation. It was something I gradually rid myself of as I grew older. Doing so I found helped me avoid considerable embarrassment. But the sight of the two corpses that day was so unnerving that my outrage could not be contained.

A serious expression came over Sunusret's face and his voice became stern to the point of anger when he spoke. "That, Thutmose, is military justice!" He shook his head and spat. "There is too much of this kind of stuff if you ask me." He paused and looked toward the corpses upon the wall. "A terrible waste of good soldiers," he said and shook his head.

"What do you think they did to deserve such terrible punishment?" My voice had lost its outrage. I felt only sadness and I could hear that sorrow in my voice.

Sunusret shrugged. "Who knows? It could have been anything." He took a deep breath. "They could have been caught stealing. Maybe they were trying to desert. It's hard to say. Maybe they killed some girl or attacked a merchant. Who knows?" He shrugged again. "Its hard to say."

I could see that Sunusret was troubled.

"Do they often execute soldiers who commit crimes?" I asked.

"Too much for my blood," he said. "Usually if the crime is not too bad they just flog the poor wretch within an inch of his life. Once I saw a soldier attack his officer. They cut the nose and ears off that poor fellow. Another who killed a comrade in a fight at an inn was blinded. Others have been branded." Sunusret sighed. "Its all up to the commander. Some of them are just and others are animals." He shrugged again to show his resignation to a system that was beyond his control.

"But surely," I said, "the crime in this case must have been very serious. They nailed their feet to the top of the wall and let them hang there until they died! Even their eyes were left open!"

Thaneni gave forth with a visible shudder and he shook his head as if trying to drive away the chills. It was the kind of gesture that any Egyptian might have made at my words. A corpse with open eyes attracted crows to pick at them. The beak of an Egyptian crow is not sharp enough to cut through the skin and so must eat only those parts that its beak can tear. Egyptian soldiers going into battle fear their fate at the beaks of the crow. To have one's eyes pecked out before the body can be preserved meant that the poor soul would stumble through eternity with blackened eyes. An eternity of darkness is more than most men can contemplate without shuddering.

"Most likely you are right, Thutmose. Even in the army this punishment is reserved for the hardest cases." He paused. The wall was behind us now as the boat sailed on. "At least we know they weren't tomb robbers," he said. There was a curious lilt to Sunusret's voice as if he had recovered from what he had seen and was no longer bothered by it.

"Why do you say that?" I asked.

He smiled now. Humor was replacing horror. It was something I saw many times in my life when men who survived a terrifying sight warded off their own fears by giddy laughter and jokes.

"Well if they had been tomb robbers they would have been impaled up the ass with a sharpened stake and raised straight up upon it until the stake worked its way deeper into the body and finally killed the victim." He paused and smiled a nervous grin. "I saw it done once. Took three hours for the man to die."

The look on Sunusret's face was so comical that for some grotesque reason it struck me funny and I blurted out a short laugh. Thaneni looked at me for a few seconds and tried to hold back his own laughter. Sunusret was grateful to have company in his outrageous behavior and laughed openly. And so it went while the little boat plied its way down the canal toward T'aru moved by a single poleman who must have thought us all mad as we laughed until our sides hurt and the vision of the rotten corpses was driven from our minds.

T'aru was another of the Delta's military towns. Its narrow streets were choked with soldiers and vehicles accompanied by the constant noise of horses, chariot wheels, and the stomp of marching feet. The fortress was located at the town's eastern boundary facing the Sinai. Two miles to the front of the walls was the smaller of the two Bitter Lakes connected to its larger brother by a natural canal running north to south and emptying into the Sea of Seth. T'aru sat astride Egypt's most vulnerable invasion route. It was the most important fortress in a system of fortresses designed to protect the Black Land from the wrath of Egypt's enemies. To Egyptians T'aru was known as the "Gate of the Barbarians," the gateway through which the dreaded Hyksos poured when they overran Egypt.

It did not take long to make our way from the landing through the town and out to the fort. A soldier directed us to the headquarters building and the office of the commanding officer. My heart beat quickly with excitement at the thought of seeing Amenemhab again. We had not set eyes upon each other in more than four years and my heart ached for the sight of my oldest friend. A staff officer guided the three of us into an anteroom and showed us to some chairs. He disappeared into the adjoining room and closed the door behind him. Battle flags of the various regiments hung from poles all along the side wall. The red and white standard of Egypt fashioned as a fan of ostrich feathers stood on one side of the doorway. The standard of the Army of Ptah in the form of a painting of the sacred Apis Bull attached to a wooden staff stood on the other.

The door flew open without warning and Amenemhab came barrelling through it like a great chariot wheel turning out of control. His eyes found me in a second and a broad grin spread across his face while his voice boomed with laughter. He rushed toward me. I had barely risen from my seat before his powerful arms took me in their grasp and raised me off my feet in an embrace as powerful as that of a great Syrian bear.

"A-ha!" his voice boomed off the walls. "At last we meet again, my prince!" Amenemhab swung me around and put me down gently. He stepped back folded his arms and looked pleasingly at me. Trapped in that affectionate gaze for a few precious seconds, I felt that I was a child again. From deep within my heart the familiar words took shape. "Captain, Captain! Show me your eye!"

It was what I always had said to him whenever I rushed to him in the Garden and I almost blurted them out then and there. But I said nothing and all I could do was grin like a fool to show Amenemhab how pleased I was to see him.

"By Seth's balls you have grown!" he roared. "When I last left you you were but a stripling!" He paused and spread his hands. "But now, look at you. You are almost full grown, a man with powerful limbs and strong features." He meant my nose of course, the feature for which the Thutmosides were famous! Amenemhab winked at me. "No mistaking who your father was!" He threw his great head back and a hearty laugh came from his throat. He put his arm around my shoulder and pulled me close. I could feel his warm breath on my face. "Come, my prince. We have much to

talk about," he said and led me into his office leaving Sunusret
and Thaneni sitting there with their mouths open.

Streaks of gray ran through his asiatic beard. But except for
that Amenemhab had not changed much. He was still the gruff
commander whose presence could not be ignored whenever he
was in a room. He always had a soft spot in his heart for me and
even now sitting there watching him speak it was difficult to
remember that here was a man who had killed an enemy with his
teeth and whose subordinates walked in fear of his anger. We
talked for quite a long time and I enjoyed telling him of my adventures. Finally I presented him with my letter from Senenmut which
he read with great interest.

"I think it a good idea in light of the circumstances,
Thutumose. There is nothing but danger for you in Thebes. Here
at least you will be safe. Besides, the life of a young officer can be
very exciting." He smiled. "And you never know about things,
how things will turn around after time has had a chance to do its
work. At least in the army you will make friends. Should the
opportunity present itself they can be very helpful. You are still
regent and the queen will not live forever." His words were spoken lightly but there was a serious intent behind them. He was
telling me to bide my time, to make something of myself and perhaps, just perhaps, the gods would notice and cast their favor
upon me. It was good advice as things turned out.

Amenemhab arranged for Thaneni and me to be billeted with the
other young officers in the garrison and entrusted my training to the
careful tutoring of an old sergeant named Merykare. Amenemhab
had been a common soldier himself before his bravery raised him to
an officer. He carried with him a belief that young officers should be
trained by experienced soldiers like Merykare. Far too many of the
young officers these days came from wealthy and privileged backgrounds and lacked the discipline and commitment to the military

life to make good leaders. In Amenemhab's command all young officers were trained by tough old sergeants, although this was certainly not common practice elsewhere in the army. Amenemhab believed that before a man could lead he first had to know what it was like to follow. And so my fate was entrusted to sergeant Merykare, a grizzled veteran of many campaigns and a man of no illusions whatsoever.

I was not Merykare's only student. He was in charge of the group of officer aspirants that had been sent to T'aru for training. I was simply added to the group. We were to be trained first as infantry officers and then, if we did well, the better among us would be trained further as chariot commanders. Officers who performed poorly were sent home to their families, although this was not regarded as a disgrace by the nobility who, after all, had more important and lucrative things to do in any case. Others who performed adequately were permitted to serve in the infantry. From what I could tell of my comrades they were no more prepared for the likes of Merykare than I was.

Horus' rays had not yet crept over the horizon to give birth to the new day when Merykare and his sergeants woke the group of us from our slumber and assembled us in double ranks on the parade ground of the T'aru fortress.

"Good morning to you gentlemen," he said. His voice was even with no trace of harshness. He cracked a thin smile. "Welcome to T'aru." The skin on his face looked like old papyrus browned and deeply lined by years of exposure to the sun. Merykare was of normal height and quite muscular. Powerful legs held his back rigidly erect as he spoke.

"My name is Merykare and my job is to make officers of you fine young men." He paused. "As long as you do as you are told we will have no problems. My advice is that you pay close attention to the lessons we will teach you. If you do you will succeed. If not, you will fail."

A grin like the smile of a crocodile appeared on Merykare's face.

"And try to remember that when you fail in battle you die!"

He paused and smiled again.

"So, gentlemen, if you are going to fail do it here where you won't cause anyone else's death but your own."

Merykare's words pierced my consciousness. I struggled to rid my mind of the cobwebs of sleep. The next thing I knew Merykare was shouting at us while he and the sergeants formed us four abreast into several ranks to practice the first skill of soldiers in all armies, marching drill! And so it began. Merykare marched us first in one direction and then another over and over again until our little group began to show some semblance of military order. Marching in step was difficult to learn or so it seemed to me then. After an hour or so of continuous effort our bodies were soaked with sweat and the toe loop of my sandals had cut through the skin between my toes. And still it went on over and over again. By now the sun had risen above the fortress wall and beat down upon us without relief. My throat was dry. Dust covered me from head to foot and my feet felt as if they were on fire. As tired as I was some of my comrades seemed to be suffering more. And then Merykare brought our group to a halt. He stood before us watching the dust settle on our clothes. Behind him I could see a group of soldiers laughing at us as they passed by. Merykare's voice grabbed my full attention.

"Not bad for the first day," he said.

Our tormentor actually sounded sincere! I waited for what he had to say next.

"Good soldiers have to eat," he said. "Follow me!"

He led us to the edge of the drill ground to a long table that had been set up against the outside wall of the common room where the soldiers took their meals. We each picked up a wooden plate and clay cup from the end of the table and moved down to where soldiers were serving food. I stuck my plate in front of him and the soldier placed two pieces of fish on it. Another soldier poured me a cup of milk and another threw a piece of bread upon my plate. I was famished. For a moment I thought of asking for more food. But my hesitation brought a glare from the server and I said nothing. I sat down on the dusty ground along with the others and rested my plate in my lap.

Never had I tasted such terrible food in my life! The fish was dried and heavily salted. It tasted like thick papyrus. Were it not for the overpowering flavor of salt, it would have had no taste at all. The milk was warm and already sour. Only the gods knew when it had been taken from the teat! And the bread! Even by Egyptian standards the bread was terrible and hard enough to break a tooth! Merykare had turned eating into another torment. A few of my comrades would have none of it and simply threw the salted fish and milk upon the ground. The sneer on Merykare's face when he saw this was enough to dissuade me from doing it. Besides, I was hungry and thirsty. If the soldiers could somehow manage to swallow it I could too. I took two big bites of my fish and washed it down with a quick swallow of the soured milk. To my surprise my belly did not throw it back at me and in a few minutes the fish was gone. I settled down to gnawing upon my bread in hopes of somehow getting it inside me.

The temporary respite was followed with more drill practice. At midday we were given water and a short rest. Then back again to the parade field. Up and down, up and down we went, soaked with sweat and becoming more uncomfortable with every step. Merykare was like the sun and gave us no relief for hours on end. Many of us had bleeding feet, for the sandals we had were not up to the punishment that hours of marching inflicted upon them. At some point one of our number could no longer endure the punishment and simply lost consciousness and fell face down in the dust. Merykare was unaffected by this and marched us around the fallen man. One of the assistants drew a bucket of water from a horse trough and threw it over the fellow. But it did little good. At last Merykare ordered him dragged from the field and immersed in the horse trough. That did the trick and our comrade began to come around. Good thing too. For a time I thought he might actually be dead!

At last Merykare brought us to a halt. Standing there in the hot sun I was beginning to feel like I might lose my wits. Clay jugs of cold water were passed among us and we drank our fill. Some drank too much too quickly and within minutes their stomachs gave them great pains. We were allowed to move into the shade against the wall and sit down. We were all exhausted.

Merykare stood before us with a broad smile upon his face. "Well, gentlemen," he said pleasantly, "I trust your first day of military life has been a rewarding one for you." It was a remark that did not strike me just then as humorous. He must have seen the expression of displeasure upon my face for he seemed to look straight at me when he spoke.

"Your first lesson is that you must learn to endure hardship, to persevere when your body aches and your mind is tired. Today you have had your first taste of discomfort." His tone of voice told us clearly what he was thinking, that we had come from lives of comfort where effort and physical pain were remote things. "And that is what you are going to learn to do over the next few weeks, to suffer, to endure and still keep going." He smiled sarcastically. "It might be a new experience for you. But I can assure you it is one that your soldiers are very familiar with!" With that he turned and walked away leaving us there sitting in the dust.

I made my way back to my room. Thaneni was appalled at my appearance. After moaning about it for a few minutes, he supplied me with a basin of cold water and some wash cloths. I tore one of the cloths into strips and tied it around my big toe to comfort the skin on my feet rubbed raw by my sandals. Thaneni appeared with some proper food and beer and over dinner I recounted the day's events for my friend who, I must confess, counted himself lucky to be my scribe instead of my suffering comrade in arms.

The next day and the next and the next Merykare drilled us again and again until we finally began to move together. By week's end we could march reasonably well. But our achievement brought no end to the suffering we endured at Merykare's hands as he fed us poor food and deprived us of sufficient water. In one thing, however, he did see to our needs and had us all supplied with military sandals. Their soles were fashioned of thick leather, not the stuff of papyrus or thin animal skin that was usually worn by Egyptian civilians. Besides the thong between the toes and the instep strap our new sandals had a third strap that passed around the heel and held the sandal tightly against the foot making it easier to run with. As much an improvement as they were over what we had brought with us I found that even these sandals worked well only so long as we were in the soft desert sands. On rocky ground they were not much good at protecting our feet and foot injuries were a common feature of the Egyptian army on the march. Later, when I could do with the armies as I wished, I ordered the soles of the sandals to be made thicker. I copied the experience of the people of the land bridge and the Lebanon who lived in cold and rocky mountains and ordered that our sandals have sides put on them so that they could be wrapped around the foot and held in place by the instep strap. My armies find this to be a great improvement and my officers lose fewer men to injuries.

Such devices, however, do little to put an end to the injuries caused by horses and mules stepping on the soldiers' feet.

We had been in Merykare's strong grip for two weeks and had not been permitted to venture beyond the fortress walls. All our training, mostly marching and running in the heat to build our endurance, had been accomplished on the parade field. One morning Merykare assembled us as usual. As always his voice was sarcastically pleasant.

"This is a water canteen. Next to his spear and *kopesh* it is the infantryman's most important friend. Even when your weapons fail you and your men are scattered across the desert by the enemy, this will keep you alive."

One of Merykare's assistants distributed the canteens. The water canteen was a leather bottle whose inside had been sealed with wax. The thin neck was fitted with a clay stopper tied by a leather string. Leather thongs wrapped around the bottle permitted it to be tied to our belts so that the canteen rested comfortably upon the hip. The bottle held enough water for a day's ration. In the Egyptian desert heat even this amount had to be used carefully to last this long. For marches we were given a larger water container that looked like a long leather bag much like the skins used for carrying wine. These water bags had a strap that permitted them to be carried across the chest. There was sufficient water in one of these bags to keep a soldier going for another two days if he used it sparingly.

With our canteens filled and our water bags left behind Merykare led us out the front gate of the fortress. Our direction of march was to the south. An hour later we stood at the desert's edge where the farmlands of the Goshen Valley gave way to the bleak sands. It required but a single step to leave one world and enter another. It was Merykare's plan to teach us how to survive in this hostile world.

Merykare himself set the pace and we marched straight into the desert. The land was uneven and changed from harsh rocky soil that made our feet hurt to places where the sand was as soft and flowing as crushed wheat. Here footing was difficult and it took a great deal of strength just to put one foot in front of the other and not loose one's balance. As always the sun gave us no peace. One of Merykare's assistants soaked a piece of cloth with water from his canteen and placed it on his head. Seeing this many of my comrades did the same. Some of them had arrived at T'aru with shaven heads and the sun's rays burned their skin raw. Most military men wore their hair closely cropped but long enough to provide protection from Horus's rays. The shaven skull of the priest or Egyptian nobility was a rare sight in the infantry.

The sun's heat was taken in by the desert sands and given back with a vengeance so that it surrounded us the way the heat of a stove surrounds and bakes bread. I watched as time and again my comrades drank from their canteen bottles. Others wet the cloths on their heads with the precious liquid. I was surprised that Merykare remained silent when they did this. I kept a close eye on him as we slogged our way forward. I resolved to drink only when he did. The old fox was up to some trick or other and I was determined not to be taken by surprise.

Four hours later we halted in the shade of a large boulder and were allowed to rest. One of Merykare's assistants passed among us distributing rations. Each soldier was given half a pigeon that had been salted and dried, an onion, some bread, and two dried figs. We were hungry from our morning labors and the food went quickly. Usually the taste of salt was overpowering. This time I welcomed the normally unpleasant salt and it sat calmly upon my tongue and stomach. The Egyptian heat makes fresh food inedible in only a few hours so most of what the army consumes on campaign is dried, salted, pickled or pressed to keep it from rotting.

Game birds, meat, fish and gooseflesh are usually dried and salted. Meat, too, is pickled and smoked. Egypt grows little fruit besides figs and dates and these are packed and dried when used as army rations. Thin flat bread baked in mud ovens is a common staple since it is easy to make and transport. Vegetables like onions, leeks, turnips, cucumbers and radishes are usually eaten raw unless the army is encamped and permitted cooking fires. From time to time we would get melons that grew wild in the desert. It was always a time for joking when we received these. They were called *bedded-kau*, and were said to come from the seed of Seth who ejaculated onto the barren ground!

Merykare marched us further into the desert for another hour before turning us around and marching us back in the direction from which we had come. Now the heat and exhaustion began to take its toll. Some of my comrades had consumed all their water. By watching Merykare and drinking only when he did I still had half my water bottle left. One fellow raised his bottle to his mouth and began to drink. Suddenly another man was upon him knocking the bottle from his hand and scurrying after it as it spilled its precious liquid on the sand. Another man flew at him and the two struggled to possess the prize. The first man rose to his feet and attacked the other two. There was death in his eyes. If he had a dagger he would surely have slain his comrades. I glanced at Merykare who stood off to one side watching the fight go on. A perverse smile crossed his lips. He glanced at his assistants who smiled back at him. At last heat and exhaustion put an end to the struggle and the three men lay in the sun gasping for breath. Merykare gathered us around them.

"Take a good look at these fools!" His words were venomous and full of anger. "This is what happens when you fail to keep water discipline. First you become an animal and then you die!"

He raised his eyes and looked at me when he spoke.

"These men will be dead in a few hours. If this were a campaign march we would leave them behind."

He shook his head in disgust.

"Which of you will share your water with them?"

Merykare's evil grin crawled across his face. He snickered as he saw each of us touch his water bottle to make certain it was safe from the others. He began to laugh.

"Remember this lesson," he said. "Always plan for sufficient water. Make certain you have a map showing what waterholes are of use to you."

He lowered his eyes to the three men on the ground.

"Otherwise you'll end up like these assholes!" He spat at them and walked away.

Merykare's assistants gave the three men some water and forced them to their feet. None had much strength left and we had to take turns holding them up as we made our way back to the fortress. Still I watched Merykare and drank only when he did. By the time we reached the Goshen canal and were permitted to drink our fill I checked my water bottle and discovered that there was still some water left in it. I had done it! I made my water last the full day like any veteran soldier would have. The three men were never again accepted into our little group. They had proven them-selves ill disciplined and selfish and were of little use should it come to a fight. We did nothing to punish them directly. They were simply gnored by the rest of their comrades. One day Merykare announced to us that the three had been sent back to their families. I am certain they were better for it. We certainly were.

On other forays into the desert we were taught how to use the sun to maintain direction. Lessons in tracking helped us learn to look for the signs of ambush. Merykare taught us how to calculate distance by using the shadow clock. The clock was little more than a stick with marked intervals and a crossbar with a peg in it attached to one end. When the cross bar was aligned properly the peg threw a shadow down the length of the bar and the hour could be read at the marked intervals. After the noon hour the clock was reversed so that the shadow lengthened the further the hour was from noon. By knowing how fast a man could march and how much time had passed since the last measurement it was possible to figure how long it took to march from one place to another. Gradually we were becoming soldiers and gaining confidence in the skills Merykare taught us. We even began to regard the old fox with some affection. We were, after all, becoming like him!

As for me, I was enjoying myself. Much to my surprise I discovered that I enjoyed the outdoor life. Once my body adjusted and I became accustomed to marching I even enjoyed that unless, of course, Merykare played one of his tricks on us and we suffered. Whatever was left of my childhood disappeared. My body felt fit and my muscles strong, and the disturbing squeak in my voice had not been heard in months. But mostly my travails in the desert bequeathed me a sense of confidence that I had never felt before. No longer did I require long intervals to think things through and to make up my mind. I was less given to procrastination, second-guessing, and doubt in my thinking. Perhaps this came from living the life of an infantryman where, after all, almost everything about you constricted your choices so that whatever remained seemed obvious. Why I changed did not seem to matter to me as much as that I changed and for the better. Perhaps it was only that I was a man now and on my way to becoming a soldier that made the difference.

Weeks of drill and marching sleeping on the ground and eating bad food had made us an angry lot, especially so since after all this time none of us had even seen a spear or shield. I, too, was anxious to get on with the real business of soldiering, learning how to fight. Merykare was an old hand at training soldiers and sensed our impatience. The next day we were taken to the practice fields and given weapons.

There are two types of infantry in the Egyptian army, the *megau* or "shooters" who use the bow and the *nakhtu-aa* or "strong arm boys" trained in close order hand-to-hand fighting. Merykare did not think much of archers and we were trained as *nakhtu-aa*. We were first given a wooden shield covered with bull hide. It weighs about fifteen pounds and is flat on the bottom and rounded at the top so that it can be rested on the ground when used to form a wall of shields. Merykare made us carry the thing around at arms length for a while to get us accustomed to its weight. Its weight and the single handgrip make the shield difficult to use if you try to push the other fellow around with it. Instead, as Merykare showed us, it is best used as a barrier to the other fellow's weapons. If you crouch a bit the shield covers most of your body. From this position you can lash out at the enemy with your spear. The spear or *dja* is a meter long shaft of wood tipped with a bronze blade and socket cast in one piece and fastened to the shaft with rivets. Merykare taught us to resist the temptation to throw the weapon at the enemy. Most of the time you missed and found yourself without a spear to counter an attack. The proper way to use the *dja*, Merykare said, was to use it overhand as a stabbing weapon striking out from behind your own shield either over or around your opponent's shield. It all seemed simple enough until you realized that your enemy was trying to do the same thing! Once we began to train in mock combat with each other it became clear that a good spearman needed strength, endurance, and plenty of courage to do his job well providing, of course, you cared whether or not he lived or died!

Merykare was an expert in all the weapons of the infantry, whether the sickle sword, the socket axe, or the dagger. He took great delight in engaging us in mock combat with these deadly devices to show us the proper way to use each one. He was a master of every maneuver and dirty trick and applied them all with equal ease. Merykare particularly liked the socket axe which, he said, could split a shield in two if you hit it right and he could wield the *kopesh* or sickle-sword with deadly grace and speed. It was difficult for me to imagine anyone who was better at his work. All of us agreed that if we had to go into battle we wanted Merykare next to us! In those days the infantry fought with little armor. We wore thick bands of stiff linen criss-crossed over the chest that held a leather or bronze breast plate in place. A piece of thick fabric stiff with starch protected our balls and the leather belt from which our weapons hung helped protect our belly. Officers and charioteers wore helmets of bronze while the infantry wore a cloth hat that looked like the linen *nemset* headdress worn by Pharaoh. I have seen enough Egyptian heads split open to know that while this headdress helped keep the sun from our skulls it did little to soften the blow of a battle axe.

It required a long time and a great deal of hard training to become proficient with these weapons. But no matter how long one trained one could never be certain of the most important weapon in the arsenal of the soldier, his courage to stand and fight. As I became more practiced with my weapons the more I wondered what it would be like to fight another human being and kill him. The more I thought about it the more unpleasant the whole thing seemed. The truth was that the thought of killing held a strange fascination for us all. The very idea was always before us. Merykare saw to that. No lesson went by without the admonition to "stick him in the guts!" or "smash the bastard in the face!" Whenever one of us was vanquished by our instructors in mock combat or committed some error or other we were reminded that if we did that in battle we would be dead and left as food for the flies and hyenas! Over and over again images of death motivated us to train hard. It was, as all soldiers find out sooner or later, a cruel deception, a theater play to convince young men uncertain of their courage that they could endure the terrible reality of personal combat.

Infantry fighting is very different. The archer does not have to look into the eyes of the man he slays. To the charioteer the javelin or the arrow takes down his prey bloodlessly and at a distance. But the infantryman does his work with his sandals covered in the blood of men whose terror at being struck down screams from their mouths and leaps from their eyes. Death is always close by and never its own witness. In the infantry there is no hiding what one has done or what one has become once the sword has been buried to its hilt in the warm flesh of another man's body. One is truly never the same.

But all this was hidden from us young officers as it must be. Once we became good enough with our weapons we practiced close order drill again and again, this time in full kit to get used to moving under the weight of our equipment. Chariots fight alone much of the time. But the infantryman who finds himself alone is slain as easily as a young gazelle. There is strength in numbers, and day after day we practiced marching in line and wheeling into position until it became second nature for us to maneuver as a unit.

And then it was done. We had been in the care of Merykare for three months when he assembled us as usual one morning. This time he stood before us in his full battle kilt flanked by a scribe on one side and the *idnu* or adjutant on the other. Merykare stepped forward.

"Well, gentleman, this will be our last meeting. Your training here is complete. I have instructed the scribe to enter your names upon the army list."

He paused and looked at us. The expression on his face was the same as it had been the day I first saw him, a mixture of matter-of-factness and sarcasm. However memorable or not our training was to us, to Merykare it was all the same.

"The adjutant has been told of your performance and has assigned you to your units. I do hope you do well." He turned toward the scribe who handed him a scroll. Merykare took it and passed it to the adjutant.

As things turned out I was assigned to the chariot corps along with about half my comrades. This came as no surprise. Officers from good families always went to the chariot corps unless poor performance or bad politics kept them from it. Then, of course, they went to the infantry. From the corner of my eye I caught a glimpse of Thaneni standing with Amenemhab. Both were smiling as they listened to Merykare bid us farewell. With a simple "good fortune to you," Merykare strode from the parade ground and disappeared into his quarters. It was left to the scribe to dismiss us.

I made my way to where Thaneni and Amenemhab were waiting. Both my old friends embraced me.

"I see you have been assigned to the chariot corps," Amenemhab said with a laugh. "Well, just as well. The infantry is not for everyone." He paused and a snide grin appeared on his face. "But it is for the best!" he shouted and threw back his huge head and laughed loudly.

Thaneni enjoyed the joke too and smiled broadly. I watched the old soldier enjoy himself. He came by his pride in the infantry honestly enough. He was, after all, the commander of a unit of the King's Braves, the most elite soldiers in the army. Each soldier in the regiment is selected only after he has performed a notable act of bravery on the battlefield. Every soldier is a seasoned fighter. As their commander Amenemhab was regarded as the best soldier in the regiment. Here was a man who had earned the respect of all who knew him. Watching him laugh at his own words, I felt happy to be with my old friend again.

Amenemhab draped his arm over my shoulder in an affectionate gesture."Come walk with me," he said. He led Thaneni and me over to the stairway that led to the ramparts atop the front wall of the great fortress. The stairway zig-zagged from landing to landing until it reached the top of the forty foot high wall. From here I could see for miles across the barren Sinai desert that led to the land of the Retjennu and beyond. The fortress stood on the edge of the green fields of Goshen more than a mile back from one of the smaller forts that guarded the bridge over the canal connecting the Bitter Lakes. Each place where the canal narrowed a fortified compound guarded the crossing. To the south the barren desert presented the invader with a formidable barrier to surprise attack. The main coastal road to the northeast passed before the fortress towns of Pela, Migdol, and Sile, each of which possessed a strong garrison to deal with any attack. Together these forts and barriers formed the Wall of Princes.

Amenemhab stared off into the distance for a few minutes gathering his thoughts. Thaneni and I stood beside him silently taking in the beautiful view. After a few minutes the old soldier turned to me and spoke.

"I wanted you to see it from up here where you can get a sense of how it fits together," he said. "The world is changing, Thutmose, and you would do well to understand it as best you can." He sighed. "It was the invasion that changed it all," he said. "The damned Hyksos shook our faith in everything from how we tilled the land to how we fought our wars." He paused for a moment. "Two hundred years! They sat upon this land for two hundred years! And when we finally drove them from it we were left with a great sense of uncertainty about the world and ourselves." Amenemhab shook his head slowly. "It changed how we saw everything." His voice trailed off and he stared at the horizon again. A few moments later he shook off his somber mood.

"Your wars will be very different from mine, Thutmose." He turned back to the horizon. "There'll be no more chewing off of noses I can tell you!" He laughed. "No. From now on it's speed and maneuver. We have the chariot to thank for that."

I looked at him and nodded as if I understood. But Amenemhab must have seen the confusion on my face and wasn't fooled.

"Look at this place," he said. He turned and pointed to the back wall. "Notice how much lower it is than the front wall," he instructed. "The front gate has been widened and there are new gates in the rear and on each side. These changes have been made only in the last few years," he said. "The gates aren't designed to keep the enemy from getting in! They're designed to let our chariots out! The gates are wide enough to allow three machines at a time to pass through them." He paused for a few moments. "Forts are used differently now, "he said. "The idea is to force the enemy to gather around them in an attack. Once they do you can use your chariots to sweep out and attack their flanks and rear. If you do it right you can crush the enemy against your own walls like a hammer upon an anvil." Amenemhab sighed. "You have chosen well, Thutmose. The future is with the chariot, not with old foot soldiers like me."

The desert terrain around T'aru was suitable for training charioteers and the army had established a training "stable" as they were called at the fortress. A few days after completing my infantry training I reported to the officer in charge of the "stable." He was a gruff sort and he asked me if I knew how to handle a bow. When I replied that I didn't, he shook his head almost in disbelief.

"We can't have you running around on a chariot throwing stones at the enemy now can we?" he said sarcastically. "A chariot without an archer isn't much use you know." He breathed a deep sigh then directed me to report to the section of the "stable" that trained archers. There I introduced myself to a sergeant named Khu who, as it turned out, could hit a bird on the wing with an arrow from a hundred paces and taught me how to shoot.

Khu's first words were encouraging enough. "It's not very difficult to shoot a bow," he said pleasantly. "The hard part is hitting something!" From the expression on his face I guessed that he had used this same joke on every officer who was sent to him. I smiled obligingly. Khu took a bow case from its place in a rack of cases and placed it upon the table. He opened it and carefully lifted the bow and handed it to me.

"Here," he said, "get the feel of it."

I took it and examined the instrument closely. It was about a yard and a half long and somewhat heavier than I had imagined although, as I later learned, this weight helped steady the weapon when aiming it. Khu drew my attention to the center of the bow, what he called the "belly."

"A good bow starts with a stiff wooden stave that can be carved flat." He ran his finger along the flat part of the staff. "Look at the center," he continued. There were several thin layers of what seemed to be ram's horn glued together over the belly and wrapped tightly with thin leather strips. "That's what gives it its power," he said pointing to the thick center of the bow. Khu told me that the bows had to be kept in their cases much of the time. If there was too much moisture in the air the glue that held the horn strips weakened and made the weapon useless. Archers took great care with these fine instruments and many even gave them names!

"Here let me have it," Khu said.

Using his knee Khu pressed the bow outward slipping the bow-string's loop over the notch at the end of the bow. He relaxed the pressure of his knee against the wood and plucked the string as one would a lute. The bowstring was made of two strands of twisted gut that made a low buzzing sound when plucked. Khu handed the bow back to me.

"See if you can draw the string to your ear."

It took more strength than I had thought to draw the bowstring all the way back. The force needed to keep my arm rigid made it impossible for me to aim straight. I wondered how I would ever learn to hit anything with this thing, never mind hit anything while I was standing on a chariot moving along at full gallop! Khu chuckled at my difficulty as I relaxed my grip on the bowstring.

"Don't worry. You'll get it with practice," he said. "You'll be surprised at its power. A good bow can put an arrow through five pine boards or a copper ingot three inches thick." He turned and picked a quiver of arrows from the rack and took a single arrow from the quiver and handed it to me.

The arrow was a yard long and fashioned from a reed shaft. It had a hardwood tip with a bronze arrowhead fastened to it with a single rivet. The rear or nock was made of hardwood as well and gave the bowstring excellent purchase against the arrow. Three fletched feathers on the rear of the shaft kept the arrow stable in flight.

"How far can one of these arrows fly," I asked.

"A good archer can send an arrow more than three hundred yards if he shoots on an arc," he said. Khu frowned. "But you don't have to worry about that. A good driver can get a chariot archer much closer." He paused. "If you can hit something at twenty yards you'll be able to do your job when the time comes."

Khu took me to the target range and showed me how to draw and release the bow. And then he left me to myself for the next few days as I practiced getting the hang of the deadly instrument. At first I managed only to get sore fingers and a bruised forearm from the bowstring snapping against it each time I released an arrow. But eventually I caught on to it and by week's end I could hit the target with some regularity and Khu pronounced me marginally fit to use the weapon.

I returned to the officer in charge of the "stable" who seemed satisfied with my slow progress and assigned me to a pair of grooms named Kheti and Abu whose task it was to make a charioteer of me. If I had known then that it would take a year before I was sufficiently competent to be assigned to a chariot squadron I would have ignored Amenemhab's advice and stayed in the infantry! Still, it was what I wanted to do and much of the training was quite fun. I learned much about these magnificent war machines that served me well when my armies fought against the Mitanni at the Great Bend of the Euphrates.

Each chariot fell to the care of two grooms to see to the horses and a repairman whose task it was to make sure the machine was in working order. I spent the first week in the stables listening to Kheti and Abu tell me how to care for the horses. Kheti made it clear from the start that he considered his horses of more value than any chariot commander. He had seen too many fine animals driven into the ground or their legs broken in a fall or killed outright in battle not to regard any charioteer as little more than a two legged fool who kept putting his beauties in harm's way. In those days our horses were small, no more than thirteen hands high or about six feet. When our armies finally brought Syria under our control years later we were able to purchase fine Mitanni and Hittite horses. These were taller and stronger beasts. We took them to Egypt where we bred them as our own. A stallion and a gelding were paired together to a single machine. Unless one of the animals died or was killed the pair always remained together. The horses were black, gray, bay and chestnut, and it was common for chariot squadrons to have the same color horses for every machine in the squadron.

Once, at the end of a day of feeding, washing, and grooming the horses, Abu approached me. He was an older man and had spent his life in the army taking care of horses and charioteers from one end of the empire to another. He had participated in many campaigns and seen many young charioteers he had trained foray into battle and acquit themselves reasonably well. There was a calmness about him that came from doing what he liked and did best. We chatted a bit and then Abu told me that if I felt up to it tomorrow I could take my first ride in a chariot. I was thrilled at the idea. Memories of that heroic ride with Mersu in the Libyan desert flooded my mind and kept me from my sleep.

To my surprise Abu was waiting for me when I arrived at the stables. Kheti was there too and a small group of assistants that I had never seen before. Abu greeted me warmly.

"Well, sir. I trust you are well-rested" he said.

I nodded and smiled. I was ready to begin and looked to Kheti for help in deciding which horses to use. I was about to ask when Abu broke in.

"Sir, I have hitched up the animals and the machine awaits you outside." He smiled warmly again revealing not a trace of what was about to happen. "Why don't you go ahead and I will catch up in a few minutes."

I nodded and strode through the gathering and out the door ready to begin my adventure. I had not taken ten steps before I saw it. The loud sound of coarse laughter suddenly fell around me like the clatter of pottery being shattered. The old nag turned his head and looked at me. For a moment I thought that he, too, was laughing at me! Swaybacked and scarred this was *Soleb,* "He Who Shines In Truth," an old warhorse who had witnessed more battles than any ten horses in the regiment. As a reward for his courage he had been put to pasture and permitted to spend his remaining days in comfort. As it turned out he was only put back in service for "special occasions" such as breaking in a new officer! His ears twitched and he shook his cheeks making a rumbling sound as he stared into my eyes waiting for me to do something.

Whatever confusion filled my mind left me quickly when I saw the "chariot" that Abu had hitched *Soleb* to. It was a small two-wheeled cart with thick wooden wheels. The reins ran over the races and attached to a halter on the animal's head. The whole rig looked ridiculous, and the sound of laughter crashing over me didn't help one bit. I turned in anger about to give the grooms a piece of my mind and found myself staring straight into Abu's face.

He was so close to me that I could smell his breath and count the missing teeth that his broad smile revealed. Before I could speak he grabbed me by the shoulders.

"Ah now, sir. Don't be taking this serious. Its just a little joke that me and the other grooms play on the officers from time to time." He shrugged. "You know we don't mean anything by it."

The laughter had stopped and over Abu's shoulder I could see the other grooms starting to leave having had their joke for the day.

"Besides, sir, it's no joke really. All charioteers start on the training cart."

I glared at Abu.

"You expect me to drive that thing around do you?" My voice was harsh and Abu's face turned serious.

"Yes indeed sir," he said. He paused for a few seconds. "Give it a try. I think you'll find it a bit more difficult than you think."

When it came to chariots Abu knew his business. I had great difficulty making the cart go where I wanted. More than once I turned it over and had to jump free. Every time I stopped to right the cart *Soleb* looked at me over his shoulder with an expression of glib tolerance that was almost human. Of course none of this was new to him. Age had granted him the gift of tolerance of stupid humans who couldn't seem to learn the simple lesson of how to control a horse-drawn cart! And so it went. After several attempts I was finally able to ride around the training ground making gentle turns and changes of direction without toppling the cart.

The larger machine with two horses proved only slightly more difficult to get the hang of than the training cart. One reason was that the machine itself was expertly designed. Egyptian chariots are lighter than those of other armies and are fashioned almost entirely of woods selected for their springiness and strength. Two men can easily carry a chariot across a stream or over rough ground. The floor of chariot iss made of a single stave of wood bent round almost to a half-circle to form the frame. Leather strips are stretched over the frame and covered with hides or woolen or canvas carpet. The cab itself is formed in the same manner and covered on the outside with bull hide and inside with sheepskin. The cab of my chariot measured 1 meter wide, a half meter deep and a meter high. A belly bar across the cab and a leather leg loop helped steady the archer at high speed. Setting the axle far back on the cab keeps the machine stable and maneuverable even at full gallop. Wooden wheels fashioned and interlocked in sections are held together by bronze bands that run completely around the rim and are fastened to it by metal studs whose heads give the wheels good traction over the ground. Wooden spokes held in the center by bronze hubs have to be frequently oiled to prevent the wood from becoming brittle in the heat and shattering at speed. Mutton fat keeps the hub turning smoothly around the axle without wearing it thin.

As balanced and stable as the Egyptian chariot is, it still required practice to aim and fire the bow even at slow speeds. Once I mastered driving the machine I then had to learn how to

hit something with the bow while my driver manuevered the chariot into position. Abu had spent his life around chariots. He was
an accomplished driver and he and I spent many hours on the
practice range with me shooting at targets. Targets the size and
shape of a man and made of copper were arranged in a long row
ten or so yards apart. At first Abu walked our team of horses
down the length of the range while I tried to remain upright, take
an arrow from the quiver, nock the bowstring, aim and fire. It
came as no surprise to Abu that even at a walk I couldn't manage
to hit a single target.

Abu's face wore a look of pleasant boredom as time after time I
tried to load and shoot while the chariot bounced around underneath me. After a few attempts he turned to me.

"Try putting your leg through the loop and pulling the cinch
tight." He shifted his body so I could see his leg fastened against
the front of the chariot in a similar manner. "Once you are tied on
press your body hard against the belly bar as you draw and aim the
bow." He laughed. "Its a lot like being a sailor," he said. "Once
you get your balance you won't pay any more attention to the
bumps in the road." He smiled broadly. "And don't rush. Take
your time. The only thing that matters is where the arrow strikes!"

It was good advice. After a few attempts I became steadier on
my feet. Our horses were tired from so many trips down the range
that Abu suggested we return to the stable and call it a day.

"Once more," I said. "I want one more chance at the damned
things!"

Abu sighed and shook his head in resignation. He snapped the
reins against the animals' rump and brought the chariot around to
the starting line.

"Are you ready?" he asked.

I nodded my head and felt the horses tug at the races. The
machine moved under me. Slowly we moved along the row of

targets. I set an arrow in the nock and drew the bow to my ear using my stiff left arm to track the target as we approached. My body acted like a cushion and the bumps of the machine were taken up by my legs while the rest of me remained steady. The target slid into view at a wide angle and I let the arrow loose. The bowstring hummed in my ear. I felt the slap of the string on my leather wrist guard as the instrument gave up its power to the arrow. The shaft flew straight and took the target high in the head. Excitement ran through me. A hit! I was so pleased with myself that the next two targets passed before I could nock another arrow. Again the bow bent back and the gut string hummed, and again the arrow flew, this time wide of its mark. At slow speeds the wheel's metal rims made an irritating crunching sound as they ground their way over the earth. The noise drowned out the pleasant hum of the bowstring as I loosed another arrow at yet another ellusive target. A hit! This time square in the body. And then we passed the last target and my last arrow flew striking the target square even though I rushed the shot. It was a beginning and I was pleased with myself.

"Now " I said slapping Abu on the shoulder "we can call it a day!"

The old groom turned around and smiled and snapped the reins across the animals' rump. Instantly the horses broke into a brisk trot and headed for the barn.

Several more months were required before I became proficient enough with chariot and bow to be assigned to a regular unit where I spent the next year practicing my trade as a soldier. Amenemhab saw to it that I was assigned to one of the small forts ten miles forward of the T'aru garrison. Here I couldn't get into too much difficulty and I took up my post as member of a chariot troop or *Sa* of ten machines. The troop was commanded by the *kedjen-tepy* or First Charioteer. He was only a year or two older than I, perhaps eighteen, but was clearly an excellent horseman and archer, as were most of the troop all of which had more experience than I. Still I found my place within the unit and in a few weeks was accepted by my comrades and felt quite comfortable to be among them.

Our troop was part of one of the two chariot regiments stationed at T'aru. One of these was billeted in the main fortress itself. The other was scattered among several forts, bridge crossings, and forward posts forming a screen in the shape of a wide semi-circle that ran in front of the main defenses. A full regiment, two-hundred and fifty machines organized into five squadrons of fifty machines each, was deployed forward of the T'aru fortress and the canal bridges. The squadrons, in their turn, were dispersed further into troops responsible for patrolling a section of the desert that separated Egypt's frontier from the lands across the Sinai.

Egypt was at peace with the city-states across the Sinai so that the only trouble was caused by marauding bands of "sand-dwellers" who raided whatever caravans could be had. Sometimes these bandits grew brave enough to attack one of the copper mines that we Egyptians had opened in the Sinai, but that was rare. The Sinai offered few opportunities for theft. But in the settlements across the desert the pickings were better, and some of these groups of bandits were a hundred men strong and even had chariots. They caused difficulties for our other units to the northeast at Migdol and Sile who had a tough time of it keeping the coastal road to Sharuhen open and safe. But it was calmer things for me and I soon grew bored with the daily patrols. I would often leave my driver behind and take the chariot deep into the desert by myself.

I had been with my troop for about six months when one day I struck out on one of these solitary journeys. The day was cooler than normal for the Sinai at this time of year and I took that as an omen that I might spend a restful day alone with my thoughts. I had not slept well for several days and felt as though I might be ill. From time to time I was overcome by feelings of sadness that I could not drive from my mind. I felt trapped by my own circumstances which day by day I found less and less interesting and worthwhile. Almost two years had passed since leaving Memphis. During that time I had finished my training and taken up my first posting as a soldier. But for some reason the joy of it had fled. There was, as far as I could see, not much else for me to do. I could, of course, remain in the army and go from posting to posting hoping for a war to start so that I might test my skills against the enemy. In due time I would be promoted. But then what? For this I had no answer. Whatever purpose my life once had seemed to have vanished.

The desert's quiet enveloped me. The sky filled with flat grey clouds like those that sometimes brought rain to the high mountains that lie far to the south and east. A cool wind blew steadily against my face. I lost myself in my thoughts and permitted the horses to follow the well-worn track that marked the usual route of my patrol. By noon I reached where our patrols normally turned around and headed back. The horses, too, recognized the spot and stopped without being told. Thick clouds darkened the sky and the shallow light made it seem like early evening. The wind blew hard then calm, sometimes flying at me from one direction and then another, twirling itself around and around carrying the dust from the desert floor upward with it as it went. The animals fidgeted and sniffed the air turning to look at me, waiting for the command to return home and the safety of the familiar. Perhaps that was it, the safety of the familiar, that weighed upon me. I do not remember why I ordered the horses forward. I remember only that something, some strange feeling, urged me forward and drew me deeper into the desert.

The ground became uneven and rocky and the horses stumbled along picking their way across unfamiliar earth. Ahead steep gray hills rose sharply upward throwing their massive forms in my path forcing me further to the south. Hours passed as I gave myself over to the wind that blew through the narrow defiles filling the air with a howling sound like animals make when they are in pain. The horses pulled hard to carry the chariot across the rocky earth and must have been puzzled by the slack in their reins for I no longer guided them on a set path but permitted them to take me wherever it was the god's wished me to go.

The jagged slash of brilliant light flew raggedly across the sky with such force that the wind itself seemed to stand still until the bolt ran its course and filled the air with the odor of burnt flesh. The avalanche of sound that crashed around the horses a moment later frightened them to the bone. The lead horse reared back upon its legs and lifted the chariot with it to such an angle that had I not grabbed the belly-bar to steady myself I would surely have been thrown to the ground. The coupling's eyes widened in terror and he lurched forward almost causing the other horse to loose its balance and fall sideways. But the saddle yokes held fast and the horses regained their footing. Another flash of light was followed by another crash of noise. The animals could stand the terror no longer. With a great thrust of their hind legs they leapt forward at gallop speed carrying me and the machine with them.

The wild ride lasted only a few minutes until fatigue and the steep landscape brought the horses to a stop. Around me the wind howled mercilessly while the clouds pressed closer to the ground until all about me seemed like night. I jumped from the machine and grabbed the horses by their halters moving into their vision so they could see me and take some comfort from not being alone. Each time the jagged light shot across the horizon I gathered my grip on the halter to prevent the frightened animals from becoming

crazed and bolting away once more. Powerful gusts of wind flew
through the narrow canyons that were the only openings in the
range of steep stone gray hills before me driving dirt and pebbles
through the air at great speed that cut when they struck my skin.
My grip on the tugging horses weakened with each contest. I dared
not raise my head to search for shelter lest I be blinded.

And then as if it were willed by the gods I saw the opening in
the side of the canyon wall yawning at me like a great mouth. The
breach of the cave was only a few yards away. I struggled to
release the animals from their saddle yokes. With my last ounce of
strength I led them into the cave and out of the storm. I led the
horses from the cave's mouth toward the back of the cavern and
tethered each of them to a heavy stone that dragged between their
legs whenever they moved more than the length of the tether rope.
Safely out of the storm the animals calmed themselves. Outside
the wind roared and the sky filled with bolts of light that were followed each time by great crashes of noise.

The cavern walls were uneven and jagged bits of rock protruded from them at all angles. The mouth of the cave opened into
a spacious room that ran back for some distance before ending at
a solid wall of stone. Where the wall and ground met a pool of
water held by a natural cistern was fed by an underground spring.
I drank from the pool and quenched my thirst and then led the
horses to where they, too, might drink. I had no idea where this
place was. Certainly no map I had never seen showed a spring to
be here. I was very tired and looked about for some place to sit
down. Near the mouth of the cave was a flat stone whose lower
edge had been worn by sand and wind into the form of a step. I sat
upon the lip and rested my back against the step and stared into
the storm that raged just a few yards away.

A few yards from the cave opening I could see the form of my
chariot turned on its side by the force of the wind as it rocked

fitfully whenever it was struck by a strong gust. My canteen and provision bag were tied securely to the inside of the cab. For a moment I thought I might try to retrieve them. At that very instant another bolt of light lit up the sky with unusual brightness. The jagged line of light seemed to jump from one cloud to another hovering like a hawk seeking its prey. And then the bolt changed direction and sped straight down toward the stone peak of a small hill a few hundred yards in front of the cave mouth. It smashed into the tip of the hill with tremendous force cooking the very air that filled my lungs. The thick bushes covering the peak burst instantly into flame and the earth itself erupted with a force that catapulted a thick cloud of rock and dust skyward. And then the avalanche of noise struck the ground. I felt its force as a strong gust of wind on my face a second before the great crash reached my ears. Together the sensations almost knocked me over. From behind I heard a screech of terror from the animals. And then all was silent and dark again as the powerful forces of the sky retreated upward to gather their strength for another attack. The stench of burnt flesh filled my nose as if the air itself had been cooked to a crisp.

This dance of the gods went on about me for hours before it ended with the coming of night. The clouds parted revealing a bright moon. The wind, too, died leaving behind a pale shade of itself in the form of a breeze that brought no warmth with it. It was night in the desert and the air was cold. I found some twigs and a few sticks suitable for a fire and carried them back to the cave. I retrieved my provision bag from the chariot along with the grain bucket for the animals. In a short time the flames from a small fire lit the inside of the cave and I wrapped myself warmly in my cloak. There was not much grain for the animals, but they seemed grateful for what I offered them. I dined that night upon dried beef, hard bread, and radishes.

The glow from the fire flickered upon the walls of the cavern lighting its dark nooks. For no reason one of the horses shuddered and the noise drew my attention to the rear of the cavern. I was surprised to see a small altar carved from the wall that stood behind the spring. A form cast an unfamiliar shadow upon the water's surface. As I came upon it I recognized the shape of Hathor, the cow-goddess. The statue was not large, perhaps only two feet tall, and revealed a female form with a smiling human face. Upon her head the goddess carried the sun disk held fast between two horns. A small statue of pharaoh for whom Hathor received the setting sun and protected it for the god-king stood between her legs. It was Hathor who raised the sun to the horizon each morning with her golden horns so Horus might accompany it upon his journey. A large sistrum rattle lay on the altar. I picked it up and shook it. The shooshing sound of the beating wings of the *Ba* filled the cave. One of the animals whinnied at the strange sound and I replaced the instrument upon the altar. Hathor was the goddess of human destiny. It was she who showed the way through life's valleys urging us onward toward the light of the sun. Hathor caused us to dream. It was her priests who foretold the future. She had been worshiped in Egypt since very ancient times, and as I examined the statue the light from the fire played upon her face making it seem that she was smiling at me. How long the goddess had been worshiped in this place I do not know. But for this moment Hathor stood before me radiating her grace upon me. I went back to the fire and wrapped my cloak about my body and lay down upon the earth. I was tired and calm descended over me. I closed my eyes and drifted toward sleep comforted by Hathor's smiling face whose vision lingered in my mind.

The goddess of slumber drew me close to her breast and my troubles were carried from my mind by her tender caress. Pleasant visions of Ese and my childhood came and went without effort bringing happiness and calm to my sleep, drawing me deeper and deeper into the goddess' embrace until it seemed I might never wake again.

I saw myself standing upon a mountain. Spread below me was a great plain where many walled cities stood. Tongues of flame leapt from the buildings within the walls, dark clouds of smoke rising like great smudges on the cloudless sky. Everywhere people ran in panic, everywhere the soldiers of an army as numerous as ants marched forward covering the ground so thickly with their numbers that even the desert sands could not be seen. A chariot of gold and electrum pulled by a pair of white horses raced across the plain at great speed throwing up clouds of dust behind it. The horses flew as if they had wings, for their chariot carried the great warrior king into battle against the enemies of Egypt. And from the mountain I saw the face of this great king before whom all of *Kemit's* foes fell like stalks of grain before a sickle. It was my face.

Out of the confusion rose the sound of a voice that I had heard many times.

"That is your destiny, Thutmose. To lead Egypt's armies against her enemies and to slay all who oppose her. For only then can the land of the gods be safe."

I beheld the form of my father standing next to me. He stood there in full battle uniform, the crown of war upon his head. *Uraeus's* body stood erect against the gold band that held it to the war helmet. Its garnet eyes gleamed with fire ready to strike all who raised their hands against Pharaoh. The armored corslet of thin bronze plates returned Horus' rays to the heavens brighter than when they fell upon it. My father's face was as I remembered it as a boy, strong and full with eyes gleaming with the spark of life. His body was young and powerful again. He stood before me with legs apart and arms folded just as I had seen him when he stood before the great throne of Egypt that night many years ago when I had almost been killed by the panther.

"Do not permit your doubts to rule your thoughts Thutmose. Take no counsel from your fears, for fear has no place in the deeds of great warriors." His arm swept the horizon and the wide plain below. "All this will you do in the name of Amun," he said as if the Hidden One himself had willed it. "Do not be troubled by what awaits you. You are Thutmose, the son of the god your father, and the third of our line. Always remember this, Thutmose, and no man can stand before your will."

I looked upon his face and felt my gloom disappear into the air about us as does the Nile mist when Horus's heat frees its waters from the deadening grasp of the cold. My father's words lifted me from the pit in which I had dwelled for these many weeks. His eyes met mine and again his arm swept over the plain.

Before me the great king in the electrum chariot bore down upon the shepherd warrior before him with sword and shield drawn ready to meet the charge. The bronze helmet could not conceal his coarse black hair that hung in ringlets from beneath the rim. A thick black beard arranged neatly in rows of curls hid his face. Armor painted the color of blood surrounded his body as if it were a wall of clay brick. Tight lips showed no fear and defiance flashed from his eyes. Onward the steeds of the electrum chariot came drawing the great king nearer his enemy. With powerful arms the great king drew back his bow and loosed an arrow. The shaft moved as a bolt of light across the stormy desert sky and struck the dark warrior square in the throat. The arrow tore through the flesh. Hard bone resisted its assault but could only slow the deadly thrust. When its fury was spent the bloodied shaft came to rest with half its length protruding from the back of the warrior's neck.

There was no pain. Only the look of surprise crossed over the soldier's face. His mouth opened to cry out but his throat offered only silence. The warrior's eyes rolled heavenward and he stared into the sun. His great body fell to the earth with the force of a cedar toppled from a mountainside in Lebanon. Still the mighty horses came on and the king in the electrum chariot stood straight and strong while he guided the reins to drive the chariot over the body of the Asiatic and grind him into the dust so that even in death he might know the power of the Mighty Bull of the Nile.

Around me I watched the carnage and slaughter of battle until the flames of destruction consumed all before me. The smoke rose and covered the sun turning day to night until even from the mountain top I could no longer see what horrors were happening below me. I looked to my father and once more his arm swept the horizon.

The royal barge appeared before me out of a warm mist. The great king of the electrum chariot sat upon his throne on the deck as the *Star of Two Countries* glided slowly past the royal palace in Thebes. From the bow of the ship, their heads toward the Nile's waters, hung the bodies of seven asiatic princes who had dared raise their hands against the power of Pharaoh and whom the electrum king had slain as a warning to others.

And then my father stood before me, the man whose life flowed in me and whose eyes glowed with a confidence that had often escaped me in my life. He had come to me in my uncertainty to remind me of who I was, to permit me to remember that I had sprung from the loins of the Lion of Egypt himself. For a time I had forgotten that and with it had gone my vision of a destiny to rule Egypt. I stared at him wanting to offer my gratitude for so precious a gift.

From behind him arose bright light that glowed brighter with every second until I could no longer look upon him. My father seemed to dissolve in the glow around him. I shaded my eyes from the magnificent light that carried him with it to the Marshes of Horus where he dwelled beyond death. But my hands could not keep the light from my eyes and I thought I might be blinded. I buried my eyes in my hands and sought safety in the dark until, at last, even the darkness parted. I woke from my dream on the floor of the cave staring into the morning light.

# Eighteen

The room was as I remembered it. I hadn't seen Amenemhab for more than three months. The battle pennants of the T'aru garrison's regiments lined the walls. The national standard of Egypt framed the doorway to Amenemhab's office on one side and the standard of the Apis bull of the Army of Ptah stood on the other. I sat in one of the chairs alone with my thoughts wondering why Amenemhab had sent for me. I hoped that I had not disappointed him with my performance. For several minutes I tried to recall what mistake might have brought me to the attention of the garrison commander, but I could think of nothing. Amenemhab's adjutant greeted me warmly enough when I arrived so that if there was trouble he gave no hint of it. My eyes wandered around the room while I sat there waiting to be summoned.

The door opened and the adjutant came out. He looked at me and nodded toward the open door to Amenemhab's office. I stood somewhat uncertain as to what to do next, but the adjutant pointed toward the door and nodded again. I gave him a quick smile and walked past him into the room. Amenemhab was sitting behind a large desk covered with papers and a map. He raised his eyes as I approached, stopped, and saluted. For a few seconds my old friend sat there looking at me and saying nothing. Then a broad smile broke over his face.

"Thutmose!" His voice had a pleasant tone to it as if he was surprised to see me which, of course, could not have been the case since he had sent for me.

Amenemhab rose from his chair. "You look well, my prince." He moved the few steps to the side of the desk and pointed toward a chair. "Here," he said. "Sit down and take the burden from your chariot officer's feet!" He laughed at his own joke. I sat down pleased to see my friend again.

"I see you are well too, Amenemhab," I said. "It seems a long time since we have seen each other," I added.

A frown appeared on his face.

"Yes," he said with a sigh. "The work of a commander is never done you know. There is always something to attend to."

He sighed again and took the chair next to me.

"But I must tell you that I am very pleased with your perform-ance, Thutmose." He smiled warmly. "Your commander's reports speak of you as a solid officer. He seems to think that you have a natural talent for soldiering."

He paused and looked at me. "That is good, Thutmose. Egypt will have need of good soldiers soon." There was a somber qual-ity to his words. And then he flashed a quick smile and changed his mood.

"Can I offer you some wine, my prince?" He pointed to a jug on a side table. "It is from the vineyards at Inut near Tanis. The wine from the Delta is the best in all Egypt and the very best comes from Inut. They say these vineyards were the personal property of one of the Hyksos kings. What do you say? Can I offer you a cup?"

I smiled at my old friend. "Certainly," I said. Then an impish look crossed my face. "But I'm surprised that you prefer wine to beer. Beer is the infantryman's drink. Wine is the drink of charioteers!"

Amenemhab's face lit up.

"Of course, of course!" he said. "But there are good reasons for the infantry to drink beer." he added with a laugh. "We don't have horses to carry us where we have to go." He slapped his legs. "These are our horses!" he sneered in mock outrage. "Egyptian beer is thick and sweet and the infantryman thinks of it as food, as well he might. It'll fill an empty belly and keep you going. Besides," he went on, "when you're living on the land beer is better than water. Bad water will bring an army to its knees in a day. But beer never makes you sick."

Amenemhab paused and smiled and handed me a cup of Delta wine.

"Remember that, Thutmose. Always take along enough beer when you make a long march. The troops will be happier and their asses won't look like jars from purging the sickness in their bellies!"

He raised his glass and smiled at me over the rim.

"To old friends, fallen comrades, and Egypt," he said.

I lifted my glass and nodded. We raised our glasses to our lips and tasted the sweet wine.

We chatted about military life for a few minutes and enjoyed the wine. And then Amenemhab's voice became serious. He put down his cup and drew his chair closer to mine and spoke.

"I have reassigned you from your platoon to my headquarter's staff, Thutmose." He paused but his words brought no reaction to my face. I was learning to control my expressions and remained impassive before him.

"You have done well with your unit, but there is nothing more to be learned by long service in a chariot platoon." His voice was steady and professional and his tone was what he would have used with any junior officer.

"Assigned to my staff you will have more opportunity to see the army at work, to get some idea of the larger problems we face here on the frontier." He paused. "If you keep your eyes and ears open it will be a valuable education."

The expression on his face softened and a sly smirk crossed his lips.

"After all you will not be a junior officer forever, my prince. There are more important goals for you to seek. Besides, I can always use a good messenger!" The thin smirk turned into a broad smile accompanied by the snort of a short laugh.

I joined in the humor of it all though in my mind I did not fail to notice Amenemhab's reference to my position or my destiny to do important things. Watching him there I had the vague feeling that somewhere events were taking shape that would alter my life in significant ways although I confess I had no idea what these events might be.

Amenemhab stood and returned to the chair behind his desk. He ruffled through the piles of paper strewn across the desk as if they had been blown there by the wind. At last he found what he was looking for and leaned back holding a papyrus envelope in his hands.

"What I want you to do, Thutmose, is to take this report to General Rekhmire at Sharuhen. It is the latest assessment of our situation in the Sinai. Sharuhen is our most forward garrison and Rekhmire will be pleased to receive it." He stopped speaking and his eyes narrowed. "Rekhmire is an important person and it is important for the two of you to meet. Both of you have much to give Egypt," he said. His voice was low and I could tell from its tone that Amenemhab was about serious business even if I did not understand what it was.

"When do you want me to leave, sir" I asked falling back into military formality. There was something about the way military orders were given that seemed to provoke a formal response even without thinking. Amenemhab nodded as if he approved of my question.

"I should think tomorrow or the next day would be soon enough," he said. "The envelope also contains a letter of introduction to Rekhmire verifying your identity and suggesting a number of things that you need not concern yourself with now," he added. Amenemhab reached over the desk and handed me the thick papyrus envelope. It was sealed beneath the official seal of the commander of the T'aru garrison as proof against tampering.

I rose to take the envelope and stepped back from the desk and brought my hand up in the military salute. Amenemhab smiled and returned my salute. When he spoke it was more with the tone of a father than of a commanding officer.

"Take due care on your journey, Thutmose. The road to Sharuhen is not like the deserted desert trails you are accustomed to patrolling. There is always the risk of danger so go well armed and take an experienced driver."

He paused and looked deeply into my eyes.

"You are the son of the Lion of Egypt, my prince. Do not squander your life in some senseless act. Think, always think. But when you act, act decisively and without hesitation. And may the gods protect you."

The next morning I visited the stables to choose a team and driver for my journey to Sharuhen. The Captain of the Stable suggested that I take along one of his more experienced drivers, a certain Djamu who knew the roads to Sharuhen well. He summoned Djamu and I went off with him to examine the horses and equip the chariot for the next day's journey. Djamu was tall and thin and looked as if he weighed less than a willow's branch. His face was long and drawn and among his comrades in the stable he was known behind his back as "the horse" because, it was said, he actually looked like one! Large eyes bulged from bony sockets and a wide mouth made him look what a horse would look like if it could smile! For all of this, though, I found Djamu competent and a pleasant companion to have along.

Djamu took me to the corral to select a pair of animals. Egyptian chariot horses were trained in pairs from early on and the pairs were never separated unless one of the animals was injured or killed.

"They all look fine to me Djamu," I said. In fact I had no great experience in selecting teams of horses and it seemed wise to have Djamu choose since he knew each of the horses from long experience. Djamu smiled and nodded.

"There," he said pointing into the pack of horses. "We'll take that pair of blacks."

I nodded my head in agreement.

"What are their names?" I asked. Egyptian soldiers seemed to give everything a name, even their weapons and chariots. It was surprising to me how often these warriors gave tender names to their animals, names like "Gentle One" and "Blue Eye," instead of names associated with war and killing. This was not, however, one of those instances.

"The stallion is called *Ptah's Victory* and the gelding's name is *Slasher*," he answered. Egyptian chariot teams always pair a stallion and a gelding together. Two stallions are impossible to control. Great care is always taken around the corrals to make certain that mares are kept far from the stallions. Once, Djamu told me, a young soldier had turned a mare loose near the corral. The stallions were crazed by her scent. Some began fighting among themselves and others crashed into the corral fence trying to get at the mare.

I smiled as Djamu told me the story and shook my head in mock disbelief as he finished. "Well, let us see to a machine," I said.

The stable had a number of chariots that had been recently repaired. I examined the axles, wheel hubs, spokes, and rims to make sure they were in good condition. The wheels were a chariot's weakness. It required considerable work for the repair shops to keep the machines ready for use. Djamu said nothing as he watched me inspect the chariot.

"It seems fine to me, Djamu. The wheels are recently repaired and the spokes new and well oiled." I paused and gave the chariot one more look. "This will do." Djamu shrugged and nodded.

"Now for the equipment," I said. My voice became serious. "I don't expect any trouble along the way but if it comes I want to be prepared." Djamu's eyes narrowed and he paid attention. "I want a good bow and two quivers of arrows aboard. We will also carry twelve javelins, six to a quiver." Djamu was looking at me seriously now. It was obvious that he hadn't expected the journey to require so many weapons.

"Make sure your shield is aboard, Djamu. If we run into trouble I don't want you shot out from under me!" I gave a short laugh. "No need for full battle dress, but I think it a good idea to bring along your armored corslet and bronze helmet. If it gets too hot we can stow them in the provision bag."

Djamu could tell from my tone of voice that I was not asking his advice on these matters but instructing him as to my wishes. We looked at each other for a few seconds neither of us saying anything. Then Djamu spoke.

"It will be as you say, sir. Is there anything else?"

I ran over things again in my mind.

"No. No, I don't think so," I said. "We are never more than a day's ride between wells so we won't require extra water." I paused for a few seconds. "I think that will be all, Djamu. We'll leave at first light so have the team harnessed and ready to go by then."

Djamu nodded and offered a salute. I returned it and walked off back to my quarters to examine my maps and prepare for the journey to Sharuhen.

The journey from T'aru to Pela three miles inland from the coast of the Great Green was easy on the horses who pulled the machine over forty miles of hard packed dirt road. The route took us by the fortress towns of Sile and Migdol where we stopped for water and food and rested the horses. Pela was a military town and we had no difficulty finding lodging for us and the animals. After a good night's rest we set out the next morning on the coastal road to Sharuhen.

The road ran parallel to the Great Green as it made its way due east. In places it ran within a few hundred feet of the ocean itself. Whenever we came upon one of these places I left the road and drove the chariot over the beach. The sound of the foamy surf rushing against the shore was pleasant and the smell of the salt air was a refreshing change from the harsh heat of the day that accompanied us everywhere along the road. It was nearly seventy miles from Pela to Sharuhen, and I planned to make the journey with a single stop at Arisha, a little more than half-way to our destination.

The coastal road was a major strategic highway connecting the frontier of the Sinai to the in-depth defenses of the Wall of Princes. It was regularly patrolled and had small infantry garrisons assigned to every fresh-water well along the way. Some of these wells were located in villages a few miles inland from the road. Often no more than a ten man squad was assigned to protect the well and the village that had sprung up around it. What danger there was came from the shepherd bandits who preyed upon the coastal road's considerable commercial traffic.

We had gone about twenty miles when Djamu brought the horses to a halt. He turned back to me and pointed to the sky off to the south.

"Look there," he said.

My eyes followed the sweep of his arm until I saw what he was pointing at. The sky was alive with vultures circling overhead. They swept low over the desert then rose on the heat to turn and circle back again. They turned over a column of smoke rising straight up in the calm air.

"What do you make of that?" I asked.

Djamu shrugged and his voice was heavy with worry. "I don't know, sir. But the smoke is coming from the village where one of our small garrisons is stationed. Perhaps there has been some trouble."

I nodded. "Let's go see Djamu."

Djamu nodded and snapped the reins. He guided the chariot off the road and in a few moments we were moving toward the column of smoke at a brisk trot. The machine moved quickly over the sandy desert plain. As it did I unpacked my armor and helmet and took the bow from its case. Djamu saw what I was doing and smiled at me. I took Djamu's helmet from its peg and handed it to him. He wrapped the reins around his waist and used his free hands to put the helmet on his head. Then he slipped the shield strap over his shoulder so the shield hung on his left side. He unwrapped the reins from his waist and guided the machine toward the column of smoke. I slipped my armored corslet over my head and secured it around my body with the leather cinch straps. The quiver of arrows slipped easily over my back and I tied my helmet with its plume of green ostrich feathers securely around my chin. Overhead the vultures circled and dipped above their prey as if awaiting one last signal from the dying to begin their odious meal.

As we approached the village I could see flames shooting from the garrison storehouse creating a column of black smoke that rose first thickly and then as mere wisps of darkness against the blue sky. I tapped Djamu on the shoulder and he looked back at me and winked. He adjusted his shield and drove the chariot straight for the burning storehouse. I took an arrow from the quiver and set its nock against the bowstring. My mind was moving at great speed and my eyes roamed over the landscape searching for targets.

Djamu quickened the speed and closed on the storehouse. Dust flew from behind us while I tried to make sense of what lay in front of us. Djamu suddenly swerved the machine to the left and my eye caught sight of a corpse. As we went racing past I recognized the body as that of an Egyptian soldier. We reached the storehouse a few seconds later and Djamu swung the chariot wide and drove completely around the storehouse having to swerve the machine again and again to avoid the corpses strewn about the sand. Djamu changed direction again, passed completely through the village, and brought the chariot to a halt. I relaxed the grip on the bow and we both looked back at the village.

"Whatever happened back there happened quickly. They took the garrison by surprise and slaughtered them where they stood," Djamu said shaking his head. He turned and looked southward. "The attackers left in this direction," he said. "Probably bandits." He took a deep breath. "There is no danger from them now," he said. "We can return to the village and see to the dead. We can report it when we get to Arisha." He turned his face to the front without waiting for me to reply and snapped the reins. The horses moved off immediately at a fast walk toward the village.

Djamu brought the team to a halt in front of the storehouse and I dismounted. I left the bow in the chariot but still carried my *kopesh* and dagger. Djamu stayed with the chariot keeping his eyes alert. I walked carefully through the village while Djamu kept the chariot close by. If we were attacked and had to fight or run, the chariot would help us make our escape. The flames subsided as the fire consumed its last fuel and the vultures grew bolder sweeping lower and lower. One of them landed close to a nearby corpse as if to defy me to slay it. I swung at it with my sword, but the great bird jumped back and flew upwards unharmed. I walked from body to body counting nine corpses in all. The number made no sense. Egyptian squads came in tens. Perhaps one of them survived and was hiding or had been taken prisoner. If so, he was their officer. None of the corpses wore the rank of an officer. The bodies had not yet begun to swell or discolor in the heat and I thought that the attack could not have happened more than an hour or so ago.

Slowly the villagers emerged from their houses and places of hiding and clustered about in little groups. Djamu and I gathered the males together and instructed them to open the earth with sticks and plow blades to bury the dead soldiers. One by one the corpses were dragged to the shallow holes, dropped inside, and covered with sand. It was how common soldiers have always been buried, without mummification or ceremony. Sometimes, if the jackals did not dig them up, these bodies were preserved by the hot sand that sucked the moisture from the flesh leaving the corpse dried and wizened like jerky. But mostly this did not happen and the bodies rotted into dust.

It was almost midday and the corpses had been laid in the earth when one of the village women came toward me waving her arms. She chatted excitedly and it was difficult to gather what she was saying. At last Djamu calmed her and we followed her to the edge of a ditch behind the village. There, laying face down in the dust, was the last corpse. I could tell from its clothing that it was the unit's officer. I made my way down the side of the ditch. The air in the trench was hot. The beginnings of a strangely sweet smell

reached my nose. The corpse's arms were slashed open as if someone had inflicted pointless wounds upon it after death. I knelt next
to the body of my fellow officer and slowly turned him over so
that his face was bathed in Horus' rays. Carefully I brushed the
dirt that covered his features from his face. As I did the man's features took shape until even without thinking they filled my eyes so
that I recognized the image that was emerging in my mind. Lying
on the sand still in death eyes open to greet Horus was Sunusret,
the young infantry officer who had accompanied me to T'aru and
taught me how to read a map.

I was stunned at the sight. Sunusret's face looked strangely
peaceful even with his eyes open. There was not a mark on it.
What had killed him was the gaping wound above his heart. And
dead he was! Staring at his lifeless body he seemed so young, and
in my mind's eye I could not recall him ever looking like that.
When I had met him he was the older more experienced officer. I
will probably always think of him that way. But here, sprawled in
the sand with his blood marking a deep wine stain beneath his
body, he looked as if he were a child.

Only the gods knew why he had died in this lonely place or
what last thoughts sped through his mind as he felt the *kopesh*
bite deeply into his chest. Did he know, I wondered, when he was
struck that the wound would take his life? Was the pain great?
Had he fought bravely or had he cowered under the assault? Only
Sunusret knew the answers and his lips would never give voice to
his thoughts again. But the memory of him that day stayed within
me for many years. Whenever I saw the fields of corpses left in the
wake of my armies I was not troubled. But the face of a single
corpse looked upon too closely always brought the vision of
Sunusret's face to my mind. Numbers make human tragedy
abstract. Individuals make it human again. It is wise never to

inquire too closely into the death of a comrade unless you are prepared to endure the pain that it brings with it.

I ordered some men from the village to lift the corpse from the ditch and place it upon a table where I commanded that linen sheets be found and Sunusret's body be wrapped tightly within them. Blood and other liquids ran from his body and several layers of linen were required to keep the ooze from soaking through. The sheets were bound with strong cord. Then to Djamu's utter horror I ordered the corpse placed aboard the chariot and tied with rope so that the machine's movement would not cause the corpse to fall from the riding platform. It was late afternoon when Djamu, myself, and Senusret's corpse resumed the journey to Arisha. Djamu, like most Egyptians, feared the night spirits and could barely contain his fright when the sun finally fled beyond the horizon leaving him alone with me and a dead body. To his credit he kept on. Two hours after darkness we drove through the front gate of the garrison at Arisha.

We released the horses from their harness and Djamu saw to their feeding and watering. It was late so we decided to spend the night in the stable so Sunusret's corpse could remain where it was until morning when it could be properly turned over to headquarters who could then see to its disposition. The priests of Anubis always had good relations with military outposts and it would be a matter of only a few days before someone would come for the corpse, hurriedly embalm it, and then offer to sell it back to Sunusret's family for proper burial. To my surprise I slept well enough. When morning came I was rested and ready to be on my way. Only a few hours were required to make my report to the garrison commander and relinquish Sunusret's body to the proper authorities. With nothing further to be done, Djamu readied the chariot and we were on our way by midday.

It was only twenty five miles to Sharuhen and we arrived there by late afternoon. The fortress sat on the border between the Sinai's eastern edge and the land of Retjennu, the name we Egyptians gave to the land-bridge between Sinai and the Lebanon. The fort squatted amidst a large area of lush farmland and date palms given life by a spring whose waters flowed from the ground in such plenty that they formed a wide stream that the local people called the River of Egypt. Although Sharuhen had been fortified for more than three hundred years, the Egyptian fortifications were of the new style. They consisted of a large rectangle with low walls no higher than twenty feet through which were cut many wide gates so that chariots might rush from within the fort or retreat to it with great speed. The fortress itself existed only to house the chariot force. When it came to fighting, the chariots forayed against the enemy using the fort as a base of operations. Sharuhen was the major defensive position between the border and the Wall of Princes and any attack could be expected to fall upon it first. We Egyptians kept a strong garrison here for just this reason. Sharuhen was one of the largest military posts in imperial Egypt comprising three regiments of chariotry or a full brigade of nine hundred and fifty machines supported by a regiment of infantry of twelve hundred and fifty men. Its commander was Rekhmire, one of Egypt's most famous generals, and the man to whom I was to deliver Amenemhab's letter.

I was given quarters with the junior officers. Djamu saw to it that the animals were properly cared for and the chariot safely stored. He then found his way to the sergeants barracks where he spent the next few days in relative comfort. I went to my room and refreshed myself and set out to find the commander's office. General Rekhmire's headquarters was only a short walk from my quarters, but I arrived after the general had departed for the day.

His adjutant told me to return in the morning. Left to myself I wandered over to the officers' mess and had something to eat.

After my meal I strolled about the fortress grounds for a hour or so and let my thoughts wander to the events of the past few days. There is so much that is false in soldiering that it sometimes takes the death of a comrade to bring us face-to-face with its delusions. One of these is that death comes to soldiers in a glorious way or at least in a manner that makes it seem as if it has some purpose. We all believe it at first. We must, or none of us would venture beyond the gate of the garrison! But one look at the slaughtered corpse of a friend reveals that the death of the young is always a tragedy no matter how noble the cause for which he has fallen.

The next morning found me in the general's anteroom waiting for the adjutant to show me in. I sat there until late in the morning when, at last, the adjutant escorted me into the general's office. The general returned my salute, took the letter, and motioned me to a chair. I sat down and waited while he read Amenemhab's report and the letter that accompanied it. He finished reading and laid the letter on the top of the desk and sat back in his large chair. His voice was strong and carried with it a tone of command as befitted his position.

"Amenemhab tells me that you have become an officer that Egypt can be proud of, highness." A slight smile crossed his face. "He recommends that you be promoted to the rank of Leader of Ten," he added nodding his head in agreement. "I trust you have no objections, highness?"

I squirmed in my seat not knowing what to say. I had been a serving officer for more than two years. But with the exception of my experience two days earlier at the village on the coastal road I had never been near a fight. Still I was not your average officer by any means given my lineage. In the long run that would matter far more than any military rank I might be given.

"Thank you, sir. I hope I will not disappoint the trust you and Colonel Amenemhab have placed in me."

The general smiled formally and his eyes narrowed while he held me in their gaze. He stood and walked from behind his desk and looked down at me. He took a deep breath and began to speak.

"Highness, I am pleased that we have finally been given the opportunity to meet one another. There is much between us in what we can do to serve Egypt." He paused. "Perhaps we should begin with the dangers that face this sweet land of ours. This is your first visit to Sharuhen I take it?" he asked.

I nodded in agreement.

"Good," he responded. "Then what I have to say will be new to you. I trust you will find it to be as important as I and Amenemhab and many other officers believe it is."

And with that Rekhmire launched into an explanation of the threats facing Egypt. Just across the border, he said, were the many city-states of Retjennu, each equipped with a sizeable military force. Individually they presented no problem. But if forged into a coalition they had the ability to eject Egyptian influence from the area. These states often came to blows with each other and threatened to draw Egypt into their conflicts. The states furthest to the north were even more powerful and even farther away from Egyptian forces. They sat across important trade routes and could block the flow of important materials like horses and the straight timbers of the Lebanon to Egypt. Beyond the Lebanon were the powerful cities of the nation of the Mitanni. The Mitanni were a great power that occupied the land beyond the Great Bend of the Euphrates river and regarded the city-states of the Upper Retjenuu as their vassals.

"And so you see, my prince, that the land bridge between the Sinai and the Euphrates has become the place where two great powers, Egypt and the Mitanni, compete for political and economic influence. The gains of one side are seen by the other as a threat to the other's security."

He paused and took a deep breath which he let out slowly in a sigh.

"Sooner or later, highness, there is going to be a war here and Egypt will be in the thick of it I assure you."

I offered the general a serious look to assure him that I shared his concern although I hadn't a single notion what he expected me to do about it. With some trepidation I offered my opinion.

"Surely, general, our rulers in Thebes are aware of this problem." I tried to hide my disgust of Hatshepsut from my voice. No use in expressing an opinion until I knew where the good general stood.

He looked at me through half-closed eyes as if I were demented. I could see the expression of disappointment upon his face.

"Of course," he said with a tone of mockery in his voice. "I hadn't thought of that!" The look he gave me had daggers in it. He sighed deeply and went on.

"Even if we could handle the problem here, there is still the difficulty in Nubia," he said. "We have ruled Nubia off and on for a thousand years. Whenever the Nubians have found a strong leader we have had to fight to remain in control. Just such a leader has appeared, and if we don't do something soon an Egyptian army will have to be sent to put down a powerful revolt. One thing we cannot afford is a war on two fronts at the same time. That would spell disaster."

Again I nodded that I understood. The general went on.

"The bandits in the eastern desert are out of control again. They are looting our gold mines and attacking our caravans. Just last month they launched a raid against Taphta, our port on Seth's Sea. Their raids go unpunished and each time they grow bolder and bolder in their attacks." He folded his arms and went silent as he looked at me sitting in the chair before him.

I summoned what courage I had left not wanting to be the object of ridicule again.

"Excuse me, general. But if what you say is true, how was such a state of affairs allowed to develop in the first place? Surely Egypt is capable of keeping her enemies at bay. All that seems to be lacking is the will to do so." I stopped and swallowed hard to quell my nervousness and let my eyes relax as I stared at the expression on the general's face.

Rekhmire shook his head slowly from side to side in an expression of serious concern as he spoke.

"What you say is true, highness. Egypt has lost her will. Our queen sits upon the throne of Egypt and concerns herself with other things like the construction of her tomb." Rekhmire's eyes flashed in unconcealed anger. "Already she has ordered the construction of her tomb in the Valley of the Kings!" He sucked in his breath in an effort to control his rising voice. "I am told that Senenmut supervises the construction of her mortuary temple and spends hours with the queen discussing construction plans." He shook his head again. "Egypt is not well served by this," he added.

He stopped talking for a few moments and calmed himself. When he began speaking again he was more clearly in control of his emotions.

"The queen has had several special ships constructed so that they may sail upon Seth's Sea and around the Horns of the Earth to Punt to obtain strange plants, spices, and animals to decorate her court and bestow upon her favorites. This, too, occupies her attention for long hours. I am told that the military commanders cannot obtain an appointment with her to inform her of the difficulties facing the country." Again he sighed and again he shook his head in a gesture of disgust.

As I watched Rekhmire pace back and forth giving voice to some of his most closely held thoughts and fears I wondered where this was all leading. Rekhmire, after all, had earned his position through his family's connections more than his own performance on the battlefield. It seemed strange that he should be criticizing the very hand that fed him so to speak! But then advancement by lineage was hardly a new story in Egypt and is, no doubt, as old a practice as Egypt herself. Rekhmire came from one of Egypt's oldest noble families, a family that had survived and prospered equally well under the old order and the New Kingdom. So skilled were these aristocrats that they had even done well under the Hyksos overlords! However sincere Rekhmire was in his opinions one thing was certain, and that was that he was a patriot first and an opportunist second. He gave not a *deben* who sat upon the throne of Egypt as long as Egypt was safe and he and his family prospered. And why not? Personal interests are more certain motivations than most and great men are not always moved by great or noble motives. As he continued to talk I came to the conclusion that Rekhmire was telling me all this because he had come to believe that Hatshepsut was leading Egypt into trouble. But what, I asked myself, did he intend to do about it?

The general stopped pacing and pulled a chair directly across from me and sat down where he could look directly into my eyes. For a few moments he examined my face and said nothing. Then he spoke in a serious voice.

"Highness," he said, "there are dark times ahead for the land of Egypt," he said with great emotion. "The time may come when Egypt will seek her rightful ruler, the true Lion of Egypt." He paused and looked straight at me. "Should the sun ever rise on that day, my prince, the Lion of Egypt can count on the loyalties of my officers."

His words filled my ears as a strong wind and the meaning of what he was saying made me uneasy. What he said was treasonous. I knew that. But he also spoke the truth. For I owed the queen nothing, and less so if she placed Egypt in danger. I looked into Rekhmire's broad face.

"Egypt is fortunate to have generals like you, sir," I said. "Should events warrant it would be my greatest wish to serve by your side in keeping Egypt safe from those who would harm her."

I smiled my most sincere smile and stood up to leave. The general understood my meaning and rose to his feet also.

"I am pleased, highness, that we have had this opportunity to meet. Unless events intervene it will be some time before we see each other again." He paused and let out a deep breath. "In a few weeks I shall relinquish my command here at Sharuhen. I am to be transferred to the garrison at Thebes." He shrugged and his mouth formed into a wry smile. "Who knows what the future holds?"

I took my leave from the general and went in search of Djamu. I had had enough of Sharuhen and I was eager to return to T'aru. At least there I knew who my friends were and my world made more sense. Besides, I had many questions about what Rekhmire had said and I was anxious to seek Amenemhab's advice.

I spent the next few months serving on Amenemhab's staff. This gave me the opportunity to read the reports of senior commanders and to listen in on important conversations whenever visiting officers passed through T'aru and came to see Amenemhab. From time to time Amenemhab invited me into his office and we would talk about many things, but mostly the problems confronting Egypt. I learned much from these conversations and my experience on the staff.

I learned that the senior commanders were concerned that Egypt was at risk as a consequence of the queen's inattention to matters of state. This they found particularly puzzling since Hatshepsut's father and husband had both been great warrior pharaohs. It was suggested more than once that her lack of interest was due to her sex. Military men tend very much to regard feminine traits with a sort of curious contempt. The very idea that the queen sat upon the throne of Egypt while assuming the titles and dress of a male struck them as curious at best and perverted at worst. In their minds Egypt needed a ruler who had a real pair of balls and a good sized cock, a real male and not some silly woman who strapped on the royal beard in the morning to make her look like a man!

Hatshepsut's interest in the strange plants and animals of the Divine Lands that lay to the east and south of the Sea of Seth had led her to spend large sums on the construction of ocean-going cargo ships to travel to Punt and elsewhere in search of these goods. It was said that the navy had difficulty obtaining large timbers for their ships because the best lumber was assigned to Hatshepsut's cargo vessels. And then there was Hatshepsut's tomb. The very notion that a woman would presume to have her tomb constructed in the Valley of the Kings bordered on sacrilege. It was land reserved for the *sons* of the gods. Whatever else the queen pretended to be, she was certainly not that! The generals even complained that she was spending huge sums on the construction of her mortuary temple. This struck me as humorous. Pharaohs have always lavished large sums on their temples. It was my view that for whatever reasons the generals had come to hate Hatshepsut and it no longer mattered at all what she did or didn't do. There was serious discontent in the upper ranks of the army and it did not bode well for Egypt.

After a while I grew tired of the politics and turned to reading the field reports that arrived from some of our companies that had been sent into the eastern desert to deal with the raids of the *Ente* bandits. I recalled having watched the execution of some of these bandits during my stop at Gebtu when I travelled with Ra-hotep on the Nile from Thebes to Memphis. They were a problem. Judging from the reports they had become bolder and attacked the caravans and the gold mines almost at will. A few company-sized units from T'aru had been sent to Taphta where they were joined by other units sent from Thebes to put an end to the banditry. Since then a number of skirmishes had been fought and some soldiers killed. But the problem persisted with no end in sight. Now requests for additional units had been received and I planned to use them to get assigned to my first real war!

A few days after receiving the request I entered Amenemhab's office and placed the letter before him. He was busy reading something else and barely took notice of my presence.

"What's this, Thutmose?" he asked without looking up.

"It's from the commander at Taphta, sir." I paused hoping my silence would draw Amenemhab's attention. He continued to read. The silence grew until at last he raised his head.

"Well?" he asked. "What about the commander at Taphta?" he said. He looked at me standing there and a quizzical expression appeared on his face. He was looking at me as if something was wrong.

"Well, Thutmose, what is it for Seth's sake?"

I put on my best professional voice and spoke up.

"The Taphta garrison is having difficulty dealing with the *Ente* and requests that you send them three more companies to augment their force."

Amenemhab put downs his pen and leaned back in his chair. There was an impish twinkle in his eye and a sly smile formed upon his lips.

"And what do you think, Thutmose? Should I send this fool at Taphta more troops or have we thrown enough manpower at the problem with no result?" His eyes narrowed, but the impish gleam did not disappear. Amenemhab was having great fun although I didn't know why.

"It is my opinion, sir, that the Taphta commander has good reason for needing more men. The eastern desert is vast with many places for the *Ente* to hide," I said. "Also, the bandits move by mule and foot. To catch them we need to move faster than they do. What we need is chariots, sir, to run them down." I was about to dig myself in even deeper when Amenemhab broke in.

"And how do you propose to use chariots in that miserable terrain? From what I remember of it there isn't a flat place large enough to build a house on never mind maneuver chariots in! By Horus, Thutmose, the eastern desert is one of the most miserable places on earth!" Despite his words his eyes flashed and the smile remained. I stood there not saying a word. Then Amenemhab threw back his head and gave out with a roar of laughter that took me by surprise. I could do nothing but watch. At last his laughter subsided and he spoke.

"The answer is yes, Thutmose. You have my permission to go to the eastern desert and seek your adventure!" It was the kind of answer that a father might give to a son who wanted something very much but was afraid to ask for it directly.

"But there will be no three companies! That fellow at Taphta is like all commanders. Everyone of them sees his problem as the most important facing Egypt." He smiled. "Besides, the *Ente* were there long before you or I were born and they will still be raiding our caravans long after we are both dead! You may trust me that

Egypt will survive their predatory habits. But, Thutmose, you may take your ten-man squad of chariots and go seek your war."

Amenemhab rose from his chair and walked from behind the desk and stood before me. Our eyes met and much passed between us in the few moments that we looked at each other although not a word passed our lips. In my mind I had become a young lion whose time had come to seek his prey and test himself against his own expectations and the expectations of other lions. And there was no better testing ground than war, although I must admit upon reflection that chasing bandits is not exactly the kind of war I recall having in mind. But, as is always the case with young lions, you take the war that the gods give you and get on with it. But however I saw myself, the look in Amenemhab's eyes was quite different. There was a strange depth to them as if some sorrow were hiding within them for what was about to be. There was at the same time a sense that my going to battle was necessary if ever I was to lead Egypt. To command generals to war requires the king to have had his own war or so it seemed to me then. So Amenemhab looked at me with resignation on his face and a concern for my life in his eyes that any father would have for his son, as my father would have had for me if he still lived.

In less than a week I had formed my squad of ten chariots, planned for adequate provisions, and made ready to move along the road from T'aru to the port where the Bitter Lakes empty into the Sea of Seth. From there we would put aboard one of the freighters that the navy operated and sail the four hundred miles to Taphta hugging the coastline of the eastern desert along the way. These freighters were designed for ocean sailing and had the new post and rudders to steer with. Enormous sails pushed the ships along at good speed. I calculated it would be less than ten days for me and my unit to reach our destination. As things turned out when we finally tied up to the quay at Taphta we had been at sea for almost two weeks.

Taphta is one of those towns that we Egyptians had to tear from the grasp of nature. By all accounts it has no right to exist in such a barren place, and should we cease our efforts to keep it alive Taphta would die a quiet death in a few weeks. It sits on the shore of Seth's Sea hard against the granite mountains that rise steeply upward to meet the barren limestone plateau that runs westward until it drops to the floor of the valley of the Nile two hundred miles away. Nothing lives on the plateau that cannot carry with it its own food and water. Even trees and lowly bushes cannot survive in the harsh glare and heat of the sun. To the east the plateau ends in a range of mountains some as high as six thousand feet whose steep sides drop sharply away pressing against the thin shores of the Sea of Seth. Taphta was fashioned from nothingness to serve as a port for Egypt's trade with the Divine Lands to the south and east. The ground yields no food and there is no natural water here. All that men eat or drink must be transported overland by caravan from the town of Gebtu that sits on the Great Bend of the Nile one hundred and fifty miles to the west. Not a single tree of any size lives in Taphta. Even the beams for the mud brick houses had to be transported overland. Taphta is where Hatshepsut ordered her large ships to be constructed so that they could sail to Punt. Every stick of wood, every piece of canvas, and every inch of rope had to be carried by pack mule or ox-cart from the Nile to the shore of the sea. And when these great ships return from their miraculous journeys laden with ivory, ebony, fruits, spice trees, and rare animals, all these must be carted back to the Nile on the same pack mules and ox-carts.

As barren as its sands are to the eye, still the eastern desert holds treasures beyond measure for those with the strength and endurance to search them out and strip them from the hostile earth. The eastern desert supplies almost all of Egypt's flint with which to light our fires and fashion our sickles and scythes. Our women adorn their bodies with the precious stones of garnet, agate, rock crystal and carnelian, all of which are found here. Granite is to be had in abundance and the beautiful *bekhen* stone, that gray-blue graywacke prized for its mirror-like finish, comes from this harsh land. The *bekhen* is most prized by our kings and nobles, for in its substance are to be found the many statues that fill the monuments and temples. Copper for mirrors and arrow-heads and malachite for cosmetics and potions to cure the sick are found here too. But of all the treasures gold is the one most sought and the one that extracts the highest price in body and bone.

Taphta was teeming with human life attracted by the prospect of wealth. I sent Djamu and the rest of the squad out to the fort on the southern edge of the town while I spent the next hour walking through it getting the smell of the place. Taphta held forth no pretense, only rough promise. No building had more than two floors to it and all were made of the same rough mud brick. There was not a single coat of whitewash or paint to be seen anywhere. Everything was the color of mud dust. What passed for streets were mere alleys and most were filled with refuse of all descriptions. Not that it mattered. The climate was so unrelentingly hot that anything made of flesh or pulp dried to a crisp in a matter of a few hours taking with it any stench it might once have harbored. There were people everywhere, not one of whom could not have done with a bath! Everyone seemed dressed in workman's clothes of one sort or another. This was truly the frontier, rough and ready for anything, and filled with hard men willing to do what had to be done to survive and become wealthy.

I made my way through the narrow streets always keeping south in my direction. In this way sooner or later I would pass through the town and come upon the fortress that guarded the road from the port through the mountain pass upward to the desert plateau. Moving through the streets I noticed that almost everyone who passed had a weapon in his belt. Not a good place to get involved in some brawl, I thought to myself. As I wandered along taking in the sights I had this feeling that something was missing. For the longest time I couldn't quite put my finger on what it was until I saw the old crone hobbling along with her water jars. And then it struck me. No women! From what I had seen the entire population of Taphta consisted of adult males and most of them armed to the teeth at that!

The street passed between the last two buildings at the town's edge and led into the open desert. Straight ahead about a half-mile beyond the town were the walls of the fort. The garrison was the largest in the eastern desert but by no means as large as T'aru. It comprised two regiments of infantry and a company of chariots. The troops were used to guard the gold mines and to provide military escorts for the rich caravans that traveled between Taphta and Gebtu. Soldiers also accompanied the caravans that kept the gold mines supplied with provisions. The commander welcomed my arrival, especially so since I had brought ten chariots and horse teams with me. His own chariots were in sorry need of repair and the horses had been worn to a frazzle from overwork in the harsh climate. I tried not to show my disappointment when my equipment was turned over to the chariot troop and I and my men assigned to an infantry company!

A few days later I was given command of a platoon to which my men were also assigned that was to accompany a supply train to the gold mines at Eshuranib. Once there I was to relieve the platoon that had been guarding the place for the last six months and remain at Eshuranib until my unit was relieved in its turn. Usually this was at six month intervals. But as one of the other officers told me sometimes it took as long as a year! None of this made me very happy, but orders were orders and there was nothing to be done about my circumstances except to try and make the best of them. I had volunteered to fight a war. Now it looked like I was going to spend my time guarding a gold mine hundreds of miles from the nearest human comforts.

One day while walking across the parade ground on my way to the stables I was approached by a curious fellow dressed only in a loin cloth and with no sandals on his feet. His thick curly closely cropped hair and black skin marked him as a Nubian. He wore a native headdress fashioned of animal skin and reeds and a dagger and *kopesh* hung from his military-style belt. I moved to pass by him when he came to a sudden halt and raised his hand in a salute.

"Sir," he said. "My name is Setau and I will be going with you to Eshuranib." He paused. "I thought it might be wise if we had a chance to meet and talk about the journey" I was surprised by this. No one had told to me that anyone else was to come along. Nonetheless I returned the salute and gave him a slight smile.

"Very well, Setau," I said. "If we are going to be travelling together it is indeed a good idea for us to meet and get to know one another. My name is Thutmose." I wiped the moisture from my brow. It was still only morning and already the sun was making the earth as hot as an oven. "Let us at least get out of the sun," I said. "I was going to the stable. Why don't you come along." Setau smiled and the two of us walked toward the shade of the overhang that jutted out from the stable's roof.

Setau was the first negro I had ever met and was surprised at his skill and intelligence. He was a *medjay*, those Nubian mercenaries that had served in Egypt's armies for more than five hundred years. The *medjay* were desert tribesmen that lived in the eastern deserts around Aswan and Upper Nubia. They were known for their fierceness in war and for their loyalty to Egypt's pharaohs. *Medjay* were used as policemen in Egypt's largest cities and formed the special necropolis guard in the Valley of the Kings where they pledged their lives to guarding the tombs of the pharaohs for all eternity. As scouts and skirmishers they had no equal, and no one was more at home or knew how to survive in the barren desert more than the *medjay*. Setau told me that two companies of his soldiers were coming along to Eshuranib.

"You see, sir, I am their chief. When we get to Eshuranib my men and I will take over the job of guarding the mines and the prisoners there," he said.

All of which meant, I said to myself, that there will be several times as many *medjay* as there are Egyptians. I was beginning to feel uncomfortable and it must have shown on my face for Setau immediately set my mind at ease.

"No need to worry, sir. It is the same arrangement that our people have had for centuries. We supply the troops and you supply a small contingent of Egyptians and some officers to see to it that we don't get out of hand!" He smiled a broad smile as he spoke and waited to see if I saw the humor in it all.

I cracked a thin smile for I was not yet entirely certain of how this arrangement might work. I nodded to show him I understood and set an even tone in my voice when I spoke.

"So I will be in command of the supply train as it travels to Eshuranib, is that right?" I asked.

Setau smiled and nodded. "Yes."

"And when we get there? Your men will be under my orders, is that correct?"

Again he smiled. "Yes sir. That is correct."

I nodded and gave Setau my best serious expression as if something of great importance had just been agreed to.

Setau spoke. "I am here to serve you, sir, the way my people have served yours for so many centuries," he said. He allowed a long pause to rise between us. "There is nothing to fear, sir...and perhaps very much to learn."

There was indeed very much to learn, and I have never forgotten my debt to Setau for teaching me how to survive and fight in the desert. My instruction began immediately.

"I understand the journey will take more than a week," I said. I looked up at the sun and shook my head. "Quite a walk in this heat."

A puzzled look crossed Setau's face as he spoke. "Why would we walk, sir?"

Now I was puzzled. "The chariots are useless in this broken terrain. We'll have to leave the horses behind." I paused. "Besides, my horse teams and machines have already been taken by the chariot company."

Setau's face broke into a smile as he finally understood what I was saying.

"We never use horses here sir," he said. "We use mules." He paused and looked around. "Look," he said with a sweep of his arm. "Over there."

I turned toward where he was pointing. Across the parade ground I saw a mule walking toward us. A *medjay* warrior armed with a bow and a quiver of arrows was perched upon the animal's back. A dagger and *kopesh* hung from the warriors belt. Two reins ran from his hand to the animals's mouth. By pulling on the reins and pressing the animal's sides with his legs the *medjay* easily controlled the animal. The negro's sweaty skin glistened in the sunlight like polished ebony and contrasted sharply with the dull dried brown color of the animal's hide. Sitting upon the mule's back with his head topped by the curious headdress the *medjay* looked comical. Seeing him there few would have guessed that these native warriors were ruthless killers and formidable enemies.

Setau saw my confusion and spoke up.

"Don't worry sir," he said, "you and your men will get the hang of riding the mules in a short time. I suppose your training on the chariot will help you to shoot the bow from the back of the animal, but that might take a bit more practice." He paused and waited for me to acknowledge what he was saying. I nodded and turned back to look at the mule. Setau continued.

"Infantry armed with bows set atop mules is a good combination, sir. The mule can go more places and has more endurance than a horse in these conditions. It's how the *Ente* travel and fight. If we want to catch them this is the only way to do it."

As strange as it seemed it made sense. We Egyptians only used the mule for drawing carts and carrying cargo. This was the first time I had ever seen a soldier set upon one to do battle. It was something I remembered for many years and often thought of forming such units in my armies. Nothing ever came of it and to this day we Egyptians still use the mule the way we always have.

At last the time came to get the supply train underway. I ordered it assembled on the parade ground early in the morning. Thirty pairs of oxen drawing carts loaded to the rails with food and other supplies led the way. The oxen were much slower than the pack mules so putting them in front set the pace of the column at about twenty miles a day. Behind them came scores of pack mules, some with cargo saddles and others with side panniers to carry their loads. Civilian merchants who had been contracted to deliver the supplies to the mines came along to insure that their wares arrived safely and they were properly paid for them. The commander of the garrison assigned a physician's assistant to see to our injuries. The regular camp physician, of course, stayed behind to tend whatever ills might befall the garrison. Of some interest to me were the half-dozen women who accompanied us. No shy flowers these, they were prostitutes—what we used to call "Daughters of Bes"—who intended to make a tidy sum selling their wares to the soldiers along the way. The soldiers at the mine had not seen a woman in many months so there was sure to be a healthy market for their favors no matter how shopworn or tattered they were. And then, of course, there was the trip back where business would not be as brisk, but where a *deben* or two could still be made.

For their own safety I placed my men halfway back in the column. They were still unsteady on their animals and would be useless in any fight. At the head of the column they might panic at the first sign of trouble. In the middle they would be safe, and if one fell from his animal someone behind him was sure to notice and give him a hand! Setau and I took the lead supported by two squads of Setau's *medjay* warriors. Except for a small contingent that ranged far ahead as scouts, the remainder of his men anchored the middle of the column and formed its rear guard. It took several hours to get everyone in their assigned places. It was almost noon before I gave the command to move out and the column slithered out the fortress gate like some great snake moving out from under a rock.

The desert journey was more difficult than I imagined. Had it not been for Setau's sound advice the column might not have reached its destination at all. It was he who suggested that a guard be placed around the water supply to prevent looting. Fights broke out over the women and I was compelled to have two fellows whipped for their part in the commotion. Fortunately they were civilians. To my surprise my own men performed well under the circumstances, and by journey's end had grown accustomed to riding their mules. Whether they could yet hit anything with their bows, however, I confess was another matter. Setau's men, of course, were at home in the desert and performed without complaint even though the conditions under which we lived were harsh. Day after day the column moved over the rocky and barren land dependent only upon itself to survive. One day from the top of a small hill the mining town of Eshuranib came into view. The journey had taken four days longer than I had calculated it would. When the last of the column finally arrived at the town we were down to our last day's supply of food and water.

Eshuranib turned out to be the worst place I had ever seen. To call it a town was to give it a dignity that it truly lacked. It was, if anything, a collection of mud huts arranged randomly over the landscape. Few of the huts even had doors. Not a speck of paint or color of any kind disturbed the universally mud colored buildings. Rows and rows of open stalls arranged in the manner of stables seemed to be the most common type of building few of which had any roofs and all of which had strong metal rings anchored to their earthen floors. When I inquired where my troops were to be billeted I was shown to an old barracks that had not been lived in for months. It would only be for a few days I was assured until the troops vacated the other barracks for the trip back to Taphta. Then I could move my men in there.

As dismal as Eshuranib was it was one of Egypt's richest gold mines, the place where the finest quality gold, the "gold of thrice," was mined. Setau had been here many times and showed me around the place that was to be my home for the next six months. We walked aimlessly through the compound. A pile of leather sacks neatly arranged in parallel rows caught my attention. The openings to the sacks had been sewn shut.

"What are those, Setau?" I asked pointing to the pile.

The *medjay* smiled. "That is the result of six months labor, sir. It is gold ore waiting to be transported to Taphta on your ox-carts."

I was amazed.

"You mean each of those sacks is full of gold!"

There was an excited incredulity in my voice. So much gold in one place seemed an impossibility even for me who grew up in a royal palace where gold furnishings were commonplace.

Setau shook his head and laughed.

"It is not as you believe, sir. No. What is in there is a fine mixture of crushed gold ore and the gold itself." He looked at me and saw the puzzled look on my face. "I see you don't know much about gold mining," he said pleasantly.

I shook my head. "What you say is true Setau." I paused and smiled. "Tell me, how does this wretched place turn a profit."

"Well, sir, it turns a profit alright, but only because it does not care about the costs. Look over there."

I turned to where he was pointing. A line of naked men chained together at the ankles slogged slowly over the burning ground. Their hair was filthy and hung below their shoulders. Skin parched and burnt by the harsh sun covered their bodies except where deep pale scars caused by the whip had healed without color. Next to the men walked an armed *medjay* soldier with a whip in his hand. No words passed between the men and their guard as they made their way in the direction of the stalls.

Setau turned to me and his lips tightened.

"Those are the laborers who work the mines. They are convicted criminals, slaves, prisoners of war, and any other poor wretch who was sent here at the command of pharaoh's courts. They work every day without rest. If they fall ill there is no physician to tend to their sickness. They are not even given clothes. They live on bread and thin beer and they are worked until they die. Not one will ever leave this place."

It was a miserable sight, this collection of human suffering that passed before us. "And him," I said gesturing in the direction of the *medjay* guarding the others.

Setau laughed. "It is as I told you sir. We *medjay* watch the prisoners and you Egyptians keep watch on us! It has been that way
for centuries." He snorted. "Who else could you hire to come to
this place? The prisoners have no choice and for us *medjay* the
eastern desert is our home. At least we can come and go as we
please. There are so many prisoners and so few guards that the
poor wretches are never free of their chains. They are chained to
one another in groups of six when they are at work in the mines
and chained to the rings in the floors of their stalls when they are
not working."

Setau shook his head again. He seemed to be wondering how
any man could live like this and not prefer to find a way to take his
own life. He said nothing but I could see his thoughts in his eyes.

The compound squatted in the middle of a flat piece of rocky
ground surrounded on three sides by steep mountains. From
where we stood I could see several tunnels that had been cut into
the solid rock of the mountainside. The opening of the shaft
looked like the gaping mouth of a rock tomb such as I had seen in
the Valley of the Kings. The shaft reached hundreds of feet inside
the mountain. Small rooms ran off either side of these shafts
where the gold ore was chopped from the walls with chisels and
mallets. Often the ceilings of these "gold rooms" were so low that
workers labored on their knees. The dust inside these chambers
was so thick that laborers wore rags around their mouths to help
them breathe. Still, the workers suffered from coughs and difficulty breathing. Chipping ore from the inside of a mountain was
dangerous work in other ways. Sometimes the chisels sent small
sharp pieces of rock flying from the wall that could cause blindness if they struck an eye. Many workers that I saw had lost their
sight this way.

The ore from the "gold rooms" was pushed to the central shaft
where it was collected twice each day. Teams of men harnessed

like mules dragged wooden sleds laden with the ore out of the tunnels. This rough ore was deposited in a huge pile. Workers chained to the ground sat in a rough semi-circle around the pile of ore. These were the "millers." Each of these workers sat with a granite hand mill in front of him. The mill was nothing more than a flat piece of granite worn in the middle much like the mills used by women to crush barley or emmer. Pieces of ore were placed on the granite stone. Using the other piece of granite like a roller, the worker ground the ore down to a fine sand which was then collected in sacks for transport to Taphta in the empty ox-carts that had carried our supplies. Except for the large nuggets that could be easily taken from the ore with a chisel or hammer, the mines at Eshuranib produced no refined gold at all. What the mines produced was the ground ore from the mills. Water was far too precious at Eshuranib to be used to extract gold! The ore had to be sent to Gebtu where the Nile provided an abundance of water to wash the gold from the sand that held it.

Eshuranib was such a terrible place that even the soldiers of the garrison felt that they were being punished for some unknown wrong. Certainly the commander of the garrison had every reason to think he had been forgotten by his superiors. He had been in command of the garrison here for three years and except for an occasional visit to Taphta had never been relieved. When I met him he was drunk and his uniform ill-kept. It was clear from our conversation that he cared little for his responsibilities. The compound was run by the commander of the *medjay* troops. This was fortunate for me since Setau was to be the new commander of the native troops. We had gotten along well over the duration of our journey.

And so I remained at Eshuranib for the next six months, one of three officers in charge of a company of Egyptian troops whose task it was to protect the garrison from the *Ente* raiders. In fact the *medjay* kept the compound safe. From time to time I would ride patrol with Setau and a few of his men hoping to run across a raiding party. I had, after all, come to the eastern desert to find my war. But we never encountered any of these bandits. Still I became proficient at sitting a mule, and with some practice became quite a good shot with my bow even while firing from the moving animal. Once we came upon a merchant who made his living visiting *medjay* and bedouin villages with a collection of prostitutes. Setau convinced him that there was a profit to be made at Eshuranib and we saw the caravan safely to the mines where they were welcomed with open arms and open purses by the soldiers. Having long grown accustomed to the prostitutes that had arrived with the supply train months ago, the soldiers took to the new women as if they were all fresh beauties. It was a wild night of drinking and fornicating. By dawn almost the entire garrison had exhausted itself. Setau and I kept our distance from the revelry as a matter of professional responsibility. Too, the prostitutes were hardly the comely "serpents of the Nile" that I had seen in the inns and pubs of Egyptian military towns. Dirty and unkept, they did little to raise any desire in my body although I confess that the thought of the ladies brought to mind pleasant memories of Nefurure and the time we spent together so long ago.

And then one day a soldier spotted a column of dust rising from the approaching supply train and I knew it would be only a few more days before I could leave Eshuranib and return to Taphta. Perhaps orders were waiting for me there and I could leave the harsh desert for a more pleasant and exciting assignment. Djamu and the rest of the members of my chariot squad were also ready to leave, the sooner the better. Duty at the mines had been particularly difficult on them. They regarded life in the infantry as dirty and uncomfortable compared to duty in the chariot corps. Forcing them to go on patrols with the *medjay* and their mules earned me few friends. But were it not for these patrols the men would have had nothing to do at all and would have gotten into all sorts of trouble. A few days after the column arrived I told Djamu to make the men ready to depart. I said my farewells to Setau and the garrison commander and prepared to accompany the supply column on its return journey to Taphta were I hoped I might yet find an opportunity for adventure.

The difficult trek back in addition to the six months of hard duty in the harsh surroundings of Eshuranib had weakened my health and I fell ill near the end of the journey. The garrison physician examined me and prescribed plenty of good food and rest. I had lost considerable weight that my thin frame could ill afford and the chance to rebuild my strength came as a welcomed reward for the miserable days and weeks I had spent baking in the desert like a loaf of bread upon a hot stove. For the first week I rarely left my bed and then only to eat and bathe. I felt myself growing stronger with each day. By the end of the second week I was feeling my old self again and beginning to get bored.

The first thing I did upon my return to duty was to assemble the men, machines, and horses that I had originally brought with me and reform my platoon. Djamu and the soldiers were overjoyed at being relieved from infantry duty and threw themselves into their training with renewed vigor. At the end of two weeks the platoon was in fine fighting fettle and their skills were as good as they had been before we left T'aru. And a good thing too, for we had just finished our training when the garrison commander assigned me and my platoon to a squadron of twenty-five machines to accompany the next gold caravan to Gebtu.

The size of the caravan dwarfed the supply column that I had escorted to Eshuranib. This one was a true treasure caravan with three hundred ox-carts and two hundred mules transporting all sorts of valuables. Many of the ox-carts hauled the heavy leather sacks of crushed gold ore to be washed and refined in the Nile's waters at Gebtu. Others carried cargoes of ebony wood and ivory that had been brought to Taphta on Hatshepsut's great sailing ships from the Divine Lands far to the south. Precious plants from which aromatic spices and healing balms could be taken filled the mule's panniers. The panniers were an ideal way to carry the sacks of gold nuggets. Other sacks on cargo saddles were filled with garnets, rubies, agates, and other precious jewels that were part of the rich harvest of the eastern desert. Two ox-carts carried cages of the kind that would normally hold wild animals. But these cages each held a pair of pygmy dwarfs taken from some strange land south of the Horns of the Earth. Upon seeing them a vision of the pygmy who let the panther loose upon me in the menagerie flashed into my mind! A cold shudder ran up my back when I thought how close I had come to being killed at the hands of one of these little fellows.

The caravan's treasures made it a fine target for the *Ente* bandits and the garrison commander assigned a sizeable force to escort the column. A full company of infantry, two hundred and fifty men, in five platoons of fifty men each led by a commander called the Greatest of Fifty accompanied the column. Three of the platoons were "strong arm boys," heavy infantry armed with *kopesh*, shield, and spear, and the other two platoons were archers or "shooters." The bandits were infantry accompanied by archers mounted on mules so a strong infantry force was needed to deal with them if they attempted to attack the caravan. I and my platoon of charioteers were assigned to a squadron of twenty-five machines under command of a Standard Bearer. Each platoon of ten machines had an officer in command. The chariots were used as scouts, flank security, and as advance and rear guards. Unless the bandits attacked the column in open country, my machines and men were not likely to be very much help in any infantry melee that developed.

It was more than a hundred and fifty miles from Taphta to Gebtu along a broad and flat road that connected the two cities. The road began its climb from the shore of Seth's Sea and wound its way upward through the mountains until it gained the flat limestone plateau that stood between the eastern mountains and the edge of the Nile Valley where the plateau dropped away again down to the city of Gebtu. For most of the journey the road ran over open country that made it difficult for bandits to approach the column without being discovered by our scouts. But there were several places where it ran through narrow canyons that afforded excellent opportunities for ambush. Our chariot scouts made special efforts to make sure that these canyons were clear before the column passed through them.

For the first two days of the journey my platoon brought up the rear of the column as it wended its way through the eastern mountains to reach the edge of the plateau. The dust made life miserable for the rear guard and I permitted my men to drop a good distance behind the column to avoid being choked by the dust. I had ordered my men into full battle gear at the start of the trek, but by the second day the heat of the metal armor and bronze helmets threatened to overwhelm them and I ordered the battle gear removed and kept handy should it be needed. I noticed that the infantry commander had done the same with his men, although I thought it a bad idea that the spears and shields were carried on the ox-carts out of easy reach. The third day out from Taphta my platoon was assigned as scouts and forward screen for the column. I ordered three chariots a mile to the front and another two to the flanks. The remainder of my platoon, five machines, I kept with me a half mile to the front of the column. We had passed through two canyons that day without incident and I had no reason to expect that the canyon up ahead would be any different. Still, for reasons I cannot explain I was uneasy the way an animal sometimes senses the presence of the hunter and ordered my men to put on their helmets and body armor and string their bows. Djamu had a puzzled look on his face as he looked at me. I guessed he was trying to decide whether or not to trust my instincts. With the platoon arrayed for battle I raised my arm and ordered the scouts into the canyon.

A few minutes later the rest of my platoon followed. The canyon was different from the others we had passed through. There were no steep walls rising straight up to great heights. Steep walls made an ambush difficult. Here all around me were short rocky hills, more like piles of rubble than walls, that hemmed in the track so tightly that once the column was within it there was hardly sufficient room for a chariot to fit and turn between the column and the canyon walls. My eyes searched the rocky hills for any signs of the *Ente* even as I made rough calculations to determine the length of the canyon. By the time my platoon reached the exit I reckoned its length to be a little more than two miles. This meant that the column would be completely inside the canyon just as its advance guard was emerging from it and its rear guard had not yet entered. The column was completely within the canyon now and I remembered looking at the sky and thinking that by the time we cleared the canyon walls it would be close to dark and we would have to camp somewhere near the exit. Since we Egyptians feared the night and never mounted military operations in the dark, the time of day lessened my fears of an ambush. It was then that the *Ente* struck.

A sudden whistling of wind shot by my ear. I caught sight of the arrow as it passed close to my head and struck the ground to my left. Instinctively I turned toward the direction from which it had come only to see another arrow just miss my head and strike the side of Djamu's shield. Djamu's felt the impact and turned toward me with a puzzled look on his face. In less than a second we had been fired upon from two directions!

"Move!" I yelled and shoved Djamu in the back. The force of my arm turned him around and in a single movement he snapped the reins sending the horses lurching forward at great speed. The wheels dug into the earth, gained purchase, and the cab shot forward almost throwing me from the rear of the chariot. "Move! Move!" I yelled as we passed the other machines. I wanted them in motion to make more difficult targets. As Djamu guided the machine past one of the others I saw the chariot commander fall from the cab clutching an arrow that had struck him in the chest. The frightened driver drove the horses forward and made no attempt to retrieve his fallen comrade. In a second I was in front of the platoon leading them away from the canyon exit. I signalled for the others to pull behind me in a line and then led them around in a wide circle until we had reversed direction and brought them to a halt facing the canyon exit.

A few hundred yards in front of us were scores of *Ente* swarming down from the rubble piles that formed the canyon walls. Their sudden attack had separated my advance guard of chariots from the column they had trapped in the canyon. I did not know it at the time but a simultaneous attack had taken place at the other end of the canyon isolating the rear guard as well. While I examined the situation three scout machines pulled up and wheeled into line. Inside the canyon the *Ente* showered arrows on the column taking a heavy toll of our infantry who were caught with their weapons and shields stored on the ox-carts. Men scrambled around in great panic unable to protect themselves. At last they retrieved their shields, but not before some had been killed or wounded by the hail of arrows. Every soldier hit meant one less that could fight when the bandits rushed down and slaughtered everyone at close range.

I looked at the line of nine chariots formed on either side of me. Their commanders looked to me awaiting my orders. Djamu, too, looked over his shoulder waiting for me to do something. My heart was pounding as I tried to picture the canyon in my mind. There was little space between the column and the walls, enough for one machine at a time to move through, but with no space to turn around and maneuver. Chariots moving through that space at speed might be able to kill as they went. But if they stopped they would be quickly overwhelmed and their crews slaughtered. But if the chariots could cut their way along the entire length of the canyon and break through to the rear exit, the rear guard would be able to join the battle from the other end. A chariot charge even in single file would also buy the hard pressed infantry time to regroup and counter-attack. As my mind raced Djamu stared at me with eyes wide with the familiar combination of excitement and fear. As I looked at him I had no idea whether my plan would work. With the sounds of battle coming from yards away I had to do something. I had found my war at last and the pounding of my heart urged me on.

With a sweep of my hand I brought four of my chariots abreast with me and yelled to their commanders at the top of my voice.

"Form a single file and attack through the enemy to your front staying to the far left canyon wall. Drive through the canyon and relieve the pressure on the rear guard at the other end. If you make it join with the rear guard's chariots and attack back through."

I saw their heads move up and down that they understood my order. I raised my hand and yelled.

"Horus, Great Hawk of Egypt, guide the talons of our arrows!"

My hand dropped and the chariots moved forward one behind the other in single file as they prepared to attack. I signaled the rest of the platoon to follow me in single file as I lined up to lead the attack down the right canyon wall. For a second all was calm as the chariots held their positions awaiting my signal. Up ahead the *Ente* stood their ground. My heart raced and my head pounded. I felt a weakness in my belly that made me fear that I might foul myself. And then from deep within my mind I heard the sound of my father's voice.

"Do not be afraid, Thutmose. Take no counsel of your fear for this is your destiny. Find the courage my son and this day you will triumph!"

And then all about me grew calm. Even the *Ente* appeared to stand as still as stone statues. Djamu looked at me and I smiled at him. I turned toward my other commanders and raised my arm for them to see. With a great voice that required all my strength, I gave the order.

"ATTACK!"

Djamu snapped the reins and the haunches of the horses tightened like springs only to uncoil with great force propelling the chariot forward. Again and again Djamu snapped the reins until *Slasher* and *Ptah* were carrying us along at gallop speed. From the corner of my eye I saw the first chariot off to my left begin to move as he charged straight toward the bandits guarding the mouth of the canyon. I pulled an arrow from my quiver and set the nock to the bowstring. Underneath me the chariot flew over the hard ground with a steadiness that I did not expect. Djamu adjusted his shield and drove the horses straight at the bandits. I was still forty yards away when I drew the bowstring to my ear and let fly my first arrow. The fletches hummed as the string slipped from my fingers and sped by my ear. Straight as the wind the arrow flew taking one of the bandits in the chest. I watched the arrow strike and the *Ente*'s body buckle and fall. A warm flood of excitement rushed over me. It was a lucky shot but it was a kill!

My eyes widened and every muscle in my body went taut. I set another arrow to the bow. The targets were closer now and the bowstring hummed again as my second arrow flew true to its target. Another hit! Horus was guiding my arrows! Djamu drove the horses so hard that the wind passing my ears seemed a roar. Straight for the canyon mouth we came. There was time for one more shot before we were upon them. I made the great bow ready and searched the group of bandits for a sure target. There! A tall man with a red shield. I yelled to Djamu who moved the horses slightly off the track so that I would pass close to my victim. In a flash I was upon him and saw the look of terror in his eyes as I held him in my stare. I let fly the deadly shaft. The *Ente* seemed rooted in place and had not even the presence of mind to raise his shield. My arrow leapt at him like an angry lion and struck him square in the throat. I had no time to look at him again when Djamu sent the horses crashing over the bodies of the bandits who bared the way to the canyon.

There was a sudden thud and the chariot's wheels left the ground. I heard the sound of their spinning through the air. I grabbed for the belly-bar and hung on while Djamu did the best he could to keep the machine upright. The spinning wheels found the earth again and dug their bronze studs into the ground sending the chariot shooting straight and true once more down the narrow space between the trapped column and the canyon wall. Behind us the second of my chariots had begun its charge and already its commander's arrows were landing amidst the stunned bandits.

Djamu spurred the horses into the canyon's mouth. For a few seconds we were alone and I could see what was happening. Our infantry had found its weapons and regrouped and our archers were answering the bandits' arrows with good effect. Infantry platoon leaders rallied their troops using the ox-carts for cover. But most of our infantry were strong arm boys and were useless unless they could close with the bandits in hand-to-hand fighting. The sky was growing dimmer with the onset of dusk. Already long shadows crept along the canyon floor making it difficult for the bandit archers to hit their targets. As far as I could see the lane between the column and the canyon wall was clear. Above me and to my right the hills crawled with the enemy. Suddenly it seemed that every arrow from those hills was aimed at me!

I set an arrow to its nock and sent it upward in the direction of a bandit, but the steep angle and the speed of the chariot made the shaft fly wide of its mark. Another try and another miss. I realized that further attempts were useless. Djamu kept the chariot on the narrow lane as we galloped straight for the rear of the canyon more than a mile in front of us while arrows fell thickly around us as we went. I glanced behind me and saw that the other chariot, too, was on course. I realized that we had stumbled into a battle that was only going to be won by infantry. As far as anyone in the canyon was concerned I and my chariots could keep on going right out the rear of the canyon! I had found my war at last, but was fast running away from its first battle. And that, I said to myself, would not do!

As we came abreast of the middle of the column I caught sight of one of the infantry officers with whom I had a passing acquaintance in the garrison. I ordered Djamu to bring the machine to a stop. Grabbing the javelins, I jumped from the chariot and made my way to the cover of an upturned ox-cart. Djamu, not knowing what else to do, stayed where he was until I yelled at him to make for the canyon exit and see to the horses' safety. The officer and his men gaped at me as if I might be mad. My fellow officer shook his head in disbelief when I asked to join his unit for the coming fight. He ordered that I be given a shield taken from one of the dead. I thanked him and drew my *kopesh* to face the attack I was certain would come.

Blocked by the rim of the canyon wall the sun's rays cast only a dim light as the day prepared to give itself up to the night. It was darker on the canyon floor than on the hills above it and glow of the setting sun provided a background against which the bandits stood out as targets. I looked up at the hills. They were crawling with bandits who had left the cover of their hiding places and prepared for an assault against the column. All around me infantry and archers made ready their shields, helmets, and weapons. I, too, found myself fidgeting with my *kopesh* as I felt fear rise within me. Then the silence of the canyon was shattered by the screams of the *Ente* soldiers who rushed down upon us. I watched them swarm toward us. It was as if we were about to be overwhelmed by ants.

Our men rose from their hiding places behind and under the ox-carts and rushed to meet the enemy. I was already standing and found myself in the front rank of the infantry. Blood flooded into my head and my senses sharpened. Every muscle tightened while my eyes widened as excitement and fear combined to prepare my body for combat. I rubbed my thumb over the hilt of the *kopesh* until I felt the sting of a fresh cut. Noise filled my ears with the general din of swords banging against shields and the sound of screaming men rushing over the narrow ground that separated me from them. For a second I felt rooted to the earth. A warm liquid ran from my body and trickled down my leg like a hot stream. Out of the rushing tide of screaming men came one with shield lowered and sword arm raised, the gleam of lethal metal flashing from his fist. His eyes shown red with anger or fear, I could not tell which. And when our eyes met it seemed to me that our destinies were locked together, and that by day's end one of us would be dead.

Within seconds the space between the column and the narrow sloping canyon walls was filled with the crush of screaming sweating agonized humanity crashing into one another. All up and down the canyon the air filled with the force of the raw emotion of fear disguising itself as courage as the two groups of antagonists closed with one another in deadly earnest. The noise of shields crashing against other shields and of swords against helmets and javelins against armor made the hot air ring with the sounds of a thousand blacksmiths and foundries. Screams of frightened men mixed with the noise of clashing weapons until all about me was a roaring cacophony of sound that drowned all but the noises of my own body as my adversary crashed into my shield.

Merykare's lessons flashed through my mind and I met the attack by dropping to one knee and catching the enemy on my shield throwing my full weight upward to force him off balance and follow him to the ground. We crashed into the earth like falling stones and I felt the breath go out of him as my full weight landed upon his body with a great force. With my shield I pressed against the back of his head forcing his face into the sand. Even as I did this I rose to my feet using the press of my shield against his shoulders to steady myself. As soon as I gained my feet he turned face up in the sand. In one quick motion he reached for his sword that had fallen from his grip.

Every sense focused on my prey while all about me the press of other combatants swirled almost unnoticed. The terrified mules danced in the dust lifting and dropping their hooves as they tried to escape the madness that went on beneath them. Strong tether and harness held them fast to a few feet of ground. Unable to flee, the terrified animals whinnied and screamed and swung their heads in a pointless display of their own madness. My eyes bored in upon the helpless bandit struggling in the dust and I fixed my target in my mind. The grip of my *kopesh* was slippery with my own sweat and I had barely sufficient room to wield its deadly edge. My arm drew back. I turned the curved blade outward with a twist of my wrist as Merykare had taught me. The weapon reached the top of my arm's arc and had begun its deadly descent toward the neck of the *Ente* when my consciousness opened into a great white light accompanied by the heavy thud of a sword blade smashing against my helmet.

The force of the blow sent me crashing to the ground, spots of blue-white light danced before my eyes robbing my vision of any focus. The great melee' of men maiming men roiled above me. The stamp of trampling feet danced about me raising dust so thick that each breath only made the next one more difficult. Lying on my back I rolled back and forth to avoid being trampled while I struggled to clear my head in the dusty stifling heat that clung to the canyon floor. I dragged my body under an ox-cart and lay there wiping my eyes and gasping for air. My shield and weapons were gone, knocked from my grasp by the impact of the sword blow to my head. Slowly my head cleared. From underneath the wagon I caught sight of my *kopesh* lying in the dust a few yards from me. I lunged for it and my hand skittered through the sand coming to rest on the weapon's handle. My fingers closed around it and I drew it toward me. I knelt in the swirling dust of the battle that raged around me wondering where the next blow would come from.

Not five yards distant to my right lay my prey still stunned from the force of my attack. Like the crabs on the shores of the Great Green, I scuttled toward him on my hands and knees. He was raising himself when I smashed into him and slipped one arm around his throat and forced him back into the dirt. The *Ente* was bigger than me and struggled like a trapped animal bucking himself off the ground trying to free himself from my deadly grip. Under these circumstances my *kopesh* was of no use and I let it fall from my hand. The two of us rolled in the sand. For the first time I understood how it was that Amenemhab had killed that fellow by biting off his face! Both of us were terrified of the other so that if it took

tearing the other apart with bare teeth to free ourselves from the
fear, then both of us would have surely done it without hesitation.

I tightened my arm around the *Ente*'s throat and reached for
my dagger with my other hand. My fingers found the ball of the
weapon's handle and closed around it drawing the weapon from
its sheath. My breath came in short gasps and my mouth filled
with dust. Sweat poured into my eyes distorting my vision. My
heart pounded like a drum and the roar of noise filled my ears.
And yet my mind, if not my senses, was clear. With my last
strength I squeezed the bandit's neck against my arm and chest
and rolled to one side taking his body with me as I did so that he
ended up on top of me with his face toward the sky. The maneuver took him by surprise. For a few seconds he relaxed his struggle. That was when my dagger found its mark. A quick movement
brought the knife from my right side up and over his chest where
it hovered for a split-second like the hawk above its victim. And
then I plunged the dagger into the *Ente*'s chest.

I felt the tip of the dagger strike bone, hesitate a second, and
then slide off to finish its plunge through soft flesh until the hilt
pressed hard against the body's outer skin and brought an end to
the weapon's travel. The *Ente*'s head was pressed close to mine by
the force of my arm and the rush of air that flew from his lungs
made the sound of a sistrum. His body arched upward as the
shock of pain ran through it while tightened muscles held it at the
top of the arc for a second until it fell upon me with great force.
The bandit's arm moved for his throat, his hand grasping in a
claw-like fashion as if to grab his windpipe. But the force of life
was fleeting. Half-way through the movement his arm fell limply
to his side. Still I held him in a strong grip with one arm and my
hand held firmly to the dagger's ball. I did not know what to do.
But I dared not let him free before I was certain he was finished
lest he rise up from some ghastly charade and strike me down in

my turn. Besides, lying there beneath the *Ente*'s corpse I was safe from the harm of the battle that raged above me.

I would have stayed there until it was finished were it not for the sensation of warm stinking shit flowing from the corpse onto my stomach! Merykare had told us that the dead loose their bowels and piss when they expire. Some, he said, even died with their pricks stiff as the organ filled with one last flood of blood before death stilled it forever. The stench and slippery feeling on my body made my stomach wretch. I threw the *Ente*'s corpse from me and struggled to my feet. Anger at being fouled flooded through me and I flew into a rage. I reached for a *kopesh* lying in the dust and raised it with both hands. The canyon floor was covered with dead and dying men. The once pale sand had turned red black in splotches of color. The din raged without end and the moaning of the wounded was carried away in the howls of those freshly struck with metal weapons. My senses were enraged. Whatever conscious ability to think remained in this terrible place was driven from me by the great anger that swelled inside me. I rose to my feet both hands gripping the handle of the sickle-sword and looked for the nearest enemy to kill.

All around me men were locked in deadly embrace. They struggled against each other for advantage in the contest of life or death. What was left of the dying sun glinted off sword blades as they rose and fell completing their fatal work. So great was the press of bodies that I barely had room to move and little to swing a sword. But through the screaming squirming crowd my eyes fell upon the figure of an *Ente* standing over a soldier he had stricken down with the blow of a club. The bandit stood erect, his back to me, head turned to body writhing in pain at his feet. My hands tightened their grip on the handle of my *kopesh*. I pressed my way through the struggling tangle of bodies until I was no more than two yards behind him. In the confusion and noise he did not see

me turn my wrist to set the edge of the blade facing outward nor
see me draw the weapon back and set it swinging at his legs.

The *kopesh*'s blade cut deeply into the *Ente*'s legs severing his
ham muscles in an instant. The blade had passed completely
through the thick muscle before the bolt of pain thrust itself into
the soldier's consciousness and he turned his head to look. Before
his eyes reached the sight of his bloodied legs the pain of the
wound found its mark and overwhelmed his senses. The soldier's
head snapped back and a great scream rushed forth from his
throat. His weapon fell from his hand as he reached behind him
and clutched his wounded legs. The bloodied legs quivered and
bent under his weight and the *Ente* sank to his knees.

Two quick steps and I was upon him. He knelt helplessly in the
sand, his eyes filled with an expression of pain and fear that bordered on madness. Behind him the sand grew damp with the
spreading stain of the man's blood. He was not much older than
me. Though the pain distorted his features his face was not
unpleasant, a young man in his prime with much life left in him.
When he turned to look at me I tried not to look into his eyes for
fear that I would see my own fate this day. Still, for a few seconds,
we could not avoid each other's gaze. From nowhere an arrow
pierced the sand next to me and a falling body crashed behind me.
I drew my *kopesh* back and set the blade outward. My body
coiled its strength as a cobra does before it strikes. The *Ente*'s eyes
widened at the sight of the blade and his arms rose in a cross
before him to ward off the blow that would surely take his life.
My ears filled with the din of battle around me and my parched
throat burned like fire as I threw my last strength into the sweep
of the blade.

My muscles uncoiled like the snap of a whip and the blade cut
through the air with the silence of a falcon diving upon its prey.
The sharp edge sped straight for the junction of the *Ente*'s head

and neck where it passed so cleanly through that I barely felt the impact in my hands before my eye caught the bloodied blade of bronze pass out the other side. Thick neck veins that a moment ago pulsed with life now stood upright as the force of the man's blood spurted in a grotesque fountain of red that formed a mist and then poured forth in torrents. Blood was everywhere and spatters of the warm liquid struck my face and arms. The horror sent my own blood to pounding while I watched the *Ente*'s head, its lifeless eyes still open in shock, jump from the stump of his neck and tumble sideways onto the sand. The headless body pitched forward into the dust. Its arms and legs jerked violently the way people taken by the fits jerk. The foot of a soldier occupied by the press of the fight kicked the *Ente*'s head as it lay in the sand and sent it rolling into the melee where it was struck by another foot and yet another until what had once been the soul of a man was no more than another piece of torn flesh littering a pitiless battlefield.

I turned from the sight to better see what was going on about me lest I, too, be struck from behind by some unseen enemy. The blast of an *Ente* trumpet covered the battlefield with a blanket of noise. Another loud note bounced off the canyon walls. All along the line of battle *Ente* soldiers broke off the fight and scrambled up the rocky canyon walls in retreat. It was almost dark and our archers picked off what few they could in the dim light. But there was no thought of following them. We had had a difficult time of it and many of us were satisfied just to be alive. Everywhere our soldiers put down their weapons and sank to the ground in exhaustion where some fell quickly into a deep sleep. Others held their faces in their hands. Except for the occasional bray of a mule or bellow of an ox there was no sound. Those who had escaped death sat silently upon the canyon floor alone with their thoughts.

Darkness filled the canyon broken only by the light of the quarter moon and the stars. I walked toward the rear of the canyon in search of Djamu and the rest of my platoon. It had been a bloody battle. Everywhere the bodies of the dead were strewn upon the ground where they fell. Morning would give us a better idea, but from what I saw that evening it seemed that both sides had suffered badly. Only a few of the corpses had arrow wounds, proof enough of Merykare's dictum that when it came to slaughter, archers weren't much use. It had been a typical infantry battle and the missing arms and hands and gaping slashing wounds revealed all the signs that the deadly *kopesh* had been at work.

Few had been wounded. Close combat is always to the death. Only those struck seconds before the trumpet had sounded were left unkilled as their opponents followed the command to retreat. Normally a wound led to a quick death unless the victim fled the field. But in this fight there was nowhere to flee so the wounded had been slain. Still, there were a small number on both sides. Any wounded *Ente* who could not be salvaged for the slavers was killed on the spot. I was surprised to see that some of our own men who had been wounded badly and were in great pain begged their officers to kill them quickly to relieve their misery. This task was usually left to the junior officers who, it was believed, would become more hardened to death for the experience. Fortunately I was not asked to kill my comrades. Had I been, I don't know that I would have done it in any case. Those whose wounds were not so severe were gathered together and placed on ox-carts for carrying to Gebtu. Their moans and cries of pain echoed through the canyon all night long and many were found dead in the morning. A good number of those who survived that painful night nonetheless succumbed to the rough journey. All in all less than twenty of the wounded survived to reach Gebtu.

I found Djamu about three quarters the way down the canyon. He had turned *Slasher* and *Ptah* loose to fend for themselves. Both horses had made straight for the rear of the canyon and managed to break through where they were corralled by the charioteers of the rear guard. When the fight was over Djamu retrieved the horses and hitched them to the chariot and waited until I found him. One charioteer and a driver of my platoon had been killed. It was the fellow who followed me in the charge down the canyon wall. Seeing the bandits attack in force and witnessing the death of one of their comrades, the rest of the platoon had remained where they were and waited for the battle to end. It was not what I had expected of them and plainly told them so. But having been frightened to death myself, I wondered if they detected the uncertainty in my voice.

There was little firewood to be had on the canyon floor so only a few campfires flickered in the darkness. The enemy corpses were stripped and we burned their clothes and sandals to make the fires last a bit longer. Through the darkness the moans of the suffering wounded could be heard. But as the night passed there was remarkable quiet as men kept to themselves and thought about the day. Once I heard the sound of sobbing and the other sounds men make when they choke back tears. But except for this, all was still that night.

Early the next morning the chariots formed at the front of the column beyond the canyon's mouth while the infantry units formed beside the column itself. While preparations were being made to begin our journey, squads of soldiers gathered up our dead and placed them one atop the other in shallow graves. Stones were placed on the freshly disturbed earth to hinder the hunger of jackals and vultures. The *Ente* were stripped of their weapons and any possessions that we found useful and were left where they had fallen to provide food for the flocks of vultures that had already begun to gather overhead. By mid-morning all these tasks had been accomplished and the column was given the order to march. The next few days passed without incident. It was early afternoon of the third day when my platoon finally passed through the gates of Gebtu.

It was two days later when I awoke from my exhausted slumber disturbed by the loud knocking on the door of my quarters. My hands rubbed the sleep from my eyes as I made my way to the door.

"Thutmose! Here you are. We have been looking for you for days!"

Refu's voice smashed into my consciousness and its braying quality set my teeth on edge. He had commanded the infantry platoon that I had fought with in the canyon and Seth only knew what he was doing standing in my bedroom late this afternoon. I yawned right in his face, turned, walked back to the disheveled bed and threw my tired body upon it.

Refu followed me while the three other officers entered the room and stood near the door. I felt Refu's arm grab my shoulder and shake me until I could no longer ignore my annoyance that I made no effort to conceal.

"What in Seth's balls do you want, Refu? Can't you see I am trying to sleep." I paused and looked at the others standing by the door. "Who are they?" I demanded.

Refu smiled. "They, you idiot, are the officers of the other platoons who fought next to us in the ambush." He paused. "A sorry lot I grant you, and with poor judgement. I took them here to meet you because they didn't believe what I told them about you." Refu paused and waited for me to speak.

"What did you tell them?"

"That even for a chariot driver you did a good job that day. Killed your share of bandits and held up well." He smiled affectionately at me. "They came along to see who you were, that's all." His voice took on a tone of mock seriousness. "Now that they have seen you, get your worn out ass out of the bed and get dressed."

My eyes were clear now and I saw the look of youthful enthusiasm on Refu's face. There was no point in arguing with him.

"Why? I said. "Where are we going?"

Refu brought his face close to mine.

"Were off to feed our faces, my boy, and then to take care of anything else we might need." He laughed. "Hurry up! My stomach is growling and we have the whole night before us!"

It took some time for me to bathe and shave the stubble from my face. While I was at it I shaved the hair from my crotch and under my arms. Egyptians are a clean people and we bathe daily if we can and shave our body hair. I had not done so since leaving for Eshuranib and I had quite a crop to get rid of. The four of them were waiting for me at the bottom of the staircase. After a few jokes about how I smelled, we were off to Gebtu to sample its delights.

We followed after Refu who led us to the section of shops and houses near the Temple of Min that dominated the religious life of Gebtu. Min is the god of fertility and it should have come as no surprise that the best inns and "blue houses" were located nearest the temple. Refu led us around a corner toward the brightly lit building across the street. A large sign hung from a post beside the door. The figure of Min, his legs tightly wrapped together, skull cap on his head and sporting a huge erect prick, left little to the imagination as to the delights that could be purchased inside. The inn, fittingly enough, was named *Min's Garden*. At the feet of the portrait of Min on the sign was a bed of lettuce, a plant that we Egyptians believed has the power of an aphrodisiac. Next to the god was a life-like portrayal of female genitals, the *Kat*, that advertised another earthly delight that could be purchased inside.

The sign itself was sufficient to set us all laughing as we stood outside the door.

"What did I tell you, Thutmose? This is the best house in
Gebtu."

Refu laughed and took a deep breath as if he had just conveyed
some important truth. He turned to me and raised his eyebrows as
a thin snicker crossed his lips.

"I am told the women here are among the finest in Egypt!" He
paused and his eyes flickered again like some imp of Bes. "And,"
he said, "they have the juiciest *keniw* in the land!"

Refu's vulgar description of the vagina sent the rest of us into
hysterical laughter. Laughing like drunks and slapping one
another on the back, we pushed through the doors of the "blue
house" ready to consume all the delights offered there.

The main room was brightly lit. We found ourselves a table
near a window where we could avail ourselves of the slight
evening breeze. The sound of music filled the place and I caught
sight of a group of half-nude women clothed in sheer dresses
through which one could easily see their shaven crotches. They
were playing musical instruments. The only male musician was a
blind harpist! I smiled at Refu who returned the gesture. It always
came as a surprise to foreigners in Egypt that our music was usually made by half-naked women. Even the best of families used
these orchestras at social gatherings so that their presence in this
place was not surprising. But it was pleasant and I rather enjoyed
myself as I compared their bodies and features with my eyes.

Refu ordered the best wine in the house and we drank cup after
cup while we waited for our meal of roast goose, slabs of meat,
bread, and figs. Good natured banter passed among us as we
relived the day of the ambush. The end of the meal was not the
end of the wine and we drank as we talked more and more about
our experiences. It was my first such experience with men reliving

the tales of their battles and I was surprised to hear events retold with such calmness and bravado. To hear my comrades tell it all was clear from the start. There was no panic nor uncertainty, every thrust of the *kopesh* or shot of the bow found its mark, and apparently no one but me had lost control of his piss! So when it came my turn to tell of how it was for me I lied and my story followed much like the others as I left from its retelling my great fear and the uncertainty that plagued me that terrible day. My comrades laughed at the right places and shook their heads solemnly whenever it was required by the tale. But the wine was doing its work. In all truth I probably told my tale as if I, too, believed it! I never trusted the truth of war tales again.

It was late and we were drunk. Still the wine came and still we drank. One of our fellows slept with his face buried deep in his arms right there on the table. Refu, too, was drunk and had fallen into a somber mood. He raised himself half from his chair and waved his arm calling to someone across the room. I turned to see what he was waiving at and my eyes fell upon a beautiful creature! Her name was Marit. She glided across the room with the movement of a sleek boat upon the waters of the Nile. She was thin with small firm breasts that fit well with her delicate features and tanned skin. Fine hair from her wig draped casually about her shoulders setting off the green cosmetic around her dark eyes. Her thin nose added to the fragile quality of her face. Shapely lips painted red parted sensuously when she smiled and her teeth were clean and white. Marit wore the blue Bes tatoo on her thigh. Bes was the goddess of a woman's private parts and blue was her color. Marit had tinted the nipples of her breasts blue as well so when she walked they moved up and down and drew the eye to them. Her hips were shapely and her flat hard stomach ended in the bow of her shaven crotch that revealed lips as thick and full as her mouth. Around her waist was a string of beads, a *menat*, that rubbed together when she walked making a smooth clicking sound that seemed the essence of passion itself. It was said that it was possible to measure the skill of a women at love by how loud and how long these beads made sound during love making!

Marit stopped next to Refu and draped her arm over his shoulder. With a toss of her head she rearranged the cascade of curls that framed her beautiful face and offered me a smile through barely parted lips. I saw her tongue slide sensually over her moist teeth. My eyes filled with her beauty and I felt a tingling in my loins.

"Here she is, Thutmose. Marit. The very best of a very good lot, if I do say so myself."

Rafu laughed and gently pushed Marit toward me. A few steps and she was beside me pressing her hips against me. The smell of her perfumed breath was delicious. She flicked her tongue in my ear and my body shuddered.

My comrades all had broad smiles on their faces.

"She is our gift to you, Thutmose. You have fought and killed with us and we have shared the bond of battle among men." His voice turned serious. "It was your first fight and your first kill." His eyes met mine and there was a sadness in them that offered a strange comfort to me. "Such things are not easy, my friend," he said. "You will carry with you the burdens of battle for a long time. But for tonight take this woman and lose yourself in her charms. The dawn will come soon enough. But for the moment take her and celebrate the fact that you still live even as the men you slew are dead. Celebrate life, my comrade, for death is never far away."

The others drank their wine quietly and nodded their heads in solemn agreement as Rafu spoke. A long silence followed his words and none among us looked into the eyes of the others. At last Rafu downed his wine and bellowed.

"Well you chariot driver are you going to sit here all night or are you going to take her!"

The spell was broken and laughter tumbled from our mouths. Marit covered my mouth with her own warm lips and her tongue danced within my throat. I pulled her toward me and felt her hand reach under my kilt and take me in her hand. Smoothly and gently she moved her hand up and down my staff while excitement rose within me. Rafu's voice filled my ears.

"Not here, by Isis' sweet tits! Have you no shame!"

Rafu's bellowing voice filled the room and drew the attention of the other patrons.

"Not here you randy goat! Upstairs!"

A crescendo of laughter filled the inn as a hundred patrons joined the joke. Marit smiled at me and took my hand. I rose to follow her only to find my prick standing straight out against my kilt. Rafu pointed to it for all to see and the laughter grew louder until my only escape was to stumble up the stairs behind the beautiful Marit and follow her into the room.

After a while the laughter died away and we stood there looking at one another. Marit seemed a vision of life itself, of all that pulsated and moved, of all that felt pleasure and pain. I took her in my arms and pressed my lips against her. I felt her life pour into me and fill that dark space in my soul that I had put there with my own hand when I killed my enemy and changed my life forever.

# Nineteen

I spent much of the next year traveling back and forth between Taphta and Gebtu escorting the caravans with my platoon of chariots. After the ambush we strengthened the escort with more chariots and infantry and that seemed to convince the *Ente* that it was too costly to raid another caravan. For the rest of the time I was with the Taphta garrison there were no more bandit attacks on the gold trains. Thaneni had not been with me when we were ambushed and felt that he had missed a great adventure. This provoked him to come along on many of the other trips where he often expressed the hope that the *Ente* would attack us! I thought this strange coming from a fellow who made no secret of his dislike for what he called the hapless misery of military life and who complained the entire time we were together in Eshuranib. But as I was to learn over the years it is common enough for men who had missed the opportunity to test themselves in war to bemoan this circumstance as their lives went on.

War is most fit for the young. Only they have the sense of invulnerability that permits them to dare death safe in the belief that they will always escape it. Older men, even veterans, have had their enthusiasm and confidence soured by experience and make poor warriors. Their bodies shake and their fears hold them back.

Thoughts of being killed are foremost in their minds. Anyone who has experienced war does not long for it the way those who have not do. And so Thaneni accompanied me on many of my trips to Gebtu searching for the taste of war thinking it would be sweet upon his tongue. It was much later, after we had left Taphta, that Thaneni finally drank from that cup. And when he did he found the drink was sour and left his mouth bitter.

The regular treks to Gebtu served some purpose though and that was to allow Thaneni to acquire more books. He read all the time. The walls of his quarters were filled from floor to ceiling with shelves upon which he kept his growing collection of manuscripts, papers, and books. Thaneni read mostly history, and over the years we had known each other he had become quite a scholar on the history of Egypt. He even acquired considerable knowledge about the countries and peoples who lived in the lands that bordered upon Egypt. He often astonished me with tales about their customs. Thaneni had taken to military life well enough, although he was often appalled at the conditions under which soldiers were expected to live. His stay at Eshuranib had been particularly difficult and he fell ill for several days. Still he had recovered and returned with me to Taphta where he threw himself once again into his studies.

One day he announced that he was keeping a journal of our lives together and asked me to read it. He had to reconstruct the early years of our friendship from memory and wanted to see if I remembered those years as he did. To my astonishment most of the journal was about me with little devoted to Thaneni himself. When I asked him about this he replied that history would not be interested in the life of the scribe of a great pharaoh, but only in the life of the great pharaoh himself. Keeping the journal was Thaneni's way of reminding me of my heritage. He had fully come to expect that I would rule Egypt someday and Thaneni, the lover of history, intended to be present to write everything down. He often observed that tombs were only one way for a pharaoh to achieve immortality. History was another.

The flood had just begun to drive the summer heat from the air and replenish the soil with new life when I received orders that brought my term of service at Taphta to an end. An envelope bearing the seal of the commander of the Army of Amun at Thebes arrived for me at Gebtu. The envelope contained a personal letter from General Rekhmire who had now been given command of the army at Thebes. I was to report to his headquarters in Thebes at once where I had been assigned to his staff. I was excited at this new opportunity. I immediately drafted a reply in which I thanked the general for his confidence in me and informed him I would not be able to come to Thebes for at least a month. I had to fulfill my duty to escort the column back to Taphta and then inform my commander of my new assignment. Then Thaneni and I had to return to Gebtu where we could obtain passage on the first boat bound for Thebes. All in all it would take a month or so to complete these arrangements. Still, I was excited at the prospect of being assigned to the staff of a general officer and of seeing Thebes again. The weeks until my departure passed quickly.

It was only a day's sail from Gebtu to Thebes and there were plenty of boats hauling cargo and passengers to the capital on which to book passage. We stayed one night in Gebtu before setting sail the next morning for Thebes. The conversation among the merchants and government officials in the inn that evening was about the coming war with Nubia. Three times in the past years Hatshepsut had sent small expeditions into Nubia to punish the population for its raids against Egyptian settlements. Each time the Egyptian army moved from village to village slaughtering whomever it could get its hands on regardless of guilt or innocence. Occasionally some rebel leader or bandit was captured and publicly executed. For a time the raids would cease and the army would withdraw. Within months the raids would start up again. Now the pleas of Egyptian merchants could no longer be ignored. Hatshepsut was making ready to send a large expedition to the south to deal with the Nubian rebels once and for all.

Thaneni and I stood by the rail of the boat watching the crew untie the ropes holding her fast to the quay. The captain ordered his men to the oars to maneuver the boat away from the quay and take her into mid-channel. It was the time of the flood and the Nile flowed swiftly and deep. Even with the north wind at our back the current was sufficiently strong to require the crews to work the oars for the boat to make any headway. The cool air of the early morning refreshed me and the gentle breeze caressed my skin making me aware of my body and how good I felt to be free from the heat and dust of my desert outpost. The Nile looked fresh and green. Everywhere along the river banks the land was coming awake once more. The water moved silently under the hull and the oarsmen barely rippled the river's surface as they dipped their oars again and again into the water pulling the boat forward to give the wind some help. I turned toward Thaneni who leaned with his back against the rail staring skyward at the bright white sail trimmed in green that puffed out its great breast above us catching the wind and holding it to push us upstream.

"What do you make of that talk at the inn last night?" I asked.

Thaneni shaded his eyes and kept looking at the sail.

"You mean the merchants and their talk about Nubia?" Thaneni answered.

I nodded.

"Do you think Egypt will send an army against Nubia?" I said.

There was an edge to my voice. I reckoned that if there was to be a war with Nubia it would fall to the Army of Amun in Thebes to fight it. And here I was making my way to the commanding

general's staff for a new assignment. Having tasted battle in a
dusty desert canyon I found myself less than excited about the
prospect of having to risk my life again, even for Egypt.

Thaneni stopped looking at the sail and let his eyes fall across
my face. He smiled.

"We have been involved in Nubia for more than five hundred
years, Thutmose. It would be foolish to think that Egypt would
turn its back upon so rich a place." He gave out a short laugh and
shook his head.

"Even the name of the place—*Nub*—means "gold" in Egyptian.
We call it Nubia or "the land of gold." We also call it the land of
Kush. The richest mines in the world are located there. Just like
Eshuranib in the eastern desert, Egypt takes great riches from these
mines."

A grin appeared on my face. "No wonder the merchants were
the first to know!" I said with a laugh. "If there is gold or wealth
to be had you can bet that the merchants will be the first to know
about it."

Thaneni laughed. "True enough. Wars are always good business. I have no doubt that the merchants will turn a tidy *deben* on
this one as well."

"But," he continued, "in the case of Nubia there are more
important reasons than gold for Egypt to be wary of her black
neighbors to the south."

A look of puzzlement came over my face that Thaneni, ever the
scholar, took as a sign of encouragement to go on as he always
did. As it had so many times in the past, my lack of knowledge
provided an opportunity for my scholarly companion to enlighten
me about some subject or other about which I had unwittingly
revealed my ignorance. I looked at him and saw the familiar smile
of pleasure came over his face as he began to speak.

"Egypt first invaded Nubia more than five hundred years ago when Amenemhet I sailed down the river past the great cataracts at Aswan raiding and burning Nubian villages and towns along the river. His son, Usertsen I, pressed an Egyptian army all the way to Buhen and Semna on the second cataract where he built the first fortresses. And we have been there ever since!"

As was his habit, Thaneni paused to make certain he had my attention. I nodded dutifully and he continued.

"From this time on Egyptian merchants and military men have sought their fortunes in Nubia. Gold mines run by the military were worked by Nubians who had been forced into the mines under one pretext or another. In those days the Nubians lived in tribes in villages along the river. They lived by cattle raising and trading with one another. Their canoes ranged far to the south where they obtained ivory and ebony and other goods to trade with each other and, eventually, with us Egyptians. But these tribes had proud chieftains who refused to carry the Egyptian yoke about their shoulders. And so they raised armies armed with bows and spears and great war canoes to war against their Egyptian colonizers. So fierce are these warriors that they are called the "crocodiles of Kush." And so the pattern was set. Egyptian control is broken by tribal uprisings only to be restored again by an Egyptian army until the next revolt when the pattern begins all over again. The cost in lives to both Nubia and Egypt over these many centuries has been very high indeed!"

Thaneni took a deep breath and let it out in a sigh.

"One of the greatest of our pharaohs, Usertsen III, tried to solve the problem once and for all. From Aswan to Semna he built thirteen large fortresses at key places along the river. From here Egypt controlled the river and deprived the Nubians of their ability to move about in their war canoes. Having done this he loosed upon the land of Kush a great slaughter of women and children and the destruction and burning of villages. Those who survived he sent into the mines. Their leaders he killed or imprisoned. At Buhen he caused a great stele to be raised as a warning."

Thaneni closed his eyes as if lost in thought. I saw his lips tighten as if he was searching among his many shelves of books for some piece of information. For a few seconds he said nothing. Then his face relaxed and a smile came over it.

"I think I can remember the inscription," he said. He closed his eyes again and began to recite from memory the words that the great Usertsen had caused to be carved into the rock at Semna.

> *"I have ravaged the land of Kush by my hand. I carried off their women, I carried off their subjects, went forth to their wells, and smote their bulls: I reaped their grain and what I did not take I destroyed by fire. I established this stone as a warning so that no negro might pass it, neither by water or by land, neither with boats nor herds of the negro. Those who come after me and keep this boundary from the negro are my sons, of him whom I begat. For he who shall not keep it nor fight for it, he is not my son, he is not born to me."*

Thaneni finished his recitation and his eyes opened slowly and his body relaxed. The sun shone straight into his eyes and he squinted using his hand to shade them. To avoid the glare he moved his body a bit so that he could now look at me without being discomforted by Horus' bright rays. Thaneni went on with his story.

"As brutal as Usertsen's policy was, it worked well. For almost two hundred years there was no trouble with the Nubians from Aswan to Semna. We built many towns along the river and Egyptians moved into them and lived side by side with Nubians who went back to their herds and hired themselves out to the townspeople to make a living. Some adopted Egyptian ways. Others, it is said, even made our gods their own. But south of Semna things were different. Here, from the city of Kerma, powerful chieftains controlled large tribes of warriors who raided the Egyptan forts while biding their time and waiting for their chance to revenge themselves on Egypt."

"Their chance came when the Hyksos overran Egypt. Egypt was weakened by defeat. A great Nubian king called Nedja attacked Semna and Buhen driving the Egyptians from their fortresses until the Nubians controlled the land from Kerma to Elephantine. The Nubians who had lived next to the Egyptian towns rose in revolt and a great slaughter took place. And for more than two hundred years the Nubians sat upon the land even in Elephantine, Aswan, and Philae while it was Egypt's turn to wear the conqueror's yoke."

"And then the mighty liberator, Ahmose, drove the Hyksos from the land of Egypt. And when this had been done he turned his anger against the Nubians whom he drove back from the first cataract. His son, Amenophis I, who was called, "He Who Inspires Great Terror," pushed the Nubians further south until Buhen and Semna, the two great fortresses on the second cataract, were once again in Egyptian hands. To govern the area he appointed a viceroy, one Turi, to keep the lands safe. But south of the cataract things remained as they had always been, with strong armies and proud chieftains who raided the border at will and kept watch for their chance to drive the Egyptian conqueror from their land."

Thaneni's eyes brightened as he told me the rest of the story. He knew that what he had to say would come as a surprise to me. With a broad smile on his face my old friend continued.

"And then there was your grandfather who could stand the predations of the vile Kush no longer and sent a powerful expedition down the Nile beyond Semna and captured the city of Sai. It is said that he even went further and burned the rebel capital at Kerma and captured one of the kings. Your grandfather hung the king over the prow of his royal barge and sailed into the harbor at Thebes with his enemy hanging there like a hunting trophy. This was after he caused a great slaughter to flood over the land of Nubia."

Thaneni saw my eyes widen as he told his tale. It was with obvious delight that he went on.

"The Nubians did not escape the wrath of your father either," he said. "Early in his reign the vile Nubians attacked the frontier fortresses and again Pharaoh sent forth his army. This time it was an army led by your father. The texts and monuments record that he was as angry as a panther at the rebels and he swore "that I will not let live anyone among their males." It is said he killed many of their men so that they could never again lift up their hands against pharaoh."

Thaneni paused and took a deep breath. He shook his head as if trying to explain a problem for which there was no solution.

"Now even Hatshepsut has found it necessary to bring the Nubian rebels to heel and another Egyptian army prepares to move south yet again to do what it has done so many times before to no permanent solution." He flashed me a broad smile and his voice had laughter in it. "That is what is pleasant about history," he said. "It seems to repeat itself often!" He laughed.

I was grateful to Thaneni for his knowledge that he so readily bequeathed me. Now I would not stand as some ignorant fool before General Rekhmire when I reported to his headquarters. If an army was to be sent to Nubia, I had no great wish to be in the thick of things. Perhaps a knowledge of the country that Thaneni had provided might serve me well in keeping out of the fighting.

Thebes was still Thebes. As I made my way to the headquarters of the Army of Amun everything about my surroundings felt familiar. The headquarters building was located in the outer palace compound. I had to present General Rekhmire's letter with its official seal to gain entrance. Once inside it was a simple matter to find the general's office and to introduce myself to his adjutant. The room was festooned with military flags and symbols displayed on each side of the official standard of the Army of Amun with its head of a sacred ram surmounted by a solar disk above a small statue of pharaoh himself. My military experience had accustomed me to waiting and I settled down in a large chair to await Rekhmire's summons.

Much to my surprise it was only a few minutes before the door swung open and the general himself filled the doorway with his bulk. I rose to my feet and raised my hand in the military salute. The general returned the salute.

"I see you have arrived safely," he said with a smile. "Come in, come in." He extended his arm as if to drape it around my shoulder as he escorted me into his office and closed the door behind us. Rekhmire showed me to a chair and took his own place in a chair opposite me. He spoke in an even voice that had a quality of officiousness to it that suited his position as commander well.

"I trust that you find your new assignment to your liking, highness?" His eyes held me in their gaze as he awaited my answer.

"I owe you a debt of gratitude for rescuing me from my posting at Taphta," I said smiling. Not wanting him to think I could not stand the rigors of military life I quickly added that I had learned much from the assignment but was now ready to move on. The general's letter had come at just the time I had concluded that there was no more to learn escorting caravans. Rekhmire listened politely and smiled thinly as I spoke.

"I am grateful for the opportunity to serve on your staff, general. I hope that I will be worthy of the confidence you have placed in me."

It was the kind of exchange that often passed for conversation between a junior officer and his superior in the military and required just the right amount of disingenuous fawning to succeed. The general nodded. It struck me he was impatient to move beyond the normal pleasantries and get down to business. Impatience is a trait common to military men.

"Highness, let me come directly to the point. Egypt is about to send an army into Nubia to deal with the rebels. Your assignment to my staff provides you with a good excuse to return to Thebes without arousing the suspicions of the queen or her advisors. As of now only a few trusted officers know of your presence here and in a few days you will be on your way again under my orders. For the short time that you remain in Thebes I think it wise that you be my guest at my villa outside the city, that you do nothing to draw attention to yourself. During your stay I will arrange for you to meet some officers who could be of great service to you in the future and whose loyalty to Egypt is beyond question." The general let his voice trail off even while his eyes held me fast with his own.

Thoughts flew quickly through my head as I attempted to surmise what Rekhmire was telling me without him saying it in so many words. It was clear enough that the reason behind my assignment to Thebes had little to do with the Nubian expedition. It had far more to do with politics. Not knowing what the general had in mind, I thought it best to say little and keep my own counsel.

"I take it from your words, general, that circumstances at the palace have changed since last we spoke?" It was one of those vague questions that permitted Rekhmire to tell me as much or as little as he wished.

"Yes, my prince, some things have changed."

I nodded and smiled as if to say by my gestures that I might find these changes of some interest.

"A number of advisors have fallen from favor in the past few months," Rekhmire said in a serious tone. "The vile Senenmut has been removed. It is said he lives in poverty as a commoner in the very village from which he came."

I could hardly believe my ears! Senenmut! A broad smile beamed from my face at the news that my tormentor had been driven from the palace. Rekhmire saw the smile and offered a smirk of his own. He was not a man to resist gloating over the demise of his enemies.

"The man went too far," Rekhmire said. "Even one so brilliant and skilled at deception and treachery as Senenmut was in the end brought down by his feelings for a woman." He shook his head in genuine disbelief.

"It had been rumored for years that Senenmut and the queen were lovers. Some even believed that she had come to Senenmut before your father died." Rekhmire chose his words carefully and watched my face for any hint of a reaction. I remained impassive and he went on.

"There was also much talk from the priests that the queen was committing a sacrilege by constructing her tomb in the Valley of the Kings. While the queen's tomb was being built Senenmut constructed his own in the hill directly behind the one in which her architect had carved Hatshepsut's tomb. One day a priest charged with keeping the queen's tomb in readiness happened to open a door to one of the niche shrines lining the main corridor. To his horror he discovered that someone had painted Senenmut's likeness on the inside of the doors of all the shrines so that Senenmut's face not the queen's was presented always before the gods! It was a great sacrilege, and like a grassfire the story spread through the priesthood and finally to the court itself. Senenmut was brought forth to explain himself before the queen. Once suspicion fell over him everything he had done was subject to examination as his enemies gathered for the kill. It was soon discovered that his tomb had been built in such a fashion that the burial chamber rested directly beneath the floor of the queen's tomb! He had caused a tunnel to be built through the rock so that it reached beneath the queen's burial chamber. When confronted with the evidence of this outrage Senenmut admitted everything, collapsed, and broke into tears, murmuring some nonesense about wishing to lie with his beloved for all eternity!"

Rekmire shook his head in disgust.

"Men's pricks always get them into trouble," he snapped. "The man's a fool!" The anger in his eyes flickered for a second and then a wry smile appeared on his lips.

"Of course only a fool like Senenmut would tunnel into the queen's chamber from the rear!" Rekhmire exploded in laughter at his own words. His humor proved contagious and I, too, fell into a fit of laughter at the joke.

"Others, too, have been removed. Inebni, the Chief Viceroy of Kush, has fallen from favor. The queen blames him for not dealing with the situation in Nubia. Now that events are out of hand she is forced to send an army to put things right. This detracts from her interest in developing more trade with the land of Punt."

Rekhmire took a deep breath and let it out slowly.

"The court is full of toadies," he said with no effort to conceal his anger. "And now they are going to send an army to fight the crocodiles of Kush." He paused. "Events have a way of getting beyond the control of those who set them in motion."

His eyes fell on me in a way that I had not witnessed before.

"We who have sworn to defend Egypt from her enemies must never fail to see those enemies clearly, highness, no matter where they dwell. For it is an old Egyptian proverb that the asp kills quickest when held closely at the breast."

Rekhmire was anxious to get me to the villa without arousing notice and he sent me along in the company of his adjutant without telling me of my military assignment. When I raised the issue with his adjutant I was told that everything was in order. I would be informed in due course of what the general wanted of me. The *ka'tana* made its way through the streets of Thebes with little effort and soon we reached the gate of Rekhmire's villa. The single sentry came to attention as he recognized the adjutant and saluted while the wagon rolled past into the compound. The gate opened upon a small courtyard facing a raised platform upon which the main house stood set back from the steps that led to it. The adjutant's knock on the front door quickly brought a servant who took my bags and showed me to my room. I was given a large suite of rooms that were equipped with every Egyptian luxury. Many months of living in military quarters had caused me to forget the luxury in which many of Egypt's wealthy classes lived. The adjutant left to return to headquarters and I took advantage of my surroundings to refresh myself with a short nap and a long bath. It was mid-afternoon before I put on fresh clothes and left my room to walk on the villa's grounds.

The villa's formal garden was much like the Garden of the royal palace where I had spent my early childhood and the fragrant smells of the flowers and lush green of the trees that gave it shade from the sun brought back memories of Webkhet, Amenemhab, and my mother. Strolling through the cool shaded lanes it was as if I were a child again. I lost myself in these pleasant surroundings. Without planning I found myself standing before the pool watching the sun dance upon the waters rippled from the disturbance of a frog swimming to a lotus pad. The water lilies floated gently upon the tranquil surface, their flowers reaching skyward to catch the rays of the sun. The pungent sweaty smell of the blue lotus reached my nostrils and a smile crossed my lips. I remembered being told that to Egyptians the smell of the blue lotus is the smell of a woman. In my thoughts I wondered how many young men had been told that just as I had been only to discover how true it was once they grew older and gained some experience with women. The shimmer of the sun on the water calmed me and the gentle liquid movement of the lily pads drew me into their motion until I felt myself slipping into a relaxed daze as all these sensations enveloped me in a gentle embrace. Had it not been for the sound of her voice I should surely have fallen peacefully asleep on the banks of the enticing waters.

"You'd best be careful or you'll fall in and hurt yourself," she said.

For a few moments the pleasant voice seemed to be coming from a great distance with barely enough sound to strike my ears. I was not truly certain that I had heard a voice at all.

"Have you no ears!" This time the voice was louder. "Or do you usually not answer people who speak to you?"

The sarcasm in her voice was more playful than real and I turned to see who it was that had intruded upon my restful mood.

Her features were typically Egyptian except for her light green eyes that were the color of the waters of the Great Green. One could not help being drawn to those eyes that glistened against her tanned skin like precious stones set in tawny gold. Shapely lips held the promise of passion and her thin nose set against high cheek bones gave her face the delicate cast of fragile alabaster. A shapely body was visible through the thin sheer of her dress and her bare arms revealed a moist skin whose softness could be easily imagined without touching it. Bracelets of gold and electrum graced her wrists. A wide faience necklace of brightly colored beads surrounded her throat so that light bounced off the colors and upon her skin in the way light enhances a waterfall. She was short even by Egyptian standards, a feature that made her equal in height with me and which, I confess, I found very attractive. She was younger than me, perhaps only fifteen years or so, and stood there smiling while the sun danced through her black hair.

"Well," she said. "Just who are you and what are you doing in my garden?" Again her tone was playful.

"My name is Thutmose." I said, "I am General Rekhmire's guest in his fine house." I thought it wise to tell her no more than this for the moment. I offered her my most sophisticated smile.

"And who are you?"

I attempted to put some lightness in my voice to attract this beauty. The truth is that I had not much experience with women, at least not this kind of women, and I did not want to drive her off by the tone of my voice.

"I don't really see why I should answer that question from a stranger in my garden," she said. Some of the playfulness was gone from her voice, but still its tone was not truly serious. She stared at me with those green eyes for a few moments. I felt myself suddenly uncomfortable in the presence of her strange beauty.

"I suppose I have to tell you if my father invited you," she said. "My name is Merytre and General Rekhmire is my father." She paused and then extended her hand for me to take.

"Welcome to our home, Thutmose" she said.

I took her hand and felt my hard callouses rub against her soft pliant skin. It seemed like such a long time since I had caressed anything so feminine that I held her hand longer than was appropriate. Yet she did nothing to pull her hand from mine. All the while her red lips parted in a gentle smile and her magic eyes caressed my face with their movements. At last I permitted her hand to fall from mine.

"Have you seen the rest of the garden?" Merytre asked. Her playful tone had returned.

"No," I said.

"Then you must permit me to show you the grounds."

I had barely begun to nod my head in agreement when she stepped closer and moved next to me wrapping her arm through mine. The smell of cinnamon wafted in the air, a sweet odor of her perfume raised from her body by the warmth of the sun. Arm and arm we strolled slowly through the garden while Merytre told me about the villa and her life as the daughter of a general.

The next two hours passed deliciously slowly in the company of this entrancing woman. I found her to be quite unlike other Egyptian women in many ways. Her father had seen to her education and Merytre could read and write. She told me that she was particularly fond of poetry and had even tried her hand at writing poems. I found, too, that she often listened in upon her father's conversations and was well-informed about many important subjects. Merytre was Rekhmire's youngest daughter, the third of three children. The general's first born, a son, had been killed in a skirmish with the sand-bandits in Retjennu. The death of her son plunged Merytre's mother into such sorrow that she refused to eat. Overcome with grief, the general's wife spent her days in her bed, rarely speaking with anyone. Egypt's best physicians could do nothing to remedy her condition, and six months after the death of her son her servants found her dead in her bed. The other child, Merytre's older sister, was married to one of the general's officers who commanded the palace guard. I was impressed with the manner in which Merytre spoke of the great sorrow of her family and of the pain that her father carried as the consequence of his son's death. We walked and laughed and talked with one another in passing the most pleasant afternoon I could recall.

It was late afternoon and we found ourselves standing once again on the banks of the pool. We had spoken of many things. Merytre had told me much about her family and her father. When she asked about me I made an effort to hide myself from her and did not tell her who I was. She asked many questions about my circumstances and how I had come to be in the army. Though I answered all her questions, my answers concealed myself from her. Despite my deceit, in the space of a single afternoon I had become thoroughly enthralled with this beautiful young woman and was determined to see more of her at every opportunity.

She caught me looking at her and turned toward me with a broad smile.

"What is it, Thutmose? Why do you stare at me so?"

She made no effort to conceal the flirtatious giggle in her young voice. I was about to answer when the loud voice of the general fell upon my ears.

"I see that the two of you have already met," he said.

I turned and saw Rekhmire walking toward us. The general walked with the authority of his rank, taking big confident strides that quickly covered the distance between us. He was met by a smile of genuine affection on his daughter's face. She threw her arms around him in a loving hug.

"Hello father," she said stepping back from him and looking into his eyes with the kind of adoration that only the father of a daughter can know.

"Hello little one," the general replied. His voice was soft and comforting as if he had spoken to his child in this manner for many years. Rekhmire turned to me and smiled.

"You see how beautiful she is, Thutmose!" It was a father's proud boast.

"She gets her beauty from her mother. Looks just like her." He glanced at Merytre who seemed embarrassed at her father's words but made no protest to stop him. I surmised that she was enjoying the praise.

"Don't let that beauty fool you, Thutmose. Beneath that smile resides the temperament of her father." Again he flashed a smile at Merytre. "If anyone in this family is more headstrong and strong willed than me it's my little girl here."

"Father!" Merytre snapped. "What a horrible thing to say!" Her face formed into a pout and she folded her arms as if she was greatly displeased. Rekhmire was not fooled by the performance and threw his head back and laughed heartily.

"See!" he said laughingly. "What did I tell you!" Rekhmire stopped laughing and turned to me.

"I have invited some guests for dinner who I think might be valuable for you to meet," he said. He turned to Merytre. "Would you mind acting as my hostess again, Merytre?" He didn't wait for her to answer. "Even if the wine is bad, at least they shall be treated to the sight of my daughter's beauty," he laughed. Merytre smiled at him.

"If there is to be a dinner tonight I had best see to the cooks and servants," she said. She hugged her father again and then turned to me offering her hand.

"I hope to see you this evening, Thutmose. Perhaps we will have another chance to talk."

She slowly pulled her hand free from mine and walked off across the courtyard that separated the garden from the main house. I watched her body move with the grace of a gazelle and felt a pang of desire rise quickly within me. The sound of her father's voice brought me to my senses again.

Rekhmire steered me to a stone bench and we sat down. A servant appeared carrying cool beer in clay mugs for us to drink. It was Rekhmire's daily ritual to arrive home and sit in the garden for a while and have beer brought to him. It helped him make sense of the day's events he said. The general took a deep draught of the cool sweet liquid and set the cup down on his leg.

"My adjutant tells me you are curious about what I have in mind to do with you now that you are assigned to my staff" he said. He was relaxed, but his voice still carried with it the aura of authority.

I nodded. "Yes, general," I said. "I assumed that it has something to do with the Nubian expedition but…" my voice trailed off as I waited for Rekhmire to tell me what it was he wished of me.

"An advance party of staff and supply officers will leave Thebes for Semna in about two weeks. Their task will be to prepare the forward fortresses to receive and support the main body of the invasion force." He paused. "We intend to send a force of five thousand men, mostly infantry with chariot support. What I want you to do is to travel down the Nile in advance of the staff and make and record any observations that you think might be of use to them and the expedition commander when he and the army arrive. Most importantly, Thutmose, I want you to be my eyes and ears and to tell me all you witness that is important for Egypt's well-being and success." He leaned against the back of the bench and took a drink of beer.

I looked at Rekhmire and could see that he was troubled. I took great care to choose my words carefully before I spoke.

"With all due respect, sir. But why send a junior officer to Nubia on such a mission?" I paused and let my words sink in.

Rekhmire sighed and put down his cup on the side table. He leaned back in the bench and let his body relax as if he had tired of carrying a great burden. His eyes narrowed and he spoke with a seriousness that I had come to respect in the man.

"The reason, Thutmose, is that you will not always be a junior officer!"

He paused and a smile creased his face.

"We have been fighting the Nubians for centuries and never with clear result. The solution to our difficulties there will never be achieved by force of arms. Some other way must be found. It has never been possible to convince our kings of that fact. Nubia provided rich opportunity for glory at small risk. If I can convince you to search for another way, one day when you are Pharaoh perhaps you will seek that other way."

I was astounded at the matter-of-factness with which Rekhmire expressed his conviction that I would some day rule the land of Egypt. What he said about Nubia made sense. The convictions of a powerful ruler can often change things, that much was true. But to leap from that to my ascension as king was a very long jump indeed! At the moment it seemed all I could do to grasp the task before me in Nubia.

"If I am to record my observations in Nubia I will require my scribe to come along if that is permissible," I said.

The general nodded his approval.

"When would I leave for Nubia?"

"In about two day's time. A boat will be waiting for you at the quay. The Nile is in flood so that some of the more difficult passages will be easier to navigate. South of Thebes the Nile is a far different river than you are used to. The main body of the army will leave Thebes in a month when the full flood will ease the passage of the large troop and supply boats."

I nodded and remained silent. For a few moments the two of us sat there looking at each other not saying a word. Rekhmire took the last drops from his cup, placed it on the side table, and rose from his chair. I stood immediately in the presence of my superior officer.

"We shall be dining in two hours, Thutmose. Perhaps you want to refresh yourself and rest before this evening." The general paused. "Be on your best behavior, my prince. Much rests on this night." With that he turned in the direction of the villa and walked away leaving me to wonder about the meaning of the words he had just spoken.

I waited in my room while the guests arrived until a servant summoned me to join the others. The large central dining room of the villa with its open ceiling reaching to the clerestory roof was ablaze in light from scores of oil lamps whose flames illuminated the brightly colored murals that adorn the walls of the country houses of the wealthy. Servants carrying food and drink moved about the room being careful not to jostle the guests. Cups of wine and beer carried on gold trays kept the guests refreshed. A small orchestra sat in chairs on the patio tuning their instruments. Their dress was not the usual dress of Egyptian female musicians. Instead they were adorned in the colorful flowing gowns common to Asiatic women. Rekhmire's long posting at Sharuhen and other garrisons on the land bridge of Retjennu had given him a taste for things Asiatic. Dinner was served from a single large table Asiatic style instead of the individual small tables normally used by Egyptians. Standing there looking at the small group of guests clustered around Rekhmire, I wondered whether the good general had also imported barbarian dancers for our amusement. Egyptian dancers performed almost naked with little more than a crotch string to hide their privacy. Asiatic dancers hid their bodies through layers of sheer veils and left much more to the imagination. Egyptians who had seen the barbarian dancers were often quite taken by them.

I stood at the foot of the stairs looking across the room searching for Merytre. I felt a gentle touch on my elbow and turned to find myself looking into Merytre's eyes. She smiled warmly as she kept her hand on my elbow.

"You look confused," she said in a pleasant voice. "Don't worry, we will take good care of you."

Her words brought a smile to my face and I glanced at her hand still resting on my elbow. She watched me do it and our eyes met for a few seconds. Touching the elbow of the opposite sex is an Egyptian gesture of affection and sexual interest. The longer I looked into Merytre's eyes the clearer it was that she intended it to be exactly that as she cupped my elbow in her hand. Then she smiled shyly although I felt it difficult to believe that there was much genuine shyness in this woman, and let her hand fall to her side.

"There," she said gesturing with her eyes toward the dinning room, "My father is trying to get your attention."

I turned and saw the general gesturing with raised hand for me to join him and the group of six officers around him. As I approached the group I felt their eyes fall upon me as if they were watching my every movement. These were important men and my every sense warned me to be cautious. Rekhmire placed his hand around my shoulder and drew me into the half-circle of officers who arranged themselves around him.

"This, gentlemen, is one of my junior officers. A fine example of the kind of officer that Egypt must have if she is to defend herself from her enemies."

Rekhmire's voice was jovial and his words brought smiles to the others' faces. I bowed my head slightly and smiled at my superiors not knowing what else to do. I had no idea if Rekhmire had told the generals who I was. For that matter I had no idea what he expected of me. I stood silent and Rekhmire continued.

"This young man has already faced Egypt's enemies in battle. He has taken two hands from the vile *Ente*!"

The senior officers bobbed their heads and smiled with great approval at learning of my experience in battle. Rekhmire's voice boomed on.

"Had one of us been witness to the event our young fellow here would surely have been awarded the Gold of Valor. As it was only lower ranking officers that were present, there was no one of sufficient rank to swear to his deeds." He paused. "Still, his superiors find him a man of courage and endurance, one who fights equally well from a chariot or on foot."

Again the assembled officers smiled and bobbed their heads. One of them raised his glass to me in a silent toast and the others followed. All I could do was smile back and look to Rekhmire for some clue as to what he wanted me to do. Off to the side I saw Merytre standing alone straining to catch every word. She beamed at me but said nothing. Finally the silence in the group became embarrassing and I spoke.

"The general exaggerates my contribution to a small skirmish, sirs," I said. "I did only what any officer would have done under the circumstances."

A serious expression came over their faces as I spoke. "What is important is that Egypt always be prepared to grapple with her enemies and emerge victorious."

I paused and saw that they were all intently focused upon my words.

"It is to her generals that Egypt looks for guidance and example in keeping her safe."

I raised my glass to the group.

"May the gods always bless Egypt with great generals!"

They all drank to their own health. From the corner of my eye I caught Rekhmire's wink and knew I had done well.

A servant appeared and struck a small cymbal indicating that the meal was ready. Rekhmire herded the group around the table.

He placed me beside him with Merytre next to me. We all sat down and, as if on cue, the servants began bringing food. Out on the patio the musicians took up their instruments filling the background of the room with low music. The meal began with wine. Plates of stuffed dates and Nile figs passed from person to person. Next came three kinds of bread with which to eat the roast goose and duck. Plates of warm meat in dark gravy appeared followed by bowls of radishes, lettuce, and peas. Desert melons, turtle cakes, dom dates, honey covered pastries and two fruits called apples and pomegranates not grown in Egypt but which Rekhmire had imported from Syria finished the feast to everyone's great content.

During the meal the talk had turned to war and the coming expedition against Nubia. The generals were united in their support of the war but agreed that it had to be accomplished quickly. By far the greater threat lay in the land of the Retjennu where the Mitanni were provoking trouble among the city states in Syria, urging them into an alliance against Egypt. The Nubian expedition could not be permitted to drag on without resolution lest Egypt be attacked in the land bridge and find herself with a war on two fronts. I sat through it all without comment for no one asked me and I would not have known what to say had they asked. I confess that what they had to say seemed to make a great deal of sense to me.

And then the talk turned to politics. I could see Rekhmire's eyes narrow and his body grow tense as carefully the generals ventured into deep and treacherous waters. One officer, the commander of the city garrison, offered the view that Egypt had encouraged her enemies by not remaining sufficiently vigilant so that events had proceeded way too far already. Another, the commander of the stables, thought that the court was filled with treacherous toads who enriched themselves at the expense of Egypt. The commander of the military stores offered the view that Egypt would always be at risk until once more it was ruled by a warrior king. And so the conversation went. Good food and plenty of wine and beer had allowed their true feelings to reveal themselves. Through it all Rekhmire remained silent, glancing at me from time to time as if things were going exactly as he had planned.

At last the conversation slowed and faded leaving us all in a silence that hung heavily around the table. I glanced at Merytre who seemed puzzled by all this. I saw her looking at me as if she were attempting to fathom my role in this whole business. And then, quite without warning, the commander of the stables looked straight at me.

"And you," he said. "I have not even been given your name."

He looked at his fellow officers who also turned their gazes toward me as if suddenly becoming suspicious that Rekhmire had played some dangerous trick upon them.

"What do you think about all this?"

It was not the kind of question that I could avoid and I glanced at Rekhmire before answering only to see him looking intently at me himself as if some curious element of his confidence in me was suddenly absent.

"First, sir, my name is Thutmose." I let my words die in the air so that they took on the character of a mild rebuke as if it had been the general's fault that he had not asked it before rather than mine for not offering it to begin with. The general offered no visible response to my words.

"As to the rest of it, I am sure you appreciate my lack of experience in these matters makes my views of no value at all."

I paused and watched the officer sit back in his chair as if he were disappointed already in my answer. I continued with a firmer voice.

"It seems to me that there is one concern for a soldier and one only, and that is the safety of his country. From what you say

Egypt has been put at risk by some failure of its leaders. If so it is our job to make it right and insure that Egypt is not punished for the stupidity of its leaders."

My words brought knowing nods from some of the officers. Others remained impassive.

"But one thing is certain. It is our responsibility to make sure that the court sees to it that Egypt is protected. Sometimes generals must instruct their leaders."

And here I paused and looked at Rekhmire who nodded his head slowly as if in approval of what I had been saying.

"Sometimes for the good of Egypt we must instruct our leaders even when they do not wish to be instructed."

My words fell upon the table with great weight. There was silence. One by one the eyes of the generals rose to meet mine until each in this own time nodded his head in agreement. All this passed between us and not a word was spoken aloud. Rekhmire, too, nodded his head and fixed me with his eyes that shone with an approval that was more appropriate to a father than a superior officer. Merytre continued to stare at me, the expression on her face more confused than before. At last Rekhmire summoned a servant to fill the glasses of the generals with fresh wine. This having been done he rose from his chair and lifted his glass.

"Gentlemen, with your permission, I give you the future of Egypt. Let us drink to our fine young companion."

Smiles broke out on their faces as the generals reached for their wine cups to join the toast. Rekhmire went on.

"Gentleman, let us toast Thutmose, Son of Pharaoh, the rightful heir to the throne of Egypt, and man enough to be the lion to defend *Kemit* against all her enemies!"

The look of shock on their faces was a wonder to behold. They quickly turned to one another in disbelief as if asking to be told that what they had heard was indeed the truth. Abruptly the commander of the stores rose from his seat and fell immediately upon his knees touching his forehead to the floor. The others, fearing to offend the son of god who sat before them, did the same thing. In a few seconds all the generals were on their knees afraid to lift their eyes to my face. Rekhmire, too, understood what had to be done and began to fall to one knee. Wishing to spare him embarrassment I commanded them all to rise and retake their seats. I glanced at Merytre whose pretty mouth hung open in an expression of shocked disbelief at what she had witnessed. I smiled at her to put her at ease, but her expression remained unchanged. She sat there next to me arms folded in her lap, her eyes downcast for fear that she too might somehow offend me. I turned to Rekhmire who nodded and then turned toward his fellow officers and spoke.

"I wanted you all to meet his highness to give you cause to believe in Egypt's greatness once again. The Lion of Egypt is among us. Should the gods will it, he is prepared to take his rightful place and govern Egypt in peace and power."

He paused and looked into the eyes of each officer before continuing. The generals could not take their eyes from Rekhmire and hung on every word he spoke.

"We have been comrades for a very long time," he continued. "Each of you I trust with my life. I have brought you here so you could see for yourself the kind of man Thutmose is. He has served among us and endured the hardships of military life without complaint. His superiors have judged him a fit leader of men and he has shown his courage in battle even as he has slain the enemies of this land. The spirits of his grandfather and father live in him. Egypt has been given yet another great warrior pharaoh. It shall be your honor to serve under him when the time arrives."

Rekhmire stole a quick glance at me and found my face appropriately expressionless as he spoke. He turned back to the generals and spoke in a solemn tone.

"None of you are to speak of what you have seen or heard here tonight. To do so is to put our Lion in danger."

He paused to let the seriousness of what he was saying take hold in their minds.

"Is there any one of you who will not be with his brothers as they stand with the Lion of Egypt to protect this land from its enemies?"

With great solemnity each of the generals raised his eyes until they fell first on Rekhmire and then upon my face. And then each after another slowly shook his head. With this act they had chosen freely to serve me and Egypt and turned their backs upon those who had made themselves my enemies. When all had shown their loyalty, I rose from my chair and looked upon each of them until the sight of my gaze forced each to drop his eyes to the floor. And then I took my leave of these powerful men, confident of their commitment to Egypt and to me, and walked boldly across the room onto the patio and out into the warm Egyptian night.

I leaned against the stone railing and looked into the moonless sky. I felt the darkness envelop me like the tender embrace of a woman. The murmur of conversation among the generals as they prepared to depart reached my ears as formless chatter that I easily ignored. I stood there alone with my thoughts for what seemed a long time trying to make sense of what had transpired, trying to understand Rekhmire's motives in bringing me here to meet the generals. What had been said was perilously close to treason. Should word of it reach the queen or her advisers, some of the men I met tonight would pay with their heads. But in that fear lay our greatest security. Our words had bound us all together in some vague undirected conspiracy rooted in the best of motives to protect Egypt from those who would weaken and destroy her. The confusion boggled my mind and I made an effort to push these thoughts from me.

The house had grown quiet. Servants extinguished all but a few of the lamps in the dinning room leaving it in a dim glow wrapped in heavy shadows. The quiet fell easily upon me. For the first time all evening a peace came over me as I stood alone on the patio wrapped in the warm air of the night.

"May I come near, highness?" The soft voice came from behind me and I recognized it immediately. I turned toward Merytre.

"Of course," I said. The warmth in my voice did nothing to hide my pleasure at seeing her. I was completely taken by this young woman and there seemed little point in trying to conceal my feelings.

"Thank you, highness," she said and walked slowly toward me with her eyes averted so as not to offend me by looking upon my face.

"Please," I said, "There is no need to look away. When you do I am deprived of the pleasure of your eyes."

I laughed playfully.

"And you may not deny your beauty to pharaoh." It was a joke and the smile upon her face as she lifted her eyes told me she was more at ease now.

She leaned on the railing next to me and looked up at the night sky as she spoke.

"I came to see if you were alright. There was a troubled look upon your face when you left as if you were carrying a great burden." She paused and took a deep breath. "Things are not well for Egypt, are they?"

I shook my head. "No Merytre they are not."

Without warning she turned to me and her eyes filled as if tears would come to them.

"Are you in any danger?" Before I could answer she went on. "I don't want anything to happen to you."

She pushed herself against me and threw her arms around my neck pulling me tightly against her body. I felt her take a deep breath and shudder as she permitted her breath to escape. My arms enveloped her and the two of us stood there in the warm night not saying a word permitting our bodies to tell us of our affection for one another. For a long time we held each other tightly until Merytre pulled away to allow her face to look longingly into mine. For a second I was lost again in her eyes. Then she brushed my mouth with her lips and drew me toward her until our lips met in a lingering kiss of passion whose heat flowed through my body coming to rest in my loins. I pressed my hardness against her and felt her hips thrust against mine. My breathing came quickly. I felt Merytre's hot breath against my neck as she pressed her breasts against my chest. My hand dropped from her back and ran along her hip until it found the space between her legs. Her breath came in deep sighs as my hand caressed her lotus. For a moment I feared that she might be so overtaken by her passion as to slip from consciousness.

But this was not to be. Suddenly she pushed me away and escaped my embrace. Her face glistened from the sweat her passion had evoked and her body trembled. Merytre's eyes smoldered with desire as she stood before me mouth open and wet lips forming words that had no sounds. She bolted past me with the movement of a young gazelle frightened by some unseen terror and disappeared into the darkness that shrouded the villa's empty rooms. I was alone again in the warm night. My body heaved with unspent passion trying to cool itself from the great heat that Merytre's body had kindled within it. After a while quiet returned to my body and mind but did little to help me understand why Merytre had run away. But she had seared her memory into my mind. For the whole time I was in Nubia I was never able to completely free myself from remembrances of that night.

Dawn came early and I joined Rekhmire for breakfast. Merytre was nowhere to be found. Neither the general nor I commented upon her absence. The general and I rode in the coach together to his headquarters. We talked of the Nubian expedition and he repeated once more what he wished me to do. I followed Rekhmire to his office and took the chair he offered me. He sat down behind his desk and ruffled through some papers while I waited. A few minutes later a sharp knock was followed by Rekhmire's adjutant opening the door.

"Captain Tekhet is here sir, as you ordered," the adjutant said.

Rekhmire nodded and the adjutant gestured to someone in the outer office. A moment later a tall muscular man with black skin dressed in the uniform of a captain in the Egyptian army walked through the door, stopped in front of the general's desk and offered a salute. Rekhmire returned the salute and pointed to a chair next to mine.

"Take a chair, captain," Rekhmire said. He leaned forward over his desk.

"Thutmose I want you to meet Tekhet. He will accompany you on your journey to Nubia."

I nodded in Tekhet's direction and my smile was met by a similar nod and smile from him in return. We both looked at Rekmire. He must have noticed the puzzled expression on my face. Why did I need another officer with me? And who was this negro officer? We Egyptians employed native troops of all kinds throughout the empire. But I had never seen one in the uniform of an Egyptian officer. And how trustworthy was a negro officer going to be in Nubia? All of these questions rushed through my head as I waited for Rekhmire to explain what he had in mind.

Rekmire rose from his chair and walked to the front of his desk and leaned back upon it as if it were a seat.

"Gentlemen," he said, "you will trust one another even as I trust both of you to do what is asked of you." His voice was stern and his words carried the character of a military order in them. "Otherwise you will be of no use to Egypt and even less use to me. Do you understand?"

It was the kind of rhetorical question that in the military demanded an answer and both Tekhet and I nodded our agreement.

"Good. Then we understand each other," Rekhmire said. He turned toward me.

"Thutmose, it is important that you understand who Tekhet is. Years ago when Thutmose II had been Pharaoh for only a few years, Egypt was compelled to put down another Nubian revolt. This time Pharaoh ordered his army to bring about a great slaughter as an example to the Nubians and many thousands were killed. One of these was a great chief of the Nubians called Toshka whom Pharaoh captured and carried back to Thebes as a war trophy. Eventually Toshka was executed. But Pharaoh in his mercy spared his family and Toshka's only son, a child, was taken to Thebes and raised in the court by one of Pharaoh's concubines. He grew to manhood and entered the service of his adopted country where he became a loyal and trusted officer."

Rekhmire paused to allow his words to fix themselves in my mind. Then he spoke again.

"Thutmose, this is Toshka's son," he said pointing to Tekhet. "And together I hope you will be able to do for Egypt and Nubia what all the wars of the past have failed to do, to help construct a lasting peace between the lands."

To say I was stunned by Rekhmire's words was not to do justice to my feelings. I looked at Rekhmire in silence. He turned toward Tekhet and continued speaking.

"And you, captain, must know that Thutmose is the son of the pharaoh whose name he bears. It was his father, Thutmose II, who killed your father and brought you to Thebes as a child." The look of shock on Tekhet's face was no less than my own had been. Rekhmire said nothing as his words took hold in Tekhet's mind.

"Were that not in itself sufficient to confuse you, captain, you might also keep in mind that if events warrant your brother officer Thutmose could well rise to the throne of Egypt as her next pharaoh." His eyes narrowed and his voice became solemn. "You are entrusted to each other's fate and with you are entrusted the fates of two nations."

Tekhet and I looked at each other, each a prisoner of the other's history, each unable to escape it even if we wished to. Rekhmire went on to explain the details of our journey to Nubia. It was four hundred miles from Thebes to Semna at the second cataract and Tekhet and I would have plenty of time to get to know one another before we reached our destination. Neither of us knew then what events our actions would wreak upon our native lands.

Thaneni and I arrived at the harbor by daybreak and stowed our baggage in the shallow hold of the boat that Rekhmire had ordered the navy to provide for our journey. She was named *Amun's Glory* and was typical of the small entrepot boats the navy operated up and down the Nile for transporting special cargo and important people. Thaneni and I had taken possession of two beds in the deck house and were unpacking when the door opened and Tekhet entered. I had told Thaneni about Tekhet when I discussed with him the events that had transpired at the villa the night before so that he was not surprised when he met him. Thaneni became more of the scholar with each book he read. By now his natural prejudices had been almost completely replaced with impassioned curiosity about the differences among men. He took to Tekhet as if he were some long lost friend. It took

Tekhet a bit longer to warm to Thaneni and his infernal list of questions. But by journey's end the two had become close enough to call each other friend. Perhaps it was a good omen for both countries that man's natural tendency toward suspicion and hatred could be conquered so easily by a knowledge of how similar we all are under our skins.

The cool air of morning still hung over the harbor as *Glory* pushed off from the quay under power of her oarsmen and pointed her bow upstream against the current. The square sail rose smartly up the mast, its belly quickly catching the north wind and setting the boat on its southward course. Sailing against the flood even with the north wind at our back required the power of the oars to make much headway. In the short time it took us to reach Inuy south of Luxor the strain of the labor was beginning to show on the sailors' faces. The boat put in to the pier to take on water and provisions that were cheaper to purchase here than in Thebes. From the quay I could see the red sandstone temple dedicated to Montu, the local god of war. Montu had once rivaled Amun for followers in Thebes. But more and more as the pharaohs attributed their victories to Amun Montu was eclipsed. But warrior pharaohs are above all practical men and they saw to it that the temple of Montu was preserved and honored. Both my father and grandfather had lavished significant sums on its priests to insure that Montu oversaw their military exploits with favor.

Two day's sail brought us to Nekhen, the Red Mound, where stood one of Egypt's oldest and most magnificent fortresses. Its location here, as Tekhet pointed out to me, was to protect what was then the small country town of Thebes from the predations of the Nubians who sailed up the Nile in large war canoes burning Egyptian towns as they went. So important was the Nekhen fortress that the commander was on equal standing with the Theban royal princes. Nekhen was home to the beautiful temple of the vulture goddess, "The White One of Nekhen," that the Theban princes adopted as their own royal symbol and which adorned the crown of Egypt along with the snake goddess of the Delta.

Our next stop was Khenu, the closest place to Thebes where sandstone was quarried for buildings and temples. Here the Nile narrows, forced between tall cliffs of sandstone that mark the end of the limestone plateau and the beginning of sandstone bluffs that hold the river to its bed all the way to Nubia. The river runs shallow and swift through the gateway of cliffs often throwing boats up on sandbars. Strong winds trapped by the high cliff walls force the wind downward upon the water so that it strikes the river surface in gusts of great force. A boat making its way through this "place of the rowing" as it is called, for only the power and steering of oars can navigate the shoals, risks being spun about and smashed into the walls. Surprisingly, our captain navigated the narrows with little difficulty. It is, he says, due to the height of the flood that carried the boat safely over the submerged rocks and sandbars.

Fourteen miles later we tied up at the pier in Nubit. Thaneni drew my attention to the large number of crocodiles that swam unmolested in the harbor. Others, some with their great mouths open to the sun, slept on the river banks apparently without fear of being hunted and killed by the town's inhabitants. Tekhet had visited Nubit several times and was quick to tell us that here the crocodile was sacred and worshiped as a god. A beautiful temple raised to Sobek the crocodile god stood in the center of the town. The town made its living from the pilgrims who came to the temple. I had visited the temple to Sobek in Crocodile City in the Lakeland when I was a boy and was anxious to see the sanctuary in Nubit. I found the temple easily, but was disappointed at its size and at how much in need of repair it was. After a few minute's visit I returned to the inn where we were staying and joined Thaneni and Takhet for the evening meal.

We resumed our journey at mid-morning the next day. The captain explained that it was only twenty-five miles to Elephantine where we would stay the night so a late start would still bring us into the quay before dusk. Elephantine marked the boundary between Egypt and Nubia, the beginning of seven miles of rapids and rough water that formed the first cataract of the Nile. The town was built on an island close to the west bank. It was originally a place where Egyptians met and traded with Nubians for ivory that the Nubians obtained from their elephant hunts. The city was founded more than a thousand years ago and was originally called Abu or "Ivory Town" in the old language. Here for the first time were the large outcroppings of black, red, and gray granite that revealed the presence of the granite quarries across from the town on the east bank. From here came the stone for the splendid red granite obelisks that stand before so many of our temples and government buildings. It was to protect these quarries and to control the land routes around the rapids northward to Thebes that we Egyptians built the fortified city of Aswan, turning the top of the cataract into a double fortification to prevent the Nubians from moving further north.

The first cataract of the Nile runs for seven miles over black and gray granite boulders that force the river into swift flowing streams that forge their passage over and between narrow gorges and rapids. Except during the flood, even a small boat such as the *Glory* finds it impossible to pass here just as the war canoes of the Nubians could not pass. The cataract was an excellent strategic obstacle. When Egypt grew strong under Usertsen III three hundred years ago, he ordered a canal to be cut along the cataract so that his fleet might pass the obstacle at will to support the Egyptian fortresses that lay along the river from Elephantine to

Semna. It was through this canal that our boat passed the next morning on our way to the island of Philae. With his fine soldier's eye for military advantage Tekhet pointed out the huge granite blocks that rested at intervals across from each other on the canal's banks. Should things go badly for us Egyptians in Nubia, our engineers had placed these blocks on the banks so that they could be easily and quickly levered into the water denying the use of the canal to any Nubian fleet. With the canal blocked the fleet was useless and a Nubian army would have to make its way overland passing under the fortifications of Elephantine on the west bank or Aswan on the east bank where Egyptian infantry and chariots had the advantage. Tekhet shook his head in mock admiration for the brilliance of Egyptian military thinking and had to admit that the plan was a sound one.

Our boat slid by the small island of Sehel and from the deck I could see the temple that held the nilometer that was the first to measure the height of the flood each season. Just beyond was Philae that we Egyptians called "the island of the time of Ra" which many Egyptians believed was the original site of creation. It was here at the southern end of the island that the grave of Osiris could be found. Tekhet took some pride in telling me that the island was our first stop in Nubia itself for the Nubians had considered the island a sacred place from a time long out of memory. The *Glory* made fast to the quay near dusk and the three of us decided to spend the night aboard rather than at an inn. It seemed fitting that we should spend our first night in Nubia on the sturdy little craft that had carried us there. Come morning it would carry us further into the land that would soon feel the flail of Egypt upon its back.

The Nile cuts through Nubia the same way it slices its way through Egypt, cutting a river valley through stone. South of the first cataract the sandstone plateau has been worn down by the force of the rushing river creating a valley much narrower than the Nile valley in Egypt. In most places the valley is no wider than five miles, and in only a few places does it expand to even nine miles. High cliffs meet the edges of the valley floor cutting it off from the plateau above. Just as the limestone plateau above the Nile valley is a barren lifeless place, so it is in Nubia where the sandstone plateau is home only to the wind and a few hardy plants.

Most of the Nubian settlements rest on the banks of the river or are within sight of the Nile's waters. As we sailed from Philae to Baki over the next four days, Tekhet pointed out the Nubian villages with their round huts of mud and reed. Egyptian settlements existed side by side all along the river bank. The Egyptian settlements were walled compounds of mud brick with watch towers and strong gates giving the impression of military strongpoints rather than civilian towns. Tekhet explained that although Nubians and Egyptians lived closely to one another, at nightfall each withdrew to their own villages and towns out of fear of the other. Centuries of rebellion and slaughter had made each side wary and the imposition of Egyptian viceroys to govern Nubia did little to change the perception that Egypt controlled Nubia through military occupation.

Baki was a fortress town that controlled the junction of the Nile and the road to the eastern desert and the valuable gold mines that Egypt exploited for centuries. We spent an uneventful night there and resumed our journey the next day. Four days later we approached Mi'am the military capital from which Egyptian forces were supplied and coordinated in controlling the country.

"You Egyptians seem to build nothing but fortresses," Tekhet said with a sarcastic laugh. His arm swept the horizon to draw my attention to the steep brick walls that rose almost forty feet from the river bank to form the front wall of the fortification.

I nodded and shook my head in agreement for there was no doubt that Tekhet was right. He went on.

"Since we left Aswan we have sailed past a half dozen fortresses." He sighed. "In the next fifty miles between Mi'am and Buehn there are no fewer than eleven major fortifications, most built in pairs to control both sides of the river and the major roads that run northward along the riverbank. What few towns you have constructed you surround with walls and gate towers so they, too, become fortifications."

He paused and looked at me.

"Thutmose, you Egyptians will never control this country until you convince the people here that you do not come to enslave and slaughter them. Only when they become like you, only when you allow them in your temples, and only when you permit them to live among you, will the fear of the Egyptian sword cease." He took a deep breath and let it out slowly. "Only then will you have peace."

We stayed two days in Mi'am where we introduced ourselves to the commander and were shown the preparations that had been undertaken to receive the expeditionary force that would sail from Thebes in about a month. All seemed in order. There would be little to report to Rekhmire except that the local commander seemed diligent and competent and was carrying out his duties with the usual Egyptian military efficiency. I noticed that there was a large force of chariot troops in residence. The commander explained that the flat terrain of the narrow valley made them particularly useful in a fight. The Nubians fought on foot and could be easily overtaken by our chariots and herded together where our infantry could finish them off. Too, the chariots were an excellent means of intelligence gathering through patrols while making regular communication among the fortresses up and down the Nile easy to accomplish.

From Mi'am to Buhen was two day's sail and we were never out of sight of one fortress before another came into view. On this stretch of the river the valley was narrower than usual. I could easily imagine that lookouts atop the battlement walls could see from one wall of the valley to another making it impossible for any sizeable force to slip by without being discovered. Once discovered, chariot forces could be dispatched to harass and engage the enemy until the heavy infantry arrived. Should the enemy prove to be particularly strong, units from the other forts could be rapidly dispatched as reinforcements. It was a strong defense in depth that would be difficult to defeat under any circumstances.

Buhen was as far as *Glory* could take us. The second cataract of the Nile that lay below the city itself was a narrow field of rapids through which the river descended amid a chaos of glistening black boulders wet from the foamy spray thrown up by the river current as it sped through the steeply sloped gorge threading its way more than three miles distant between the massive twin fortresses at Semna that marked the southern boundary of Egyptian control of Nubia. Here was a fortress built half a millennium earlier as the first line of defense against the war canoes of the Nubian chieftains. Its brick walls were eight yards thick and forty feet high and reinforced by heavy timbers. Each corner mounted a raised bastion of even greater height, and watch towers ran along the walls at regular intervals. On three sides ran a ditch more than thirty yards wide and twenty feet deep revetted with mud brick on the near side to make scaling difficult. The fourth side fronted the river itself and sat atop tall cliffs that formed a sheer wall more than two hundred feet high against which no attack was possible. From the battlement wall I could see Semna's sister fort across the river where it sat astride the main road that ran north along the riverbank. Each of these fortresses held a garrison of fifteen hundred men. Often the officers were accompanied by their families. As long as one remained within the compound itself or nearby there was no real danger from the Nubians.

We had been at Semna for about a week when Tekhet came to see Thaneni and me in our quarters. He seemed unsettled at the prospect of remaining inside the fortress while the expedition made its way from Thebes.

"You know, Thutmose, if we are ever to learn about this country we are not going to do it from behind Egyptian fortifications," he said.

I nodded my head in agreement. Thaneni remained silent, but I could tell from the expression on his face that he thought the idea of leaving the fort at least something worth considering.

"What we need to do is get out among the people, learn how they think, see what fears they harbor."

Tekhet's voice was impatient and I knew that his interest in Nubia was genuine. After all, he was a Nubian too, even though he had spent most of his life in Egypt. Even if he wished to forget his people, we Egyptians would remind him of his origins every time we saw his black skin. I did not completely understand what Tekhet thought he might achieve here, but I found his yearning to know more about his people quite natural.

"What do you suggest, Tekhet?" I asked and shot a glance at Thaneni who was listening with great interest.

"Let us do what we were sent here to do. How are we to advise the commander of the expedition or even Rekhmire about circumstances here if we have done nothing more than sail past a few Nubian villages as we journeyed from one fortress to another!"

There was sarcasm in his voice and I saw Thaneni smile at Tekhet's words. Tekhet went on.

"We need to journey south along the river, deeper into Nubia where Egyptian power does not run and see the Nubian as he is. At the very least we would be able to advise the expedition commander on terrain and other matters to the immediate south of Semna."

I looked at Teket whose excitement for adventure was beginning to infect me as well. "We could move along the river by mule," I said suddenly becoming Tekhet's accomplice in convincing myself and Thaneni. "It is unlikely that there are any enemy forces this close to the fort." I paused. "Once we began the journey we could proceed slowly with due care for any dangers we might encounter."

I smiled at Thaneni who was beginning to doubt my sincerity.

"After all, we are soldiers and soldiers go where the enemy is. If things worked out we might learn something of great value to help the expedition."

Tekhet's head bobbed up and down in enthusiastic agreement and his face broke out in a smile.

Thaneni was listening to all this with interest and at last offered his opinion.

"I suppose that if I am to keep a journal of the great deeds of the future pharaoh of Egypt you expect me to come along don't you?"

It was said lightly, but I had known Thaneni long enough to know that his tone hid genuine concerns for his safety. He was not trained as a soldier and had not taken to life in the field with great success. He had followed me everywhere, but always with some fear and usually with complaint. Tekhet's eyes met mine and we both broke into laughter.

"Of course you must come!" Tekhet said.

"If we are slain by the vile Kush who will be left to tell the tale if you don't come along?" It was a poor joke and did little to allay Thaneni's fears. Nonetheless my boyhood friend would not hear of me risking my hide without him to protect me as he had so many times when we had been students together at the temple.

And so reluctantly and with great complaining Thaneni agreed to accompany me into the land of the crocodiles of Kush.

Tekhet and Thaneni were having some difficulty controlling the mules as we made our way south on the narrow road that ran along the river. We had abandoned our military uniforms and equipment for ordinary clothes, although it was unlikely that anyone would take us for anything other than Egyptians. We counted on Tekhet's ebony-colored skin to ease our passage through any difficulty. We had agreed to tell anyone who challenged us that we were merchants from Elephantine who had come south to purchase monkeys to sell to the Egyptian nobility for their amusement. It was a thin tale indeed, but no better or worse than any other. South of Semna was dangerous country for any Egyptian and Thaneni and I knew we were relying upon Tekhet to free us from any difficulty in which we found ourselves.

In the three days that we had been traveling we passed through several small villages. It was Tekhet who was the first to notice that there were unusually large numbers of cattle in the villages even though there were no young men. The animals were tended by boys. Women and children were found in the usual numbers, but what few men there were seemed to be old and infirm.

"Their men are with the rebels," Tekhet said matter-of-factly, "It is the large number of animals so close to the border that makes me concerned." I saw Thaneni nod his head that he understood even while I didn't. There must have been a puzzled look on my face because Tekhet turned and spoke to me.

"The herds are large enough to provide food for great numbers of men," he said. "Somewhere close by in the valley it is likely that a contingent of Nubian warriors are assembling for a raid across the border." He paused. "It would be foolish to assault Semna. I don't think they would attempt it."

It crossed my mind that if Tekhet was right then it was also likely that the rebels were aware of our presence as well. Three Egyptian monkey traders would hardly go unnoticed in these troubled times, at least not by any warrior chief worth his title.

Two hours later we approached another village. It was near dusk and Tekhet thought we ought to seek lodging and see what we could learn by talking with the inhabitants. If this one was like the others there would be only boys, old men, and women to contend with and there was no danger from them. Much to my surprise Tekhet was welcomed as a native although his command of the Nubian language raised some suspicions. But after a while we were brought to one of the older men of the village who bid us join him for milk and cheese and fresh water. It was thin but refreshing fare and the old man's courtesy was undeniable. The conversation was pleasant and turned to trade in ebony and monkeys and other matters of commerce that I hoped helped convince him that we were what we said we were. It grew late and the three of us were shown to a small hut that Nubian villages maintain for guests and visiting relatives. We began to make ourselves comfortable for the night.

I had just begun to do doze when the movement of a shadow rushing through the open door of the hut startled me into the sudden awareness that a man was moving toward me at great speed. My hand lunged for the dagger that I had placed next to my sleeping mat. I felt my fingers touch the handle, but my attempt to close my grasp around it was met with a sharp pain in my wrist as the calloused foot of the Nubian warrior came down hard upon my arm. I rolled toward the pain as my body lurched from the floor in a movment calculated to catch my attacker behind the knees and bring him down only to see the sharp tip of a spear hover over my chest and force me down upon my back. The Nubian straddled me keeping the spear barely above my flesh as he fixed me with a malevolent stare. From out of the corner of my eye I saw that Thaneni and Tekhet had both been taken too. There was nothing more to do but lie there and hope that the gods were kind.

Our attackers forced us to our feet while others bound our hands behind our backs. Strong hands shoved us forward through the door of the hut and walked us at the point of spears in the direction of the house of the old man who had fed us earlier that night. Through the darkness I saw the old man standing in front of a group of Nubian warriors. Next to him was a warrior adorned in the uniform and headdress of a tribal chieftain. Thaneni, Tekhet and I were forced to kneel in the dirt in front of him.

"The old man says you are Egyptian spies," the chieftain said in a somber voice. "Is this so?" It was not a serious question and he did not wait for a response. "For if it is I shall have no reason not to kill you."

I raised my eyes and saw the broad features of the negro. He was enormous, perhaps over six feet tall, and as thick as a wall. His eyes possessed a yellow cast to them and flickered with a pitiless coldness that I suppose he found useful in frightening enemies. Thaneni and I kept silent. Anything we might say would only make matters worse. We looked at Tekhet who seemed the least frightened of the three of us. He raised his head and spoke.

"We are not spies," he said. "I am of your people. I, too, am of this land." He paused. "Do not your eyes see the color of my skin?" Teket's eyes stared straight at the chieftain and showed no weakness.

The chieftain looked closely at Tekhet for a few moments.

"Untie him," he ordered.

A warrior moved behind Tekhet and slashed his bonds with a knife. Tekhet's arms fell to this side and he rubbed his muscles with his hands to sooth the pain from the cuts in his skin made by the ropes.

"And who are your friends, brother?" the chieftain asked.

Tekhet looked at Thaneni and me.

"They are merchants as they say they are. Nothing more. They are harmless. Soon the land will be covered with dead Egyptians and Nubians. What difference would two more make? I ask you to spare them for they are of use to me."

The chieftain examined Thaneni and me looking for some sign that Tekhet was not telling the truth. Finally he gave orders to release us. He turned to Tekhet.

"Who are you?" He paused to allow his words to hang in the air. His eyes narrowed and his body tensed as signs that he had not yet accepted Tekhet's story. All of us were still in danger.

There was no trace of fear or tension in Tekhet's voice when he answered.

"My name is Tekhet, son of Toshka, warrior chief of the Nubians. Our village is far from here, near Sai. My father fell in battle with the Egyptians many years before. I was taken hostage and held against my will in Thebes. Now I return to my land and I bring you warning that a great army is being sent from Thebes to punish the Nubians. You would do well to prepare for war."

The chieftain's huge head tilted back and laughter bellowed from his throat. Soon all the warriors were laughing and even Thaneni and I found ourselves smiling more out of fear than any comprehension of what was going on.

"The sons of Seth come to their graves!"

It was almost a curse and the other warriors repeated the words out loud again and again.

"Do they think they come without our knowing?" the chieftain said. "Then it will be they who will be surprised when our armies swarm over them like the red ants of the African plains. We will eat their flesh and leave their bones to turn white in the sun."

The chieftain let loose another mighty roar of laughter then ordered us to follow him into the hut. The four of us sat around a smoldering fire and a servant brought us cups of bitter Nubian beer.

"Drink!" The chieftain ordered. Thaneni and I followed Tekhet as he raised his cup to his lips and drank a toast to our host.

Tekhet lowered the cup and looked at the chieftain.

"I have spent many years away from my land," he said with a hint of genuine sorrow in his voice. "During that time I have learned much about the Egyptians, but know little of my own people. Why do the Nubians and Egyptians war against each other?"

Tekhet's words fell upon the chieftain's ears with the honesty of a priest. Had I not known better I would have sworn his words carried no deception with them. But Tekhet was the son of a warrior chieftain himself and his words sought to pierce the mind of the negro and fathom why he fought. Perhaps in this way, Tekhet reckoned, he would learn of ways to halt the slaughter that had gone on between the two peoples for more than five hundred years.

The chieftain drank deeply from his beer and wiped his lips with the back of his hand.

"The sons of Seth have sat upon this land as conquerors for too long. Their forts block the Nile from our canoes. Once we sailed freely up the Nile to Elephantine and traded with them in a time long past. Then they blocked the river to us and much of what we had to sell we could no longer sell. Our merchants were forced to sell at the price of the Egyptians at Semna or the other forts who then resold our goods to their own people at far more than they pay us."

Tekhet nodded his head slowly as if to give solemn effect to his understanding of the chieftain's complaint. His gesture had the result of encouraging the chieftain to go on talking.

"The Egyptians treat us as animals. Even in the northern towns where our two peoples live side by side there are two laws, one for Egyptians and one for the "crocodiles of Kush" as they call us. The authorities always take the side of the Egyptian in disputes. Many times lands are taken from Nubians without payment. They send us to the mines for the slightest infraction of the law where we are worked as animals. Many of our people have died in those mines and not a *deben* of the profit from them is given to the chiefs or people of Nubia in return."

The chieftain spat.

"We are not animals!"

His voice was almost a screech.

"We will teach these vile sons of Seth how we Nubians deal with those who would enslave us!" he said.

Tekhet glanced toward Thaneni and me. In the darkness I saw the look of concern on his face. Later he told me that he feared that the chieftain had drunk too much beer and was unable to contain his anger. Tekhet feared that the outraged Nubian might well take out his anger upon Thaneni and me. Cautiously Tekhet spoke.

"Do not we Nubians flail at ghosts?" he said.

The chieftain looked at him with narrowed eyes as if he found suspicion in Tekhet's words. Tekhet went on.

"This land has seen many wars, some so long ago that none alive today can recall why they were fought. The sons of Seth and the sons of Kush flail at each other fighting the wars of their fathers even as they do not know why they fight. Cannot the two peoples live together in peace? Must there always be war?"

The chieftain stared at Tekhet not knowing what to make of his words for they were the words of the Egyptians but from the mouth of a Nubian. They made the chieftain suspicious all over again.

"It is our land," he said. "We must have a share in determining its destiny. If we are to live in peace, then Egyptian must give way to Nubian in some things as we have had to give way in many things. The law must be the same for all."

He paused and shook his head.

"You speak as if in a dream. It will never be."

Time passed and the fire died slowly. The chieftain having drunk too much stretched out upon the floor and fell into a deep sleep. Soon most of the warriors were asleep on the ground. I could hardly keep my eyes open and at last gave myself over to a much needed rest. Thaneni, too, I saw lie down to sleep. Only Tekhet remained awake even as slumber overcame me and I drifted off into blackness.

Morning came quickly. It seemed that I had been asleep only a few brief moments before the stirring of Nubian warriors all about me in the hut awakened me. I staggered to my feet and shook Thaneni until he, too, woke. After a few minutes to drive the cobwebs from our minds, we left the hut into the sunshine where, despite the blinding brightness of the early daylight, I could make out the figures of Tekhet and the chieftain talking together. I started to walk toward them when I saw Tekhet and the chieftain grasp each other's forearms in the Nubian gesture of friendship. A broad smile rested on their faces. Tekhet turned from the chieftain and came toward me.

"Good morning, Thutmose!" Tekhet said in a voice whose cheerful tone surprised me. We were still in the middle of a Nubian camp and as far as I knew still being held prisoner, circumstances it seemed to me that did not easily lend themselves to cheerfulness.

"What are we going to do?" I said anxiously not thinking to respond to Tekhet's greeting.

Tekhet smiled and the anxious tone of his voice the night before seemed to have left him.

"We are going back to Semna," he said. "That's what we are going to do."

He must have seen the stunned look that his words brought to my face.

"The chieftain sees no danger in permitting us to leave. In fact it was he who suggested we return to Semna instead of journeying further south to Sai. If there is to be a war, it will be fought here. Egyptian forces are too strong north of Semna to deal with in any way except small raids. So we will journey north and stay out of the way until Egypt has laid her flail once more upon the back of Kush."

Tekhet took a deep breath and sighed as he let it escape from his lungs. He had been in Nubia for only a short while and already I sensed a sadness in him for his people and what would happen to them. Tekhet was after all a royal prince of Nubia, as I was a royal prince of Thebes, and he ached for his people the way I would have ached for mine had things been turned about. Together we travelled the river road back to Semna. The three of us talked long into the night to find some way to avert the tragedy that was soon to befall the land of Nub. Days later when the battlements of the Semna fortress came into view we had worked out the semblance of a plan.

It was six weeks before the troop ships carrying the advance guard began to arrive at Semna and disgorged their cargo of soldiers, horses, and equipment upon the river's banks. An army of five thousand men is a huge beast that takes up a great space and consumes all before it. For weeks the garrison at Semna had been gathering food from the farms in the countryside to feed the army.

Once it began to move south into Nubia the army would carry as many of its own supplies as it could and confiscate whatever else it needed from the Nubian villages along the way. Within days the area around the Semna forts had been transformed into a military camp with soldiers, chariots, supply wagons, oxen, horses, and mules everywhere. There was room within the fortress only for the senior officers and scribes. Junior officers and other ranks lived in tents outside the walls. The great mass of civilian hangers-on—the whores, servants, barbers, physicians, grooms, and wives of the soldiers—made do as best they could on the open ground.

The expedition commander was General Horemb, and as soon as he arrived I made an effort to see him. Horemb was one of the generals I had met at Rekhmire's villa and I hoped he would be receptive to what I planned to tell him. It took Horemb a few days to oversee the landing of his army. When this had been accomplished he sent for me. He had taken over the garrison commander's office and seemed in a good mood when I arrived.

"Good day, General" I said. "It is good to see you again." I paused. "Is there any news from General Rekhmire?" I asked.

Horemb smiled and walked from behind his desk and placed his hand on my shoulder.

"Thank you, highness. General Rekhmire sends his regards and his hope that your efforts can be of some help to my expedition."

His words seemed genuine enough. But Horemb was a soldier and what I was about to tell him was not likely to please him. He let his arm drop from my shoulder and pointed to an empty chair near the desk. Horemb returned to the chair behind his desk and sat down. He sighed and looked right at me with narrowed eyes. His manner was all seriousness.

"Tell me," he said. "What have you learned about these Nubians that can be of value to me?"

He paused to let his words sink in and then leaned back in his chair and waited for me to answer. I sat silently for a few moments gathering my thoughts. I was remembering what Tekhet and I had agreed that I should tell the general. There was, of course, no point to bringing Tekhet into this. He was a Nubian and that was that. Anything that he might say would be dismissed immediately by this or any other Egyptian general. Finally I spoke.

"General I have spent some time among the Nubians and have come to believe that there may be a way to avoid the slaughter that will fall upon this land."

I permitted my voice to trail off. I studied the general's face for any sign of a positive reaction. There was none and his face curled up in a scowl as if I had uttered some sacrilegious oath that offended the gods. Still he said nothing and I went on. I told him about being taken prisoner by the Nubian chieftain and what I had learned about the Nubian view of things. Horemb listened with what seemed genuine interest and then spoke.

"And what do you conclude from all this, highness?" he said. A flicker of suspicion passed over his face as he sat there waiting for my answer.

"What I think, general, is that we can avoid this war if we have the patience to permit diplomacy to seek its course. If we approach the chieftains one at a time at first and listen to their complaints, it seems to me there are some things we can agree to do that might remove some of the reasons for their hatred of us. They see us as invaders, that much is certain. But we have sat upon this land for so long that it is way beyond the time for Egyptians and Nubians to learn to live together."

The expression on the general's face gave me hope that he was giving my words some consideration and so I went on.

"In truth, what they ask would be easy to accomplish. Much of what they say of our treatment of them is true. We have allowed

Egyptian policy here to be driven by the interests of merchants and cattle breeders who get into trouble with the local population by dishonest dealings and then rely upon the army or police to get them out of it by using the laws and courts unfairly. They want an end to the enslavement of their people in the mines and want to be permitted to travel freely again up the Nile to the first cataract as they had done for millennia before we Egyptians came to sit upon the land. None of this is impossible to achieve and with it would come peace and an end to the slaughter from which no one benefits."

I saw the general stroke his chin as if he were in deep thought. I was encouraged by this for it seemed to me that he was giving my words serious consideration. After a few seconds when we both sat silently Horemb looked at me, smiled, and began to speak.

"No doubt what you say has merit, highness, and perhaps some day it might succeed. But the time is not now."

His words had a finality to them that I did not expect.

"Queen Hatshepsut has neglected the situation in Nubia for too long. It has been several years since an Egyptian army has ravaged the land and broken the spirit of the Nubian chiefs. In that time they have grown stronger and bolder until even our gracious queen was forced to follow the advice of her generals and turn her thoughts to Nubia."

He sighed and drew a deep breath.

"Even if we wanted diplomacy to take a hand in these events it would still be better to use it after we have punished the Nubians. That way we would have the advantage in negotiations. Your advice is sound, but it comes at the wrong time."

He offered me a slight smile. I was about to answer him when he put up his hand to stop me.

"Please let me finish, highness," he said. "There are other reasons for doing what we are about to do. Nubia is the easiest of two difficulties. The neglect of matters of state by the queen and her advisors has emboldened the Mitanni and their allied city-states on the land bridge between the Sinai and Lebanon. Even now Egyptian commercial interests are seized and harassed. The prince of Kadesh, one of the most powerful city-states in Retjennu, plots to form an alliance of cities to drive us from the land-bridge by force."

Horemb paused and I saw that his words bore the seriousness of much thought behind them. What he was telling me were not only his thoughts, but those of his superiors who had already advised the queen.

"There is going to be a war on the land-bridge and it will happen soon, perhaps in less than a year. Egypt cannot afford to have her resources or attention diverted by circumstances in Nubia. If we are engaged in Retjennu, the Nubian chieftains will take advantage of the war on one front to attempt to drive us from our positions on the second front."

He stopped and looked right into my eyes.

"Highness, this is not the time for peace. I have been ordered to lay waste the land south of Semna and damage the Nubian chieftains so that they will be unable to challenge our hold north of Semna while we are at war on the land-bridge. There is no question of either peace or long term solutions. That will be for others to accomplish in calmer times. Right now I intend to cripple the military power of the Nubian chieftains and to return to Thebes as quickly as possible so that the army can be reequipped and made ready for transport to Retjennu and the coming war."

He stopped speaking but kept my eyes fixed by his stare for several moments until he was certain by the expression on my face that I understood the meaning of what he had just told me. Horemb was teaching me an important lesson, one that I carried with me for the rest of my life and that served me well again and again. Sometimes events took on a life of their own and created realities from which there was no escape where to choose one course of action negates another. The realities were such that even were I Pharaoh I, too, would have done what Horemb planned to do. I looked at the general who continued to stare at me. I nodded my head solemnly that I understood what had to be done. I stood up and came to attention before the general and offered the military salute.

"I would appreciate the opportunity to accompany you on the campaign, general." I paused and the general offered a slight tilt of his head in agreement. "Thank you," I said. "Now I had best be about preparing myself for my duties."

Three weeks later I turned eighteen years old. The next day the great beast of the army stirred from its lair and began to amble southward along both banks of the Nile devouring every living thing in its path. It was slaughter pure and simple. Each day was the same. Chariots moved out ahead of the infantry and threw a cordon of archers around the village to prevent the inhabitants from escaping. Then the infantry attacked killing men, women, and children without distinction. Whatever livestock or harvest was found was confiscated for the use of the army and the village set to fire. Every Nubian village from Semna to Sai, a hundred miles to the south, was destroyed. Columns of black smoke from the burning rubble warned the villagers in the next town and some fled before us. But there was no sign of the Nubian warriors even as our army drew near to Sai.

My reaction to all this was more sadness than anything else. Thousands met their death for reasons they never knew nor, perhaps, would comprehend even if they did. Armies are pitiless things, more like humans than animals in that regard, and slay all that resists them even when for their own good mercy would be the better policy. Thaneni took refuge from the bloodletting in his sense of history. It had, after all, all happened so many times before! Yet I confess to being disappointed at my friend's unemotional reaction to the suffering, and I feared that Thaneni might have become one of those scholars without a soul from whom the world learned only how to create suffering and injustice in pursuit of goals that seemed to have an existence only in their minds.

The most human of us was Tekhet who seemed to suffer the pain of every slain Nubian whose corpse he saw. At times he would break into tears and sob quietly. At others he would simply turn his back and remove himself from the place of horror. By the time we reached Sai, Tekhet's compassion had turned to a smoldering anger barely held in check by his own instincts for survival. We two had sworn when the killing had begun that someday when I was pharaoh and he a noble prince of Nubia we would never permit such horror to occur again between our peoples. Now, examining the look of hatred etched upon his face by the experience of war, I wondered if I would ever again be able to trust this man who had become my friend. Had events moved so far beyond us both that his heart harbored only vengeance for us Egyptians who had butchered his homeland?

It was, finally, a few miles before the city walls of Sai that we found the Nubian warriors we had been searching for. Horemb was growing impatient. The destruction of the villages denied the enemy the food and supplies he would require to attack beyond Semna. But the seasons would restore them in a year's time and all would be as it was before. Egypt needed more breathing room to deal with the Mitanni and Horemb knew he had to find and destroy the Nubian tribal armies. His laying waste the villages had been his way of drawing these armies to battle. They decided to stand at Sai, a fortified town with good defenses and the main Nubian city north of the capital. Our army was within two miles of the city when it came under ferocious attack by Nubian infantry.

The chariot scouts failed to detect the enemy who concealed themselves and permitted the scouts to pass through their lines so as not to give the alarm. The advance guard was right in the middle of a major concentration of Nubian soldiers when the Nubians pounced upon them killing them in great numbers. A commander of a chariot company saw the slaughter and ordered his unit into the attack. Within minutes they were surrounded by hordes of infantry, pulled from their machines, and slain. Another unit, this one a company of infantry, committed the same mistake and dashed into the fray. It, too, was overwhelmed and cut down with great loss of life. By now Horemb had moved forward to assess the situation. He immediately ordered a halt to the army behind him, sending not a single soldier forward to rescue those who had already been lost or wounded. It was the act of an experienced soldier who recognized the futility of attacking a sizeable force in piecemeal fashion. But the enemy had finally shown itself and Horemb decided to kill it then and there if he could.

The signals from the Egyptian force across the river showed it to be unmolested. Horemb ordered it to move swiftly down the riverbank and cross behind the city to cut off a retreat and prevent reinforcement. Then using the river to guard his flank he spread his army wide across the valley floor throwing sizeable chariot forces furthest out on the flanks to pivot inward like a great fan and join up with the units moving northward from behind the town. The fighting was fiercest right along the riverbank. The Egyptian infantry pressed the Nubians hard forcing them back upon Sai itself. The two Egyptian forces joined up just past midday and Horemb ordered them to close the noose and drive everything they could not slay before them until the Nubian army retreated behind the city's wall. By nightfall Sai was surrounded on three sides with no possibility of reenforcement or retreat. Horemb settled his army around the town and brought it to siege.

Horemb could ill afford a long siege of a year or more. His orders were to destroy the Nubians and return to Thebes with his army so that it could be used against the states of Retjennu. After a few weeks he undertook to subdue the city by storm and elite troops—the Braves—were thrown against the walls. Logs with huge metal blades were fashioned by engineers to pry loose the mud brick of the walls. Fire arrows set the buildings in the city alight. Tunnellers dug under the walls to weaken the earth and bring the casements down of their own weight. All of these means failed. After more than three months the Egyptian army still surrounded the city and the Nubians held forth within it.

Horemb began to despair of being successful. The country-side had been stripped bare to feed the army. The supply of beer was exhausted and sickness broke out among the troops as they were forced to drink the local water. And then the gods took a hand and smiled upon Egypt. A great epidemic broke out within Sai and took the lives of many of the defenders. Within a few days hundreds had died or become sick. So numerous were the dead that their corpses were flung from the battlements into the river below attracting hundreds of crocodiles to the funeral feast. Seeing this, Horemb ordered his own men to do nothing until, after a time, he concluded that the garrison was reduced enough to be unable to resist an attack. He launched a number of small assaults at different points along the walls so that the defenders were forced to rush from one point to another in their defense. After several attempts one of our units of Braves succeeded in fighting their way inside and opening a gate that the Nubians had left undefended. Within a short time Egyptian infantry rushed through the opening and attacked the garrison in force. Our soldiers fought their way to the main gate and forced it open and our men poured through in great numbers. The fighting raged for two days and hundreds of Nubian warriors, many weakened by disease, met their deaths.

When the last of them had surrendered, Horemb ordered a great slaughter to commence and thousands—many of them old men, women and children—were put to death and their corpses thrown over the walls into the Nile as food for the crocodiles.

The great pitiless beast then loosened its coils from around Sai and slithered upstream to its lair in Semna where it rested and healed its wounds before preparing to begin the journey to Thebes where its masters were preparing yet another meal for it. Horemb's army had done its job well. It would be years before another Nubian army grew strong enough to attack Egyptian towns and forts. In that time Egypt was free to concentrate on the greater threat that was developing beyond the Sinai frontier. The flood was now three months gone and the Nile remained high enough for effortless travel. Thaneni, Tekhet, and I prepared to return to Thebes along with the army.

It was a few weeks before the army could begin to move and I spent my time in pointless activity wandering around the fortress and generally doing nothing. After a few days of this nonsense I was bored to my bones and glad to be summoned to Horemb's office. His adjutant showed me in and I presented myself to the general.

"You are looking well, highness," he said pleasantly.

Generals are always pleasant when things are going well and events certainly had conspired to put Horemb in a good mood. Back at Thebes there would be honors and gold waiting for him. I sensed he was as anxious to return as was I.

He reached across his desk and handed me an envelope that had the seal of the Army of Amun, *Mighty of Bows*, across its front. It was from Rekhmire and I found it difficult to contain my excitement as I opened it. I read it quickly and then turned to Horemb.

"It is from General Rekhmire," I said flatly. "He wishes me to return to Thebes as soon as possible." There was no explanation for the order, but it was accompanied by authorization to have one of the smaller naval boats take me home.

Horemb stood up.

"Highness, I hope your trip to Thebes will be a safe one," he said. "I am grateful for your presence during this time of difficulty in Nubia" he continued. "I hope we will see each other in Thebes upon my return and that we will once again dine together at General Rekhmire's villa."

He paused and his eyes narrowed producing a deep furrow upon his broad forehead. His tone was deep and serious. There was warning in his voice.

"It will be my honor to serve the common destiny that you and Egypt share," he said.

And then Horemb did a strange thing. He brought himself to attention and offered a military salute as if I were his superior and he my junior. As I returned his formal gesture of respect with my own salute, unspoken feelings of loyalty and respect passed between us so that we came to feel in that moment that each could depend upon the other to serve Egypt.

I walked from the building into the courtyard and found a small plot of shade in which to take refuge from the terrible Nubian heat. My hand slipped inside the envelope and I withdrew from it a smaller envelope of the kind that Egyptians use in common correspondence. I opened it and took from it a single sheet of paper folded in two and read the words written there in a delicate hand.

Come swiftly to your love,
As a royal messenger spurred on by the
Impatience of his master. That is, if

Royal messengers are to be believed.
Come swiftly,
The entire stable is at your disposal.
The chariot ready.
No headlong horses
When you meet her
Will match the stampede of your heart.
Come headlong
To your mistress' house
Like the pride of the king's stable,
Chosen from a thousand thoroughbreds,
Trained on special feed,
Who breaks into unrivalled gallop
At the mere mention of the word stirrup
So that not even the head trainer
Can hold him in
How well he knows her heart

The words flooded my soul with emotion and drew my eye to where the poet had written an author's name. In fragile script I saw her name, *Merytre*, and my heart leapt.

# Twenty

I reached Thebes barely ahead of the main body of the returning army. Thaneni was struck by a mysterious illness whose seriousness was such that I was not disposed to abandon my friend for fear that the gods might take him from me in my absence. For more than two weeks Thaneni lingered in his bed racked with fever and pain. At times the heat of his body was so great that the physicians poured water over him to soak his bedclothes before they fanned cooling air over him. Other times Thaneni became so cold that he shook violently and his teeth clattered until it seemed they would shatter. The illness that possessed his body also affected his mind and sometimes he would fall into a state of near madness where his eyes bulged and he rambled on making no sense.

One day while attending to Thaneni Tekhet came see me. Tekhet had been spending more and more time among the Nubians and had taken to affecting Nubian dress instead of his uniform. He recognized Thaneni's illness immediately, having seen it among the Nubians. He became concerned that Thaneni was not recovering and, like me, feared that he would die. The next day Tekhet returned with a Nubian physician. The man was short and very thin with folds of excess skin hanging from his arms. The bones in his face stuck out from beneath his skin stretching it taut.

Deep hollows held yellow tinged eyes making the Nubian look both ancient and ill. He carried with him a leather pouch upon which were painted magical signs. The physician examined Thaneni who had taken to a fit of shivering and then stepped back. He muttered something in the gibberish that was his native tongue. Tekhet nodded solemnly.

"Bring water," Tekhet said translating the physician's wishes into Egyptian.

A few moments later a servant arrived with a jug of water and placed it on the night table along with a cup. The physician took a pinch of grayish powder from his leather pouch and mixed it with the water in the cup. He slipped his arm behind Thaneni's neck and raised him from the bed holding the cup to his parched lips and bid him drink. Thaneni took a swallow and his face curled from the terrible taste of the potion. A broad smile crossed the Nubian's face and he pressed the cup to Thaneni's lips again. Thaneni was forced to drink until he had consumed the entire contents. The physician gently laid him down upon the bed. Thaneni's eyes met mine and he smiled wanly at me. I smiled back at my sick friend and hoped that my expression did not betray the concern I felt for him. Off in the corner Tekhet and the Nubian were talking. I saw the physician bow to Tekhet and hand his leather pouch to him. Tekhet smiled and bowed and walked toward me.

"Here," he said handing me the pouch. "Make certain your friend consumes two potions each day until the contents of the pouch are gone."

Tekhet smiled.

"Don't worry. The Nubians know how to cure this illness. They call it the "sickness that comes from the swamps." Their potions were given to them by the ancient ones. Thaneni will recover if you force him to swallow the potion."

Thaneni began to show signs of improvement within a few days. When another week had passed he was eating and laughing like his old self and the fear of losing him finally passed from my mind.

The great beast of the army had finished loading its equipment and supplies aboard the fleet of boats when Thaneni, Tekhet and I departed Semna for the journey to Thebes aboard one of the navy's small boats. The journey itself was uneventful and we arrived in Thebes two weeks later and about a week ahead of the first boats of the flotilla carrying Horemb and his victorious army. As soon as our boat put into the harbor the three of us made straight for Rekhmire's headquarters. The news of the events in Nubia had reached Thebes long before and the city was preparing for a great victory celebration. The city was more crowded than expected and it took us longer than usual to make our way to army headquarters. Rekhmire was pleased to see us and invited Tekhet and me into his office. Thaneni was left to wait in the adjutant's office. It was a slight for which he never forgave Rekhmire.

We spent most of the afternoon telling Rekhmire about our experiences, of the great slaughter named victory, and of the difficulty of forging a peaceful solution without first changing Egyptian policy there. Rekhmire listened attentively nodding here and there to show that he agreed with what we were telling him. We finished our report and Rekhmire rose from his chair, walked over to the window and stretched, bringing forth a great yawn. Slowly he turned and walked back to his chair and sat down.

"It is as I thought it would be," he said seriously. He took a deep breath.

"Still there is hope that we can change things when the time is right."

He paused and nodded his head slowly.

"But that time is not now," he said. "For the present we have far more important things to deal with."

Rekhmire smiled a formal smile.

"Captain Tekhet, I want you to return to your staff duties for the time being," Rekhmire said.

His voice was official but lacked the sharp edge that commanders sometimes reserved for subordinates. Instead Rekhmire seemed pleased.

"You both have performed your duty well," he said.

He looked at Tekhet.

"Captain, you have served your people and your country and both are grateful as am I for your service. The day will come, I am certain of it, when Nubian and Egyptian will live in peace. And when it does you can be certain that you will play your part in bringing that hope to fruition."

Rekhmire stood up and both of us sprang to our feet in response. He turned to Tekhet and spoke.

"You are dismissed, Captain."

He paused while Tekhet came to attention and offered a salute. Rekhmire returned it and Tekhet left the room. Rekhmire sat down across from me and leaned back in his chair. He seemed suddenly more relaxed now that we were alone.

"Well, Thutmose, its nice to have you home safely. No one knows of your presence in the city I trust?" he said. I nodded.

"Good," Rekhmire said with a smile.

"I think it sound advice that you remain inconspicuous." He paused.

"I have arranged for you and your scribe to take quarters at my villa. You will be safe there and there is much I have to tell you about the situation in Thebes since your absence."

A deep frown wrinkled his forehead. "Things have become very serious," he said solemnly. "Very serious indeed." He shook his head in a gesture of confusion and worry.

"The time is fast coming when something must be done or Egypt will be put in mortal danger."

A ray of sunlight danced over Rekhmire's face revealing the expression of a man who was nearly exhausted. He looked as if he had not slept well in many weeks, distracted by affairs of state that his office required him to deal with. I looked at him as he stared off into the distance, his eyes closed, looking as if he were on the edge of sleep and lost in his own thoughts. I sat there in silence waiting for him to speak. At last he opened his eyes and shook his head to clear it of the spiderwebs of slumber. He turned to me and spoke. With his words came a genuine smile of affection that seemed to lift the burdens from his mind if only for a few moments.

"I have been instructed by my daughter, highness, to deliver her regards to you and to inform you that she is pleased that you have returned to Thebes safely."

He spoke the words with a mock formality that did little to hide the playful humor that they gave him.

"Merytre further instructs," and here he rolled his eyes at the thought that the general was being given orders by his daughter, "that you are to accept my invitation to reside at the villa."

He laughed.

"She is so much like her mother!"

The general's words brought a warm smile to my face as my mind recalled the vision of Merytre standing before me with smoldering eyes and wet lips that night upon the patio. I had not been able to rid myself of her memory during all the time in Nubia. Now that I had returned to Thebes I wanted nothing so much as to see this beauty again and take her in my arms and feel her body against mine.

"I accept your invitation with gratitude, general" I said with a smile.

That evening I accompanied the general in his coach to his villa. As the *ka'tana* rolled through the villa's main gate my eyes searched the familiar surroundings for a glimpse of the beautiful Merytre.

I installed myself in the same suite of rooms that I had been given before while Thaneni was given a smaller suite on the backside of the villa overlooking the garden. Despite being the closest friend of the heir to the throne, Thaneni was still the son of a glass factory worker and was always taken with the surroundings of the wealthy, especially so whenever he had the opportunity to indulge himself in them. And so Thaneni was quite content with our new circumstances. He busied himself with reading, keeping his journal, and exploring the villa.

It was the season of *Shemu*, the time when the Nile dies and the heat rests upon Egypt like a woolen cloak and Egyptians avoid the outdoors except during the cooler evenings. But the heat of the day was not equal to the passion that Merytre and I found in one another, a passion that shaped our bodies and souls during that first season of our love. At first Merytre retained her formal stature, especially so whenever her father was near. I began to fear that I had somehow offended her or done something to drive her away. We spent many days together and often traveled in a coach to places in the valley where the air was cooler. We had picnics in the gathering dusk. Although my body burned with desire for her there had been no repeat of that delicious night on the patio the evening before I left for Nubia. All this did nothing to quench my desire for her and, in a curious way that women know, my passion grew.

One night I lay tossing in my bed unable to sleep from the oppressive heat. The visions of Merytre that danced through my head brought my body to such a state that I could not bear the covers to touch my skin. Outside the heat began to stir and move about in heavy gusts that came and went as in a gathering storm filling the window frame with the motion of the curtain there to resist the wanderings of the Night Demons. The wind blew stronger and the intervals between gusts grew shorter but it brought no relief to my stifling bedroom. This night's wind carried no coolness upon its wings filling the air instead with blasts of shouting heat like those that fly from a furnace when the door is opened. Sweat covered my naked form. I rose to tear back the night curtain and look upon the evening sky in search of the rest that the elements and my body denied me.

I drew the curtain aside and the sky filled with the rumble of a heavy noise like that of a huge sled loaded heavy with granite blocks running crazily down hill on wooden rollers crushing the pavement stones with its weight. The roaring noise grew louder and louder as if it were closing upon my very room with some evil intent that I could not determine. The noise crashed over me and my body was struck by a blast of wind so powerful it stung my bare chest with its force. And then the sky broke brightly open in a multitude of jagged flashes of white light shooting across the sky touching horizon to horizon before spindly spidery legs thin as string exploded in thickening brightness dragging the hot bolts to the ground.

I stood at the window watching the power of the rainless storm that seemed to live and writhe upon the heat itself taking from it the power to illuminate the sky with streaks of light that brought the wind behind them in powerful gusts that cooled nothing and made everything hotter than before. It was as if my passion for Merytre was exploding upon the night sky but granting no relief from my tormented senses. The storm raged filling the darkened room with gusts of wind, waterfalls of noise, and stiletto flashes of light that fell all around me until, as if from a distance, I heard Merytre call my name.

"Thutmose."

The sound fell gently around me like the call of a mother to her child.

"Thutmose," I heard again. "Come to me, my love."

My body turned before my mind could stop it and I stared back into the darkness of my room toward where my bed stood. For moments all was silent and dark. And then the wind threw a great gust upon the night and the rumble of the crashing noise began far distant and rushed toward me as a great spear that knew its destination with no one to tell it only to be discovered in a bright blast of light given off by the jagged bolts flying across the heavens. And in that light and wind and sound I saw Merytre standing there, her beautiful body covered only by her arms in a gesture so innocent as to be unforgettable. Still, now, many years later, whenever I am alone and think of Merytre, I see her as she was that night, wrapped in an innocence and beauty that I cannot forget. Forever she stands there in my mind.

"Thutmose, my beloved. Come to me."

Merytre's voice was as sultry as the warm Egyptian night and held the promise of a passion harbored within for many years finally released. A few steps brought me next to her. She tilted her head back and closed her eyes in a gesture of submission while upon her parted lips the moisture of her mouth had gathered in anticipation of a kiss. My arms opened and she stepped into them without effort or fear and gently pressed her nude body against mine. Her very gentleness made my passion grow. It was with the same gentleness that I pressed my body against hers until it seemed we had become one in the way molten wax clings to a hard form only to soften it as it does so. We kissed once and then again and again until our mouths never parted except to say those endearing things that lovers say to one another when the enthrall-ment is complete.

We lay next to each other for a moment catching our breath for the passion and heat had made us dizzy. I watched the light and wind play upon the ceiling and listened for the coming of the rum-bling from the distance. Merytre slowly turned to me and pulled me close. I rolled toward her and her legs parted permitting my body to fall between them as if I had rested there a thousand times before. She lay beneath me, her eyes closed as her mouth parted and her tongue ran wetly over her teeth. Her hand guided me so that I paused at the mouth of her lotus for a second before, as slowly and gently as I was able, I pressed myself home and entered her body.

When I was completely within her Merytre's green eyes opened slowly to reveal the moist look of passion that gave them the look of drowsy slumber. Her mouth widened into a sweet smile of con-tentment. But when I began to move, to thrust inside and out, her expression changed and a wildness overcame her that for a moment made me fear that I had hurt her. Her hips rose to meet my every thrust even as her arms fell across my back to pull me closer to her. Her throat gave birth to low groaning sounds that rose and fell with her body until the sounds came together in a passionate cry that came in spurts as quickly as her breath. She grabbed me with a strength that she had until that moment kept hidden while our bodies moved in entangled unison until I could resist my passion no longer. I let my fluid spend itself within her and fell upon her warm wet skin in exhausted pleasure. Around me the wind and light continued their dance. Outside, the thun-derous noise crashed again and again. Merytre, already half-asleep, crept upon my chest like a naked infant upon the breast of its mother. Her breathing gave evidence of her own contentment. I looked at her gentle features and sighed. Then I gave myself over to my own exhaustion and slipped into a deep sleep.

When I awoke I was alone.

The next day was as the others so that whenever we met or dined together with her father not a word or expression passed between us that would have hinted at our secret. And then night came. When sufficient time had passed for me to fall asleep I was awakened by the gentle touch of Merytre who lay down with me again. With slumber gone with the morning sun Merytre left me once more. And so the season passed with Merytre coming to me when she chose and always deeply in the night so that no one, not even the usually observant Thaneni, knew of our trysts or the growing love for each other that was blossoming in our breasts.

The season of *Akhet* when the Nile's waters flood the soil was almost upon us when one evening at dinner I was introduced to Kheteb, General Rekhmire's son-in-law and husband of Merytre's oldest sister, Kiya, who to my eye lacked the beauty of her younger sister in that she shared too many of her father's harsh features and seemed as well to lack his sense of humor. She was a serious woman, the kind who makes a good attendant to a husband's ambition even though she was not expert at concealing it. We had finished eating when Rekhmire turned the conversation to circumstances at court.

"My son-in-law is commander of the palace guard," Rehkmire said with some pride, although it had been through his influence that he had secured the post for his relative.

I nodded and gave Kheteb a sincere smile. Kheteb looked every inch the soldier, from his strong frame to his short military haircut. He was an infantry officer and had some battle under his belt. When Rekhmire told him of my own fight in the canyon he smiled warmly and offered his admiration. When he was told who I was he was even more pleased to learn that the son of Pharaoh had experienced the sting of battle. I sensed from that very moment that here was a man who had already sworn his loyalty to me out of common experience even though he spoke not a word to that effect. Sometimes it happens that way. Men take other men to themselves as comrades. When this is the case they are loyal even unto death, for what they have given out of love and honor only death can retrieve.

"So you command the *Eaters of Hearts,* do you Kheteb?" I said jovially the way one comrade might joke with another.

Kheteb nodded.

"And there is no better regiment in the army!" he said with obvious pride.

I nodded.

"It is a good regiment indeed," I said. "It was my father's regiment when he fought in Nubia. One of my oldest friends, my bodyguard as a child, served in its ranks."

I paused and took a sip of wine from my cup.

Rekhmire sat across from us watching the banter of his two young lions. At times I saw a look of genuine affection cross his face as he listened to Kheteb carry on about something or other. It was, I surmised, the pride of a man who had lost his own son and hoped to gain another through the attraction of his daughters. Sometimes Rekhmire looked at me in the same way, like a father studying his son, searching for clues to his character, as if character were a gift of blood and training that only a father could bequeath. Kheteb had finished talking when Rekhmire spoke.

"There is something I think you might wish to know Thutmose," he said.

His tone had turned serious.

"It regards your mother Ese."

The mention of my mother's name started my heart to beat and I felt a flush of blood run to my face. Ese! The tone of Rekhmire's words suggested trouble. My mind raced. Ese! Was she safe? I had not seen her in more than five years! I had been an ungrateful son, and now I feared that something had happened to her and I was to blame.

I tried to calm myself.

"What is it? Is my mother safe?"

There was a sharp edge to my voice that bespoke of terrible vengeance if any harm had come to Ese.

Rekhmire shook his head as if to say that all was well.

"Your mother is alive, Thutmose. But she now requires your attention as never before."

He paused.

"Kheteb can tell you more."

His voice trailed off and he looked directly at Kheteb and nodded as if granting him permission to speak.

Kheteb glanced at Rekhmire then turned his eyes toward me. There was an expression of sorrow upon his face as he spoke.

"My prince, the queen has taken revenge upon your mother and all the other concubines."

He paused and looked at Rekhmire again.

"The queen has become fearful of everyone now that Senenmut has been driven from her comfort. She trusts no one and has few skilled advisers to place her fears at rest. Hatshepsut sees conspiracy everywhere and no more so than where you are concerned. She hates your mother as the one who gave life to him who would take from her the throne of Egypt. She has ordered that your mother be driven from the apartments in the Garden and turned out upon the streets as a common woman."

Upon hearing these words I formed my hand into a fist and I brought it smashing down upon the table with a great crash. The women who had been chatting quietly at the far end of the table were startled into sudden silence by the violence of the sound. Merytre's eyes found my mine and saw my rage and was taken back by the hate that streamed from them. It was a side of her lover that she had never witnessed and it frightened her.

"Easy Thutmose," Rekhmire said softly. He reached across the table and touched my arm in a gesture to calm me.

"All is well, my prince. Calm yourself."

His words reassured me and I looked at Kheteb who continued his story.

"Your mother lives in a small house at the outskirts of the city," Kheteb said with a reassuring tone. "All this happened while you were in Nubia and you have General Rekhmire to thank for looking after her. The court was buzzing with the news of Ise's eviction and I happened to mention it to the general. At once he made sure she was safe and her needs met."

He glanced at Rekhmire who sat silently across from me.

"Now that you have returned to Thebes she will be happy to see you, highness. But you must be careful, for it is unlikely that the queen has abandoned her efforts to have her watched. You must take precautions or your presence here in the city will be discovered.

Kheteb sighed and measured his next words carefully.

"The queen sees enemies everywhere. Should she discover you in Thebes your life may be in danger, highness. It is a time for great care."

I thanked Kheteb and the general for their kindness to my mother and made it clear that I wished to see Ese as soon as possible. It was decided that I would visit her the next night. Merytre came to me that evening and in the wonder of her flesh I found relief from my fear. But when the dawn came and Merytre had gone my fear returned. I knew it would remain until I saw my mother safe once more.

Thaneni agreed to act as my scout. Using the directions given him by Kheteb, he found the house where my mother lived without difficulty. It was, as he described it, little more than a hovel of mud brick with no whitewash on the walls and a door of thin palm wood barely held in place by leather hinges. The house sat in the midst of a shabby neighborhood of other rundown hovels and the stench of burning horse dung covered the houses when the smoke of the cooking fires filled the evening air. Faithful Thaneni spent the entire day perched on the edge of an alley from where he had a good view of the house watching for any sign that the queen's agents were about. Every now and then he would rise and walk down the street like some casual stroller, ever alert for any sign that he was being watched, only to return from another direction some time later to catch anyone off guard who might be watching. By dusk Thaneni was convinced that there were no spies and that I might safely approach the house. He hurried back to the villa and told me of these things.

Dressed in old clothes borrowed from the servants, Thaneni and I made our way down the dusty street. It was dark and the streets were empty. The jumbled mass of houses and shops looked different in the dark and Thaneni had some difficulty finding the right door. Finding the house at last we stood across the street taking a few minutes to make certain no one else was about. The glow from an oil lamp lit the second floor window. I saw the shadow of someone moving around inside the room. Thaneni tugged at my arm to draw my attention and gestured for me to cross the street. I nodded and walked quickly to the door and knocked sharply. After a few moments I heard the shuffling sound of someone making their way to the door. Behind me Thaneni slipped into the shadows where he waited to give the alarm should any danger arise while I was inside. The glow from a lamp leaked through the thin cracks in the wooden door and from the other side came a woman's weak voice.

"Who is it?" the voice asked. There was a tremor in the woman's words put there by fear. For a few moments I said nothing.

"Who's there?" the voice came again. "Who comes to my door at this hour and for what purpose."

The voice had gained some strength as if trying to intimidate whoever it was that was disturbing it. But its strength was not genuine and it would have done little to drive away an intruder who might have evil intent. My words reached my lips cast in a soft tone for I wished to cause my mother no further difficulty.

"Mother, it is your son, and I have come to comfort you and protect you for you were the one who brought me into this world, who gave me life, and who will love me until you breath no longer."

My voice broke from the emotions that welled up in my breast. I felt at that moment that I had failed in my duty to protect Ese and was responsible for the suffering she endured on my behalf.

"Ese...mother...It is your son."

For some time there was no answer from the other side of the door. Even the ribbons of light from the lamp cast through the cracks did not move as if she who held the lamp was cast in stone unable to move or give voice to her thoughts. And then I heard the bronze bolt slide back and strike the block. A moment later the door opened and I gazed upon my mother's face.

Ese looked at me adoringly. Her smile of surprise turned quickly to a worried frown as tears of joy rushed from her eyes. She threw her arms around my neck. I held my mother close and listened to her sobbing and tried to comfort her with assurances that she was safe and no harm would come to her. It was then that I swore that I would take my revenge upon the vile Hatshepsut should the gods permit and make her suffer the way my mother suffered. At last Ese stopped sobbing and led me up the stairs to a small room sparsely furnished with cheap furniture. She bid me sit at the table while she brought a jug of common wine from the kitchen, a few figs, and some bread. She placed them upon the table with a shrug that bordered on an apology and sat down across from me.

She began to tell me the tale of how she had come to this place. I listened without interruption. Ese was in her mid-thirties, the beginning of old age for an Egyptian woman. Her beautiful black hair had streaks of silver in it when I had last seen her. Now, so many years later, her hair was almost completely gray. Still, it draped itself smoothly around her face and shoulders forming a frame within which her beauty was portrayed. There was still a softness about her even as the wrinkles around her mouth and eyes had deepened, and her dark eyes still sparkled with life while they roamed over my face searching for the features of my youth that only mothers remember. Her smile made her face beam, but the straight row of white teeth was broken by the black spaces of missing ones, and the way she chewed her bread told me her back teeth were worn to the gums and sometimes gave her pain. Still, she seemed the most beautiful woman in the world to me. The years had taken their toll but had done nothing to dim the love that passed between us as we sat there taking in every detail of each other's presence.

We sat together for a long time talking and smiling and reassuring each other with smiles, touches, gestures and words that each possessed someone in this world who cared for the other as much as we cared for our own lives. It grew late and Ese had difficulty staying awake. Her circumstances had worn heavily upon her. Now that my presence promised some relief, Ese permitted herself the relaxation that comes from another's willingness to carry the burden so that the desire to sleep was irresistible. I assured Ese that she would want for nothing and that Thaneni or others would visit her regularly and see to her needs. She thanked me but I could see it was not enough. Ese wished to be free of the hovel, wished her old life to be returned, things I could not give her now. And so I explained that she would have to remain here for some while yet until a solution could be found. To move her would arouse the suspicion of the queen and place her in danger. After much talking Ese shook her head more in defeat than agreement and made me promise to return soon. I stepped into the deserted street and searched for Thaneni who walked quickly to my side. Together we walked noiselessly through the dark streets of the shambled neighborhood and made our way back to the villa.

The inundation had begun and the coolness that was the gift of the north wind filled the evening air so that nighttime on the patio of the villa became even more pleasant. Over the past weeks Rekhmire and I had acquired the habit of sitting together in the evening discussing the difficulties confronting Egypt. These discussions were a valuable education for me and gave me an insight into the manner in which our generals saw the world beyond Egypt's borders. It was a world of greater complexity than I had imagined, one that presented grave challenges to any pharaoh. I was fortunate to have such an experienced teacher as Rekhmire.

Hardly a week went by when Rekhmire did not return to the villa without another tale of some incident that had happened in Retjennu involving Egyptian interests. At first the pressure had been economic and Egyptian cargoes were seized. Then Egyptian diplomats and consuls were harassed. Once, near Gaza, an Egyptian military unit moving toward Joppa to repair its chariots was trapped and attacked by a mob. Several civilians and a soldier were killed. At last the army commander in Memphis ordered the border garrisons and the Wall of Princes reinforced. He had done this on his own authority. When news of his actions reached the queen the officer was severely reprimanded. But he had refused to rescind his order and the garrisons remained at full strength.

One evening Rekhmire brought another officer to our discussion. He was General Shepsekaf, Keeper of the King's Secrets, the chief of military intelligence. His task was to keep an eye on Egypt's allies and enemies and to collect and analyze information so as to know the intentions of Egypt's neighbors at all times. Rekhmire had brought him along so I might learn first hand of the situation in Retjennu and learn from the general's own words the urgency in which he held the situation. Shepsekaf was a short fat man with balding head and squinty eyes that made him look more like a scholar than a soldier. Indeed, it had been his keen intellect that had propelled him up the ranks, for certainly his body was of little use in war. He spoke in short sentences, a man of facts and measurements, not given to speculation if there were other choices. The high tinny voice that escaped from the round body at first struck listeners as comic. But comic or not, a few minutes of listening to this man convinced most men that they were in the presence of a brilliant intellect.

Rekhmire introduced us and we sat down on the patio. A servant poured wine and then vanished. Shepsekaf drank from his cup and licked his lips. His eyes beamed with delight at the fine quality of the wine Rekhmire provided. He took another swallow, smiled, and put the cup down on the table.

"General, things are getting beyond our control in Retjennu."

Rekhmire glanced at me.

"The incidents over the past few months are part of a pattern of harassment by the princes of the city-states. They are carefully calculated to embarrass us, but not sufficiently serious to provoke a military response." He paused. "And in that they are very cleverly done. Very!" he said.

I looked at Rekhmire who asked the general to go on.

"These are not military incidents, general. They are part of a pattern to garner support among the princes of those states who remain our allies and pay tribute to Thebes. Each time we are provoked and do not respond, each time our enemies point to our allies and say that Egyptian power is weak and of no use in protecting them. The goal is to convince our allies to abandon their commitments to Egypt."

He paused to let his words take hold.

Rekhmire took a deep breath and let it out slowly.

"If there is a pattern, general, surely you have discovered who is behind it and why?" he said.

Shepsekaf nodded and glanced in my direction and then back to the general asking with his eyes for permission to continue. He was an intelligence officer, the most suspicious of the military breed, and he had no idea, or at least never let on that he knew, who I was. He wished to be certain that Rekhmire approved his talking frankly in front of me. Rekhmire caught the gesture and smiled.

"Its all right Shepsekaf. Please tell us more," Rekhmire said.

"The troublemaker is the prince of Kadesh in the north of Retjennu. He seeks to extend the influence of his city southward across the River of the Dogs. To do this he must weaken the influence of Egypt among her allies so that one by one he can intimidate them into submission. The harassment is designed to weaken our pledges to our allied cities. Once we prove that we are not willing to come to their aid, they can be plucked from our tree like ripe dates."

I studied Shepsekaf as he spoke. All that he said made sense except for one thing. It struck me that any city-state, even one as powerful as Kadesh, would never take it upon its own to challenge the power of Egypt. If the bluff failed and Egypt took to arms, we would make short work of the army of the prince of Kadesh. Certainly, I reasoned, Kadesh's rulers must have made common cause with some other greater power to come to their aid. Only in this way could Kadesh avoid destruction at the hands of Egyptian arms if it miscalculated and provoked our anger. When Shepsekaf paused to swallow some wine I offered my question with my own answer and waited for him to reply. The general nodded his head and offered a slight smile as if in appreciation for my thoughts.

"What you say is true," he said nodding his head for emphasis. "The prince of Kadesh is the patron of the King of the Mitanni who rules a great empire beyond the Euphrates and who covets a larger presence in Retjennu for a share of the trade and riches there." He smiled. "The biggest fish sets the large fish upon the minnows only to consume the large fish in its turn when the time is right! The Mitanni support the prince of Kadesh to serve its own interests. I have no doubt that a treaty exists between them to the effect that if Egypt attacks Kadesh the Mitanni will come to her aid." He paused. "The question is, how good is the pledge of the Mitanni?"

Rekhmire leaned back in his chair and sighed.

"How do you live in this world made of mirrors Shepsekaf? Its complexity and uncertainty would drive me mad in a short time." He exhaled loudly. "Is there nothing certain anymore?"

He shook his head in disgust and looked back to Shepsekaf who looked at me and shrugged as if to say, "Why blame me?" I smiled at the antics of both generals who were acting like young officers. I nodded my agreement to Shehsekaf.

"What you say is of great interest, general. I assume the queen has been informed of this?"

I paused and glanced at Rekhmire.

"How does she see these events and is she prepared to act?"

The question made Shepsekaf uneasy. Once again he looked to
Rekhmire for permission to answer. Again Rekhmire smiled and
nodded his head telling him it was all right. Shepsekaf took a deep
breath and sighed.

"It is not a happy circumstance," he said. "At the suggestion of
her advisers the queen remains unconvinced that circumstances in
Retjennu are anything more than the usual complaints and incidents that happen to any great power when it becomes involved in
the politics of small states. Whenever it is reported that some
ambassador has been insulted or a cargo stolen or a soldier killed,
her response is always that Egypt is far too great a power to worry
about such small things. Egypt, she says, has a bright future elsewhere than among the "sand-peoples" of Retjennu as she calls
them. Egypt's future lies in trade with Punt and other countries
near the Horns of the Earth."

He shook his head and curled his lips as if what he had said had
given him great distress.

"I fear that Egypt will not be permitted to respond until events
have moved too far. Then there will be no other choice than a war
against a powerful coalition of city-states led by Kadesh and
strongly supported by the Mitanni. Under these circumstances
much of our empire on the land bridge could be lost."

Shepsekaf's tone left no doubt as to the seriousness of what he
was saying. I could see by the expression on Rekhmire's face that
he, too, was convinced Egypt was facing a grave crisis. The three
of us sat there for a while longer and the conversation turned to
other things until Rekhmire brought the discussion to an end. The
general and I saw Shepsekaf to his coach.

"General, if you have any influence with the queen, I beg you to
try to get her to see how wrong she is and how grave is the threat
to Egypt. Perhaps there is still time. My fear is that Retjennu will
burst into flame if our queen does not act. Then time works

against us. It is one thing to prevent a situation. It is a far more difficult thing to restore a situation."

Shepsekaf paused and his voice grew solemn.

"It is my judgement that we have less than a month. After that there will be no stopping things. Try, general, try to make her see the light. Otherwise..."

His voice trailed off. He stared at Rekhmire and me for a few moments and then sat back in his seat. The two of us stepped back to avoid the coach's wheels as the driver snapped the reins and the horses carried the *ka'tana* across the courtyard through the gate and down the road toward Thebes.

Shepsekaf proved as good as his word. A few weeks later Retjennu burst into the conflagration that the general had predicted. Events began with the seizure and looting of an Egyptian merchant ship in the harbor at Byblos carried out by the local authorities. There was some resistance and the ship's captain was slain. When the Egyptian consul general at Byblos lodged a protest, he was told that he would be better advised to direct his protest to Kadesh. Without waiting for instructions the consul travelled overland to Kadesh only to be ambushed and killed on the road outside the city. Egyptian agents in several ports from Gaza to Byblos reported the unloading of caches of weapons, armor, and chariots and their transport to the authorities of several cities in Retjennu. Within a week these cities exploded in revolt and Egyptian merchants, soldiers, and civilians were attacked, beaten and slain. With the few small Egyptian units pinned in their garrisons by these disturbances, a large contingent of troops sent by the prince of Kadesh appeared outside the fortress city of Megiddo. The authorities threw open the gates and welcomed them as allies. From Gaza to Kadesh and even further north Egyptian influence and power was reduced to shards in less than a month.

Rekhmire assembled his staff and asked for an appointment with the queen only to be told that she would not be available for two days. The queen's advisors continued to insist that the circumstances in Retjennu were not unusual, that small trade delegations no longer constituted Egypt's vital interest. Rekhmire and his officers pleaded for permission to counter the situation with a strong show of force. Egyptian garrisons in Sharuhen could be dispatched immediately to the border and reenforced within a few weeks by sea using the units along the Wall of Princes. Reserve forces from Memphis, Avaris and Tanis could be used to fill out the rear defenses in case of reverses. The queen and her advisors refused to change their minds. Rekhmire lost his patience and flew into a rage, an act that prompted the queen to threaten him and his staff with imprisonment. Rekhmire was dragged from the queen's sight by his own officers who sought to save his freedom. Two days later Rekhmire and his officers assembled at his villa late in the evening.

I watched the coaches arrive one by one as I stood looking down from my window. Rekhmire himself had not been at the villa for the evening meal so that we had not seen each other that day. Merytre, too, had gone off late in the afternoon so that only Thaneni and myself dined together. The presence of Rekhmire's generals at the villa this late in the evening suggested that something very important was about to happen. Perhaps the queen had changed her mind and Egypt was preparing to go to war. Or maybe there was dire news from Retjennu to be dealt with. Had things changed for the worse in Nubia? All of these were possibilities. I mulled them over in my mind when a knock came at the door.

"Highness," Rekhmire's voice said. "May I enter?"

I walked to the door and opened it and let the general in. He walked quickly across the room and looked out the window at the activity below. After a few moments he turned and stood before me.

"My prince," he began in a somber tone, "Egypt is at great risk. Those who love her can no longer stand aside and watch her suffer at the hands of simpletons and traitors."

He fixed me fast with his eyes and searched my face for a reaction to his words. Not knowing what else to do I nodded solemnly to encourage Rekhmire to go on. The general's face was haggard from exhaustion and lack of sleep. He appeared fidgety and tense. The dark shadow of his unshaven beard gave his face the expression of someone on the brink of collapse. He began to pace about the room as he spoke.

"Highness, it is the duty of the army to serve Egypt. I have gathered my officers together tonight to discuss a plan that will rescue our country from the talons of those who have betrayed her."

And then Rekhmire began to tell of me of the events that had occurred in Retjennu and how he had to attempted to convince Hatshepsut to take strong action to preserve the eastern frontier only to be threatened with prison. Rekhmire told me of the fears he had for his family now that he had placed himself in opposition to the queen and her advisers. It would be only a matter of time before he would be removed from his command. How vicious would be the queen's revenge depended upon many things, but Rekhmire felt certain that he was in danger. Finally he spoke of his officers, of those men who had served Egypt in peace and war for many years and who, because of their desire to protect their country, had placed everything at risk and now were in danger too. When he finished Rekhmire was on the verge of tears. He sat down and permitted his body to slouch. It looked as if the weight of a thousand pyramids were upon his shoulders.

I walked over to him and placed my hand upon his shoulder in a gesture of affection for I had truly come to care for and respect this man. Now, in an hour of torment, I tried to help.

"General," I began, "What is it you require from your lieutenant?"

It was a strange thing to say, but it was my way of offering my help. Whatever Rekhmire had in mind it was likely to involve me in one way or another. Better that it should do so right from the beginning. It was a dangerous stratagem, but I cast my lot with the officers. After all I was one of them, or certainly more so than I was one of the toadies at court. I had lived the soldier's life, eaten their bread and salt, fought with them, and watched men die with them. Whatever else, I was more one of them than I was of anyone else. This night Rekhmire seemed more my brother, my comrade on the eve of battle, than my superior officer, and I cast my fate with him.

Rekhmire turned his face up at me. A worried smile creased his lips. With his last strength I saw his eyes flash with excitement and gratitude at my words. He reached up and took my hand in his and squeezed it firmly in a gesture of affection and respect. With that single act we sealed our fates. He let my hand fall from his and began to speak.

"What I wish, highness, is that you listen to what I propose. I have gathered my officers here tonight to suggest a plan to save Egypt. These are serious men, highness. If they think the solution sound, they will be prepared to act upon it. If they think it foolish, they will say so. But a sound military plan needs a larger purpose, a reason for men to risk all they have for a higher cause, to risk it all for something larger than themselves. And that means, my prince, that you, too, must come to Egypt's side. You, sire, are the larger cause for which we do what we are about to do."

And then Rekhmire told me of his plan. As I listened to him it was clear that he and the others had been thinking about this for some time. In good military fashion they had prepared a plan to deal with something that might happen so as to be well prepared when it did. Now their worst fears had been realized and Rekhmire and his officers were ready to deal with it. When he finished he looked at me in pleading silence and waited for my response. For a few moments the silence hung between us.

"Go tell your officers that the prayers of their pharaoh go with them in their quest to save Egypt!"

My voice was strong and firm as I had trained it to be when addressing troops.

"Tell them that what they do they do with my blessing and that of the gods. I stand with you and those who serve you, Rekhmire. Let your victory be my victory. Let your danger be my danger. Above all, let us act to save Egypt!"

Rekhmire rose quickly from his chair as if his body and mind had found new strength. He stood before me in silence, his eyes filled with tears barely held in check by sheer will. Weaker men less sure of themselves would have fallen to their knees before their pharaoh. Rekhmire was made of sterner stuff. He stood before me with no sign of fear or uncertainty. And then he smiled broadly as if, somehow, the weight of his burdens had been lifted from him. He walked past me and left to join his officers who awaited his arrival in the room below.

Several hours later the noise of the officers' coaches leaving the villa awakened me from my shallow slumber. Over and over again I thought of what Rekhmire had told me until I knew the details of the plan by heart. The whole affair, I confess, left me frightened. And while I could control my unease, it remained always just beneath the surface of my thoughts. I drove these things from my mind and turned on my side to seek the comfort of sleep and the brief respite from my fears that it promised and was slowly borne away upon it like a small boat upon the Nile uncertain of its destination.

Thaneni and I passed the next day uneventfully while we waited for sunset. The first indication that something was in the wind was the increase in the strength of the guard around Rekhmire's villa. As soon as evening's cloak shrouded the city two platoons of infantry arrived at the villa and threw a cordon around the compound sealing it off from the outside. No one was allowed to enter or leave. I learned later that all the villas of Rekhmire's generals had been reinforced in the same way. It was a precaution against failure. If things went badly the troops would be able to buy some time while the generals and their families escaped. In truth, there was nowhere to escape to. Had the conspiracy failed, some of the officers would more likely have taken their own lives than fled. Others who lacked the courage would be arrested and executed.

Later that evening while Thebes slept the commander of the Thebes garrison doubled the sentries at each of the city's many gates, bared the wooden doors, and closed off the city. Smaller units were deployed across every road that led to the city with orders to stop and hold anyone foolish enough to be on the road at that time of night. Some of the other garrisons were outside the city and their commanders were not privy to the plot. There was always the possibility that one of them might take it in his head to rescue the queen and try to force his way into the city. The outlying units would delay any such attack until events had proceeded so far as to be irreversible. The most important reason for sealing off the city was to prevent the escape of any members of the court who slipped through the net.

Shepsekaf's intelligence officers led units of elite troops to the villas of some of the oldest noble families in Egypt who had long been supporters of Hatshepsut. Many of these families provided the advisers, priests, and high government officials who ran the government. They could be counted upon to protect their investments and remain loyal to the queen. The raids began at midnight.

Scores of these people were dragged from their beds, bound, and taken to military compounds where they were held prisoner. In a few instances things got out of hand and people were injured and killed.

It was several hours past midnight when I heard the sound of a coach pull up outside the main door of the villa. I looked out the window and saw Rekhmire climb down and stride quickly up the main steps. I turned to Thaneni who sat half asleep at the table. I heard the sound of the general's footsteps coming down the hall. A few moments later Rekhmire walked through the door. He was wide awake and had a broad smile on his face. His excitement concealed the fatigue that showed around his eyes.

"Highness, things move quickly and just as we planned them," he said. "The city is sealed, the opposition is imprisoned, and we have achieved complete surprise."

He glanced at Thaneni who had awakened fully and was paying close attention.

"Is that beer in that jug?" Rekhmire asked with a grin.

Thaneni nodded and passed the general an empty cup. Rekhmire filled his cup with the cool amber-colored liquid, raised it to his lips, and drank the entire contents without stopping. He wiped his mouth and let out a quiet burp. Refreshed, he smiled at Thaneni and me.

"Now is the time for you to go to the palace highness and take your rightful place as Egypt's protector," he said solemnly.

"All Egypt awaits her new pharaoh!"

I stared at Rekhmire without speaking. His words struck my mind with great force. At last the day had come to fulfill my father's testament! At last his will was to be done. I glanced up at Rekhmire. For some reason Thaneni rose to his feet. I looked at him and he bowed his head and uttered a single word.

"Pharaoh!"

I nodded and turned to Rekhmire.

"Let us go general," I said. "Egypt awaits her king."

The ride to the palace was swift as the driver guided the horses at lope speed through the empty streets. Before us a squad of chariots rode advance guard to intercept and deal with any trouble. Behind us other chariots protected the rear. Before I left the villa I changed into my military uniform at Rekhmire's suggestion. Now as I climbed down from the *ka'tana* that had halted before the main stairway of the palace a double row of palace guards, Kheteb's men, snapped to attention and presented their weapons in salute as I walked quickly up the stairway accompanied by Rekhmire and Thaneni. Khebteb greeted me at the top of the staircase with a salute.

"All is in order, highness," he said with a smile. "I will take you to the queen."

Kheteb and his men of the palace guard played the crucial role in the plan. He had carefully selected the queen's guards from his most loyal men so that they could be relied upon to follow the orders of their officers. As events proceeded outside the palace, Kheteb's men swiftly rounded up the high government officials whose privilege it was to live at the palace and imprisoned them in one of the storehouses at the rear of the compound. Kheteb arrested the queen himself not completely trusting even his most loyal officers to resist a royal command. Two hours before I arrived Kheteb and two of his officers had marched straight into the queen's bedroom and awakened her from her sleep. She was permitted to dress and sit in one of the large overstuffed chairs that were a favorite of hers. Her servants, all women and one portly eunuch, were locked in one of the rooms and placed under guard. As Rekhmire, Thaneni, Kheteb, and I approached the sentry guarding the queen's sitting room I felt my heart begin to beat quickly and the blood rush through my veins.

Hatshepsut slouched in the huge chair that seemed to surround her with its bulk and make her appear smaller than she really was. The shock of the night's events lingered on her face. Hatshepsut was almost fifty, ancient by Egyptian lifespans, and sitting there in her disheveled gown with her balding head unconcealed by a wig my aunt seemed as old and worn as the pyramids themselves. Wrinkles no longer hidden by thick white makeup ravaged her face so it resembled an overripe plum. Without lipstick to give her lips the glow of life, they seemed thin lifeless sticks. Only her eyes remained as they always had been, sunken now in deep sockets, but still capable of vigorous emotion. And in them I saw the hatred that filled her soul this night.

"So, nephew," she said. "This is your doing!"

The words flowed from Hatshepsut's mouth in the same manner that a cobra spits venom to blind its victim to the attack.

I offered a thin smile to my aunt.

"Yes," I said formally. "I have come to fulfill my father's testament. I have come to sit upon the throne of Egypt as was his wish."

I stared straight into her eyes meeting her hatred with a determination of my own.

Hatshepsut threw her head back and laughed.

"You are as much a fool as your father!"

She laughed again.

"Take it, then! Sit upon the golden throne."

She waved her hand as if to push the throne from her.

"I am done with it. Do what you will."

Rekhmire and Thaneni looked at each other and both turned toward me. Hatshepsut, seeing the gesture, looked at me.

"I see you have not yet decided what to do with me nephew."

There was sarcasm in her voice.

"Am I to be killed?" she asked. She spoke without fear.

I shook my head slowly.

"You did not slay me when you could have done so and I will not take your life from you. But I will have the name of Paremheb's assassin and all who were involved in the murder."

I paused and watched my words cause my aunt to narrow her eyes as if preparing for some important contest in which the stakes were her life.

"And I would have the names of those who helped the vile Intef kill Mentuhotep. Give me their identities and no harm will come to you."

I spoke sternly so as to make it certain my aunt understood my meaning. If she wished to live she had to deliver into my hands her most trusted henchmen. I stared at my aunt awaiting her answer.

For a few seconds our eyes met. Then she nodded her head slowly in a gesture of exhausted defeat.

"It will be as you wish, nephew" she said with a deep sigh. "And now if there is nothing more, I wish to rest."

And without saying another word Hatshepsut rose from her chair, turned her back on us in a gesture of almost magnificent contempt, and walked silently into her bedroom closing the door behind her.

Rekhmire, Thaneni and I walked from the queen's apartment down the long corridor to the main receiving hall. Along the way Rekhmire seemed bothered.

"Is it wise to permit the queen to live, highness?"

It was not a rhetorical question. Rekhmire was an intelligent man and accustomed to making certain that loose ends were tied up neatly. I glanced at Thaneni who had a sly smile upon his face. He was enjoying my discomfort.

"General," I said, "there is nothing to be gained by killing the queen. Permitting her to live shows mercy, and a good pharaoh must be merciful. I shall do to her what she did to my mother. She shall be given a small house in a poor neighborhood and be given enough to live on. There she will spend her last years deprived of the wealth and privilege that she valued so highly all her life."

Thaneni's smile turned to a beaming grin and he gave forth with a short sharp laugh that drew a dirty look from Rekhmire. The general was not a humorless man but this was serious business and he was not pleased by the snickering interruptions of some factory workers son! Rekhmire was about to speak when I raised my hand and cut him off.

"When she dies she will be buried in a common grave. Neither her first tomb nor her other in the Valley of the Kings shall hold her body. Her name is to be removed from the statues and paintings that adorn that monstrosity of a temple that is nothing more than a testament to her vanity. Let the gods themselves search the earth for her corpse!"

Rekhmire listened and, finally, nodded his assent. The issue was closed. Pharaoh had spoken.

We entered the great hall and the sound of our footsteps echoed through the empty chamber. I suddenly felt exhausted. Outside, the first hope of dawn was rising over the eastern horizon as Horus took wing to bring the new day to life. Overhead the first pink rays of the early dawn poured through the clerestory windows and lit the second level of the hall drawing our eyes to the stepped ramp that led from where we stood to the platform above. The sun's bright glow fell upon the golden throne and made it seem aflame so that all else in the great hall faded into shadow. The three of us stood in wonder at the sight, for it was as if that great seat of power were itself alive, drawing to it those of proper sacredness and magnificence.

Rekhmire's voice broke the silence.

"The throne of Egypt awaits, highness."

And with that he and Thaneni bowed their heads and backed away as if they were in the presence of someone they did not know but for whom the gods had reserved this special place. I watched my old comrades bow before me. A feeling of unexplained sadness came over me, for few men would ever be as close to me again.

I turned and walked to the foot of the stairs that led to the golden chair. With deliberate steps I climbed the staircase until I stood before my father's throne returned at last to his rightful son. My body trembled. For a moment I wished for all the world that I might be only myself once again. But I was who I was. I was Thutmose, prince of Egypt, the third of my line, and chosen by the gods to walk this path and fulfill the destiny they had set for me. The sun streamed through the windows, its power and heat grown stronger with the fading darkness. Hot rays caressed my body as if they were the golden feathers of Horus himself. I sat upon the golden throne and let the sun's glow envelop me and draw me to itself. I stared into its light and became part of the new day that was dawning for Egypt.

Printed in the United States
141515LV00002B/237/A